WESTWARD GO!

Fremont, Randy, and Kit Carson Open Wide the Oregon Trail

Dramatized Events of
John C. Fremont's Report
describing his 1842 Map-Making Expedition
from St. Louis, Missouri, to
South Pass in the Rocky Mountains
with a crew that included Kit Carson and
12-year-old Randy Benton

by
T. L. Loftin

Illustrations by Beth Berryman

100 pictures, many based on works by artists of the mid-1800's, show
historical scenes, events, and characters: Fremont...Randy...Kit
Carson...Indians...Buffalo...Buffalo surround...Son of Sacajawea...
Mountainmen Lucien Maxwell, Jim Beckwourth, Basil Lajeunesse...
Fort St.Vrain in Colorado...Fort Laramie in Wyoming...The Platte River, and both the
North and South Forks...The Sweetwater River
leading to South Pass, Wyoming...13-year-old Cheyenne boy who became
Randy's close friend. One exciting adventure after another!

History comes alive for you!
U.S. Geography becomes real!

Tee Loftin Publishers
685 Gonzales Road
Santa Fe, New Mexico 87501

Tel/FAX 505-989-1931

ISBN 0-934812-05

ABOUT THE AUTHOR:

T.L. Loftin during 20 years as researcher-writer in National Geographic Society's Special Publications Division, Washington, D.C., authored as Tee Loftin Snell AMERICA'S BEGINNINGS: THE WILD SHORES. (Check the public library for one of the 350,000 sold.) She also wrote chapters for a number of books about diverse subjects. Before joining the National Geographic staff, she wrote for radio, TV, and for her hometown newspaper, The Kinston (N.C.) Daily Free Press. In 1980, she edited-wrote-published trapper Andy Nault's adventure book, STAYING ALIVE IN ALASKA'S WILD, best-seller in Alaska 1981. In 1989, after retiring from the Geographic, she completed and published CONTEST FOR A CAPITAL, true story in novel form of our founding fathers' 8-year fight with each other over where to locate the national capital city. Bookstores in the Smithsonian, Archives, D.C.Historical Society, commercial bookstores in D.C., and DisneyWorld in Orlando, FL, sold the book. Her picturemap of Civil War Washington sold at Ford's Theater for 25 years, her picturemap of Washington 1800 still sells at Octagon House. Ms.Loftin has a Bachelor of Journalism from the University of Missouri, an M.A. in Journalism from American University, Washington, D.C. Since 1992, she has lived in Santa Fe, New Mexico.

ABOUT THE ILLUSTRATOR:

Beth Berryman has illustrated books for various writers and publishers since receiving her Bachelor of Fine Arts from North Texas State University in Denton, Texas. Her constant companions-friends for many years have been her daughter, Haley, now 15, and her mules Walter, Claire, Hillary, Belle, the late Great Frank and Emma. Her Mule Dance Ranch at Glorieta, N. M., on the Old Santa Fe Trail, merged in 1998 with nearby Stage One, a service for movie-makers, when she married Stage One owner Dan Berryman of Pecos.

Contributing artists
Steven Henneman, San Rafael,CA
E.Barrie Kavasch, Bridgewater, CN
T.L. Loftin composed the illustrations.
Computer graphics:
Jim Jennings

Special Adviser:
Dr. James L. Snell
Seattle, Washington

CONSULTANTS

Jeff Hengesbaugh:
Historian, lecturer, relic-collector, authority on 1820-1845 mountainmen, U.S. tools, guns, clothing, transport, outdoor life, customs, he is co-author of "Mountainmen Dress and Equipage." Descendant of Zebulon Pike of Pike's Peak fame, he lives near Santa Fe and Glorieta Pass, New Mexico, and is an authority on their Civil War events.

Dr. Robert Shlaer:
"The World's Only Full-Time Professional Daguerreotypist" travels in a "daguerrean saloon" van based in Santa Fe. For his just-published book about Fremont's daguerreotype pictures of the American West, he has retraced Fremont's Fifth Expedition route to make his own daguerreotypes of the same scenes. Some 150 will be exhibited in the Palace of the Governors Museum, Santa Fe, during the year 2000. Dr. Shlaer's PhD. from the University of Rochester is in Sensory Psychology and Neurophysiology.

Dr. Peter Ifland:
The author of "Taking the Stars,"which is illustrated with color photos of his noted collection of sextants and other historical navigation instruments, is a retired business executive living in Cincinnati, Ohio.

Trapper's Trail
Lee Whiteley, Littleton, CO

Spanish language:
Robert Ortiz, Viet Nam War seaman on U.S. destroyer Coral Sea, is retired from the Santa Fe Fire Department.

Mule behavior:
Estelle Whaley Hardison, daughter of the late noted mule trader, Kenyon Whaley, of Kinston, North Carolina;
Beth Berryman, book illustrator, owner of Mule Dance Ranch, Glorieta, N. M.;
Dr. T.C. Jones, Santa Fe, Professor of Comparative Pathology (emeritus), Harvard University.

Historical forts and trails:
Fort Laramie, WY, Nat. Historical Park
Bent's Fort Hist. Pk., LaJunta, CO
Oregon-California Trail Association, Independence, MO

WESTWARD GO!

It's a book for readers age 10 to 100 who love the Oregon Trail story, want to know details of Fremont's famous expedition in 1842 to map for everybody the feared, mysterious trail across the Great Plains, making it known to all, possible for all. By 1852, some 250,000 people had traveled by Fremont's map and day-by-day guide to the Rockies, and beyond.

It's a book for readers who want to know in detail what the Plains were like before covered wagons by the thousands began rolling across them.

It's especially for readers who "hate boring history lessons," and need to see that history is actually a series of exciting stories full of surprising information about people and places.

WESTWARD GO! looks like, reads like a novel, with its main character a 12-year-old boy—and, of course, John Fremont. While the events are dramatized, personalized, enhanced by conversation, expanded to include many sights and details Randy and Fremont would have seen but Fremont had no space for in his Report,WESTWARD GO! closely reflects the stories in Fremont's famous Report. WESTWARD GO!—history in you-are-there style!

Sights and details I have added come from reports of other people who lived in or visited the West in the mid-1800's. In seven years of research and writing, I've consulted about 100 biographies, autobiographies, and historical books and magazines. Some unrecorded stories I've drawn out of circumstances in Fremont's writings where they were embedded. I have also added episodes to fill holes—logically, of course—in his Report. "Hole-fillers" and added episodes are identified as such in margin notes. Other margin notes give sources for the adjacent text—an informal bibliography.

Other books about Fremont's first expedition give only a passing glance at the unusual fact that a 12-year-old boy went on this historical adventure. In this book, WESTWARD GO! you'll find him in every chapter. One whole chapter describes his 6-week stay in Fort Laramie while Fremont and crew rode to the Rockies on a trail that dire warnings insisted would be swarming with hostile Indians. Fort life details in this Randy-chapter come not from Fremont but from accounts by trappers, traders, soldiers, European visitors—and a Fremont crewman whose secret diary surfaced after 110 years!

Fremont's mention of Randy is scant. Only a sentence tells of the friendship that developed between him and a 13-year-old Cheyenne Indian boy who traveled with the Expedition for almost two weeks: "(The boys) eyed each other suspiciously and curiously, (but) soon became intimate friends." A lot of story bound up in those words! How did they talk to each other? In WESTWARD GO! you'll learn from pictures how to "talk" silently to your friends in Universal Indian Sign Language. The Boy Scouts learn it, but you can say Randy, a Cheyenne and Kit Carson taught you!

Throughout WESTWARD GO! the focus is upon a boy's reactions, interest, or point of view. At the same time, I have kept to the point of view of 1842 Fremont, and of 1842 mountainmen, not softening the rough edges of those illiterate, used-to-violence trappers. They speak like backwoodsmen, many with French-Canadian or Cajun accents."The way it was then" comes from first-hand or scholars' accounts—named in the margin—of trappers and their outdoor lives in vast, isolated wildernesses where danger of dying, of fighting and killing Indians were daily possibilities.

One more special feature of WESTWARD GO! You'll find it has exciting stories from Fremont's Report that are left out or barely mentioned in the many books describing Fremont's journey. A day with Sacajawea's son! 200 Indians on horses racing toward you—and halted! Buffalo surround! Wild horses herd! Great storytellers Jim Beckwourth, black ex-chief of the Crow Indians, and Maxwell who lived with Arapahoes! Fremont's experiences on the SOUTH Platte may not be "important" since they didn't happen on the NORTH Platte Oregon Trail, but they're mighty exciting—and WESTWARD GO! has them all!

Now, get started on your Randy adventures!

T L Loftin

CHRISTOPHER "KIT" CARSON
Age 33

RANDOLPH "RANDY" BENTON
Age 12

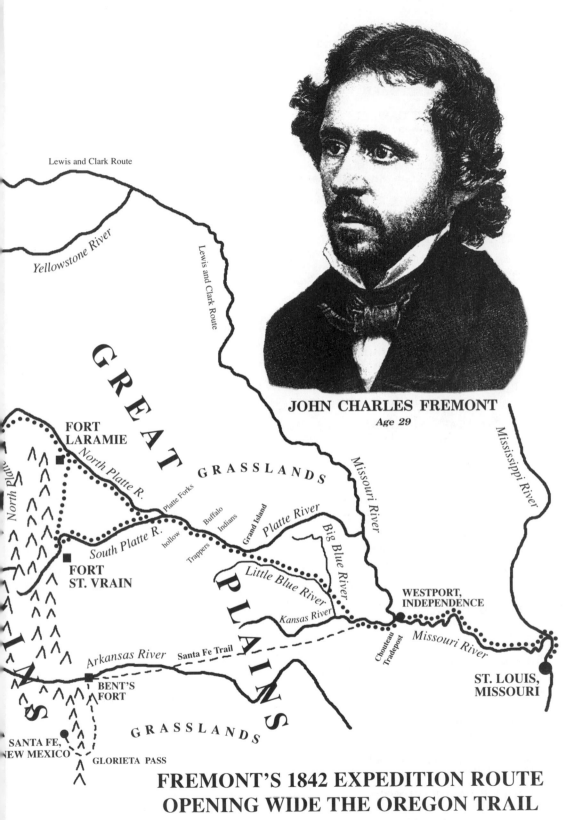

Lewis and Clark Route

Yellowstone River

Lewis and Clark Route

GREAT

FORT LARAMIE

North Platte R.

North Platte

GRASSLANDS

Platte Forks

Buffalo

Indians

Grand Island

Platte River

hollow

Trappers

South Platte R.

FORT ST. VRAIN

PLAINS

Little Blue River

Big Blue River

Kansas River

Missouri River

Mississippi River

WESTPORT, INDEPENDENCE

Chouteau Tradepost

Missouri River

ST. LOUIS, MISSOURI

Arkansas River

Santa Fe Trail

BENT'S FORT

GRASSLANDS

SANTA FE, NEW MEXICO

GLORIETA PASS

JOHN CHARLES FREMONT
Age 29

FREMONT'S 1842 EXPEDITION ROUTE
OPENING WIDE THE OREGON TRAIL
from Missouri to South Pass (Wyoming) June 1 - August 8

TABLE OF CONTENTS
and Index

Standing on steamboat Rowena's deck, Lieutenant John Fremont, his 12-year-old
brother-in-law Randolph Benton, and mountainmen hired as part of Fremont's expedition crew,
watch roustabouts unload freight and load furnace firewood at a lonely Missouri River landing.
By this June day in 1842, steamboats have for 20 years carried passengers and freight from St.
Louis on the Mississippi to Westport trading post, later called Kansas City, up the Missouri River.
A few miles short of Westport, Fremont and his crew will leave steamboat Rowena at the wilderness landing where the Kansas River enters the Missouri. There, they'll join Expedition crew,
carts, provisions, mules, and horses that made the trip by land, and begin a thousand-mile journey
west to map the Oregon trail to the Rocky Mountains.

CHAPTER 1

FREMONT HIRES KIT CARSON

June 1 - 4, 1842, Missouri River Steamboat
June 4 -14, Kansas camps, Kansas River crossing

JF Report
June 1-2, 1842

CLANG! CLANG! CLANG! Steamboat Rowena's big bell voice overpowered the rhythmic sloshing of sidewheel paddles scooping water, the rumble of propelling machinery, the loud coughs of black clouds from tall, spectacular smokestacks. In the plain workaday dining room on the main deck, CLANG CLANG CLANG drowned out all human conversation among a scattering of people, all male, seated on benches at a dozen long tables. One conversation included the last half of a redheaded, frecklefaced young passenger's sentence.

"I'm Randy, I'm twelve years old and I'm on my way with Lieutenant John—"CLANG-CLANG-CLANG!!

The clean-shaven tradesman he was speaking to across the table leaned forward. "John who did you say?"

"Lieutenant John Fremont—my sister Jessie married him. Everybody said he was the best-looking man in Washington. We're on our way to the Rocky Mountains."

J.C. Fremont

The man drew back, flicked a crumb from his white shirt-front, his expression skeptical. "Now how can that be, young man. The Rockies are a thousand miles away and across the Great American Desert. You and Mister—what's his name, again—?"

"LIEUTENANT John Fremont. He's standing right over there by the door with Max and somebody Max knows, somebody he wanted John to meet. I was hungry and they sent me on to the dinner table."

The man stared at the men across the room. "Umm. He's in uniform. I haven't seen any other soldiers among the trapper fellows on this boat. Just him and you off to the Rockies?"

"No, sir. Nobody in our expedition's a soldier. John's not either. He's a Scientific Celestial Navigation Map-maker. But he has to wear a uniform and be a Lieutenant because he makes maps for the Army. The rest of the men—uh, twenty, I think—all of 'um, used to be trappers in the Rockies. About half of 'um are sitting together over there at the end of the dining room."

Randy Benton
(Artist's Conception)

Fremont,
Path Marker.
A. Nevins

JF Report
p.1,trappers

C.Preuss
Exploring
With Fremont.
(Journal)
E.G./E.K.
Gudde

Old Bullion
Benton.
W.Chambers

The man twisted around to take a look. "Well, I'll be dog-goned. Pretty scraggly looking bunch to be going to the mountains with a, what did you call him? a scientist something or other. Where'd your Lieutenant pick up with them trappers?"

"At Mr. Chouteau's big store in St. Louis. Mr. Chouteau knew all of them, except Mr. 'Proyse'—that's German. See that old man with a lot of kinky yellow hair sitting by himself at a table by the window? He hates listening to 'mountain men' tell stories—low-class Creole and Canadian lies, he says, 'specially 'cause they tell 'um in French. Mr. Preuss is real-high educated but he's fault-finding and grumpy. He's near-'bout 40—lots older'n John—and's gonna help John draw a map of an old trail John says we'll ride all the way to the Rockies. My father says the country needs the map so anybody who wants to go to Oregon can go on his own in a wagon with his family."

The man gazed at the freckled face, pink and bright with enthusiasm, telling him such amazing news. He shook his head disapprovingly. "It's one thing that your Papa and the Army send a mapmaker to the Rocky Mountains. It's something else for them to send a child along—bait for the Indians? They love to snatch white children. I'm shocked that your papa would allow you to go off on such a dangerous trip so far away from home. Who IS your Papa?"

"Senator Thomas Benton, elected four times."

"Ohh...Well, if you don't come back alive, I'll know Missouri has a fool in Congress, one I won't vote for again. Mighty poor judgment, Senator Benton, mighty poor. I have a boy nearly 'bout your age, son, and I would never risk sending HIM off to deserts 'n' mountains swarming with savages. It's like Abraham sacrificing his son Isaac, and I'm sure God hasn't spoken to Senator Benton asking him to do such a thing. Tell your Papa I said so."

Thomas H. Benton

"Yes, sir. What's your name so I can tell him."

Riverboats
of America.
(Mo.River)
F.Donovan

"Just say I'm a voting tradesman in St. Charles, Missouri, on the muddiest, swiftiest, crookedest, shiftiest river in the west—the mad Missouri, just for this minute or two letting our steamboat float peacefully on top of it.

"Listen, son, that clanging bell said we're about twenty minutes from pulling up to the St. Charles landing. That's where I get off. You can get off, too, if you've got any

3

sense. I'll look after you, put you on the next steamer going back to St. Louis, and LEND your Papa a dollar for you to ride on this twisty river and the Mississippi 40 miles to St. Louis. You got kinfolks in St. Louis, I reckon."

"Um-huh, Cousin Henry's Mama—that's Henry over there with the mountainmen. He's 18, and got sent on our expedition to help look after me," Randy answered politely. "And thank you, sir, but I don't WANT to go home! We're going to hunt buffalo and see a lot of Indians and maybe grizzly bears in the Rocky Mountains! John says we have men and guns enough—I know how to shoot a pistol to scare off, fight off the Indians we might run into, and Father let me come on the trip 'cause it'll prove that people with children needn't be afraid to start out, go to Oregon and out-people the British. Besides, Father said I could stand some toughening up. Besides THAT, I'm nearly 13, just a few days younger than 'Gus Chouteau was when he helped old Laclede pick a spot on the Mississippi to start Saint Louis!"

"You're some talker. Uh-oh..Here's the Lieutenant and the two men he was talking to," the Voting Tradesman said, straightening in his chair and hastily mopping up gravy from his plate with half a biscuit. "Now, his two friends in fringed buckskin and mocassins, they look like mountain men, too," he mumbled as he swallowed the last bite and pushed his chair out to leave, "but like CLEAN mountain men, chins and cheeks shaved'n' smooth." Eyeballs rolling toward the approaching men, he sidled off.

Arriving at Randy's side, Fremont leaned toward the seated boy to announce that he and Maxwell, the 21-year-old mustached strongman beside him, were leaving for a few minutes again. "I need to go out on deck—more private—and talk business with Max's friend here," Fremont said, gesturing behind him at a short but broad-shouldered man with shoulder-length light brown hair. "Come around here, Mr. Carson, meet Randy Benton, crew member—and my brother-in-law.

"Randy, this is Christopher—'Kit'—Carson from Taos, New Mexico, same as Max. He's a long-time friend of Max. Max says Kit's a scout, trail guide, trapper, mountain man for 17 years, known among whites and Indians for quick thinking and decisive acting. Kit says he was brought up in Howard County, Missouri. BUT, he can speak Spanish, French, and half-dozen Indian languages. Remarkable!"

"Howdy, Mr. Randy."

"Howdy, Mr. Kit."

Steamboaters.
H.Drago

Auguste Chouteau, age 13, helped step-father Pierre Laclede choose site, found, town of St. Louis in 1763.
Am. Fur Trade, I, p100
H.M. Chittenden

JF Report p.1,1842 exp.

Lucien Maxwell.
L.Murphy

Kit Carson.
T.Guild/ H.Carter

4

"When Max saw him just as we came in," Fremont went on, "he said to me 'What luck to find Kit Carson on the boat with us! You MUST meet him!' We've talked enough now for me to know I want to talk to him much more. So, Randy, you go on with your supper and we'll be back about the time you're finishing your apple pie."

JF Report.
JF Memoirs.

"No," Randy answered as he began pushing his chair from the table and standing, "I'm all done—don't want pie—want to go with you." Fremont beckoned him to come.

Mountain Men,
Fur Traders.
L. Hafen,
H. Carter

Up on the deck as Fremont and Kit talked and walked slowly past barrels, bags, boxes, and piles of freight, Randy had a long look at Mr. Carson. He liked this man's looks, his big chest and shoulders, his plain, square face, calm, even gentle. "Just a head taller'n me," Randy saw, "and 'bout up to John's nose—and John's not tall as Max—or Father.

"I like his name, too," Randy thought, "and the way he talks, quiet, sort of a drawl. Mama would say 'backwoodsy.' He looked straight at me, too, when he said 'Howdy, MR. Randy.'" Randy even liked the way he walked—a little bow-legged but loose, light, quick.

John was talking a lot. Randy heard words he'd heard a hundred times before, or so it seemed to him. "Oregon... British...Congress...Platte River...Fort Laramie...South Pass...emigrants..."

Randy's face lighted up when he heard John say, "Mr. Carson, I'm well impressed with your experience, knowledge of the country, the people, and their languages—as well as your hunting skill—all of which the hunter I've hired, your friend Maxwell, vouches for.

"I'm inclined to act on this impression rather than take a chance that the mountainman, Capt. Drips, will receive a letter I addressed to him weeks ago. I was offering him the job as guide to the expedition, and requesting that he join my party on the Missouri River at the Kansas River's mouth. That's where this steamboat will bring us. I've heard nothing from him."

Maxwell's powerful voice interrupted. "Lieutenant, it's a one-in-a-million chance that Drips ever got your letter, which he couldn't've read anyway—or that he'll be awaiting us at Choutou's Kansas River trad'n post!"

"I know Drips well," Carson said, "and at this time of year he's more'n likely taking it easy at one of the forts, Bent's or Laramie. He's a good man, but Lieutenant, I've been working the country west of here for near 20 years,

Lucien Maxwell

and I can guide you to any place you have in mind. It happens that I wuz going home to Taos to settle in for the summer, but the work you're going to do interests me considerably."

Impulsively, Fremont answered, "The fact is, I cannot risk making this journey without a guide—a man who knows the prairie and the mountains. Mr. Carson, you and Max have convinced me that you will be reliable and dependable as my guide, and as my interpreter and adviser when we meet Indians. I can offer you $100 a month, beginning today, June first, for four months, possibly five, same as I was offering Drips. Is this satisfactory? Will you accept?"

"Yessir, Lieutenant Fremont," Carson answered, his grey-blue eyes looking steadily into Fremont's intensely blue ones. "I thank you and I do accept."

Kit Carson

As they shook hands, Fremont said, "On YOUR competence the success of this expedition depends a great deal. I believe I've by chance found the best man to guide us safely to the Rocky Mountains."

"And the best to keep us from going hungry, too!" boomed Maxwell. "He's a much better shot than I am!"

Randy put out his hand and shook the new man's. "Mr. Kit, I'm sure glad you're going to be our guide. I'm gonna like saying and hearing 'Kit Carson' all day in camp instead of 'Cap'n Drips' or just 'DRIPS!'"

All three men chortled, "Mr. Randy," Carson said, "Capt. Drips is right-smart-old, but he knows his business and he's not too hard to get along with. After a few days of hearing his name over and over, you'd've stop noticing that it's a word with a meaning—it just becomes a sound, meaning 'the guide.'"

"Well!" Fremont said, "now that you're one of our crew, I'll point out our boxes of freight in this collection here. We'll probably be called on to help move it to shore ourselves—unless our cart drivers meet the boat in time to do it. This pile of saddles and harnesses is ours. About half my crew has gone by land on horseback, or as mule drivers hauling most of our supplies in eight, two-wheel French-carts.

"Stacked right over here are thirteen boxes of scientific instruments—near 500 pounds of sextants and chronometers, compasses, barometers, thermometers, sperm and spirit lanterns, folding tables, chairs, tripod, paper, pencils—everything for measuring and recording for Congress all the information to make a scientific map of the trail to South Pass in the Rocky Mountains."

JF Report.
(Accounts)
Items bought,
costs.

"Rowena"
new side-
wheeler.
Murphy
Library
steamboat
list, U. Wis.
LaCrosse, WI

Voices on
the River.
W.Havighurst
p.158, 209

Steamboat Rowena, one of nearly 500 steamboats puffing up and down the Mississippi and Missouri, had pushed some 15 miles up the Mississippi from St. Louis, then into the turbulent entrance of the Missouri River under calm, sunny skies by day and a bright moon in an unclouded night sky. Water three feet above sandbars and snags, was quite high enough for a flatboat needing less than 30 inches depth to float above such lurking disasters. An easy trip. At 10 miles an hour pushing upstream, even with two stops a day to load on wood for the furnaces, and ten more stops a day at landings to let off and pick up passengers or freight, Rowena, brand new, would in four days cross Missouri's 400-miles from St. Louis to Chouteau's Landing at the mouth of the Kansas River. A few miles more up the Missouri, and it would pull up to landings at fast-growing Independence and Westport.

Riverboats
of America.
F.Donovan,
p144-5
p155-6

At St. Charles, a riverside village in a semi-circular clearing at the forest-edge, Rowena noisily eased up close to the dock where most everybody in the settlement and beyond had gathered and was shouting welcomes. Roustabouts shouldered boxes, rolled barrels down the gangplank. Two-man teams toted to shore crates, kegs, bundles, and sacks, many of them belonging to Mr. Voting Tradesman. They brought back armsful of wood for the furnace, or freight labeled for Westport. With short, warning bell-clangs, the boat pulled away, smokestacks puffing, and sidewheel paddles pushing Rowena westward.

Old Bullion
Benton.
W.Chambers

Randy hadn't traveled the Missouri River before. He'd only read about it in the account of the trip made by Meriwether Lewis and Capt. William Clark, who had been a friend of Randy's father. But Randy had gone back and forth year after year on steamboats from St. Louis on the Mississippi, down to the Ohio River, and up to Pittsburg on the way home to Washington, D.C.

Strangers Guide to
Washington,D.C.,
1865
by T.L.Loftin
(poster-map)

From Pittsburg, he and his family took a canal boat to Harrisburg, Pennsylvania, boarded an oversize coach-and-six for a jostling ride to Philadelphia. There, a steamboat took them a hundred miles to Baltimore. For as long as Randy could remember, he and his family had then taken a train pulled by a steam locomotive to Washington's station. The last mile coming in, when he looked out the train window across an open, wide meadow, he always felt a tiny shivery thrill at the sight of the low hill holding the small, white Capitol building with its flat little dome.

But there wasn't any thrill in spending days moving slowly along any river where there's nothing much to see but water and trees at a distance along low banks. Some bigger settlements might have docks where something interesting was going on, but after the twentieth trip and twentieth look at them from the boat deck, Randy's feeling about steamboats was that they took too long to get anywhere.

Days of boredom on board listening to the grind of turning paddlewheels, the splash of falling water boxed out of sight...saying 'Hi!' to the pilot in his cabin—he didn't want you lingering—eating ham, corn, and boiled beans three times a day...peering into the boiler room, the engine room...yawn. Still, on one or two trips, the pilot had let him pull the bell rope a few times—wish that could've been a steady job!

Riverboats.
F.Donovan
p152, food

At least Rowena was one of the fast, new boats that could move up to 11 miles an hour against the current! And the Rowena cook made apple pie every day, the best ever, strong in sugar and cinnamon! And at the dining table, this new man Kit Carson told exciting stories about Indians! The rest of the day, Kit, John, and Max—Mr. Preuss, too, sometimes—talked "business," or Kit talked with the other trappers. All of them knew about Kit, he knew some of them.

Bell (1842)
Voices on
the River.
W. Havighurst

At long last, on June fourth, the moment Randy had been longing for, came. When he saw the ten bearded mountain men, a small herd of horses, and an empty cart waiting on the riverbank by a simple landing platform, he began to shout, "We're here! We're here!" All Fremont's men on shore and on boat deck cheered, waved, and joyfully fisted the air.

JF Report
June 4, 1842

Freight loaded into the carts, saddles strapped onto horses, they rode 12 miles into Indian Territory to the Kansas River trading post of Cyprian Choutou, half-Indian son of Pierre Chouteau, Senior, son of Gus, cofounder of St. Louis. Cyprian had a spacious log house and invited Fremont to sleep and dine there.

In the front yard rose Fremont's camp of 20 white canvas Army tents and eight carts beside a rail-fenced corral for more than 60 horses and mules. Fremont, his 26 men and one 12-year-old boy began practicing camp routines, and enduring murky weather.

Randy rode "Spots," his small horse—"Indian pony"—hours every day, to condition his seat muscles against saddle soreness. At night he wished for softer ground to sleep upon.

Steven Henneman

Fremont and Randy, followed by Kit Carson and mustachio'd Maxwell, lead the column across the prairie.

9

At meal-time, he ate as much fried pork and bread as any grown man, no matter Mr. Preuss told him the cooking at all four "messes" was dirty.

Journal.
C.Preuss.
June 6,1842

Finally after six days, having bought a few horses and mules, and having tucked into the carts the extras bought in the store of Cyprian's brother in Westport across the river and six miles upshore, Fremont's expedition column formed and began to move. Cyprian led them to an Indian he'd hired to lead them 30 miles farther through Kansas woodlands to the edge of the prairie.

JF Report
June 10

"That ocean of prairie stretches without interruption to the base of the Rocky Mountains," Cyprian told them, bade them farewell, good luck with weather and Indians—"and hunting, since you plan to feed yourselves with wild game, except for your four oxen."

Randy rode with Maxwell and camp director Lambert behind Fremont and Carson at the head of the column. At first amazed by treeless, green-grass lumpy plains stretching endlessly to the far horizon, Randy after a few days was wishing something would happen besides fording streams.

Water made his wish come true. First a midnight downpour of rain soaked through all the canvas tents, drenching everybody, everything. Then it was the cold, rushing water of the deep, wide Kansas River when the column forded it a hundred miles west of Chouteau's trading post.

Journal.
Preuss,
June 12

"This here is the usual place, the best place, to cross," Carson advised. "The banks on both sides are low, the river not quite so wide—'bout 200 yards or so. Horses 'n' riders just swim across easy, usually. But Max and me better test that."

Shoeless, they sat firmly in their saddles. By words and reins and heels they ordered their mounts into the moving stream. Their horses splashed into the shallows. Soon their powerful legs began propelling them through deep water, with only their heads lifted above the surface. When they returned, Carson, wet to the waist, reported the water was deeper and swifter than expected, but safe.

"With Max riding out ahead on a mare that the mules, the other horses, and the oxen accept as a trusted leader, with me following behind to keep stragglers and wanderers in line, and ha'f-dozen more riders holding the herd edges together, we can easy herd across all the animals and secure them on the other riverbank. You come with us, Mr. Preuss. Just sit tight on your horse and talk to her calm whilst she swims. Even mules are good swimmers when

Jeff Hengesbaugh,
consultant

JF Report,
Preuss Journal
June 14

they see it's a belle mare leading them into the water."

Fremont sent Randy's pony across with the herd. "You can help us here to pump up the rubber boat and load it with carts and supplies. You and I will ride on the eighth and last trip across. Men, you've learned how to assemble the carts—you did it in St. Louis. Now you're to disassemble them for laying in the boat once we get it inflated. Bring out the big bellows. Bring out the rolled-up rubber boat! We're the first to use this new invention of India rubber cloth to cross a western river!"

In a few minutes, horses with riders and the herd of loose animals, had all reached the opposite shore in safety— all except the oxen. Wily beasts, they had drifted into the downriver current, bumped into a hidden snag, threshed the water mightily to turn back, swum to the shore they'd just left, and clambered up the bank.

While the horses and mules were swimming, Randy helped Fremont, Basil Lajeunesse, Carson, and big-strapping Honore Ayot, "Yo," haul out the heavy rubber boat and big bellows from a cart. The India rubber was still smelling strongly "chemical," but not as strong as it had in Washington the day Fremont brought this air-inflatable boat made of new, wondrous material, inside the house. He'd rushed it outside to air when its breath-taking odor overpowered Mama Benton, made his pregnant wife Jessie vomit, and clogged the house air. It took the smoke of many pounds of smouldering coffee-grounds to chase away the smell.

Randy paired with "Yo" to do a turn at pulling, releasing, the top handles of the Randy-height, accordian-like bellows. Down and up, down and up dozens of times. Puff by puff, air pumped by changing pairs of men expanded and expanded the rubberized-cloth boat. Finally, it looked like a black raft twenty feet long with a five-foot-wide bottom and rounded sides two feet high, all parts swollen round and hard with air.

All the while, cart drivers had begun unloading carts one by one, disassembling each, stacking its own load beside it. When at last the boat, tightly fat with air, was dragged up to the water's edge, the men, suppressing their doubts, carefully loaded into it one flattened cart, five-foot-tall wheels, the barrels, boxes, cans, kegs, and bundles the cart had transported, plus the load of a packmule.

At Fremont's instructions, three men picked up paddles and a long pole that came with the boat, and took their places—helmsman with pole to keep it heading toward the opposite shore, two to paddle the boat forward. "All together—SHOVE!" Off they went!

The other men stopped work to watch. Would it float? Carry a ton of weight? Could three men match the force of the river current? Was there any danger of a puncture? Were the air valves stronger than the added pressure of the load? Basil Lajeunesse saw some answers at once. The swift river current was snatching the boat, and the boatmen could do little to counter, being pinned down by the freight, unable to move to where rowing and poling were needed. Without a second lost, Basil, a strong swimmer, romped into the water to grab a line at the helm. Walking in the shallows, he pulled the boat to head toward the opposite bank, fighting the surging current. In deeper water, he slid swimming into the river. Holding, pulling on the line, he tried to swim with one arm.

No good. He needed both arms. He brought the line to his mouth. "Look, John!" Randy cried. "He's pulling the boat with his teeth!" Head almost continuously underwater, Basil began his powerful swimming strokes, teeth and jaws hauling the boat, keeping it on course despite the current. Fremont, Randy, men on both sides of the river, all watched transfixed, silent.

JF Report
June 14
"(Basil)
pulled the boat
with his teeth.."

Almost two hundred yards—and his feet touched bottom forty feet from shore. Men splashed into the shallow water, pulled him, the boat and crew onto land. Cheers resounded on both sides of the river.

"But the boat has to come back!" Randy cried out, still shaking with excitement and fear. "Then SEVEN MORE carts and loads for him to pull across! His teeth won't last that long!"

Kit and Basil took turns, a cart an hour. Five carts, their loads, three boatmen—five trips guided by the swimmer, rope tied to his body. Then the swim back with the empty boat. Their wet deerskin shirts and trousers clung tight as skin.

"You'll never get out of them," joked Fremont. "Can't afford to while they're wet," answered Kit. "Got to stay in 'um whilst they do their drying and shrinking to our size and shape."

Now the sun was going down, Carson and Lajeunesse were shivering tired, and two more carts, their boxes and barrels, cans and bags awaited ferrying. Should the seventh cart and load go now, and the eighth wait until morning?

Basil arrived with the empty raft and the question. The prevailing answer was, "Sure would like to have this overwith TODAY, by dark." Fremont observed that with dark less than two hours away, one boatload would have to take TWO carts and supplies, "then come back for us men left behind, and take us across. Think you can do all that before it gets dark?" They wanted to try, they'd learned how to pack faster with more in less space. "Timing'll be close but we'll make it."

They fitted and fitted, stacked and stacked. "No room for full crew," Basil said, "so I'll leave two boatmen here wid you t'ree, Lieutenant, just take a helmsman. I'll move dis stuff across in minutes. Enough hands over dere to unload in no time, so I should be back in 'bout haf'n-hour to pick you up."

They set out. Randy could see Lajeunesse's black hair bobbing in the water now and again as the boat moved slowly toward the other shore. "He's having some trouble with the current and a load twice as heavy as the others," Fremont fretted. But slowly, slowly the overloaded raft crossed the river at an angle. "Five more minutes at the most," Fremont said when he saw Basil had only 50 yards to go.

Suddenly, Randy screamed. "WATCH OUT! WATCH OUT!" Stacktop boxes were sliding off, splashing into the water. The weight-shifting was dragging other boxes, bundles—the whole boat was rocking and leaning! A barrel tumbled, rolled, struck the raised edge of the raft, and slid off when the raft tilted! Boxes, cart-sections began sliding with the tilt. The helmsman lost his nerve, splashed overboard. Randy heard his scream just as he saw more tumbling cargo leap across the boat's side—flip it upside down! "OH LORDY!! IT'S TURNED OVER!! BASIL! BASIL!"

JF Report
June 14.
Overloaded
boat capsizes,
the rescues.

Where WAS Basil?! The boat and boxes were floating away in the current. A commotion ruffled the water near the helm. Randy saw Basil's black hair appear in the middle of the ruffle, while the helmsman's head moved away, his arms threshing the water.

Randy watched and shivered, biting his knuckles, making low groaning noises that held back screams. He saw men on the opposite river bank running downstream, jumping into the water, reaching for, swimming for, boxes, kegs, cans and sections of carts, dragging them to shore. He saw

13

the boat moving bottom-up closer to shore, and Basil's black hair again. Men ran toward the boat, quick-strode into the shallows to reach it, Basil, and the helmsman, haul them all in.

Fremont watching shocked and silent, could not take his eyes away from the scene on the opposite side of the river. He cried out with relief when he saw Max, then Looie Guion, cook-turned-scared helmsman, coming out of the water. He saw the boat, still inflated, dragged onto land, righted, and Basil's hauling rope untied from his waist.

His deep sigh was cut short when Randy shouted, "Somebody's drowning downriver where stuff's a-floating! River's carrying away everybody—everything!   *JF Report*

Teeth gripping the rope of a newly invented, air-filled India-rubber raft, Basil Lajeunesse pulls a ton of Expedition equipment and supplies safety across the swift current of the Kansas River, Fremont reports. But hours later, Lajeunesse pulling the seventh raft piled high with a double load, will disappear in the water when boxes and barrels topple, overturning the raft. Randy, horror-stricken, will watch during ten minues of terror as swimmers from the opposite bank frantically grab at men and supplies.

15

CHAPTER 2

FIRST DIP INTO THE WILDERNESS

June 14-23, Kansas River to the Little Blue

Fremont was leaning forward, his face contorted in horror. Luck, oh luck, don't let it happen—the expedition has just begun—to lose a man now—to lose a man any time—it must NOT HAPPEN !

The men on the other side of the river were not letting it happen. Four of them had seen the flailing arms of TWO men being swept downstream by the powerful current, had heard them yell, and swum to grab them. "They've got 'um!"

JF Report
June 14
(rescues)

"Oh thank you, thank you! thank you!!" moaned Fremont. Randy panted, "They're pulling them to the shallows—look, one of them is standing—now the other one is, too!"

Fremont was nervously wiping his forehead, his cheeks, his neck, breathing hard, sighing his relief. "Two near-disasters in fifteen minutes! I feel as if I've been running up a steep hill for a whole day. I owe much to those two rescuers for the wonderful scene at the end—four men on the river bank, the rescued and the rescuers. Can't tell from this distance who they are—I wish I could tell them how happy I am to see them there, all four OUT of the water!"

"I'll tell'um!" Randy said, and yelled in his piercing, high soprano voice, enlarged by cupped hands, "BRAAV-OOOH!" They heard and waved.

Carson and Basil, too worn out for another round-trip with the boat, sent horsemen leading five horses across the river to fetch the stranded men and boy. When Randy on his mount reached the mid-river depths, and felt water creeping up his spine, saw the horse's head barely above the fast-flowing current, he thought briefly of his wish not long ago for "something to happen." He sighed, "But NOT NOW!" In a moment, he felt the water begin to recede. Then he felt the horse's hooves touch muddy bottom and heard himself murmuring in a surge of relief, "Bravo!"

Fremont's first questions were, "Who were the rescuers and rescued—what supplies were lost?" A jumble of voices answered: Len Benoist and Honore Ayot pulled non-swimmers Ben Potra, cook, and Moise Chardonnais, blacksmith, out of the river. Half the coffee, some of the sugar were the only losses from the boat spill. "The coffee we'll mourn weeks from now when we're weary and famished and badly need it," Fremont observed. "But mostly we rejoice that non-swimmers are alive, and we honor the swimmers who saved them."

They camped an extra day on shore under the trees to rest, to dry out everything, to bully the oxen into swimming to the camp from the far shore, and to watch over Carson and Basil's recovery from exhaustion and chill. "It must be all that river water I swallowed that makes me feel weak and unsettled inside, and 'course my jaws are right smart sore," Basil said. Carson hardly said a word, just lay sleeping under a blanket.

JF Report
June 15-16

Randy, taking his turn at staying close by the two men, kept seeing some mostly-naked brown people slipping among the trees, stooping, squatting, peering over bushes, watching the camp. After a while, one wearing deerskin trousers walked boldly up to Basil and spoke in French as good as Basil's.

"Bonjour—we see you whites had many difficulties crossing the high water. We will trade you food—beans, pumpkins, onions, lettuce, butter—for two of your oxen."

"How is it that you speak French?" asked Basil, "and how is it you have butter?"

"I was brought up in St. Louis, and we have a cow full of milk for her calf."

"Umm. Our Chief, over there—"Basil pointed to Fremont—"perhaps will consider a trade, two oxen for cow, calf, vegetables, and butter. Randy, escort him to the Lieutenant. Mention this offer to him."

The trade was made. Two oxen stayed on the Kansas River, Fremont's camp had cream if not much sugar in its coffee, butter for bread, and milk for a growing boy.

JF Report
Packs on
mule, horses,
carts had
India rubber
cloth covers

Fremont ordered the camp moved out of the woods and onto the sunny prairie for still another day of rest and recuperation. Carts were reassembled, then painted with oil paint, a work that brought the title of "prairie artist" to Mike Descouteau. Reloaded, the carts were draped with their India-rubber covers ready to be tied down. Target practice got going noisily. The sound of gunshots guided to the camp a lone horseman coming from the west.

He was an ex-trapper a couple of the men knew, and he was on his way to St. Louis. While he gobbled Indian vegetables and the camp's fried pork, he told his story. Fremont and Mr. Preuss used the hour to write to wives—letters the visitor would mail in St. Louis, one to Washington, the other to New York.

"See," the visitor said, "I needed a job since the price of beavers, which're hard to find anyway, has come down from $6 to $1 a pelt. So I hired on with this Preacher White

17

who's the leader of more'n a hundred folks—men, women, children—some riding horses, some walking, to Oregon. They're about three weeks ahead of you. Driving a big herd of cattle, too. And hauling big wagons full of furniture. Real unpractical folks. And they had big troubles, like some getting sick, and some children dying. So, I decided to drop out and get on back to St. Louis."

"The children DIED?" Randy asked, eyes wide. "Why?"

"Oh, probably typhoid, dysentery. Don't know if they were big children like you, Randy, or babies." When he left, Randy wasn't the only one feeling uneasy.

Once the mile-long column got on the move, the days passed in just the way Randy heard Mr. Preuss describe them. "Monotonous prairie behind us, monotonous prairie ahead." He could've added monotonous food, and a monotonous list of daily events—fording creeks and small rivers, plodding up low grassy swells and down, camping by brooks or springs, riding in silence under a blazing sun, or slapping mosquitoes in damp, hot, still air, drying out after a downpour. He was so tired at supper, he didn't take out his guitar but once to play for the men to sing. He almost wished he hadn't insisted on dragging the clumsy instrument along.

Every day, the streams were smaller, the trees along them fewer, the grass sparser. Nothing loomed in the landscape except the rump of the horse just ahead. Only the sight of emigrants' wagonwheel ruts, and the sound of Fremont calling attention to spots of purple flower clusters, patches of pink wild roses "scattered like bouquets," and yellow flowers he called by forgettable Latin names, relieved the daylong tedium.

The first new, exciting anything was almost a week in coming. Cousin Henry found a pack of playing cards left behind by an emigrant at a campsite! That same day, Kit Carson pointed out a Pawnee Indian trail, deep ruts in the sandy earth dug by the bottom ends of long sidepoles on narrow platforms loaded with household goods. Dogs or horses pulled these "travois," Carson said. "Indians didn't know about wheels until white men brought'um."

But the next day, fewer plants, deeper sand, hotter sun, ten hours riding without rest—no water in creek beds, only prickly-pear cacti. Desert! How long would this last? The men mumbled the question to each other.

"Over the next rise—maybe two—I bleeve we'll see a line of trees along the banks of the Blue River," Carson finally

JF Report
June 17

Journal.
C.Preuss
June 17-18

Guitar not mentioned in *JF Report.* *But July 21, JF described Randy as" the life of the camp," whose "bouyant spirits" might well have included guitar music (a family skill) "afford(ing) great amusement (to the men)."*

"After a hard day's march of 28 miles (without finding water in any creek bed since noon) we encamped a 5 o'clock on the Little Blue River (Kansas), where our arrival made a scene of the Arabian desert. As fast as they arrived, men and horses rushed into the stream, where they bathed and drank together in common enjoyment... "We were now in the range of the Pawnee Indians. For the first time, therefore, guard was mounted tonight."

(Fremont Report)

19

said, "and we'll ford its shallows just above where the Little Blue enters it. In no time we'll be on a bank of that pretty little river. Good place to camp—and SWIM!"

Shortly, Randy was shouting and laughing with the others, "Water! Water!" "Regardez La Petite Bleu—une belle riviere—mon Dieu!" Twenty horsemen, eight drivers of carts, their sixteen mules, a herd of spare animals including a cow (the calf had long been digested), and one ox (the other recently digested), raced through a line of cottonwoods to the edge of the Little Blue.

JF Report
June 23

In seconds, men's legs were swinging over saddles, riders jumping to the ground, jerking off boots or mocassins, shoving down stiff deerskin or rough cotton trousers, yanking off hats, stripping off shirts—their all—and leaping into the stream. Their horses, led to the bank, began drawing up water noisily. With cries of enjoyment, the men were kicking and splashing, drinking their fill. Turning to float on their backs, they began spraying water, whooshing like small whales.

"Make way for the mulesters!" yelled Francois Badeau, "the hairy one," a burly man whose black, curly hair darkened his head, cheeks, arms, legs, chest, and upper back. Running naked to the river edge, he bellylanded into the water. At the same instant, Randy, kicking and paddling a yard away, heard a shout, "Watch out, petit garcon!" He glanced left, saw, heard, a half-dozen other cart drivers bellyplopping on the four-feet-deep water behind Badeau. Suddenly, bursts of spray and waves rolling high and hard crashed into Randy. His arms flew up, his head went under, his legs threshed wildly.

All at once he felt a strong hand under his arm lifting, holding him up. His head broke the surface, his toes touched bottom. He gasped a deep breath, opened his eyes— and looked into the black eyes and wet smile of the mulatto "Johnny" Janisse.

"Let me go! I don't need any help!" blubbered Randy, now standing head and shoulders out of the water. "I wasn't about to drown! "

"Oh but little red-head," Johnny said, "we can't risk having our petit garcon drink up the Little Blue River!" and slid away on his back.

Frowning, Randy looked around to see how many others had been watching, might have heard "petit garcon" and laughed at him. He noticed Fremont standing on the river bank, pulling on his sturdy cotton trousers. Randy quickly decided it was time to speak to him about a matter that had been bothering him ever since they left Chouteau's trading post two weeks before. Hastily he scrambled out of the river, onto the weed-covered bank.

"John—Lieutenant," he said—he still had to remind himself to call his sister Jessie's husband, and his idol, John Fremont "Lieutenant" as head of the expedition. Randy's father, had made that an order before they left Washington. "NO ONE in Lieutenant Fremont's expedition," the Senator had said, "can be exempted, EVER, from showing the leader proper respect."

"Lieutenant," Randy said, wiping water from his chin, "Can't you order the men to stop calling me 'little boy'—I know that's what 'petit garcon' means. And tell them to stop thinking they have to save me from something all the time. I'm a real good swimmer, and I know how to saddle, bridle, groom, hobble or stake my horse to graze, which is more than old Preuss does!"

"Now Randy—"

"I know how to pack my saddle bag right, too," Randy charged on, "but they keep on acting as if I don't know how to do ANYthing right. Sometimes they look at me as if I oughtn't even to be here—old Preuss does that all the time. Can't you tell him—them—what Father said about why he let me come with you—how my traveling the trail to the Rockies is IMPORTANT 'cause if I can do it safely, then families with children will know they can do it—?"

Lieutenant Fremont interrupted in his calm, polite manner to tell the naked, wet boy to call the cartographer "MISTER Preuss," not "old Preuss." He added that he thought he might be able to get the "petite garcon" message across to the men so they would not use that phrase to tease. "I know they like you, Randy, even if a few French voyageurs seem to make fun of you sometimes. They admire your knowing how to play the guitar. It might help if you played more often so they could sing to your music—that makes everybody feel better, livens up the whole camp."

Fremont sat down on the grass to pull on his boots while continuing his talk to Randy, who, frowning, stood shaking water off his arms and legs. "I doubt that any of these men have ever lived with or traveled with a 12-year-old boy," Fremont said. "Certainly these trappers who've lived in the woods for 20 years haven't known a 12-year-old like YOU!—a boy who's always lived in a big city, who's gone to school, can read and write. All but one or two of them write X for their names—Kit Carson, too!

"They like you, I'm sure of that. Their sort of clumsy,

teasing kind of attention may be what they think is the way to show they like you. Calling you 'petit garcon' may mean to them 'my young friend' or even what your sister Jessie calls you–'my pet.'"

JF Report
July 21
"petit garcon"

Fremont got to his feet, picked his cotton blouse from a bush, and began pushing his arms through the sleeves. As he pulled it over his head, he reminded Randy that all the men–from Kit Carson, guide and hunter, to the French Canadian and Creole workhands and mule-team drivers–had traveled and worked in Indian territory many years."They know by experience–some of it terrifying–the dangers we could face on this journey. They also know, for I have told them quite emphatically, that we must bring Randolph Benton back home safe and sound."

Fremont reached out to pat Randy's shoulder affection- ately. With a smile, he added, "So all of us are watching out for you–by my order keeping an eye on you every minute. Danger isn't just attacks by wild animals or Indians. Accidents and bad luck can happen. If they do, and you're five hundred miles from the nearest help, you can easily die. Our two-dozen watchful companions can pre- vent your having accidents and most bad luck."

Fremont paused, picked up his broad-brimmed Army hat and settled it over his dark curls. "And Randy, these men also know this is your first time away from family and home in Washington or St. Louis. This is your first time to live out-of-doors day and night, ride a horse ten hours a day, do everything for yourself, no servants. They know that until recently, a stableman saddled and bridled your horse–"

"Buuut!" burst out Randy, "Our stableman gave me lessons and I've been practicing since New Year's! I know I'm really good–he said I am!"

Fremont took Randy by the arm and began walking. "You practiced with an English-type bridle and a hornless saddle on a full-size horse. Here you have a Spanish saddle and gear on an Indian pony. It's safer for you to have a sec- ond or third pair of eyes checking all the details before you mount. Might save you from a broken leg. Suppose you didn't wait until your pony exhaled so you could pull the girthstrap tight around its belly? When it DID exhale, your saddle would slip when you're mounting. You'd go tumbling to the ground. A bad injury could dog you the rest of your life.

Jeff Hengesbaugh,
consultant,
Mountainman
historian.
Glorieta, N.M.
Horses, gear,
camping

"Come now–where are your clothes? By that big cotton- wood? I see your pony was tied up there after someone took him to drink. Quick now, you go get dressed. Everybody's out of the water, so we'll soon move. We're making camp about a mile from here on a little rise Carson has chosen close to the river but away from the trees. It's safer."

Randy walked fast to keep up, and tried to get interested in Fremont's explanation of the importance of a hill for a camp, how on the flat prairie, a small height lets you see approaching enemies sooner, gives you an advantage if they attack.

As Randy and Fremont approached the boy's heap of clothes, Randy sighed. "Well, so I have to get used to being called 'petit garcon' since you say it's like my sister calling me 'my pet.' But will they never stop TREATING me like a little boy?—stop laughing while they un-do what I just did, or just don't let me do ANYthing?"

He stumbled, and Fremont reached out to steady him, stopped, and said, "Suppose I assign you to a responsible job, a hard job even for an experienced man. Suppose you stuck to it, showed you're reliable and competent—and brave. It's my guess that'll speed things up for you."

Cautiously, Randy said, "A HARD job? Like what?"

"I will announce at supper that beginning tonight we will have guards throughout every night from now on. I could assign you a two-hour guard duty."

Randy drew in a quick breath, his freckled face pink and beaming. "Guard duty! You'll let me do that? You mean it?! Whooo! What'll I be guarding against? Bears? Wolves? Will I have a gun?"

Fremont looked at him with a serious, unsmiling face. "Your clothes are on the ground just there. Must I order you to go get into them?" As soon as Randy was tugging on pants, boots, and shirt, Fremont said quietly, "You'd guard against Indians."

Randy cocked his head to glance up, questioningly. "Indians? We haven't seen any since we left the Kansas River where one of the Indians spoke French. We didn't guard against them. They gave us beans 'n pumpkins 'n butter, and a cow 'n calf. Are Indians on Little Blue River different—bad Indians?"

Fremont explained that they were near Nebraska Indian Territory, and only a day or so from the Nebraska River. "We call it the Platte River. Indian 'Nebraska' and French 'Platte' both mean 'flat.' Pawnee Indians ride south from their river villages to steal horses—everything—from travelers like us. Pawnees know that whites crossing the prairie to the Rocky Mountains come up this trail to the Platte, then follow the river west. Warriors in a surprise attack can steal our horses, goods, provisions. Sometimes they kill us travelers."

"They always come at night?" Randy asked intently.

"That's not predictable," Fremont said, "but if they do, and all of us are asleep, they could unstake our horses and run off with the whole herd. If they steal our transport, we'll be stranded, and in great danger in every way.

"So, we must guard the animals and the camp through-out the night from now on. We're not in the United States any more, we're in Indian Territory according to a law made by Congress five years before you were born. The Missouri River where we began our march is the boundary—forever, Congress said, and whites can't settle on the Indians' side. But with times so hard and so many poor people wanting cheap, maybe free, land, it's my guess that this Indian Territory 'forever' won't last many more years."

Randy, puzzled, rubbed his damp, red hair. "But WE are here in Indian Territory—and the trappers have been here a long time and made this trail, didn't they?"

"Yes—but Congress sent us. If Congress says do it, it's all right to do it. And we're not staying—just passing through. As for trappers, they just took their chances. They were scattered and roaming over hundreds, thousands, of miles—trapping beavers for St. Louis merchants like our friend Mr. Chouteau. Merchants paid the trappers and sent them sup-plies. So horses hooves and wheels of a yearly wagon train are what marked this faint trail we're following."

Randy persisted. "Indians didn't bother them?"

Fremont hesitated. "Well.....I wouldn't say that. It depended on—it still depends on—how eager the Indians are for horses and white man's goods, or how angry the Indians feel about whites taking—stealing, Indians say—beavers in the creeks. It depends on how angry trappers feel about Indians stealing their horses, and killing trappers during raids. It depends on what trappers do—like destroy Indian villages—to take back horses, or avenge deaths of friends.

"Still, most of the time, most of the trappers and traders have gotten along—get along—well with SOME of the tribes. Even so, they fear Indian treachery from all of them. You've heard our men tell of surprise attacks by Indians who had pretended to be friends, lone trappers killed—"

"—and scalped?!" Randy's eyes stared into Fremont's.

"And scalped. But a party as big as ours, well armed, with even the youngest able to hit a target, we'll go our thousand miles and return with all our hair quite secure on our heads, I believe—and so does your Father. Now, untie your pony and mount. Time to move on."

Fremont walked away briskly toward his own horse. His thoughts went back to his first encounters with Indians a

JF Memoirs
p59-61 Indian Territory

Pictorial History of the American Indian. *p40,104,230 O. LaFarge*

American Heritage Pictorial Atlas. *p149(Indian Re-moval Bill-1825)*

History of the American Frontier *F.L. Paxton chap2,p12*

24

half-dozen years before. Just out of college in Charleston, South Carolina, he surveyed land for the U.S. Army—land farmed by North Carolina and Tennessee Cherokee Indians living in good houses they'd built. It was the Government's first step to take the land and force thousands of Cherokees, Choctaws, Creeks, and Chicksaws to walk hundreds of miles west—"the Trail of Tears" they call it—to grasslands north of Texas, prairie lands of the Oklahoma Indian Territory created by Congress.

Fremont,Pathmarker.
p19-28 A.Nevins
(JF youth)

President Jefferson had set the policy and President Jackson had completed it. Fremont believed it a wise and humane policy, as they said. The few thousand Indians remaining east of the Mississippi would join the 300,000 Indians already on the "great central desert" hunting their food among the millions of buffalo. They'd have no need for good farmland. White farmers growing crops on the former Indian land, would help feed 17,000,000 American citizens.

Northern Indian tribes had already occupied the north and central parts of the "desert territory," pushed there gradually during many decades, both by eastern enemy tribes and white settlers, then by the United States Army.

As for the towering Rocky Mountains rising on the western edge of the grassy plains, they walled off Spanish, Mexican, and Russian settlements along a Pacific oceanside strip of land. Some Americans, Fremont mused, couldn't see that Jefferson's "Louisiana Purchase," mostly of desert and mountains, had gained them much. Their view changed after revolutionaries had thrown out Mexico's French rulers 20 years ago and opened New Mexico to American trade at Santa Fe.

French took it
from Spanish,
Mexican
revolutionaries
executed
Maximilian,
the French
govenor,
1820

"What an exciting twenty years while I was growing up," Fremont thought. "Every trader and footloose man in the country beat a trail across the 'Great American Desert' to Santa Fe to grab a piece of the 500% profits for American trade goods. Hundreds of them ended up in the beaver trapping business in the mountains. Traders and trappers explored, made trails through the Rockies to fertile Oregon on the Pacific Ocean. Can't blame poor people for wanting to go to that land, empty—except for a few Indians and a little British trading post.

"But Americans don't know how to get across the 'great desert' or Rocky Mountains. They fear the trappers' trail will be as impractical for families in wagons as the Lewis and Clark trail to the north. I'm the one to make them a map and a day-by-day guide! I'm the one because my father-in-law, Senator Thomas Benton wanted this expedition and squeezed money for it into the Army budget. He argued that the United States must have settlers from ocean to ocean—and he's RIGHT! no matter Daniel Webster and Henry Clay roaring in Congress 'the country's complete—we should draw a line at the edge of Missouri and never go farther!'"

Old Bullion Benton
W. Chambers

Lieutenant John Fremont, surveyor of land by celestial navigation instruments, smiled to himself. "I am the luckiest man alive," he said aloud as he mounted his horse by Little Blue River. He looked with deep pleasure and pride at the wooded stream and open grassland, the former mountainmen under his command, the eight carts crammed full of supplies, the little army of mules to pull them, the herd of horses for his men. "My surveying, exploring, and mapping are bound to change my country's history," he whispered. "Who could ask for a better life?"

He glanced back to see how Randy was progressing. He heard the boy voicing an urgent question. "What kind of gun will I have—a pistol?" His face reflected an imagination running at high speed. "Is my guard duty tonight?" he added.

"Ohh...I think not—not the first night. Tomorrow night, perhaps. I'll see about a pistol for you."

Fremont moving out from the trees, saw the line of carts and men on horseback forming ahead. He urged his horse forward. Shortly, he saw Mr. Preuss sitting alone under a cottonwood tree, watching his horse nibble grass. "Hallo! Come join me!" Fremont called. Hastily, Preuss mounted. Blushing and stuttering thanks for this personal favor, he took his place beside the Lieutenant.

Randy on his Indian pony followed close behind. Picturing himself guarding his sleeping companions against harm—a man's duty—had stirred in him the most grownup sensations he had ever felt. He passed most of the next mile imagining himself minute by minute on guard duty.

How would an approaching Pawnee sound in the dark—footsteps swishing the grass? Should he call, "Who goes there?" No, he'd just fire his pistol. The Indian would yell, horses neigh, mules bellow. Running-feet sounds would fade away. Next morning, John, Kit, maybe even Mr. Preuss would shake his hand for saving the camp. Nobody would call him "petit garcon."

Beth Berryman

Hobbling the horses, all 60 of them, and 20 or so mules, keeps most of the work crew busy for an hour or more–depending on animal mood–morning, noon, and night. Tying the ends of a yard-long rope to the front feet of an animal won't automatically gain its submission or even reluctant cooperation. Randy, excused from this dangerous job, and from staking animals with a long rope to a circle of grass, observes that camping mostly means animal-tending–feeding, watering, tying them up to keep them from running away or stolen by Indians, saddling and unsaddling them. "But," Kit reminds him, "our 27 man-power, plus one boypower, has to keep our 90 horse'n-mulepower healthy'n hitched if we're gonna move our expedition across half a continent and back."

CHAPTER 3

PISTOL-TOTING JOB FOR RANDY

June 23, 1842, Little Blue River, Kansas

The trail followed the course of the Little Blue except for short-cutting its bends and curves. Ignoring the line of trees along the riverbanks, Mr. Preuss was again complaining there was nothing to see in "zis monotonous prairie. Iss no 'grand view' as you say. Iss flat, flat—viss busy-busy tall grass tvisting, making vaves in busy-busy vind. I do not onderstand your en-tOO-zee-eesm for hundreds miles of nuzzing but GRASS!" His mouth twisted in disdain, he squinted his bulgy blue eyes to gaze across a green, slightly rippled landspace to the edge-of-the-world horizon, a line almost as uninterrupted as the horizon of a slightly restless ocean.

Journal. C.Preuss June 19

"It's clearly not the Alps, Mr. Preuss," Fremont said with a small, tolerant smile, taking pains to pronounce "Preuss" as "Proyse," the German way. "But I love this open country, this space unobstructed—no trees, no houses for hundreds of miles—except once in a while there's a low, thin line of dark green marking the course of a creek or a river, just like on a map. And the sky! The big, dramatic scenery of the prairie moves high above us—clouds roaming, cavorting, warring. When they're not, and the clear black sky becomes the backdrop for a trillion dots of light, nothing below in the prairie's landscape blocks my view of those heavenly bodies.

"The heavenly bodies! What would we do without them for finding out where we're located on this Earth! It's quite miraculous that night after night wherever I am, I can EXACTLY measure with a sextant the angle made by the fixed North Star in the clear sky and my feet on solid earth. North of the Equator, that angle translates into a number telling us where to put a dot on our map for our camp—tonight in Kansas, next week in Nebraska."

Journal. C.Preuss June 19 (critical of JF's star "manipulations")

"EXACTLY measure?" mapmaker Preuss murmured, turning his head away.

In no more than a second, the 29-year-old Lieutenant had reined his horse to a stop and spoken stiffly but quietly to the 39-year-old cartographer-artist. "What exactly do you mean, sir?" His action came so suddenly that Randy's pony, close behind, almost bumped its nose against Fremont's horse, while Preuss on his mount kept moving ahead. Fremont's voice penetrated, jolted, Preuss's train of silent scoffing, for when he looked around at Fremont, his face had the expression of one who has been unpleasantly startled into wakefulness. He pulled his horse into a half-turn and faced the intense gaze of his youthful leader's shiny blue eyes.

"Explain yourself, sir," commanded Fremont calmly.

Randy had always thought Mr. Preuss's head looked, well,

JF Memoirs.
Description
of Preuss.

unlike in color and parts any head he'd ever seen. Blond, very curly hair stood up high across the top, and, in the three weeks of camping, tight blond curls had grown like a thick mossy carpet over the lower half of his face. He

Preuss Journal.
Photo portrait

blushed easily, often, when he was even slightly agitated, and his whole face stayed red a long time at the smallest suggestion that he was in error about anything.

But a red face from time to time made less of an impression on Randy than Mr. Preuss's black eyebrows. They stood out like two bushy, out-of-place dark mustaches in the wrong place. Lying between blond hair and beard, and over slightly bulging, large, transparent-blue eyes made them even more startling. "And his eyes look at you suspicious-like," Randy thought. "Feeling suspicious of everybody maybe makes the corners of his mouth droop."

Now red-faced Preuss was sounding strange as well as looking his worst. He could scarcely speak, and when a sound did come out, anxiety kept it stuck and repeating.

"V-v-v-vhy uhuhuh, Lieutenant, I-I-I vas only re-mmmembering zat your chro-nnnometer vas asleep on Sunday ven you set it at 12 o'clock as ze sun reached its highest altitude...SSir."

Charles Preuss

Fremont, his shoulders still tense, replied that after Preuss left that noon, he had wound and reset the clock, adjusted it for time lost, redone the longitude calculations of time and distance from Washington-Greenwich base-time. "I recorded our EXACT location on June 19, 1842, as longitude 96 degrees, 48 minutes and 5 seconds according to the difference between English and Kansas time. As you may

JF Report
June 19
(location)

remember, I found our latitude height measured by the sextant the night before as 39 degrees, 39 minutes and 47 seconds....exactly.

"Now, I recall, sir," he added, "that when you applied to me—in some desperation, you'll remember—for work some months ago in Washington, you made it clear that you had no training in determining latitudes or longitudes by using

Mulatto Johnny Janisse lets the German cartographer Mr. Preuss take a turn holding the mule's reins. Mr. Preuss usually rides a horse, but hates the discomfort the saddle gives his seat. His complaints gain Fremont's consent to sit with driver Johnny on the scientific instruments cart. It carries Fremont's sextants, chronometers, barometers, daguerreotype equipment, and papers as well as his personal baggage and tent-office furniture. Seven other carts carry baggage, tents, barrels and boxes, kegs and bundles of food—flour, salt pork and hams, pilot bread and crackers, coffee, sugar, rice and macaroni—as well as tobacco, cooking pots, pans, various tools and necessaries, including a bulky folded rubber raft.

JF Memoirs.
(Preuss limited
skills)
celestial navigation instruments. You are an artist, able to record on paper topographical facts—a mapmaker, a cartographer. That is the one skill you trained for in Germany, as you yourself have said."

As abruptly as he had halted his horse, Fremont now abruptly clucked it to go.

Preuss followed, stammering, "Eexxxcuse me, excuse me, I didn't see you adjust zee chronnnometer and recalculate, I did not mean—but, but I have done every dday, every one of zee topographical surveys and sketches for zee map, and zey are all drawn on paper, up-to-date, every one...Sir."

Randy moved closer, ears alert, shoulders taut, wondering what he'd hear next. He was guessing Fremont would put Preuss deeper in his place by holding himself to silence and a cold shoulder—when he heard Fremont speak. "I must teach you, Mr. Preuss, how to 'shoot the stars' with the sextant, how to use time from two chronometers, and records of moon and star movements in astronomical tables—teach you as the great French cartographer and mathematician Nicolas Nicollet taught me on my first expeditions to the American West.

"It was four years ago, in Minnesota-Dakota Territory. He mapped all the Upper Mississippi River area for our Topographical Survey. He needed an assistant, so he taught me. For me, it was better than going to a University.

"My job now is to map our trail with scientific pinpointing—latitudes and longitudes—of places from the Missouri River in Kansas to South Pass in the Rocky Mountains. It will be better if more than one of us knows how to make accurate observations of important stars, of the moon, some planets—and to do needed calculations.

"We must always keep in mind the main purpose of our journey—to bring back to Washington a scientific map showing the old trapper-trader route to the great pass into the Rockies—a reliable guide for anybody who wants to journey across the continent to Oregon. So, tonight, weather permitting, we will begin shooting the stars together to determine our latitude.

Journal.
Preuss,
June 23
"Oh—since your new duties will require extra time and effort, I will instruct Raphael Proue to saddle, groom, and feed your horse beginning today."

Preuss's back had gradually straightened. His face, redder than ever, had begun a tight smile, and he was answering in a tumble of words without stammering.

Randy's surprise turned into a tingle of pride that his Lieutenant had turned a bad moment into a surprisingly good one. And the minutes of absorbing drama had halted his imagining and rehearsing for his coming guard duty.

But now that Fremont and Mr. Preuss were moving on silently, Randy went back to seeing himself riding around the camp in the dark, hearing a small sound, cocking his pistol-hammer. He was assessing the effect a shaking hand might have on his aim when a call from Fremont banished the thought—"Randy! Hunters in view! Come!"

Randy clucked his pony to move faster, catch up with Fremont and Mr. Preuss. In a moment, he could see a little rise on the plain, just a small bump stretching out a few hundred yards or so ahead. Coming past that knoll were Kit and Maxwell galloping toward the column—hunters bringing fresh meat for supper.

But where was the meat? Neither man had a dead antelope or even a jack rabbit behind his saddle. "We had a chance at only one 'lope, no matter we saw a good herd of 'um just before starting out," Carson told Fremont a minute later. "Both shot at the critter, both missed. It disappeared into tall grass. Has to be another supper of pickled pork."

The long column coming up had been moving briskly toward the knoll, each man anticipating a dinner of fresh, roasted meat. Sixteen cartwheels had been squeaking energetically in a joyous end-of-the-day chorus as the drivers watched for the hunters' return. Then the words "pickled pork" hit the ears of the mule driver on the first cart. All carts slowed as "pickled pork" was shouted down the line.

When the carts reached the top of the little knoll, the drivers guided their mules to the usual locations for marking off a large, circular campground. "Eight carts some distance apart ain't like a barricade of fifty big wagons," Clement Lambert, the camp conductor, had noted their first night on the trail. "But eight carts distributed around a big circle means eight sheltered positions to shoot from if, God forbid, we're ever attacked."

J.Hengesbaugh (camp set-up)

Just outside the circle, each man was hobbling one or two animals so as to let them graze beside the camp, but limiting how far they could roam. The ends of a short rope tied above the front hoofs of an animal allowed it enough slack to take a step by lifting both feet at the same time, but not allowing it to run, or to stray more than a mile or so from camp. Free of harnesses and saddles, all 90 horses

Wah-To-Yah. L. Garrard p.76(hobbling horses) chap3,p6

and mules, one ox, and a cow bent their necks low to crunch off a supper of tall, still-green grass.

Randy gave his hobbled brown-and-white pony, "Spots," an affectionate cheek pat and a quick scratching between the ears, before sauntering to the baggage cart whose driver was the mulatto Augustin Janisse— "Johnny." He had the tailgate down and was pulling out bundles, boxes, and sacks, each with a large-size name initial or two painted on it.

Mr. Preuss stood by Johnny, hurrying him along. "Zis sack I vant iss not so big, just full of dirty clo'se. To vash I have no skill, no desire to learn, no time. Maybe no matter. Lice and fleas ve shall get from ze Indians anyvay. I could imitate Maxvell and Ze Kid Carson by keeping my shirt on my body until it falls off. But—I am just now lucky to engage Registe Larente for 10 cents a shirt to do my laundry. Tomorrow I vill enjoy ze feel of putting on a clean shirt—if you don't take all night, Johnny, to pull out my sack."

Journal.
Preuss,
June 21,24

Johnny stopped and slowly wiped sweat from his brow. "Yassuh, Mr. Pro-sey. You goan have yo bag in a second. Ze smell of yo' dirty laundry iss rising to ze top." He leaned into the cart, dug, pushed, tugged and jerked out a not-so-big sack marked CP. "Zat's goot," Mr. Charles Preuss mumbled, and marched off.

As Johnny threw up his arms and made a stretch-mouth face, his eyes happened to meet Randy's. Both burst out laughing.

"Randy-boy, come on, get busy and HURRY me up!" he begged, and began a sing-song with no more rhythm than tune as he hauled out the baggage. "Oh ho ho! Gotta wait yo turn—a lonnng lonnng time—yo blongins be's deeeep—all kivvered up wid a hunn-errrrrd—baaagsssss—boxxxessss—blaaanketsss—an' buuug-ssssss!"

"Aww! What bugs? You're just making that up, Johnny!" Randy laughed.

"I caught some bugs in somebody's hair—I ain't saying who—dis morning and I saved 'um fo' you, Randy. And here dey BE!" he exclaimed and tossed out Randy's rolled tent. "See? See?! There's a big Indian louse—just like Mr. Pro-sey said! It's crawling on your tent—see?—gonna jump on you!"

"Yeah, yeah! I got him!" shrilled Randy, picking up an invisible critter, impulsively leaning to tap it onto the neck of Jean Lefevre who just then was bending to pick up his tent roll. "What wuz dat?" snapped 'Fev, big, raw-boned Canadian boatman turned roustabout. His first job for

Fremont had been to lead a crew of men with 19 horses and 16 mules pulling thousand-pound loads in carts across the whole state of Missouri—St. Louis to Chouteau's trading post on the Kansas River.

"It's a tent bug! A bed partner!" Two more men, just arriving to collect their bundles, laughed at the joke and one brushed a finger on the back of 'Fev's neck—just in time to bump into 'Fev's hand. "Whass DAT?!" he hissed, and swung a huge, muscular arm around so fast he almost knocked the tickler down.

"Whoa, Fev! Whoa! Pas si vite—not so fast! C'est une petite comedie du Petit Garcon!"

Randy, not waiting to see or hear more, trudged off with his tent roll. "Petit garcon, petit garcon," he grumbled.

His regular spot for pitching the tent, which he shared with his cousin Henry Brant, was in the line-up of tents near the cart padded to carry chronometers, barometers, sextants and Randy's guitar. Some days he moved fast enough to capture one of the spaces next to Fremont's big, India-rubber cloth tent. His competitors were Mr. Preuss, Maxwell who shared a tent with Carson, although Kit slept mostly out-of-doors "under the stars," and camp conductor Lambert.

Winning the race, especially beating Mr. Preuss, became a big goal of the day for Randy. Cousin Henry, uninterested in such, arrived after Randy had pounded tent stakes into the ground, lugged Necessaries Bag, blankets, and saddle inside. Like Kit Carson, Randy used his saddle as a pillow.

Today, Randy won the race because Mr. Preuss had stopped to talk to head cook Jean Dumes. Randy could hear the complaining tune of his voice but no words, and he could see that Jean Dumes was not bothering to hear them either. Instead, the cook pressed his full attention upon a little fire shooting pointed flames through a tiny cage of kindling.

Journal. Preuss, June 21 (complains about cook)

Randy heard another familiar voice, Henry's, and saw his cousin nearby playing at fisticuffs with another 18-year-old in the party, Ben Cadot. Ben drove one of the mule carts, and Henry rode his horse alongside talking loud and laughing all day. "They just want to talk about girls all the time," Randy fumed. He and Cousin Henry, Aunt Sarah Brant's son, used to play together when Randy, his Father, his Mother, his sisters Jessie, Susan, Liz, and Sara came to St. Louis to spend the time between sessions of Congress.

But since Henry got to be sixteen a couple of years ago, he went off "to do things" with boys his age. He hadn't

(Probable reason Brant came with JF's expedition.)

wanted to spend this summer camping with John Fremont, but Senator Benton had quieted Mrs. Benton's weeping and pleading against Randy's going by promising her that Henry would go too and look after him. So here was Henry, scuffling and rolling in the grass with a wiry Canadian voyageur, strong and motley from a winter of trapping.

In the big campground circle of grass, twenty tents were going up, Fremont's and four others by the scientific instruments cart, and two or three tents by each of the other carts. Men pounded and pushed on Y-shaped poles to hold the center ridgepole, and hammered stakes in the ground to hold down the edges of the Army tent canvas. Inside, each man had his sack of clothes and bag of necessaries, and two blankets—one to spread on the grass for a bed, the other for cover. No one undressed for sleeping. Staying wrapped in shirt, britches, and a sweater for the chill of the prairie night added a noticeable softness to a grassy-earth mattress, saved time and fumbling to dress in the dark if an alarm sounded in the middle of the night.

J.Hengesbaugh (camp details)

Randy took one last look at the Henry and Ben scuffle as he came out of his tent and turned toward the big black tent where he hoped to find Fremont.

Only the Lieutenant and Mr. Preuss had more than a two-blanket bed in their tents. Expedition leader and the mapmaker each rated a sturdy box to sit on, lantern with a sperm-oil candle, an alcohol "spirit lamp," and a table with folding legs. Fremont also had a folding chair. He had to write his journal every night, shoot stars, moon, and planets every clear night, read almanacs and tables, check latitude and longitude figures, keep daily records of weather, land heights, air temperatures. He also pressed flowers, leaves, and grass, preserved insects and small creatures like lizards, boxed soil or rock samples, all for the government's official collection.

Mr. Preuss had to record the daily distance they traveled, and all along the way make a survey and record location, size, and height of hills and rivers, convert those heights and shapes into lines and circles drawn in the right place on the all-important map. If he had energy left, Mr. Preuss sketched landscapes with his pencils.

Randy, arriving at the doorway of Fremont's tent, saw Fremont sitting at his table, writing. "John?"

"Randy! Come in! I need to talk to you!" Fremont cheerfully welcomed his young brother-in-law. "I've just written out the names and hours for guard duty beginning tonight. I'll announce them at supper, but I wanted to tell you ahead of time that your turn will be tomorrow night, 10 o'clock to midnight. You'll be stationed by the scientific instruments cart near my tent. Kit Carson will be two carts away on one side, Cousin Henry will be two carts away on the other side.

"You'll stand watch on the outside edge of the camp circle, each of you staying in the shadow of the cart. No, you don't walk or ride about. Kit will give you further instructions."

Randy could feel his face flushing red and warm with excitement, felt the heat spreading through his scalp and ears. "John," he whispered, "what about my weapon?"

Fremont smiled, rose from his seat and put his arm around Randy's shoulders. "You've done so well with the pistol during target practice, of course it's a pistol you should carry. Kit will loan you one of his when you and he and Henry get together after supper tomorrow.

"Now one word of advice: You can expect the trappers and voyageurs to spend the next few hours after the guard duty announcement telling you gruesome stories about Indian attacks they or some good friend have lived through. Just listen. Keep a straight face. No questions. You may feel a little scared, but keep telling yourself that even if we are attacked—which is not likely—with sharp shooters like Kit and Maxwell and Basil—"

JF Report
June23-24
(scary stories aimed at Randy)

"—and you!" interrupted Randy, who had seen his idol shoot five bulls'-eyes in a row with a pistol, and a skinny, wriggling weasel at 50 feet with a rifle—

"—and with two dozen more men, all experienced at wielding rifles and pistols, we can well protect ourselves, our horses, and carts of supplies. Now, go to supper. I'll come shortly..." He walked Randy to the tent opening, and gave a parting squeeze to the shoulders of a soon-to-be pistol-toting, midnight protector of the camp.

Based on Alfred Miller (top)

"Seems I'm hungry all the time." Randy tells Chief Cook Dumas. Smells from the boiling coffee, the frying bread and fat salt pork–"bacon"–make him even hungrier, no matter he ate the same fare three times yesterday, and several days before. But this morning, a big change! Cook made a pot of rice to dribble with fat drippings–gravy!

CHAPTER 4

SCARY TRAINING FOR GUARD DUTY

June 23, Little Blue River Valley camp

Twenty-seven hungry men!

To quickly cook and serve a meal so no one would have
to wait, four two-part fires had been built a few yards apart
near the cart in which the flour barrel and pickled pork barrel were sitting. At all four "messes," coffee pots did their
boiling on one bed of coals, frying pans sizzled, or stewpots
simmered on the other. Four watercarriers and four firewood gatherers—Randy occasionally volunteered to be one or
the other—hurried to and from the river and its trees.

*J.Hengesbaugh
(camp cooking,
dining)*

At Fremont's mess for six sitting-on-the-ground diners,
including Randy, and two never-sitting cooks, Cook Tessier
sliced salty pork—"bacon"—on top of the pork barrel, threw
the pieces into a huge frying pan to cook. In between forking the sizzling bacon slices to turn them over, Cook
Dumes stirred flour, water, and lard into bread dough,
pinched off chunks, slapped them into flat pancakes, and
threw them into a huge frying pan of fat he poured off the
frying bacon. When the stack of hard fried bacon matched
in height the stack of hot pancakes, and the giant coffee
pots—first things put on the fire—sang with steam rolling
off a hard boil, the cooks declared the game won, struck
their hands together, and yelled, "Come and git it!!" One,
two, or three minutes later, they'd hear the same call at
other messes.

The hot crusty bread and crisp strips of meat washed
down with boiled, sweetened and creamed coffee tasted
good, filled empty middles, gave such a satisfied feeling
that the men and boy could almost forget they had eaten,
would eat, the same fare for breakfast, midday, and supper
for days. That is, all men except Mr. Preuss who grumped
to himself as he chewed, "Meat'n'bread, meat'n'bread,
nuzzin but meat'n'bread."

*Journal.
C. Preuss
June 19*

A tin plate apiece to lay hot, greasy bread and pork
upon, and a few spoons to pass around for stirring sugar
into tincups full of hot coffee, aided the primary eating
tools—fingers. Whether the diner did his chewing while
standing knee-deep in grass, leaning against a cart, or, like
Fremont, Mr. Preuss, Carson, Maxwell, Lambert, and

Randy, sitting on the ground around a sun-whitened buffalo-skin "tablecloth," in five minutes the diner's stack of fried bread and meat slices were all swallowed. Drinking a second cup of hot coffee, smoking a pipeful of tobacco could take another half-hour.

To call the attention of everyone to Lieutenant Fremont now standing beside the "tablecloth," Basil Lajeunesse began blowing an Indian hunting whistle used for luring deer. "Bleee-eet, bleee-eet, bleeeet!" sounded like a mama deer calling her young. "Dis is a call for you to come close, listen to Lieutenant Fremont! He has somet'ing important to say!" Basil's voice boomed. "He'll read de list of names for guard duty tonight and tomorry night!"

Journal.
Preuss,
June 21
(Bleet,bleet)

Fremont repeated what they all knew—that Pawnee Indians in this area close to the Platte River were daring thieves, that the camp's horses were in far more danger than the men. Beginning at 8 o'clock tonight, three men, one at each of three carts, would keep armed watch for two hours when they'd be relieved by the next team of three. The fifth and last shift would serve from six in the morning all the rest of the day as horseguards.

When the name "Randy" was read after Carson's and Brant's for 10 o'clock the next night, handslapping and knee whacking mingled with scattered cries of "Bravo!" "Tres bon!" "Grand garcon!"

And as Fremont had predicted, Randy was quickly approached by several men with extra-wide smiles. First they slapped his shoulder and said, "Un petit garcon tres brave!" then teasingly asked him in French mixed with Frenchized English, about his experiences doing guard duty in Washington.

Frances Stadler,
curator, retired, Mo.
Historical Society. St.
Louis history

Randy understood the good French part of their French, and part of the slang. In the half-years he spent in St. Louis at his Grandma Benton's house, then after she died, at the Brants, Randy had heard French every day on the streets, in the shops. When he was ten, his father hired a tutor to teach him to speak properly the language of the city's founders and many of its present residents. Local French, and Creole French from downriver Mississippi, as well as Canadian voyageur French, Randy had heard in St. Louis as frequently as American English. No Spanish despite Spain's 40-year hold on St. Louis—until Napoleon of France reclaimed all "Louisiana" before selling it to the United States. That had happened only 35 or so years ago.

"Pas de sauvages a Washington, eh? No savages in Washington?" Francois Badeau, "the hairy one," queried Randy. "Well, uh," answered Randy, "I've seen Indian chiefs with feather bonnets, and some bald Senators that looked scalped. Nobody guards anybody in Washington, so I never got any experience. Is it hard to sit real still in the dark for two hours listening for Indians? Don't you get sleepy?"

"Ef you ain't never done no sitting in the dark list'nen fer savages," chimed in 22-year-old Michel Marly of St. Louis, "I jes' better tell you it ain't no little boy job. Cain't keep your eyes open one minute, scared to jitters the next. A mule snuffles—you know they's somebody close by. Yer trigger finger tightens up—but you first make sure t'ain't one o'yer own men draining hisself—"

Basil Lajeunesse's lively voice interrupted, "Mon ami, it all depends." The young trappers leaned forward respectfully. Basil, age 39, had Indian stories from 20-some years back, for he'd done trapping in the Rockies since he was 17. Among trappers, hired or independent, he was known as quick to size things up, accurate with bullet and story, strong as an ox, and, as Fremont had been heard to remark, "spry as a mountain goat."

"Oui. I learned 'it all depends' from Jim Beckwit' not long after I come west. We werz in de first bunch of 100 men working for General Ashley of St. Looie. De General got dis Rocky Mountain beaver trapping going as a business, you know. Jim Beckwit' had took me under his wing—I wuz a lad just run away from home—Jim he always called me 'brudder.' One night when we and some ot'ers werz sleeping on nearly 200 packs of furs wort' $1000 apiece—our year's work, dem packs, and dey werz to start by cart for St. Looie next day—we werz woke by de guard.

Adventures of James Beckwourth (autobiography)p51,13 76,142,404,586

"He whispered he'd heard somet'ing he bleev'd wuz Indians. We raised up, peered into de dark and werz satisfied he wuz right. We raised two men next to us. Wi'hout a speck of noise we all took aim de best we could at de suspect bushes. When Jim said 'psst' we all fired. In de dark we heard some rustling and t'umps, den not'ing.

"In no time, everybody in camp had come running to us. Even General Ashley. He hisself had led de 20-wagon train of supplies across de prairie for our next year's stay, and would lead back his carts loaded wit' $200,000 wort'o furs. He said to Jim, 'What werz you firing at?' and Jim said, 'I bleeve it wuz uh Indian.' 'Well,' said de General, 'any time

40

you T'INK an Indian is in de camp at night, you do right to start shooting.' Dat night, no more Indian sounds. Camp went back to sleep.

"At daylight we found TWO dead Indians lying in de area we had shot at in de dark. One had a rifle ball t'rough his head. De ot'er had a ball t'rough his arm and body. Well, Jim and me had shot rifle balls. De ot'er two men had fired shotgun pellets."

"Bon! Bon!" cheered the young trappers. "Bull's eyes wid your eyes closed!" "Did you take scalps? Were dey dem bad Blackfeet?" All three young men talked at once in a tangle of gnarled French and chawed English. "Naw—dey werz good Crows," said Basil. "Friend or foe, dey's all hoss t'ieves. So are we if we need hosses. Didn't scalp. Easy to scalp warm bodies, cold'uns not so easy. We just stripped de buckskin leggings off'n one—real pretty leggings dey werz—and Jim wore dem a good while."

Randy, mouth dropped open, was wondering how much of Basil's storytelling was lies like Mr. Preuss had said, then he was forgetting Fremont's advice to keep quiet, no questions, and was inquiring in his boy-soprano, "Who is Jim Beckwit?"

"You never hear of Jim Beckwit', boy? Kit Carson didn't tell you 'bout Jim? I didn't see Jim since a long time ago at a Rondyvoo on Green River. He went off to de Powder River, fork of de Yellowstone, wit' a party of trappers headed by Jim Bridger. You never hear of Jim Bridger? Dat's only because you've been on eart' too few years. Dere's not a mountainman dat didn't hear a hundred stories 'bout Jim Bridger—he's a Number One—like Kit Carson, like Tom 'Broken Hand' Fitzpatrick, like Charlie Bent, Jedediah Smith, and my 'brudder' Jim Beckwit'.

"About a year or so after me and Jim parted, my 'brudder' begun living wit' de Crow Indians. Pretty soon he wuz deir Chief! Many a tale has circulated 'roundabout Chief Jim. De Crows done real good de six'r seven years he led dem—it's said he killed at least a t'ousand of deir enemies, married I don't know how many Crow girls. I hear he tells folks he quit de Chief job 'cause he got tired of killing, scalping, and listening to Crow women howl day and night for WEEKS after deir warriors got killed whilst stealing another tribe's horses.

"Jim looked like an Indian, 'bout the same brown color. Had long black hair, but curly whereas Indian hair's straight. No, he wuzn't no Indian. He wuz a mulatto. He told me his Papa wuz a white man and his Mama a black slave in Virginia. When his papa moved to St. Louis he brought all his t'irteen young'uns wid him, whatever color dey werz. But let me tell you somet'ing: Wuzn't no man smarter dan Jim Beckwit' and probably no ot'er man fought as many Indians, killed as many, scalped as many as my 'brudder' Jim, or so I'm told. He left de Crows in '36—dat's six years ago.

"Last time I heard anyt'ing 'bout him, he and his latest wife, a white woman, werz trading white man's goods for furs'n'robes wid Indians between de Sout' Fork of de Platte River and Bent's Fort on de Arkansas. Jim for a while worked outta de big fort dat Mr. Bent and Mr. St. Vrain built on de Sout' Platte. You can see de Rockies from dat fort."

The keen ears of Lieutenant Fremont, just walking up, caught the names "Bent" and "St. Vrain." Although he had come to rescue Randy from gory tales of attacking Indians, his first remark was a question. "Fort St. Vrain, you say? You've been there?"

Lajeunesse had been there, worked there. "How far is it—how many days' march is it, say, from the North and South Platte river fork?" "Oh, 'bout 150 miles, 'bout a five-day hard ride. Pretty level." "Is it level north from there to Fort Laramie?" "Yep."

"St. Vrain's keeps a good stock of provisions?" "Most times." "Mules and horses to sell?" "Prob'ly. Indians bring stolen horses, trade'um for red cloth and beads."

Bent's Fort.
D.Lavender.
Fort St.Vrain

"Indians friendly?" "'Rapahoes 'n' Cheyennes—yep. St. Vrain boss—de booshway—always treats'um honest."

Fremont smiled, his gaze holding Lajeunesse's eyes for a moment. "Arapahoes? Maxwell mentioned something about living in an Arapahoe village while working out of St. Vrain's Fort just before he came to St. Louis where I met him. You two at the fort about the same time?" Basil nodded.

Turning away, Fremont said to Randy, "Oh—Kit Carson's waiting for us! He said he'd walk right now with you and Henry—if you can find him—to see where he, you, and Henry will be stationed tomorrow night. So come along—Kit's waiting for us at my tent. Good evening, men. You'll all get your turn at this unpopular, and I hope boring, night duty from now on. But your friends can sleep sounder knowing you're wide awake, watching, listening for Pawnees."

On their way to Fremont's tent, they looked around for Henry. Randy spotted him sitting on the grass playing cards with Ben Cadot and two other muleteers. "Well," Fremont said, "they're in the middle of a hand. You can show him around later—before dark. It's always better to do your looking around when it's light and the weather's friendly. I feel the wind rising, see clouds gathering, rain coming."

Longitude
Dava Sobel.

Kit Carson was waiting in front of Fremont's tent, and the three of them strolled to the cart, Randy's station, a few minutes' walk behind Fremont's tent. Fremont opened a padlock on the tailgate, reached in to get a hat-size box. "Inside this well-padded, spring-seated box is a Chronometer—a clock—showing Washington, D.C. time," he said. "With the hour it shows when our clock here shows noontime, I can count the difference in hours and calculate our longitude. That's our distance west of baseline longitude at Greenwich, England. I'll take the box to my tent and give this large-size watch its regular winding. It mustn't run down, or we'll hardly be able to tell where we are along our line of latitude!"

When Fremont went off, Carson asked Randy if he knew how a clock figured into longitude, whatever that was. "No," Randy said, "I think you have to be a Scientific Celestial Navigation Mapmaker to know mysterious things like that."

Kit gazed after Fremont and rubbed his chin. "Well, son, the onlyest thing you need to know from me right now is where to stand, lean, or squat—you'll do all of 'um in two hours' guard duty—and that place is here between the cartwheel and the cart's tongueshaft. You see how the tongue is slanted to the ground and pointing out toward the nearest tent. It'll shadow and hide you, and the wheel will give you sum'um to prop against.

"Whilst you're doing that, keep in mind that the reason you're staying awake is to hear suspicious sounds and see little give-away movements in the dark. You can see a lot in the dark out here on the prairie just by starlight when the sky's clear—or just by a little moonlight when there's clouds. You have to keep still and quiet yourself—don't even breathe or yawn in a hurry.

J.Hengesbaugh
(guard duty,
instructions)

"Your movin' will catch an Indian's eye same as his movin' ought to catch your eye—though Indians can move silent n'still as ghosts. But if you do hear a little noise like grass swishing, you should lean down close to the ground, look toward the swish and the sky above it for a black silhouette against the stars—the shape of a man standing or crouching.

"That's when you pull the trigger of your gun. Aim straight up in the air. Just the noise nearby will scare him

43

off. Usually at a camp like this, only one or two Indians on foot will try to sneak up to staked horses, cut one or two loose, jump on them, and race off. One shot before a rope is cut or a stake pried up will change the Indian's mind."

"Or kill him, like Basil did," Randy said, wide-eyed.

"Well...more'n likely you won't have a story to tell like that," Kit answered in his gentle drawl.

Randy looked toward the second cart on his left, then at the second cart on his right. "I have to sit still by my cart, watch all that distance between me and four other carts? They're a long ways off!"

Kit nodded. "Your eyes haf'ta keep sweeping the open space out beyond all them carts, being that's the grassy space where the horses are staked for the night. But like I told you, even with nothing but starlight, you can see grass swaying when anybody's walking in a crouch, or even slithering through it on his belly."

Kit saw Randy's expression of dismay at the word "slithering" and hastily added, "When an Indian gets real close to the camp, he'll slither like a snake, not walk upright, but you can hear him. The animals, especially mules, can hear him even better. They'll snuffle, snort, whinny, and they'll dance around, move their heads quick, startled like, when somebody suddenly comes close in the dark. BUT—a thief will need to stand up to grab-ahold a horse and leap on. Then YOU can see him. Don't think of aiming your shot at the thief and the horse—you're likely to hit the horse.

"Now don't you worry a whole lot, Randy. I'll be at the second cart on the right there. I'll be close enough you can holler at me if you think you see sum'um. The Lieutenant's closer and will prob'ly hear you, too. Holler loud. Shriek. You'll prob'ly scare off any thief."

But Randy couldn't help worrying "a whole lot." Inside his head, over and over he saw pictures of oddly moving grass—an Indian slithering toward him, then a man's shape in the sky, blotting out stars. He hardly slept longer than five minutes at a time all night.

With his guard duty only one night away, Randy's imagination, fired by cartdrivers' tales of Indian attacks, flames with scary pictures. He sees himself alone in the night facing Indians with long scalping knives, hearing horse thieves slithering toward him through tall, breeze-murmuring grass.

CHAPTER 5

EXTREMELY DANGEROUS JOB!

June 24, 1842, Little Blue River, Kansas

"TURN OUT!!" called camp conductor Lambert.
Randy jerked half awake, alarmed. A boot-toe nudged his
foot. He heard Henry growl, "Up!"

"I'm too tired." How weary a body can get from threshing about in bed trying to stay asleep while slithering
Indians worry his mind. Randy sighed to himself. In the
tense grayness of the hour before sunrise, he could hardly
bear thinking of lifting his head and shoulders from the
warm bed of blanket, grass, and ground, so restful now that
it was time to get up. Dreamily he felt for one wink of a
second that his bed on Kansas earth was as soft as his bed
at home.

But then he heard the deep voices of men, their cough-
ing and throat-clearing and nose-blowing, the cooks' rat-
tlings of coffeepot lids, the neighing of horses beyond the
camp circle, the faint, soothing murmurs of the horse
guards changing night-time stakes to daytime hobbles for
each animal and leading them to fresh patches of grass.
Randy pushed his blanket cover aside.

*J.Hengesbaugh
(starting a day
in camp)*

Eyes still closed, he sat up. Slowly he rose to his knees.
With a yawn so deep it drew apart his eyelids, he levered
himself upright with an elbow. Shivering when a chilly gust
of wind puffed through the tent flap, he pulled his boots
on. He stuck his head out the door. Camp conductor
Lambert, passing by, yelled, "Turnout, sluggards!" and suddenly everybody was rolling blankets, moving baggage to
carts, taking down tents. Cooks shouted "Come git it!" then
began beating pans impatiently, calling, "Caff-aye! Caff-aye!
Plenny sugar 'n' rich, new-skimmed-off cream !"

Barely had a fiery red glow of the sun topped the naked,
faraway horizon when the caravan of horsemen, carts, and
animals began to move from the camp site. Fremont and
Carson headed the column as usual, the Lieutenant on a
horse with such a reliable number of steps per minute and
miles per hour, it automatically measured distance traveled
during a day. Just behind Fremont and Carson, Randy's
somewhat smaller Indian pony stepped dutifully along.
Beside him, Maxwell's over-lively mount was requiring much

hauling on the reins.

Camp conductor Lambert roamed up and down the line looking for problems—packloads coming loose, slow-poke riders, animals allowed to meander out of line. At least twice a day, he could be heard voicing the law of his life, "ORDER! ORDER! The Good Lord and Lambert love ORDER!"

Near the end of the line, between the spare mules and the ox and cow, rode Mr. Preuss, the corners of his mouth drooping lower than usual. Up until today he had been permitted to ride as far as a mile in advance of the column to do topographical surveying and sketching of land features, their shapes, sizes, heights, and depths. But this morning at breakfast, "HE," as Mr. Preuss privately referred to Fremont, had told him to move to a place near the end of the column "for protection in this area of hostile Pawnees."

Journal.
Preuss,
June 24

"Stay in line wiz ze cow," Mr. Preuss mumbled in German. "HE said it vas too dangerous to ride on ahead, alone. Ach! Stupid! I hate being stuck here wiz zese animals and horse guards, zis Frenchy rabble around me. Ze littered track of ze column smells like a stable. Ugh! Stupid! If I just had someone to talk to in my language! Ach! Zen I vish I had a bottle of good wine. Oh vell, I must take SUCH a journey as zis to remember to enjoy consciously at home ze comforts I ordinarily pay no attention to."

Overhead, a thick layer of white and gray clouds had moved across the vast dome of the sky, leaving a border of bright blue all around the horizon. The wind, however, persisted in pushing eastward this friendly cloud umbrella, allowing darker clouds to crawl menacingly if slowly from the west. "Glad for a cloudy, cool day," Fremont said to Carson, then to Maxwell and Randy behind him. "No rain last night after all—just clouds keeping me from star-gazing.

"But rain tonight wouldn't surprise me. Did either of you ask Moise Chardonnais, our master cloud reader, what news he sees in the sky?"

Carson and Maxwell answered something about the Intuitive Method of Moise, a combination blacksmith and self-taught animal doctor. The three men laughed—but not Randy. His thoughts had begun fading into dreams.

Wide-brimmed hat pulled low on his forehead, he had kept his eyes open long enough to knot together the pony's reins and slip the loop over the horn of his saddle. With his hands resting atop the horn, he imagined himself secure and gave-in to an overwhelming desire to sink into the sleep

47

that had refused to envelope him during the night.

Through his mind flickered pictures of horses, trees—and his mother sitting in the grass in front of the house on C Street within sight of Pennsylvania Avenue and the Capitol in Washington, D.C.. Sister Jessie was standing close by her.

Mother seemed to be pinning something on a skirt Jessie was wearing, and Randy knew Jessie was getting ready to go to a reception at President Tyler's house across the street, except the White House wasn't that close to the Benton's except in dreams. Jessie looked very pretty with her dark red hair rolled into a bun at the back of her head. She was saying, "But Mother, the daughter of a Senator can't go to the reception without an escort!"

Jessie Fremont
P. Herr

Then she grabbed Randy's arm and said, "Oh, but Randy's a grand garcon—come, my pet, escort me to the President's House!" Randy saw himself in his everyday clothes—knee pants, a floppy shirt, no shoes—being grabbed and hauled across the street. Jessie WAS bossy even if she was his favorite sister of four.

Randy heard himself say, "But Jessie! I can't go! I have to stand guard for two hours in case Indians come to steal Mother!" Jessie snatched away her hand and swished off, half-running. Randy watched her all the way to the front door of the White House. He saw Father was waiting for her there, big and majestic in his full blue cloak and his broad-brim, high crown hat. Randy wanted to run to him and tell him about his guard duty against Pawnees, but his mother was calling. "Randy! Come to the table! Your pancakes are ready!" Then Cook was plopping hot pancakes on his plate, and he was pouring on a flood of syrup and melted butter.

Maxwell, straining to hear what Fremont and Carson were talking about, was paying no attention to the boy beside him. But Lambert on his trouble-checking tour arrived alongside Randy's pony just in time to see the rider's head slump forward and his relaxed hands jerk to tighten their hold on the saddle horn. Quietly, Lambert reached out to grasp a limp rein and gently tug it to lead the pony and sleeping boy slowly out of the advancing line. He turned the pony in a wide curve heading toward the end of the line.

J.Hengesbaugh
(riding asleep
in circles)

Lead cart driver Janisse began a whooping laugh, smothered it with his hand when he saw Lambert's forefinger rise to his lips, shhh. Into the wide space between Janisse's cart

48

and the mules pulling the next, Lambert gently led Randy's pony, then led it into a turn back toward the head of the line. Lambert suddenly called loudly to Janisse, "Hey! Think this fellow's dreaming about riding a merry-go-round?!"

Janisse's laughter made Maxwell look around—and yelp with laughter at the sleep-circle joke Lambert was playing. Carson and Fremont glanced behind. Their faces broke into wide smiles just as Lambert called out loudly, "Which way to Fort Laramie, Mr. Benton?!" Randy's head jerked up, his eyes wide with surprise and half-awake puzzlement at finding himself on the left side of Maxwell, and five men around him laughing hard.

"What happened?" he asked, bewildered. Then he saw Lambert wagging a finger at him and saying, "When your eyes are closed, being led in circles to strange places beats tumbling from saddle to ground!" Randy blushed, felt foolish, began laughing, too. He said to himself he'd never, never be sleepy again—at least not sitting on top of a moving horse.

The trail they plodded along lay within sight of the Little Blue River and its large cottonwoods, and was well-marked by many hooves and wagon wheels. Fremont commented that if the clouds did drop some rain, the wheel ruts and

JF Report
June 21

tracks of horses and cattle herd would be washed away. "I'll miss them," Fremont said. "Riding over the footprints of the Oregon-bound missionary folks relieves the loneliness of the road a little. Camping at two of their stopping places some days ago gave me the warm feeling they were fellow travelers, no matter they're two, three, weeks gone."

Suddenly, Randy heard a wild cackling noise. It grew louder and louder and LOUDER. "Kit! What kind of animals make such a noise?! Hyenas? They must be over there by the river, hiding in the trees! Don't you need to get your rifle ready?!"

*Journal
Preuss,
June 24*

Carson, who'd made no move to raise his gun, looked behind him at Randy and answered with a broad grin. "Not hyenas out here in Kansas, Randy. Just big, fat, scared turkeys, probably a flock of a hundred or two. They're sitting up high in the big trees by the river quite a ways down the slope. What's bothering them? Probably us. Our horses and squeaky cartwheels sound menacing, so they scream in a cackling chorus to scare us away. "

*JF Report
June 24
(turkeys,
botanicals)*

On the prairie side, Fremont called attention to "botanicals" and their beauty—bouquets of wild roses shining through the grass, purple clusters of amorpha, and more and more silver-leafed wild sage.

"The slopes on the low, grassy hills over there bordering our valley on the east look uncommonly bright and beautiful this morning," Fremont observed. "Yes," said Carson, "and if we moved a little off trail and closer to them later today, we could bring our animals to some extrafine forage. About 20 miles ahead, we'll come to a creeklet that runs into Little Blue, and if we turn east along that creek, follow it about an hour toward the hills, we'd come to a big acreage of prele–or horsetail herb.

JF Report
June 24
(prele)

"It's real good for animals. It grows in tree shade all over a low wet area around the creek, brightest light-green plants you ever saw. They're shaped like foot-high Christmas trees— but folks who call it 'horsetail' think they're shaped like a horse's tail. Prele plants don't have leaves–just stem-like branches, smooth and crunchy as an apple. Horses love it. Right now it's at its best–crisp, juicy. Very strong food for animals. Ours need it after two weeks of working their way across hot Kansas, swimming big and little streams, crossing drylands. It's worth going out of our way, adding a few miles to the day, to strengthen the animals."

Growing, Using,
Healing with Herbs.
G/S Weiss, p165

Maxwell's excited voice broke in. "Loook! Look up there on our right–on top of that long, low rise–an elk! No, three elks! Kit, we're bound to eat a good supper tonight!" Kit looked, judged the elks were too far away, and made no move to go after them. "Now, Max you know distances out here in these big spaces fool you," he said in his soft drawl. "T'would take us a half-hour to gallop to where the elks are now. By then they'd be long gone n' miles away."

Miles and hours later, they made their midday stop under the great oaks of a large grove by the river. Water splashed cool and wet on faces, filled cupped hands and was drawn into dry mouths in one breath. Animals slupped up water by the gallon. The cooks began building fires, filling kettles with water and ground coffee, and slicing saltpork for the frypans. When horses and mules, cow and ox had been led to nearby grass to feed, the men gulped down their rations and settled under the big oaks for the next hour to stretch out and nap, play card games, tell stories of narrow escapes, forget about riding a horse six hours to cover 18 miles of flat, monotonously blank landscape.

Randy resisted taking a nap, and instead watched Fremont and Mr. Preuss do their mid-day chore of recording the heights of mercury columns on barometer and thermometer. That didn't look hard, he thought. But finding the instant when the sun was at it highest point overhead—noon—and comparing 12 o'clock in Kansas with Washington and English time—or so John had told him—on the special chronometer looked mysterious.

His attention flitted to Cousin Henry. Had he talked to Kit Carson about how a guard watches for and SEES Indians in the night? Henry had stayed in the muleteers' tent until late last night "just talking," and slipped into his own tent and bed so silently he hadn't interrupted Randy's many anxious thoughts.

Did Henry have any idea that Indians slither through the grass on their bellies like snakes? Randy pondered. Maybe he ought to tell Henry. Randy left Fremont talking to Mr. Preuss about minutes and seconds and degrees of longitude, and began wandering the campground looking for his cousin. He found him in a circle of card players.

"Henry, did Kit tell you—"

"Good lordy, Cuz Randy, m'boy, guard duty is hours and hours away—plenty of time to find out what I'm supposed to watch for, where I'm going to stand, what I do if and when I see a suspicious anything. Now you go play your guitar and dance a jig—we've got a life and death game going on here." He took a puff on his pipe and turned back to his card game with the young muleteers from St. Louis and Taos who had become his special friends—Ben Cadotte, Dan Simonds, and Mike Marly.

Clenching his fist, Randy said fiercely as he walked away, "Well, anyway, you shoulda gone with Kit and me last night! You're gonna be sorry when an Indian slithers up and you feel a knife cutting a circle on your skull!"

Nearby, two young French Canadians, one short and round, one a muscular rail, both in fringed deerskin britches bought in St. Louis, stood leaning against a tree watching the card game, listening. They snickered. The round one poked the slim one. Both quickly knocked the tobacco ash from their pipes and followed Randy.

Just past a big willow tree, they caught up with him. "Hi, Randy, we heard what was said back dere," said Tessier, the tall "rail." He was a "dark Frenchman" who may have had an Indian mother though he denied it. He patted Randy's shoulder and said "You shouldn't worry so much, petit garcon. Trut' is you're not going to see a t'ing while you're on

51

duty tonight. De only t'ing you'll hear is crickets. De only place where a guard ought to worry is Blackfeet Indian country, way fart'er west. You'll be going dere."

"Oui!" Larent said. "Francois knows all about Indians! He's had beaucoup experience guarding camps!"

Tessier nodded. "Pawnees are rabbits compared to Blackfeet—Piednoires. Dey hate whites, and in de first place dey're just plain mean—t'ieves, killers, treacherous—and second, dey've got good guns'n'powder, balls'n' flints. Most Indians have bad guns dey bought wid beaver pelts from whites, but de Piednoires STOLE de trappers' and traders' BEST guns. Know how to use'um, too."

Journal of a Trapper.
Osborne Russell
(Blackfeet)

"Oui, oui!" Larent exclaimed, nodding vigorously.

"When dey go on a raid," Tessier went on, "dey ride de best horses, all of 'um stole. I've seen'um charge full gallop into our camps, broad daylight AND middle of de night, screaming and screeching most terrible—dat's scary. No slit'ering at night on deir bellies. Dey werz after our horses a'course but dey werz after our scalps, too. You're lucky dere's only Pawnees 'round here."

Larent agreed, "C'est vrai! True, true!"

"Lemme tell you, Randy," Tessier said, leaning down, his hand on Randy's shoulder, "when twenty or more Piednoires on horses crash into your camp, you'll be so scared you'll forget how to load your gun—"

"Ahh—c'est terrible—oui,oui—"

"Last fall, I was trapping in de Rockies wid a group of about 40 men when one night we woke up to mos' dreadful screeching, yelling, and de pounding of what sounded like a hundred horses' hooves on de ground INSIDE our camp circle! Piednoires werz firing into our TENTS 'fore we could jump to our feet! I wuz shaking—like dis—I wuz so scared." Tessier held out his vibrating hands.

"Mon Dieu—" breathed Larent.

"It didn't matter dat guards had been watching around de camp edge—dey didn't see ner hear not'n 'til de Indians werz on top of us and shooting. It wuz a skinny-moon night, we couldn't see much, but neit'er could dey, so dere wuz a lot of up-in-de-air gun firing. Went on a long, long time. Den dey alla-sudden left. Dey might've seen dere wuz more of us dan expected—or dey may have fired all deir loaded guns and couldn't reload in de dark while dey rode and yelled. Or dey noticed t'ree of deir men fall, and ot'ers hurt. So dey just herded away 14 of our horses, killed five more, wounded t'ree ot'ers."

"Terrible!" whispered Larent.

"We men fared better dan de horses—only one of us hurt. But you see, even if guards keep good watch, a pack of raiding Indians can all a-sudden crash in, steal, kill your horses, wreck your supplies. Everybody knows Indians are like fleas—liable to jump on you any time, any place, no matter what. Guards get blamed sometimes, accused of sleeping, sentenced to walk de trail ALL next day. But dey ain't to blame. Trut' is, Indians sneak up like ghosts—"

"Oui! oui! vraiment! really! tout invisible—!"

"—and guards have no chance to warn de camp!"

Tessier ended his story with a sharp intake of air. Larent nodded sympathetically, hastily began the tale he had impatiently held back while his partner finished his. Larent was a short butterball of a man, known for going back to the cooks for seconds or thirds, eating all scroungeable scraps.

Adventures of a Trapper in the Rockies. p.8,9,10 *Zenas Leonard*

"Oui, oui—de night guard's always taking a lot of risk! One night when I wuz doing guard duty, I had to go outside camp where de horses werz and move de stakes so de animals could feed more. A hundred horses! But t'ree ot'er guards helped wid de staking. All a-sudden, I heard CRACK! CRACK! ZING! and Indian shrieks.

"De 'zing' ball had hit my arm—right here. I hadn't been on de ground long enough to holler when an Indian dropped from nowhere on top of me and ketched aholt of my topknot. He was pulling HARD, and I was twisting and yelling, terrrrfied—I felt a cut on my forehead—see, right here, a little scar—I knowed my skin wuz 'bout to rip off quicker'n a jackrabbit can jump, when alluva sudden he let go, said 'ungh' and fell off me, a knife in his back. My friend Baptiste had killed him! Just as quick, he grabbed my arm right where dat bullet had hit—hurt like hell—and pulled me in a run back inside de campground.

"We heard shooting, screaming, yelling all'round—de whole camp had rushed out dere. Dey werz too late to save de other guard who wuz hit, or to keep de Indians from herding off 15 horses. Dey left two Indians dead, one hurt. We helped him get dead as de ot'ers, den kilt two hurt horses. We didn't go after de stolen 15. Wish we had."

This story was so vivid that Randy and both men stopped walking in the middle of it, stood stock-still to hear better. "Do you mean you sometimes DO chase them—kill the Indians, take the horses?" Randy gasped.

"Naturellement! Once we went 40 miles, fought and won and took about 30 horses back to camp. Ot'erwise we'd've been stranded a hundred miles from anybody wid no transportation. Kit Carson one time chased some Indian horse t'ieves 100 miles! Burned a whole village, took his horses and deir herd, too!"

Randy, heart pounding, face red, teeth clenched, couldn't take his staring gaze from the man's plump round face. It wore a faint smile. Its owner half-whispered, "REAL scary, huh, petit garcon?"

Tessier, with a quick toss of his head said, "Hey, let's move on, Reggie, not overdo dis t'ing. I want to go down to de river before de call to mount."

"I want to see your bullet scar," Randy said quickly, pressingly to Larent. But he was already walking away fast toward the river. "It's not much—pretty well faded after two years," he called over his shoulder.

Nerves taut, face flushed, his mind replaying the near-scalping scene, Randy stared after the two men. A new worry! Would John blame him if during his guard-duty a swarm of Indians swept in, stole the horses, and killed somebody? Oh lordy.

54

Steven Henneman

Kit Carson's story during the day's march, telling how he and two Indian companions crawled over the snow to capture their stolen horses from Indians celebrating in temporary pole-forts, keeps Randy's thoughts from dwelling on guard duty coming up at midnight. "We had to throw snowballs at the horses to get'um heading the right way and moving fast after we cut'um loose," Carson said. Randy's camp-guarding that night will hold two big surprises, but no Indians.

CHAPTER 6

"KIT! YOU HEAR ANYTHING?"

June 24, Little Blue River, Kansas

When the column began to move after lunch, Randy eased his pony to a place beside Carson. "Kit," he ventured after a while, "if somehow I don't see the Pawnees when they slither through the grass tonight to steal our horses—or if I don't hear them before they ride into the camp to steal everything, maybe scalp somebody, will anybody blame ME? Will you think—will the Lieutenant think—that I'm a little boy who shouldn't have the job of guarding the camp?"

Carson's wide, thin-lipped mouth stretched into a big smile. "That slithering really got stuck in your mind, didn't it? Also sounds like some of the fellows with scary stories got to you. Well, you can put aside Indian scares for tonight at least. Moise the Weather See-All says a storm will hit tonight, so I predict no Pawnee will slither or charge in on a horse or even stick his head out his teepee to face the terrible prairie lightning."

A short silence. "Why do I have to sit outside by the cart and face the terrible lightning since there won't be any Indians coming?"

Carson's mouth stretched wide open and across his face into a full-volume laugh. "Randy, if the wind and the rain and the lightning hit during our watch, you and me and Henry will do like Indians do when the sky flashes and pours—run to the nearest tent!"

Then Carson's voice became serious. "But we're really horse guards, you know, and even in the tent we'll be keep'n eye on the nervous animals out there in the storm. 'Course, everybody'll be watching—and if it looks like there's trouble— horses rearing 'n plunging in fear, pulling their stakes, running—everybody will run after'um, storm or no."

J.Hengesbaugh
(horses in storm)

Randy winced. He squirmed in the saddle, glanced up at the clouds.

"Well, some other night when I'm on guard, if the Indians slith—get to our horses and run off with a lot of them, will you chase them for a hundred miles the way Registe Larente said you did one time all by yourself? Are you going to kill the Indians, burn their village, take our horses and bring them back?"

"Is that what Larente told you? Of course I'd go after any thieves that run off with expedition horses. But Larente got it wrong, this story he told you about me. What he did wuz mix n'stretch two stories. Seems to me I ought to untangle them for you. I wouldn't like to think that you might tell your Father or your friends in Washington something that's not true.

Kit Carson's Autobiography. M.Quaife,ed. p.36(horses)

"Larente told you I went by myself a hundred miles following some Indians to their village, took the horses, and burned the village? Well, the time I kept after the thief 100 miles—it wuz actually 130 miles—I wuz following ONE Indian. When I caught up with him, he wuz by himself on a mountain trail. Seeing me by myself, the man showed fight. I wuz under the necessity of killing him. He wuz a California Indian who had joined up and come east with the Robidoux group I wuz with. We had to wait out winter snowstorms in Utah country, and during the wait, this California Indian disappeared with six valuable horses. Some werz worth $200 a head! Mr. Robidoux asked me to go after them and bring'um back.

"For the first 100 miles, I had the company of a Utah Indian. Then his horse gave out. Since I'd come that far, I decided to keep on. Thirty miles later, I overtook the thief with the six horses, killed him, and walked the horses back to Mr. Robidoux. No village burned.

"Now, as to the other story Larente scrambled with the first, that took place another winter, and it took place in a different territory. This time the thieves numbered 50, and they werz Crows. This time a dozen of us in our winter camp went after them Crows. We rode through deep snow for 40 miles. It took us 12 hours.

"At dark we saw the Indians' camp fires. We tied our wore-out horses to trees, began walking, then crawling toward the camp. When we come within about a hundred yards of it, we could see the Indians werz in two forts of about equal strength. A temporary Indian 'fort' is a big teepee made of saplings set almost bark to bark. Inside, the Indians werz dancing and singing and passing the night jovially in honor of their robbery of us whites. We saw our horses, all six of 'um, tied to trees near the entrance of one of the forts.

"Let come what would, we werz bound to get'um. We remained concealed in the brush, lying in the snow, and suffering severely from the cold for what seemed like half the

57

night. When we thought the Indians werz all asleep, six of us crawled toward our animals, leaving the others for us to fall back on in case we didn't meet with success. Two of us crawling in the snow werz Cheyenne Indians we called Pat and Mike—who'd been trapping with us.

"We hid behind logs and crawled silently towards the fort, the snow being a great help for us to crawl without making any noise. Finally we reached the horses, cut their ropes. To get'um moving and in the right direction, Pat began throwing snow balls at them, so we did, too, and drove the horses to where our other six men werz."

Kit Carson's Autobiography. p.24(snowballs)

"Snowballs!" Randy laughed.

"Not the fun kind," said Carson grimly. "Nearly lost some fingers to frostbite. So when we twelve men got to talking about what to do now that we had our horses, there werz three of us who didn't agree to just go on back to our own camp. No sir, after all the trouble and hardship we'd gone through, we three wanted satisfaction. One wuz myself, Christopher Carson. I hadn't never before lost a horse to thieves, and neither had the other two. We three just felt a powerful urge to go back and punish them Crows, even if we risked getting ourselves killed. Finally the others agreed to join us.

"We secured the animals, left guards, and nine of us marched to the forts. We werz within a few steps of the first one when a dog began to bark. Right off, the sleeping Indians inside began to rouse up and come to the door. We opened a deadly fire, each ball taking its victim. We killed nearly every one."

"How many?" Randy breathlessly interrupted.

"I'd say 20. Then the Crows in the other fort, which wuz only a few yards away, began firing at us. We moved back behind some trees, firing only when we werz sure of our object. Now it began to be light and the Indians got the idea that we werz such a small force they could wipe us out in a charge. We kept calm and let them get close. Then we fired, killing five. The rest ran back.

"Next time they charged, we werz out of balls, so we retreated in a run through the woods, back to our horses. We waited but no Crows came. We got home 12 hours later in time for a late supper. But 30 or more redskins—that's not a whole village—had gone to their final home. That wuz our satisfaction."

Randy stared wordlessly at Carson for some time as their

horses plodded along the trail. Finally he asked the question that had come to the top of his thinking about Kit's wanting to go back to fight the Indians when he didn't have to.

"Kit," he said, "Don't you ever feel scared?"

Carson's laugh made a noise in his throat behind tight lips. "Randy, one day when we're riding along the Platte River bored to numbness with nothing in view but grass and sand hills, I'll tell you about the occasion when I wuz the wust scared in my life. Right now I'm moving up ahead. Maxwell and the Lieutenant look to be talking about our going after some fresh meat for supper. You fall back in line next to Mr. Lambert. It may be that me and Max will spend the next coupla hours looking for an elk."

But they didn't. Instead, the three men talked back and forth for a while, stayed in line, and fell as silent as the prairie. Overhead, the white cloud umbrella shading the caravan from the sun was becoming rumpled with invading gray billows, advance army for darker forces pressing slowly, relentlessly from the southwest. Winds were quickening and Fremont quickened his horse's pace. Hour by hour the clouds grew blacker, thicker, more menacing, the wind stronger. Tension grew. All eyes scanned the sky.

At last, the landscape was broken by a line of trees some miles ahead. Like a straight avenue of planted cottonwoods leading to a plantation mansion, it crossed the open plains of green to the foot of a low grass-covered hill a few miles east.

"That's the creeklet leading to the prele pasture," Carson said."We can probably make it to the prele before the storm breaks. Me and Max can run ahead and look for an elk. Seems like some elk might right now be dining not far from the prele patch." After some talking, hand waving, and pointing toward the hill, the two hunters galloped off.

Fremont beckoned to Lambert and Randy to come ride beside him. "It's a bad sign that we've seen no elk, no antelope this afternoon, but our hunters wanted to try," he confided. "If they have no luck, I shall tell the cooks to kill our last ox for supper, and tomorrow's meals. Four days we've eaten only fried pork, fried bread, and coffee. We must have fresh meat. Besides that, we'll shortly need to set up camp in a sheltered place like under the trees at the prele patch."

Within minutes, the plodding animals seemed to smell the prele, for they began to step livelier and lift their heads. When, in a low wooded hollow, damp with moisture from the creek, acres of the odd looking, stemmy, bright-green plant came in sight, the cow began to low and the mules to bray.

Soon, sixteen mules taxed the muscles and tempers of eight drivers trying to park the carts, unhitch the hungry, eager animals, lead or drag them to the creek for a drink before staking them in the midst of their lucious, crunchy, herby dinner. None of the 28 riding horses, three dozen 'loose' horses, 10 pack mules, 16 cart-mules, nor even the cow or ox lingered at the water's edge, but impatiently turned quivering noses and muzzles toward the prele.

The men were just as hungry as the animals, and when Carson and Maxwell rode elkless into camp, the stew pots were already boiling, the butchers' knives sharpened, and the ends of dozens of long roasting-sticks trimmed to points. At Fremont's signal, a bullet ripped through the ox's neck and head below one ear.

Small chunks of beef soon sizzled along half the length of dozens of sticks, ends anchored into the ground, a circle of them leaning over a half-dozen fires. Chief cook Dumes declared a Beef Festival and threw a few handsful of macaroni into each of four pots of boiling beef. Randy, standing by his two sticks to turn them so the meat chunks sizzled and browned evenly, gulped mouthsful of delicious smells to temporarily feed his hunger.

Cooking and eating went on for two hours. Four times Randy filled his pointed sticks with squares of beef, three times he filled his cup with beef and macaroni stew, three times he picked up a handful of griddle cakes. He'd never had such a good dinner nor eaten so much in all his life he told everybody.

By the end of the meal, more than half the ox was digesting in 28 contented men. Leftover cooked chunks and stews would make breakfast and mid-day meal tomorrow. Two shoulder-quarters hanging on the back of a cart wouldn't have time to spoil by end-of-next-day, Cook Dumes assured Fremont. "Wash off the dust, cook one more banquet, and poof! 300 pounds of beef, gone!"

Spirits rose high. To eat well tonight and know they'd eat well at least one more day, maybe longer, was enough to make a man—or a boy—forget the sky was growling, tumbling black clouds had turned daylight into dusk and he was hundreds of miles from everybody—except Indians.

Indians! Guard duty! Tonight! Randy was suddenly reminded when he heard Lambert's call for the first three men doing guard duty from 8 to 10 o'clock. Camp had been set up on a high spot a little distance from the low, damp prele patch where the animals would be eating all night. Randy glanced at the cart behind Fremont's tent, at the carts at some distance on either side of it, and grimaced. Just two hours before he, Cousin Henry and Kit would take their places by those carts!

He saw Carson call Henry away from his friends and speak to him a minute. Then both began walking towards Randy. Each step they took seemed to him like doom slowly approaching.

A great roll of thunder and a gust of wind underscored the feeling. Carson hardly looked up. "You two," he said on arrival at Randy's side, "need to load your guns so as to have them ready before dark—and rain. Come on to your tent."

J.Hengesbaugh
(gun loading)

When Randy had in hand his pistol—on loan from Kit—and Henry had his rifle, ramrod, and powder-horn hanging from one shoulder, war-bag holding lead balls, cloth patches, and flints hanging from the other shoulder, Carson said, "You fellows've been practicing gun-loading and target-shooting off'n'on the past coupla weeks, so you don't need to be told how to aim and fire.

"Randy, your pistol's ready-loaded with powder and bullet. Henry, let me see how FAST you can measure powder from the horn...pour it down the muzzle...seat the lead ball on the cloth patch...push it a ways down the muzzle...trim off excess cloth with your knife...ramrod the ball all the way down the muzzle to sit right on top of the powder...pour a little powder in the pan...close the frizzen.

"Hmm. About two minutes. You need to do it in half the time—or less. Takes practice to get faster at it. Now put your rifle back in its scabbard, cap the end of your powder-horn, and put everything where you can lay your hands on 'um quick in the dark. Now let's move along before it starts to rain."

Carson's plan was for them to walk around the outside of the camp circle while there was still some light. "Today's next-to the longest day of the year," he remarked, "but with this black cloud rolling over us, and cooking fires dead, we won't have a bitta light by the time we start for our guard posts near 10 o'clock. We need to go-over how to find our way in the dark and how to get back to our tents at midnight. Besides that, it's better to speak now to the men we'll be relieving so they'll know our voices in the night."

Before they completed their tour, the thick, black clouds

had blocked out all but dusky light. Suddenly a violent wind struck. Pushing hard to move against its strength, Carson locked arms with the boys to lead them to their tent. Hard gusts of wind grabbed at their breath, pressed it out, then sucked it away. Randy sheltered his mouth and nose behind a hand to capture some quiet air to breathe.

JF Report, and *Preuss Journal* June 24 *(superstorm)*

Lightning flashed through the thick blackness of the cloud, tearing white-hot streaks all the way to the horizon. A monstrous, reverberating roar of thunder sounded like ten cannons firing while the whole sky began sparkling and trembling with lightning. On and on thunder rolled— GROWWWLL! CRAAASH! BOOOOM!

Rain poured from the sky just as the trio stumbled into Randy and Henry's tent. Whirling sheets of rain beat against the tent sides, lifted the bottom edge to spray water across the blanket-beds on the ground. A minute later, the tent roof, drenched, streamed water inside. "So everybody gets his monthly bath tonight!" joked Carson whose soaked clothes were clinging to his body. His audience didn't answer. "We shoulda dug a little drain-trench around the tent," he grunted.

The two cousins stood close together, bewildered, staring into the darkness. "Ain't this pure damnation on our guard duty night!" Henry blurted. The noises and flashes above them, the sky gone mad, the winds attacking the tent, which looked as if it would dissolve in the next column of water that struck it, the steady shower soaking and resoaking them, the pool of water leaking into their boots, chilling their feet—was this what they had to endure on their watch? For two hours!? Then come "home" to sleep on wet blankets lying in running water?

"Kit.."

"I'm right here." Randy felt a wet arm fold around his shoulders.

"How much longer will this go on?"

"Don't know for sure. Storms out here on the prairie are ripsnorters like nowhere else. Sometimes you think thunder and lightning intend to split apart the earth. But sometimes, after an hour they move on, 'specially if a big wind's a-hurrying stormclouds to somewhere else."

"So maybe by 10 o'clock, it'll be gone?"

"If Moise Chardonnais wuz here, his intuitive weather predicting might let him say a definite yes or no. But I can't say more than 'maybe.'"

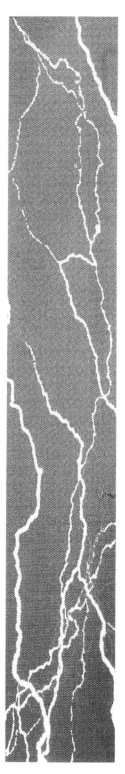

FLASH! A nerve jangling crack of lightning shone in zig-zagged brilliance through the tent fabric for an intense second, long enough for Randy to see water falling like a veil from the wide brim of Carson's hat. Overhead the BOOM! of thunder that followed pressed like a solid weight upon Randy's head.

He was literally thunderstruck, wordless for a long time while the storm continued its noisy war, its angry driving winds and water sprays. Then, "Kit, what do you do when you get tired of standing but there's water under your feet?"

"You sit down...in the water." No answer. "It's not that bad, Randy. We don't have to see to bring the four blankets together, make one fat roll of 'um, and all of us sit on it. It'll be wet, but better than sitting flat down in a puddle."

The storm cloud, grumbling and nipping the horizon with small defiant flashes, did move on after an hour, taking water and wind with it but leaving pitch darkness under a thick, quiet cloud cover. Randy heard the men in close-by tents come out to wring water from their blankets and to pour dissolved muck from their mocassins.

"I bleeve we have 'bout a half-hour before we go to our guard posts," Carson told his fellow guardsmen in the blackness of their tent. "I'm goin' to feel my way to my tent, get into some dry clothes. You do likewise, if you've got any. You'll get pretty cold if you're in wet clothes standing outside for two hours. I'll be back shortly and go with you to your guard posts."

As soon as he was gone, Henry broke into a string of "damns" and "sacres", wishing he'd run away for a few days in St. Louis and come back only when the Fremont expedition was well out of sight. He fussed when Randy called on him to help wring out their blankets—"in pitch dark?! And what difference will it make when the ground in here is still a lake?!" But he took a-hold, helped roll one blanket at a time, twisted his end while Randy twisted his in the opposite direction to squeeze out streams of water. They spread open all four on top of the tent to dry a little during guard duty hours.

Both guards-to-be found a dry shirt and cotton pants in their India rubber clothes bags, both leaned their boots upside down against the tent side and slipped on mocassins pulled from deep within their packs. At that moment, Carson called to them from the tent door.

"Let's get going. Got your guns?'

"Just a minute...Yeah." "Think your powder's dry?" "Can't tell without shooting." "Can you see me?" "Not really." "Then hold onto my shirttail—here—and Henry you take aholt of Randy's. Done? Randy, I'll deliver you first since your guard post is closest by—the cart behind the Lieutenant's tent. As soon as we get close to his tent, we'll have a speck of light. He's still up, probably doing his journal. His India rubber tent don't leak, else his papers and instruments 'ould be ruin't."

Slowly, quietly, they groped their way through wet grass, mushy ground and puddles, past Fremont's water-tight tent and its tiny sliver of light from a door crack. At last they bumped into the instruments cart. Carson heard an ominous snap of metal. "Carson here with Randy, Johnny," he near-whispered. "How wet are you?"

Johnny Annisse went "heh-heh-heh" and whispered in his soft Virginia accent that he wasn't Johnny, he was the Dripping Ghost of Fremont's Mule Carts in the Wilds of Pawneeland. "Here, take my hand, Randy—if you can find it in this pitchydark place—and I'll help you to your guard-seat. It's the old oaken bucket turned upside down, but I've kept one little spot on top dry for you no matter how the wind pushed me and the rain beat me and the fire bolts in the sky scared the wind outa me.

"Here, take your seat and park your gun, you're about to start the most boring two hours of your young life. No Indians, no interesting goings-on in the sky for you—just sitting still in the dark by yourself listening to a B-I-I-G quiet space. Bye, bye, I'm gone."

Assuring Randy again that he was within hollering distance in case Randy saw or heard anything suspicious, and would come running ready to fight and rouse the camp, Carson departed with Henry.

Randy listened hard for awhile. Nothing. The pistol began to weigh heavy in his hand. He secured it in his belt. He looked to the right, then to the left. Nothing but blackness. He shuddered. He had never before sat alone surrounded by, wrapped up in, an endless quantity of blackness.

He wanted to close his eyes against it. But then how could he keep himself awake? Kit had said Indians probably would stay home in a bad storm. Randy imagined them, envied them, in their teepees, dry and warm, sleeping soundly. He wondered if they had a petit garcon outside keeping guard.

Maybe he could kill a lot of time thinking about playing his guitar. He'd heard about a man who made up tunes in his head while he was in prison, and, having no piano, practiced fingering in the air the notes of tunes.

Randy pictured himself taking the guitar out of the cart he was leaning against. He made the movements of taking it from its case. Fingers wriggling in the air, he tuned it. That took a lot of time—even Father took a lot of time when he tuned it for Randy or his sisters.

Fremont Memoirs (biographical sketch of Senator Benton, by Jessie Benton: "Papa Benton played the guitar and sang."

A good sounding old guitar even if it wasn't as big as some of the new ones. Father's sisters had played it—so Father said—and Father played "a little" once upon a time. Hmm. What to play..? How about "Turkey in the Straw," an old song Mother especially liked.

For some time, Randy fingered strings in the air, strummed and plucked tunes, whispered the words softly until he almost put himself to sleep. He stood up, stretched and woggled his shoulders. What a lot of supper he'd eaten....He noticed the clouds had left part of the sky clear. A few stars and a glow from a still-hidden moon were diluting the intense darkness. It must be close to midnight. All at once, he heard Something. Was that a slithering sound—a WET slithering sound? It was still too dark to see the grass. He pulled out the pistol tucked under his belt and held his breath to hear better. It was not a slithering sound. It was more like "grinnnt...grinnt." Footsteps? Should he shoot at the place it was coming from like Basil said he did? But what if it was a ghost? Or one of our men? Carson..?

JF Report June 24 "Randy called out twice"

He cupped his hands and called a high-pitched, "Kit!" After a second, he heard a soft whistle. "Kit! You hear anything?"

Silence. Then much closer by, Carson, a bulk in the darkness, whispered hoarsely, "Animals cropping grass." "Is it midnight?" "No."

Randy spent a little time counting the horse's grint-grint bites of grass. Not a bit interesting once he knew what it was. Suddenly, he heard a different sound—and woke up.

Eennnggg.....Mosquitoes! A whole colony had flown in on a soft, surprisingly warm wind, singing with hungry anticipation. Randy swatted the air, slapped his arms, face, neck, ankles. He began to itch and scratch, which seemed to invite more and more piercing mouths, increasing the singing volume of a thousand, a hundred thousand, hateful, humming wings.

"KIT!" Ten slaps and a minute of wild hand-flinging, and again Kit's voice not far away said softly, "Whas matter?"

"'Skeeters! I'm making noise swatting 'um. Can I go get my netting? I can see my way. Moon's coming out."

"Remember—all the bedding's wet, netting, too. Won't do you any good. You'll have to tough it out—won't be long." "How long?" "Half an hour." "I'll be dead."

When Moise Chardonnais walked up to relieve him, he said softly, "Comment ca va, Randy—any Indians?"

No, Randy answered, no Indians. No danger of being scalped—just of being eaten alive.

In his tent, lying between wet blankets, listening to Henry's breathing, he prayed that all guard duty wouldn't be like this one. Could a slithering Indian on a starlit night be worse than lightning, thunder, whirling wind and rain, thick darkness, wet clothes, going to bed in a cold, wet blanket, itching with a hundred 'skeeter bites?

Fascinated with buffalo bones and skulls scattered over acres of prairie, Randy longs to put together a whole skeleton. But too many essential bones are missing. Moise, the intuitive weather predictor, explains that Indians who camped at this spot maybe a year ago after their hunters surrounded and killed a hundred or more buffalo for food, cracked many big bones to eat the marrow inside. They also took shoulder blades and ribs to make into tools. Randy hides three souvenir skulls in his tent and conspires with Moise on a plan to send them to St. Louis.

CHAPTER 7

ELKS! BEAVERS! BEARS! BUFFALO SKULLS!

June 25, 1842, Little Blue River Valley, Kansas

Sleeping in wet blankets all night after the drenching storm seemed to have driven out of the men's memories smaller details like Randy's standing guard. Nobody made a remark on that subject at breakfast, nobody asked a question. The sliced roast beef and pots of hot stew held their attention and silenced their food-busy tongues.

Finally, Lajeunesse, as he was wiping his mouth with his sleeve and muffling a burp in the same motion, caught Randy's eye and said, "How yo' guardin' go, garcon?"

Randy had prepared an offhand remark for any such question. "Oh, I killed 475 enemies with my bare hands, and they drew only a few drops of blood from me." Lajeunesse laughed loud and heartily, slapped his hands together, kicked up a bit of dirt with his boot heel and hollered Randy's retort for all to hear. "Yo' lees'un wha' dees garcon say 'bout dem MUS-sqweetoes!" The men close by waved their coffee tins, laughed and answered, "Hey hey!"

It was almost as good as hearing the Lieutenant say that he'd been brave, guarded the camp well, kept everyone safe all night.

So Randy was smiling and repicturing the scene some hours later as his pony plodded from the prele patch west under scorching sun along the creekside trail, then north within sight of the Little Blue River.

In the middle of the best repictured scene—Basil Lajeunesse doing his jig—Randy heard Fremont call "WHOA!" to his horse, saw him hauling on the reins. Fremont was staring intently towards the river now at the bottom of the ridge they'd begun traveling to shortcut a wide river bend. His gaze focused on the top of a ridge on the other side of the river and visible over the riverside cottonwoods and willows.

"Look there!" Fremont said to Carson and Maxwell. The two friends broke off their mumbled conversation comparing Josepha Jaramillo and Maria de la Luz Beaubien of Taos. Kit had been saying that after this trip with Fremont, he was going home to marry 14-year-old Josepha, which would connect him with TWO important families—Jaramillo AND Bent of Bent's Fort. Charlie Bent had married one of the beautiful Jaramillo girls, "so," Kit was figuring, "one day he'll be my brother-in-law." Maxwell was answering that his bride of this past March, 13-year-old Maria Luz, was French aristocracy, being the daughter of Carlos sieur de Beaubien, a rich trader in Taos about to get the Mexican government to deed to him a huge tract of land north of Taos. "He dies, Maria inherits. As my wife, what's hers is mine—"

Bent's Fort.
D.Lavender,
p175-6,p200

Maxwell-Beaubien
N.M./Colo.
land-grant
Smithsonian
Magazine
John Neary

"LOOK!" Fremont repeated more urgently. "There—across the river—on top of that ridge! Do you see something moving? Indians perhaps?"

Carson and Maxwell whoa-ed their horses and stared squint-eyed over the tops of the trees toward the distant ridge. "Any glasses handy, Lieutenant?" Fremont said no, his Army binoculars and telescope were so big and heavy he'd left them in the cart with the scientific instruments. "We need," he added, "the half-breed who worked with me during the Dakota expedition—Louison Freniere. He could tell at an amazing distance whether a moving object was an antelope, buffalo, elk, Indian, whatever. If it was an Indian, he could tell whether he was friend or foe."

Fremont, Path
Marker, p40
ANevins
(Freniere)

"Maxwell, your eyes are years younger than mine—what do you see?" Carson asked. Maxwell thought he saw elk legs, not men's.

Just as the words left his lips, a man from the rear spurred up in great haste shouting, "INDIANS! INDIANS!" He was pointing emphatically at the ridge across the river. "Are you SURE it's Indians over there, Cousin Henry?" exclaimed Fremont.

JF Report
June 25
(Brant's "Indians")

"YES! YES! I counted them—27 Indians! Probably on war path!"

Carson looked skeptical, Maxwell laughed. But Fremont declared they couldn't take a chance and ordered the carts, all of which were draped with blankets needing drying out, to form a small defensive circle, all horses inside it. The men, guns ready, would position themselves by the carts. During the flurry to carry out Fremont's orders, Carson, who'd kept an eye on the ridge, suddenly leaped on his just-unsaddled horse, and bounded off to the river.

They splashed through the shallow stream and galloped through the tall prairie grass toward the moving objects on the ridge.

With an admiring smile, Fremont watched Carson.

"Look at that man!" he murmured. "No saddle, no hat, hair flying, moving in rhythm with the horse. What a picture! Finest horseman I've ever seen!"

JF Report
June25
(Kit,horseman)

Randy was trembling with excitement. "Lieutenant! What if the Indians shoot at Kit?! He'd have to fight them all by himself! Shouldn't we saddle up, go help him?!"

Fremont didn't answer for a moment. Then, looking away from Carson briefly, he said, "I think Kit felt sure Maxwell was right, Randy. He wasn't putting himself in any danger by running out to take a look. Ahhh—there's Max racing off to help Kit—if he needs any help. But see there, Max won't get far—Kit's turning back—and nobody's following him."

Shortly, Maxwell and Carson braked their horses to a halt beside Fremont and Randy. "Not a War party?" inquired Fremont. "Elk, sir. Six elk. Real peaceful."

The men, who had rushed to Fremont to hear Carson's news, whacked Henry Brant on the back, laughed, called him Eagle-Eye Henry, Harry Six Elks, Twenty-seven Harry Legs. Henry cringed and took fist pokes at his young friends when they danced around him, whooping like Indians.

Mr. Preuss, standing close by Randy, said quite loudly, "What a silly, silly boy. Such a fool. Worzless for such an expedition as zis. Better his Mama had kept him at home wiz her—" and added some short, rough German words. Randy balled up his fists and glared, but he couldn't think of anything he wanted to say in Henry's defense except, "Henry's my—my Cousin!" Mr. Preuss glared back and said more gutteral words. "Bet he's saying I'm worse than Cousin Henry," Randy thought, and stalked off.

Diary.June 25
Preuss
(Silly boy)

It now being close to mid-day mealtime, Fremont ordered the carts, animals, and men to move the carts close to the river bank where trees could shade everyone from the broiling sun while they ate, and river water could revive, wash, and cool everybody. Under a great cottonwood, cooks started their fires, sat pots of water on to boil coffee, and began searching supply carts for the cooked beef left over from breakfast. But where was it? Only Chief Cook Dumes, who had stored it, knew where.

And where was Dumes? Nobody remembered seeing him since arriving at the river bank. A hunt for the man began. Fremont, much annoyed, remarked that Dumes had become slower each day, delaying meals and marches. He called to Mike Descouteau, who had painted the carts, and whose previous job had been cook on a river steamboat. "Prairie

Artist," Fremont said, "I'm appointing you assistant cook to Monsieur Dumes. I want you to start moving fast at doing whatever needs doing, all of which should stir Dumes to move faster, and be on time."

At last, Dumes ambled out of the woods. He had gone exploring, he said, looking to see if the river had any fish. He looked around in puzzlement at the men asking why he'd stayed so long, and didn't he hear everybody calling his name, didn't he remember no one else knew where the beef was stored among the supply boxes and barrels, didn't he know the Lieutenant was noticing how slack he'd gotten to be and how he was holding up the whole camp?

Dumes said not a word. When Fremont approached him and told him calmly but firmly that the kitchen work must be speeded up, that Descouteau would be his co-headcook, Dumes only pressed his lips tighter.

Descouteau had Dumes' fires going and coffee boiling. Dumes sullenly ordered him to bring out the cooked beef from a keg underneath the macaroni keg. He ordered him to find the butcher block. He ordered him to find the big butcher knife, sharpen it, carve the cooked meat for all four messes. He ordered him to search the kitchen cart for griddles to cook bread dough Dumes was stirring up.

JF Report
June 25
(New cook.
Pan-fight later,
Preuss Journal)

"Not the small griddles you're holding, you lummox! Why does the Lieutenant try making a cook out of a prairie artist with clouds in his head—?" at which Descouteau lifted one griddle head-high, glared at Dumes, rumbled a string of French swear words, and declared he was a better cook than Dumes."You threaten me?!" Dumes shouted. Infuriated, he grabbed the handle of a mammoth frying-pan and swung it at the griddle.

Whang! At the sound and sight, Randy ran to Fremont who was busy with Preuss and a barometer. "John! The cooks! They're dueling!"

Whang!

Fremont started toward the cooks. Carson joined him, saying, "Lieutenant, 'scuse me, but my advice is to leave them be. Your stopping them won't settle nothing. They ought to have the natural freedom to thresh out differences when they're of no importance to anybody else, or anything else. That's the way these men are used to having it. They don't want no interfering in what they more'n likely consider their amusement."

JF Report
June 25
(not interfering)

Fremont stopped, watched the two cooks menace each

71

other but not join their weapons again. They blathered in French until Descouteau dropped his griddle on the ground and walked away.

"Mon Dieu, nobody can say today's march across the prairie was monotonous!" declared Lajeunesse who was just coming up from the river. "Elks looking like Indians! Cooks battling with griddles and frypans!"

For the morning part of the day, that was true, but the afternoon plod of four hours under a blistering sun relieved only by a scattering of hand-size white clouds, became monotony in slow motion. Randy, determined not to close his eyes and risk going to sleep, pushed his hat high on his forehead, and began to count aloud each step his pony made. Tap-tap-tap-tap, how-much-far-ther, they seemed to repeat in steady four-four time.

"Randy?" Randy looked around. Kit's blue eyes smiled at him. "I said t'other day I'd tell you sometime about when I wuz the wust scared I've ever been. Seems like now is a good time. Might stir us both into sitting up straight, get our thinking parts to run faster."

Randy straightened, tugged at his hat brim. His freckled face, glowing red from the heat, beamed at Carson. "Man, I sure can stand a stir-up-ing!" Carson laughed and began.

"Well, acourse this happened some time back when me and three other men werz hunting all summer long 'round the head of the Laramie River and its tributary creeks, a place with beavers a-plenny at that time. But we had to camp in the mountains since we werz just four men, too few to risk venturing out on the open plains where Indians werz roaming. One evenin' after I had picked a camp site for the night, I turned my horse over to one of the men for him to tend, and I started on foot to kill sump'um for supper seeing that we hadn't on hand a particle o' sum'um t'eat.

"I had gone about a mile when I saw some elk on the side of a ridge. I shot one. As soon as I fired, I heard a noise behind me. I turned 'round—two of the biggest grizzly bears I ever saw werz a-making fer me, and my gun wuz unloaded! Them bears werz so close, I couldn't possibly reload in time to fire—even though I can reload a rifle in 20 seconds flat. I had to do sumthing else—fast. I ran! I'd seen some trees right close by and I made fer'um, the bears so close behind I could hear breathing 'n' snorting at my heels, almost smell their breath."

"I made it to a big, tall tree, dropped my gun so I could

Kit Carson's
Autobiography,
p37(bear scare)

72

climb, and went up the trunk about five seconds ahead of the bears' claws and teeth. I got up about fifteen feet, putting about six feet betwixt me and the bears standing on their hind legs.

Staying Alive in Alaska's Wild. Andy Nault, trapper

"BIG bears can't climb trees—they're too heavy. But they can stand against a tree fer hours, snap their teeth, and keep you plenny scared. One bear left after a while, but the other one—prob'ly the hungriest one—stayed the rest of the afternoon. He tried climbing my tree ever' once in a while, but ever' time he brought his hind legs up high enough to

Kit Carson Autobiography

reach a claw closer to where I wuz, he'd fall back'erds he was so heavy. When he got tired of doing that, he took to making like he'd climb some small aspens growing next to my tree, get at me that way. He bent and broke them, he clawed at their roots and the ground with his long, curved nails—they're razor-sharp on all edges—until he nearly uprooted every little tree.

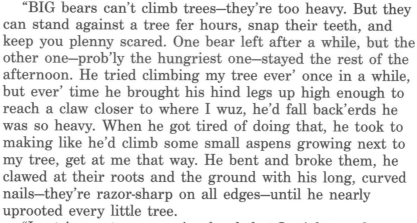

"I sat in my tree worrying hard that I might need to hang up there all night long. But at sundown, the bear finally concluded to leave. He just all-of-a-sudden walked off. It wuz one of the purtiest sights I've ever seen!—fer I wuz scared like never before—ner since."

Randy's shoulders twitched in a little quiver of excitement. "I bet you jumped down and ran all the way back to camp!" he ventured.

No, Carson said, he stayed in the tree another half-hour or so, long enough for the bear to walk at least a mile. Then he backed down the tree trunk and grabbed his gun, loaded it before hurrying to camp. "It wuz dark when I got there. I didn't have the heart to send anybody out to get the elk I'd killed, so we went without supper. Didn't sleep much either. Instead, during the night we went trapping, caught some handy beaver, so we had sum'um t'eat for breakfast."

"BEAVER?! I never heard that trappers ATE those beaver," Randy said, his face showing mild revulsion and surprise. "I thought the only good thing about a beaver was its soft, thick fur."

Carson gave a little laughing snort. "Trappers practically lived off'n beaver meat since they had a heap of it on hand after skinning the animals caught in their traps. When we

Kit Carson's Autobiography p38 (beaver)

got tired of its musky taste, we went after an elk or antelope or, on the prairie, a buffalo. Or a bear—bear meat's good. But beaver wuz a mainstay—until a year or so ago that is, when they got to be sca'ce. I'll bet we trapped a million in 20 years. Most times, we had so much beaver meat, we cooked only the tail—"

"The TAIL?" gasped Randy.

"The tail. It's what I'd call a great dainty. It's about this long—" Carson held his hands a foot and more apart—"'bout this wide"—he measured four inches—"it's flat, has an oval shape, and scales like a fish instead of fur. Ole beaver uses it as a rudder when he swims, but he slaps it BLAP!! on top of the water to sound a warning to other beavers. But a-course it's the body fur that's valuable for making hats."

Scales on its tail? Randy wondered if they had to be scraped off the way fish scales had to be.

"I reckon you could. But the best way is to sharpen the end of a stick, push it into the end of the beaver tail, scales and all. Then you stand the stick in front of the fire and let the beaver tail roast through. The scaly skin rises up in blisters, and you pull it all off. Then you see rich white meat. Umm-amh! It's sooo deelicious! One tail's big enough to feed two hungry men a-plenny."

Randy's face stayed in a tight grimace while he digested the unfamiliar culinary details silently.

"But wait a minute," he said, "Doesn't a beaver hat have a beaver tail hanging down at the back? I remember seeing a man wearing a fur hat with a bushy tail at the back. He came to see Father at our house in Washington, and he wore his hat all the time through dinner."

Carson gave a short laugh. "Now that sounds like Davy Crockett when he wuz a Congressman. He liked RACCOON hats—probably made'um hisself, wouldn'tna been caught in one of them tall shiny beaver hats like politicians wear. Don't your papa have one?"

"Stovepipe hats don't look like beaver FUR!!"

Carson, with a small introductory cough, said yes, they were fur after a fashion—that is, it was the fashion to shave the fur off the skin and paste it on a cardboard hat. "You see, Randy, beaver fur's double thick. There's a bottom, short fur layer soft as can be, and a long, coarse, top layer like hair. It's the soft layer the hat makers want.

"They yank out the hairs, shave off the soft fuzz, and blow it onto cardboard hats all sticky with glue. When it dries, the hatmaker rubs the hat until it shines, sells it for $50 to rich men in New York, Washington, Paris

—lotsa places. Fifty dollars! Shows you there's a large number of rich men in the world, 'cause we sure caught and our bosses sold a large number of beavers. They priced at about $6 a pelt at first—that wuz 20 years ago. Now a pelt sells for no more'n $1.50—if you can find a beaver to trap.

"Mr. Chouteau in St. Louis told me he paid $50 for his beaver hat some years ago. That was when a hired trapper got paid $150 and some supplies for a year's work living outdoors amongst Indians and bears in the Rockies. A third of his pay to buy one hat! But then he wouldn't've had any use for a shiny top hat, would he. The other week, Mr. Chouteau showed me his NEWEST stovepipe hat, said it cost MORE'n $50. It's not covered with beaver fur, it's covered with SILK from China. So far-away China helped put me out of a job."

Carson turned his head to look pensively across the endless grassland, now motionless in calm air. Randy leaned forward to look, too. He thought he could see heat waves rising, he knew he could smell the grass cooking in the sun. Finally Carson looked back around at him. "So like I said a while back, that, 'after a fashion' wuz why I wuz looking a job when Lieutenant Fremont met me that day on the Missouri River steamboat.

"Actually, Randy, I can't think of any job that might've come along that I'd enjoy as much as this one. The Lieutenant treats a man like he's as much a Somebody as himself. We all know he's the Boss but he don't lift his voice, don't cuss and swear to REMIND us he's the Head Man. He don't have to. He's no sluggard ner deadhead. He's a SCIENTIST—first one I ever knowed. See how he goes out in the grass where the patches of flowers and weeds is blooming? Look at him out there now, pulling up a sample of every kind to show gov'ment people zackly what-all's growing on the prairie."

Just at that moment they saw Fremont vigorously waving one hand and arm. Carson thought he heard his name. He and Randy began standing in their stirrups, waving both their hands and arms. Fremont began waving both of his, then beckoning with them.

"Let's go!" Carson said, heading his horse out of line, clucking it into a trot. Randy decided Fremont's TWO-arm beckon did include him, and made Spots speed after Kit.

Fremont wanted a little help, he said, a strong man with a large hunting knife to cut through the sod mat. He wanted a sample of sod and of the soil underneath—AND he needed Randy's big pants pockets to take the sod and soil to camp. "We should be stopping in another hour, shouldn't we, Carson? From this little rise, we can see where the river begins to bend west. You said we should camp tonight near the bend so tomorrow we can strike north 25 miles to the Platte River. At last we'll be on the highway to the Rockies. Randy, the riverside trail goes west for hundreds of miles!"

"Yes," said Carson, "that's right. Today we've marched less than 25 miles, and tomorrow will be a little longer—harder, too, on account of the sun will probably be as hot as it's been today, and there won't be a drop of water anywhere until we get to the Platte. Everybody should have a long soak in Little Blue tonight, and in the morning, we must fill every water cask, canteen, and bottle we have."

As Carson dug, Fremont on his knees watched the sod and soil the knife was bringing forth. He closely examined some of it. "Yes," he said, "this soil beneath the sod is a sandy loam. I'm sure it will prove to be as fertile as eastern soil that today grows corn and wheat. This grass growing here, and the sod built up during past centuries surely must prove that there's enough rainfall for grain crops. All of this tells me that before long, farmers may start for Oregon but many will choose to stop here, measure for themselves a few hundred acres of this grassland, build their homes by a prairie stream, plow up the sod-mat, and plant corn in the rich soil below."

JF Report
June 25
(dig sod)

Carson glanced at Fremont and gave an almost invisible shake of his head. He had cut through 12 inches of the tough mat of grass roots before reaching the soft sandy loam.

Story of the Great American West
(Readers Digest book)
p310-12, rich prairie

Randy turned around in a circle looking across the tree-less miles of grass. Build houses without wood? His eyebrows and mouth drew together. Like Carson, he couldn't see corn growing there either. But the Lieutenant was a scientist, he decided, and knew a lot more about such things than a mountainman trapper or a boy whose voice wouldn't deepen for a couple of years yet.

In an hour, the column reached a riverside place where Indians had once camped. Randy saw many big bones lying on the ground, and some rough bark sapling frames standing here and there. All the men cheered at the sight. "Buffalo bones! We're in buffalo country!"

Carson said the campground was Pawnee, was about a

year old, and some wooden frames were to stretch buffalo hides, others to hang meat strips on to dry. "Looks like they killed upwards of 50 or more in a surround here. Big buffalo herds don't often come over this far east. We probably won't see one before a couple of days' march west along the Platte River."

Nearby was a fine place for a camp. Randy hurriedly put up his tent and tossed his blankets and belongings inside. All the while his mind was picturing bones, the bone field they'd just passed, the animals those bones once held together, though he'd never seen a live one. Chores done, he ran back a quarter-mile to the acre of scattered bones. Buffalo! Buffalo bones! Randy began picking them up, putting them in a pile, thinking about putting them together to make a whole buffalo skeleton. The pile grew high with bones of every length, enough bones, Randy thought, to make at least the animals whose hides had been stretched in the wooden frames.

But when he separated them into piles of ribs, spines, legs, and pelvics, there weren't enough of some kinds, he decided, to make even one complete buffalo. Undaunted, he began searching for more bones in the underbrush next to the trees on the riverbank. Finding nothing, he looked up with a sigh—and saw three skulls hanging on a tree branch!

At that moment, he heard his name—"Randy!!"—looked up and saw bushy-headed Moise Chardonnais, blacksmith and weatherman coming toward him. "The Lieutenant says to come eat some beef stew before it's all gone!" Moise called. "I can't go now—I've just found some buffalo skulls! I need them to make a whole skeleton! I need a lot of other bones, too—more backbones, 'specially. And ribs. Wonder why there're fewer of them?"

"Probably wolves and coyotes toted off a lot," Moise said, "and a lot wuz cooked soft enough to be chewed up 'n' swallowed by a hundred dogs. Dem camp-dogs are work dogs dat drag de Pawnees' loaded racks. Dey're always hungry, eat anyt'ing. You're gonna end up hungry, too, if you don't come on to supper. Dese ain't de only bones you'll come across. In about 48 hours you'll begin seeing so many buffalo bones, buffalo herds, buffalo hunts, buffalo carcasses, buffalo meat cooking on sticks, piles of bones—"

"Moise!" Randy interrupted, "I don't care about them, I just want these right here! Help me get the skulls out of the tree! PLEASE!"

In a few minutes, Moise was carrying a skull in each hand and Randy was hugging the smallest buffalo skull to his chest. All the way to camp he was wondering what John would say if asked about loading the skulls on one of the carts and taking them to Washington....

BARRIE KAVASCH

Surreptiously, Randy's co-conspirator, Moise, with two buffalo skulls in hand, hurries to hide them in a tree by the Platte River. Behind him, a pressed-into-service friend of a friend hugs and lugs a huge but one-horned bull skull. They expect to enlist skull-transport service from the first passing traveler, one on his way to St. Louis where Randy's aunt lives. But hidden Somebodies watching the skull-toters will shatter Randy's plan.

CHAPTER 8

SKULLS A-WEIGH—UP A TREE

June 25 - 26, Little Blue to the Platte

They hadn't walked far when Moise all of a sudden stopped and faced Randy. His face, a deep-lined, browned record of decades of sun, wind, cold, danger, catch-as-catch-can eating, broke into an open-mouth smile. "I bet I know what you been t'inking, young 'un! You'd like to hang dese skulls in your house back in de big city o' Washington, wouldn't you!"

Randy's smile matched the Cloud Watcher's. "YES! That's just what I want, Mwasey! But we're a long ways from home, and I don't know how to get them there." Moise's sparkling eyes clouded over. "Well, now, it be's dat— a long, long ways, skulls big and heavy. Dey'd have to travel wid us all de way to de Rockies and back again. I t'ink de Lieutenant might not smile on dat. I 'spect you best give ole Buffalo Bull here a pat, tell'm' goodbye, den look for anudder skull close by de Missouri where you're closer to home." He set the skulls down.

"Aww-www—ww. Kit said hardly any buffalo get this far, so I'll bet none get as far as the Missouri, so no skulls there, Mwasey! Besides, these are special, being the first we've seen, and one very big, even with just one horn. Can't I at least keep them in my tent tonight and say good-bye in the morning?"

Moise answered by reaching down to grab two skulls by a horn, and starting to walk. Randy, hands locked together across the smaller skull's face, hugged it to his chest all the way to camp.

"It's a good t'ing everybody else is eating all de beef stew on de o'ter side of camp, paying no mind to dis side," Moise mumbled. "We can slip in your tent, put de skulls to bed, and miss out on a lot of teasing and jokes."

When the skulls lay out of sight under Randy's blankets and saddle and clothes bag, Moise declared that Randy could tell everybody back home how he slept beside "de beautiful faces o' t'ree buffalo—it'll impress de President even! Gotta leave'um now and run to de stew pot."

Arapahoes.
L.Fowler
p18 (bones)
Skull episode
not in JF Report.
But bones found at
old campsite would
have excited intense
interest in a
12-year-old.

But as soon as Randy had swallowed his share of beef stew, griddle cakes, and "cowbrewed" warm milk, he ran back to the hidden skulls in his bed. Having never been well acquainted with buffalo, the size and heaviness of the head-bones surprised him. He lifted the biggest skull by its horn. "Bigger and heavier than my saddle!" He sat it down, fingered the lone horn, so broad where it was attached to the skull, so quickly becoming sharp-pointed as it curved out, then up. What scary monsters buffalo bulls must be! Look at how thick the bone is, he was saying to himself when he heard Moise's voice.

Account of an Expedition from Pittsburg to the Rocky Mts. *Maj.Stephen Long* p.311(buffalo skull)

"Bullets bounce right off'n dat headbone, dat dey do." The "gentle bear," as Fremont called him for his size, muscles, mass of curly hair covering all his head except for nose and eyes, had slipped into the tent silently, and was kneeling on one knee beside Randy. His eyes were sparkling with interest when they met Randy's buffalo-struck gaze. He kept talking, not waiting for a response.

"See, garcon, dere ain't no jawbones left on dis skull. Indians can easy unhinge'um, and make sum t'ings out-n'um, specially for playing games, like tied to a stick, to hit a ball along de ground. Bones're so useful here on de prairie where der's no wood much, dat's de BEST reason you won't find what you need to put together a whole skeleton. Take de buffalo's long curved ribs—de Indians'll lay five of 'um side by side, tie deir ends to a stick laid 'cross'um, and slide on dis sled down snowy hills faster dan a horse can run! I've seen'um do dat!

Black Elk Speaks. *J.Neihart, p.52* (bones used for games, sleds)

"Take odder bones, like de shoulder blade an' de big rib. Indians rub dem down til dey have a knife edge sharp enough to cut t'rue buffalo hide. See? De GOOD bones wuz gone from dat boneyard. Yo' little stack wuz not'ing but gnawed or broken discards."

Arapahoes *L.Fowler* p18 (bones)

"Not little, Mwasey! It was a BIG pile!"

"Aww, it'ud take a pile of'um twice tall as me to make one buffalo. And de right pieces, which der wuzn't. I'm s'prised any kinda skull, even a broken bull skull, got left. Indians hang up good'uns inside deir teepees and all 'round camps for good luck. Dat's after dey take out de brains for tanning de buffalo hides, and tongue to eat.

"Now come on, wrap up de skulls good so Henry won't notice'um if he happens in. Let's go get your guitar and bring it to de campfire fer a leetle chording so as we can brace ourselves fer tomorry—fer I'm predicting dat tomorry will be Meanday. At breakfast time, a BAD but short storm. Lotsa rain, so wrap up good. Den, 'bout midday stop after we turn nort' away from Little Blue, we march de afternoon across a desert wid no water, no firewood. Ready y'self for cold rations and a dry mouf."

"But what can I do with my skulls, Mawsey? How can we take them, too? If I ask the Lieutenant, I think, and you said you think, he'll say I can't. Could we hide them some way—like in my clothesbag? 'cept it's stuffed already. Aw, Mawsey, come on, think hard!"

Moise scratched his head with one finger and grimaced. "Well, I can't think hard enough in the next five minutes to do you any good. You come on, now—let's get dat guitar or der won't be time for a tune to set the men singing."

They walked to the scientific instrument cart behind Fremont's tent. With Moise's slow limp from a stiff knee—"got a piece knicked off by a bullet"—they had time for the question Moise's weather talk had just raised. "How can you tell today," Randy asked, "what the weather's going to be like tomorrow? Do you really figure it out by studying clouds up there? Is that why the Lieutenant and Kit call you Cloud-Watcher?"

"Oh, sooo—I've acquired a reputation! But—I doubt dey look at my wedder predicting as 'scientific,' do dey? And dey ought'n't. It be's a mystic, pure and simple. In my head dere's a wind vane, and a rain sniffer, and a detector of de temper of de air. Not 'temper-a-ture,' garcon—'temper,' like anger. When all of dem begin to whirr at de same time, it's like I be visited by a dream. I see it coming, dis wedder. I see de exact time dis wedder will hit. You don't bleeve de dream knows all dat? Dey don't eeder, so don't tell'um, hear?"

When Randy appeared with his guitar, scattered cheers welcomed him. When he struck the first chord, the men circled around him and helped him sing Moise's request, "I had an old dog with a cold wet nose, too-ray-too-ray, foddy-linky-di-do!" Then came sentimental songs, French or English, noisy with feeling—"Louisiana Belle," "Sur le Pont d'Avignon," "Oh Dear, What Can the Matter Be!" "I've Something Sweet to Tell You," and finally a raucus "Turkey

Overland Journal, *Ore./ Calif.Trail Association, Spring 1986. (Music)*

in the Straw!"

"Now that'll carry them light-hearted through the storm," Moise whispered to Randy when dusk signaled bedtime and the men went off humming tunes to their two-blanket beds on the ground.

In his tent, Randy stroked the big skull in the dark and worked through the details of one scheme, then another, finally a good one, for transporting the skulls to Washington—if not tomorrow, then on the way back to Missouri. He'd have to ask Moise to help. No use to ask Henry, who'd taken to spending all his nights and days with his friends. Randy went over his plan in detail, step by step, minute by minute what he'd do, then over it again to make sure he'd have it all down-pat when the time came. In the dark his hands measured the size, horntip to missing-horntip, of the big skull. BIG. Moise just HAD to help carry three skulls.

He was about to drop off to sleep when morning camp noises brought him to his feet. He hurried to Moise's tent, scratched at the tent flap, calling his name. Moise came out, listened intently to Randy's excited whispering of the main parts of his plan, shook his head, whispered several reasons why it wouldn't work, and went inside his tent.

By breakfast time, Randy had another plan. Moise's head-shaking sent Randy away clenching his teeth. When he saw a mule cart moving toward line-up, he confronted Moise again. "No, dat won't work," he said, "BUT—maybe dis way I've been t'inking 'bout WILL work."

They hurried to the cart where driver Johnny Janisse, today driving a cart without a hoop-raised top, was draping the India-rubber cloth cover from side to side. He nodded agreement to Moise's plan—IF they could carry it out without Johnny's noticing what they were doing. In minutes, Moise had a rope long enough to throw across the width of the cart and hang down both sides. Quickly he peeled back the cart cover and put rope and skulls in place, the big skull on one end of the rope, the two smaller skulls on the other end. He tied the skulls with rawhide shoelaces to the cart sides "so de bones won't bounce."

With the cart cover back in place and its long sides tied down, the skulls were only ordinary mysterious bulges. Johnny drove the mules and cart to their place in the line-up without stirring a single glance from anybody.

Right on Moise's weather schedule, 7 o'clock, when the mile-long column of mounted horses, mules and carts, pack-horses, extra mules and horses, and the cow had moved along a mile or so, a cold northwest wind hauling dark-edged clouds blew in.

By 9 o'clock, black, roiling cloud masses covered the sky dome like heavy smoke from an invisible, horizon-to-horizon fire—invisible fire except for startling flashes of electrical flame spearing down toward the prairie. Thunder boomed at shorter and shorter intervals, squalls of rain streaked sections of the sky, first in the north, then east, reappeared in the west, jumped south, moved directly overhead and poured. Randy and the men wrapped hand-outs of India rubbercloth covers around their head and shoulders—the Lieutenant had taken Moise's prediction seriously, scientific or not.

Suddenly, a FLASH! A loud crackling, stabbing sound! Randy's eyes felt scorched for the half-second before his lids snapped shut—but not before he saw a column of dust rising where the lightning had stabbed the earth a little distance away! Then upon their ears fell a numbing clap of thunder like the clang of a million-ton bell hidden behind the dark curtain above.

The column stopped with horses rearing and neighing, mules kicking the carts and bellowing, the cow lowing and crying. Rain gushed while men's voices shouted reassuring words to the animals, flung coarse words at the raincloth sliding from their head and shoulders.

Randy, trembling with fear and cold and excitement, hung onto his cover of raincloth with one hand and the pony's reins with the other, hoping and praying that Moise's other prediction would come true, and in a hurry. "Short—it won't last long, dis rain," he'd said. "It'll move on wid de fast wind."

Rain did move on after a few minutes, a column of liquid streaks led across the prairie by the hypnotic light of electrical bolts and noisy crashes of turbulent air.

For a half hour or so, the column remained where it was to recompose animals and men, to check covers on carts, and packs on horses and mules. Overhead, the black turmoil, quick flashes, rumbling and growling moved steadily

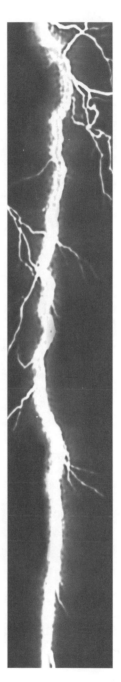

JF Report
June 26
(lightning stab, storm)

away, and clear sunlight filtering in through a cloud-crack in the west began diluting the gloom. Fremont, Lambert, and Carson rode down the line, asking after everyone and everything, listening to the comments—"Never seen anything like that BOLT hitting the ground!"—and seeking out Moise for his latest weather news.

Moise was smiling. "Dere'll be more sunshine dan anybody likes in an hour, Sir. So much, such a bearing-down heat, Randy better cover his head wid a hat over a kerchief—don't risk sunstroke," he said. While he spoke, Moise moved this way and that, same as Fremont moved, blocking Fremont's view of the skull bulges on the sides of Johnny's cart.

"Moise Chardonnais knows what he's doing!" Fremont declared, which caused Moise a slight twinge of conscience and a nervous smile until the Lieutenant added, "so I'm going to pass the word that, to hurry across the dry, hot sand desert you predict, we'll make no mid-day stop. We'll take 30 more minutes right here, before we leave the Little Blue, for the cooks to distribute good helpings of hard bread. Every man must check his water supply, refill if needed. Each man must immediately take his own mount, and any he has charge of, to drink their fill of river water. If there's any time left, lead the animals to nearby grass.

JF Report
June 26
(no-water trek)

"We've seven or eight more hours of march to reach the Platte River. There'll be no more stops to re-fill water containers, since, as you were told yesterday, there is NO water on this barren ridge we must cross. Carson says grass gets scarcer and scarcer the farther we go."

Time and the animals' walking pace went slower and slower during the next hours when the sky had cleared and the sun bore down. Tufts of grass grew farther and farther apart after they began ascending the long if slight incline upon leaving the Little Blue Valley. Across the bleak landscape, which became more and more sandy, the trail faded into barely visible hoof-and-wagonwheel lines of the emigrants. Other, deeper, lines crossed it from time to time, the biggest—the only—diverting sight on the long, tedious, sun-burning march.

"Same as the lines we saw back a few days," Carson told Fremont. "Pawnee trails. These look kinda like eight or ten wagonwheel ruts side-by-side and close together, but they're not. They're ruts dug by hundreds of loaded travois poles.

Great Platte River Road.

Whole Pawnee villages move southwest to the Arkansas River in the general direction of Santa Fe, looking for buffalo, or for horses to steal, or for Sioux and Cheyenne Indians to kill. Mortal enemies, they are."

Looking across the blank distances all around him, and hearing in the same moment Carson's talk about Pawnees, made hot, thirsty, bored Randy feel that Pawnees didn't really exist. They were just talked about. "Look, there's no place for them to come FROM. Not a teepee dot from here to the edge of the world maybe a hundred or a thousand miles away." Still, the talk, the word "Pawnee," reminded him that his night for guard duty was soon rolling up again.

He had just about decided to speak to Kit about that when he heard him say, "Maxwell! Look to your left! Antelope! Let's go!" and begin reining his horse out of the line. Impulsively, Randy cried out, "Let me go!" thought he heard Kit Carson say, "Come on!"

Randy reined his pony out of line, too, poked it with his heels, clucked a "Gittyup!" felt the pony's muscles tense, its legs begin a galloping rhythm. In the near distance, he saw three tan, four-legged shapes, heads down, paying no attention. He saw the hunters rapidly closing in.

Rather leisurely, one pronghorned antelope lifted its head. It seemed to look with great interest and little concern directly at Randy. A second antelope looked up and stared at Carson and Maxwell. In another second or so, all three antelopes were leaping in the opposite direction of the huge, fast-moving objects that at first had merely aroused curiosity.

Randy saw two antelopes falter, fall. Then the gun-noise arrived—two bangs but so close together they were almost one. The two hunters, their horses neck and neck, manes and tails bouncing and flying rapidly to the movement and speed of the gallop, reached the fallen pronghorns. The men reined their mounts to a stop, slid off. Randy's pony ran up as the hunters were cutting the throats of the wounded animals.

"Randy! What are YOU doing here?!!" Carson shouted. For a moment, Randy felt afraid he had done something terribly wrong, terribly stupid, shameful even. His face expressed his fears. Carson immediately waved a hand and worked up a half-smile. Relieved, Randy said, "I heard 'Come on,' and I wanted to come!"

Maxwell said, "Aw, it's all right for the boy to have a lit-

J.M.Mattes
(travois)

JF

Pawnee
Based on G. Catlin

Report
June 26
(antelope hunt, Kit
and Max)

86

tle adventure, ain't it, Kit? Must be right hard for a 12-year-old to sit all day in a saddle with nothing to do, hardly anything to see. Remember how we at that age couldn't bear to sit still for long, kept itching to DO something? Still do, wouldn't you say? Lord knows I was hoping just now for something to start happening—even a Pawnee war whoop would've been welcome. Just before you yelled 'antelope!' I was about to offer you five dollars to kick my horse and start a ruckus."

Carson began laughing, so Randy did, too. "Besides, this boy brought us luck!" Maxwell went on. "Remember I missed my shot last time we went after that elk—but this time, that big red bandana flapping 'round Randy's head fascinated the 'lopes just long enough for me to aim, fire, and make a hit."

Squinting, Carson looked hard at Randy's head and drawled, "If I'd knowed that was a red bandana, I wouldn'na said a word. I thought it was all hair."

Puzzled, Randy asked, "My bandana fascinated the 'lopes?" Maxwell, his eyes shining merrily, said that some hunters swear waving a red cloth at the antelopes will cause them to stand still and study it, favoring their strong curiosity instead of their instinct to scamper away. "Looks like your red-top proved that's true, Randy!"

They were still laughing when Kit said, "Grab a hind leg there, Max, and help throw dinner behind our saddles." In great, good humor, the three hunters trotted back to a whooping line of men happy to see fresh meat arriving for the next meal.

But a few hours more of working across deeper and deeper sand remained before antelope steaks could roast on campfires.

About five o'clock—"o'chronometer" as Fremont liked to say—they approached what had for some time seemed to be a range of high and broken hills. They turned out to be

JF Report
June 26
(sand dunes,
Platte Coast)

sand dunes blown into peaks, and shaded light green in color by prairie grass. "They're not as high as they looked," Fremont said after taking an angle and working the arithmetic. "Maybe 50 feet. And speaking of altitudes, the barometer tells me, Randy, that you're now standing 2,000 feet above Washington, D.C. at near-sea level!"

"All downhill to home!" called Johnny Janisse who had

left his cart for a look-around when the column stopped. "My Grandma's there. She's in your big capital city—25,000 folks, and Grandma and de ot'er slaves."

They went through low spots between the sand mounds on the Platte River "shore," descending slowly, sand dragging at the animals' feet and the cartwheels for two miles. Emerging from the last line of dunes, they shouted, waved, reined their horses in circles at the thrilling sight of the expanse of water—"like a big lake"—the wide, flat, shallow Platte River, roadway to the Rockies!

Great Platte River Road,p153,161. J.M.Mattes

Across the sandy "beach" to a strip of lush grass, flowers and cacti, through a thin fringe of now-and-again willows and ancient, big-branched cottonwoods along the low river bank, horsemen raced into the river's edge. They jumped to the ground, scooped up water by hand. Before it touched their lips, they let it spill, and called out almost in chorus, "Lordy, it's half sand!" Then, like singing a rehearsed second verse, "Whole river's four inches deep!"

JF Report June 27 ("scattered fringe of trees on bank.." Also,June 28 trappers put furs in trees by river.

While Randy and the horsemen explored the water and trees at the river's edge, the mule drivers, directed by Lambert, were parking to form the cart-circle of the camp. Moise made it his business to trot along close to Johnny Janisse and the skulls.

Suddenly, Francois Tessier ran up on the opposite side of the cart, said something to Johnny while leaping up to sit beside him on the driver's seat. Moise thought fast about what to do if Francois didn't quickly finish his business, jump off, and go away.

Skull episode not from JF account.

Johnny's cart in the camp circle was on the river side. As Johnny began persuading the two mules to turn and straighten the cart to head toward the central circle, Francois hopped off to help guide the mules.

Moise decided young Francois looked to be close friend to Johnny—so, chances were good that what Johnny did or said about the skulls, his friend Francois would, too.

Johnny, jumping off the cart on Moise's side, said "Hi" to Moise, rolled his eyes at a bulge under the cart cover, and hurried around the mules to Francois' side of the cart. Moise heard Francois say, "Whatcha got under dis bulging cover over here, Johnny?"

"Oh, just a little undercover business of Moise's dat I don't know not'ing about," Johnny said blithely. "Moise's on the other side, and, uh, I wouldn't be s'prised if he'd be glad of a trusty hand if you have one to offer. But better be quick, EVERYbody'll be rushing over in a minute for tents and bags—including nya-nya Proyyyce!"

Francois climbed up and over the cart seat. "Moise! Whatcha up to?" he asked, jumping to the ground. Moise decided to open up. He needed help to move fast. Still untying rawhide strings holding the cart cover, he told Francois in voyageur French that he was helping Randy with the first stage of moving three buffalo skulls to Washington, D.C.

"I've got to get'um off and hung high in a tree here by de Platte so dat de first traveler we meet who's going east can be asked to pick'um up and take'um to Randy's folks in St. Looie. I want dat de rest of dis camp don't know not'in 'bout it."

Quick-witted Francois set to with Moise standing guard, and a quarter-second before the first camper strolled up asking for tent and sack, Francois was out of sight climbing the biggest cottonwood tree by the river. In another two minutes, the three skulls were tied to a tree limb. "Snug up against de trunk on de side away from de trail, dey'll be plenny hard for passersby to see," Moise agreed.

A hundred yards upriver, Randy was wading in the yellowish, murky water along the edge of the river. Nearby, Carson was busy dissuading Henry and three of his pals from wading their horses across the wide stretch of shallow water to big trees growing on what looked like the opposite bank. "But it's actually the bank of an island—a big island.

JF Report
June 26
(river,island)
To get there, you could ruin your horses. Bottom's mighty treacherous," he was saying. "Quicksand in spots. Holes that'll break a horse's leg and send you flying. You might even break your neck landing on river bottom that's so close to the surface. Water's barely four inches—hardly above Randy's ankles."

Henry interrupted impatiently. "Awww—in that case, we could wade out there if it's so risky for the horses." Carson agreed. "Well, you probably can. Platte means 'flat' in Indian and French, and a flat river means spread out wide and shallow. What you see here is not even half its width. The rest is on the other side of Grand Island. It splits the Platte in two.

"Grand Island is LONG," Carson told them. "Some folks say it's 100 miles long. Other folks say it starts God knows

89

where and ends God knows where. I judge that we're about 20 miles west of its eastern end, and we'll be seeing it all day tomorry as we go on thirty miles. That don't add up to a hundred."

Henry jumped off his horse. "An island, you say? Ha! That makes the woods even more interesting! What say, fellows—let's tie our horses to the trees and cool off our feet in the big Platte pool on our way to the island!"

Before Randy and Carson departed for camp, they watched Henry and his friends Cadot, Ruelle, and Marly wading alongside the riverbank, heading for the narrowest stretch of water between themselves and the alluring island.

"Pssst!" Henry suddenly hissed to the other three. "You see somebody climbing that big ole cottonwood on the riverbank? Look right up ahead!"

"Hohoho! It's Francois Tessier. That's Moise on the ground handing him—what? Wonder what's going on. Let's watch. Get down behind the bushes, out of sight."

Great Platte River Road.
J.M.Mattes
p61-4, p161
(Platte River, Grand Island)

Sextant in hand, Fremont kneels behind the artificial horizon box. Randy expects him to lift the sextant, bring its telescope to his right eye, and train it on the North Star, Polaris, shining way out beyond the Big Dipper's lip-star. Instead, Fremont stares through the telescope at the pool of mercury lying under the glass roof of the artificial horizon! Randy sets his lantern down, leans to peer at the silvery liquid metal, sees in it the twinkling reflection of the North Star! This is how John "shoots a star" with a sextant to find out how far north of the Equator the campsite is? Randy settles down by Mr. Preuss to watch silent, intent Fremont.

91

CHAPTER 9

SHOOTING STARS, SHOOTING BULLS' EYES

June 26, Grand Island, Platte River

Ravishing smells of roasting meat from a successful hunt, then the good feeling spreading from tongue to toe from the first taste of hot, juicy, right-off-the-smoky-fire antelope steaks, turned the arrival at the Platte River Coast into a festive day of triumph.

Even the water of the Platte tasted delicious after the cooks had let the sand settle to the bottom of the buckets. Only Mr.Preuss strained it through his handkerchief, then asked the cook to boil it with coffee grounds to improve the flavor and kill "the wiggly inhabitants" he claimed to see.

Randy had searched out Moise first thing when he came into camp from the river. "Tell me quick," he whispered, "how'd you unload the you-know-whats, and what did you do with them?" Moise looked around at the men pressing close to pick deer steaks from the grill. "Dis no place to talk, Randy," he muttered, "Tell you when we sit down by ourselves to eat."

Randy was bursting with questions and hurried to collect meat, bread, n'coffee before running outside the camp circle to an isolated grassy place.

Moise was taking a long time. Politely waiting to eat, Randy lay back on the grass. Into the blue, blue bowl of sky, a sudden swarm of swallows darted, swirled, and whizzed away. He heard a horse snort and blow, saw its back shining like burnished gold in the late afternoon sun. "I'm getting to like this prairie, all this wide open sky and land. John says big space expands the mind, gives it room to roam, so maybe I'll roam past the horizon to—"

But Moises' baritone was saying as he limped up, "Dat first big cottonwood by de river—sit up and look over dere. See dat old tree wid big branches close to de ground? You can a'most see from here where de skulls is tied to a branch big around as your head, Randy. Tessier—you know, de voyageur dat checks de carts every day, puts grease in de axle boxes, mends and fixes everyt'ing—he done de tree climbing and skull tying. Just happened he jumped on de cart wid his friend Johnny, and den, just naturally hap-

June 27
Skull episode not in
JF Report

92

pened dat he lent a hand to me, de friend of his friend Johnny."

"Can we go over to the tree?" Randy wanted to know. "I'd sure like to see exactly where the skulls are. Are you sure nobody will steal them before our St. Louis trapper— the one you say we're bound to meet in a day or two—gets here and takes them to my aunt?"

Moise didn't see how in the world a passing stranger from any direction could see the skulls the way they were tied to the tree branch. "But after we finish eating, we'll take a little walk over dere."

Moise took his time sipping coffee, filling his pipe with a mixture of tobacco and kinnikinik, lighting it, slowly puffing, and telling Randy all the details of "de time-immemorial" smoking plants of de Indians. "Kinnikinik's de inner bark of de red willow tree," he said, "wid a little dried sumac leaf added. It smells good, but de smoke tastes a whole lot better when it comes-off a mix dat's half REAL tabacky."

Half of Randy's attention heard Moise. The other half went to clouds hovered at the horizon waiting to cushion the sinking fireball, soak up its red, pink, orange, and lavender lights, flare them magnified across the horizon. "Now that's really pretty," Randy thought. "Mother would like that. She might'n like all the prairie space but I know she'd like these pretty sunsets."

Moise had just begun to expand on what Indians smoke— "all kinds of plants—rose bark, lobelia"—when they heard a rifle shot.

They looked at each other questioningly. "Dat shot come from down river," Moise said, nodding his head toward the east. "Pawnee villages dat way."

Then they heard a pistol shot. "Dat don't sound like Indians—or all de camp would be commotioning. I t'ink it's some fellas target shooting. But I better go investigate. You better run find out if de Lieutenant give anybody permission to shoot." Moise had scrambled to his feet and was fast-limping toward the river.

"But I haven't seen the skull tree, Moise!"

"I'll take you first t'ing in de morning!"

As he ran to Fremont's tent, Randy heard more shots, one accompanied by a splintering sound. "Sounds like a bull's-eye," he thought. Fremont's tent flap was wide open and Randy ran through it, blurted out his message and question, "Gunfire! Indians?"

Fremont laughed, rose from his desk and put his arm around Randy's shoulder. "Calm down, my boy! No Indians! Just some of our men—Cousin Henry included—doing a little target practice. They rushed in from wading in the river, gobbled their meat and ran, wanted to practice target-shooting before daylight fades. Too bad you weren't around.

"Well, as it happens, Randy, I'm glad you're missing target practice. I have an important job for you tonight. You'll find it much more interesting than staring at a bull's-eye. Wouldn't you rather shoot stars with a sextant than shoot targets with a gun?

"Besides, you should see what I must do every evening the sky is clear to carry out the main work of this expedition—make a scientific map—not just a guesswork we-camped-here sketch of the trail from Missouri to South Pass in the Rockies. Our scientific map showing lines of latitude and longitude will precisely, accurately, locate the trail on a reliable map for families wanting to cross the continent and settle in Oregon.

"So, every clear night, I must go out after sunset, find the North Star in the sky, position myself and the sextant so that I see—

"What's a sextant? A celestial navigation instrument, Randy. It's in this box I've just brought in from the instruments cart."

He began opening a large-booksize wooden box on the table. "We're going to have a perfect night for viewing the heavens—clear, almost cloudless, a small moon. Soon after sunset, we'll take the sextant outside. We can begin our star-gazing as early as twilight—dark enough for the North Star's reflection to be seen twinkling both in the mirror-like mercury pool in an artificial horizon at my feet, AND in a small mirror on the sextant's pointed top."

"Artificial horizon?" Randy said, surprised. He declared he'd been seeing a REAL horizon every day across the flat prairie. Fremont smiled. "An absolutely flat, unobstructed horizontal line? At sea—yes. But on land—hardly ever. Too many things and land shapes in the way. Even on the flat prairie, bumps and ridges in the land rumple the horizon's straightness."

Fremont lifted the foot-high sextant—two brass bars, ends joined into a point at the top and spread wide at the bottom to form an inverted V shape—from its padded box. "Here," he said, holding the sextant out to Randy. "Take ahold of the handle on this bar, and raise the sextant high

Consultant for historical navcigation instruments: Dr. Peter Ifland, Cincinnati, Ohio. Author of Taking the Stars, Celestial Navigation from Argonauts to Astronauts. Published 1998, The Mariners' Museum, Newport News, VA. and Krieger Pub. Co, Malabar, FL.

enough that you can look through the eyepiece of the little telescope attached horizontally midway a bar of the triangle. Point the telescope at the sky. What do you see?"

Randy squinted a look through the telescope. "Well, uh, a rectangular something is standing right in the way. The left half is glass, so, I can see through it to a wall of your tent. The right half—well, it's a mirror. Don't see anything in that except some fuzzy light."

"Yes!" Fremont nodded. "This two-inch half-glass, half-mirror rectangle attached to the sextant right in front of the telescope is an ingenious way to bring together the ends of two sides of a Heaven-Earth triangle. Where the sides come together on Earth, an angle is formed. If we can measure the angle's size, we can calculate where we're standing above the Equator on our globe.

"But how do you bring the star-line down to Earth to form an angle where you're standing? Before you can measure an angle's size, Starlight and your Earth horizon must meet to create the angle!

"You need a Celestial Navigation instrument to help you. For thousands of years the instrument was simple, using it was an art. But a hundred years ago, the invention of a triangular sextant with mirrors made the job quick and easy by bringing the star's REFLECTION down to the horizon!"

"How does it work? Our sextant's TOP mirror FACES THE STAR, catches the reflection of its starlight. Then the mirror is turned a little so it reflects its captured starlight downward to the mirror BESIDE the little, clear glass window you saw when you looked through the telescope. With the glass window trained on a view of the horizon, you've got them side by side—horizontal Earth-line and the slanting starlight from the sky! The angle is framed in the sextant!"

Fremont was smiling broadly. But Randy frowned. "Somehow I still can't see what angles have to do with the Equator or where I'm camping in Nebraska—"

"—or any other place on Earth's northern half," Fremont added. "Think of the North Star as a tall lamp-post at the top of the Earth. Imagine you're standing on the Equator, Earth's fat, middle bulge. You look for the light of the North Star—but at the Equator it's so low on the horizon it's out of sight!

"What's happened? Earth's mid-section bulges out so far it stops North Star's light, it can't get past! So, Zero North Starlight—perfect starting point for measuring latitudes—distances—all along the line-of-starlight, all the way from mid-globe to the top of the world! Every point along that slanting line forms an angle with Earth.

"Travel north from Equator's Zero Latitude and you'll see the North Star shining a little higher above the horizon each night, so the Earth-Star angle increases, too.

"When you reach the top of the globe, the North Star will be shining directly overhead—90 degrees Latitude—height—above the Equator. The sextant will see the Earth-Star angle there as a right angle—90 degrees! Half-way there would be 45 degrees—Nebraska!

"No, Randy, the angle's size can't be in miles. It must be in 'degrees' of CIRCLE measurement, the Earth being round, a globe—not a box of straight lines!"

Randy grimaced, looked puzzled as he stared at the brass triangle in his hands. "Well, all right. But how can you measure Nebraska's Earth-star angle? Do you need a circle-drawing compass? Or do the sextant mirrors have some magic in them?"

"There IS a mirror connection, Randy! Yes—the sextant itself does the measuring—as its top mirror turns!" Fremont exclaimed. "See this long Index Arm, its top end attached to the top mirror? The other end points to a flat metal arc at the bottom of the sextant. Degree marks on this curved arc measure Earth-Star angles. So, the Arm's TIP-END moving across the arc is measuring YOUR Earth-Star angle at the same time the TOP of the arm is turning the top mirror! It must turn until the star in the top mirror shows up in the low mirror. A RE-reflection!

"When you, looking through the sextant telescope, see that doubly reflected starlight in the mirror beside the glass window showing the Earth-horizon, you can be sure the Index Arm tip has stopped on a number that will reveal your latitude!"

Randy thought hard for a moment before saying, "I think I've got the picture pieces fitted together. Such a lot of 'um—but I still haven't heard what makes the top mirror turn! And where's the horizon—that 'artificial horizon' you said we have to use instead of the real horizon?"

"Very close by!" Fremont exclaimed, "as close as the top of a wooden box near your feet. The iron 'horizon' trough sitting atop the box must be high enough that I can comfortably aim the sextant telescope to see the trough and the mercury I pour into it under the glass cover. I'll be looking for the North Star's reflection in the mirror-like mercury—

starlight marking the horizon!

"When I see that light twinkling through the glass window in front of the telescope, I have only to hold steady as the top mirror turns. Suddenly, I see top mirror's star reflection moving into, re-reflecting into, the mirror beside the glass window showing the horizon star-light! An exciting moment!

"There they are! The angle is formed—and automatically measured as it formed! Now we know where we're tenting between the Equator and the top of the globe!"

Randy looked impressed but still puzzled. "But you didn't tell me yet what pushes the arm so it can turn the top mirror. There must be another magic something-or-other on the sextant for that job—isn't there?"

Fremont patted Randy's shoulder approvingly. "Yes! You're right, and the something-or-other is ME! To turn the mirror, my finger gently pushes the Index Arm's TIP, sliding it along the measuring arc!"

"So the magic's mostly in your finger!" Randy declared. "And when it stops pushing, our latitude is a mark on the measuring arc! I'll bet nobody else in our camp knows we're sleeping tonight on a line with a number in Nebraska. Can't ever SEE a latitude line on the ground—can you?"

"True you won't see a signpost by the road—but you can see latitude lines on a map," Fremont said. "Here—look at my Atlas cover showing latitudes on a GLOBAL map. Any trouble finding the Equator zero line?"

"Oh no. I had to learn by heart in school, 'The Equator is an imaginary line that circles Earth exactly midway between the North and South Poles!' "

Fremont pointed to the zero next to the Equator, then to each line circling the earth east-west, 10, 20, 30, 40—above the Equator all the way to 90 at the North Pole.

Randy, intently staring at the Atlas as he leaned over it, murmured, "Hmmm. I never understood all these lines on a map before. Lines circling the globe mark off slices all the way to the top! No slice at the top—just a dot marked '90 degrees.' But 80 degrees is a flat little circle. Like a bald spot on a round head!

"Oh, and 'way down here, sort of crossing the middle of our country, I see line 40. A river's close to it going a long ways west from the Missouri River. It must be the Platte!"

"Good!" Fremont said. "About half-way between the Equator and the North Pole! Randy, I think you might become a fine cartographer—mapmaker—like Mr. Preuss! Or a celestial navigator like me! I can see that you'll enjoy going outside with Mr. Preuss and me tonight to help us find the North Star, catch it in the mirrors of our sextant and artificial horizon."

Randy's beaming face had dissolved into a scowl when he heard "Mr. Preuss." His eyes toured the tent and found Mr. Preuss sitting in a dim corner. He and Randy gave each other a glance of disappointment.

"Amazing, isn't it, Randy, that this odd-looking metal triangle can bring us a message from faraway objects in the sky!" Fremont went on. "But I must tell you that doing what must be done to capture that message isn't as simple as my brief explanations may sound. We must do every step slowly, with exactness—often a tedious business—if we want to get from the twinkle of a heavenly body an accurate answer to 'Where on Earth are we ?'"

Randy heaved a deep sigh and shook his head. "I think it's really really HARD being a celestial navigator. I'm not sure I want to try learning much more."

Fremont laughed sympathetically. "It's true there's lots more to learn. But it's EASY compared to what celestial navigators had to learn before the invention of this sextant! For thousands of years, navigators used an 'astrolabe,' a flat disk they held vertically, letting it swing freely. Persians invented it for sighting a star—including our sun—along a pointer attached to its center. The navigator, usually on a heaving ship at sea, read the star—or sun—angle off of a 'scale of degrees' painted or carved on the astrolabe's face.

"Four hundred years ago, a big improvement—the cross-staff, a long flat stick with a sliding crossbar.

"It took three hundred more years, until about 1730, for the idea of using reflection—mirrors—to bring the star down to Earth resulted in the building of the kind of sextant you've been holding in your hands.

"Curiously, not one but TWO men, John Hadley in England, and Thomas Godfrey in Philadelphia, sketched out the same design for using mirrors to double-reflect starlight—an easy way to bring star and horizon together.

"No, Randy, they didn't know each other. Thousands of miles apart, both added two small mirrors to a metal triangle, attached to the frame a small telescope that allows the viewer to see when the twice-reflected North Star's light and Earth's horizon come together. Quite remarkable!"

"Why's it always the North Star?" Randy murmured.

"Not quite 'always,'" said Fremont. "Some other stars can be used, but the North Star is the most convenient, easy to find. Stars that continually move across the sky complicate observations and calculations. The North Star is always found in the same place, and stays there. Just as important, it's where we who live above the Equator need for it to be— hanging high above the north top of the world! A center post to shoot at!"

Randy giggled."You said the North Star comes down to Earth in the sextant mirror. It's shooting us! "

Even Mr. Preuss laughed.

"Well, it can shoot only as far as the Equator, Randy!" Fremont said. "As I've mentioned before, folks below the Equator's bulge can't see our North Star."

Randy pointed to the Atlas globe map. "But I see latitude circles BELOW the Equator. Do star-shooters down there have a South Star at the bottom of the world?" Mr. Preuss shook his head. "Zey're not so lucky as ve are. Zey don't have a fixed star as conveniently located as our Nort' Star. Zey use sextants to measure angles, but finding latitude by stars zat change position isn't so easy."

Fremont nodded and added, "Mr. Preuss, I've told Randy that Nebraska is about Latitude 45 degrees. Actually, as we were nearing the Platte, we recorded our latitude as about 40 degrees. Show him, please, where to put a dot locating us on our Atlas map of the globe."

Even in the now dim light Randy could see the fiery red glow of Mr. Preuss's face. "But I-I-I-, yo-y-y-you—"

"You're the cartographer, the map maker, Mr. Preuss. I know you can explain quite clearly. But hold off a minute. I need to light the spirit lantern. It's beginning to get dark in this tent. The sun's almost down."

From a small box wrapped in oil cloth, he took a short, thin wooden stick. One end had a gray blob. "I'll use a new French 'locofoco match' instead of going for a lighted splint from the campfire," Fremont said. He raked the match head across sandpaper on a wooden block. With a flare of white phosphorus that made Randy jump, and a smell of sulphur that made him sneeze, the match flame lighted the wick of the alcohol spirit-lantern.

"There now," Fremont sighed, relieved that making fire by "the new method" had gone well.

"Vell," Mr. Preuss began after much noisy throat-clearing, "zee Lieutenant gives ze number 40 for our Latitude, and you vant to know vhere to put it. Vell, a few minutes ago, you found ze 40 degree latitude line across zis country. Find it again."

Quickly, Randy answered, "Here—the fourth line above the Equator!"

"Dahs iss goot!" Both were smiling broadly, looking at each other. "So, YOU put ze dot on zis map."

Randy took the pencil eagerly. He bent over the map, pencil poised for dot-making. He looked up, puzzled. "Here's the 40-degree line near the Platte River. But where ON the line should I put the dot?"

"Exactly ze right question! You are not so stu—vacant as I t'ought—ach—heh heh—vell—yah. Ze Lieutenant says ve have traveled 328 miles from Vestport, but not all 328 miles vent vest. Many miles ve came nort' to find ze Platte River. Vee need OZZER map lines to find how FAR vest ve are ALONG zee Platte River. Vee must find out vich of zeese LONGITUDE lines running Norse Pole to Souse Pole CROSSES our 40-degree latitude line—yah?"

"I see them!" Randy exclaimed, "they have numbers, too, and the ones crossing the Platte are 98, 99, 100—my favorites, 'specially for school grades!"

"You see, I hope, zat Longitude lines make ze Eart' look like a peeled orange viz all ze section seams showing. But maybe you've never seen an orange."

Randy had seen one and even eaten it. "Sweet and juicy, and orange inside and out. Somebody gave my Father one. He said it came from Hispaniola Island and that Columbus brought oranges there from Spain."

"So? Vell. Ze Longitude seams—ah,lines—start on ze map at zero degrees in Greenwich, England. See it? Ze lines are numbered from ZERO to 180 VEST, and in ze ozzer direction ZERO to 180 EAST—all togezer a global circle of 360 degrees. You told me ze map shows several Longitude lines cross our 40-degree Latitude area. But vich one is nearest to us—98? 99? or 100?"

Randy, grimacing, shrugged his shoulders.

"Zis time, TIME vill tell—heh,heh. Yah, but vee need time from TWO clocks—chronometers—special clocks, STAY-ACCURATE clocks, no matter how hot or cold, how rough ze road. Can't forget to vind zem up every day, yah, Lieutenant? Ze sextant shows us precisely when ze sun has reached its highest ascent and vhen it begins its decline. Zat's vhen ve set OUR chronometer at 12 o'clock.

"Ze ozzer clock needs to show Royal Observatory time in GREENVICH, England, zero degrees Longitude, like Equator iss zero degrees Latitude. But to bring Greenvich time on a clock set in England iss not practical. Ve can use just as vell ze clock time of a place vhere ve know for sure ze longitude.

"For us, zat's Vashington, D.C., our home base. Zo, in Vashington, ve set ze exact Vashington time, co-ordinated viz Greenvich time, on our special chronometer. It looks like a big vatch, but iss very special, very accurate—"

"—and very expensive! $300!" exclaimed Fremont.

"But he pays! Vee need zat special, accurate clock! Ze reason? To locate vhere you are east or vest on land or sea, you measure distance by time!"

"But using MAN-made CLOCKS instead of a SKY-CLOCK of moon and stars to determine east-west distance is rather new," Fremont interrupted. "It's only 70 or so years old—no older than your Grandpa, Randy! Navigators and astronomers had long known that time was the way to measure east-west distances. But not by clocks, even after small wind-up clocks came into use in the 1500's. Too inaccurate.

"The moon is more reliable, astronomers thought. It moves like a clock HAND at a steady rate across the sky, sweeps past certain stars along its path. The moon seemed a Heaven-sent, natural time-mechanism for calculating earth distances and locations. Measure the angle between the edge of the moon and the star it's passing, then calculate, calculate, for three or four hours to determine the time and east-west position on Earth.

"Well, if you had a copy of the book filled with astronomers' records of moon travel for every day of the year—its path is a little different each night—your calculating took less time. Even so, answers too often sent ships crashing into unexpected shorelines."

"Zo—"

"Hold on a minute, Mr. Preuss—let me tell Randy an amazing story—how CLOCK-time finally replaced moon-time to determine east-west locations.

"In the mid-1700's—about the same time the sextant with mirrors was invented—John Harrison, a village carpenter and clockmaker in England invented a clock that would keep accurate time no matter the motion of the sea, or degree of heat, cold, or dampness. Tests at sea proved Harrison's 'chrononmeter'—time measurer—would stay accurate for months, making it the quick, simple, reliable way to determine longitude.

"But for 40 years, distinguished, powerful astronomers and scientists in England, clinging to their sky-bound methods, ridiculed his chronometer, calling it a 'tick-tock' solution. However, sea captains, including Captain Cook, used and praised Harrison-type clocks.

"Finally about 1770, the astronomers began accepting that the village clockmaker's chronometer was more practical and reliable for finding longitudes than their lunar-time tables and charts. So, the celestial clock requiring four hours of trigonometry and logarithm calculations and much faith gave way to fast-figuring of clocktime.

"Still, it took the determined intervention of King George III—'By God, Harrison, I will see you righted!'—and an act of Parliament in 1772 to get Harrison, village clockmaker, the prize money his clock had rightly won.

"Now, Mr. Preuss, tell Randy why calculating longitude by chronometer-time works so well."

"Yah—it vorks because ze Eart' makes one complete turn every 24 hours! Zo, ze Globe has been marked off into 24 sections, one for each hour of a day. Every section iss 15-degrees of east-vest distance.

"How to find out vhere ve are? Ve sight ze sun for noon, zen see vhat time it iss in Greenvich, England, ze longitude-zero line—OR—as I've told you—ze time in our home base, Vashington, vhere ve know vhat iss ze exact longitude. It's— but let's say it simply—77 degrees.

"Zo. Here in our Platte River camp on ze Norse American central prairie, ve set our clock vhen ze sextant shows ze sun iss at its highest position, noon. Ve look at ze Vashington, D.C., clock. It says ze time iss almost one-zirty! One hour and a half hours later zan our time! "

Randy's questioning voice interrupted. "But how do—"

"Don't interrupt! I am coming to zat point. One and a half hours—zat's one and a half SECTIONS between longitude lines! You know how to multiply one and a half by 15? Yah, by 15. Don't you remember zat's ze number of degrees in each section? Ze eart'z 360-degree circle divided by 24 hours?"

Randy mumbled, multipled quickly, then blurted, "Fifteen by one-and-a-half is 22 and a half!"

"Goot! Zo, zat's how far ve, and ze sun, have traveled from Vashington. Zo, add zat number to Vashington's 77 degrees longitude position."

"99 and a half!"

"Good, Randy! 99 and a half degrees is quite close to the number I expect tomorrow when I work out our longitude to the minute and second!" Fremont said.

"Goot! Zo! Now, you must find on ze Atlas globe-map ze norse-souse longitude line marked 99 zat crosses ze Platte River in ze 40-degree latitude section...Goot! Put a dot by ze Platte River..hmmm...it's such a small map...zere, west of ze meridian—ze line—marked 99 degrees."

Nervously, Randy pressed the pencil point into the spot, then lifted the pencil with a triumphant flourish. "Zat's our camp!"

Fremont quietly applauded. "Excellent, Mr. Preuss. But we must emphasize to Randy that we often need to check accuracy of our Washington clock to the minute and second. We do that by observing what time the moon passes Mars, comparing it with the time for our angular distance given in a record book. So you see, to correct a too-slow or too-fast Harrison-type tick-tock timepiece, I use some of the 'lunar distance' tables of Harrison's foes! Those tables are still being updated and printed!"

"Zo vee must not forget to vind ze clocks every day, or ve'll need zose lunar figures every night, eh, Lieutenant?"

"Yah, Mr. Preuss—I'll wind them tonight, AND wrap blankets around them in their well-padded, spring-seated boxes before we go bumping along the trail. We must protect them extra well. A clock that slows down for any reason means a map mistake of many miles for travelers.

"But now the light is dim enough for us to start work with the sextant outside. Randy, you can take the first look through the telescope, admire the North Star. You know how to find it by looking for the Big Dipper in the northern sky? You know the lip of the Big Dipper points to the North Star? It's a faint, faraway twinkler for such an important use on Earth.

"Now let's quickly pack up and move outside to do this evening's work. You carry the lantern, Randy, and this knee-high wooden box to set the artificial horizon upon. I'll carry the sextant in its box. Mr. Preuss, please take the box holding the artificial horizon's iron trough, glass roof, and iron bottle full of mercury."

Outside, looking at the pale North Star twinkling at some distance beyond the lip of the Big Dipper, seeing it enlarged by the telescope into a bigger, fuzzier twinkling light, Randy secretly decided he'd rather be an astronomer than a navigator or mapmaker.

Preparing and arranging everything for sky-watching and angle-measuring took a long time. First, they'd had to find a quiet, level spot away from the camp and the grazing animals. Then Fremont poured mercury into the artificial horizon trough, secured the inverted-V glass roof over it, and carefully positioned the box and trough to catch the North Star's reflection in the mercury's mirror-like surface.

Fremont then knelt in front of the glass pitched-roof. He looked through the sextant's telescope into the small clear glass window in front of it. He saw a star twinkling on the mercury's surface—the horizon. Holding onto this telescope view, he pushed forward with one finger the tip-end of the Index Arm. The top mirror began to move, angling slowly downward. Patiently he watched for its starlight to re-reflect in the empty mirror beside the starlit horizon he was seeing through the glass window.

In the tense silence, only Randy seemed to notice the deepening darkness, or how the flickering lantern light was attracting tribes of whining mosquitoes.

Suddenly Fremont called out, "I've got it! The star reflections in the top mirror and the mercury mirror are side-by-side in front of the telescope! Randy! Come here and look at them! Yes—you can take my place, though you may need to stand a little closer to the mercury trough. The mirrors are set and will hold the star reflections as long as we stay here! Anyone, short or tall can hold the telescope to his eye and see the starlight meeting of Heaven and Earth!"

Randy held the sextant handle tightly and peered into the telescope. "They really are side by side!" The sight gave him a shivery thrill "maybe like the inventors felt the first time they saw the mirrors on their inventions actually worked!"

Fremont held the lantern for Randy to see the Index Arm. "Look where the tip is pointing, the mark it's pointing at. That mark's number works out to mean latitude 40 and a little more than a half. "

After looking, checking, discussing, and number scribbling while Randy held the lantern high, Fremont announced, "Our latitude is 40 degrees, 39 minutes, 32 seconds." Mr. Preuss wrote it down in the record book.

It WAS amazing, Randy thought, that this star-shooting instrument could do so much. It must be a little bit magical since it showed you with mirrors what you wanted to see.

Now Fremont had more work to do. He observed the moon, measured the angle it made with Mars. Then he took long minutes to carefully pour the horizon mercury back into its bottle. Mr. Preuss packed the sextant and the artficial horizon into their boxes. Randy fought off pricking, singing insects with one hand and held the lantern with the other.

Both men had become so absorbed in heavenly bodies they had forgotten Randy's earthly body. Suddenly Fremont exclaimed, "Randy! We must get you to bed or you'll be falling off your horse tomorrow!"

Carrying the star-shooting equipment, they walked him to his tent. Even as Fremont was spreading a mosquito net over him, Randy dropped off into dreamless, starless sleep.

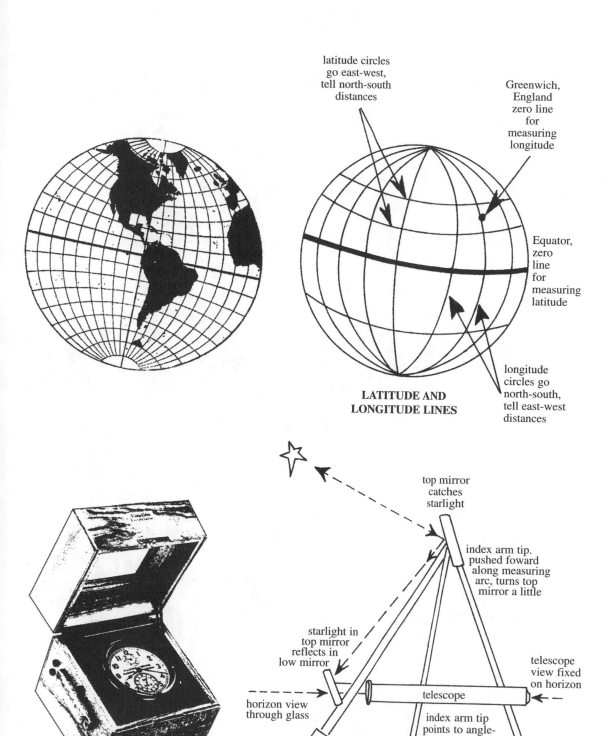

latitude circles go east-west, tell north-south distances

Greenwich, England zero line for measuring longitude

Equator, zero line for measuring latitude

longitude circles go north-south, tell east-west distances

LATITUDE AND LONGITUDE LINES

top mirror catches starlight

index arm tip. pushed foward along measuring arc, turns top mirror a little

starlight in top mirror reflects in low mirror

telescope view fixed on horizon

telescope

horizon view through glass

index arm tip points to angle-degree marks on measuring arc

CHRONOMETER,
about the size of a large watch, spring-cushioned in its carrying box

SEXTANT
about 12 inches high

106

Randy pleads the case of his hidden, now shattered, buffalo skulls before Judge Fremont
in an open hearing at camp. Co-conspirator Moise listens raptly. Opposite him, the four
accused skull-smashers, Cousin Henry among them, stare Moise down as they await
their chance to deny, accuse, defend, excuse their behavior. What will Fremont decide?
Who will be punished?

CHAPTER 10

SUNRISE JUSTICE

June 27, Camp by Grand Island, Platte River

Moise aroused him with a shoulder shake at daybreak. "Randy garcon, open your eyes. Moise must speak to you."

His voice muffled by a yawn, Randy asked, "What...you say?" and sat up. "Cousin Henry slept out again, seems."

*June 27
Skull episode not in
JF account.*

"He's in wid his mule-driver pals, and I hope he and Cadot, Ruelle, and Marly are showing wid black eyes and bruises, 'cause I shore laid some hard blows on 'um after supper—after I left you yesterday."

"You had a big fight with Henry and his friends? Why? What about, Moise?" Randy stifled another yawn. Moise squatted beside him and answered, "De whole story I hate to tell you, Randy, but you got to know, and you got to know first t'ing dis morning 'fore we all meet at breakfast. De story begins wid de buffalo skulls—"

"The buffalo skulls—you're gonna take me to see'um this morning." Randy was now wide awake.

"Randy, dis what I hate to tell you—de buffalo skulls wuz stole."

Randy wailed, "Ohhh nooooo!" He threw aside the blanket and began getting up, but Moise held him back. "Hold on, hold on. Dere's a lot more o'dis story to tell you. When you set off to check wid de Lieutenant, I headed for where it seemed to me de gunfire was coming from. Randy, I'm right at de part I hate to tell you. I wuz heading for de old, old tree wid de barrel-size trunk and long, thick limbs close to the ground—de one me and Francois hung de skulls in. Closer I got to it, better I wuz hearing wood splinter wid de shots.

"Den it come to me in a flash! Dis is DRY splinter sounds! Dis is NOT live cottonwood! Dem splinters is dry BONE! Skulls!"

Randy's cry was almost a sob.

"I run to where I could see 'um—Brant, Cadot, Ruelle, and Marly, and pieces of a skull on de ground. Brant was pulling his rifle trigger. CRACK! SMASH! De bottom part of a skull hanging on a little branch of the limb flew apart in splinters—"

"Awooowww!"

108

"—and two of 'um wuz laughing and slapping Brant on de back. De ot'er one, Marly, was taking aim at anot'er skull tied t'rou de eye sockets to de same branch. I started running toward 'um, hollering 'Stop! Stop!' but de rifle fired. Dat skull's face-bones scattered ever' which a-way!"

"NO! NO!" Face distorted with anger and grief, fists balled, Randy leaped up and ran out the tent door. He headed for the tent where Henry was sure to have spent the night with his pals. But Moise had sprung up, too, and his legs were longer and faster. He grabbed the boy and held him, kicking and protesting.

"Now listen to me, young man," Moise said, half-dragging him back to his tent, out of sight and hearing of his neighbors. "Running over dere and giving dem a few whacks ain't de way to do. Look at my eye, look at my lip—I tried knocking dem fellas, I wuz so mad, but de four of dem knocked me—me a man at least twice as big as you, and dey knocked me worse dan I done dem—and den dey said 'go pour horse liniment on yo'self and keep yo' mouth shut.'"

Randy stared at Moise's face. Even in the dim light, he could see the swellings. "Aww, Moise. They hurt you bad."

"Bad enough it'll be noticed by de Lieutenant. So we gonna be asked questions. Now even if you hit and bit and scratched and kicked dem fellas, if you done'um some harm before dey swatted you down, wouldn't dat put you in worse wid de Lieutenant?—I mean, seeing as how YOU de one gonna START dis fight now. He might see dat as bad—maybe worse dan Brant's taking and destroying your property.

"We already enough in de bad—sneaking de skulls like dat onto de cart. Dem fellas'll say you didn't get de Lieutenant's permission—which we didn't. Dey gonna say dey wuz worried 'bout de extra weight being a hardship for de poor mules, and how dey wuz only getting rid of a ton of useless baggage. Dey'll say, if de Lieutenant lets one person put on useless souvenirs, all de ot'ers will say dey can do it, too.

"And on top o'all dat, dey'll fault me for starting de pushing, shoving, 'n' fisting when dey wuz target practicing on de skulls, and I won't deny dat."

Randy was shocked into silence. It didn't sound right, or not as right as it ought to be. "But THEY'RE the bad ones—at least they're a lot worse than we are. You make US sound more awful than they are, and we're NOT!"

"DEY'LL make us sound awful—dey're like anybody in

109

trouble—dey zaggerate, make up stories, plain lie, say anyt'ing to try 'n' get demselves outta trouble."

"That's not fair!" Randy cried.

"Fair? Boy, 'fair' ain't naturally built into anyt'ing dat happens. 'Fair' is sum'um man-made. OUR man is Lieutenant John Fremont, so we have a good chance to see some man-made 'fair.'

"Tell you what we better do," Moise said. In the growing light, Randy saw Moise's swollen eye and lip were looking worse. "De best way for us," Moise went on, "is to go right now to tell de Lieutenant—tell him EVER't'ing—you, me, bot'. He'll do de right t'ing. He'll sort out what we say wid what dey say, and he'll wind it up like it oughta be.

"Now you get ahold of yourself. Straighten your face. We'll start dis minute for de big tent. But let me tell you sum'um else. Don't ask de Lieutenant to do sum'um real bad to Brant and dose pals o'his. We got to have'um go on working to get where we're going, and we got to have dem doing deir jobs willing, not shirky or sullen.

"Well, here's de Big Man's tent. De front flap is open, so he's up and about. Let's get dis job done."

Moise cleared his throat loudly. "Lieutenant, Sir!"

"Come in, Moise—and Randy, too, I see. What have you two come to report?" Fremont, seated at his table to write by lantern light, laid down his pen.

Moise took the lead. Standing arms akimbo, he told their story, taking all the blame for the idea of loading Randy's buffalo skulls onto the cart, hiding them in a tree after the arrival at this campsite yesterday—and for striking the first blow at the men he caught shooting Randy's skulls to bits as targets for rifle practice.

Randy explained that he'd never seen a buffalo skull before, he wanted really bad to take them back home to Washington for his Father and his sisters and all his friends to see, too, that these skulls were special because they were his first find, and that he felt bad about Moise's getting hurt when he tried to stop the men from shooting their bullets at real bull's eyes.

He skipped over his fear that if he'd asked for permission, Fremont might have said "no" to taking three heavy skulls on a cart even one day, much less three months. But he did mention that he was sure a trapper on his way back to St. Louis "would be glad to take the skulls to my Aunt, and get paid by her for doing it."

Fremont had listened attentively as he sat elbow propped on the table, chin in the palm of his hand.

Moise and Randy, having finished confessing, waited expectantly for Fremont's response, sympathetic, Randy felt sure.

But after a silent minute, they heard him say, "Men, I want you to go to your tents, get your things ready for our departure, and have your breakfast. I will send word to the four men you've named to do the same.

"As breakfast is ending, I will call all the men together. I expect that this incident has been noisy, violent, and visible enough to come to the attention of most of them. So, we will do the accounting and judging where all can hear instead of leaving it to hearsay and gossip. If anyone approaches you with questions between now and the hearing, you are not to talk to them except to say that they can hear all the details themselves very shortly. Now off to your work."

Outside, in the light of sunrise, Randy examined the blue color around Moise's eye and the swollen, broken skin of his lip. Moise noticed the red flush in Randy's cheeks, his teeth biting his lip. "You're nervous, Randy-boy? De Lieutenant knows what he's doing, so dis must be de right way."

Randy half-moaned. "But doing it where EVERYBODY can see and hear us! We have to stand up in front of the whole camp! Everybody'll be looking at me!"

Moise, Fremont's "gentle bear," put his arm about Randy's shoulder. "Don't use up your worrying on de matter of telling ever't'ing out in de open. All de men and 'specially de Lieutenant hearing de whole story is zactly what dem skull-busters DON'T want. Remember dey told me to keep my mout' shut? Dey didn't want anybody to know de true facts 'bout what dey done.

"In about ten minutes, dey'll know HE KNOWS, and in anot'er hour, ever'body's gonna know, and de Lieutenant's gonna pronounce JUDGMENT. Dey know he's gonna see deir meanness is 'way worse dan our little mis-step. Petit ami, dem boys' worrying now and after dis hearing is gonna be multiplied by four, 'cause deir's four o'dem!

"Come on now, let's bag our stuff, take our tents down, and get our nerves ready for standing up to face de public."

But Randy couldn't halt the worry questions running around in his thoughts. Why hadn't John looked at him with a little—even a tiny—smile? Not getting permission to lay three skulls on a cart was as bad as stealing and shooting the skulls to bits? Or was it WORSE because Moise

111

started a fight? Was there a law that said so, and that was why John hadn't smiled? What kind of punishment were they in for? Wouldn't Henry get punished, too? Would John tell Father? Henry's mama? Oh lordy me.

Moise rumbled a few words of cheer when they finished packing and walked to where the cooks were dishing up fried bacon and bread. The hot food and sweet coffee was tasting good until Randy glanced up at a hissing noise and saw Henry, Cadot, Ruelle, and Marly ten steps away glaring at him. They didn't look scared at all

They didn't look worried either. Henry made a motion with his hands like wringing somebody's neck, the other three laughed. One of Marly's forefingers blipped his bottom lip to make it look swollen, while his other hand squeezed an eye almost shut. Loud laughter as the four turned away. Randy, stiff and still, stared after them. Henry didn't seem a bit like the cousin he played ball with two years ago in St. Louis. Does the way Henry acts now happen to everybody at age eighteen? Randy wondered.

Moise saw the questions in Randy's eyes, still staring after Henry and his friends. "A mean streak in a man will come out on de prairie," he mumbled past his bruised lips, and put into Randy's hand a cup of milk the cook had handed him. "But de time is fast coming when dem fellows can't scare up one smile amongst 'um."

They sat apart from everyone to avoid questions. Hardly had Randy forced down a last bite of bread when he heard the head cook's iron serving-spoon beating a copper pan. Randy shuddered. He heard Kit Carson's voice calling loudly, "This is a call for a hearing, Lieutenant John Fremont presiding! The hearing concerns three buffalo skulls. Involved persons will come forward! Benton! Chardonnais! Brant! Cadot! Ruelle! Marly! All other men gather 'round! Lieutenant Fremont instructs you to silence—no pro or con noises during the hearing."

"Everybody's looking at me," Randy thought, and stood rooted to the ground. "Coming!" roared Moise, giving Randy a quick nudge with his elbow and striding ahead. Staring at the fringe on Moise's shirtsleeves, Randy followed numbly in his shadow to the row of six "involved men" facing the Lieutenant. Fremont, erect and solemn, imposing in his blue Army jacket with shiny brass buttons and belt buckle, spoke first to Randy, asking him to "relate what part you had in bringing the buffalo skulls to this camp."

Randy took a deep breath and glanced sideways at Moise. How could he keep his friend Moise from looking bad because he found a way for the buffalo skulls to travel, first to the Platte, then to Washington, and tried to save them from being blown to bits? How would the other 20 men treat him, Randolph Benton, if he was punished, and treat Moise if Moise was punished for helping him? In a flash, Randy knew he ought to make his own blame as big as he could.

He'd already told John his story—the short version. Now John would hear the long version. "Not to lie," he told himself, "just make my blame stand out big so it weighs more than Moise's—by telling every little detail about my thinking, no matter it sounds stupid, dumb, or foolish."

Randy began hesitantly, in the voice of a petit garcon, with a list of all the people in Washington he had wanted to show the skulls to because they might never get to see one if he didn't. In a stronger voice, he began describing how he couldn't sleep all night for trying to think of a way to carry the skulls to the Rockies then all the way back home—to St. Louis at least. He couldn't think of a workable way.

He'd have to bury them. Two nights ago, he'd turned and twisted for hours seeing himself five or six times digging a hole, putting the skulls into the hole, shoveling in the dirt, marking the place with rocks, finding it on the way home, moving the rocks, digging out the dirt, pulling up the skulls.

His voice strong now that words, whole sentences, were flowing easy and fast on the breath of excitement for the picture he was creating, Randy described jumping from his blanket, straining to lift the big skull, measuring it in the dark to find out how big a hole he'd have to dig—"one THIS WIDE!" Randy exclaimed, and stretched his arms as wide as they'd go. He heard some nearby snickers.

Unshaken, he declared, "I just had to have some help. I went out of the tent, and there was Moise coming out of his tent, so I asked him to help me. He said there weren't any rocks on the prairie, just grass, and besides, Indians would find the fresh-dug dirt and dig, thinking they'd uncover something valuable. Right then it was real plain that I had to find a way to take the skulls with me, maybe in my sack.

"But I didn't have room in my sack. The skulls had to have a ride—but on what? I had just my horse and saddle.

113

That had to be it—leave two skulls behind, tie the best and biggest on my saddle, and walk leading the horse."

Randy saw the smallest smile twitch a corner of John's mouth.

With a deep breath and bolstered confidence, Randy went on. "Just before leaving-time, when I was DESperate! when I was wondering how I could lift the big skull onto the saddle—it's REAL heavy! when I was 'magining myself walking to the Rockies and back—worrying about what you'd say when you saw a skull in my saddle instead of me—I all of a sudden remembered Kit once said that lotsa trappers go home from the Rockies along this river.

"I made up my mind to beg you to let the skull stay in the saddle, let me walk just a day or two, to give me a chance to meet some trappers. I could hire one to take the buffalo skull to my aunt's house in St. Louis—" (Randy's eyes rolled briefly in the direction of Henry)—"and she'd pay him and keep the skull safe until my Father came.

"But what if you wouldn't let me walk even a day or two? Right then, I saw the mule-cart drivers were starting to get in line—and I hadn't even saddled my horse. I was TERRI-BLE desperate then! I ran all around looking for Moise—found him—asked him how he thought you'd feel about my walking. He said you wouldn't like that. Besides, the skull's shape wasn't right to ride in a saddle. I was WORSE than desperate then! But then he said MAYBE the skull didn't have to ride in my saddle for those two days. MAYBE all three could ride on a cart for one day!

"He thought they could be hidden in a tree at our next camping place, which would be by the Platte River, easy for a trapper going home to find. I said I'd also thought of meeting a trapper, I'd help him get the skulls on a cart—"

As Randy had warmed up, become immersed in telling his story, his words had dissolved his fears, his awareness of Henry and his friends, or the little crowd behind him. Moise had slowly turned, gazing at him in wonder. When Randy said "help him get the skulls on a cart," Fremont quickly interrupted, "Thank you Randy!" Immediately he called, "Charbonnais!"

Moise, chortling, turned from Randy, and looked with smiling good humor at the Lieutenant standing in front of them. Hand on hip, he looked Fremont in the eye and said, "I've done confessed to you, sir, dat all de blame is mine for de idea and de muscle of loading de skulls on de cart, hiding dem in de tree by de Platte. I take de blame for not asking you or even telling you anyt'ing about bringing dem along, t'ough I couldn't see any serious reason against it. Chances are, dem skulls could've made it all de way to Sout'Pass and back home even if'n we didn't meet up wid any homebound trappers—and if de skulls weren't stole from de tree, turned into targets, and shot to pieces wrongly and secretly."

"Stolen?" Fremont inquired. "You said 'stolen?'"

"Dey werz Randy's, dey werz hid, dey werz took out o'hiding, hung up and shot to pieces without Randy's knowing 'bout it—he hadn't give 'um to anybody. Dat means dey werz stole."

Suddenly, to everyone's startlement, Mr.Preuss spoke up quite loudly, "And I saw zose men wiz zere rifles, heard zere talk of stealing ze skulls!"

Over the murmur rising from the listening men, Fremont said sharply, "How did that happen, sir?! Come forward!"

Mr.Preuss, his face all crimson, spluttered his answer. "It vas s-supper yesterday. I vas standing by zee tailboard of zat cart over z-zere"—he pointed vaguely west—"and I vas using zat tail b-board for a desk to 'rite a letter to my vife. Zen, I heard low voices coming near. I looked around and saw Brant, Marley, Cadot, and Ruelle. Zey had guns and vere joking about who'd climb ze tree to bring down Cuz Randy's REAL bull's-eye targets."

Fremont had listened with a puzzled frown."Mr. Preuss, why didn't you report this incident to me right away?"

Mr. Preuss flushed a deeper red, waved his hands in helpless little circles, opened his mouth to speak, but didn't.

Instead, Henry shouted in a loud, angry voice, "WE weren't talking about bull's-eyeing skulls—UNTIL Preuss gave us the idea! He said, 'You're going after BUFFALO SKULL bull's-eyes?' or something like that. Until then, all we'd intended was pitching into the river the silly skulls we saw Moise and Francois hanging in a tree!"

"Oh—Mr. Preuss and you did speak to each other. And you had your guns, having just gotten my permission for target practice. You knew the skulls you saw Moise and Francois hanging in the tree didn't belong to you, but to your cousin. Why did you think you had a right to take someone else's hidden skulls and destroy them in ANY fashion?" Fremont asked sternly.

"Lieutenant," Henry said stiffly, "we wanted to help your

chances of success on this expedition. See, when we saw the size of the skulls in the tree, we knew they'd put an extra load of 100 pounds or more for already overloaded mules to pull all day long. We wanted to make sure our mules wouldn't have that burden for the next two or three months. Useless pounds to haul to the Rockies and back! Worst kind of souvenir, big and heavy! Had to be Randy's—we saw him play for hours with the buffalo bones at the last Little Blue campsite.

"Being Randy's, we figured you might weaken, let him keep them. What we were trying to do was what was best for the expedition! What does it matter HOW we got rid of them?! Using them for targets made rifle practice more interesting, made us better marksmen—important when we have to fight Indians!"

"So!" Fremont's sharp voice stopped Henry. "You DID take the skulls you knew belonged to another, and you DID destroy them! That YOU have now confirmed!"

Henry shouted, "It wasn't OUR idea! We wouldn't have shot at them if the old German here hadn't said 'buffalo BULL'S EYE' and sicced us on!"

"I did NOT sic!" Preuss shouted back. Together, the four young men yelled, "YES YOU DID!"

A loud POP! and five startled arguefiers found themselves looking at Fremont's pointing finger, jabbing forward from a hard hand clap. "ORDER!" he commanded. "You will wait to speak until I have called upon you to speak—and you will not shout."

In the dead silence of the next seconds, Randy felt a gentle message from Moise's elbow.

The silence continued while Fremont, arms by his side, fingers clenched, body at military attention, considered the men one by one. Then he began his judgment. "Since the responsibility for the welfare of this party and the success of this expedition rests on my shoulders, no other member of the party can take it on himself to make any decision or carry out any act affecting the expedition without my knowledge and consent.

"Randy Benton should have consulted me about his intense desire to bring along the skulls, even if he foresaw disappointment. To help him remember this throughout the trip, I will assign him extra guard-duties until we arrive at Fort Laramie."

Randy clenched his teeth, stared at the ground in misery

and relief.

"Moise Chardonnais, voyageur and mountainman for many, many years, for failing to guide Randy with your better judgment but instead aiding, abetting, and defending him in ways that led to misguided if not detrimental acts, I assign you to be in charge of a crew consisting of Michel Marly, Benjamin Cadot, and Joseph Ruelle, which, for the next month, beginning tonight, will do the midnight restaking of our numerous animals.

"Midnight restaking is now necessary since, as we move west, the prairie grass will become shorter and less plentiful though more nutritious. The three men just named will pay due respect and obedience to their crew supervisor, Moise Chardonnais."

Moise rolled his eyes and cast a doleful glance at the world at large. His crew passed a feeble grimace among themselves.

"Henry Brant," Fremont was saying, "the leader of any group of men should think of himself as a model of good sense and decency for the others to follow. You are well-educated, you have had a good family upbringing, you undoubtedly have been taught that stealing, then destroying another's property for the fun of it is a sin. I will give you time to think about this. Until we reach Fort Laramie, you are assigned to remain at the end of the column, in company with Mr. Preuss, whose regular station is there for cartographic purposes.

"You are to aid him in his work, and you are to learn well the training in surveying that I now assign him the duty to give you. At all other times you will attend the cow, including learning from Moise how to milk her and taking every other turn. You will also assist in loading and attending the packmules—which will be a lesson in patience and temper control. You already know that I do not tolerate swearing, nor cruelty to animals. During the day, you are to keep to these duties, refraining from your usual routine of moving up the line to socialize with the cart drivers.

"I have considered confiscating your pack of playing cards, Henry, but decided against that—provided that you carry out your duties well by day, return to your own tent by bedtime, and sleep there every night. In all situations, I expect you to maintain the good manners and politeness I know you have been taught. Above all, you will bring to me any questions or ideas you have about what is best for the

117

expedition."

All eyes had been turned upon Henry during this sentencing. Tight-lipped, he had looked from under lowered brow at no one but Fremont. Hands in pockets, he shifted weight from one foot to the other, but clamped his teeth, and kept his poise.

"Do all of you whose names I called understand your assignments and have registered them firmly in your minds?" Fremont asked. A mumbled chorus of, "Yes, sir."

"Then this hearing is closed. It is now well past our usual leaving time. There are some tents still up, and much cleaning and packing remains for the kitchen crews. Lambert will be calling 'line up' in half an hour. Dismissed! To your places!"

Twenty-eight men, including Fremont and Randy, worked quickly and in near-silence, all weighing in their thoughts and feelings the justice of what Fremont had parceled out. Even after the mile-long line of horsemen, carts, pack animals, cow, and Brant-Preuss rearguard was well on its way, the subdued mood of the whole party prevailed.

"But," Kit Carson told Fremont when they stopped for fried pork and crackers about noon, "it's not a sullen mood, sir. I don't feel any undercurrent of disapproval among the men, or resentment agitating the seven involved. I think they think same as I do—that you done it like it ought to've been done: just, without hard shameing. And, sir, the sorting out you done was, well...ju-di-cious. Putting them to work together like that, with your instructions for them to live up to, might even square them around for the rest of the trip."

They pitched camp early, ending the day's march of only 18 miles alongside Platte River and Grand Island. Even so, it seemed to Randy that the hours had hung in slow motion for a long, long time, stretched by his busy mind and everyone's quiet. Only after he and silent Henry, who wouldn't look at him, had put up the tent did Randy remember it was their night for 8 o'clock guard duty—again...!

Beth Berryman

Down and out, footsore and ragged, unarmed, their treasure of buffalo robes left in sand
pits, 14 trappers walking from the Rocky Mountains to St. Louis make a stop at
Fremont's camp by the Platte River. Some of the Mountainmen had become buffalo
robe traders with the Indians when Rocky Mountain streams had no more beavers to
trap. On this trip to market their robes, they've joined another crew bringing robes to
Chouteau's St. Louis fur company."They're on their way to St. Louis!" Randy bemoans.
"Moise! Help me find another buffalo skull!"

CHAPTER 11

NO INDIANS—JUST TRAMPING TRAPPERS

June 27-28, Platte River camp (Nebraska)

Being alone was like a sleep signal to Randy's mind and body. Cutting short his regrets about guard duty, he fell asleep despite the afternoon sun shining into the tent's open flap. His sleep the night before had been cut short at both ends—Fremont at one end showing him how to shoot a star, Moise at daybreak showing him his battered lip and eye. Neither the supper gong nor Cousin Henry's digging through his pouch for his playing cards interrupted the soothing quietness of Randy's blank, unconscious brain.

But Danny Simonds did. "Hey you lying in there! You gotta go stand guard, same as me in half'n'hour! I'm taking Henry's place tonight—we swapped time so he can mould shot. Paid me fifty cents. Told me to let you know. How 'bout if I sit down in here 'til it's time to go?"

Danny was a skinny, slow-moving fellow who didn't look you in the eyes when he talked. About the same age as Henry, he'd left home in Taos the year before to go as a common hand with a scouting party through the Rockies. He'd had some adventures and he'd had little chance to brag about them.

"You know sum'um, Randy, this guard duty can get real dangerous...." and he sat down in the doorway to tell Randy about the night when he was on guard duty and his camp was completely surrounded by Indians yelling and firing guns for an hour or so, and how he and the others managed to slip out, get away with just their lives, leaving behind all their valuables—

At that point, Randy, now on his feet, interrupted to say he had to leave and find Kit Carson. "He's got my pistol!" he explained, stepped over Danny's legs and hurried off toward Fremont's tent. Carson and Fremont greeted him warmly. "Randy! You're a half-hour early!"

"I came for my pistol—and to get away from stories about yelling Indians attacking a camp in the middle of the night. Nearly everybody who talks to me starts off with another guard'n'Indian story!

"I bet they make up more'n half of it, just trying to

Fremont Report
June 27
(*"Randy took a regular turn of guard duty"*)

120

Journal of a Trapper
Osborne Russell

Kit Carson's Autobiog.
M. Quaife, ed.

Kit Carson
T.S. Guild/ H.L. Carter

scare me. And they aren't even INTERESTING stories."
Carson smiled, saying he knew a REAL interesting guard
duty story, and it didn't have a single dead man in it.

"It goes like this," he said, "and it happened about five
years ago when I was trapping with Jim Bridger. He and
sixty of us trappers had set up camp on a bluff when a
lookout saw a THOUSAND—yeah, THOUSAND—Black
Feet Indians on foot swarming across the plain below.
Bridger set us men to building a circle of logs and brush
around the camp. We worked hard and fast to complete it
by dark. A double guard wuz mounted. Bitter cold, it wuz,
trees cracking like pistols. No moon, stars shining bright.

"'Long'bout ten o'clock, the Northern Lights, light green
mostly, commenced flashing, darting, rushing to and fro
like curtains across the sky. Finally they began to calm
down. But the lights in the farther half of the sky turned a
deep, steady red while the closer lights faded. The red lights
lasted a coupla hours before disappearing.

"All this time, perfect quiet down on the plain. Next day,
we worked hard dawn 'til dusk cutting down big trees to
reinforce our fort. Still no attack. Another night passed.
Nothing happened. We began to worry that all our work
would go for nothing.

"But the next morning at sunrise, a guard passed the
word, 'Indians coming!' We saw them down on the plain,
marching 'round the river bend, a thousand or more in close
columns. The Chief, wearing a white blanket, came forward
a few steps, stopped, raised his eyes toward the fort. With
sign language he said they wouldn't attack—they werz going
back to their village. They turned and WALKED AWAY!

"Some of us men thought the Indians had seen the forti-
fications we'd built, and that wuz why they didn't attack.
But Bridger and most of the rest of us said it wuz the wonderful appearance of the lights in the sky. The Great Spirit
had shown the the Indians that when the shooting and
flashing ended, the Chief's side of the Heavens wuz bloody
red, whilst the trappers' side wuz clear and serene. What
do you think, Randy?"

Randy looked left, then right, then up, before answering.
"I think, with the trappers up high and the Indians down
low, the Chief was lucky he had a Great Spirit to tell him
he was going to lose."

Carson and Fremont had a big laugh, with Carson saying
that Randy would grow up and become an Army General.

"No, a wily politician," Fremont said.

He noted that the chronometer was saying it would be 8 o'clock in a few minutes. "Here, take this mosquito net and drape it over your head while you're on guard duty. 'Squeeters will fly in soon. Plenty of 'um around this river."

Randy said "Thanks!" twice. "All forty bushels of 'um gonna be disappointed when they bump into this net. They can sniff me but not taste me. Well, I'm on my way to the cart over there. At least half my guard-time's in daylight so it'll be easy to see slithering Indians."

The netting wasn't long enough to cover his legs below the knees unless he sat on the ground, legs folded under him. "Bet I'll look like a ghost to an Indian—that'll scare him off before he can get to the horses."

With this comforting thought, he stared through the thin, white veiling at the grassy area where a dozen or so horses were cropping their dinner. Brilliant light streaming from the setting sun lay like a fine net of golden threads across the wide river.

From then until the sun was out of sight, until the sunset's colors had faded, until the mosquitoes were zinging, and a gentle light was drifting down from a thin moon, Randy practiced expanding his thoughts beyond the cart, and beyond his sat-upon legs now going to sleep.

He decided he would expand by asking questions and making up answers...How did people find out what those lights are up there in the sky?....Who first noticed pale little North Star—and that it sat in the same place every night, all night?....Would he really LIKE being a stargazer like John?....Was anybody mad at him and his buffalo skulls for causing such a camp stir?....He couldn't make up answers to any of his questions.

Suddenly, it was dark and he heard noises...just good horse noises. He felt pleased with himself for not hollering for Kit the way he did last time. "It might help if I did get a little scared so I wouldn't feel so drowsy...."

At last, a hundred years later, the shadowy figure of his relief guard, good ole Basil Lajeunesse, came near and softly called his name.

An hour or two into the next morning's march, Randy was asking Kit Carson, "Do you think anybody—everybody— is mad at me about the skulls and the hearing, and what John did about everything?"

"Now what makes you ask a question like that? Did anybody say or do anything bothersome to you?"

"No," Randy said,"It's just that nobody's talking much to anybody. I mean—it's so QUIET."

Kit looked back towards the carts."Well, THERE'S much of the answer to that."

Randy turned to look. "I don't see anything."

"That's just it," Kit mumbled. "Until the Lieutenant's pronouncement yesterday, Henry spent his time horsing around the carts, laughing and loud-talking with the drivers. They're all right close to the same age, and boys that age just naturally like to whoop and holler. In camp they play noisy card games, wrassel, throw horseshoes—whatever they do, they're noisy about it.

"Now with Henry 'way down at the end of the line and no longer a loose horseman riding up and down the column, the noise level is way down. I like it this way. Less likely Indians will notice us. Them boys' voices and cackling carry across this open country for miles. It's a wonder we didn't have some Pawnee visitors."

"Kit, we haven't seen a single Indian since those who traded with us—their cow for our ox team. You said the travois tracks we saw mean the Pawnees've gone buffalo hunting. Where? How far away?"

"O, probably as much as a week west to find the big herds. Villages of two, three hundred people—and dogs—move out to the prairie as far as they have to go to meet up with a buffalo herd."

Randy frowned. "If they're not around here, then why do we have to have guards at night? I've got to do it extra nights, John said, until we get to Fort Laramie."

"Well, for one thing," Carson said, "it's your penalty pronounced by the Lieutenant. For another thing, we can't know if every single Pawnee in the area is out to the west killing buffalo—or, if he is, when he'll be coming back this way. It don't take but ONE wild man with a gun on a horse to wreck a whole camp when we're all asleep."

Randy tried again. "Nobody in sight for a hundred miles, Kit, in any direction right now. There's nobody out there. Also, I've noticed there's short grass now, no long grass to slither through. Seems to me that I shouldn't have to sit up at night watching for NOBODY to come."

No answer. Silence for several dreary minutes of listening to the dull plodding rhythm of horses' hooves on the grassy, sandy trail.

123

"Kit, if I did see an Indian anywhere around, could he hear us talking?"

"Not 'less you yelled—or cackled like Henry."

"Then tell me a story—one about nearly getting killed."

"Randy-boy, I'm not feeling like telling an old story. I've got a good case of shut-mouth like 'most everybody else in the column—'cept you."

Moise had a good case of shut-mouth, too, Randy found out at mid-day when the column stopped for food and rest within a short walk of the riverbank. He recognized his friend's bushy hair and bulky figure kneeling at the river's edge, and ran to join him. He was sloshing water on his face. "Hey Moise! You'll get sand in your eyes! How's the eye that's swollen?"

Moise barely looked up and shook his head. "My lip hurts. It don't want to talk. Hurt last night, too—but I had to get up anyway, put dose boys to work re-staking de animals at midnight."

"You mad at me?" A head shake and grunt answered. Randy gazed at the river. Now that they'd passed the western end of Grand Island, he could see the full lake-size sprawl of the gold-colored Platte, fast-moving though shallow. Beyond, grassy prairie spreading for a few miles north stopped at the edge of low sandhills—huge old sand dunes. They looked green, too, their tops a series of scoops and peaks like stiff ocean waves. Randy had seen hills like that at the prairie's edge on the south side of the trail, too, but they seemed bigger, maybe for being closer.

A breeze ruffling the river's surface made the sandy water look cool and tempting. Randy knelt beside Moise and began pulling off his mocassins.

"Moise! Wouldn't it make your whole face feel better and cooler if you came wading? Come on! I've got my shoes off! Here goes!" He ran into the ankle-deep water.

Moise rose to his feet calling, "Randy-boy! DON'T DO DAT! Bottoms's got holes! Come back!"

But Randy was running and laughing, calling, "See how shallow it is? Just above my ankles!"

Moise had started a limping run into the river to catch Randy when he heard the cook's gong and stopped. "Come on back here, Randy! Hurry up! We gonna miss de fried meat and griddle cakes! Lieutenant's not goin' wait for you nor me nor anybody—he's in a hurry to move on!"

"Oh, all right," Randy said, slowly turning around.

Moise, reaching dry land, was stepping into his mocassins when suddenly he stopped, shaded his eyes to look up at the bank and beyond. All at once, Moise's booming voice stopped Randy in fear and startlement. What was Moise yelling!?

"DU MONDE!! DU MONDE!!" Strangers!

"STRANGERS?? WHERE? WHERE?" Randy yelled.

JF Report
June 28
(strangers)

"DU MONDE!" Moise repeated, cupping his mouth with his hands, directing his voice toward camp. Now the horse guards were shouting it, too—"DU MONDE!"—and were running to unhobble animals grazing near the river, lead them toward safety inside the camp.

All at once, Randy heard and saw Kit Carson and Maxwell on horses pounding out of camp, leading four armed horsemen upriver to confront the strangers. Who could they be?? Dangerous?? Would they shoot Kit?? Randy, splashing toward Moise and the river's edge could see nothing upriver, no horses, no approaching anybody. "Who is it? Where?"

Moise yelled back, "I seen 'um! I seen 'um when dey werz walking past a big opening between de trees! Dere wuz a whole buncha men walking togedder toward us! Couldn't tell if dey got guns, couldn't tell what kinda men dey are, why dey walking, where dey left deir horses! "

When Randy reached Moise on the riverbank, he could see Kit, Maxwell, and the other horsemen stopping not far away by some cottonwoods beside the river. They were pulling up short in front of a sizeable group of men. Nobody was raising a rifle or pistol.

"Dem strangers don't look like Indians," Moise rumbled, his sore lip forgotten. "Dey're carrying big packs on deir backs...dey could be lost so'jers...But dey not in uniforms. Dey're in crazy looking ragged clot'es. Yeah, dey look bad-off enough to be trappers! Lord a-mercy—dem's trappers walking to Saint Looie!"

"TRAPPERS! TO SAINT LOOIE!!!" Randy cried. "I've got to find a buffalo skull before the trappers leave—"

"HOLD ON, BOY!" Moise commanded. "We're not hunting for anot'er skull! Dese men don't have animals to ride or to carry deir belongings! Dey couldn't lug even one buffalo skull to Saint Looie. When dey come closer, you'll see what worn-out, bone-tired, ragged fellows you'd be asking to carry de dead-weight of a buffalo skull on deir back. Dey'd just laugh at you—if dey had de strengt'."

Rhythmic thuds of galloping hoofs, duddle-lup duddle-lup, came closer and closer—Kit Carson and Maxwell hastening back to tell Fremont the camp need have no fear. "Who ARE dose men?" Moise called out as the two horses flew past. "Trappers! American Fur Company!" Kit yelled.

JF Report
June 28

"Well, I'll be a dog's hind leg," Moise laughed. "I'll bet I know some of 'um, and I'll bet when dey pulled out'n de Rockies, dey was de last—not a trapper, not a beaver left in dem mountains. Just t'ree years ago, Randy, dere wuz hundreds working for, making lotsa money for y'r folks's friend Mr. Chouteau, Big Man of de American Fur Company in Saint Looie. Now dese trappers outa de Rockies is traders demselves wid buffalo robes, I betcha. C'mon—let's go see if I know any amongst dese on-foot fellows."

The closer they came to the men, 14 by count, the more ridiculously tattered they looked. Draped in ragged clothes, heavily bearded, the grimy vagabonds had only one rifle among them. A wild-gamey odor seeped from them. Randy stared, then began to snicker, pointing to a small man whose waist-long beard was the only cover of his chest, his wide spread of neck hair the only drape on his back. "He's wrapped for hot weather," Randy giggled. "Even his feet!" His mocassins had worn apart, and he'd tied them to his feet with leather strings, fringe snapped from someone else's trouser-seam.

"Don't you go laughing, Randy. Dis may be 'bout de way we'll look when we get back here heading home a coupla months from now."

"Dis confounded Platte River! We ruined ourselves dragging our barges and rafts on river bottom sand covered wid no more'n four inches of water! Takes six inches to float a barge carrying a ton or more of buffalo robes! Dragging'um, we didn't make more'n three miles a day for three weeks! Finally we all give out, couldn't do such pulling'n'hauling any more. We left dem robes behind in sand pits or hid'um under canvas, started walking 200 miles to de Missouri, our best chance to stay alive."

CHAPTER 12

FIGHTING THE PLATTE

June 28, Platte River, Nebraska

Moise stepped forward quickly, announced his name and offered a handshake to the leader, a sleeveless, muscular man whose biceps looked like fists. "John Lee here," he said, "in the position of worrying along these men to Missouri." His strong Southern accent sounded like Carolina mountain talk when he asked Moise if he happened to have a chaw of terbaccy on him.

"We're slam out of anything to chaw or smoke. Made the 10 miles we walked today seem like 50, and the day's only half gone. You say your camp might spare us some pipe stuffings? Halley-LU-yah! We've got 15 more miles to walk today—200 more to the Missouri River—a mighty long ways to be traveling without the comfort of a pipe or a chaw."

The other men, who had been gathered 'round the remaining horsemen from Fremont's camp, now turned their attention to Moise and "le petit garcon," asking what this poor child was doing 'way out here on the prairie. Not waiting for an answer, they exploded into talk of their joy upon sighting a camp of maybe traders, maybe emigrants, their added joy upon hearing it was a government-sent expedition.

Moise assured them they'd be welcomed, fed, and their terbaccy pouches refilled. John Lee assured Moise that, although they'd had only greens and roots to eat for days before reaching the forking of the Platte, since then they'd killed buffalo, eaten regular, had cooked meat enough in their backpacks to offer some to the camp to pay for any bread it could spare. "Your camp got plenny-a flour for bread? Good! Long time since we tasted bread."

"So let's get going to the camp cook!" John Lee called to everybody, and waved a beckoning arm. The little crowd of men, limping, shuffling, bending to carry their provisions and bundles, hurried as fast as they could behind the camp's horsemen.

As they moved along, John Lee and a tall man with a spread-eagle mustache, Canadian voyageur Francois LaTulippe, took turns telling Moise and Randy what had

128

happened to the group. "My bunch has been 60 days getting this far," Lee said. "Come 300 miles! Started out with the annual flood on the western end of Laramie River. Thought the Platte would have enough water to float barges carrying us, hundreds of buffalo robes belonging to Mr. Chouteau, and a few furs of each man, to Sarpy's trading post on the Missouri. Floating from the Rockies to St. Louis saves time, work, cost of carts and mules, and steamboat fare."

"But no," LaTulippe took up the story, "dis devilish Platte River fooled us independents, too, and upsot us after we floated as far as Scott's Bluff on de North Fork, just 100 miles sout' of Fort Laramie. Yeah—we stopped at Laramie. We left there a week after Lee did. Caught up wid'um just a few days ago. At Laramie, all'uv saw bot' Fitzpatrick and Jim Bridger—you know dem, everybody knows dem—fer 20 years dey headed-up plenny men sent west outta St. Louis to trap for de Fur Companies."

Broken Hand,
p180
L.R.Hafen
(emigrants, Bridger)

"At the Fort, we also saw a hundred or so folks Oregon-bound—men AND women AND young'uns," John Lee added, looking around at Randy.

Randy said, "Yes sir, we know about them. We met a man who'd left the emigrants and was going back to St. Louis. We've been seeing their wheel tracks and camp sites. John—our Lieutenant, says they're traveling three weeks ahead of us."

"Yeah—they got horses pulling 18 wagons!" Lee said. "And they had hundreds of cattle! The leader sounded like the preacher kind. He wanted a guide to lead 'um to Oregon from Fort Laramie. Looked like Fitzpatrick might do it, seeing as how guiding folks through the Rockies is the best paying job around. But 'big-neck' Jim Bridger and upwards of hundred trappers 'n' traders told us they were still getting ready to ride on to Saint Looie. You might even meet 'um twixt here and Laramie."

LaTulippe interrupted. "Dis expedition of yours—it's set up to do what kind of work, and who is your head man, your booshway?"

"Dis is a scientific surveying and mapping expedition," Moise said proudly. "Our leader is wid de Corps of Topographical Engineers, United States Army, and his name is Lieutenant John Charles Fremont!"

LaTulippe's eyes and mouth widened. "Oohhh!! Mon Dieu!! Fremont!! My old friend! My companion on de nort'ern prairie back in '38! C'est un miracle! Let's get a move on! I'm in a hurry to see him!! C'est un moment extraordinaire!" The lanky man whose lined, scarred, and weathered face labeled him a veteran of unsheltered life took off at a run, ragged shirt and trousers flapping.

"Well," said Moise to John Lee, "Dat's a surprise. Anot'er surprise is dat I don't know ANY of your men. Wish I did 'cause I'd like news of anybody we'd bot' know. Some of dese fellows wid you have a young, greenhorn look. Must be Saint Looie town-boys."

"Yeah—except that fellow over there with the rifle," Lee said. "He's a New England town-boy, a newspaper reporter. Been out in the Rockies living like a mountain man trapping, trading, living with Indians, Cheyennes mostly, so he can write a book about all that, he says. Name's Rufus Sage. He and five trappers—independents including Tulip here—joined us some days after they unloaded their boats, left 600 robes on the Platte riverbank. We soon did the same with our 900—"

Scenes in the Rocky Mountains. Rufus Sage

"Sacre!" Moise interrupted."Yours wid de ot'ers would toget'er sell for more'n $15,000 in Saint Looie!"

"BUT, it couldn't be helped—all of us was exhausted from dragging boats and barges down a river with hardly four inches o' water in it," John Lee said. "Such work! Blistered hands, worn out backs, shoes, feet, clothes—everything—AND a stretcha starving. Made New Englander-Sage look mighty bent and no-account, but betcha he'll enjoy writing about our slaving and stumbling 500 miles!"

Moise twisted his head around to stare at Rufus Sage. "He can make a living writing stories 'bout us trappers?" Moise, who'd never been taught to write even his name, scratched an itchy spot on his neck. For the thousandth time he wondered how long it 'oud take him to learn to make "dose mysterious marks and remember what dey meant."

Just then, Randy called, "Look, Moise! There's John— Lieutenant—coming out of the camp to meet us—Do you suppose he really knows the Tulip man??"

"We'll find out in a minute—I see Tulip running toward him—Ohhhhyes! Dey know each ot'er! Dey're bear hugging— I hear 'um talking!"

"Moise! I want to hear what they're saying!" Moise waved Randy on.

He sprinted ahead, arriving at Fremont's side in time to hear him say, "I'm VERY glad to see you again, Tulip! And VERY glad to hear you say that buffalo are abundant a day or two's march west—my men are ready for a change from salt pork!

"But you've changed in four years. Tell me how you got that scar on your brow—and there's one on your cheek, too! You've added them since our north-prairie days working with Nicollet. You look like one of Napoleon's Old Guard who's fought in six sabre battles! Did a b'ar get ahold of you, Tulip, old friend?"

JF Report
June 28
("Tulip like
Napoleon Old Guard")

LaTulippe slapped the side of his leg, threw back his head, laughed so loud and boisterously that approaching fellow travelers slowed, and mouths agape, looked to see what could cause such a racket. They heard LaTulippe bellow, "Not a b'ar, Fremont! T'war Rondy-voo!

"You've heard 'bout dem wild frolics when de wagons wid firewater and pay-day goods arrived in the Rockies from Saint Looie! Well, in '40, dere come to de Green River 'n' Horse Creek junction for de sixteent' Rondy just a few wagons o' goods, not much firewater, hundreds not t'ousands o'Indians and trappers and traders.

Rocky Mountain
Rendezvous.
F.R.Gowans
(rondy scenes)

"The fun program was a parade of 300 Shoshony warriors painted and ornamented from head to toe, ready to go off, find and kill hundreds o' Blackfeet. Next wuz a daily missionary sermon, den a Cat'olic mass. De most exciting events happened to ME, and only because I wuz luckily standing in deir pat' and I became LaTulippe of the Wounded Chin. An arrow kissed me in whizzing past, sent by an unseen bow!

"Also, I became LaTulippe of the Singe'd Brow! Dat wuz when a bullet on its way to some ot'er target zinged by me, skimmed off a lee-tle string of hairline, flew on to greater glory!

"Ahhhh—and dis cheek scar half-hiding under dis side of la moustache, oh, I became Tulippe of de Insulted Mule Foot when de critter slapped my face—but softly—wit' its sharp little hoof. Ot'erwise, dis Rondey wuz so tame, de Saint Looie fur companies called it deir last!"

Now everybody was laughing—the ragged arrivals, Fremont, Randy, Fremont's crew, especially Kit Carson.

Kit Carson's
Autobiography
(Shunar fight)

"Your story reminds me of the Green River Rondy in '35," he drawled, "when I shot it out with the bully Shunar. His bullet went wild—fer all I know skimmed off the hairline of some lucky skull like yours!"

Fremont waved his arm for quiet and welcomed the trappers as guests. "But our shipwrecked guests, despite their rags and tatters, offer us a buffalo hump already roasted!

131

For us it's DESSERT! A buffalo wafer'll taste sweet to us saltpork diners. Randy, run ahead and tell the cooks to throw some chips on the coals and start frying bread for 14 trappers walking home from the Rockies!"

In minutes, cooks were handing out hot bread and everyone was nibbling thin slices of buffalo hump roasts. The mood of the camp, visitors and all, had shifted into high spirits. Laughter, talk, and, when Randy brought out his guitar, singing, melted dejection and fatigue.

Fremont excused himself after a bit, and walked with John Lee to his tent. Fremont wanted to write a letter to his wife, Randy's sister, who was with their family, the Bentons, in Washington. Fremont imagined her becoming more visibly pregnant every day, watching out windows for someone bringing a letter, feeling disappointed when no one came. He had just enough time to write her that all was well, Randy and Brant in good health doing their share of work, that in a day or two, they'd see buffalo—and that he loved her dearly. Lee had agreed to take the letter to St. Louis, stamp it, put in the post office.

Jessie Fremont.
P.Herr

While Fremont wrote the letter at his table, John Lee paced back and forth reciting the hateful character of the Platte River and how it had piled misery on him and his men. Fremont looked up and nodded from to time to keep Lee going but not paying close attention to his tale of woe.

"We done all right floating on our three barges 'til the water quit under us and went sprawling. Crazy River—a monster puddle divided into strips by sandbars....four-inches-deep water—boat needs SIX to float...quick sand...holes that drop you neck-deep in muddy soup..."

He paced and talked about backtracking ten-mile mistakes—"dern-near kilt me...had to go on all the same, dragging three barges loaded with more'n a ton of robes apiece. Went on fer days and days...After awhile there'uz nothin' t'eat...got weaker 'n' weaker...et grass 'n' roots..."

JF Report
June 28,
and R.Sage
account,
Scenes in
the Rocky
Mountains
(low river toiling)

Fremont now laid down his pen and was listening intently. "Where are the three barges and all Mr. Chouteau's buffalo robes now?" he asked.

"Well, we'd ruin't ourselves dragging them big barges and their four tons of robes over river bottom for three weeks. Didn't make no more'n three miles a day. Then we couldn't do that any more. So we dug a huge pit in a sandbank, put all 900 robes in it, laid canvas over 'um, covered 'um with sand. Three men volunteered as guards. Rest of us went on, pulling the empty barges for another 20 days. Didn't want to leave 'um beached for fear Indians seeing 'um would steal 'um, then, thinking we were toting valuable goods, would hunt us down, rob, maybe kill us.

"But finally we just couldn't drag 'um another step even though we now had plenny buffalo meat to eat. What to do?

"Before we decided, here comes six men, independent trapper-traders, dragging a flatboat. No robes. Sage, the newspaperman said they'd stacked 600 under canvas on the riverbank near Scott's Bluff, left two guards, sent two men back to Laramie to get carts and mules. The six we met dragging the flatboat were collapsing, ready to quit.

"All of us agreed the best chance for staying ALIVE was to sink barges and flatboat out of sight, and start walking to St. Louis with no more'n we could back pack. Well, every one of us still had his own canvas-wrapped package of small furs—fox, weasel, sheep, jackrabbit. But nobody had the strength to add a 25-pound fur bundle to his backpack for a 200-mile walk.

"So we hung'um high in big cottonwoods by the river, hoping Indians wouldn't see'um before Mr. Chouteau sent a wagon to pick up his 900 buried robes and our bundles as well. Last thing, we probed the river bed 'til we found deep holes, pushed flatboat and barges under water.

"That was early this morning. We might've covered 10 miles when we saw your camp. We've got to walk 15 MORE today if we're gonna make it to Sarpy's on the Missouri in a week....if we last that long."

John Lee wiped his nose with the back of his hand. "If 'n' when we get to St. Louis, or even to Sarpy's, we might be worse off than we are now. We've no money for grub and a raft to float down the Missouri. If we ever get home, Chouteau'll be mad 'cause we didn't bring his 900 robes and he's lost a whole winter's buffalo-robe sale. He maybe won't pay us, so we'll have nothing—not even our little furs—only blisters and rags for our slaving and misery."

Fremont nodded in sympathy. He rose, went to his necessaries bag and brought forth a small bottle. He filled the cap with liquid and handed it to John Lee. "This is French brandy, Mr. Lee. Good for relieving disappointment—and maybe good for forgetting foot blisters, too."

While John Lee sipped and savored, Fremont completed writing the letter to his wife. Then he wrote a sentence on separate paper, addressed it, asked John Lee to kindly take it to Henry Brant's mother in St. Louis. "She'll no doubt invite you for an excellent dinner."

On their way to rejoin the feasting men, Fremont stopped rather abruptly and asked John Lee if he had any objection to LaTulippe's leaving his party and joining Fremont's.

"Tulip told me he'd like to turn back, go with us west. He's a man I've worked with, he's a personality that will add humor and liveliness to the camp, and he's a strong man in every way, one I can rely on."

JF Report
June 28
(Latulippe
joins JF party)

John Lee said it was all up to LaTulippe. "He's one of the flatboat independent trappers. He said he wasn't glad about going to the States, just came along with the others. I'm not surprised he's asking to go back with you, sir— especially since you and he are old friends."

When Fremont told LaTulippe and offered him a dollar a day for pay, LaTulippe let out one of his loud whoops of joy, grabbed Fremont's hand, shook it long and hard until Fremont cried, "Spare my bones for another day, Tulip!" The ragged mountainmen drained their coffee cups and heaved their backpacks to their shoulders. "Fifteen miles more to walk today!"

"Yes, visiting hour is up for all of us," Fremont said. "We much enjoyed your buffalo meat dessert, you've a replenishment of chewing and smoking materials that should make your journey seem shorter—so all of us are better equipped for continuing upon our different ways. Last handshakes— gentle ones, please—before my men mount their horses! Good journey on foot, good sirs, and farewell!"

Fremont swung into his saddle, saluted the visitors, and took the lead of his caravan riding westward.

Based on a Frederic Remington drawing, published 1897

Who are the three Indians watching the Fremont column from a distant ridge? Friends?
Or a scouting party for a hundred hostile warriors out of sight behind the hill? Kit
Carson thinks he knows, and races his horse toward them. As he comes near them, he
sees the two men repeat the hand signs he's made to them–"Friend! Stop!"

135

CHAPTER 13

FUR-LINED TREES, INDIAN BOY

June 28-29, Platte River camp (Nebraska)

During the hot afternoon, there was plenty of talk among the men bunched near Fremont at the head of the caravan—the new man LaTulippe, plump Lambert, loud-voice Maxwell, reserved Kit Carson, and Randy. For quite a while, Tulip was answering questions about the ragged trappers from whose company he'd chosen to depart.

JF Report
June 28

"Are John Lee's men counting on meeting only good Pawnees, the kind dat don't attack unarmed men? Well, unarmed except for Mr. Sage. But he told me his rifle didn't work," Moise said.

Tulip nodded. "John Lee told us he wuz sure us men's ragged and wort'less looks would protect us from de Pawnees. Mr. Sage plans to give de rifle to de first Pawnee dat holds out his hand to take it. Pawnees will see how nobody in dis bunch is carrying anyt'ing wort' stealing, 'specially deir dirty, ragged, stinking clot'es."

What chance is there for rescuing the robes? "Well, not much for Mr. Chouteau's 900—unless one of de men goes ahead fast to St. Louis, like in two weeks, and Chouteau sends carts on a day-and-night run de next two weeks."

Carson said, "Hmmph. A month's a long time to expect guards to hang around the sandbank where you men buried them 900 robes by the river. Some big hole you musta dug. I'd say the two men left to guard the independent trappers' 600 robes on the North Fork ain't there any more either, nor the robes, being they weren't buried out of sight, just covered with a canvas. Seems to me you fellows musta been too tired to think, to keep in mind you werz in the Platte Forks area, square in the favorite path of roaming buffalo herds and Oglala Sioux hunters. Leaving two or three men there might have been a sentence of death for 'um."

"But," Tulip countered, "there's a small chance dat we independents may see our 600 robes again since de men we sent back to Laramie may have returned in a week or so wid carts. In dat case, dey'd now be on deir way to Saint Looie—we might soon be meeting 'um!"

Randy's face lit up. He clapped his hands, started to

speak, but Moise on his right and LaTulippe on his left held up warning fingers. "Maybe!" Moise declared. "BIG maybe! Chances are we'll pass by two skeletons picked clean by wolves and buzzards, and de robes gone wit'out a trace. A coupla WEEKS is a long time for two men to camp by a big pile of buffalo robes in plain sight of every passing Sioux."

Randy said breathlessly, "You mean Indians might have killed and scalped the guards?"

"Maybe, again," answered Tulip, "but maybe not. Two men MIGHT not be noticed by passing Indians if dey kept out of sight." Carson grunted "hungh."

"Besides," Tulip continued, "de Platte sees traders and traders coming and going right often—some of 'um could've rescued dem men and some of de robes wit'in a few days, taken'um to Laramie." Carson muttered, "Ha!"

"Now, GOOD news, wid no maybe's!" cried Tulippe, and turned loose his big raucous laugh. "Dere was ONE lucky man among all dose in de barges and boats! ME! Francois LaTulippe! I am NOT walking East, I am NOT standing guard for weeks on a riverbank where Indians roam! No! LaTulippe is riding a horse West wid his friend John Fremont and a well-provisioned expedition—AND getting paid for it!" Tulip's dramatic, arm-waving presentation had the men laughing again. "Even the horses are grinning, showing their teeth," Maxwell said.

LaTulippe had more to say. "T'ank you once more, friend Fremont, for saving me from Saint Looie. What would I'd'a done in dat town? I'd'a headed for one of de outfitter stores, maybe Mr. Chouteau's, begged for credit to buy grub, clot'es, a place to sleep. Maybe I'd get some rough work, den after awhile I'd get an offer to go back West and round up buffalo robes from de Indians. I'd jump at dat, tickled to leave. I'd hit the trail smiling. But joining dis expedition is de best.

Rocky Mountain Rendezvous. F.Gowans p190 (miss danger)

"I tell you life in de city is all burden and no jig—got to work INSIDE at somet'ing you hate, got to be somewhere and leave someplace by somebody else's clock, got to have MONEY to eat, sleep, or have fun. Besides all dem 'got to's', cities STINK wid horse manure! It's so deep on de streets you need to put down a board to walk across widout ruining your foot gear!

"I'd drut'er eat free b'ar meat I killed in de mountains, 'n' buffalo on de prairie, freeze in icy water, stomp t'rough snow, dodge or fight off Indians who want my hair, run all

137

kinds of scary risks 24 hours of de day—dan to live in de city grubbing, grubbing, grubbing.

"Fact is—" and Tulippe stopped for another whooping laugh—"I MISS my daily danger o' Injuns, b'ars, 'n' weat'er—excitement every day! I love working a t'ousand miles from a Big Boss! And fact is, in de city, you can't look up and see snowy peaks, or walk outta da woods and face a hundred miles of valleys and hills nobody but Indians has seen before! You can't explore, swim, ride a horse a hundred miles at de drop of a hat!"

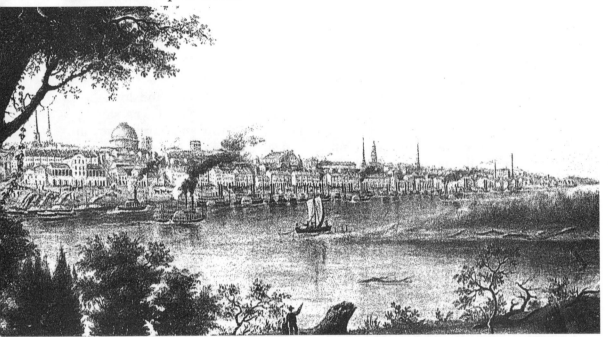

Gateway to the Oregon Trail after 1842, St.Louis, Missouri, will grow from 16,000 residents to 80,000 by 1850.

Fremont looked around at Tulippe with a smile and said he too loved the outdoor life, and hoped to spend a good part of his life exploring America. "I learned from my first job out-of-doors six years ago that I wanted the occupation of my prime of life to be among Indians and in unknown places. I loved every day's novelty, adventure, hardships. I knew then that the path of the explorer, hard as it might be, was the one I wanted to walk."

Randy, like all the others, leaned toward Fremont, listening closely, wanting to hear well all he said.

"Later in Washington, an interview with Senator Benton, Randy's father, was decisive. His talk dwelt on the unoccupied country beyond the Missouri, the uncertain, incomplete knowledge concerning the vast space called 'The Great American Desert' south of Lewis and Clark's explorations. The thought of penetrating into the recesses of that mysterious region filled me with visions of my life as the explorer who would secure that knowledge, make it known.

JF Memoirs, p65
(happy as explorer)

"Since college, I had devoted myself to my profession of engineering, but now I saw myself working with Nature where in all her features there was still aboriginal freshness. I would travel across unknown lands, learn at first hand from Nature, be the first to drink at her unknown springs.

"But it was unreasonable, I then felt, to expect this pleasure—to expect that it might happen that I would be among the few to whom the chance would fall to live this life. But it did happen, and I am a happy, happy man."

Maxwell immediately spoke up with strong—and loud—warmth. "Lieutenant, you've said exactly what I was saying to myself ten years ago. I ran away from an easy life set up

Lucien Maxwell.
L.R.Murphy

for me by my grandfather, once Lieutenant Governor of Illinois. I took up a life like the one he was famous for in his youth—fur trader in the wilderness. Good ole Charlie Bent gave me my first job in his fort, trading calico and beads for Indian furs. Turned me into an independent trader and trapper. Never regretted it a day. I expect Kit, and Lambert, too, can tell pretty much the same story."

Lambert nodded, but Kit Carson shook his head. "Not meaning I regret coming west, but the reasons werz mighty

Kit Carson's
Autobiography.

different. I did run away—and the saddler I wuz apprenticed to valued me so much he offered ONE cent reward to anybody who'd bring me back! But my reason for leaving wuz not so much about how I'd enjoy nature, or living in the woods, or trapping animals, as it wuz to get away from Howard County, Missouri, to travel, see different places, make some money—not easy for a farm boy who didn't go to school.

"I'd heard a lot of tales about the Rockies and how you could go out there and make a dollar a day, which sounded to me like a lot of money. In August 1826 when I wuz 15 years old, I heard of a party about to start from St. Louis for Santa Fe. Charlie Bent—the same Charlie Bent of Bent's Fort where you worked years later, Max—hired me as a cavvyboy to tend spare mules and oxen in the caravans hauling his trade goods to Santa Fe.

"That wuz six years before he built his fort on the Arkansas River at the edge of the prairie, near the tail end

The fabled Santa Fe Trail from Missouri to New Mexico ends in Santa Fe's central plaza.

of the Rockies. From the fort, Santa Fe wuz a turn to the south, a climb through Raton Pass to get back onto the prairie, then another hundred miles to Glorieta Pass. Out of the pass, to get to Santa Fe you turn back north, ride 25 prairie miles along the west side of the Sangre de Cristo mountains. When I first come there, Santa Fe wuz just a dirt adobe Mexican town, real small—but the onlyest real town for nearbout a thousand miles."

LaTulippe, Lambert, Maxwell, and Fremont as well as Randy strained to catch Carson's every soft-spoken word. All had heard second-to-tenth-hand bits of stories about Carson. Now to hear Carson tell about Carson!

"It took me some time to get to driving a wagon team and make a dollar a day. I actually started East real dis-couraged a coupla times but turned back. By the time I wuz 20, I had fought Indians and trapped beavers in streams all the way to southern California and back. When I got paid at the end of 20 months, I had several hundred dollars, the most I'd ever had in my hands at one time. The next move I made wuz to get myself hired by Jim Bridger to join his sizeable crew of men to go trap beavers in the big Rockies north of Santa Fe and Taos.

"Of course I enjoyed the scenery, the exploring, and all, but the main thing wuz making a living. I'd say that most of the men I knew when I first went to Santa Fe, and later to the Rockies, werz there for about the same reason.

"Now that this source of money—beaver fur—is gone, where can a poor boy with no schooling dream of going,

140

A.L. Dick engraver, E. Didler artist, published 1845

At the end of the Trail, the adobe town of Santa Fe in view, traders bringing goods from St. Louis fire their guns for joy. Traveling six weeks or so across the Great Plains, they're eager for their 500% profits.

hoping to make a living? Sure would help if we could find something valuable as beavers in the Rockies, more valuable than pretty scenery—" LaTulippe growled, "Amen"—"though I love to look at pretty scenery," Carson added, "and to live in it like an Indian." LaTulippe said, "Amen again!"

Then all of a sudden, Tulip announced loudly, "Hey! Look! We're coming to de little grove of cottonwoods where we trappers hung our fur bundles!" Expectantly he looked at Fremont, his face aglow with excitement. "Lieutenant! My bundles 'r' in one of dem trees, and I'm going to go over dere, climb up and get'um! I'll catch de column in just a little while!" Before all his words were in the air, Tulip had pulled his horse out of line and was galloping away toward some large trees by the river.

Fremont watched him for a minute. Turning to Lambert, he said, "Call a halt down the line."

With a glance at the sky, Fremont observed that there were less than four hours of daylight left, "and I doubt we've moved ahead more than five miles since we left the trappers. That means if we stop here an hour or so to deal with the bundles-in-the-trees question, it'll be about time for us to set up camp—ending a day of only 17 miles. I'd like to

141

hear what you have to say, Kit, about what, if anything, we had best do about those bundles."

"Well, sir—" Carson pushed his hat back from his forehead, exhaled noisily, then inquired, "Did John Lee ASK you to do anything about the bundles?" Fremont shook his head and said, "No."

Carson grimaced. "Well, seems to me he should've. Them men, in my opinion, have not been thinking sensible for some days. It's like this, sir, about the furs: If we, the first passersby don't take charge of these bundles, the next passerby, or the next wind and rain storm, will. If we take charge of 'um, we can leave'um at Laramie. Maybe some day, one way or another, the owners will git'um back, cash 'um in, have a little pay for their work."

Shortly, they spotted Tulip trotting his horse toward the column. At his saddle front and back lay bundles as long as Randy, and bigger around. "Good Lord!" Lambert exploded. "If all 14 men had two bundles apiece like that, I don't see how in the world we can load 'n' carry them!"

Tulip rode up, his face one big smile. "Dey're all dere!" he cried out. "Just the way we left 'um!"

"How many?" Fremont demanded.

"Ohhh—well...you see dere wuz 19 of us when we two parties started out. A few had three bundles..." Tulip's expression had changed from joy to wide-eyed hope and lips pursed in doubt and fear.

Fremont's eyes measured Tulip's bundles. "Forty—50? bundles big as yours? How heavy are yours?"

"Well, uh—see, easy to lift..."

"We have only eight carts, Tulip—five bundles piled on top of each, that's at least a hundred pounds extra for each pair of mules to pull. A few days ago, there was some worry about adding three much less weighty objects. Carson, what do you say?"

Carson looked at the carts, at Tulip's puckered face. "Let's try, Sir. May be their only pay for a winter's work." Immediately, Fremont called, "Make camp!" Carts rolled into their circle positions, tents went up. A dozen young men and Randy then raced to the cottonwoods.

When Randy stood under a big cottonwood, looked up into its huge outstretched arms, saw bundles wedged in their joints or tied to leafy branches, he clapped his hands, waved his arms, and called to Johnny Janisse already climbing out on a limb, "A Christmas present tree, Johnny! A birthday-present tree! That's what I'm gonna ask for in November for my birthday party!"

Quickly, he grabbed a low tree arm and swung up. All around he heard THUD! and THUD! and THUD! as men in a half-dozen trees dropped bundles to the ground. "Presents are ripe and falling!" he shouted, yanked loose a bundle, gave it a push, heard it smack the ground.

Collecting packages in trees not in JF account. But would this crew of trappers have left these furs to be stolen by others?

In a half-hour, the bundle-rescuers had tumbled 46 bundles out of the trees, picked them up, and carried three or four bundles each to camp. Stacked, the Randy-size packages made a small mountain. Fremont shook his head. "We may have to hang some back in the trees."

The loading waited until the fried bacon and bread were swallowed and washed down with coffee, and then until Carson and Fremont, with Randy at their heels, had inventoried cart space, measured, squeezed bundles for softness, made a plan for fitting them inside the carts. It still being an hour before first guard duty, Fremont called for "a mighty effort" to pack all the bundles into the carts.

"We've shown you where the space is. Put the bundles into it anyway they'll go—standing, lying, crammed in as padding, where they might even do some good. Also, put them so we won't have to take them off at every camp site to get at tents and bags, or reload them every morning. "

Randy could best help by bringing out his guitar and leading the bundle-heavers in a lively song, Fremont said. By the twentieth verse and shouted chorus of an old sea chant—"Heave ho! and up she rises!" all bundles had been hoisted into the carts, pressed into place, Fremont was smiling, and Tulip's laughter was everywhere.

They were just sprawling on the grass, drinking a second cup of coffee and lighting their pipes, when a cry went up from Cousin Henry. "Lieutenant! I see three men on horses coming toward us from a hill on the south! They look naked! One has a feather in his hair! I think they're Indians! I'm sure they're not elks!"

Carson jumped to his feet. "Yes, you're right, they're Indians. No rifles—just bows, arrows, and wooden spears. They look like Cheyennes—tall, slender men—not broad and plump like Pawnees. Usually friendly. I'll ride out, see who they are, learn their intentions."

Standing close by the carts, guns ready, Fremont and his men watched Kit Carson trot his horse toward the slow-moving Indians. They saw him stop short of them by a hundred yards, raise his right hand, palm forward, then push it back and forth.

"What's he doing?" Randy whispered to Lajeunesse beside whom he was crouching next to a cart wheel. "Indian sign language. Means 'halt.'" Lajeunesse said. "See, the Indians have stopped. That shows they'd rather talk than attack. Now one of 'um is signing 'halt' to Kit."

Carson stopped, raised his upright hand palm forward, twisted his wrist to the right, then left. "He's asking 'Who're you?'" Lajeunesse told Randy. They saw the Indian with the feather in his hair draw the edge of his right hand across his left arm and wrist as if slashing it with a knife. Randy caught his breath, thinking the Indian was giving some kind of warning.

But Lajeunesse said, "Kit was right, Randy. They're Cheyennes—known among Indians as 'Cut-Wrists' or 'Slashers.' Their men cut strips from an arm before going on warpath, women slash their arms to mourn men killed. I know Kit talks and understands Cheyenne. They're moving closer together. There's Kit holding up his hand with two fingers extended—and now one Indian's making the same sign—'friend.'"

Kit was now close enough to the Indians for talk and it appeared they were having a lively conversation. "Really talking together?" Randy whispered. Lajeunesse nodded. "Really talking together. Kit can talk TEN Indian languages, and sign language to every tribe."

Carson wheeled his horse around and started back. Feathered-Indian guided his spotted pony to Carson's side. The other two pulled in their ponies behind them. Unhurried, all came toward the camp.

Fremont's voice shouting, "Attention!" made Randy jump. He looked toward the sound and saw Fremont standing near the center of the camp circle. "Precautions only!" he called. "Stay alert 'til we see Carson's smile!"

The horsemen approached. Kit and his companion, both with little smiles, led the other two directly to Fremont. Kit saluted. "I know these men, Lieutenant! We've trapped beaver together. They're Cheyennes."

Randy, watching from his cartwheel station, suddenly cried out, "Look! Look! One of them is a BOY!"

QUESTION

FRIEND

JF Report
June 28
(two Indian men, one boy appear)

Randy and the Cheyenne Indian boy look each other over while Fremont,
interpreter Maxwell, and Cheyenne-speaking Carson smoke the peace pipe with two
Indians Carson knows as Pat and Mike. "Remember my story about throwing
snowballs at our just-recaptured horses to get them moving in the right
direction?" Carson reminds Randy. "Well, these two Cheyennes here are the same Pat
and Mike that werz with me on that occasion."
But are they trustworthy now–enough to live in Fremont's camp, travel with the Fremont
Expedition? "And how," Randy asks himself, "does Kit know the boy is 13 years old?
How can we get to be friends when we can't understand each other's words?"

145

CHAPTER 14

INDIAN HAND-TALKING

June 28, Platte River (Nebraska)

Randy, without thinking, ran straight to Fremont from the cart where he had been peering around Basil Lajeunesse and his rifle. As he ran, he could not take his eyes from the bare-skinned, slender Indian boy, a little taller than himself, standing proudly straight and solemn with his adult companions in front of the Lieutenant.

Like his companions, the boy's long black hair, parted in the middle, hung in two long locks, one in front of each ear. Dust of gray earth and clay mottled the medium brown color of his skin. His breechcloth of deerskin, hanging on a fold from a waist-cord, covered his groin. Another such apron covered his buttocks. At his bare feet lay a wooden spear, a bow, an arm-size leather tube with a top fringe of arrow feathers.

Cheyennes.
E.A.Hoebel
p63,90

Pictorial History
of American
Indians.
Oliver .LaFarge
p32,162
(men's dress)

When Randy ran up and stopped beside Fremont, the Indian boy saw him for the first time. His facial expression did not change, but his glittering black eyes held their gaze upon the freckled pink face and red hair of the stranger, a young "wi'hio." Anything or body with mysterious powers Cheyennes called "wi'hio"—spider—a creature skillful in creating nets to catch their food, in moving themselves in the air, down and up again, seemingly on nothing—magic power, Big Medicine. The strange white-skinned people were wi'hios with mysterious Big Medicine, powerful ways of doing everything from grinding corn to killing enemies.

Cheyennes (II)
G.Grinnell
p88 (wi' hio)

Randy stared, too, now that he was close and looking, not at the boy's profile, but straight into his face. "He's better looking than I am," Randy thought with a twinge of envy. "I'd like having a long, bony face, neat nose, and dark suntan skin. I'd look more like John. But I like my blue eyes—they're already like John's. I think long red curly hair would look silly bunched in front of my ears, 'specially if I couldn't comb it but once a week—or month. And Mother would never let me go anywhere wearing nothing but a short apron. He has a little bag on a string around his neck. Something's in it. Wonder what?"

In St. Louis and even in Washington, he had seen on the

JF Report
June 28 "Randolph
and the young
Cheyenne,who had
been eyeing each
other suspiciously
and curiously, soon
became intimate
friends."

Warriors of the Plains, p38-9
Colin Taylor
(pouch)

street a few Indian men all dressed up in beaded and fringed leather shirts and leggings, their heads crowned with colorful feather bonnets. But he'd never seen a near-naked Indian, especially a near-naked boy about his own age, and especially not within arm's reach. Was he—were they—"wild! savage!" like Grandma Benton and Aunt Sarah had said? They looked naked-wild, but their manner was calm, not scary. They'd put all their weapons on the ground and were standing like wooden statues, arms folded, waiting.

Kit Carson's Autobiography
p24,28ff
(Cheyennes, his co-workers,1833)

Fremont's blue eyes were looking them over as he listened to what Carson was telling him. Randy moved closer to Fremont to hear better. "We can trust these men in our camp, Lieutenant. I know them well!

"They're brothers—both of them trapped with me and my party for some weeks a few years back. Remember how me and a dozen others rode in deep snow for 40 miles to catch up with a bunch of Crows who'd stole our horses? And how we crawled through deep snow when we found them in their teepee forts, cut loose our horses, throwed snowballs at 'um to get 'um moving?

"Well, two of our party werz Indians—these Cheyennes men standing here! They have long Indian names, so we called this one with the feather in his hair 'Pat' and his brother 'Mike.' We trusted them with our lives every day and night. They took hardships in silence, they never tricked or deceived us. With Cheyennes, once yer their friend, they treat you like one of their family. If they're up against enemies, they're bold, brave, savage killers.

Cheyennes.
E.A.Hoebel.
p92 *(rules)*

"But in family camp they live by rules their parents—their whole band—has pressed on them all their lives: 'Be BRAVE. Be honest. Be industrious. Be generous. Don't quarrel. If you behave bad, you'll be shamed in camp. Nobody'll respect you. Listen to us and grow up to be a good person.' Sir, I've lived with these men, and them's the rules they, and this boy—Pat's son—go by."

Fremont nodded, but caution still drew tense lines around his eyes and mouth. "What are they doing out here alone on the prairie? Could they be outcasts—men who broke those Cheyenne rules? How far from their people are they? How long have they been away from their camp? They and their horses look in poor condition, even the man with a feather in his hair and beads on his breechcloth. Their horses look like wild ponies they lassoed on the plains. True, they have amiable, honest-looking faces but you and many others've told us ALL Indians have a treacherous streak. To allow these men to stay in our camp even one night, I must know more about their circumstances."

Maxwell had moved up next to Carson to remind him that during the same two years Carson worked at Bent's Fort, he was working at St.Vrain's Fort on the South Platte, living for weeks at a time with Arapahoes, close friends and neighbors of Cheyennes. "If you want to question these men, I know Indian sign language same as Kit, and understand Cheyenne talk. So, if you'll think up the questions, Kit'll ask them, and when Pat and Mike answer, I'll quick translate talk and hand signs for you, Lieutenant."

The Indians, however, were not ready to talk. "Smoke peace pipe," Pat hand-signed. He drew from his quiver a long-stemmed pipe. Carson hastened to bring forth his tobacco pouch, fill the pipe bowl, call to the cook at the nearest mess fire to bring a hot coal. The Indian men and boy sat down side by side, legs crossed under them. Fremont, Maxwell, Kit, and Randy sat to face them. The two boys stared at each other, examining each other from head to toe.

After pointing the end of the pipestem to the god in the sky, Heamma Wihio, the Wise One Above, then to the Power of the Earth, Ahk tun o'Wihio, then to the powerful spirits of the east, the south, the west, the north, calling out all their names and inviting them to smoke, Pat took the mouthpiece between his lips. He drew a deep breath, exhaled smoke through his nose. He passed the pipe to his brother, who repeated the ritual, handed the pipe to the boy.

Randy, startled, expected to see him put the pipestem to his lips and puff smoke. Instead, the boy rose, stepped forward, and with a slight bow handed Fremont the pipe. Fremont took a quick draw of smoke and blew it out his lips while passing the pipe to Maxwell and Carson.

When Carson returned the pipe to Pat, the Indian solemnly pressed a thumb into the pipe bowl to kill the fire and compress the ashes—enough tobacco fragments for a later smoke.

Fremont broke an awkward silence with a cheerful "Welcome, friends of Kit Carson, and now our friends, too, since we have smoked with them the pipe of peace." His warm voice and expression had a visible effect on the three visitors. Their stiff faces relaxed as they unfolded their arms and nodded in response.

Bent's Fort.
D.Lavender.
Maxwell:189,
197-8,201

Lucien Maxwell
L.R. Murphy

JF Report
June 28
(smoke pipe)

Cheyennes.
E.A. Hoebel

JF Report
June 28
(smoke pipe)

JF Report
June 28

Carson immediately leaned forward and began speaking in Cheyenne language. At the same time he made Indian hand-signs for the words. As fast as Carson asked questions and Pat answered, Maxwell half-whispering gave Fremont the translation. "He says," Maxwell began, "their people are camping on the prairie by the South Platte River a few days ride east of the foothills of the great mountains. That could be maybe 75 miles east of Fort St. Vrain on the South Platte. From here, it's about a ten-day ride—say, about 250 miles.

"He says they're on their way home....been on a horse-stealing raid...ashamed—couldn't steal even one Pawnee horse...Pawnees are cowards—they shut up their horses in their teepees at night...He says two other Cheyennes in the raiding party left them and went on—they didn't want to climb with Pat and Mike to top of the hill over there to spy out the land.

"From the hilltop, Pat saw our camp...He says he and his brother had always had good treatment...and food from the whites...They felt confident we'd treat them well...so they hurried toward our camp...were overjoyed to see that the rider galloping toward them was their old friend Kit Carson.

JF Report
June 28

"Pat says they'd like to travel with us...that if they travel alone and the Pawnees see them, they can't possibly escape being killed. They left home a month ago...their horses are worn out...the men ate the last of their dried buffalo strips SIX days ago. SIX DAYS! No wonder their ribs are showing!"

Suddenly, another voice was pressing a question. All eyes turned toward—Mr. Preuss. He had come from behind the Indians' scrawy horses and was standing to face the boy.

Journal
C. Preuss
June 28

"Zis boy," he said, pointing, "will be afraid to lie about how zey vander about zee prairie to steal—how zey first KILL zee owner of zee horse, ZIN take his horse—yah, boy?!"

Carson quickly answered, "Indians do steal horses—from their enemies and, if needs be, kill their enemies rather than be killed!"

"How do ve know ZESE Indians don't plan to kill us vhile ve sleep, and run off viss all our horses?" Mr. Preuss demanded.

Fremont abruptly stood up, startling the Indians into jumping to their feet. "Carson! "he said, smiling at the Indians. "Tell these men that I invite them to eat bread, rice, coffee, and fried pork with us!" Carson told them by hand and voice. "Hawagh! Hawagh! Hawagh!" the Indians chorused, beaming satisfaction. Raising his voice, Fremont called out to the men still waiting, rifles ready, by the carts. "At ease, men! Come to supper!"

Carson moved closer to Fremont to say quickly, "Lieutenant, I sure do thank you—for myself and for Pat and Mike. You can fire me, turn me 'round for St. Louis, if these men don't live up in every way to my esty-mate uv'um. Now about supper, Lieutenant. These men is starving and I know they're happy to eat with us.

"However, there's one thing they won't eat. If'n I wuz hungry as I know they are, I'd eat fried dog if'n that wuz the offering—but these Cheyennes will let their insides shrivel before they eat PIG meat. So I jus' mentioned bread and rice to them.

JF Report
July 3

"Also, I better tell you, they'll keep eating bread and rice no matter how many hours the cooks hand it out. They can go for days without eating, but when they get a chance at plenty of food, they fill up—fo'ce down food until their bellies bulge, skin stretching 'til it thins out from brown to white."

Kit Carson's
Autobiography
(Indian appetite)

Fremont laughed, the Indians relaxed, looked relieved at the pleasant outcome of so many words, and followed Fremont when he waved them on toward the cooks.

Randy grabbed Carson by the arm. "You didn't say ANYTHING about the BOY, except Pat's his papa!" he accused in a fierce half-whisper. "You didn't even tell his name! Or how old he is!"

Carson put his arm around Randy's shoulders and answered as he guided him firmly toward the cooks' campfires. "Well, Randy, I haven't heard the boy's name myself, so I couldn't tell you. But anyway, it'll be something like—I mean a long Cheyenne sound—meaning 'Sticks-Everything-Under-His-Belt,' or 'Lying-on-his-Back-With-His Legs-Flexed.' "That's why we trappers renamed these men here 'Pat' and 'Mike.' They told us they liked their 'white' names, and most likely the boy'll be happy to have a name you pick out for him. Got any ideas?"

Cheyennes.
Hoebel. p54-5
(Indian names

Randy shook his head. Carson advised him to keep his thoughts running 'round looking for a name, and after awhile he'd bump into one.

Randy persisted. "But how old he is—is he the same age as me?" Carson said Pat had told him this raid to steal horses was the boy's first—"and I know this big event takes place when a Cheyenne boy is thirteen. He's ready, old enough, for real hunting and real war—no more playing with children, girls as well as boys, at pretend-grown-up camp

Cheyennes.
Hoebel
p93.(Age 13)

150

life. So he's a year older than you. He could be fourteen—Indians don't keep track of time all that close. When we hear him talk, if his voice is changing from boy to man, we'll know he's fourteen."

A half-hour later, Carson was saying to Maxwell, "The rice is all et up, and the cooks keep on frying bread—which our three Indian friends is still eat'n' as fast as cakes come outa the pans, like one every minute, running up the total to about a hundred."

Maxwell said, "No, Kit, that's not the way to count the cakes. The accurate way is to count how many times a minute Pat swallows. I've been counting and it's 12 times, no stops. Multiply 12 by 30 minutes and you get 360 bites, which amounts to 180 griddle cakes for one Indian, two bites to a cake. Multiply 180 by three starving Indians—FIVE HUNDRED and FORTY cakes! More'n a THOUSAND bites!"

Both men were slapping their legs and bending over in laughter. Then, wiping his eyes with the back of his hand, Maxwell added, "So I was stretching it a bit—but only a bit. You and I have both seen Indians eat steadily for hours—all day, through the night. In that time, 20 of 'um can cook and gulp down a whole buffalo, guts and all."

Carson wagged his head in agreement, said he'd noticed that Pat and Mike and the boy HADN'T noticed they'd each eaten a cup'a PORK fat the cakes soaked up while cooking!"

They smothered their laughs behind a hand and watched another minute or two. "Max, you know how an Indian can tell when he's full and sated? It's when the cook turns the flour barrel upside-down and bangs on it to show him there ain't no more."

Behind them, the cooks began using their own sign language to get the "no more" message across. Seeing their signals, Fremont called to Carson and Maxwell, hurried to the Indians, who were saying, "Hawagh! Hawagh! Hawagh!" rapidly to thank the cooks, express their pleasure. Fremont invited them with a beckoning hand to come sit with him and their old friend Kit.

"And me, too?" Randy queried. "Especially you, Randy, because you will be bringing to me from the table in my tent a pencil and the biggest sheet of paper you can find. I hope the Indians can draw a simple map to show the rivers and creeks that lie between here and their family."

Mr. Preuss, sitting close by, scrambled to his feet, saying, "I have some big sheets of paper for map-making and sketching—and a trimmed pencil. I'll bring zem!" and ran off. Randy, just starting his run, stopped, looked back at Fremont, his face expressing his irritation, annoyance, disappointment. Fremont beckoned to him. When Randy had sulkily stalked back, the Lieutenant said quietly, "Straighten up. He has more and larger paper than I do—better to save my supply."

Mr. Preuss rushed up panting. He had brought his hard drawing board, too, and laid it and the oversize sheet of paper on the ground in front of Fremont. Pencil in hand, Fremont knelt by the paper and beckoned to the Indians to kneel beside him. "Tell them," he said to Carson, "to make marks with this pencil to show the course of the Platte, all the waters flowing into it, good camping places where there's plentiful grass and water, the location of their home camp, the foothills and high mountains—AND—very important—where St. Vrain's Fort is on the South Platte."

JF Report
June 28
(Indian map)

Guided by Carson's voice and hands signs, Pat and Mike drew the lines, laughing at the novelty of using the wi'hio stick as one or the other made x's for camp sites, small and large up-side-down V's for hills and mountains, circles for the Cheyenne camp, a square for St.Vrain's Fort. "We'll need the names of the places written on the paper," Fremont said after admiring the map. Without mentioning that Carson could not write or read, he turned to Randy. "I've seen how you print by hand very well, Randy. Give him the pencil, Carson, and tell him what names to write where."

Glowing with pride and excitement, Randy sat down by Carson and propped board and map against his own bent knees. Carefully he printed place names where Carson pointed. Squatting behind him to watch, the Indian boy made little noises of admiration, and began talking energetically with Pat and Mike.

Randy noted with relief that his voice did not break from soprano to tenor or baritone. He was still a boy, not soon turning into somebody different the way Cousin Henry did.

Mr. Preuss had been watching, too. When Randy had printed the last name, Preuss barked, "Now put zee date— you should never forget, never fail, to put zee date on a map. Today is June 28, 1842—Tuesday!"

Journal.
C.Preuss,
Tuesday,
June 28

"Tuesday!" Randy repeated. Then a smile spread across his face. He looked at Carson and again said, "TUESDAY!" cutting his eyes at the Indian boy behind him. "You know— like Robinson Crusoe named the naked man he found

152

'Friday'—I'll name my new friend for the day of the week when he came to our camp—'Tuesday'!"

When Carson told the Indians the name Randy had chosen for the boy, all three looked very pleased, almost smiling. They began murmuring among themselves. "What are they saying? They really like it?" Randy asked urgently.

Cheyennes.
Grinnell II
p171,180
(Tou-wits)
"They're pronouncing 'Tuesday' same as' Tou-Wits'—the name they call him, short for his full name Nay-Wa-Men-o-Tou-Wits, his Papa just told me. He says it means 'Quick Ornamenting.' The boy must be good at painting fancy stripes and designs on warriors' faces and bodies. Seems Pat thinks the name you're giving the boy sounds like his present name, and you knowing it without being told foretells big success for the boy.

"See, Randy, a Cheyenne boy is given his adult name if he comes home a Big Success from his first raid—or hunt. No success so far. He hasn't stolen a single horse or killed a buffalo—which means he'll just keep his 'boy' name until his luck changes. They've decided YOU will bring him luck. Randy you sure bumped into a lucky sound to call him—at least his Papa and Uncle think so!"

Mr. Preuss, standing with hands on hips watching and listening, loudly muttered, "He vouldn't have zought of 'Tuesday' had I not told him!" Randy stiffened, glared.

Carson glanced at Fremont, caught his eye, saw Fremont's elbow swing out in a nudging motion. Quickly Carson passed the nudge to Randy's ribs. Randy looked around with a questioning frown. Kit murmured, "Ignore that remark. Get up. Here, hand the map to Lieutenant. Hand Proyce his drawing board. Say 'thanks.' Do it."

Randy said 'thanks' faintly through clenched teeth. Mr. Preuss gave him a fleeting almost-smile.

Map in hand, Fremont thanked everybody. "Now, we must make arrangements for the visitors to sleep here tonight. I see halves of buffalo robes serving by day as saddle on each Indian pony. By night, no doubt they serve as beds in the open air." Carson nodded.

"The question is, Where shall the visitors lay their beds?" Fremont continued. "Since a few of our men during supper hour expressed some skepticism or anxiety about the advisability of allowing Indians to stay inside our camp, I will suggest a place within the view of everyone, especially the men taking their turn at guard duty during the night—that is, the center of the open area within our circle of

153

carts and tents. Any objections?"

When no one spoke up, Carson asked about the Indians' horses and weapons. "I think it would make the skeptics feel better if all their weapons are put for safekeeping in various tents. Our men'll take the ponies for hobbling or staking among ours outside the circle."

"Excellent!" said Fremont. "So, Carson, will you explain about the weapons and horses to our visitors—tactfully, of course—show them where they will lay their robes. Maxwell, you take charge of their horses and lead them to Moise. Mr. Preuss can collect and put away the weapons. And Carson, you should also kindly call the visitors' attention to the fact that a number of guards will be on duty throughout the night to protect us, them, and the horses from surprise Pawnee attacks. Oh—and show them where the latrine is.

"It's only a half hour before darkness ends a most eventful day. Carson, you should describe to the Cheyennes our morning routine—that they'll have a hearty breakfast of griddle cakes ('Hawagh! Hawagh! Hawagh!') before we begin the march toward the first camping spot marked on their map. It appears to be about 25 miles to the west. Ask Pat if we'll find buffalo there."

Carson asked. Pat held his right hand, forefinger extended, over his heart, and woggled the finger with twists of his wrist. Fremont laughed. "So! Indians say 'maybe yes, maybe no' with a hand sign much like the one I learned at home! Good night, Gentlemen!"

Based on
Indian Sign Language.
W.Tomkins.
(perhaps)

Randy and Tuesday exchanged friendly glances as one followed Fremont, the other followed Carson, the horses followed Maxwell on his way to find Moise, and smiling Mr. Preuss loaded down with bows, quivers, knives, and spears marched off to his tent.

1.

2.

PERHAPS

Darkness blew in on a cold wind. Randy rolled himself up into a ball to keep warm under his blanket. His thoughts about Tuesday, lying naked out there in the open, the cold wind striking him, kept him awake for a while. He wished he had an extra blanket to take to him. Then he fell asleep, only to dream about Tuesday shivering in the cold. The wind blew harder and harder, lifted Tuesday and his bed from the ground, flew them up and away. "He's going off to kill a buffalo so he can change his boy name to his grown-up name," Randy told Kit in his dream. "But how can he kill a buffalo when Mr. Preuss has his bow and arrows ?"

Yes

Friend

Brother

Together

Good

Beth Berryman

While mountainmen are telling Fremont about dealing with hostile or thieving Indian warriors, outwitting them or out-fighting them, Kit Carson and Pat Cheyenne are showing Randy how to talk with Tuesday Cheyenne in Indian sign language–a start in finding ways to become "intimate friends," as Fremont says they did during the next 10 days.

155

CHAPTER 15

TALKING ABOUT INDIANS—
TALKING WITH INDIANS

June 29, Platte River (Nebraska)

Fremont's calm voice and South Carolina accent, then Kit Carson's responses in his Missouri nasal drawl, awakened Randy. Inside his tent, darkness still concealed the form but not the moany snores of Cousin Henry, who came to bed and got out of bed as late as possible.

The strong cold wind pushing against the tent flap brought fragments of some puzzling sentences from the two passersby outside. Fremont's trailing-off voice was saying, "but what will we do with..." and Carson's mild voice answered with something like "...a mistake to..but.." As they passed out of Randy's hearing, Fremont was saying, "think of some way to—"

Randy sprang into action. They must be talking about the three Indians! He'd dreamed that Tuesday needed a blanket, now he knew Tuesday needed more than a blanket—he needed a friend to speak up for him! In the faint pre-dawn light, Randy raced toward the center of the camp circle where he'd left the Cheyennes to sleep the night before.

Nobody there! Nothing! Had they already felt the message "Not wanted"—and left?

Heart pounding with disappointment and dismay, Randy rushed toward a cook starting his mess fire. "Mike!" he called to Descouteau. "The Indians have left! Did you see them?! Where did they go?"

"Prairie artist" nodded, smiled, and jerked his thumb toward the scattering of trees by the river. A gusting wind blew away the sound, but Randy could see the word "firewood" on Prairie Artist's lips. Relieved, Randy began walking toward the river. He soon couldn't decide which way to go—the Cheyennes could have gone up or down the river. He stopped to wait upon the growing light, to look in all directions, and to think as he shivered.

"Should I tell them right off what I heard John and Kit say? But I can't—I don't know how to talk Cheyenne. Br-r-r—wish I'd wrapped up in my blanket. Well, I DO know how to sign 'friend' the way Kit showed me. If I do that, they'll

FRIEND

know I'm on their side."

He practiced holding up two fingers together on his right hand. Soon a rougher wind set him hopping back and forth on one foot, hugging himself for warmth. Across the grasslands to the east, he saw on the horizon the first flashes of the sun's fiery rim.

Shortly, he saw Tuesday and the two men, draped in their half-buffalo skins, walking toward him. Each was hugging an armful of broken, dead tree branches.

Randy met them half-way, raised his right hand with two fingers together and smiled. Tuesday's face glowed, both men began tight-lipped smiles. The man with a tall feather standing upright in the scalplock at the back of his head, suddenly spoke. "Fren'!" he said loudly.

Randy's mouth dropped open into a wide smile and quick laugh. "You know 'friend!'—English! That's going to make everything a lot easier!"

The Indian man repeated, "Fren!", then added, "Ki' Cars'n" and a shoulder shrug and grimace that seemed to mean "that's all."

Tuesday began giggling. "Fren! Ki'Cars'n!" he mimicked. Suddenly Randy saw the humor. "Tuesday!" he exclaimed, waving his hand, two fingers extended. The four of them laughed loudly, warmly, and moved on toward the campfires. "Two English names—Tuesday and Ki'Carson, one Indian sign for one English word—friend," Randy sighed to himself, "not much to start with. I've got to get Kit to teach me more signs."

Another name then flashed in his mind. He moved beside Tuesday, pointed a finger at himself. "Randy," he said. The Indian boy stopped to gaze eagerly into the blue eyes of the wi'hio and to say the strange name, "Ran-dee." It was a moment both would remember as the moment each knew he'd found a kindred spirit.

They were breaking the firewood into arm-length pieces when Kit Carson came hurrying up. He called to Pat and Mike in Cheyenne and made hand signs. They immediately dropped pieces of wood, pulled together the fronts of their buffalo cloaks against the gusting chill wind and half-ran to Carson."What is it?! What's wrong?!" cried Randy. "What are you going to do with them, Kit?!"

"Come along!" called Kit, beckoning. Both boys abandoned their jobs and ran to catch up with the three men. "Are you telling them to leave, Kit?!" Randy panted, tugging at Carson's sleeve. "No, no, Randy—we need them to do a lifting job." Randy exhaled a deep, loud breath of pent-up anxiety. "Lifting? Lifting what?"

"It's them bundles of furs we yestiddy loaded into the carts," Kit explained. "Just now, the Lieutenant showed me whereby the three biggest bundles must come out—or else there's nowheres to put all our tents. These three biggest bundles belong to Tulip, who had more than just 'small furs.' He also had three roll-ups of ten buffalo robes each! Musta been some work to drag them up a tree. He meant to leave them, they're so big and heavy, he said, but changed his mind when the Lieutenant said we'd take ALL bundles!

"He's a little shame-faced about it now since those are the ones we need to unwedge, lift up and out of each of three carts. Them bundles will weigh a hundred pounds apiece, and they're bulky, awkward to handle. The boys who brought them from the trees say their backs are sore and they daren't pull the bundles up and outta the carts.

"Pat 'n Mike by themselves can lift'um, move'um, get'um outta there. That'll show anybody a-noticing that Indian muscle is worth keeping in this camp. These Cheyennes may look skinny, but I've seen'um lift bundles bigger and heavier than these, then toss 'um to the ground yards away."

Randy thought of warm, furry buffalo robes tossed on the ground and left behind. It made his shivers stronger and his goosebumps bigger. "Can't we take along ONE robe somehow?" he shouted through chattering teeth and into a sudden blast of wind.

"Oh yes! We mean to!" Carson shouted back. "The Lieutenant is offering Tulip a silver dollar apiece for a dozen or so for cushions to put under the pack animals' loads. The rest can be bought by them folks what's been complaining— Mr. Preuss in particular—about how bare-ground beds is so hard and cold. They can spread robes out at night to sleep on, spread'um by day under their saddle to ride on. I'M gonna buy one. Maybe two."

Randy declared he had $2 and he wanted two robes—one for himself and one for Tuesday. "He's only got a halfa-robe, and when we start riding, that's the only thing he has for a saddle. So he's left naked to sit and freeze all day in this cold wind."

Carson said the Cheyenne men were in the same naked situation. "They need robes, too, though they won't complain or ask for any. They just clamp their teeth together

Loading trappers' packages of furs into Fremont's carts not part of JF's Report

JF Report Accounts (However, JF paid Tulippe $12 for 12 robes..)

158

and sit up straighter. You may not believe it, Randy, but I've seen Indians as naked as these two that kept on riding when snow wuz falling and wind cutting through my deerskins—the Indians never once wincing."

Tuesday, walking close to Randy, observing Randy's foot stampings, arm hugging, and glances at the buffalo half-robes the Indians were wearing, abruptly unfastened his own and draped it over Randy's back and shoulders.

"Hey! DON'T do that!" Randy cried out, and began pulling the robe off, meaning to hand it back. Quickly, Carson grabbed hold of it, redraped it across Randy's back. "Don't ever refuse a gift from an Indian," he said in Randy's ear. "He takes it as an insult. Here, I'll hold this robe so it won't fall off whilst you busy your hands to say 'thank you'. He's looking at you, so you put both your hands out in front of you, edge to edge like this, thumb against thumb, palms down. Fingers straight, let your wrists wave your hands up and down while you bend forward a little.

"Go on, do it. Smile. Good. Now beckon to the boy—that means 'come'—and take him with you to your tent. You put on a sweater and jacket and hat, THEN it's all right to give him back his wrap."

When the boys showed up by the cart where two of LaTulippe's bundles of buffalo robes had been opened and unrolled, Fremont, Carson, the two Indian men began to laugh, then all the other men stopped their robe-buying to laugh with them. Tuesday was wearing Randy's knitted red hat and sweater with Randy's khaki pants! Randy, still draped in Tuesday's half-robe had put on a "baseball" cap his Father had bought for him in Washington where the hit'n'run game was becoming the rage.

Giggling, they made the hand sign for "trade". Hands raised, index fingers pointing upward, each swished his right hand and arm to the left at the same time he swished his left hand and arm to the right—back and forth, quickly.

"But he can still use the half-hide for a saddle when we get started!" Randy declared. "Here's my $2 for two robes! We're going to wrap ourselves and our ponies in them and ride warm!" Randy silently added, "And I won't be wearing a smelly half-robe he's sat upon for at least a year."

When breakfast was over and the column was slowly moving westward alongside the Platte's miles-wide braid of water ribbons and sand bars, the cart drivers and a number of riders and their horses looked to be under tents. Inside

THANK YOU

COME

Encyclopedia
Britannica
11th edition
Vol.2,baseball

TRADE

Signs based on
Indian Sign
Language.
W.Tomkins and
Indians Signals and
Sign Language,
G.Fronval/ D.Dubois

them, the men silently thanked Fremont for the furside-inside deliciously warm covers around their bodies. What snuggly shields against the force of the prairie's cold, incessant, increasingly boisterous wind!

Overhead, clouds in every shade of gray and black rolled and tumbled like a thousand feather coverlets in a world-size bed. Under foot, the bare earth here and there looked sickly white with salt crystals. On the river banks, wide open spaces between trees were often dry benches where cacti, thistles, and desert peavines clung. Beyond the Platte's thin waters, miles of gray-green grass rippled frantically all the way to sandhills notching the horizon.

JF Report
June 29(cacti)

With Earth and sky both in wild motion, Mr. Preuss, head drooped, huddled in his furry robe at the end of the column. Depressed, wondering at his foolishness for taking such a job, he stared at the desolate, salty earth just beyond his stirrup. In his native language he mumbled, "All vacant—nothing to see—only sand, sand, grass, grass. Can a little lieutenant who says he ENJOYS looking across thirty miles of nothing be sane? To me, he's like someone who would prefer a book with blank pages instead of a good story."

At midday, after plodding 15 miles with only the wind's whistles and moans for company, the column stopped to rest and eat at a riverside spot where three trees not far apart might break the wind a little. The cart drivers persuaded the mules to position two carts side-to-side, so close that axlehubs of the five-foot-high wheels were touching. The lattice of wheelspokes, draped with a buffalo robe gave a tight circle of men protection from the wind at each of the four stations. Compared to bouncing in a saddle while a cold, powerful blast hit eyes and nose, the cartside dining space felt calm, even cozy.

Journal. Preuss
(blank pages) p8

Having unhitched, watered the animals at the river's edge, and staked them for a quick, grassy lunch, the men gathered first by the water bucket and the cracker barrel. "Too much wind for a fire," the cooks had said, and handed out "pilot bread," renamed "pilot shingles", since they were of the same hardness as those wooden objects. Holding water-cup and bread, the diners, some sharing buffalo robes, crouched in tight circles by the cartwheels.

Fremont, Maxwell, Lambert, Preuss, Lajeunesse, and LaTulippe sat legs crossed, knees almost touching. "It's good to hear a human voice again," Fremont said to his companions, all crunching crackers between sips of water.

*Conversation
not in JF Report,
but drawn together
from other sources.*

"Six hours pass exceedingly slowly when we ride ears in the wind and speechless as Indians."

He twisted his neck and head around to look at the next cart where Carson, Randy, Tuesday, Mike, and featherless Pat were kneeling in a circle. Fremont turned back with a smile to say that perhaps "the silent Indian" was an exaggeration. "Or maybe they just need a Carson and a Randy to get their tongues started. Hands are moving, mouths too, and not just from grinding crackers."

"I t'ink," Tulip spoke up, "our own manners toward Indians can determine de way dey talk wid us—same as happens wid anybody else. Make de air comfortable and Indians'll open up—by hand-talk if not word-talk."

"But does zat make Kit Carson's talky Indians trustworzy?" demanded Preuss.

Lajeunesse quickly answered. "Mais oui, M'sieur—you can t'row away your suspicions 'cause Kit Carson KNOWS dem—'cause he's worked wit'um, and dey know he's trustwort'y 'cause he's always done'um fair and square. So now all of us can trust dem—if we act as good and true as Kit. Oh, Kit Carson is known far and wide amongst Indians AND whites for his tru'fulness—whet'er he's talking 'bout helping you or killing you. Furt'ermore, he has de common sense to know when to help and when to kill. He'll live a long time. So will we—as long as we have Kit Carson wit' us."

Fremont nodded vigorously, agreeing. "Truth and Carson mean the same thing. So do Carson and caution, keen intuition and understanding of the thinking of Indians. He's daring, inventive, but cool-headed, especially when facing danger. A most admirable man!"

Lambert, who ordinarily was too busy directing wagon and packmule traffic, listening to complaints and requests, checking animal health, tracking supplies, and a hundred other tasks that kept the camp and men functioning sensibly if not to everyone's complete satisfaction, raised his hand like a school boy. He pounced on the pause at the end of Fremont's sentence.

"Yes sir! Kit told me about a time when 500 Indians — and I can tell you that's a VERY LARGE crowd—swarmed around his camp one day while most of his men were out visiting the beaver traps. These Indians made all the signs saying 'friend.' But Kit judged they were just pretending, seeing as how they'd come in BIG numbers—no matter he didn't see any weapons on them.

"He decided the safest way to act was not to let the Indians know he didn't trust them, but to assume a fearless MANNER—at which he is a master. He also told one of his men to look in a nearby ravine for hidden weapons, which he did, and discovered bows, arrows, and sharp-pointed poles.

"Soon as Kit heard this, he spoke in Spanish to one of the Indians who understood that language, and told him, 'Say to your warriors, You must leave this camp inside of ten minutes. If anyone stays longer, he will be shot dead.' Kit told me that long before the ten minutes were up, not one Indian was left for him to shoot."

The circle of men agreed that guns and nerve AND language in a case like that were a winning combination. "But let me tell you something else about Kit," Maxwell said. "Though he's known among the Indians as harsh to any of them who attack or trick or steal from him, he's also known for punishing Indian behavior by actions other than shooting. I give you a 'fer instance.' There was this Indian boy he'd been kind to and let have the run of the camp for a week. When camp was breaking up, and the boy would be going back home, he stole an old trapper's tin cup. He tossed it across the creek into the rushes, thinking nobody saw him.

Overland With Kit Carson
G.D.Brewerton.
p82 (tin cup)

"But somebody did. Kit grabbed the boy by the hair with one hand, grabbed a leg with the other hand, and took him to the creek. Into the water he pushed him head first. 'Swim across to the rushes, find that cup, and bring it back here to me and the old man—or ELSE!'"

In the midst of the laughter, Preuss blurted out that the Lieutenant now knew what to do if TUESDAY tried any thievery.

Fremont ignored the remark. "What I know about getting along with—managing—influencing—dominating Indians, I learned during my two seasons with Nicollet's mapping expeditions in Dakota country. My first teacher was a man about my age who had quit the study of law to become a fur trader among the Indians when John Jacob Astor owned the American Fur Company. By the time I knew him— Henry Sibley—he'd become part owner of the company when Astor sold out. The Indians of that northern area admired Sibley greatly, for he set rules of behavior and maintained discipline over a large number of white traders, clerks, and French voyageurs. In addition, he was a giant of a man with both a decisive character and amazing skill with pistols

JF Memoirs,
Fremont Path-
marker, p33-4
A.Nevins
(Sibley, Renville)

162

and rifles."

This picture excited LaTulippe to applaud, whoop with laughter, point a forefinger around like a pistol, and boom "BANGBANG!"

"Just a minute, Tulip!" Fremont continued."My second teacher, Joseph Renville, was a half-breed in that region with a different way of dealing with Indians living within a hundred miles of his place. He was like a judge-chieftain. It was his tact, insightful decisions, personal attention that gained him respect and admiration—and obedience. I learned from watching and listening to him that it pays to speak to Indians in a low-pitched, calm voice, and ALWAYS tell the truth.

Minnesota Historical Collection I "Sketch of Renville"

"Never show fear, Renville said, or else they'll think your heart—your courage—is weak, shifty, and your tongue crooked. Never appear stern or haughty, nor use more words than necessary. Show respect and listen carefully to their complaints, no matter how trifling they may seem. Show that you rule by right, that you won't give in to force or unjust demands from any source. I have witnessed many times," Fremont added, "how Indians listened with reverence to even his harshest judgments."

Maxwell was shaking his head. "Well, now," he began, "we men living out here on the prairie and in the Rockies know there's a great difference of character from one tribe to another—and there's about 30 or so tribes. The Blackfeet are merciless devils. The squat, ugly Comanches are arrogant, obsessed with horses. The moralistic Cheyenne six-footers are loyal friends of whites since William Bent more'n ten years ago saved in his fort a pair from a Comanche scalping party. Broad-faced Crows are fine-looking like Cheyennes, but love the excitement of war and killing.

Warriors of the Plains. C.Taylor, p33 (tribal character) *Bent's Fort.* D.Lavender. p123-9 (tribal character) *Zenas Leonard Trapper,* p138 (tribal character)

"With ALL of those, and with all the other tribes, WAR is THE way to glory and personal position.

"War is horse stealing. Horses are wealth and status. Indians steal from each other, they trick each other, they are sworn enemies to tribes that fought them and won—look at how the Cheyennes hate the Pawnees. As tough old trapper Zenas Leonard says, 'thar ain't more'n three tribes in that whole territory on friendly terms with each other.' That can change in a day, or an hour—if one warrior short on character and long on impulse steals a horse from a friendly neighbor.

"They don't wait on niceties like tact and calm talk. They

163

go after their horses, take back their own and the enemies', too, steal the women for slaves and kill the men, wreck and burn whole villages of teepees. They call it 'teaching them a lesson.' That's the way Indians 'deal' with enemy tribes, and 'improve' their own reputations.

"Whites are one enemy tribe among tribes that are enemies to each other. We're all competing for the fur animals, the food animals, the space of the plains, to make a living, become 'somebody important,' get rich. Tribes have long played this game of tricking, stealing, warring, and teaching each other a lesson.

"If we stay in the game, we have to play the way they play. That's the way Kit sees it, and that's the way I see it. If we try to 'influence' them to give up stealing, raiding, warring, or howling day and night for weeks grieving over their dead, we'll lose the few friends we have—and our lives, too. This is the reality we have to 'deal' with."

For a long moment after Maxwell's last words, no one spoke. The men's churning thoughts, examining the complexities of 'dealing' with Indians, rivaled the commotion of the windstorm.

"It's likely," Fremont said as he slowly began backing out of the circle, then pushing his arms and legs to rise, "that the Upper Mississippi Indian-white situation of six years ago was only for that place and time—a fort that was a marketplace, good managers, little hostility, no competition between Indians and whites over beaver streams, or horses, or buffalo hunting."

JF Memoirs (Upper Missi- ssippi years)

Lajeunesse felt compelled to say, "And de whites had ALL de guns den. Now de story's changing. Your map of de trail will bring t'ousands of whites and arguments and fights—not just about de animals of de land, but about de land itself. Even if whites t'ink dis is strange land wit' no trees, dey see it as VACANT. White farmers wid families will come, each one staking off a big, free piece of land. Dey can see it grows good grass so it's bound to grow good wheat and corn—dey's grass, too. Bullet-shooting-hell will break loose when it comes to pass dat farmers tell de world dat bloodt'irsty Indians and crop-trampling buffalo have got to go. You'll see."

Fremont had listened closely while he got to his feet. His response, "You sound like a Biblical prophet, my friend," was lost in the wind.

He was bending into the wind, a hand on his hat, the

other holding the collar of his "blue blanket" coat close about his neck, when he came to Carson's little circle of two boys and two Indian men. "Time's up!" he shouted. Carson waved a salute, then turned his attention to Randy. "In no time if you work at it, you'll know enough signs to talk to any tribe from Canada to Mexico.

Indian Sign Language W.Tomkins

"See, every tribe has its own spoken language—they can't understand each other any more than you can. Long ago, some smart Indian invented a set of hand signs to represent things, actions, ideas. All the tribes learn them and use them—a common Indian language. Now you've got a good start on sign-words for your hands to practice, Randy. Guard duty this evening is a good time to do it, specially since there'll still be daylight part of the time."

Randy grimaced. Guard duty? When he was waiting for a pilot shingle, Cousin Henry had passed by and teased him about doing guard duty tonight—"your TERRIBLE punishment for sneakiness," he sarcastically called it. Randy had hoped Henry was only teasing. He asked Kit for the truth, and he got it. "Yes, it's the extra shift you have to do this week. Lambert got so deep into the robe-buying this morning, he didn't get around to announcing the guard list. You have the 8 to 10 'twilight' shift."

But now that he'd had a few bites of something to eat, and now that Kit and the Indians had shown him the hand signs for some words—yes, no, good, bad, wait, many, few, together—he felt better about doing guard duty. Yes, he thought, as he and the Indians and Carson scrambled to their feet, those dreaded hours alone wouldn't be so scary and tedious this time.

Alone? Hastily he grabbed Kit's arm. "Kit! If Tuesday could stay with me on guard duty, he could help me practice the hand signs! We won't be talky and noisy, and he's probably a lot better at hearing slithering Indians when the wind is blowing than I am!"

Carson laughed, then shouted through the wind, "If this wind keeps up, you won't need to worry about slitherers—just horses and mules panicking! I'll check with the Lieutenant about Tuesday sitting with you, but it sounds like a good use of boypower to me!"

During the miserable afternoon of riding while the wind kept strengthening, the cold biting harder, Randy occasionally tried to hand sign "together" to Tuesday. "Together" got through, but the idea of attaching it to anything didn't.

165

Tuesday looked mystified and just signed back "together." Randy tried to imagine how "guard duty" would look in hand signs but he couldn't.

The afternoon march came to a halt early after a few raindrops were felt swirling inside miniature cyclones. Lambert led the carts to a small clump of timber by the river bank, and directed them into a circle just big enough to crowd all the tents into.

In the middle of this setting-up, when animals were noisily complaining and men were screaming orders into the wind and rain, Mr. Preuss suddenly raced between two carts into the circle, grabbed in great excitement at the arms of men in his path.

Randy, running to fetch a left-behind from a baggage cart, crashed into Preuss and fell. Preuss reached down, hauled him to his feet, and shouted in his ear, "TURDS! I've just seen enormous buffalo turds, all fresh! Finally ve've come to vere ze buffalo are!"

Journal, Preuss
June 29

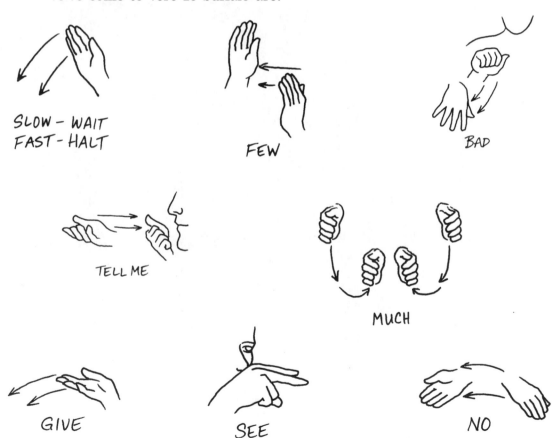

SLOW – WAIT
FAST – HALT

FEW

BAD

TELL ME

MUCH

GIVE

SEE

NO

Based on Harper's Magazine, 18--

Whar's de buffalo?! Impatient to see a herd, dash into it, make a quick kill, Basil Lajeunesse rushes on horseback to the edge of the Platte to take a look upriver. "Dey not crossing de river–dey musta come over to dis side already! Tomorrow'll be De Day!" But Lieutenant Fremont has a surprise for him.

CHAPTER 16

BUFFALO COMING!

June 29, Platte River trail (Nebraska)

"Booffaloo!" boomed Moise Chardonnais, magnifying the magic word Mr. Preuss had brought. The wind picked up the word and carried it to the far rim of the camp circle. "Come on, Randy, let's run see les animaux! Dey must be coming 'cross de river!" Moise bounded off, with Randy and Tuesday at his heels. Behind them an array of running men quickly followed—mule drivers, horse tenders, packers, musclemen, cooks, and Fremont. A minute later, Carson and Maxwell, rifles in hand, galloped on their horses out to the prairie. Close behind them two Cheyennes pressed their heels into the sides of their spotted ponies urging "faster, faster."

JF Report
June 29

Mr. Preuss yelled at all of them, but the wind swallowed the sound and nobody looked his way. "Zey won't see any animals—I told zem I saw EVIDENCE of animals! Stupid people! Zey never listen!" Mumbling to himself, he retreated to his tent, draped his newly acquired buffalo robe about him and recorded German grumbles in a notebook for his wife.

At the river's edge, Randy and Tuesday huddled together close by Moise and the Lieutenant. Without his furry robe, Randy shivered in the slowly dying but still chilly wind. "See anything up or down the riverbank?" Fremont asked. Moise shook his head but continued his sweeping gaze over the river, a small island, the river's lightly wooded shore, and the prairie expanses beyond the river's far side.

Just then, he felt a sharp tug on his jacket. He looked around quickly. Tuesday was pointing across the river to the wooded little island a short wade away. Moise stared at it but saw nothing that looked like a buffalo. "Rien," Moise grunted. Randy looked at Tuesday, translated "Nothing!" as a shrug and raised empty hands.

Tuesday grabbed Randy's arm, pointed to his own eye, then Randy's, then the island, directing Randy's gaze to the island's east end. Suddenly, Randy said, "Moise! Look! The end of the island!" He pointed to the right where he could see in the dark bushes two buffalo heads bent to the water. Moise stared hard, saw only bushes—until one buffalo raised its head and the motion caught Moise's eye.

"HALLOO! Dere dey are, Lieutenant!" Moise hallooed so loudly the buffalo turned its head to look in Moise's direction a second or so later. "De Indian boy saw dem. His young eyes can see t'rough bushes and shadows—and besides, dem eyes has had a lotta practice spotting de booffaloo."

"Yes, yes! I see them now!" exclaimed Fremont. "No matter how many times you've seen these beasts, the next first-view is always thrilling. Do you think more than two animals are over there?"

Moise's grimace said there was no way to tell for sure. "Dey may be strays from a faraway herd—or de herd might be on de prairie BEHIND de island—or de herd might be resting out of sight ON de island—or—maybe de Indian boy knows sum'um more. Lemme try getting 'cross to him de kernel of dis question."

Eyebrows arching above his questioning eyes, he faced Tuesday. Lips parted perhaps to voice a word, Moise paused to ponder, a finger rubbing the side of his neck.

Randy interrupted the pondering process. "I think I know how to say it, Moise! Let me try!" Moise and Fremont chortled and gave him handwaves of approval.

Randy caught Tuesday's eye and held up two extended fingers on his right hand. His left hand jabbed the air, pointing at the buffalo pair on the island. When Tuesday glanced toward the buffalo and nodded, Randy raised his open hand to shoulder-height, palm facing Tuesday. He twisted his wrist from side to side.

QUESTION

"Sign language for 'question,'" Randy murmured. Then, catching Tuesday's eye, he pointed at the island buffalo, raised two fingers, quickly raised five, then ten, repeated "question."

Tuesday's face lit up. Randy smiled. "He got it!"

His face taking on the confident expression of one who knows what he's about, Tuesday pointed to the small island, to the prairie beyond, turned and pointed to the prairie behind Moise, Fremont, and the camp. He completed the circle by swinging his pointing finger all the way left to the west end of the island.

Moise, having followed Tuesday's silent message with a face showing avid interest, now turned a puzzled, quizzical gaze on the boy, then on Randy. "Randy, What's he saying?" Fremont looked on, amused.

Randy frowned, lips pursed with uncertainty. "That looked like 'acted-out sign talk' to me. I know how to sign 'not', but I can't remember how to sign 'understand.' Maybe if I sign 'no'—" Randy held out his open right hand, palm down, quickly swung it out front and left, palm turning up. Pointing to his head, he shrugged.

NO

Again, Tuesday "got it." With a little smile, he repeated his buffalo message, jabbing his finger in the direction of prairies all around them. Then he raised two fingers of his right hand, held them over his heart, and woggled them from side to side.

A yelp of loud laughter exploded from Moise. "Dat's de one sign I learnt from seeing de Indians make it to answer most anyt'ing I asked 'um. It means 'peut-etre—maybe, perhaps'."

UNDERSTAND

Tuesday joined in the laughter. His buffalo message, Fremont said, showed that Indians can't predict any better than anyone else where, when, nor how many buffalo are nearby or on their way "coming toward us."

PERHAPS

Just then a rhythmic bang-bang-bang sound came from the camp. "There's the cook beating the big frying pan, calling us to supper," Fremont said. "Besides, the wind is going through Randy's jacket and making his teeth chatter. Back to camp, men! The buffalo herd will let us know with a steady rumbling roar, and fits of bellowing, when the animals are getting close enough for us to see."

All signs based on Indian Sign Language. W.Tomkins

The two boys ran a race across the hundred yards from the river to cook's dishing-up pans. On the way, Randy's thoughts raced, too. "Buffalo hunting! Will John let me go buffalo hunting when a herd comes in sight?"

In the back of such thoughts, he could hear Fremont saying, "It's too risky. You don't know how big these animals are, how fast-moving, what brute strength and dangerous actions you'd face.Your pony knows as little as you do. Your father and mother would never forgive me if I let you go out to chase buffalo and you had bad luck."

What could he say to the Lieutenant to convince him that he ought to relent a little, say at least an iffy-yes? IF Tuesday goes on his pony and I stay close to him, do what he does...IF I don't take the pistol, don't go to kill, just go to see? If I can't go at all, how can I ever know what hunting buffalo is like? Besides—IF Tuesday goes but I don't, how will that look to him? Maybe Kit will speak up for me. But maybe he'll back up the Lieutenant. I'm gonna ask Kit what he'll do—no, I'd better wait'n'see."

The cooks dished up sum-more-of-the-same for supper. "This fried fatback and bread won't keep a body warm through the night," complained Registe Larente, the always hungry cart-driver. Prairie Artist-cook Descouteau countered, "Well, this grub ain't bad enough to keep YOU from coming back for a third helping three times a day. No wonder you ask Lieutenant for a dose of Doctor Mozingo's Concentrated Fig Syrup Cleanser every night."

JF Report
(fig syrup to Larent)

Reggy's companion Francois Badeau, "the hairy one," declared that everybody would be drinking the fig remedy if buffalo meat didn't soon show up in the cookpans.

"Will we live long enough to see the day when we eat fresh meat again!?" he cried out.

A chorus answered, "YAAYY! Dat's de question! Where's dem BUFFALO! BUFFALO! BUFFALO!"

Kit Carson, Maxwell, and the Indians rode up just in time to hear the question. Carson rose in his saddle and shouted, "TOMORRY! They'll meet up with us tomorry! We rode five miles west and we saw dust clouds on this side of the river in the distance! We and our Cheyenne friends agree that a herd is eating its way to us, and we'll see it soon after we get going tomorry morning! One more meal of sum-more-of-the-same and we can gorge ourselves on the best tasting meat in the world!"

Two dozen meat-hungry men cheered and cheered. A few battered hats flew into the air—and even a piece of hard, fried "bacon." Then excited voices began buzzing, soon were babbling, about who, how many of them would have a chance to take a shot at a buffalo.

The answer came during pipe-smoking time after supper. Fremont, heralded by Lajeunesse's blowing the "bleep-bleep" antelope call on a whistle, signaled a camp meeting. With Carson and Maxwell at his side, Fremont announced to the men eagerly awaiting exciting news, "We have only 50 miles' march to reach the junction of the Platte River's North and South Forks!"

This was not what the men had been tensely listening for and they received it with grunts and shuffling feet. Fremont paused long seconds before adding, "Somewhere along tomorrow's miles, we'll encounter a vast herd of buffalo!" The listening men shrugged—they knew that already. But surely the next sentence would name hunters for the first day's sport.

"Our skilled hunters, Carson and Maxwell, will go ahead of our caravan, approach these masses of huge, wild, powerful, dangerous beasts, kill two or three—enough to keep us

171

busy for the rest of the day and night with cooking and eating!"

The men looked at each other. Did Fremont mean that only Carson and Maxwell would have the fun and excitement of going buffalo hunting? The men hardly knew whether to grumble in disappointment—or to applaud the prospect of eating great quantities of roasted meat continuously for hours.

Fremont's restricting buffalo hunting to Carson and Maxwell is not stated in JF Report, but is implied by mention of only Carson and Maxwell hunting, killing buffalo.

Fremont gave them little time to wonder. "After our hunters kill the animals, you men must be ready to take to the field when the herd has moved away.

"The dead animals must be skinned, the meat cut up and hauled on carts into camp. Immediately thereafter comes the Great Banquet of the Prairie, which will last far into the night—ALL night if it takes that long to fill you up!" The men applauded politely, but their big question remained on their faces.

Fremont continued. "I have asked our hunters to organize teams for each job. Carson and Maxwell know skillful methods for skinning these ton-size animals and how to butcher the meat to the best advantage for cooking. They will instruct anyone who needs instructing—or you can do your learning while you watch others, while you help take an animal apart.

"Now, to repeat words you've heard before! The object of this expedition authorized and paid for by the Congress of the United States is to map the trail across the prairie to South Pass in the Rocky Mountains—AND—to bring that map and ALL the men in this party home safe and sound. Keep this in mind every minute of the exciting days just ahead. Keep your eyes, ears, and attention alert to danger— there'll be much danger on hoof and on horse!

"This expedition needs every one of you—and needs you sound and vigorous in heart, limb, and head for the next three months! Take no risks with these mammoth animals whose roaming grounds we are about to cross. Resist your urges to run out among them to kill for a trophy—or to repeat a daring attack like one you perhaps made in a buffalo hunt some other year.

"You'll feel plenty of excitement in simply WATCHING this drama of the prairie! Now the two hunters have a few things to say about skinning, butchering, and bringing to camp the buffalo they kill. Carson, Maxwell, take over."

Randy turned away. So, hunting for him was definitely out. Well, they wouldn't want a boy getting in the way of their butchering. Besides—there'd be all that blood. And guts. And other inside-things.

"Come on," he said, beckoning to Tuesday and pointing to his tent. "Let's go put on another sweater or jacket." As they ambled along, he kept thinking how good he could feel in Washington IF he could tell Joey and Billy and the other boys how he rode his pony right into the herd behind Kit Carson, fired his pistol so the bullet struck the buffalo in the heart and she fell dead at his feet—when he became aware of camp conductor Lambert beside him.

"Listen, son," he was saying, "I should've told you sooner, but with all this buffalo excitement—well, what I need to tell you is that your guard shift tonight will start at seven instead of the usual eight o'clock, and that Tuesday can sit guard with you. Lieutenant and Carson agreed to that. They said you might could use that daylight time practicing your sign language while you listen for buffalo and Indians. I must run—much to do !"

He hurried away so fast that Randy, his mouth open to ask, "Is it almost seven o'clock?" had no chance to say it. For a moment he watched, amused, as the bulky former accountant bounced across the camp circle.

"Ran-dee?"

Tuesday's soft voice brought Randy back to his companion. "Hey! you called me by name!" he exclaimed, and saw by Tuesday's face that he understood the sentiment if not the words. "Heck. I wish I knew more signs. Maybe he called my name because he wanted to tell me something. What, I wonder." He made the "question" sign, right hand palm out held at shoulder height and twisted from side to side.

Tuesday made the same sign, looked expectant.

"Aww," Randy groaned. He tried again. "Question," then quickly pointed to Tuesday and back to himself while stretching his face into what felt like a very quizzical expression.

Tuesday bobbed his head—he DID have a question. How to ask it when Randy knew only a handful of signs for making an answer?

The two boys looked at each other, smiled, shook their heads, and began laughing. All at once, Tuesday stopped. He began looking around at the ground, searching for something. Not finding it, he abruptly made a slow "halt" sign—"wait"—and ran to the cooking area. He picked up one of the sharpened sticks the men had collected for roasting buffalo meat over the campfires.

Returning to Randy, he beckoned, and led him out of the camp circle to a sandy area near the river. There, he leaned toward the ground, touched the stick point to the sand and began to draw lines.

Randy watched with amazement as Fremont's life-size profile with pointed nose, short curly mustache and beard, thick, wavy hair, lips open to speak—flowed line by line from Tuesday's stick point. "Tuesday!" exclaimed Randy, "how do you do that!?" Tuesday in silent concentration kept drawing—Fremont's shoulders, one raised arm, hand open, palm up, fingers spread in a characteristic gesture, then Fremont's blue blanket jacket, his trousers and boots.

"That's John, top to bottom!" Randy exclaimed. But Tuesday was absorbed in drawing Kit Carson's big, square face lightly bearded, his wide, thin lips, straight eyebrows, nearly straight hair hanging shoulder-length over his ears. The top of his head stood level with Fremont's nose. Tuesday dressed Kit's thick shoulders and broad chest in a fringed leather jacket, his legs in fringed deerskin trousers, and mocassins.

Then he began a quick sketch of Maxwell. Tall as Fremont but heavier, with big arms, heavy features made fierce by short, thick beard and mustache, and long straight hair, he stood with one hand on a hip, a bit of a swagger in his stance.

Deftly, swiftly, Tuesday sketched a circle of men facing the three men. Beside them, he drew two smaller figures. "That's you with the long hair in front of your ears—so the other one's me!" exclaimed Randy. "But you aren't THAT much taller than I am!"

Tuesday placed the stick point close to Fremont's mouth and holding his gaze on Randy, he made the sign for "question," then moved a cupped hand by his own mouth forward again and again.

Randy mumbled to himself, "Question—long talk sign. So this picture is the camp meeting we just had. Tuesday wants to know what John talked about. Yikes! To tell him, I've gotta draw buffalo and two men with guns on horses. My buffalo will be just two circles, four stick-legs, and two curved marks for horns. Same for horses, except no horns, but stickmen Kit and Max sitting on them."

Randy did his best. With Tuesday's portraits of Kit and Maxwell to point to as the hunters, and the sign for buffalo

Episode of Tuesday Cheyenne as artist is not in JF Report. But drawing pictures would have helped communications, led to" becoming intimate friends."

LONG TALK

Based on *Indian Sign* *Language* *W. Tomkins*

174

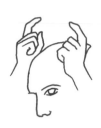

BUFFALO

WITH (AND) TOGETHER

*All signs
based on
Indian Sign
Language.*
W.Tomkins

—fists to either side of his forehead, forefingers extended and curved like horns—the message came through. It made Tuesday frown. Two fingers raised, hand then twisted in a question sign, he gave Randy a puzzled stare.

Just then, Randy heard Moise's voice trumpeting his name. Quickly he ran close to the camp circle, yelled, "Coming!" waved at Moise, and ran back to Tuesday. He signed "together"—right forefinger placed against the palm of his left hand—beckoned and started for his tent. Tuesday did not follow. Randy turned back. "I can't tell him in words or sign, nor draw a picture of 'guard duty'. What shall I do—hey, what's HE doing?!" Then he saw.

Tuesday was bending low over his drawings and sweeping the length of the long stick across the sand to erase them. Randy jumped to snatch the stick from Tuesday's hand. Tuesday whirled around and grabbed it back. Each boy held on. Glaring at each other, their faces inches apart, both let fly a stream of protesting words entirely incomprehensible to the other. When the words stopped, their tenseness hung in the air as blue eyes stared into dark brown, dark brown stared into blue.

Suddenly, both snickered—and let go of the stick at the same moment. It dropped to the ground.

"Aww, come on, let's go find Ki'Cars'n. He can explain everything to you," Randy said, beckoning.

"Ki'Cars'n," Tuesday answered, smiling.

Carson had just finished naming the buffalo "cut-up" teams, and was talking to the Cheyenne men. With hands moving quickly to keep up with the spoken Cheyenne words, Kit told them, and repeated for Tuesday when he joined them, about Fremont's plan for tomorrow's buffalo hunt. "But that's only for our men, you can hunt with your bows and arrows if you want to. Oh, and tonight, right after supper," he added, "Randy and Tuesday are going to do guard duty together—if Tuesday's willing."

Tuesday looked at Pat. Both smiled.

"Time for you boys to go now—it's close to seven o'clock," Carson said, "and Lambert's hollering for you."

"But show me how you signed 'guard duty'," Randy insisted. Carson held up his right hand, two fingers extended in front of his left eye and stared in the direction the fingers pointed—then the same with the left hand in front of the right eye.

Randy did it, Tuesday did it, laughingly Pat Cheyenne

SEE (AND) GUARD

did it, and the two boys ran off to do the duty itself.

For the next two hours, they sat silently at the guard post by Fremont's instrument cart. They wrapped in buffalo robes, for Moise had warned them that while the wind had calmed, the temperature was going down almost every minute "what wit' dis black cloud-cover ten miles thick dat's started rolling in."

Tuesday had rescued the long stick for drawing pictures on the bare ground, and Randy watched with admiration when Tuesday stood up and scribed in a bare spot of sand by the cart the animals of the plains—buffalo, antlered elk, horse, wolf, pronghorn antelope—then the animals of the stone ridges and mountains—goat and sheep, a big bear. When he sat down, he drew in the sand nearest them small pictures side by side—a teepee, a woman, a man with marks across his arm, a running horse, a man holding a peace pipe—until dark clouds had swallowed blue sky, sun, and nearly all the light.

When Tuesday laid aside his drawing stick, Randy held out his hands, edges touching. His wrists bent down, he made a little bow to say, "Thank you."

The boys pulled the buffalo robes snugly about them for the last minutes of guard duty, and sat silently in warm companionship. No practicing hand signs in the cold or dark. No slithering motions on the ground, no suspicious noises, no whinnying alarms from mules. When Ben Cadot arrived to relieve them, and said tauntingly, "Real terrible punishment, ain't it," Randy couldn't resist whining, "Worse yet," in a voice tremulous, with a tone of fake childish anger.

In his tent, Randy lying warm and sleepy inside his folded, furry buffalo robe, thought of the buffalo hunt he was going to miss. "It doesn't matter that I can't go. I'd rather stay in camp with Tuesday than chase some mean old buffalo. We can paint red stripes on our faces and arms, and I'll play my guitar for Tuesday to dance."

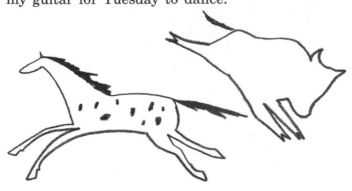

176

Randy sinks to the ground, stretching out behind a too-small rise, hoping to become invisible to the cud-chewing buffalo cow staring his way. On the prairie beyond, the herd he had so urgently wanted to see streams by. Tens of thousands of animals run toward distant hills, trying to escape Carson's rifle fire, and the threat of Maxwell and three Cheyennes galloping in a spacious lane the panicked buffalo have just vacated.

CHAPTER 17

BUFFALO! BUFFALO! CARSON HURT!

June 30, Platte River camp (Nebraska)

January chill on the last day of JUNE!? Winter had blown
in during the night. Moise was elated. He had told the
Lieutenant soon after supper that all his internal weather
wheels had slowed to a grind, grrrrr-uh. "Dat means sleep
UNDER de buffalo robe," Moise had advised Fremont. At
sunup, Fremont was showing Moise the thermometer. "Look,
Mr. Weatherman! Mercury's down to 44! Only twelve degrees
above freezing—with the Fourth of July just hours away!"

JF Report
June 30
"air at 44"

"Figger-in dis prairie wind dat never quits, and it IS
freezing," Moise said. "Just de right kind of weat'er for a
day dat's heading into an all-night cooking party! De
Greatest Buffalo Banquet of de Neeebraska Prairie!"
declared Moise, rubbing his stomach, showing every tooth
in a smile.

Several men promptly came out of their tents, looked out
across the flatlands in every direction, cupped their ears to
catch any buffalo sound the cold west wind might be bringing. Mule-driver Johnny sniffed the air for the scent of buffalo. They mumbled a few words to each other, shrugged,
slapped their shoulders to beat off the chill, and went back
into their tents.

When the crew came out for breakfast, a few men were
buttoning their overcoats, but most had draped blankets
around themselves. That was enough cover for the few minutes it took to pick up a cup of hot coffee, a few strips of
fried salt pork—"bacon"—and a handful of fried bread before
hurrying back to the warmth of their tents.

The mood of the camp was one of suppressed exasperation
at twin disappointments—unseasonable cold and a vast prairie
still empty of promise for a fresh meat banquet. Word had
slipped around that the Indians had said no buffalo herd
would show up for another two days, maybe longer. "Sacre
bleu!" fumed prairie artist-cook Descouteau. "Sum'mora same
for five or six more meals! You men only have to EAT it—
what if you had to COOK it AND eat it, like me!"

"Advance!" The crack of a whip, the heaving bellow of a

mule, and the column began its daily trudge westward along the Platte. Hardly a human voice was heard during the next two hours, and that voice was throwing an insult at a stand-still mule. "Garcon de garce! Son of a wench! Giddap! Giddap!"

In his place near Fremont at the head of the line, Randy sat on a saddle softened and warmed by half of his buffalo robe, furside out. He clutched together the edges of the other half to cover his shivering shoulders. Beside him, Tuesday rode Indian-silent. He looked warm in Randy's bright red sweater. His pony was quite warm, rump to ears, under buffalo fur.

Suddenly, a shout coming from Carson and Maxwell in the same moment shattered the monotony. "Six buffalo to the right!" Off the two hunters galloped. Randy, startled, his heart pounding, let the robe drop behind him when he saw Fremont also breaking from the line to follow the hunters. Then Lambert took after Fremont. Behind him raced two yelping Cheyennes. They barely squeezed in ahead of Lajeunesse whooping and yelling, trailed by young roustabout Raphael Proue shouldering a shotgun.

"Are buffalo attacking us?!" Randy shouted to Tuesday, forgetting that the message would move no farther than his own lips. He stood up in his stirrups and stared at the hunters. They were still strung out in a line, but moving slower. Ahead—yes!—six buffalo! "They'll be scared away!"

Journal..
C.Preuss
June 30

Randy said. But the six black animals didn't even glance up. They looked like cows calmly eating grass.

Randy suddenly became aware that he and wide-eyed, silent Tuesday were all who were left to lead the column. What was he supposed to do? Stop the column, or keep going? His pony had kept going, the line had kept up its slow, steady pace. After a moment, Randy patted "Spots" and said, "Well, Pony, the column acts as if you're doing the right thing, so keep on 'til something else happens." Randy rose to stand in his stirrups again. He saw the eight buffalo hunters slowly moving closer to the heads-to-the-ground, heedless animals. "Why don't they start shooting!?" Randy wondered to himself.

Just then he saw coming over a grassy hump near the grazers a band of a dozen or so buffalo, then another larger band. "LOOK! LOOK! JOHN! KIT! Watch out!" he yelled. The hunters stopped as if they'd heard him. The bands of

Beth Berryman

buffalo walked jauntily unaware, each animal swinging its great, furry head as it tested the grass on either side.

All at once, three men broke away from the group and trotted toward the bigger band of animals. After a moment's pause, Fremont, Carson, and Maxwell dashed after them, leaving the Cheyennes behind.

Randy, a quarter-mile distant, watching at the head of the moving column, saw puffs of smoke, then heard the crack! crack! of two rifles. He saw one band of buffalo turn away and break into a run. BOOM! from a rifle! POW! from a pistol. The bigger band quickly followed the smaller. In seconds, all the buffalo had disappeared behind the

Journal.
C.Preuss
June 30

grassy hump.

When Fremont, Carson, and Maxwell skidded to a halt beside Lambert, Lajeunesse, and Proue, the gunmen were hurriedly reloading rifles and pistol. Lajeunesse was tearing a strip from his shirt tail to use for patching under a lead ball, Proue was spilling gunpowder from his powder-horn into his rifle's flash pan, Lambert had loaded his pistols and was poised for the chase.

Randy could tell from the Lieutenant's flinging out his arm toward the rise where the buffalo had vanished, then his shaking a forefinger at the gunmen, that their excited shooting had hit nothing but Fremont displeasure and anger. The would-be hunters had ruined Carson and Maxwell's chances of a quick kill for a buffalo feast. Randy watched the three gunmen slowly holster or sling their weapon straps across their shoulders and turn their horses toward the column.

Even a 12-year-old at a distance could tell by Fremont's rigid neck and shoulder bearing that he was greatly disturbed by the thoughtless, even disobedient, "hunting" that three of his most trusted men had done. Fremont spoke for a moment to Carson, then he, Maxwell, and the Cheyennes trotted to rejoin the reprimanded men, lead them toward the moving column.

"Why is Kit staying behind? Is he going to hunt buffalo all by himself?" Randy said aloud, holding his gaze on Carson and his horse. They were galloping west on a slanting line that would eventually connect with the moving column. Carson seemed to be aiming for a low flat spot at the end of a swell.

"What IS he going to do?" Randy said aloud. Moise's voice growling beside him startled him with an answer. "He's staying away from our rumbling cart wheels and our horse and mules' drumming hoofs so he can hear buffalo rumbling and hoof-drumming. Now dat our head men are

JF Report
June 30

on deir way back, Randy, it's just for a little bit longer dat I'll keep you company at de head of de line. I come up here wid you 'cause seem like you two boys looked orphaned."

Randy hadn't time to answer. "Look at Kit! He's stopped! He's off his horse! He's crawling on his hands and knees! Moise! What's wrong with him?!" He began hauling on the reins to move his pony out of line, bumping into Moise's horse,

181

thinking only of rescuing his friend.

"Whoa-oh-o, Randy!" Moise shouted, grabbing Randy's arm. "Kit's putting his ear to de ground! He's listening for vibrations! A buffalo herd on de move will shake de eart' miles away!"

Just then, the ex-hunters rode up, Fremont in their midst speaking with a firm edge to his soft South Carolina accent. Moise muttered to Randy, "For sure he's giving dem some more words about deir deciding for demselves it was all right to shoot at a little bunch of buffalo, missing every one, just scaring'um away. De Lieutenant meant what he said—only Carson and Maxwell—and hisself, a-course—to hunt de buffalo."

A trilling, throaty cry from Tuesday drowned out Moise's voice. When Randy looked around, he saw Tuesday's fists by his ears, and forefingers curled like buffalo horns. At once, Pat and Mike slapped their ponies to spirit them toward Carson. Tuesday abruptly pulled his pony out of the column and followed them.

"Kit's coming back!" shouted Randy. "He must've heard buffalo sounds!"

Fremont, now at the front of the line with Maxwell and Lambert, led the column forward at a faster pace to meet Carson on his galloping horse.

"Look at that man ride!" Fremont said to the prairie breeze in the exhilaration of the moment. "Ahhh! Carson on a horse, the Indians, and the buffalo make poetry of life on the prairie!"

JF Report
June 30
(poetry)

Carson's horse thundered up, the Cheyennes' close behind him, horses dancing and turning they came to a halt. "They're coming!" Carson called out loudly. "The ground has the hum and the drum from a half-million hoofsteps! I could hear the murmur of growling, huffing, bellowing, snorting— even horn-clashing of fighting bulls. Sounds like a herd of a hundred thousand! They're not on the run—don't smell us, the wind is from the west. We'll smell them any minute. They're just walking and feeding—"

JF Report
"heard from a distance a dull and confused murmuring"

"How far away?!" asked a chorus of voices.

"About three miles. We'll probably see them in an hour or so from now—soon as we mount the sand humps and ridges of the next two miles."

"Lambert! Spread the word down the line!" Fremont

ordered. "We'll move sprightly, but not rush." Cheers and shouts greeted Lambert and his message all the length of the mile-long column. Songs broke out in Cajun French, Canadian voyageur French, tavern English, Mississippi steamboat rowdy, Missouri gospel revival, all quickening the rhythm of the column's forward movement.

Sunshine with winds floating away broken clouds transformed the day, confirming its festive outcome. From time to time during the next hour, word from Carson was passed along for the line to stop, keep silent. "Listen, alla-you! Listen for a low murmuring, like a crowd of people talking. When you first hear it, the buffalo herd will be less than two miles away! The closer we come, the louder the rumble! You may even feel the earth tremble when 100,000 tons of buffalo stomp on it!"

Cheers and renewed singing and clapping greeted the barely audible hum of buffalo voices during the first stop. Randy longed for his guitar as he beat chords and fingered strings in the air to accompany a male chorus roaring out a jumbled rendition of an old Erie Canal tune everybody knew—"Buffalo Gals won'tcha come out tonight! And dance by the light of the moon!" Tuesday watched with a look of puzzled amusement, uncertain why Randy was hand-flinging, intrigued by the strange vocalizing.

Two stops later, when the men heard the steady, loud hum and rumble, the shrieks of a mighty mass of buffalo, all the column's singing merged into a resounding cry of joy. Hustling to the top of a long, wide grassy bulge of sand, they saw a few hundred yards away scattered loners on the outskirts of three separate, mile-wide, black carpets, one after the other, on the plain. Each undulated, vibrated, with the jostling and noise of the masses of huge, wild animals.

"Such a quantity of life, all in motion!" Fremont said to Carson. "I have a strange feeling of—grandeur—the grandeur of this vast, untamed land."

JF Report
June 30

"Good for us they're eating, moving slow," Carson said. "Seems a day or so ago, they crossed the river to the bank on our side. You can tell where they werz yessidy—on the north side of the Platte—look 'way over there—all brown. Ain't hardly a green blade left standing. They wander, eating their way across the plains from Canada to Texas, following good grass.

"This herd's about a half-mile away now, moving slow, thinking of nothing but eating—a good time for a hunt. Right over there close to the riverbank should be safe for our camp—let's not wait 'til mid-day. Me and Max will take off in a hurry to hunt soon as camp's set up. We've got a crowd of half-starved men here who need a fresh meat banquet mighty bad and pretty quick."

As the column arrived near the river and began forming the camp circle, Mr. Preuss's mount trotted up to Fremont at the head of the line. Stuttering with excitement at the news he brought, Preuss pointed west to a dark mass on the prairie and advised the Lieutenant of a strange and exciting feature he had seen in the landscape.

"You see over zere on ze left in zee distance is a row of big l-lumpy hills? You'd probably call zem 'mountains.' And just in front of zem you see zree dark sections of forest? Spruce, I zink—zee first ve've encountered in zis treeless country. Extremely unusual! Important f-f-feature for my topographical m-m-map, yah?"

Journal. Preuss, June 30

"Well, Mr. Preuss," Fremont laughed, "you missed all the celebrating about the fact that those dark 'tree' masses have legs and move! Buffalo, my worthy map-maker, BUFFALO! You strayed so far behind the end of the column today to do your sketching, you didn't hear all the excitement? And our joyful singing and shouting?" Mr. Preuss blushed deep red, mumbled something to himself, jerked the reins to turn his horse toward the end of the line, and gave the animal a heavy heel kick.

JF Report June 30

Sidling out of line, Randy flung excited words in the direction of Tuesday. "Look! Look over there at that cloud of dust! Two great big buffalo are fighting—oouuww! One's knocked the other down! He's rolling over—trying to get up—he's got his front legs half up—now his back legs—the other one is coming at him—hurry up, hurry up! He's up, he's up! Aww.. He's running away!"

Tuesday was shouting and pointing at other dust clouds, other fights, other chases, imitating the clumsy side-rocking of huge animals on the dusty ground, when Randy heard the command faintly through the din of excited talk and singing—"Make camp!"

Randy and Tuesday raced Carson and Maxwell in tent-raising and baggage toteing. "I'm winning!" shouted Randy, lugging in and dropping his saddle and buffalo robe on the grassy ground of his tent. "Oh no! The clothes sack!" He dived through the tent's door flap to run back to the baggage cart. Where was everybody?

It took a few minutes to uncover his sack, haul it out, and run back to his tent. He threw the sack inside and yelled, "Kit! Max!"

They had vanished from next door. He looked all around and called loudly, "Tuesday!?" No answer. He had disappeared, too. And then Randy saw his red sweater at the side of the tent where Tuesday, peeling it off, had dropped it.

Turning round and round to look in every direction, seeing no sign of Tuesday anywhere, he felt the keen pang of being deserted, not-wanted. Puzzled, and a little angry that Tuesday hadn't waited for him, Randy ran to Fremont's instruments cart where he'd seen Kit and Max tie their still-saddled horses. They weren't there.

He was only in time to see the two men galloping upriver a little distance beyond the camp circle, leaning their heads close to the necks of the hard-working horses, urging them up a ridge obscuring the view of dark acres of buffalo spreading beyond.

Where had Tuesday gone? Where were Pat and Mike? Feeling abandoned, deeply disappointed that Tuesday would leave him with no explanation, Randy began running, stepping soon on the lumps of earth kicked up by Kit Carson's horse as it had climbed the ridge. Now he could hear the buffaloes' bellowing, snorting, and horn clashing as a jumbled roar.

He paused, wondering whether he wanted to go alone any closer or not. He had just decided he would just so he could see Kit Carson chase and kill a buffalo, when the movement of three spotted Indian ponies on his right caught his eye. They were fast-trotting by the riverbank, a hundred yards away.

"TUESDAY!" he shouted, turned, began running toward them. They saw him, waved, and slapped their ponies' flanks to make them gallop. They had their bows and quivers of arrows. They had stripped bare-bodied for action, and were headed for the buffalo herds. Randy, panting, blinking fast to keep back tears, stopped. They knew the Lieutenant had told him he wasn't to hunt. Of course the Cheyenne

Episode not in JF Report. Did the Cheyennes hunt buffalo that day? Fremont, knowing they had much experience in buffalo hunting, probably would not have held them back if they wanted their bows and arrows and wished to go.

185

MEN didn't want him tagging along.

But they had let Tuesday, a boy not much older than himself, tag along! And Tuesday hadn't told him—just disappeared. A friend would have told him, not just run off... wouldn't he? Of course, Tuesday didn't have words to tell him, did he. Slowly walking back to Carson's horse tracks, Randy tried to think of hand signs Tuesday could have used to tell him that he was going off buffalo hunting. Did Tuesday think he wouldn't've understood his signs? What a hateful business having no words for giving important messages!

Maybe Tuesday didn't know until the last second whether his papa—and John—would let him go or not—no time to try signing any message. "I bet that's it!" Randy said aloud. "He knew I couldn't go with him, so—" The thought made him feel a little better.

He helped the idea along by also saying aloud, "John didn't say Tuesday shouldn't go hunting. His Papa wanted him to go, 'cause Tuesday's 13 and he needs to do something important so he can change his name. I'm only 12—and a half. Even if I killed the biggest buffalo out there, it wouldn't get me a new name...but I bet the men would start calling me a name like 'BUFFALO Garcon.' That would sound really GRAND to the boys back home."

With a deep sigh, he began walking again. "I'll go over the ridge top just far enough to see a live buffalo. I've only seen what a skull looks like. Maybe I'll see Kit riding his horse smack into the middle of the herd the way he said he liked to do. He shoots once—and a buffalo falls over dead. I'd sure like to see that!"

The ridge leveled out and he walked on uneven land, sand held together by a mat of still green short grass. But now and again the sand had piled in low peaks and knolls and ridges, miniature versions of the distant, grass-covered sand hills—Fremont did call them "mountains"—a wavy line on each side of the seven-mile-wide valley of the Platte. The prairie's lumps and rises occasionally blocked Randy's view of the buffalo herds, but not their noise. "Nor their dusty, sweaty animal smell," Randy grunted as a breeze wafted in from the west.

Episode not in JF Report.

He was mounting a grassy knoll when he saw just beyond the top a solitary buffalo cow biting off grass. She was so close he could hear her snuffle. Quickly he sank to the ground, stretching out so that only his eyes were peering over the top of the knoll. He suddenly pictured how red his hair must look sticking out of dry, half-green grass. Would she notice? When the cow lifted her head to chew, Randy was sure she was looking straight at him.

Her eyes were black, glittering, though not very big. She stared and chewed steadily. Randy, heart pounding, held very still, not daring to blink. He hoped buffalo, like bears, don't see you unless you move. He stared at her.

BuffaloBook.
D.C. Dary

"She's so BIG! And look at all that pile of curly hair on her head and forehead! And long, shaggy hair hanging down from her chin! and neck! and shoulders! She looks like pictures of lions—except buffaloes are real dark—and dirty—and bigger than lions, I think. And they have black horns curving out of that curly topknot! Mean face!" Randy shuddered. "Better slide down the ridge slope clear out of sight—I hope!"

Expedition from
Pittsburg to the
Rocky Moun-
tains, *p331*
Maj.Stephen Long
(buffalo described)

But just then, Randy saw a much bigger buffalo running fiercely toward the cow—"and maybe toward ME!" Had the beast—a bull—seen him? Was he about to be attacked? His heart beating wildly, Randy began to squirm his body backwards, hoping he was disappearing from the sight of both buffalo. When he lifted his head, he could still see the cud-chewing cow. She was still looking vacantly his way, as if she were dreaming of endless expanses of lush green grass, unaware of the closer and closer approach of violence that Randy saw behind her.

His heart in his throat, Randy stretched backwards farther down the slope, buried his head in his arms, rubbing his nose in the grass. Trembling, he lay expecting the worst. The pounding of running hooves bringing a ton of buffalo bull came closer, closer, vibrating the earth beneath Randy's ears.

Abruptly, a double rhythm of pounding feet began vibrating. Randy squeezed his eyelids together, clenched his teeth, preparing for the moment of horror. He felt a spray of sand on his hair, but in the same moment he heard the hoofbeats turn away. In disbelief, he heard them fade and fade. Cautiously he raised his head and shoulders. He saw the cow buffalo running in the distance toward the herd, her pursuer close behind her. They had almost reached the herd when a mammoth protector charged from it, head bent low to collide with the mammoth pursuer. Randy heard the crash of horns and skulls. He sat up to take his first deep breath in what seemed like a week.

Big sighs of relief and joy surged through him. He gratefully gazed at the heavenly blue sky, the endless miles of green grass, the points on the sand hills across the sprawling river. How beautiful....how well everything fitted together. What a pleasure to see again the golden sparkle of sunlit mica flakes floating in the river's sandy water. He felt affection well up for the river's scattered sand-bars, its green, wooded islands, its birds, its weeds—everything!

He even felt a new, friendlier interest in the animal noises rising from the herds. He was deciding he could possibly learn to like buffalo, not be afraid of them—if they didn't come too close—when he heard a familiar, longed-for sound. CRACK!

A rifle shot! Kit Carson! Where was he?!

Randy jumped to his feet, his eyes scanning the open plain to the edge of the massive herd, and then to a sudden milling and churning of animals beyond the edge. He saw a curl of smoke and Kit Carson on his horse charging through the crowded beasts. They moved aside to let him pass, even to let him turn back toward the animal he had shot. Then, beyond Carson, Randy saw Maxwell, his horse racing along a clear lane in between two lines of galloping buffalo—and behind him at a little distance the three Cheyennes, all running full speed.

But it was Carson whose gun had fired, and Carson who had make the kill! Good ole Kit! Randy jumped up and down shouting, "Hurray! Hurray! Ray-ray-ray!"

Sudden chaos! Without a thought about danger, Randy runs screaming toward the spot on the ground where Kit has just flown head-first from his somersaulting horse. In seconds, Maxwell reaches Kit, hears him yell, "Go after my horse!" and gallops away. In seconds more, Pat Cheyenne kneels at Kit's side, Tuesday and his uncle Mike race furiously toward them, Mike on the way letting fly an arrow to stop a charging cow. Randy arrives shouting, "Kit! Kit! you're bad hurt!" Bewildered Kit gasps, "Randy! What'r you doing here?"

189

CHAPTER 18

POPPED SHOULDER and MAGIC ARROW

June 30, Platte River camp (Nebraska)

Randy was still shouting, "Hurray, hurray!" when he saw Carson's horse suddenly sink on its left foreleg so forcefully that its body flipped headdown and sideways, its backlegs—and rider—rising, arcing through the air and falling. Randy screamed in disbelief, began running toward his friend. The buffalo herd began breaking apart into long lines of frightened animals running away from danger to the safety of nearby sandhills.

Stretching his legs into faster, longer steps, arms pumping, chest heaving air in and out noisily, Randy ran the hardest race he'd ever run, a race to his friend lying facedown on the ground, hurt. Randy could see him struggling to turn over and sit up. On both sides of Carson, the buffalo in orderly single-file lines were cantering past at high speed despite the clumsy, unbalanced look of their head-heavy bodies. In one of those lines, Carson's horse was running hard toward the sandhills and freedom.

Suddenly a horse and rider, appearing from nowhere, it seemed to Randy, were rushing toward Carson, miraculously crossing through line after line of buffalo, dashing headlong in-between the running animals. "Maxwell!" The name came from Randy's throat as a gasping sob.

Just then, a commotion and a long, high-pitched yell, "O-HO-o-o-o-HY-A-A!" made Randy look to the right toward the river. Three Indian ponies and riders were bearing down upon a cluster of buffalo, breaking it up, scattering it into running lines. Pat's pony in the lead pounded rapidly ahead to Carson's side. Pat jumped from his mount, bow and quiver still dangling from his shoulder, and knelt beside the injured man. At almost the same moment, Maxwell's horse skidded to a halt by Carson's feet.

Before Maxwell could shout a question, Carson yelled at him, "Don't stop! Go after my horse! He's in a line of buffalo heading THAT way!" He wagged his head toward the highest sandhill. Without wasting a second in talk, Maxwell spurred his horse and sprang away.

JF Report
"(Carson's) horse fell headlong...(Carson) considerable hurt (but broke) no bones..."

JF Report
June 30
("Carson's horse) sprang up, joined buffalo band ..Maxwell chased horse."

"Oh that's terrible!"
"Oho-o-ohy-aa"
(Cheyenne cry)
Cheyennes.
Grinnell II, p155

190

"Kit! You're bad hurt!" Randy's breathless voice shouted as he ran up.

"Randy! What are YOU doing here!?" Carson grunted, then clenched his teeth in pain and turned all his attention to his right arm trying to lever his body up enough to release his oddly twisted left arm.

"Kit! You're bad hurt!" Randy cried out again and dropped to his knees beside Carson and Pat.

Presence of Randy and the Cheyennes not in JF Report. But who else could have been at hand to take injured Carson from buffalo running field to camp? JF Report says nothing more about Carson's injury.

But it was Pat's voice that answered—in excited Cheyenne words as he pointed to a bellowing buffalo lumbering frantically across nearby grass, heading directly toward the man on the ground and his friends. Close behind the angry animal charged Mike, his horse's legs flying as fast as the buffalo's, its tail as straight out in the wind.

In a burst of speed, the horse drew alongside the buffalo's flank. Mike pulled tight the string of his bow, aimed the arrow at a spot between the shoulder and belly, released the bow's stored power. The arrow flashed to its target.

F.O.C. Darley, Harper's Magazine, 18--

Mike's arrow goes all the way through the cow to the grass on its other side.

Randy saw the arrow sailing away from the opposite side of the buffalo. "Oh lordy, he missed!" Randy cried out. "Kit's gonna be trampled!"

But suddenly, the buffalo stumbled, toppled, fell forward on its massive head. Mike's horse sped past the dying beast. In less than ten seconds, triumphant Mike brought his mount to a halt near Carson. As the Indian slid off the animal's back, he raised his bow high and shouted a long, joyous cry. Pat jumped to his feet, shook his fists toward the sky and howled.

Carson glanced up at Randy's wide-open mouth and eyes and said, "He says the arrow went all the way through that buffalo." Tuesday, just riding up on his pony, was slapping his arms and yipping like a coyote, rejoicing.

Carson called out Cheyenne words to the Indians. They hurried to his side, eager to hear his praise. As his voice faltered with pain, the men quieted, and began to talk to each other, and to Carson. In a moment, they had decided what they needed to do.

With one on either side of Carson, they slipped their arms beneath his shoulders and middle to help him to his feet. He tested his legs with his weight. No pain, no weakness, no break. But the left arm hanging at an angle swung uselessly from the shoulder socket. Carson, wincing with pain, clasped his right hand over his left to steady it, take its weight from the shoulder.

Quickly Pat barked words at Tuesday, sitting stiff and silent on his pony. He jumped to the ground, led the pony close to Carson and held its bridle. Deftly Pat and Mike lifted Carson, put his legs astraddle the low back of the pony, braced him while he balanced himself to sit.

Carson's face became contorted from the pain of moving and resettling his dislocated shoulder. Randy's face contorted in sympathy, and he cried out again, "Kit! You're bad hurt!"

After a moment, Carson made an effort to smile at the boy. "It's a wonder I didn't break my neck," he answered. "Lucky to hit the ground with this shoulder. Nothing's broken. Arm's just out of its socket. Pat's gonna lead the pony and me to camp. Maybe somebody there can work it back in." Carson hunched his shoulders, still steadying his dangling arm with his right hand.

Suddenly, Carson's head jerked up, his face set in a wild,

Cheyenne kills buffalo episode not in JF Report. However, JF reports 3 cows killed, 1 by Carson, none by Maxwell. Indians were experts with bows and arrows.

Cheyennes.Grinnell I, p264
"Arrow shot all the way through 2 running buffalo. Arrow found standing free in the ground."

Among the Indians. H.Boller, p237 (arrow all way through buffalo)

Oregon Trail. F.Parkman,p206 Boy hunter kills buffalo

"Considerable hurt," JF says, but Carson went hunting the next day, killed, cut up a cow. So his bad hurt was fixed quickly. Shoulder dislocation a likely injury when rider is thrown head-long from a horse going 30 miles an hour and stopping suddenly. Episode of fixing Kit's injury is not in JF Report.

192

shocked expression, his eyes glaring. "MY RIFLE!" his tense voice croaked. "My bulletpouch and powder horn! Where are they?!" It looked to Randy as if Carson was about to swing off the pony's back to go look for his weaponry. Randy reached out quickly and pressed both hands against Carson's leg. "Kit! Kit! Don't get off! We'll find them!" Carson's face relaxed, and he spoke several words to Pat.

The three Indians hurried to search the spot where Carson had fallen, to search the nearby ground—and then farther and farther away. Rifle, pouch, and powder horn had flown from Carson at the same speed the horse had been galloping before it tumbled hoofs over head.

In a few minutes, the Indians brought Carson all his belongings. He wanted them draped by their straps across his good shoulder. "That shoulder feels empty without their weight, and the rest of me would feel near-naked without their cover," he said. "I'm good and ready now for Pat to lead the pony and me to camp. You come along with Pat, Randy. Tuesday'll ride with Mike on his horse."

Tuesday handed his pony's reins to Pat waiting on his own pony. As Tuesday turned away, he finally stood face to face with Randy. He looked uncertain about what to do or say. In an instant, Randy knew what HE wanted to do. But what sign-word did he know that would tell Tuesday he wasn't peeved at him? Or how glad he felt instead that Tuesday had run off with his father and uncle to hunt buffalo—and so could bring all three on their horses close by when Kit needed help! Would "good" say it all?

Quickly he said, "Kit Carson," and quickly he pointed to Pat, to Mike, to Tuesday, then extended his open right hand, palm down, in front of himself before sweeping it horizonally to the left—"Good!" Immediately he extended both hands edge-to-edge, and with a little bow swept them outward and down—"Thank you."

All three Indians smiled broadly and waved two fingers of friendship high above their heads.

Pat gestured an invitation to Randy to sit behind him and ride to camp. But Randy decided to walk by Carson's side just in case he might need a hand to steady him once in a while. Tuesday would be in sight, riding with Mike on his horse.

Randy kept looking back to see them, and what he saw

puzzled him. Mike and Tuesday were sitting on the horse, but the horse was turning in the wrong direction. Why were they heading back to the buffalo herd? His eyes followed them until he saw a bulky black body lying in their path—and in a flash understood. They were going to the dead buffalo to recover Mike's almost magical arrow, the one that passed through the whole body of the animal.

He wanted to tell Kit—"Kit—" but at the same instant, Carson said, "Randy—do you see Maxwell anywhere? Is there any sign of my horse? I would sure hate to lose that horse, it would pain me bad in a half-dozen ways. Stop and look hard at the running buffalo, Randy. My horse's light brown color ought to stand out in that black herd. Look for Maxwell on his orangy-tan sorrel, too."

Randy squinted, shaded his eyes with his hand and strained to see any speck of color in the edge of the closest buffalo herd. "It just looks like a big black blanket ruffling along, Kit—don't see any other color. The lead buffaloes have gotten nearly all the way across the plain between the river and the sandhills. They're so far away from us and small now, I can't tell—'specially with the dust over there—if a head belongs to one set of legs and body or the next."

At the little rise that ended in the low knoll where Randy had stared one buffalo in the eye and felt kicked-up sand from another, Kit called a stop. Pat turned the pony around so Carson could look back at the buffalo herds himself.

After a few minutes, he shook his head, declared horses were like that, "and mules, too. They'll scour off in the midst of buffalo if they get half a chance. Usually you never see them again. I doubt Maxwell got anywherz near my horse. That horse! I trained him so long, he could get near'bout touching a running buffalo and stay cool when I fired the rifle. I trusted him so much I'd dressed him up today with a Spanish bridle mounted with silver. Lost! Horse AND valuable bridle—lost. Let's go."

"I don't see Mike and Tuesday either," Randy said quietly. "I can't see the dead buffalo any more. A whole lot of buffalo coming from the river have started running past it on both sides now."

Carson said maybe Mike decided to go by the river edge back to camp, and maybe his moving toward the river stirred up the buffalo along the way so they began running toward the sandhills fast like the others. "Mike'll probably get to camp before we do, tell the Lieutenant to send carts and butchers for two buffalo—mine and Mike's, not just mine."

Randy had no trouble walking fast enough to keep up with Carson on Tuesday's slow-moving pony, but all the way he was bothered by the grimaces of pain on Carson's face, and the question of whether or not he ought to talk to Kit—and if he did what he could talk about. "I bet he did break a bone. But that's not a good thing to tell him...I could tell him that I don't see how he can keep from groaning—but I think he wouldn't like for me to say that." Randy decided just to keep quiet.

When they came in sight of camp, Carson said, suppressing a groan, "Randy, run on ahead and tell the Lieutenant what happened."

Fremont, Lambert, Lajeunnesse, Descouteau, and Moise ran back with Randy to meet "the column of battle-wounded" as it entered the camp circle. "Defeated by a prairie dog," Carson added. "Also by a horse that knew how to step into a burrow hole without breaking a leg so he could run away and join the buffalo herd." Nobody laughed—Fremont's face was too serious, and he was saying, "My dear Kit—a near catastrophe! Are you certain no bone was broken? This expedition will be severely hampered if we lose your active participation—"

Carson interrupted. "Lieutenant, I expect to go hunting tomorrow. Right now, it looks like Mike and Tuesday haven't brought you the news that you ought to send men to butcher two buffalo, mine and Mike's, and carts to haul in the meat for our big feast."

Lambert went running with the order.

In Fremont's tent, with Carson seated in the Lieutenant's folding chair, Fremont brought out his flask of French brandy. "This will quiet your pain a little, Kit," he said as he filled the flask's sizeable cap. "Now the question is, Who among us has had any experience resetting a dislocated shoulder? All I know is, the sooner it's reset, the easier it is to do, and the less painful."

Episode of fixing Kit's injury is not in JF Report

When no one spoke up, Fremont looked at Moise. "How about you, Moise? You know about taking care of sick and injured horses and mules—didn't you ever treat a joint injury on a horse?"

"Tiens...well...yes, oui."

"Good! What did you do, Moise?"

"I shot him." A little cry of dismay from Randy broke through the men's laughter. Moise shushed them and said, "Randy, dere's hardly anyt'ing else you can do for a lame four-legged animal out on de trail. I never met up wid one dat had a dislocation—it's sprains or breaks dey have, and dey can't handle crutches or walk wid a leg in a sling." The men chuckled and said, "That's right," and Fremont added, "Of course."

Carson had laughed a little, but it made him double over with pain "in every muscle from breast-bone to shoulder blade and back again." Fremont refilled the brandy cup. "This is the only help we have for pain, Kit. Drink up."

As he sipped the pain soother, Carson, speaking slowly, said this need for a doctor in camp made him think of his first journey to the West when he was fifteen. "One of the men in the party accidentally shot his own arm, and when it didn't heal but instead began to mortify, we looked around to see who would amputate it. One fellow came forward and said he would. He set to work. He cut the flesh with a razor and parted the bone with a saw."

Kit Carson's Autobiography. p5-6 (trail-side amputation)

Randy's face drew into a frown of horror but he kept himself from making any sound as Carson went on with the worst part of his story.

"The arteries being cut," he said, "to stop the bleeding, the surgeon heated a kingbolt from one of the wagons and burned the affected parts. Then he applied a plaster of tar taken off the wheel of a wagon. His patient didn't have any French brandy to help him out, and he made much noise though he tried not to. I helped three others hold him still. Well, he survived all that and was perfectly healed up by the time we got to Santa Fe, New Mexico.

"So you see, one of you just has to be a little nervy, take a-holt and fix me, for I'm not anywheres near as bad off as the man needing his arm cut and sawed." Carson's story had drawn low grunts and moans of sympathy from the five listeners, but none offered himself as nervy enough for the job.

After a minute of silent misery, Moise cleared his throat and announced in his booming baritone that he thought he remembered that Baptiste Bernier had told him about having to trap beaver one winter while his arm was in a sling. "A'course it coulda been a broken arm, not'ing to do wid a shoulder."

"Go find him and bring him here," Fremont ordered. "I've had my eye on this man Bernier," Fremont said while Moise was gone. "He's always faithful and efficient at his work, inspecting meticulously and keeping in perfect repair all the leather gear for the horses and mules. He has a good, practical intelligence, and on one occasion I saw him control our rowdiest horse with determined courage and a persuasive voice instead of a whip. I hired him on good recommedations in St. Louis. His only handicap is that hare-lip."

Carson raised his head. "Sir, talk him into using his determined courage and good, practical intelligence on me. Tell him I don't feel the least bit rowdy, so I'll be less problem than a horse."

Baptiste Bernier, "Hare Snout"—Bec-de-Lievre—to most of the camp, still wore his expression of surprise—or was it apprehension?—when he followed Moise into Fremont's tent. But when he saw Kit Carson's bare shoulder and dangling arm he moved quickly to him, his face reflecting the concern expressed in his unusually musical if hollow, nasalized voice.

Fremont leaned close to catch the young man's flow of French words. Bernier looked up into Fremont's face, and realizing that he had made a rude entrance with no acknowledgement of his leader's presence, stopped in the middle of a word. He quickly straightened and addressed Fremont. "Lieutenant, Sir! Pardonnez moi!" His voice went up and down a musical scale.

"Certainement," replied Fremont. "You see Kit Carson's problem—do you think you can move the arm back into its socket—are you willing to TRY??"

Gently, intently, Bernier began to rub his fingers over the corner of Carson's shoulder. Fremont leaned close to catch quiet French words words flowing out almost like a song. Fremont translated the message for the hovering men and Randy.

"Yes, the round head of the arm has been wrenched out of its socket, so the shoulder muscles and tendons are pulled tight, very tight. Ask those muscles to relax, M'Sieur Carson. Talk to them sweetly and they will relent enough to ease your pain a little. Close your eyes. Think how your arm must move so these tendons I'm touching at the top can pull arm and shoulder socket together—"

Alternative Therapies. J.Strobecker, p379. (talking to relax injured person. "95% of the time, shoulder can be put back in its socket in 1 minute or less without morphine.")

197

Bernier had moved close to Carson's side with the dangling arm. Abruptly, in one continuous, sudden motion, with both hands Bernier grasped the arm firmly, jerked it upward and straight out from Carson's side. Pop! The stretched tendons attached to the top of the arm bone at one end and the shoulder socket at the other, when released by the up-and-straight-out arm position, had been able to contract—snatching the ball back into its socket. Pop!

"Bone-setter often effects cures...as if by magic." Encyclopedia Britan. *11th ed., vol.15, p489*

Randy's scream—and perhaps one from Carson—merged with those from the men. But when they looked at Carson, they saw him lowering his arm and laying it across his chest. "Oh lordy! Oh lordy!" he said over and over, his eyes closed, his breath rapid.

Jeff Hengesbaugh who's had 3 dislocated shoulders jerked back in place.

Bernier's strong sudden movement of Carson's arm, his quick release at the Pop! followed by Carson's abrupt arm movement, had unbalanced Bernier and sat him on the ground. Fremont helped him to his feet, hugged him, thanked him, moved aside to let the other men and Randy hug him and thank him and slap him on the back. "When did you learn how to fix shoulders?!" Fremont asked

Shyly, his melodious, nasal voice sang, in English, "No learn. I do dee obvious." Carson stood up, embraced the dark, stocky, short-bearded, bright-eyed young man and said, "Bernier, from now on, I and this camp will call you 'Doctor Baptiste'—and I owe you a bottle of French brandy when we get back to Saint Looie."

"Dey don't hev dat at Fort Laramie?" Bernier's voice ended on its highest note. Laughing and hugging Bernier again, the men escorted him out the tent door. As Fremont and Randy came out with Kit, the just-fixed hunter was telling them the best way to get rid of any "mighty sore muscles" was to exercise them. "So I'm planning to go buffalo hunting tomorrow."

JF Report June 30 (next day) "3 cows killed, one by Carson"

They looked up to see Pat, Mike, and Tuesday hurrying toward them.

Tuesday began chanting a song at the top of his voice, his walk turning into a dance. Pat and Mike smiled and clapped to the rhythm. Randy began to clap, too, and shouted, "That means they found the magic arrow!" He ran to meet them.

He stopped short. Tuesday, bow and arrow held high, was dancing in a circle around his father and uncle. They,

Cheyenne dance episode not in JF Report.

too, began dancing step-step-hop, step-step-hop, and were taking turns singing.

Fremont and his companions stopped to watch. "What are they singing, Kit? Why are they dancing?" Randy asked, staring in wonder at his Indian friend.

Cheyennes. Grinnell 1, p118,123 (hero name for 13-year-old's success on first foray)

Carson cupped his hand around an ear to better catch the Cheyenne words. A minute or two later, he said, "I can tell you the words, but I'm thinking they must be doing a big brag. It can hardly be the truth. Pat says, 'My little boy killed a buffalo,' and Mike then says, 'He's going to be a big man and a great hunter.' Pat says, 'We have had good luck,' and Mike says, 'Not a calf but a fat cow.' Now both are saying, 'His Mother will give him the name of her warrior father.'"

Fremont listened to the Indians through another repeat, then asked Carson to interrupt them. "Ask if their chants mean exactly what they say." Kit hesitated as he puzzled over how to break into the ceremony, how to ask such a question without offending. Finally he stepped forward, raised to shoulder height his right hand palm out, fingers extended.

Several times he twisted his wrist and hand from side to side. "Question!" The chanting and dancing did not stop. He repeated the "Question!" sign, but none of the three Indians, eyes closed, paid him any attention.

BIG

In a loud but polite voice, he called out, "Ki' Carson!," made the sign for "big"—palms together prayer-like suddenly spread far apart—again, the question sign—again shouted, "Ki' Carson!" Startled, their awareness slowly returning, the Indians stopped their ceremony.

Carson called in Cheyenne, "What has happened?" All talking at the same time, they hurried to him. "Quiet down," he said by hands and words, and pointed at Pat to be the spokesman.

QUIET DOWN

For several minutes, Pat's voice and actions told their story—an exciting story, Randy could see, and Tuesday was the center of it. Did he really kill a buffalo? How could he have done it without his pony, and with only his bow and arrow? The story must be about Mike's magical arrow, how it went all the way through the cow it killed.

Oregon Trail. F.Parkman, p206 Boy hunter kills buffalo

But Kit was looking amazed. Randy breathed through clenched teeth, "Kit! Hurry up! Tell us what happened!" Suddenly, Carson began waving his hand in the air, and broke away in a run from the Indians. He had seen Maxwell's horse trotting toward them across the campground—leading Carson's runaway beast! Randy saw the silver on the bridle flashing in the sunlight!

Fremont, his companions, Randy, and the Indians began running toward Maxwell, too. Along the way, a dozen others joined them. Maxwell, encircled, told his story with flourishes. "Yessssuh! It looked for a while as if Kit's horse had vanished in that mass of running buffalo! Then I saw a flash of light bounce off the silver on the bridle!

"I went after him. Kit, you and I have argued about whose horse is the fastest runner, yours or mine. For a while out there amongst buffalo rumping along heads down, tongues lolling, eyes rolling at me, I was convinced my fleet hunter was not as fleet as yours. I just couldn't get anywhere close enough to grab the reins or bridle. I decided after awhile that the only way to stop him was to shoot him—and I thought for a minute I ought to, just to save your fine bridle."

JF Report
June 30
Maxwell caught Kit's horse.
Max almost shot Kit's horse.

The little crowd of men chorused a rumbling groan. "But you know well as I that letting Kit's horse escape meant it'd run with Kit's prize bridle to a herd of wild horses on the prairie and be gone forever. I kept up the chase—never had to shoot him—he got squeezed and slowed down in a crush of buffalo. I yelled and whacked until my horse ran like the devil in a whirlwind. The first second I got close enough to your horse, Kit, I reached out and grabbed that pretty bridle. A close race, but my horse won! Here—take your danged beast!"

The little crowd of men clapped and cheered, and Carson thanked his old friend. "Maxwell, in case you wondered how I got off the ground and back to camp, the credit goes to Pat and Mike and Tuesday here—and Randy, who showed up, too, though I have yet to hear how he got there. I want all of you in camp to know that I was considerable hurt with a dislocated shoulder, and Bernier here undertook to pop it back in. It took him about one minute to fix me. I and Lieutenant Fremont have renamed him 'Doctor Baptiste Bernier,' so from now on that's what he's to be called in this camp."

Carson interrupted the clapping and talking of the men to say, "Hold on! There's one more thing to tell you. It's

200

Tuesday/Mike buff-alo episode not in JF Report.

Cheyenne boy's buffalo kill not in JF Report.

about the Indians. If what they're telling me is true—and I'm trying to find out—there's a third dead buffalo out there needing butchering and carting to camp."

"What?!" exclaimed Fremont. "The Indians killed more than one buffalo?!"

"They say so, and that it wuzn't a man killed it, it wuz the BOY! That's why they werz singing'n dancing!"

"Do you believe that, Kit?!" demanded Fremont.

Maxwell fairly shouted, "It's true—I saw it happen as I was leading Kit's horse back through the buffalo herd! The boy—that boy standing there—crouching behind a dead buffalo, shot an arrow into a passing cow. I didn't know he was there until I saw a cow, in a line of running buffalo, stumble, stagger, sway, and fall! Then I saw close by a small person stand up behind a dead cow—not one I'd killed, either—my shot had missed the one I aimed at 'way earlier.

Overland With Kit Carson. G.Brewerton, p267 ("*Indians crawl into a herd, make a barricade of huge (dead) buffalo, secure as many beasts as required.*")

"It was definitely the boy, for I saw Mike on his horse riding to him, saw the boy leap on. By the time I rode past the two dead beasts, those two hunters were riding over the first swell. Yes!—what they've told you is true! Mike probably had a lot to do with making those buffalo run close to his dead cow. But it was the boy who waited behind Mike's cow, and it was his single arrow that brought down the third buffalo for our feast today! Three cheers for Tuesday!"

Randy threw his arms around Tuesday in a quick hug. "I saw you riding back to Mike's dead buffalo!" A sudden doubt that Indians ever hugged each other for joy was interrupted by babbling, smiling men grabbing, squeezing Tuesday's shoulders and arms as they hurried past. They were rushing to arm themselves with butcher knives, to clear two carts, unhobble four mules, hitch them to the cart shafts, and head for the butchering field.

Great Platte River Road. J.Mattes, p258. *20 minutes to skin, cut up buffalo.*

Everybody wanted to go, but Fremont decided the camp needed guarding, and chose only two cartdrivers, four crewmen, and two Indians, all experienced in buffalo skinning and meat-cutting. "Let's go!" shouted Maxwell. "Me and the Indians together can skin'n'cut up a buffalo in twenty minutes—but add another ten minutes for the Indians to eat livers'n'kidneys while they're warm, crack a bone or six for marrow. Oh! Buffalo Boy wants to go all right, Lieutenant?—to retrieve his arrow—or Mike's?"

"Of course it's Mike's," Randy said softly. "The magical

arrow." He watched the mounts of the four buffalo skinners kick up earth as they wheeled to turn, dashed past the carts, headed toward the grassy plain where three dead buffalo were waiting for them. Three Cheyennes on their ponies tore out after them.

Randy was not sorry to miss going with Tuesday to the butchering party. He was very, very glad he didn't go when he saw Tuesday come back with blood on his face, hands, arms, and belly—even in his hair.

JF Report *June 30*

Kit Carson had tried to prepare Randy for this sight by telling him how the skinner cuts the buffalo skin around

Based on Frederic Remington, 18—

With the buffalo's skin stripped away and pushed aside,
the skinners lift their knives to butcher the meat.

the neck, along the backbone from neck to tail and down the legs, then peels back the skin, pulls it free to lie open and flat. "Then he slices through the belly meat from throat to vent 'til the insides are falling out.

"That's when the Indians get mighty excited. They reach in for the liver first. It's dark red color, big as the Lieutenant's wide-brim Army hat. Drips blood when sliced for eating." Randy had made a face.

Before the first cartload of meat arrived, the men in camp had fires boiling pots of settled-out river water, fires with red-hot coals under waiting grates, fires flaming in the center of circles of upright cooking sticks. As each cart entered campground, cheering, singing men converged on it, threw the skins furside down on the ground and used them as a roast-trimming, steak-slicing, cube-cutting, bone-cracking surface. Soon, smells of roasting meat charged the men with the excitement of hunger about to be satisfied.

They began cutting off slices from "hump" roasts and pulling off sizzling chunks from their cooking sticks before the meat was half-done. They burned their too-eager lips on meat broth and tender, tasty morsels in it. They slashed off a fistful of ribs from a whole ribside hanging on sticks in front of a fire. They ate and ate and ate, licked the grease from their fingers, cut off ten more chunks for each cooking stick. The peculiar odor of bone marrow roasting over hot coals hung in the air.

Journal.
Preuss
June 30

Tuesday, now known among the men as "Buffalo Boy," tugged at Randy's sleeve and beckoned "come, come." Carson said they wanted to honor him with a feast for the luck his name for Tuesday had brought them, so Randy went. But the Indians at their own fire were roasting odd-shaped buffalo parts on their cooking sticks. When, after signing "Thank you!" over and over, they became quite insistent that Randy try their delicacies, he signed, "Thank you," pointed towards Fremont's eating circle, said, "Ki' Carson," which always seemed to explain everything, and departed.

Cheyennes.
Grinnell II
p255 (boudins)

To Kit he whispered, "Are they eating still-full GUTS?" Carson whispered back, "Only small-size ones full of half-digested grass. Very strong food. They also like buffalo nose, tongue, and raw liver sprinkled with gall bitters."

With pleasant weather, no enemy to fear, no scarcity of bread, mountains of delicious fresh meat, gallons of sweetened coffee, and plenty of tobacco, the men kept coming out of their tents throughout the night. Mostly they stood by a fire and roasted yet another stickful of choice chunks of buffalo. As they cooked and ate, they heard the continuous howls and snarls of wolves and coyotes fighting and feasting on the skeletons and offal the men had left behind on the prairie.

JF Report
(eat all night)

"...dust filled my mouth and eyes and nearly smothered me...(The buffalo) crowded
together more densely still as I came upon them, rushing along in such a compact body
that I could not obtain an entrance. The horse almost leaping upon them...the mass
divided to the left and right, horns clattering...My horse darted into the opening..."
(Fremont Report, July 1, Platte River Trail)

CHAPTER 19

FREMONT, DARING HUNTER

July 1, Platte River trail (Nebraska)

Crackling, smoking fires the men had kept going all
night cooked the lesser cuts—leg-meat, backbone loins, and
shoulder chunks—for breakfast, with enough left over for
midday. "Amazing that 28 hungry men and three Indians
can eat three buffalo in an afternoon, evening, night, morning, and next midday!" Fremont laughed as he watched
cooks store ready-to-eat left-overs in every pot and pan.
"But even I ate another dinner at midnight after shooting
the stars. So delicious, this buffalo meat! Preuss even has
come to admit buffalo tastes better than beef."

Journal.
C.Preuss,
June 30

"They're all taking on the ways of the Indians," Kit
Carson answered. "Remember the day Pat, Mike, and the
boy came? We thought they'd never stop eating. They'd
gone days with nothing t'eat and like I told you, when they
finally get a chance to eat a-plenty, they fill up with enough
to last another week.

"Takes a lot of fresh meat to quiet any long-time innards-
gnaw. We can make good use of a coupla more buffalo
today. Aside from roasting the meat right away, it'd pay us
to thin-slice a lot and hang it to dry on the cart rails for a
coupla days. Chances are we'll meet up with another buffalo
herd—or two—today."

The day was cool, the wind from the west not annoyingly
strong, and the grass would be green once the column
marched beyond the area eaten clean and befouled by yesterday's buffalo thousands.

Randy wasn't noticing. By the time he'd saddled his pony
and taken his place in line, he'd registered that he wouldn't
be seeing much of "Buffalo Boy" that day. All the afternoon
and night before, Tuesday had stayed close by his father
and uncle, eating and talking, eating and talking. They
seemed to re-live over and over, minute by minute, even second by second their buffalo killings.

Twice Randy saw Mike acting out how he pulled his magical arrow from the ground, gave it to Tuesday, showed him
where to kneel and wait behind the dead cow. Then
Tuesday acted out the killing—kneeling...holding his bow
upright...placing the noc of the arrow against the bow
string...waiting...then, with his maximum strength drawing
the bow string into its widest arc...aiming at the passing

Jeff Hengesbaugh
(bow/arrow action)
cow...releasing the taut string...hearing the arrow fly...watching it plunge into the animal's hide...seeing her pitch forward...tumble over.

This morning the Cheyennes had stopped their all-night eating and moved a short distance from the camp before Randy awakened. Carson explained that Buffalo Boy was basking in Pat and Mike's praise and pride, and the three of them *Cheyennes,*
Grinnell I,
p118,123 were making plans for their entry into their village, how the buffalo story would be told, the order of any songs and ceremonies when Tuesday's mother gave him his new name, the ceremony when he gave his horse to a deserving someone.

Randy wondered as his pony plodded in line behind Fremont whether Buffalo Boy would ever come back and ride beside him. Tuesday was not even in sight any more, but a mile away at the end of the column with his father and uncle. "Maybe he won't come back where I am. He wants to talk about his big deed. He knows I can't understand him when he tells his story, so he thinks he'd be wasting time to spend it with me. I wish...but that's silly. Kit said it took him months of listening to Cheyennes to understand their words and talk like them."

Still, the picture of Tuesday holding his bow pointing one end to the sky, letting the arrow fly, kept re-appearing in Randy's thoughts. He began to put himself in Tuesday's place in the picture just to see how it felt—and suddenly he had an idea so exciting about how to win Tuesday back that it made him laugh aloud and bounce gently in the saddle.

A whiff of a peculiar, grassy animal odor scattered his thoughts. He heard Lambert call to Moise, loudest voice in the column. "Moise! Holler the word that the next two miles *Jeff Hengesbaugh*
(smells, muck) will be over-fertilized with droppings from the hundred thousand buffalo that crossed here yesterday! Slow going, too! Four hundred thousand hoofs churned the ground so bad, it'll feel like you're riding over a plowed field."

Moise hollered the news. A groan rippled along the column.

During the hour it took to ride the "muck trail" as Johnny Janisse called it, they passed within sight of the wolf-scattered bones of a buffalo killed yesterday. Randy glimpsed the rough, black cover on the horns of a buffalo head, thought of his lost white skulls, and sighed.

The column of horses and mules stepped slowly and carefully along. A cool wind from the southwest kept the air refreshed. Sandhills two or so miles away edging the plain to the left began to look higher, more strangely shaped, more colorful. A thicker fringe of cottonwoods and willows shaded the riverbank. Above, the cloudless dome of the sky glowed radiant blue in the sunlight. Underfoot, Randy's pony finally began stepping on clean, smooth ground and short grass.

JF Report
July 1(landscape,
small herd)

Just as Randy noticed that the dry wind had hardened a scattering of buffalo droppings into buffalo-chip firewood, he heard the distant murmur of—"Oh nooo!"—a buffalo herd. With every advancing step of Randy's mount, the murmur heightened, became a rumble, turned into a noisy jumble of grunts and bullish bellows rising above the drumming of moving hooves on the ground.

All at once, as the head of the column began cresting a hillock, Randy heard Carson call out, "BUFFALO IN SIGHT!" No eager cheers this time from the column of well-fed men.

Randy quietly guided his horse ahead to walk alongside Fremont. At the top of the hillock, he looked out on open prairie between river and sandhills, but the buffalo scene was quite different from yesterday's. It was a smaller herd— "couple of thousand," Carson judged—and it was coming from the other side of the river.

The animals were crowding out of the water, drinking, pushing forward, and spreading across the path of the Fremont column. They stood a little apart from each other, slow to move, as if they were enjoying a moment of privacy. Some bent their heads down looking for a sprig of grass. A few walked lazily, showing no nervousness, ambling toward the hills. Only the bulls were noisily rowdy, butting heads, roaring at each other.

Carson was saying to Fremont that, with the wind from the southwest, "we smell them but they don't smell us, so they won't start running away 'til they see a horseman come up almost within touch. Right then's the easiest time to charge into them and shoot a couple."

Fremont silently assessed the distances, the activities of the animals, and the ground the hunters would have to cross to make the attack. "Any sign of prairie dog holes?" he asked, looking pointedly at Carson's left shoulder.

With a wry smile, Carson shook his head. Fremont studied him briefly. "Still, I think I'd best go in your place—your wound is too recent, too severe for me to risk anything happening to you today—" Fremont began.

"SIR!" exploded Carson,"I don't shoot with my left arm! My rifle's loaded and I won't need but one shot for a kill!" Quickly calming his voice and face, he added, "Yessir! You should go, TOO, Lieutenant! And ride the best hunting horse—Proveau! I'd love to eat a piece of a buffalo that

Lieutenant John Fremont killed!"

Fremont laughed merrily and gave Carson a friendly salute. "I capitulate!" he said. "It's too fine a prospect for me to say 'no' to a hunt for either of us! Call for the hunting horses!"

JF Report
July 1
(Fremont,
hunter)

Three were brought up and saddled.

Carson, Fremont, and Maxwell mounted, and the excited horses, specially trained to hunt buffalo, went forward, side by side. Randy, who had been twisting in his saddle, listening, trying to think of some way to appeal to Fremont to let him ride just a little closer to the herd, impulsively called out, "If the Indians go, will you let me go with'um?!"

Without stopping, Fremont looked back, shaking his head. "No Indians hunting today! I gave them their chance yesterday!" he called. "No Randy-hunter! Too dangerous!"

Frowning, Randy watched the hunters fast-step away. Well, at least John had given Kit permission to take the Cheyennes' bows and arrows from Mr. Preuss for yesterday's hunt, if not today's. Where were the Indians anyway?

A quarter mile ahead, half the distance to a herd still peacefully crossing the shallow river and gathering on its bank, the three hunters were proceeding stealthily.

JF Report
July 1
("sudden agitation"
No reason given)

Suddenly, some buffalo scattered along the leading edge of the gathering began galloping to and fro. Immediately Randy saw a wavering movement ripple through the herd. Had they seen or heard the hunters?

The three men had noticed the ripple, too, and at once had set their horses to galloping hard.

Spreading out, leaning forward to urge their horses on, they closed in rapidly upon the buffalo.

Randy, standing in his stirrups to watch, saw a movement to his left. It was a horse and rider a half-mile away,

Indians' action not
in JF Report

heading for the buffalo! A SPOTTED horse! Pat? Mike? Tuesday? What was he doing out there without John's permission? Couldn't he see he'd alarmed the herd, messed up the three hunters' chance for an easy kill? Why didn't he turn back?

The front edge of the now massed herd of buffalo was already in rapid motion towards the hills, and in a few seconds the whole herd was following. A crowd of bulls was bringing up the rear, and every now and then some of them faced about, then dashed on after the band. Turning again, shaking their heads, pawing, they briefly looked ready to fight.

Abruptly they gave up this show of courage and defense and leaped forward with the the rest of the herd now in full rout. "They've seen John and Kit and Max!" Randy exclaimed. "And whoever else is riding out there—ooohh—there're two more spotted ponies! ALL the Indians—so it's Tuesday, too!"

Randy looked toward Fremont—and could not tear his eyes away from the astonishing scene. All three horses and riders were crashing headlong into the side-edge of the herd! The animals were giving way, fast-moving cows knocking over bulls that were putting on a show of turning to face the attackers.

JF Report
July 1
(the hunt, p6,7,8,9)

Randy cried out when he saw two bulls toppling and scrambling to get up, the horses disappearing past them into clouds of dust. He glanced left to see what the Indians were doing—and saw they had turned, were heading back toward the end of the column. What was going on with them?!

Randy heard the crack of a rifle firing and his attention jerked back to the three hunters inside the moving buffalo herd. The dust had thinned—and the herd had galloped past one riderless horse standing beside a large black body. WHERE was the rider—WHO was he?!

"Giddup!" Randy yelled. His pony leaped away from Clement, Moise, and Tulip at the head of the column, galloped Randy and his fears toward the dead buffalo where John might be lying on the ground—and dead, too.

Suddenly he saw a flash of light on the horse as it moved its head. Silver! Carson! Not John! Now he could see it was Kit's light-colored mount, and that Kit was kneeling to tie the horse's reins to the dead buffalo's horns, a sure way to keep a horse from running off.

Good ole Kit! But John—where was John?!!

A rifle shot—CRACK! Randy hauled on the reins to stop his horse, see better. Beyond Kit, a commotion in the herd was causing the animals to part into two streams, exposing the small figure of a horse and rider circling back to a dark, writhing bulk on the ground. Was the rider John? Or Max? Too much dust cloud to tell.

Just then, Randy's eye was caught by a wreath of white smoke at a far edge of one of the streams of running buffalo. The smoke was curling away from a horse and rider! The horse was light tan—"It's Max! It's Max!" So the rider he'd seen a moment before, the rider circling the fallen, writhing buffalo, was John! Joyfully he shook a fist in the air and shouted, "Johhhnnn! You've got one! Come back!"

At that moment, the horse and John dashed after the closest stream of buffalo, and was soon out of sight within the smothering dust cloud raised by thousands of running hooves. But Randy saw Max on his sorrel coming out of the

210

F.O.C. Darley, Harper's Magazine, 18··

"Johhhnnn! You've got one! Come back!

dust! He was giving up the chase! He was trotting away
from the herd, heading across two miles for the long dark
line of the caravan slowly moving west.

But as Maxwell drew closer, he abruptly reined his horse
to turn sharply. He'd seen Carson, and began galloping his
horse to where Kit stood waving his arm and beckoning.
Just then, Randy heard a strange clattering noise coming
from the direction where he'd last seen Fremont. What was
happening over there!? Eyes widened, breath panting
between taut lips, Randy stared, and began trembling with
fear. John! John! Come away from there! he wanted to yell,
but no sound came out.

The dust cloud around the herd thinned enough that
Randy could see a mass of violently threshing animals,
horns striking horns—and John on Proveau charging them!
Look! Look! Proveau's rising on his back legs! John! Why
are you telling him to spring upon a wall of black beasts?!!
They'll kill you!"

But they moved away instead—fast—separating into left
and right sections, leaving an opening between them, all

211

heading for the hills. Proveau darted into the opening, rushing ahead wildly, paying no heed and slacking not at all
when a half-dozen bulls charged into the path—only to back
off, be left behind.

On both sides of Proveau's path, a tightly packed band of
buffalo was sweeping forward like a torrent, the horns of
one animal clashing against the horns on the head of the
one beside it—all together making the strange clatter Randy
began hearing.

But look! A smoke curl near Proveau's head! A beast
leaping high into the air! John's killed another buffalo??
NO!—the beast landed on two hindlegs, dropped its front
pair and began scouring on faster than ever! Randy expected to see Proveau take after him.

Instead, Fremont reined up the horse, turned him
around, and headed out. On both sides of them the path
stayed open between the two streams of buffalo, each with
four or five hundred animals tightly squeezed against each
other, sweeping forward as solid units.

As Fremont rode out of the herds into the open ground
away from them and turned toward the column, Randy
could not keep himself from racing his horse to meet him.
On the way, he wiped his cheeks with the back of a hand,
and dried his nose on the tail of his shirt. When he caught
up with his brave John, he had put on a smile but hadn't
thought of anything to say. Neither had John.

*Randy's ride with
Fremont not in
JF Report*

They ambled along side by side in silence for several minutes. Ahead to the right were Kit and Max working on skinning Kit's kill. A mulecart was approaching them. At
Fremont's kill on the left and farther away, two skinners
and butchers on horseback had arrived.

John finally spoke to Randy. "Out there where I just
came from is a big prairie dog village," he said. "Very thick-
ly settled. Proveau missed stepping into a hole by the width
of a hoof. No telling how far the village extends, so keep
watch of the ground as we go. The buffalo trampling will've
leveled the dirt-cone around the dog-holes, making them
hard to see. If I'd gone on with the chase, Proveau might
not've been as lucky as Kit's horse yesterday. Remember
what Moise said? A horse breaks a leg bone, you can't fix
it. You have to shoot him.

*JF Report
July 1
(prairie dogs)*

"Dangerous place, prairie dog village."

"Hahhh ayyy!" Pat and Mike Cheyenne express amazement at the Very Large britches and red flannel underwear they find among many household and personal articles scattered about an old campsite. Oregon-bound emigrants led by a missionary "disburdened themselves," Fremont deduced, "of many things not absolutely necessary" before pushing on their weary way. Randy strokes a brass bedstead like his at home.

213

CHAPTER 20

THROW-AWAY TREASURES

July 1-2, Platte River Trail by Brady's Island

Without coming close to a single prairie-dog hole—as far as they knew—Fremont and Randy crossed a hoof-churned, dung-strewn quarter-mile to the waiting column of men, horses, and carts. The men had dismounted and staked their horses on nearby unsullied grass to let them graze a few minutes.

JF Report
July 1

As the Lieutenant and boy approached, Lambert, Moise, and Basil called out greetings and compliments to Fremont. "A kill with one shot!"

"Looked like a cow!" ("Yes—a fine, fat cow.") "Gotta have daring and cool to break into a herd like that, Sir! ("Need luck more than cool.") "'Spected to see you stuck-through and tossed-up by a bull's horn!" ("The bulls couldn't face Proveau!") Basil teased Randy—"See, you didn't need to go rescue de hunter!" Randy cringed and looked at Moise, who shrugged and winked.

Fremont declared he was in no particular danger in the herd. "Carson had told me that a herd can be turned or split by a single man on a fast horse. But having fired my rifle to good effect on a cow, fired my pistol to inconclusive effect on a second cow, I had nothing else to fire. Time to come out. Also, Proveau barely missed a prairie dog hole. AND, the smells and bellows and dust in my eyes and throat worked strongly against lingering."

The men chortled, Fremont smiled, and they went on picking out and adding to every detail of the hunt. "Carson got his cow quick 'n' stopped running." "Yeah, Max shot, but didn't leave a ton-size lump lying out dere."

"Quite a funny sight when you hunters first got close to the herd—all them buffaloes starting a quick get-away, slapping their tails up and down like they need spanking to get up speed!" "And at the other end, heads down, foot-long tongues hanging out, chin beards dragging the ground!" "And didja hear the huffing'n'puffing?—like a thousand big bellows sucking in and squeezing out air!"

Oregon Trail
F.Parkman,p75
(foot-long tongue)

Randy laughed, too. The men went on with hunt-talk, but Randy stopped listening. He'd seen, heard, worried more

Buffalo Book
D.Dary, p174-8

than enough about buffalo during the past hour. Now he wanted to know about Tuesday. Where was he?

During the men's next long laugh, Randy eased his pony away from them enough to let him see to the end of the column. With the horses and mules staked out to graze and the column shortened, the Indians were not so far away. All three were still sitting on their ponies. It was easy to tell which rider was Tuesday. "His head's hanging a little, and he's probably feeling ashamed. I'll bet his papa and uncle have told him fifty times what he'd better not do again. Wonder how they'd punish him if he ever does. Huh, wonder how they'll punish him NOW."

Squeaking wheels—wheels taller than Randy—of the meat-hauling cart, the shouted greetings of the waiting men, and Maxwell's raucous laugh interrupted Randy's ponderings about the ways of Cheyennes.

A blood-smeared mule driver on a loaded cart dripping blood, followed by a packhorse with bright red rib-sections dangling by a cord on each side, arrived behind Carson and Maxwell on their hunter-horses. Some distance back, three mounted butcher-skinners were leading a pack horse over-loaded with the rest of the two dead cows—ribs from Fremont's kill making a platform for a mound of meat chunks each almost as big as Randy.

"We left the coarse meat and all the big bones for the wolves since we have cart-rails hanging with yesterday's kill," Carson informed Fremont. "Got no use, either, for a fresh-off, greasy hide weighing near a hundred pounds, nor a head 'bout as heavy. No, sir, I didn't take the brains, but I did open up the throat n'cut out the tongue."

Jeff Hengesbaugh
(hide, head weight)

"And we saved a few innards for Randy and the Cheyennes," laughed Maxwell. "Let's see—there's the liver, the heart, the kidneys, the boudins, the marrow guts, the paunch, the lungs—"

"I heard you say you werz saving them for yourself, Max," Carson broke in. "Let's package'um up in a cart cover to keep'um wet and slippery until you have a chance to cook'um—'cept for them you eat raw right now!"

Amid the laughter of the little crowd that had gathered, Lambert called for quick work on wrap-up and clean-up. "We're putting off slicing and drying any meat until after our buffalo dinner today." In short order some India-rubber sheets from several carts had become sacks for buffalo meat, been piled on spare horses and mules so the blood-

215

smeared men, animals, and cart could go to the river for a scrubbing.

Carson and Maxwell, first to return, were sent to inspect a few miles of the trail ahead for prairie dog holes. By the time Lambert was calling, "Advance!" they were returning with the news that the dogs' underground village extended west for another two miles. "But it's farther away from the river than our trail. Closer to the river, they get water in their basements."

Gr. Platte R. Rd.
J.M.Mattes,p.269

Fremont had been anxiously glancing at the sun and now announced to the men at the head of the line that he was about to set a faster pace for the column. "Tomorrow, we will arrive at the forks of the Platte, and we must get all our men, animals, and carts across a wide stretch of water. You men who have made this crossing before—Carson, Maxwell, Latulippe, and others—have told me the river bed has numerous patches of quicksand.

JF Report
July 1

"That will be treacherous for us all, but especially for mules, who hate getting into water anyway, even the Platte's shallow water. If they refuse to pull the carts fast enough, they'll bring a disastrous end to the expedition when the carts sink deep into the bottomless sand, carrying our supplies and instruments with them.

"We MUST arrive near the forks soon after noon tomorrow. Our animals must then eat and rest—they ought not to be set to the task weary and hungry. THEN, we MUST complete our crossing, camp-making, and eating before dark.

"Therefore, we must press on today 24 miles more, leaving but 20 for tomorrow. Having used up much time with the hunt this morning, we'll be marching 'til late afternoon at my horse's stepped-up pace."

"Keep in mind that we have a meat-slicing and draping job right after supper!" head cook Dumes reminded. "Cooks can't do it all! Need teams-a help!"

The Lieutenant gave a half salute to his companions, and giddi-upped his horse. Lambert walked Fremont's words down the column. For the next hours, Fremont, intent at keeping his horse's pace brisk, hardly spoke.

"Well now, Randy," Carson said after a while to Randy riding beside him, "since we'll be seeing the island out there in the river for the next 15 miles, you should know why it's called 'Brady's Island,' even if the story's got an unhappy ending."

"You mean it's a scary story?"

216

"Not exactly. It's more like...gruesome. But it happened at least ten years ago, and there ain't much chance that we'll bump into any evidences that the story is true."

"Evidences?"

"Like Brady's bones—but lemme start at the beginning. There wuz this man named Brady who wuz coming down the river on a boat with a coupla trappers and a load of furs. Brady and one of the other men had been quarreling a lot on the trip, so the third man ought to've known better than t'leave 'um together for any length of time. But that's what he did soon after they stopped and set up camp on this big island. Left'um to guard the furs."

"Where'd he go, Kit?"

"Hunting. He musta gone quite a ways off, and stayed a right smart time because when people tell the story, they never mention that he heard any gunfire. However, when this hunter got back to the camp, he found Brady lying dead—shot through the heart. 'Oh,' said the other man, 'Brady wuz checking out his gun and accidentally shot hisself.' Well, the hunter didn't believe that, but he daren't say anything."

"Why? He'd never quarreled with the man, had he?"

"Not that I know of. But the hunter wuz by hisself with this man he thought wuz a murderer, and no doubt he figured it wuz safer not to get into an argument with him. So he just said something like, 'Let's get busy and bury Brady before we roast some steaks off'n this antelope I've killed."

"You mean they just dug a grave and put Brady in it and then ate supper in the graveyard?"

"Not much else they could do, Randy—and then laid down and took turns sleeping. Have t'guard the furs, you know. But the gruesome part of the story is that, as soon as the men left, wolves tore Brady out of his grave, and had a Brady breakfast."

Randy made a face. But Carson had a little more to tell him. "Now the way some people tell this story," he said, "Brady's murderer confessed as he wuz dying in agony after accidentally shooting a hole in his leg. They say he shot hisself while trying to start a fire to drive off mosquitoes. Now his way of starting a fire wuz to kneel over a little pile of tinder, and hold close to the pile a pistol loaded with gunpowder in the flashpan but no bullets in the barrel.

"He expected to pull the trigger so the flint spark flared the gunpowder in the flashpan and set fire to the tinder. But that man forgot he'd left a bullet in the pistol. When

JF Report
July 1-2

American Fur Trade
of the Far West.
A.M.Crittenden

Gr. Platte R. Road
J.M.Mattes
p252,255

Fire-starting,
J. Hengesbaugh,
consultant

he pulled the trigger, he fired the bullet through his thigh. Gangrene put him through a painful death."

"Awww."

"So po'r Brady's fame comes from gett'n hisself kilt by that man and eaten by wolves, so all that was left of him was his name put on the Island."

It was near sundown when Fremont finally called a halt and the cooks got to work roasting all four slabs of buffalo ribs, and the big, tender shoulder humps. By the flickering light of one of the campfires, Randy sat with Moise to bite half-done meat from a handful of ribs, and gnaw down a thick slice of sweet, juicy hump roast. He avoided looking across the way at Tuesday dropping slices of raw liver into his open mouth.

Hastily the men finished eating, grabbed knives to slice meat into thin strips, drape them on the cart rails. An hour after dark, they sloshed some water on their bloody hands and arms and tumbled already half asleep onto their blankets or buffalo robes.

Randy slept so soundly he didn't hear the uninterrupted howling of the troops of wolves circling the camp. Guards at the meat-draped carts kept watch with big sticks and hoped Tulip wasn't joking when he told them that wolves were the Number One cowards of the plains.

JF Report
July 2

"TURN O-U-U-T!!"

In Randy's tent, Cousin Henry half jumped out of his blanket roaring, "Wha' tha devil!" and stuck his head out the tent flap. "TURN O-U-U-T!!" he heard again, and heard Lambert walking the message by every tent.

"Good lord, man, it's still dark as pitch. What's the rush? Must be four o'clock—middle of d'night."

But he turned back to give Randy's shoe a kick, and to growl, "Lambert says get up and get going. Fremont said we hav't get to the Forks by noon. So you can't see an inch from your nose—fumble along, stumble along anyhow. UP! Come on!"

Half asleep, Randy's ears followed the sound of Cousin Henry going past the tent flap, clearing his throat, and grumping, "B-r-r-r! it's cold!" A wolf's bark seemed to answer. Then another. And another. Randy shivered. They were still out there. A few steps later, he felt safer seeing cookfires flicker away darkness around coffee pots.

Gr. Platte R. Road
J.M.Mattes
p252,255

An hour later, when the sun began spraying its first rays over the prairie and over the line-up of men, carts, horses, and mules, Lambert called, "ADVANCE!

Seven hours to the Forks!"

The wolves didn't wait for the campers to get out of sight. A dozen big gray-whites, "buffalo trailers," loped into the camp circle as fast as the carts and mounted horses moved out. They ambled this way and that, sniffing out bones and scraps, starting fights, shrilly screaming and barking, their bushy tails swishing about like banners in the noisy battle.

Randy, looking back at the scene and shuddering at the sounds, asked Carson if wolves would be circling the camp and howling every night. "As long as we kill buffalo, eat roasted ribs, throw away bones and fat and gris'le and meat a little tougher than somebody feels like chewing—yes, we'll have wolves trailing after us day and night, same as they do a buffalo herd," Carson told him. "But you needn't be scared. The guards and their sticks can keep them at a distance. But that reminds me, Randy—won't tonight be your turn for guard duty?"

Randy gasped in dismay. "Ohhhhh NOOOOO!"

"Well now, Randy, which do you think is worse," Carson said, "a silent Indian slithering through the grass or a howling wolf that keeps his distance?"

Randy looked at Carson with a face wrinkled by skepticism. "I've been watching and listening to wolves for near twenty years," Carson added, "and I tell you what I seen. Tulip was right about wolves being cowards. Wolves only attack sick or wounded or old doddering or small animals— or dead ones. They prefer dead ones."

"I'm small," Randy answered quickly.

Carson looked him over, measuring. "You might have a worthwhile point there," he said after a moment's reflection. "Maybe I can ask the Lieutenant if you can double up with me at my guard post." Randy blew out anxiety-air so hard through his mouth that his lips fluttered noisily.

After a bit of deep breathing, he smiled gratefully at Carson. "That'll make a lot of difference," he said. He pictured what it would be like sitting out in the open with the wolves only a short distance away—and he suddenly pictured the camp's herd of mules and horses standing beyond the guardpost, nibbling grass in the dark, their long reins staked to the ground.

"Kit, what do we do when we hear a horse scream 'cause a wolf is biting him? We fire a gun? We have to go out there where they are?" Randy was wide-eyed again.

Calmly, Carson allowed it might be hard to believe that wolves would creep around among the horses near a camp and attack only the raw hide reins holding a horse to a stake. "They gnaw on them—hungry, as always—and the horses don't get upset about having the wolves around. Maybe both know from experience that one kick of a sharp hoof can seriously wound a wolf, or even kill him.

"'Course, if the moon's shining bright and you see some dark shapes creeping on all-fours around the horses, you might think it's Indians—"

"SLITHERING!"

"—slithering, but if you slither out there a short way and lie flat to watch a while, you'll soon know it's a wolf. You'll just hope the raw hide is so tough the wolf can't bite it apart, free your horse. I've lost horses that way."

Randy rolled his eyes. "Kit, what's the Indian sign for 'wolf?'" Carson held up his right hand with two fingers up and wide apart, shoved them forward in a leap outward from his shoulder. Randy mimicked the hand sign, quietly howling, "Oooo-uh!"

Not long afterwards, they came upon a sight so strange that riders began to rein their mounts out of the line to take a close look.

It was Randy who saw it first. He had been rehearsing to himself in words what he wanted to say to Tuesday if and when Tuesday ever showed any interest in him again. When he gave up trying to improvise hand signs for his thoughts, he began studying the very high conical peaks on the left side of the trail. Suddenly he caught a glimpse of a brass BEDSTEAD! It was leaning against a weed-covered bump in the flat earth ahead.

"It must be a—what did John say we'd see in the distance here on the prairie—something that looked real, only it wasn't?" he said to himself, and called, "John! I think I see a bedstead that's not really there."

"What? Where?"

"A bedstead. Ahead, over here on the left. It's lying against the mound that's almost in our way. See a sort-of gravel road coming out of the hills leading to the mound?"

"Gravel road, Randy?" Fremont leaned to the left and stretched to see better.

"Yes! It's coming from the open space by that hill over there with high, jagged rocks on top."

Oregon Trail.
F.Parkman
(Modern Lib.Ed
p56,162,176,
330-1, 347)

WOLF

Indian Sign
Language
W.Tomkins

JF Report
July 2

Carson broke in to say that wash—gravel and sand—brought down the mountains in heavy rains poured out on the plain and in time built up so it looked like a man-made road. "Some stand inches higher than the plain, some scour out a ravine—a hollow. Buffalo make use of either one to go back and forth from the hills to drink river water."

"Oh, now I see the bedstead!" Fremont suddenly exclaimed. "It IS a bedstead! Not a mirage, Randy! Let's go take a look! I think I see a chair—and other household furniture!"

As Fremont began reining his mount out of the line, he shouted, "Lambert! Call a halt! I see men leaving the line—everybody wants a look at this scene! Come on Kit, you and Maxwell—and all of you! I'm sure the emigrants traveling a couple of weeks ahead of us camped here and threw away everything they could get along without. Weight in their wagons will fatigue and slow down the animals."

Gr. Platte R. Road
J.M.Mattes
(emigrant throw-aways)

The large campsite "looks like a rummage sale," Randy thought. Carson surmised that the campers had stayed three or four days, judging from the dozen or so sizeable piles of ashes, the wide area where numerous horses and cattle had short-cropped the grass. "Looks like about 300 animals!" Carson said. "And more'n a hundred people!" he added. "Maybe half of 'um children—see all these little foot-prints? Lotta folks 'n' maybe 20 wagons.

JF Report

"Lotta pathways, rutted and packed, from camp to river. Cooked beef bones scattered all over. Wolves've gnawed 'um. So much thrown-away furniture says they and their hors-es're good'n tired. And they're not even half-way to South Pass, or a third of the way to Oregon."

A dozen mounted men were roaming the sprawling camp-ground to look at the emigrants' discards—cast-iron cook stoves, chairs, pickaxes, shovels and rakes, large iron wash-pot—"everything WE don't need and even if we did, we couldn't carry such heavy, bulky stuff away," Moise said. "Now if they'd left horse shoes and a spare cart wheel..."

Randy was first to see the trunk, a wooden box with a rounded top. He left his saddle, stooped, and lifted the lid. Clothes! On top lay a very big, heavy, dark wool overcoat. Underneath lay a very big farmer's brand-new brown linsey-woolsey coveralls. No—more than one pair. Randy had thumbed through four pairs when he heard his name spo-ken. "Ran-dee?"

"Tuesday!" he replied happily, rising quickly to face the Indian boy—and his adult companions. The Cheyennes point-

221

ed at the trunk, began leaning to look into it, then squatting to reach into it. Randy backed out of their way to
stand beside Tuesday, smiling back at his smile.

*Indian activities
not in JF Report*

How could he tell Tuesday he'd missed him a lot and
wanted to describe his exciting idea—that Tuesday could act
out for HIM how he killed the buffalo, SHOW how Randy
could do it, too—if he ever had the chance! He'd ask
Tuesday to teach him how to hunt with a bow and arrow,
too. But here they were standing just looking at each other,
no words to say anything, a few hand signs but not the
ones Randy thought he needed.

Doggone it, he WOULD say it with words—and make up
action signs to go with the words. English began to flow out
as his forefinger pointed to himself, Tuesday, their horses.
He held pretend-reins in his hands and made-like galloping.
He signed "friend." He signed, "talk to me," and "buffalo."

He began imitating Tuesday acting out how he killed the
buffalo. Crouching, he looked at Tuesday with an "Am I
doing it right?" expression. Tuesday nodded and crouched,
too, raised his arms, positioned his hands to hold the bow
and arrow. Randy copied his movements, aimed when
Tuesday aimed, released the arrow when he did, and made
a sharp cry, "Hungh!" like Tuesday's.

They looked at each other, laughed, and stood up. Randy
signed "good"—his open, palm-down, right hand swinging out
horizontally from his heart. Not knowing how to sign "brave,"
he said, "Brave! Brave!" pointed to Tuesday and shook a fist
in the air—unaware that he'd almost done it right.

BRAVE

Tuesday signed "good," then signed "together," right
index finger lying flat against the palm of his left hand. Not
sure Randy knew the sign, Tuesday pointed to himself then
to Randy, repeated the sign. Randy's head bobbed up and
down. "Yes! You and I! Together!" he said smiling happily.
His exciting idea of showing his interest, his admiration for
Tuesday's bravery and skill, had succeeded. He felt sure he
had now won back Tuesday's interest in him.

"Hungh!" A loud male voice made both boys jump—and
burst into laughter. Both Pat and Mike had pulled on coveralls several sizes too wide and long for them. They were
laughing, too. Tuesday squeezed past them to dig into the
trunk, haul out three pairs of huge work shoes, two sets of
red flannel underwear, three knitted woolen sweaters, and a
voluminous pair of thick, woolen trousers. Randy was saying that this 300-pound farmer had left home taking enough

clothes to last him ten years in Oregon—when he heard Moise's booming call, "Fall in!"

He hurried to mount, and Tuesday after some quick words with his father, mounted his pony and followed him to the front of the column. The men, still wearing their barrel-size overalls, waved and turned back to pull more clothing from the trunk.

Fremont, Lambert, and the rest of the column-head were already moving when Randy and Tuesday trotted up on their ponies and took places beside Kit and Maxwell. "You boys find anything back there worth taking?" Maxwell wanted to know. "Nope," Randy said, "all the clothes were grizzly bear size. But Pat and Mike liked them." His giggling set Tuesday to giggling.

"Must be a joke," Maxwell said. "Glad to see them together—and laughing," Carson said out of the corner of his mouth. "Haven't seen much of Tuesday since he became a famous buffalo hunter. Did you notice what he did this morning when the buffalo hunt was just starting?—I didn't— riding his pony close to the herd, Moise said, setting the buffalo to running before me, Max, and Lieutenant were close enough to shoot?

"Wonder why he did that. Moise said Pat and Mike raced out to catch him, turn him 'round, and lead him back to the line. Wonder what kind of punishment they laid on him."

"Well, ask him," Maxwell said.

So Carson leaned to get a good view of Tuesday on the other side of Randy, and, in Cheyenne words, asked him, "Son of Pat, how angry was your father today when you, all alone, rode your pony close to the buffalo herd and scared it into a run?"

Tuesday returned Carson's steady gaze with his own steady gaze and answered with a quick flow of words. Carson nodded and straightened up. "Randy, listen to what I'm about to tell Max. The boy says his pony was spooked by a rattlesnake and wouldn't stop running. His father and uncle came and caught the pony. His father was glad no one was hurt."

Randy's mouth opened in surprise—and relief. "Good!" he told Tuesday with a hand sign, and told himself, "So...when I saw him after the hunt, I just imagined he looked downcast. His papa hadn't given him even a soft talking-to."

It was an hour past midday when Fremont called a halt for a meal and a rest. Midway the cold-meat feasting, two galloping ponies brought Pat and Mike sweating in their just-captured red flannels, skittering into a stop in camp. They slid from their ponies, dragging to the ground their newly-made saddles—neatly folded and stacked wool trousers, big-man overalls, overcoat, sweaters, and bed sheets. Between bites of their fistsful of meat and bread, the two scavengers pulled from the pockets of the overcoat the few small curiosities they had picked up during their hour's roam of the emigrants' campsite.

Indian activities not in JF Report

They laid them on the ground in front of Randy and tried to chew, swallow, point, and talk all at the same time. "Ten-o-wast?" they said, pointing at a pair of scissors. "Ten-o-wast?" they said, holding up a hair brush. "Ten-o-wast?" and waved a fork.

Wah-to-Yah L.Garrard, p77 (Ten-oh-wast)

"Ten-o-wast," Randy repeated. "That must mean, 'What is it? What's its use?" he said to himself, and began to demonstrate the hair brush. The three Indians first looked puzzled, then thoughtful as they had a brief discussion. Tuesday moved closer to stare into Randy's hair. He gestured to his father that he saw no head lice.

Randy picked up the fork, stabbed a piece of meat, put it in his mouth, and pulled out the fork. The Cheyennes burst out laughing. Tuesday's fingers picked up a piece of meat, dropped it into his wide open mouth, and began chomping. The men laughed louder, gestured to Randy that he could keep the meat-jabber, a foolish thing.

"I'll bet they don't laugh at this one," Randy mumbled, and picked up the scissors. What to cut? A piece of Tuesday's hair? He might not like that. Better a piece of his own. "HAAAWWW!" the Indians chorused when Randy snipped off a finger-length of his shaggy red hair and gave it to Tuesday. Pat pulled the scissors from Randy's hand and fitted his own fingers into the handles. What to cut! He looked around, then down at the turned-up legs of his new red flannel pants. "Ni-hi-ni?" and acted out the question, "Yes? Will it cut this?" Randy nodded.

Pat quickly untied waist strings, pulled off the pants, stretched them out on the ground. On his hands and knees, he caught the cloth between the blades, looked up at Randy for a nod of approval. Snip! In less than a minute, both pants legs had been shortened, and Mike was stripping and reaching for the scissors to trim his.

"Wi-heo-kis pow-wow nash't!" declared Pat, standing regally in his better-fitting new red britches.

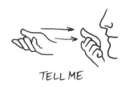

TELL ME

Wah-to-Yah
L.H.Garrard,
p77(Wiheo-kis)

Randy, puzzled, held up his open hand, woggled it from side to side—"Question!" He pointed to Pat, swept his open hand forward from his lips—"talk"—and said his just-learned Cheyenne words, "Ten-o-wast?" Tuesday clapped his hands, laughed, giggled, swept his hand in an wide arc in front of himself—"Good!"—and repeated Pat's words. "RANDY WI-HEO-KIS POW-WOW NASH'T!" Randy pieced together signs and words, decided they meant he was a VERY good white fellow. He bent his side-by-side wrists, dipped his hands—"Thanks."

"FALL IN!" The order to mount! Pat, scissors in hand, Mike swiping at his hair with the brush, rode off to the end of the line, leaving Tuesday to ride beside the Very Good Wiheo and Ki' Cars'n.

Beth Berryman

Prairie dogs, thousands of them in a "town" miles long, sit upright, front paws hanging limply in front of their breasts, and chirp warnings at Fremont's column. Tuesday chirps back, "O-noni-wonski!" Is he saying "goodbye" to the squirrel-size comics–or pointing out the rattlesnakes and owls living with them?

227

CHAPTER 21

BUFFALO BONEYARD AND DOGTOWN

July 2 afternoon, Nearing the Forks of the Platte

"Look, Kit! TREES and bushes across the trail! See?! From the hills to the river! Is this the end of the prairie?" Randy exclaimed, standing in his stirrups to see better. Carson in the row ahead looked around.

"No, just a stretch of trees edging a hollow that's across our trail. I know you've noticed the sandhills are closer, look more like rock, and are a lot higher. Rainwater flooding down from the steep pinnacles tear out deep trenches—hollows—gullies—arroyos—in the ground on the way to the river. There's more'n one. Enough soil and water comes down from the hills to grow big trees on the hollow side-slopes and top edges.

JF Report
July 2
(hollow)

"So, we'll be riding through a woods down into the hollow, 'n'coming up and out amongst trees way on t'other side. Big hills on the left—that closest, tallest lookout rock over there is 500 feet high!—and this first wooded hollow a quarter-mile across tells me we're only about 10 miles from the Forks!"

Fremont was impressed with the size of the dry water bed the column crossed after climbing down a modest slope. His companions at the head of the line declared this hollow was "a little thing" compared to The Big Hollow leading to the North Fork from a high plateau.

JF Report
July 2
(hollows)

"It's actually a canyon," Carson told Fremont.

"Traveling the length of it—about six miles—is a pleasure once you're in it," he added. "BUT—getting down in it from the plateau can end up a bust! It's a quarter-mile climb-down of a near'bout straight-down rock jumble from the top of the plateau to a sure-nuff straight-down wall. Horses and carts have the worst time. BUT once you get to where the ground flattens out between high, white walls, you have a coupla hours walk through a half-mile-wide garden—I mean a garden with groves of ash trees, flowers, birds, fresh water springs! It ends at the river, where you turn north for Fort Laramie only 200 miles away."

"Where's this ash grove hollow?" Fremont asked. "How far above the Forks?" "'Bout three days' ride."

"And a sheer rock climb-down to the hollow is the only way to get to the riverside trail?" Fremont persisted. "I

228

don't like the sound of a perpendicular wall that carts and animals must work down. Any reason we can't march along the North Platte riverbank beginning at the Forks?"

"You can—IF—" Carson said, "the river's real low and has shrunk away from some rocky projections, leaving a strip of dry shore—and if you don't get a downpour of rain bringing a flash flood in the middle of your 12-day march to Laramie. Carts could be wrecked, stuck in mud, men swept away."

JF Report
July 2
(prairie fire)

Buffalo Book
D.Dary, p39
(prairie fire)

They climbed up through the hollow's wooded slope on its west side and rode on, Fremont pensive, Carson silent, Randy drowsy. He kept smelling smoke, like leaves burning. He straightened up. "Kit, do you smell anything burning?" Carson mumbled vaguely about the prairie and Indians. "Did you say they BURN the grass? They set it AFIRE?" Randy exclaimed. "WHY?"

"It's nothing to worry about, Randy. We can hardly smell any smoke here so the fire's a good ways off. To the northwest, I think, where the grass may be drier. Lightning coulda started it. Indians could be trying to trap buffalo—or enemies." His voice faded off.

Randy went back to thought-wandering. Even Tuesday's head drooped. These tedious hours when nobody talked, when all that happened was the steady bouncing motion from the horse's walking, were the worst hours of all. Randy sighed, working at staying awake. He'd drifted through several scenes of bragging to Jerry, his best friend in Washington, about riding with Kit Carson into a buffalo herd—when Fremont's voice broke in.

"More trees ahead! Another hollow from hill to river! Pass the word!" Another careful downslope to the bottom, a quick crossing, another upslope pull, and over the edge back onto the solid grass mat. The single line reformed, with Carson riding beside Fremont in the lead ahead of Lambert and Maxwell. Carson and Fremont were discussing something in low voices. Randy stared at the back of Kit's neck, hoping he'd look around, maybe decide to come back and tell him a prairie fire story.

Instead, he felt a small tap on his arm and looked around at Tuesday. Tuesday began pointing at the ground ahead with one hand and beckoning to Randy with the other. "What is it—uh—ten-o-wast?" Randy stood in his stirrups to see.

Tuesday was pointing to dirty-white buffalo skulls scattered near piles of bones—big pelvic cups, long spines, long legs still attached to dark hooves. As they rode past, Randy

229

saw this was not the only bonepile. There were dozens! Acres of piles of bones! Randy thought of the camp site on the Little Blue River, the first time he'd seen buffalo bones, how excited he felt when he picked them up and tried to fit them together into a whole buffalo. But that was just a few scattered bones compared to these dozens of bone piles. Why were there so many ?

Buffalo bones scene not in JF Report. but a scene trail travelers often saw. Oregon Trail, Parkman, p60 Buffalo Book, Dary, p135 Expedition, Long, p304

"Maxwell?" he said. The brawny hunter looked at him. "Something wrong, boy?" "No. Just wanted you to look out there at a lot of buffalo bones—I mean a LOT—and tell me what happened, if you know."

Maxwell's eyes swept across the scene. "'Course I know, boy! Indian hunters had a BIG buffalo surround here quite a while ago." "A surround?" Randy wished Max'd stop saying "boy" to him.

"Yeah, just that, boy. Up to, say, 200 hunters on their ponies surrounded about that many buffalo and killed them all. Then the Indian women came and did the butchering, the cooking, the meat-drying, the hide scraping. The whole village, maybe a thousand people, then had enough to eat for a coupla weeks, and some dried meat during the winter.

Narratives of Exploration and Adventure, A.Nevins,p57-8 (buffalo surround)

Buffalo Book D.Darey,p90, 135(skin cleaning, tanning)

"But they'd have more than meat—the women had 200 hides to scrape clean of any flesh and any hair the buffalo hadn't shed for the summer. Big, nasty job with worse to come—smearing the skins with buffalo brains to tan them, make them soft. Women sew the skins together with buffalo sinews, make new covers to lay over teepee poles—and mocassins. In the winter when the fur's thick and strong, they leave it on, make robes. Sell'um to us."

Randy stared at the half-mile-long buffalo boneyard, trying to picture such a surround, so many dead animals, so many horses with riders shooting how many arrows—a thousand or two? And the butcher women. And 200 stacks of bloody meat. "Waghh." He saw Tuesday looking at him and grimaced as his Indian friend smiled and swept his arm out toward the killing ground—"Good!"

Lambert cleared his throat loudly and joined the conversation. "Right through here, not far from the forks, is a good stretch along the river for Indians to find big herds o'buffalo, and split off a bunch to surround. The forks of the Platte most men out here will tell you is the center of the buffalo range. Sioux bands—the Oglala, the Brules, the Hunkpapas—claim all the Forks area.

"Buffalo congregate around the sprawl of water where the North and South Plattes join. One year when I passed

Gr.Plattee R. Road,
J.M.Mattes, p253
(herds at Platte Forks)

Overland with Kit
Carson.
G.D.Brewerton,
p206(vast herd)

JF Report
July 2
(conical peaks
500 feet high)

Journal.
Preuss,
July 2
(bare peaks,
strange shapes)

(5-mile wall)
Oregon Trail,
Parkman, p61.
Gr. Platte R. Road,
J.Mattes,p265
Trail Guide, p60.
Expedition, S.Long,
p307-8
City of Saints
R.Burton, p5.

Episode not in
JF Report.
But monotony,
boredom, big
problem for trail
travelers.
Many sang to
raise spirits.

Young Voyageur.
p36 ("Turkey in the
Straw" popular
during 1820-30's)

through here, I saw the whole prairie across the Platte covered black for miles with buffalo—ten million of 'um I figured. They all were moving to drink a million gallons of water out of the river—leave it dry, you might think."

Lambert pointed to the uneven ground. "Look at that, Randy. Buffalo herds coming out of the Platte onto the prairie walk single file and always in an old track. Wears the tracks deep and packs them hard. Makes a washboard road for us, bumpity bump.

"The paths lead south across a flat mile or so to the high wall of marly sandstone you've been eyeing for a few days. Between ledges and cone-shaped peaks there're ravines leading to big grassy meadows hidden among those crazy shaped hills. Some ravines lead to the prairie on the other side."

Randy took a long look at the cone-shaped hills, rough, massive walls of bare, orangy stone topped by weird, contorted shapes. Some shapes looked like evil creatures—scary! The only trim on the gullied slopes was scattered lines of green pines and random streaks of lime-white marl.

Soon after the "buffalo surround" boneyard, a rough-faced, endless hill loomed, a massive back-drop five miles long walling off the prairie to the south. To get past it, two deadly quiet walled-in hours ahead? Hazy sky and a warm little breeze had already lulled the line of men and animals into silent, mind-numbed plodders.

"I wish I had my guitar," Randy said out loud. Maxwell beside him mumbled," Can't you sing without a guitar, boy? Most people can sing without one."

"Can YOU? I mean, WILL you, Maxwell?"

"Offer me something easy in smart time. I'd be glad of some noise around my head."

After a moment's song-title check, Randy asked, "How about 'Turkey in the Straw?' You know—" and he began to sing with a quick beat, "Turkey in the straw, turkey in the hay!" Maxwell added the higher pitched repeat, "Turkey in the straw and turkey in the hay!" and dueted with Randy through, "Roll'um up and twist'um up a high tuckahaw, And hit'um up a tune called Turkey in the Straw!"

"Sing louder!" They did, and voice after voice joined, including Canadians making up words in French and improvising on the tune. For some miles Randy and the lead men sang over and over the one verse they knew—"As I was going down the road, With a tired team and a heavy load, I cracked my whip and the leader sprung, I says hay-hay to the wagon tongue!" Up and down the line the chorus rang out, "Turkey in the straw! Turkey in the hay!" They sang it so many times, the French-Canadians mimicked, then began singing the right words, and the horses and mules perked up to march in time with the music. Tuesday, too, began making a rhythmic "hay, hay" noise.

It was the Lieutenant who finally stopped the hand clapping and raucous shouts. Without stopping the brisk forward movement of the column, he rode along the line with Lambert, who called to the singers, "Attention! Attention! Lieutenant Fremont wishes to remind you that we should quiet down before we arouse every Sioux in the Platte Valley! Lieutenant suggests a quiet kind of entertainment now—observing prairie dogs in their village just ahead. Look to your left!"

Prairie dog episode not in JF Report. But scene most trail travelers would see.

A suppressed groan of disappointment from the still moving column made Fremont declare, "Oh, but the prairie dogs will make you laugh, feel better. Then we'll have a three-hour stop. The grass will be good and river water close by, so the animals will have time to eat plenty and rest up for the river crossing late this afternoon. Call it a reward for bringing us here right on schedule!"

With an informal salute to the men, Fremont returned to the head of the line. The men mumbled to each other.

"Vous avez entendu tout ca?" You heard all that?

"Oui. Vous etes content d'observer a cet elevation du cheval les prairie dogs en passant?"

"Hmm. Oui. Better than taking a walk through their village. Les rattlesnakes live with them."

Prairie dogs:
Oregon Trail
Parkman, p68,94,275
City of Saints
R.Burton,p65-6

Fremont had repeated his speech near the head of the line, and moved back in place beside Carson.

"Prairie dogs?" Randy said. He'd heard plenty about them and the holes they made in the ground, but never seen either. Tuesday's hands and fingers busily described a circle, fingers coming up through the circle, two of them squeakily snapping together. "Prairie dogs! What's so entertaining 'bout prairie dogs?" Randy called out.

"Dog-ville's the best show on the prairie," Kit Carson called back. "Quiet down and look left!"

Randy, standing in his stirrups, looked past Tuesday at the unusual array of hundreds of wheel-size heaps of white soil. Some rose to a broad open mouth at the top of the pile, while others had been built up into chimney shapes. Atop many of these entrances into the earth, a tan, squirrel-shaped creature sat on its haunches, its two front paws side-by-side, fingers daintily drooped, in front of its white

PRAIRIE DOG

breast. Randy heard some small whistling sounds, and a constant babble of tiny squeaks from these "dog town" residents who, sitting upright defiantly stiff, quarreled at the giant creatures passing by.

TRADE

Prairie dogs:
Overland with Kit
Carson,
Brewerton,p270
Expedition,
S.Long,p301-9
Wah-To-Yah,
Garrard, p23
Great Platte River
Road, Mattes, p250.

Tuesday all of a sudden pulled his horse out of line, beckoned to Randy to come out too. Hands rapidly crossing in front of each other could only mean "trade places," Randy decided, and came out of line to make the exchange. Randy signed "good" with a smile, and now with a clear view could see that the length of the village had no end in sight.

But even the nearest mounds and "dogs" didn't give Randy the close-up view he wanted. "Lieutenant," he called politely, "could you lead the column closer to the prairie dogs for a better look, please? I'd like to see which way they go into their holes—head first or backing in."

"Yes, yes! Everybody should like that!" Fremont said. "But let me tell you first that beneath the village is even more amazing than these hundreds—maybe thousands—of mounds on top of the ground. Not only do the animals dig a hole deep into the ground for themselves, they dig tunnels to join the tunnels of their neighbors!

"If we could scrape off the top layer of earth, we'd see a maze of tunnels, miles of them, criss-crossing the whole area! They do a lot of traveling underground, and a lot of eating underground—the roots of the short buffalo grass that they eat above ground!"

"Are THEY good to eat—will the hunters hunt them?" Randy's bright blue eyes grew wide with anticipation. Fremont—and hunters Maxwell and Carson—laughed.

"They're edible, Randy, and some people do eat them, but not us. Why eat earthy-flavored prairie dog when you can have deliciously sweet buffalo meat?"

"And who'd want to eat entertainers—clowns!" Fremont added, and began turning the column, slowly edging closer to the mounds.

For the next two miles, until they saw the trees of a hollow crossing the plain, Randy and everybody else, including Mr. Preuss, laughed at the saucy, monkey-like movements of the "dogs," and their toy-puppy yippings—"Wish! Ton! Wish!"

When the animals saw the column of horses coming toward them, they somersaulted head-first into their earthy holes, heels in the air, brown backs flashing, naked string-bean tails shaking rapidly. Almost immediately, their tiny ears, then their marmot faces nosed out, challenging danger with a steady stream of fierce wish-ton-wishy chirps.

"No wonder little owls and big rattlesnakes like to live with them," Maxwell said. "Bet those owls're hooting all the time and the snakes are snickering and shaking their rattles at the dogs' silly, jerky skittering around. Fun! that must be the reason they live with the dogs! Nobody knows any other reason."

Owls? "You don't see them? They're sitting right beside some of the burrows—those little huddles with a big white ring around each eye. It's even harder to see the rattlesnakes—they're long, have skins with checkerboard patterns—and like to live IN the burrow with the dog and family. I stuck my hand down a dog hole once and bumped into the tail of a snake, so I know FIRST HAND about that."

OWL

Randy grunted "ugh," and turned away to watch dogs scampering from mound to mound, short legs working comically. A half-dozen dogs had gathered by one mound, and all were gossiping—singing?—in a chorus, "Wish-ton-wish" as they sat upright on their haunches, limp-wristed paws hanging below their chins.

"Max," Randy said, "if prairie dogs aren't good to eat, what are they good for?"

"As far as I know, they're utterly useless except for making people laugh—which is reason enough."

Randy couldn't get enough of watching the nervous, talky, irritable inhabitants of Dog Town on the Prairie. He counted them until he was up to 189, including those that immediately vanished from his sight. He looked for small prairie dogs that might be young pups but he never saw any. He wished he could take one home for a pet, but Fremont strongly assured him they were uncatchable and undig-upable.

At the end of an hour—three miles of Dog Town—Randy watched the last dog dive into the last hole.

Tuesday waved a hand at it. "O-noni-wonski," he said, and Randy guessed it was the Cheyenne way to say "goodbye" to animals.

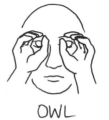

RATTLESNAKE

When he looked up, he saw that the long stone hill was ending with a definite cut-off line—trees reaching from it across the prairie to the river.

Another hollow! "Rest camp ahead!" Maxwell's voice boomed, and the news traveled quickly down the line. At the far end, French Canadians began to sing. The tune and the words rolled forward to the head of the line, increasing in volume and spirit with every voice that joined—"Turkey in the straw! Turkey in the hay! Roll'um up and twist'um up a high tucka HAWaawww—!"

Midday rest near Forks of the Platte: Critical moment of the Indian bone game arrives
when The Hider holds out both hands toward The Guesser. "Which hand holds the
marked bone?!" Randy and Moise perched on a vacant cart pay more attention to
Tuesday who brings them a clay head he's made. It looks like Randy! Suddenly, they
hear a cry of distress from the game circle. Augh! Which player bet on the wrong hand?!

235

CHAPTER 22

GAMBLING, SCULPTING, FORDING A RIVER

July 2 afternoon, Forks of the Platte (Nebraska)

Instead of calling "Halt!" and "Make camp!" just before reaching the hollow, as Randy and most of the column expected, Fremont and Carson led the line of horses, men, and carts down into, across, up, and out of the hollow. As camp was set up a little beyond the trees edging the ravine, Fremont explained that the west edge of it was closer to the Forks, "and besides, the prairie dogs have eaten most of the wonderfully nutritious 'buffalo' grass on their side of the hollow. Not enough left for our animals. As you saw, the 'dogs' have eaten clean and short the grassy roof of their miles-long underground city and a good ways on the adjacent prairie. There're thousands of them, and they need all the grass on their side of the hollow to survive and fatten before hibernation weather."

JF map
July2
Midday camp by
hollow near forks

Before the cooks had their fires going, scouts Carson and Maxwell were ready to head their horses west for the river forks five miles or so farther on. While Carson had been riding beside Fremont, the two had discussed the character of the land alongside each river fork, the depth and speed of the river waters, the river bed, the where and the how to make the crossing safely, easily. "But it's always wise to go take a look yourself, confirm ground truth of the moment, before coming face to face with the job," all three agreed.

At the last minute, while the two hunters gulped down slices of cold meat and hard pilot-bread, Fremont had listened to Lambert's advice to add himself, and brawny Honore Ayot, a crack rifleman, as well as unarmed Pat Cheyenne to the "ground truth" team.

JF Report
July 2(afternoon)
("several men
reconnoiter")

"Pawnees once held this river forks area and right on up the North Platte," Lambert said. "But seven years ago, they had a fight with the Sioux up there in the ash-tree hollow that opens out on the North Fork—the canyon we told you about. The Sioux were moving south out of Dakotaland—some folks call Sioux 'Dakotas'—and they wanted the whole length of the North Platte for themselves. They seem to'uv caught Pawnees in that canyon, and—"he drew the front edge of his hand quickly across his neck, made a hissing,

Sioux,Pawnee Platte war:
Gr. Platte R. Road.
J.Mattes,
p169,286-7
Oregon Trail
F.Parkman,
p104,136.
City /Saints,
R.Burton, p98
104, 28

slicing sound. "This is also the Indian hand sign for Sioux, y'know: Cut throats.

"So the Cut-throats beat the Pawnees. Now, the Oglala Sioux and Bruley Sioux—there're seven Sioux bands, y'know— roam the area, and their hunter-warriors kill any Pawnees they catch this side of Grand Island. I've been told several Sioux villages move about these parts, so there's something like a coupla hundred warriors close to the forks usually. Two white men meeting up with a bunch of them might not have a chance—although if there's any one man who could beat'em in a fight it's Kit Carson. But FIVE of us could hold'um off, get back to the camp where all 28 of us, counting Randy, are good shots. We can kill enough Sioux to convince them to leave us be for the rest of our march along the Platte—winning a fight here could mean long term protection for ourselves, our supplies, and your instruments, Sir."

Cheyennes,
Grinnell,I-22
Sioux friends.
of Cheyennes.

"Having Pat Cheyenne with us might even save us from any and all trouble. The Cheyennes and the Sioux are friends, strange as it sounds," Kit added.

Randy and most of the camp watched the five horsemen ride away, silhouettes against the radiantly blue sky. They cantered along a grass-green plain toward a distant converging of knobby clay heights on the left and a line of trees on the right. With the sun directly overhead in the cloudless sky, Fremont's expedition had the whole good-weather afternoon to get done the main work of the day—crossing the Platte.

"Do you think Kit and the others will meet any Sioux warriors?" Randy asked anxiously. Fremont laid a reassuring arm on Randy's shoulders as they walked toward the cook fires. "No way to tell, Randyboy. But during our six-day march along the Platte, some 120 miles, we've not seen a single Indian—"

"—except Tuesday and Pat and Mike!"

"—yes! except our Cheyennes. But no hunters, although we've seen tens of thousands of buffalo. It may well be that the Pawnee and Sioux warriors have left for other places to fight other Indians, so we will peacefully make our river crossing. Yes—I have a feeling that's the way the day will end! Now let's eat up the rest of the buffalo meat—except the hard strips that we dried on the cart rails."

Rest stop episodes
not in JF Report.

With roasted meat and hard bread in one hand, his tin cup of coffee in the other, Randy went looking for Tuesday whom he'd not seen since Pat left with the "ground truth" team. Thinking Tuesday may have gone into the hollow to relieve himself and would soon return, Randy headed for the cart closest to the hollow's tree line. He liked to "get away" sometimes and had found solitude when he climbed to the driver's seat on an unoccupied cart.

But as he turned the corner of the cart, he saw he couldn't be alone today—but he wouldn't mind, for it was Moise who had beaten him to his perch.

"Moise! All right if I sit with you?" Moise nodded vigorously, his mouth too full to speak.

Coffee, meat slices with bread, and himself safely on board by Moise, Randy said, "I'm looking for Tuesday. I'm watching the trees over there in case he's down in the hollow latrine-ing and will come out pretty soon. Have you seen him?"

Moise had. "He passed here some time ago—hey, I see him coming out now. Looks like he's picked up some rocks in dat hollow—got a yellow chunk in each hand. Wonder what he's t'inking to do wid'um."

Randy waved. Tuesday bobbed his head. When he came closer, Randy called, "Ten-o-wast?" and pointed at Tuesday's hands. "Well, of course he can't answer—I don't know his word for 'rock' and he doesn't know mine. But are they really rocks, Moise?"

Tuesday arriving at the cart, held up his golden "rocks." Moise reached for one. "I t'ink dey're chunks of real hard clay," Moise said after a hard look before handing it back. "Oh—Tuesday's trying to tell us somet'ing. See, he's pointing at his mout', den making like he's drinking from a cup. He must be terrible t'irsty. I'll give him my cup—it's still half full of coffee."

Tuesday laid his "rocks" by Randy's feet on the cart floorboard, smiled at Moise and took his cup. He looked inside it. He beckoned at Randy's cup.

"He must be VERY thirsty," Randy said, handing him a nearly full cup.

Tuesday sat the cups side by side near Randy's feet on the cart floorboard and picked up one of the rocks. Abruptly, with all his force he bashed the rock into the other, shattering it. Whack! Whack! Whack! Both rocks crumbled, and Tuesday pushed the crumbles into a heap. He poured Moise's coffee on it and began to break and press the crumbles into stiff mud. He dribbled Randy's coffee on it, squeezed it, dribbled more coffee, kneaded it into a doublefist-size ball of brownish-yellow mud-dough.

"What's he going to do with it?" Randy asked.

"Reckon we'll have to wait and see," Moise said. "But I heard about Cheyenne boys dat dey like to play wid balls of wet clay. Dey make birds and animals and figures of people out of it. Likely enough dis boy found dose pieces of hard clay in de holler—mebbe washed down from de hard clay hills—and t'ought of somet'ing he wanted to make. Den he happened onto us and enough liquid to make mud."

Cheyennes,I.
Grinnell,p65
(wet clay art)

Tuesday was rolling the mud ball round and round between his hands. He was looking at Randy and half-smiling. "Now what?" Randy said.

Suddenly, Tuesday plopped the clay ball on the board, took from behind his ear a short stick broken from a tree branch, and began to work. With stick and fingers he shaped the clay into a head, neck, and shoulders. Cleverly, he pushed up hair, ears, nose, and smiling lips, a chin, and eyebrows.When he had dug out eyes complete with irises, and added clay pinches and lines for ruffled, shaggy hair, Randy jumped to the ground, stared at the head. "Look, Moise—look! It's ME!" With a joyous laugh, he grabbed Tuesday by a shoulder, then bowed the "thank you" sign.

"Hey—dat's good!" Moise exclaimed. "Looks spittin' image of you, Randy!" he declared, "and dat's no joke!"

As Moise climbed down from the driver's seat for a closer look at Tuesday's sculpture, he saw a half-dozen men—Cheyenne Mike, Cousin Henry, and four of the cart-drivers—settling down on the ground some yards away under a big tree, three men in a row facing three others. "Hey!" Moise called, "come over here and see what de Cheyenne boy's done to dis ball of mud! Sacre bleu! It's a demn good head like Randy's!"

Mike waved but didn't move. The other men paid no attention. They talked seriously together, leaning toward each other, pointing, laying some sticks on the ground between them, gesturing, arguing mildly.

All at once, Mike Cheyenne looked up at Tuesday near the front of the cart, sprang to his feet and ran toward him. Ignoring Moise and Randy, he spoke in an intense whisper to Tuesday. The boy pointed to the small clay head sitting on the floorboards of the driver's seat. "Ahhh!" Mike exhaled admiringly, and as he examined the clay head with his eyes, he said many words that made Tuesday smile.

He turned to run back to the other men—and bumped into Cousin Henry. "I wanna see what the Indian boy made!" Henry spluttered. "Hey! That's a big surprise!—it looks like you, Randy! Say, Tuesday—you're really good! I want you to make one of me some time!"

Episode of gambling game not in <u>JF Report</u>. Hands-game preva- lent among Indians, major feature of male social life.

Mike moved past, sat down beside his two team-mates, and began to sing a lively chant. Johnny Janisse beat time, dum-dum-dum, on the ground with a heavy tent peg. Cousin Henry ran back to sit down, taking his place opposite Mike who began chanting.

"Ma-i-yun! Ma-i-yun!" Spirit! Spirit!
Dum-dum-DUM! Dum-dum-DUM!
Ma-i-yun! Ma-i-yun!"

<u>Cheyennes I,</u> Grinnell I, p80 (chant)

"Uh-oh," Moise rumbled, "no use talking to dem. Dey starting a 'hand' game—done laid down deir sticks to count wins, done picked a Bone-Hider and a Bone-Guesser for each team. Dey now making deir bets, de t'ree-men on dis side against de t'ree men o'ter side. Man on dis team bets somet'ing of value to a man on o'ter team. Dey betting dat deir team's Bone-Hider will keep de o'ter team's Guesser from knowing which one of de Hider's hands holds de spe- cial bone.

<u>Cheyenne Indians.</u> Hoebel,p45 (hand game)

"When de Hider's ready, de Guesser points to de hand he t'inks has the special bone. De Hider opens up. If de special bone is DERE, den de Hider's losing team has to pay what dey bet to de winners! What dey bet? Don't know 'bout mule drivers dat's took up dis Indian game, but Indians'll bet anyt'ing dey got—everyt'ing dey got! Dey gam- ble de quivers off deir backs, deir feat'ers, deir beaded mocassins, deir breechclo'es, all deir horses!"

"Ma-i-jun! Ma-i-jun e-tist-uh!
Spirit! Holy Big Medicine!
Dum-dum-DUM! Dum-dum-DUM! Dum-dum-DUM!
Spirit! Holy Big Medicine!"

<u>Cheyennes.</u> Grinnell I, p80 (chant)

Randy, shaking his head as Moise talked, then asked, "What did you say the Hider's hiding and the Guesser's guessing? I don't see anything!"

"BONES, Randy, bones. Two little bones! One is plain, de ot'er is marked. De Hider on dis team holds de bones hid- den in his hands. See, he switches 'um back and fort' from one hand to ano'der. He switches'um wit' hands high over his head, wit' hands down at his feet. His men make noise, sing, shout, make faces to take 'tention from de Hider's

<u>Wah-To-Yah,</u> Garrard p77 (hand game)

hands. De Guesser on de o'ter team has to figger out which hand finally has de marked bone."

"He am-ma wi'hi-o!
Give to the wise one, lucky one!"
Dum-dum-DUM! Dum-dum-DUM!

"Look dere," Moise confided, "de Hider moves every which way to confuse. Now, look! He's shoving out his arms wid hands closed, toward de Guesser on de ot'er team. Dat means, 'Which hand holds de marked bone?!' Everybody has a bet and everybody breat'es heavy! Ohhh—de Guesser is taking his time."

"I-no-o its-an-iv!
He hides something!"
Dum-dum-DUM! Dum-dum-DUM!

"Ahhh! NOW de Guesser points to de Hider's left hand! It opens! AHHH! DERE'S de marked bone, Randy! DERE'S de marked bone! Dat Guesser's really GOOD!"

The Guesser picked up a score-counting stick while his teammates shouted, clapped their hands, leaped up to jump for joy. The three losers cried out as if in pain, Mike among them, swaying, clasping his head, exclaiming "Hi-ta-i o-mon-i! Wah-he-in! Wah-he-in! All will be gone! Nothing left! Nothing!"

Suddenly, Randy noticed Tuesday had run to the players, stopped behind Mike, and stooped to speak into his ear. Mike answered, and almost nose to nose they had a tense exchange of words. Abruptly, Tuesday rose and came running back to the cart as the men began their next round of betting.

Randy heard Cousin Henry's voice, saw him pointing toward Tuesday. The singing and rhythmic thuds began again, the Hider began his hand gyrations, the noise makers their distractions, the Guesser his staring.

At the cart, Tuesday hurriedly untied, unwound the thin buckskin string securing one of his locks of hair. Holding the string ends straight and taut, he drew the string underneath the damp clay head, detaching it from the board. Carefully he picked it up. Without looking at Randy and Moise, he turned, walked evenly but quickly into the hollow.

Moise whispered, "MY bet is, Mike admitted to Tuesday dat he bet sum'um valuable—and lost it. Dem Cheyennes'r so near stark-naked, dey don't have any valuables—just worn-out mocassins, breechclot', quiver, and bow. Mike don't even wear one feat'er in his hair! Tuesday saw your cousin point dis way—"

Cheyennes,
Grinnell 1,p326
(chant)

Oregon Trail,
F.Parkman,p215
(hand game)

Tough Trip Through Paradise,
A.Garcia, p154-6
(hand game)

Cheyennes,
Grinnell 1, p188
(chant)

"Tuesday thinks Mike will want to bet the clay head!" Randy exclaimed. "I'll bet Mike told him he's already gambled away the magic arrow! He was looking for something else to bet—when Henry asked for the clay head!" Moise threw up his hands and made a face.

"And Mike just might say 'yes.' Indians any tribe go crazy when dey gamble dat Indian 'hands game'. Dey play for hours, gamble everyt'ing in de teepee, den deir horses, even deir wives—and t'ings belonging to deir kinfolks."

"You mean Mike CAN bet the clay head Tuesday made?! It's not his!" Moise nodded and shrugged.

They stayed and watched through the long play and bet, trying to tell from Mike and Henry's actions whether the clay head had been bet and lost. They became as intent on the game as the gamblers—so intent that Fremont walked up unnoticed. His strong, familiar voice jolted them and the hands-players back into the non-gaming world.

"Moise," he was saying, "please make the call to fall in." Moise strongest voice boomed, "FALL IN!! LIEUTENANT SAYS TIME TO MOVE! GET GOING!" The gambling six scrambled to their feet and scattered at a run.

The horses and mules, rested and round-bellied from a three-hour-long meal, had been brought in and resaddled, and the mules were waiting by the carts for the drivers to reharness them. Randy took his place near the head of the column. A few minutes later, he was surprised when Tuesday looking stony-faced pulled up alongside.

"No use trying to find out what or how much Mike lost," Randy decided. "He probably wouldn't tell me. No use even thinking about my clay head. It's gone for good in the hollow. Anyway, how could I have kept wet clay from getting smashed if Tuesday had given it to me?"

JF Report
July 2
(afternoon,
"marched direct-
ly for the mouth
of South Fork")

The column moved briskly along the wide, grassy plain with hardly the sound of a voice rising from the ranks. Six men were thinking of their gains or losses, and most others were visualizing several unlucky, even hair-raising, events that could possibly have happened to the ground-truth men. The next thought was what might happen soon to everybody. Fremont had said, "When we begin moving into river water, we may sink, get stuck, in QUICKSAND."

Fremont had also told them they would meet the "ground-truth" men in an hour or so, and hear their report. "They'll escort us some miles farther to the crossing they've found is best. With good luck, we can begin moving into the water at five o'chronometer, be on the other bank in less than an hour."

All turned out well, just as the Lieutenant had predicted. They soon saw the five scouts waiting in the shade of the upturned root and dry, splintered trunk of a dead giant cottonwood. Carson galloped at once to meet the column. He reported that no Indian had come in sight all afternoon, and that just west of the mouth of South Fork, then "a coupla miles" to the right off the trail, they'd found the best crossing.

"Water's so low you can see bottom, and sandbars are almost like stepping stones across 'bout 500 feet of river," Carson told Fremont.

Carson waved his hand toward the river. "This place on the South Fork," he added, "is where the trappers and traders and fur company supply wagons have been crossing the river for 20 years or so. Brings us onto the tip of the land triangle made by the joining of the North and South Platte. Good place to camp. Miles of good grass, and me and Maxwell can easy bring in a fat buffalo cow for a feast tonight."

Everybody in the column had seen during the previous hour a string of wooded islands in the Platte. Then the river appeared to turn into a shallow lake sprawling over the plain. "Well, that lake is the junction of the two rivers!" Carson advised them. "The North Platte's not as shallow as the South Platte, and that 'lake' is more'n a mile across—'bout ten times wider than where we'll cross on the South Fork!"

Randy wanted to ask if they'd be stepping into quicksand the whole way across, but the other four men had joined the head of the line and all of them and Carson were trying to talk to Fremont. Then Lajeunesse and Latulippe and Moise and Descouteau and others rode up to listen and ask questions but nobody mentioned quicksand except indirectly: "You cart drivers," Carson said, "keep them mules going, don't let'um stop or they may begin sinking."

By the time the column had crossed the plain's matted turf, made a right turn off the trail, then plunged down a loose sandbank, and finally arrived at the edge of the river, Randy's mouth was very dry. He held his pony's reins very tight. Carson called to eight horsemen to spread out along the edge of the water, start across to test the bottom for firm paths with no holes for the mules and carts. They called back and forth for a few minutes while Carson directed the drivers in lining up mules and carts to follow the watery paths the eight horsemen pointed out for stepping into and crossing the river.

"Water's shallow but moving fast and strong!" Randy heard. "Right in here's a low spot!" "Some quicksand here, but not enough to trouble a steady-walking mule!" "Start the carts! Drivers! Listen to your guide out there—keep your eyes on him! Don't let the mules slow down or stop!"

At the crack of whips over their heads, sixteen mules managed to forget they hated water and jerked the carts to a start. For a few steps they hardly got their hooves wet in inch-deep water. Whips cracked, horsemen leading the way shouted. "Keep straight behind me!" "Keep MOVING! "Keep MOVING!" "Deepest water here's only a coupla feet!"

Rushing water bounced against the tall wheels, a wheel here and there sank into a hole, tilted, pulled out, mules straining, slogging their way over churned-up sandheaps and down into holes dug by eddies. "Gee up! GEE UP!" screamed the drivers, cracking their whips.

Ten minutes walking bottom across the shimmering expanse, and they stepped on the solid sand tip of the skinny bar. A few steps more and they were in swift, three-foot deep water. Mules strained and heaved and moved slower, water half-way up their legs, and almost up to the hubs of the big cart wheels. Fast-flowing water, murky with sand, boiled through the spokes and spun in circles around the rims of moving wheels.

On shore, Randy, clenching his teeth, balling his hands into fists, kept up a hiss of encouraging words aimed at the animals in the river. "Giddap! Giddap! Keep moving! Keep moving! Pull! Pull! PULL! you mules, PULL!"

They did all he asked them to. By the end of the surprisingly brief crossing, all the carts were rolling out of the shallow edge of water in the distance. In front of them, only a long, rather high swell of sand with a wide opening lay between them and the reward for animals and men—a level, green expanse of lush grass.

"Our turn, Randy!" Fremont called with a wave and a smile. "Perfect day! Perfect crossing! Advance!"

Into the shallows a dozen horses splashed, stirring up the pale sand bottom. The riders, some leading a half-dozen horses, Cousin Henry leading the cow, shouted to their mounts, whipped their reins across their necks and set

Mule carts and herded horses follow lead horsemen across a narrow though quicksandy stretch of the shallow South Platte River. Mountainmen and supply caravans had long favored this crossing some distance west of the mile-wide junction of the North and South Forks of the Platte. Across the river, Fremont and his crew will camp in a lush pasture near the tip of the triangle formed by the two forks. To go to Fort Laramie about 200 miles north, the trail leads up the long slope of a plateau overlooking the west bank of the North Platte.

them to cantering until the drag of the deeper water slowed them down.

In the low spot where the muddy water almost reached his stirrup, Randy could feel the trembling of the sandy bottom tugging strongly at his pony's hooves. He yelled, "Come on, Spot, come on! Lift your feet faster! You can do it! You can do it!" Strong currents pushed against the pony's legs and swirled just under its belly. "Come on! Come on! Faster! Faster!"

Just ahead, Fremont's horse was speeding up as it moved out of the deep. Fremont twisted to look back at Randy, shouted, "Almost across! Keep'er moving!" Next to Randy, the three Cheyennes on their ponies looked as if they were enjoying the small sinking sensations they felt with every step of their ponies.

When they all came out upon the golden sand beach, the riders patted their horses' necks, and shouted exuberantly, "We're across! No spills! No sinkings under sand!" "And we made it by six o'chronometer!" Fremont added. Laughing and talking, they all struck out to follow the cart-tracks through the sand bank to the pasture.

"Look, Randy!" Fremont called when they arrived at the top of the rise. "We're close to the tip end of the point of land separating the two river forks. It's outlined quite clearly by a sprinkling of cottonwoods and willows around the end. Ah—I see some of our animals are already hobbled for a long evening's chomping on this rich pasture of grass."

JF Report
July 2
(camp, forks
  point of land)

By the time tents were set up and cook-fires built, Carson and Maxwell's two rifle shots had resulted in the arrival in camp of choice cuts, rib racks, and as Carson said, "a sack of choice innards" from a fat buffalo cow. Every cooking fire soon had leaning over it a circle of sharpened sticks strung with meat chunks, and each cook had additionally his own specialty sputtering or boiling on the fire. Two cooks were attending roasting sides of ribs. A third turned a bucket-size hump roast on a spit and stirred a pot of stew.

The fourth drew the most attention, comment, and lusty French-Canadian singing. The cook's wide grill held loops of "boudins" puffing up with heat and fat as they sizzled over glowing coals of wood and buffalo chips—dried dung—smokeless fuel picked up from the grass and sand.

"Moise! they look like the guts the Cheyennes were eating the other day!" Randy half-whispered when he and Moise were touring the cooking fires and luscious smells.

"Dat's right—boudins! Indian style! De little guts still stuffed wid half-digested grass. Good vegetable! Very special delicious taste. Have to tie each end of a long piece'o'gut to hold in de melting fat and everyt'ing else. But you watch! T'ain't just Indians dat likes boudins! I likes boudins! And YOU'd like boudins if you could ever get past your first try!"

Among the Indians.
H.Boller, p131,235

When the various boudins experts agreed that the right amount of steam was coming out of little punctures in the puffed up coils, two men lifted all thirty feet from the grill and heaped them on a patch of thick grass. Diners holding out their plates rushed to get their foot-long serving of the prairie cook's appetizer specialty. Fremont got his share and beckoned to Randy, who obediently but very slowly moved closer to what looked to him like a long, long, cooked snake.

Wah-To-Yah.
Gerrard,p28-9
(boudins)

Mr. Preuss strolled by, stopped, asked, "Vot have you got zere?" Cook Descouteau answered without looking up, "Sausage." Preuss held out his plate. He forked the twelve inches upward, bit off one end, chewed a moment to get the full flavor, pronounced it "good tasting, zis pudding. Very similar to a kind of German sausage."

Journal..
C.Preuss
(sausage)

Wrinkling his nose in passing the fast-shrinking heap of boudins, Randy headed for the roast ribs just being cut apart and handed out. As he bit off mouthfuls of the sweet, tender meat, juice and grease running down his chin and elbow, he caught glimpses of boudins lovers holding their pieces of long, fat-dripping "sausage" over open mouths, letting the inches slide in with the briefest of jaw and teeth action.

Buffalo Book.
Dary, p75-6
(boudins)

"I just couldn't take a bite, Kit," Randy said when shortly afterwards he and Carson were slapping mosquitoes and settling beside the instrument cart for guard duty. "Guts, still full of....Wagh." Carson assured him it was very clean, "for our cooks take only the first fifty feet of about a half-mile of small gut in a buffalo. Why, Randy, the buffalo's juices have already done a lot of the digesting work for you. Boudins do you a lotta good if you've been eating nothing but fried bacon and bread for days on end. Twelve inches of boudin grass will do away with your scurvy aches and pains."

Randy's answer was a head shake, raised brows, and a swat at a platoon of mosquitoes humming past his ears. He was about to ask a question when he saw in sundown's dimming light a dark shape, then two, then a third sneaking and slithering across the grass, stopping, sitting down, leaning on their front legs, staring toward him and Kit. One lifted its nose and mouth skyward and howled mournfully, longingly, "Owoooo-ooooo-oh-uhhh!" A second repeated the song, then all in chorus, "Owwww- oooo-oooooo-ooouhhhhh!" Distant wolf choruses answered.

"Probably smelled the boudins cooking," Carson laughed. Randy squirmed closer to Kit. He really did believe everything Kit had told him about wolves being cowards. Just the same, he was glad he wasn't standing guard by himself even on the daylight shift when the oddly sour smell of boudins hung enticingly in the air.

Beth Berryman
Based on A.J. Miller, 18--

"Lieutenant, the Cheyennes say this is the best party they ever attended, and want to know if our 'medicine days' will come often," says Carson, presiding over the brandy keg spout. Three Cheyennes suddenly whoop, begin a stomping, prancing dance, chanting and yowling, turning in a circle. Fremont's crew of mountainmen join them, dancing, cheering, celebrating America's Independence Day–until Tuesday Cheyenne suddenly sinks to the ground after sighing, "Whoop."

249

CHAPTER 23

GLORIOUS, EXPLODING FOURTH OF JULY

July 3-4, South Platte trail and camp

"Ahhhhhyy! I'll bet der's no breakfast as good as buffalo stew wit' macaroni!" Latulippe, sitting on the grass beside Randy, was holding his tin bowl near his chin, and spooning-in big mouthfuls of prairie-cook special. "Sacre bleu dis is good," he said, and spooned and spooned until nothing was left but a swallow of gravy. He drank it straight from the bowl. "Aaaaayy! dat wuz sooo good!

"Speaking of bets," he added, "word's been passing around camp as to who bet what and lost it in yesterday's 'hands' game we been hearing about." He paused and bent over a little to look into Randy's face for a sign or sound of interest. He heard two long slurps before Randy mumbled, "Bet you didn't hear anything about what Mike lost."

"Bet I did. De Indian bet against your cousin Henry and your cousin Henry was laughing and telling everybody what-all he won from de Indian. Six t'ings from playing 'hands', and a'course didn't lose not'ing hisself."

Randy said quickly, "Six things? What things?"

Latulippe snorted, "Aw—not'ing of any use to your cousin, and he won't git'um 'til de German-man brings out de arrows, and Pat hands over de feat'er on his head."

"ALL of his arrows?" Randy exclaimed. "And his BROTHER'S feather?"

"It was an eagle feat'er and Brant wanted it, wouldn't bet for not'ing but the feat'er a'ter Mike said he didn't have any more arrows. He offered Brant de clay head of you dat de boy had made—"

"WHAT?!" Randy burst out.

"—but Brant said no, didn't want dat, you'd be mad at him. So de Indian decided de big holy spirits werz whispering he sure to win de blue shirt Brant was wearing, so no risk to his brot'er's feat'er, and he bet it. Well, de holy spirits didn't tell de Guesser which of de Holder's hand he ought to point to for de marked bone. Phouff, de feat'er's lost."

Randy got to his feet. Six things? One was the feather, so five were arrows—ALL Mike's arrows? One was the magic arrow?? "I have to find Tuesday," he said, picked up

Gambling episode not in Fremont Report

his bowl and hurried off.

He was just in time to see Mr. Preuss, arrows in one hand, eagle feather in the other, and Fremont at his side, walking toward Cousin Henry and the cart drivers eating breakfast together. Randy ran until he was close enough to see Henry's red face, and to hear Fremont asking, "It was a gambling game you men were playing when I saw you yesterday during midday stop?" Mumbled "Yessir."

"You made bets, took bets?" Mumbled "Yessir." Fremont raised his voice. In the dead quiet, his words rang out sharp and clear. "In this camp, there will be no gambling! The game yesterday was against expedition rules! The work of the expedition has no room for ill feelings and other mischief brought on by gambling losses or gains!

"All goods that changed hands as a result of yesterday's gambling episode must be returned before the call to fall in! That call will be made in exactly one hour and thirty minutes! Anyone who fails to return goods by then will find himself walking all day, not riding!"

Fremont paused to let that sink in.

"During this hour and thirty minutes," he went on, "I request Proue, Larente, Badeau, Brant, and Menard to bring digging tools to a spot I have selected for a hole to be dug to cach a barrel of pork. We will dig it up in six weeks or so on our homeward bound journey to use when we're out of buffalo country and need it. The men I named should meet me in ten minutes with shovels in hand at the tall cottonwood there by the river. Thank you."

Fremont started toward his tent, Mr. Preuss at his side talking loudly with much arm waving. "You're going to hide a barrel of pork viz zese Indians vatching? You must know zey'll come back vhen ve're long gone and steal it! You know zey will! Indians are zieves!"

Fremont stopped, looked around, and asked, "Where are the Cheyennes? Under Johnny's cart? Run over there, Randy, get them, and bring them to the food cart. We'll open the barrel and let them see the salted PORK—no rich booty there. Then I'll ask them to help dig the hole for the barrel. Cheyennes don't eat pork—remember how they turned down our fried pork, even when they were starving? Go get them, Randy."

JF Report (Cheyennes shown pork)

Mr. Preuss stared at Fremont in disbelief, then followed him and spoke his mind. "You are endangering your men, Lieutenant! Zere'll be no barrel in zat hole ven ve pass zis vay again! No food for your men because ze Lieutenant has been foolish and stubborn—!"

Calmly, Fremont stopped, faced Mr. Preuss, and said, "Mr. Preuss, we're going to need a precise figure for the width of the Platte where the two forks come together—what Carson calls 'the lake.' Do you think you and a couple of the men can do the measuring job in an hour and a half? There'll be miles of walking, some in water." Mr. Preuss huffed off.

Journal.
Preuss, July 3
(measured
forks)

It was 9 o'chronometer when the call to advance started the column moving. The sour mood of wet Mr. Preuss and his two helpers had been sweetened by a swig from the brandy keg Fremont had unexpectedly offered them. "To avoid a cold," he said. Tuesday's stony face had relaxed since Fremont returned eagle feather and five arrows—no "magic" arrow. Randy tried to imagine what Tuesday, Pat, and Mike had been saying in their huddle under Johnny's cart about yesterday's "hands" game.

Journal.
Preuss, July 3
(brandy)

Fremont and Carson led the column west along the river bank. Randy, craning his head to look back at the tip of land between the two rivers, asked Lambert, riding beside him, "Aren't we going the wrong way? Isn't North Fork behind us, at the tip end ?"

"Well, son, it's like this. We go however the Lieutenant leads us," Lambert answered. "He's taking Kit Carson's advice to go west 40 miles along this South Fork to where there starts a good trail across the high plateau on our right. That diagonal trail north and east will bring us out to the North Fork by the Big Hollow—remember?—far above the junction of the river forks. We'll meet fewer Sioux that way. See?"

"We've gotta climb down that straight wall?!" Randy gasped. Lambert shrugged. "Lotsa people have done it."

Tall grass had overgrown the South Platte's bank, a plain a mile or so wide beside low hills. As horses and mules stomped it and carts rolled over it, swarms of mosquitoes, flies, and gnats flew out. Flies large as bees landed on the animals' flanks and faces, sank sharp, sucking needle-mouths through their hides and feasted on the rich, red liquid banquet arriving from half-way across the continent.

JF Report
(mosquitoes,
flies)

Bitten horses snorted, fluttering their noses, switched their tails fast and wide to sweep clean—for a second—the tormentors from their own and a close neighbor's rump. Mules twitched and tremored their hides trying to dislodge the biting varmints.

Only a friendly south wind lessened the men's torment of flying clouds of mosquitoes whining their hunger-tunes, and masses of tiny gnats fighting to sip the moisture of eyes, noses, mouths, ears.

At midday eating and rest-stop, Randy, his face dotted with red welts from itchy mosquito bites, told Carson he'd noticed that mosquitoes don't bite the Indians. "Why? Do they taste bad or smell bad to mosquitoes?" Carson, with an especially serious expression, said, "Well, I'll tell you what I heard one time from an Indian who, like the Cheyennes, wuz not bothered by mosquitoes though they werz nibbling the rest of us to misery.

"He told me that the smell your skin gives off after you eat ten stripsa raw liver fresh out of a buffalo—or antelope, or bear, or rattle-snake—" Carson stopped for a long chuckle—"will turn mosquitos away. Did you know a snake has a liver, Randy?"

No, he didn't, and the look he gave Kit said that Randolph Benton would never swallow one slice, much less ten, of ANY animal's raw, bloody liver. "I'd rather itch and scratch," Randy muttered.

JF Report
July 3
(buffalo, south prairie)

Scratching and itching, Randy gazed south across the river at the endless expanse of grassy plain. The near and far miles there were so blanketed with how-many-hundred-thousand black dots that Randy could hardly see any green. "When I get home and tell about these strange scenes, people gonna think I'm just making up crazy stories—lies—like mountain men. So I'm gonna count the black dots out there to back up what I say."

He decided to count a small group and multiply by— "What? a thousand? a million?"

Journal.
Preuss,
July 3
(buffalo killed)

Just then he saw Carson and Maxwell riding their horses so quietly across the shallow river that the nearest buffalo didn't look up. Before getting all the way across, Carson had aimed and fired.

CRACK! Randy saw the field of buffalo turning wave after wave toward the oddly shaped, high clay hills at the far left edge of the plain. The running animals formed lines, raced toward the hills, and began disappearing into dozens of ravines.

When the hunters caught up with the column, they had enough tender young meat hanging at the ends of rawhide straps across the backs of their horses to fill up 28 men at midday, evening, and breakfast, too.

Fremont allowed Randy to go wading across the shallow

Based on Alfred Miller

Outside his tent door, Randy catches his breath in wonder at a fantasy scene of beauty——buffalo quietly bathing and swimming in the shallow Platte River shimmering in the light of the moon.

river to the plain with Moise, Johnny, Yo, Latulippe, and Tuesday to pick up sacksful of fuel—"dry, and I mean DRY!"—pancakes of buffalo dung, "bois de vache," enough to cook the three meals.

JF Report July 3 (bois de vache)

In the middle of the night, overstuffed Randy, awakened by the need to unload various innards, went outside his tent. The full moon shining bright in a clear sky lit the whole world above and before him—river, endless plain, distant grotesque hill shapes—in a glowing veil of beauty. He saw movement in the water.

He caught his breath in wonder. Dozens of buffalo quietly bathing and swimming! He watched until he shivered with night-chill. At his tent door, he took one last look at a fantasy scene, a look long enough to make it a life-long memory.

At sunrise, Randy leaped up at the sound of rifle fire—CRACKCRACKCRACKCRACK—and excited shouting. Indians!?? He grabbed his pistol and sprang out the tent door. Cousin Henry and a dozen others fired off their guns again—straight up into the air! Men were coming out of tents,

JF Report July 4 (salute)

running toward the noise-makers, everybody shouting "'RAY-'RAY-'RAY!! INDEPENDENCE DAY-DAY-DAY!" Randy shouted, too, aimed at the sky, pulled the pistol trigger, "POW!"

"Great fireworks for The Fourth!" Fremont said when he brought out his secret gallon of red wine to sip with breakfast—"red fire water" Pat called it when he asked for more.

JF Report
July 4
(wine for breakfast)
(buffalo calf chase)

More excitement crashed into the breakfast scene. A buffalo calf suddenly galloped in a panic straight through the campground—followed by two wolves running like greyhounds. The men jumped up from their coffee-drinking sprawls on the grass, threw their cups at the wolves, rushed toward them waving their arms and shouting, and turned the wolves back.

The men cheered and yelled, sure that the baby buffalo, now across the river, had run far enough ahead to escape to a large herd visible at the foot of the hills some two miles distant.

But the two wolves had run around the outside of the campground circle to cross the river, take up the chase. Their barks had attracted help. First one, then another, and another wolf joined in the chase, until the calf's pursuers numbered twenty or thirty. They ran it down before it could reach its friends. An old bull galloped out, attempted a rescue. Too late. The calf was half devoured before it was dead.

Every man in camp had run to the edge of the river to watch the drama. A murmured "mon Dieu" rose from the French Canadians. Then Fremont's voice called out, "We all felt for that little calf, and had there been a saddled horse at hand, we could have helped it fare better. It should remind us of the miracle our infant country accomplished when on the Fourth of July, 1776, it ran away from the British wolves. The saddled horse that brought us help was France. Today, 67 years later, out here alone in the center of this vast continent, we will celebrate our victory with joyous feasting and singing. Vive la France! Vive the United States of America!"

"Vive! Vive! Vive!"

The mood had changed from gray to rosy so abruptly after the speech, the Cheyennes gathered around Carson to find out what the Chief had said. They still looked puzzled after Carson, with much arm-waving and a few Cheyenne words, gave them a short explanation.

On the walk back to their unfinished breakfasts Randy wanted to know what he said. "I mean, they don't know there's an ocean or British or French or anything."

"Well, Randy," Carson answered, "I hadn't even started explaining when I saw it wuz a story too far-fetched from life on the plains for me to tell 'um 'bout. So I just said they didn't need to know names, or places, or why there wuz a big fight—just that we won, and we like to remember with a feast on this Very Important Medicine Day for us white men."

Just then Carson heard his name called. It was Fremont passing by with Maxwell, Bernier, Ayot, and Lajeunesse, who were listening with rapt attention to his animated but low voice. "Kit!" he had called as they came close to Carson and Randy, and beckoned when Kit looked up. A few steps farther he called, "Lambert! Preuss!" He led all the men to his tent.

JF Report
July 4
(chooses
South Platte
crew)

"Well," Randy thought as he saw the men disappear inside, "if John is having a meeting, and it's also a holiday, I guess nobody's in a hurry to break camp and move out." He decided to find Tuesday. He had had it in mind for days to ask Tuesday to show him what he carried in a sack no bigger than the palm of his hand, a sack always hanging on a raw-hide string around his neck. But there'd been no good time to ask him. Now was his chance.

Indian
activities
not in
JF Report.

He found Tuesday next to Johnny's cart scratching pictures with a small stick on a patch of bare ground. Pat and Mike were leaning against the big cart wheel smoking cigarillos. They'd made them with crumbled tobacco sprinkled on a bit of paper, rolled into a tube, and stuck together with spit.

"Hookahay! Numwhit!" both men said, gesturing a welcome. "Hi," Randy replied. "Hi! Ran-dee!" Tuesday said. Randy smiled broadly at him—and thought, "Just his saying my name and one little word I understand makes me feel like..like we are talking a lot to each other. But then I know we're really not. I've just GOT to learn more of his words than 'ten-o-wast!'"

He squatted beside Tuesday, pointed to a wolf-shape drawn on the ground, woggled his hand for "question" and brought forth his three Cheyenne words. "Ten-o-wast?" Tuesday smiled wide enough to show all his front teeth.

"Hoh-neh. OW-oooo!" he howled. Quickly he drew another hoh-neh, and held up several fingers. "Hoh-neh HIU," he said. "Hoh-neh-hiu," Randy repeated, and said, "Wolves." "Wuvv-zz," repeated Tuesday. He pointed to his drawings of a prairie dog. "O-noni-woski," he said. Randy repeated it, laughing. "I like the name 'o-noni-woski' better—don't bother saying 'prairie dog!'"

256

Randy learned "ta-si," when Tuesday patted his heart, then Tuesday learned "heart," said it several times, smiled, pointed at Randy, touching his heart again. "I like you, too," Randy said, beaming.

Tuesday's smile vanished when he heard Randy's "Ten-oh-wast?" and saw Randy's finger pointing at the buckskin pouch hanging around his neck. "Ten-oh-wast?" Randy repeated.

Tuesday looked at his father, said something, and watched, waited for a reply. Pat tilted his head to stare at Randy's face. He took a drag from his cigarillo and let the smoke flow lazily from his nostrils. Still holding his gaze on Randy, the wihio who had shown him how to cut with scissors, he spoke to his brother. They exchanged words. Silence. Then he nodded at Tuesday. "Nihini," he said. That's 'yes!'" exclaimed Randy, nodding at Tuesday. "Yes-s-s," Tuesday said, smiling as he slipped the string over his head.

One at a time, he took from the bag six small objects, each neatly wrapped in a piece of thin deer skin, and laid them on the grass. Very carefully he unfolded each little package. Randy, on his knees for a close look, saw a bird's

feather, a small dry lizard, a chip from a horse's hoof, strands of twisted buffalo hair, a thumb-size picture of a boy on a horse drawn on a piece of white deerskin, and a folded piece of dry, shriveled, cord-like...skin?

As quickly and carefully as he had unwrapped his charms, Tuesday rewrapped them, returned them to their bag, and dropped the rawhide necklace over his head. Randy signed "thank you," and once more said, "Ten-oh-wast?" as he shrugged, hoping he was conveying his mystification.

"Hello there!" he heard just then, and saw cart driver Johnny Janisse bringing in his two mules. "Lieutenant's 'bout ready for Moise to holler 'Fall in!' Gotta hitch up my don't-wanna-ain't-gonna mules. Move out now so you won't get kicked. Time for you to get saddled up anyway."

Slowly, slowly the column moved along the river side plain below a lengthy, high, sandstone hill streaked with white marl. Its sloping sides, scarred with cracks and ravines as if scratched by giant bear claws, was the south end of the plateau reaching 20 miles north and east to the North Platte.

With each mile the column now traveled west, the space between the hill and river narrowed, became more desolate, occasionally sparkling with salt. Grassy areas, each smaller than the one before, mostly grew "salt grass" the animals refused to eat. Several "roads," some ten feet high, of sand and gravel washed down during centuries from creek beds and ravines in the hill, blocked the way and were slowly mounted and crossed.

JF Report
July 4
(10 ft.gravel ridge)

When Fremont suggested skipping midday food and rest, going on but making early camp and eating then, preparing for a feast to celebrate the day, the whole column cheered— except Mr. Preuss. He expressed disappointment that they had marched at all on "what's supposed to be a holiday, a rest day."

Journal.
Preuss
("stubborn Fremont")

To pass the time, Randy began counting the ravines and gullies in the side of the marl-streaked yellow clay hill. He had reached "one hundred and two, one hundred and three" when he noticed a cloud of dust rising from a number of the ravines.

"John!" he shouted. Fremont turned and answered, "Yes! I see! We think it's buffalo herds! Keep watching!"

JF Report
July 4
(buffalo columns)

In a few minutes, column after column of the animals came trotting out of dozens of hill openings, making for the river. By the time the lead buffalo of all the lines had reached the water, the plain was black with moving beasts except for a wide space that stayed open around the men's column as it continued to move along.

JF Report
July 4
(space left around column)

"Remarkable!" Fremont declared, looking at the animals blanketing the plain for miles ahead and the plain for miles behind the column, but all in orderly lines to the river, crossing the river, spreading over the plain beyond. The long lines melted into countless ravines in the distant hills to the southeast.

At one early moment, Fremont had estimated that 11,000 buffalo were in his view. At the end of an hour, Carson estimated that more than ten times that number had poured out of the ravines at their right. "So many buffalo moving so fast to the South hills means Indians were hunting them on the North Fork," Carson told Fremont. "If we had arrived at the junction of the Forks today instead of yesterday, we might've met up with 200 Sioux hunters. That surely would've messed up our crossing. Well, we and the herds are now nearly 40 miles farther on."

JF Report
July 4

JF Report
July 4
(Indians on North Fork)

As soon as the column had moved several miles beyond the feces-spattered area, and in sight of a patch of edible green grass, the call came, "Make camp at the grass!"

The Fourth of July feast started early—as soon as Carson

and Maxwell brought to the cooks the choicest cuts from their buffalo kill. The smell of roasting meat, stewing meat and macaroni, broiling marrow bones and boudins, bread frying in bacon fat, and boiling coffee by the gallon, soon perfumed the prairie air.

Spirits rose and rose and rose again as Fremont brought in view and distributed slices of rich fruit cake, clumps of strawberry preserves from a gallon jug, and finally dribbled brandy into each tin cup from a keg the size of a Missouri watermelon.

JF Report
July 4
(St.Louis
desserts)

"Men of this expedition!" Fremont shouted. "We have enough brandy for us to give a big cheer for America's Independence, and another for our friends in St. Louis who provided us with these excellent desserts and the keg of firewater! First—To Independence!"

"HIP, HIP, HOORAY!! "

"For Mr. Chouteau and Mrs. Brant in St. Louis!"

"HIP, HIP, HOORAY!! "

"Now, my friends, drink up! Eat hearty! Don't leave a drop or a morsel!"

Pat and Mike drained their cups. Carson, manning the

Indian activities
not in JF Report

spout, informed the crowd that the Cheyennes told him this was the best party they'd ever attended, "and they want to know if our medicine days come often!"

Tuesday, sipping firewater for the first time, had coughed after every swallow, making tears roll down his cheeks. Pat and Mike laughed and teased him to the last drop—when both men began whooping and singing, springing into a stomping, prancing dance.

Pat grabbed Tuesday by the arm, and both followed Mike around dancing, singing, and yowling. The crowd of watching men began to whoop and clap, too, in rythmn with the Indians.

Randy arrived with his guitar in the middle of the performance—just in time to see and hear an inspired Tuesday begin his own version of a buffalo dance. With forefingers crooked like buffalo horns at the sides of his head, he rocked his head back and forth, bent over and made a charging motion toward Mike, then at his father.

They made charging motions back, laughing, their feet and legs hopping. The song changed, the rhythm a pounding grunt and bellow—a dance of bulls fighting. The clapping, stomping mountainmen changed rythmn, too, shouted advice to each charging bull, even doing some charging of their own against their neighbors.

All of a sudden, Tuesday gave a big "Whoop!" sank to the ground, and toppled over. Pat and Mike kept singing, laughingly danced in circles around him, thrusting their heads and horns at him. Tuesday sat up, woggled his head, smiled foolishly, let himself be pulled up and led away by his singing, dancing, laughing parent and uncle.

JF Report
July 4
("Indian lad gets
  drunk,to his
  elders' delight")

But even that was not the climax of the day. That came soon after Pat led Tuesday from the "parade" ground. Lieutenant Fremont called for attention and made a shocking announcement.

"Friends," he said, "I have decided to divide the party. Tomorrow, most of you will proceed to Fort Laramie under Lambert's command, while I with Mr. Preuss, Maxwell, Ayot, Bernier, and Lajeunesse, proceed rapidly on the South Platte to Fort St.Vrain about 150 miles southwest of here. The Cheyennes will come with us—their band is camping near the fort, they think.

JF Report
July 4
(JF announces
plan: He and small
crew to take South
Platte to Fort St.
Vrain while main
column continues
on North.Platte)

"Carson will do the hunting for you going up the North Fork. I promise you that we six men—the Cheyennes will remain with their people—will join you at Fort Laramie on the sixteenth of July—for on that night there are some heavenly-body occulations I wish to view."

Randy couldn't believe it—he was not invited!

He fled the "parade ground" with his guitar. In his tent, he hid his muffled misery under a blanket. How could the Fourth of July turn out so miserably—Tuesday doing a drunken dance, John asking Mr. Preuss to go with him to Tuesday's camp, but not asking Tuesday's best friend Randy Benton to go, too?!

Why?! And why did John have to go off to some old faraway fort anyhow?!

Randy pours out his reasons for wanting to go with Fremont, five others, and the Cheyennes on a 10-day trip to Fort St. Vrain on the South Platte while the rest of the column proceeds to Fort Laramie on the North Platte. "I want to see where my friend Tuesday lives, maybe live the way he does for a little. I'll ride my horse dawn to dusk without complaining. Please let me go with you!"

CHAPTER 24

"I WANT TO GO WITH YOU!"

July 4, South Platte camp (Colorado)

Face down, Randy kicked the grass with his feet and
beat the blanket with his fists. He felt riled up, a knot of
disappointment in his stomach, another in his throat. Brain-
hot thoughts raced furiously. He'd just seen himself turned
into less than a petit garcon even. John Fremont wasn't
perfect after all.

Faith in John's perfection was lost, gone forever. The
realization suddenly unknotted his stomach, turned it into a
big, hollow emptiness. He pressed a fist against his mouth
to shut in sound, and let the tears flow.

He heard voices outside approaching his tent. If one of
them was Cousin Henry's—oh misery. But it wasn't. It was
Mr. Preuss talking fast and loud, and it was John, talking
calm but crisp. Randy lifted his head, propped his chin on a
fist to hear better.

"No, I do not like zis at all!" Mr. Preuss was storming.
"Up zee South Fork two hundred miles to zat fort in zee
middle of no v'ere, zen anozzer two hundred miles across
zee mountain range to Fort Laramie—all at breakleg, no,
break-bottom—speed! No, no, no! Even SLOW horseback
riding is hard enough for me. You're asking me to straddle
zee horse and bump a fast forty miles a day for ten days!
Twelve hours a day! Zat's more zan my already sore bottom
can endure!"

Fremont patiently repeated his just-finished explanation.
He needed Preuss's help with the instruments to shoot the
stars, to find latitudes and longitudes, to keep the rough
map up-to-date, to measure altitudes, to make sketches of
important landmarks or mountains or landscapes—"in short,
to help me with the important business and purpose of this
expedition! Probably the distance isn't that great or the
daily travel that long. I need you, Mr. Preuss! We'll put
extra padding on your saddle!"

Their voices had come nearer Randy's tent, become louder as they passed by, and faded as Fremont's last words
were flung at Mr. Preuss. Randy sat up and wiped his nose
on the back of his thumb. "Well," he said to himself, "Here

*Episode not in
JF Report, but it probably
happened. Small indica-
tors in the events of the
S.Platte 10-day
trip reveal that Randy,
though not named in
the record, was probably
in the small party with JF.*

*Journal.
Preuss, July 4
("don't like this")*

I am crying to go, and there's old Preuss crying NOT to go." He took a deep breath. "John let Preuss plead his case. I'm going over there to his tent and plead mine. I'm going to plead as hard as I did with Father when he said last New Year's he'd never let me come on this expedition."

It was only a few steps to Fremont's tent, and it was only minutes waiting out of sight for Mr. Preuss to leave. His voice wobbly from crying and daring and fearing, Randy called, "John..?" at the tent door.

Fremont's voice invited him in. "Randy! Come in, dear boy! Where'd you and your guitar disappear to? We were all set to sing 'Auld Lang Syne' when I looked around and you were nowhere in sight. Did you help tipsy Tuesday to his bed?"

As he ducked into the tent opening, Randy's gaze sought Fremont's while his slightly tremulous voice said, "I want to go with you."

Fremont's eyes widened while his lips parted in a smile. "You WANT to go on this arduous, bottom-numbing trip?! Ohhh, Randy! You don't know what you're asking for! But I know, and so would your father and so would your mother even more, and so would everybody in the United States who reads the report I'll write when we're back in Washington.

"It's not only a journey of physical hardship, Randy. It might also be dangerous. If any harm came to you, it would reflect on my judgment for taking you, which could destroy your parents' trust in me, destroy the expedition's value, its good impact upon all the families wanting to travel to Oregon. You DO see that, don't you?"

Randy's young, mobile face twisted, frowned, and wrinkled as he searched his thoughts for an answer. "You're talking about danger from Indian attacks?"

"Well, that's surely one danger," Fremont acknowledged. "But there are others. Rough and dangerous mountains where cougars leap on you from trees! Rattlesnakes and wolves! Hot deserts without rivers or lakes—our animals would die, then we could be stranded, die from thirst—ah! here's Kit! Come in, come in! You can tell Randy better than I about dangers we'd face out there on the South Platte! Kit's been there, Randy."

Kit shifted his weight from one foot to the other. "Well..." he began. "Well, there's dangers all right, but six men with guns and common sense have a great advantage. As for Indians, well, you have three Cheyennes whose presence will make a lot of difference. Beyond the camp of the Cheyennes— the tribe roams that whole area—when our three stay behind with their families, there's hardly any danger from other Cheyennes on account of word will've passed far and wide. It helps too that St. Vrain booshways—head men—have made strong friends with Cheyennes—and their Arapahoe allies.

"As for the terrain, I can tell you—having traveled that territory off'n'on—that you'll travel on flat land all the way and Maxwell can kill plenny buffalo for you. As for water and grass in the desert between South Platte and Laramie, there's some creeks, some dry, some not, except for a 40-mile dry stretch before Lodge Pole Creek. Well, also except for another 30-mile stretch 'tween Lodge Pole—a fine river—and a branch of Horse Creek. Once there, you'll ride 'longside the Creek with plenny water and grass all 30 miles or so to where it joins the North Platte.

Colorado Relief Map

"Still," he added after a brief pause and wave of an arm, "it WILL be hot, very hot. The land will mostly be desolate after you leave the Platte—that is, about a day after you leave Fort St. Vrain. You'll head north from the South Platte, but always bearing just a little east. Nothing much of interest to see except a limestone tower once in a while, or a white ridge or two you'll have to get around or climb, but you can easy go past a red sandstone mass that looks like a walled city. Still, I have to tell you, Randy, the hours you sit on your horse will be dawn to dusk every day."

"I can do it!" burst out Randy. The startled expressions, the explosions of choked laughter from Fremont and Carson puzzled him, and he responded with another heated announcement. "Besides! If anything BAD happens, like dying of thirst in the desert, it will happen to John, too, even if I'm not there, and that will have a worse effect on the expedition than something bad happening to me! So you shouldn't go either, John!"

Fremont, shaking his head and guffawing, declared that Randy Benton was on his way to becoming a politician like his father. "You're putting up a good argument, Randy!" he said. "Tell me—why are you so set on making this hardship journey?"

"I want to see where Tuesday lives, and maybe live the way he does for a little while. And I want to go where YOU go. And I want Kit to go, too. Why isn't he?!"

The two men looked at each other, and Carson slowly rubbed his cheek with one hand.

"It's better for Maxwell to go instead of me, Randy. It's, uh, like this...well, it may sound like a poor reason to you, but anyway, I don't feel like going to Fort St. Vrain on account of not long ago something hateful happened betwixt me and Mr. Ceran St. Vrain. He and his partner Charlie Bent of Bent's Fort own this South Platte fort."

Fremont raised an eyebrow, suppressed a smile and said quietly, "Go on, Kit, tell Randy a little about what happened so he won't wonder if St. Vrain kicked you out for wrong-doing."

(Kit's love life)
Bent's Fort.
D.Lavender
p189,192,196, 223-6

Carson winced, suppressed a smile, too, and said, "Uhm, it had to do with...a girl. Coupla summers ago when I wuz working at the fort, Mr. Ceran St. Vrain brought his 16-year-old niece, a real pretty girl, for a visit. She liked me a lot, too much it turned out, and I liked her a lot. So her uncle sent her back to St. Louis real quick, and told me in words so strong I won't mention 'um that she—and he—werz French aristocrats and I wuzn't fit to marry into their high-born St.Vrain family."

Carson paused, pressed his thin lips tightly, then blurted, "'Specially since if St. Vrain's niece had a-married me, she'd've had to take care of my then four-year-old little girl. She's half Indian and dark-skinned. Her mother, my wife, wuz an Arapaho. She died when my daughter wuz two years old."

Kit Carson.
T.Guild / H.Carter
(Adeline, daughter)

Randy caught his breath to exclaim, "You have a little girl?! How old now? Where is she? What's her name?"

"She's six now, and she's in Missouri with my people so she can go to school. I had just taken her there, was going back to Taos when I met you and the Lieutenant on the Missouri River steamboat. Her name is Adeline. Now, that's enough."

Fremont raised an admonishing finger toward Randy. "So, you must never mention Kit Carson's name even to Ceran St. Vrain's nephew, Mr. Marcellin St.Vrain. I was told in St. Louis that Marcellin is the booshway at the fort now, and I understand he's a thoughtless tease as well as a proud French pre-Revolution aristocrat. Be careful."

"You're saying I'LL BE GOING with you to the fort where he is!" Randy almost shouted.

"I didn't actually say THAT—" Fremont gasped. "I only said, 'Don't mention—' "

"Well, if you actually HAD said it, I'd back you up, Lieutenant!" Carson laughed. "The boy may never have another chance like this to visit with Indians in their camp and be shown everything by an Indian friend. There're some risks—but there're plenny risks if he travels with the other men on their way to the North Platte, then up to Fort Laramie to wait around for you. Randy's held up mighty well riding for hours every day for six weeks. Gott'n stronger I'd say. He won't be a drag on a 10-day trip, and having the Cheyennes along ought to cut way down on danger. Them's my feelings."

Fremont waved open arms in the air. "I'm outnumbered," he smiled. "Also, I expect Randy's father would agree with your feelings, Kit. He let the boy come on this expedition for the 'development of mind and body,' as the Senator said.

"But that doesn't lessen the fact that these will be harder days than any you've had so far, Randy. You'll be expected to keep up with strong, toughened, grown men, and do it without a single whimper. You'll be expected to face danger with calm control, quick attention to orders. What do you say to all this, Sir?"

Randy's blue eyes, very serious in his flushed, freckled face, stared into the blue eyes of the bearded Lieutenant. "I CAN do all you say, Sir. I WILL do all you say, Sir."

"Then we're set to go. But let it be understood that when I write my report, I will not include the name of Randy Benton in the list of men who went with me on the South Platte adventure. It would stir up criticism no matter if all goes well. We must all pray that exceptionally good luck will stay with us every day of the ten before we see you, Kit, at Laramie. For tonight, silence about this to the others, please."

By the time the sun began to break through Earth's horizon on July the fifth, wide-awake Randy Benton had already saddled and bridled his pony, bundled his extra blanket and underwear, strapped on his pistol and possibles-bag, and stood waiting for a cook to finish preparing meat, bread, coffee, and his cup of milk. Beside him, looking very pleased, smiling very knowingly, stood Tuesday. Today, his quiver of arrows hung from one shoulder, his bow from the other. He, too, was ready, eager to start for his family's village and teepee.

After breakfast, Fremont called for the South Platte crew to mount, for Ayot to lead the pack horse loaded with a box of scientific instruments, and the pack mule with the bundles of the seven men—Fremont casually included Randy's name in the list—and a small package of provisions. All the men carried on their shoulder a rifle or a double-barrel shotgun, and wore holstered pistols on their belt—Randy, too. Pat and Mike like Tuesday wore their bows and quivers hanging from their naked shoulders, while bundles of red flannel underwear and other treasures dangled from the

JF Report
July 5

back of each pony.

As Fremont raised his hand, the word "Farewell" at the edge of his lips, a sudden burst of voices yelled, "SIR!!" All eight cart drivers were pressing toward Fremont, all eight were waving their hands and talking loudly. Fremont pointed to Janisse.

"SIR!" Janisse began. "We mule-cart drivers don't want to have to go down that steep half-mile cliff into the ashtree hollow Kit Carson has told us about. EIGHT carts, Sir! TWO mules hitched to each cart! Both mules having different, wobbly footings, pulling against each other—we're in for a pile of broken-up mules and carts! We've just talked to Kit, and he says we can chance marching along the NORTH Fork's DRY bank all the way to Laramie, the river's so low and Moise predicts no rain any time soon. That's what we hope you'll let us do."

Although the route taken by the main column was not mentioned in JF Report, an Ash Hollow climbdown is also absent. Remarks by Preuss, who joined the column the next day, clearly indicate that the column turned back east, rode to Laramie along the North Platte" shore."

Carson spoke up before Fremont could ask the question. "Yes, Sir—this South Fork has shrunk 20 feet off'n its bank in this drought, so the chances are good that the North Fork has shrunk as much. I've told these men that I'll guide them through in good shape one way or another. We won't lose much time by turning back here to the North Platte. We can march north a few miles to the base of the hills we've been passing for two days, then turn back east about 20 miles to the North Fork, camp tonight some 15 miles UP the North Fork since the hill-line bears a lot toward the north, as you'll recall—"

"Why didn't you—"Fremont began.

"You wanted so strong to come 40 miles on the South Platte where you could best turn south and west toward Fort St. Vrain, and the rest of us could go across the plateau north and west toward Fort Laramie," Carson said firmly and steadily, "and we didn't know the cart-drivers had such strong worries about getting down from the plateau's steep rockpile into the hollow that opens onto the North Fork. When they told me during breakfast, I said to them, 'Say your piece to the Head Man, and I'll stand by whatever is decided.' "

Fremont's gaze held Carson's as he replied, "Your decision that the riverbank will be dry and safe is good enough for me. Cart-drivers—and all you faithful comrades—bon voyage with our trustworthy friend and guide, Kit Carson!"

Fremont reined his horse beside Maxwell and Randy at the head of the southbound line of 10 horsemen, clucked to his mount, waved his hat as the line began to move. Amid their cries of, "See you in Laramie!" and those of the two dozen turning north, "Good luck on the South Platte!"

Fremont's small party began its 150-mile walk southwest along the upper bank of the South Platte River. The only man not smiling was Mr. Preuss. He chose to ride at the end of the Fremont party BEHIND Indians armed with bows and arrows.

Underfoot, the sand whispered at every hoof's touch. Overhead, a bluish-gray line of long-legged, sandhill cranes whizzed past, sharp bills and long legs in a line as straight as painted arrows on a signpost, all pointing southwest. With a wide smile Randy watched them, his spirits speeding sky-high, flying with the birds, certain they were leading Fremont, the best man in the world, into the best part of the trip.

Randy glanced behind his shoulder at the Indians. Look at Tuesday, head up, bare chest expanded! Look at Pat, nobly dressed in almost nothing but an eagle's feather standing tall on top of his head! Look at Uncle Mike, his magic arrow's feathered end visible above all the others in the quiver! And hi-ho! Look at three usually unreadable Cheyennes who today, homeward bound, were not stone-facing their joy!

Based on Frederick Remington's, "Sun Dancer," 18--

Beth Berryman

Maxwell's story about witnessing an Arapaho warrior endure the agony of his "Sun Dance," draws a nervous inquiry from Randy. "Will Tuesday Cheyenne have to do a Sun Dance when he's a grown-up?" It's not required, Maxwell tells him, but if some-day Great Spirit saves Tuesday from a disaster after he has promised to pay back with a Sun Dance, he'll surely do it. Randy shudders as he imagines the pain Tuesday will feel while dancing with ropes hanging from the top of a pole pulling on the skew-ered flesh of his breast.

269

CHAPTER 25

DOG STEW, SUN DANCE, SADDLE TORTURE

July 5, South Platte trail (Colorado)

"Gitty-up! Gitty up a little faster, my four-footed friend!" Fremont said in between long sessions of listening and talking to Lucien Maxwell.

JF Report
July 5

"You can do better than three miles an hour! Step it up! Step it up! You can do four!" His horse's pace quickened, the other horses quickened, and the ten men felt they saw landscape details—sandy, shallow South Platte rushing downhill between miles of grassy plains on both sides, clay hills on the left, low ridge on the right—all moving past twice as fast as they had on other marching days.

Hard-eyed Maxwell, usually withdrawn, even sullen, had started the day with a talking streak about Arapahoes, and kept his story-telling going for hours. When Fremont met and hired him in St. Louis for the expedition, Maxwell had just ended a couple of years as a trader in and out of villages of Arapaho Indians close by Fort St. Vrain.

Lucien Maxwell,
L.R.Murphy
p25

Bent's Fort,
D.Lavender,
p226

He was the fort's "beads'n red cloth" trader for the Arapaho bands roaming the same area as their allies, the Cheyennes. His strong baritone voice fitted well his big-boned, muscular not quite six-foot-tall body, so Randy on Fremont's right had no trouble hearing Maxwell on Fremont's left. But catching all the words at the speed brawny, young Maxwell rushed them out became work.

The first hour, interrupted twice by Fremont's "Gitty-up," held Randy's full attention. Maxwell had watched a four-day ceremony when Arapaho warriors endured self-inflicted agony while "dancing" around in a circle and staring at the sun. Maxwell believed he was one of the few white men who'd been invited to watch this event, a sacred one since the warrior was paying with suffering for a big favor he'd previously asked for and received from a powerful Spirit.

"Did you say they cut TWO places on his chest and pushed a skewer UNDER the skin? Tied the skewer to a rope hanging from the top of a pole?!" Randy, shocked, leaning forward to ask Maxwell the question, couldn't believe he'd heard right.

Cheyennes
Grinnell, II
214-284(Sun
Dance, 5-day
ceremonies)

"That's what I said—that's what I saw," Maxwell said. "In many Indian tribes—Cheyennes among them—every year a few men do this 'Sun Dance.' First, a medicine man or chief ties rawhide strings to the skewers, cuts the chest skin, inserts the skewers, then ties the strings to the end of a rope hanging down from a pole. Now the warrior is ready to stare at the sun and DANCE while he pulls against the rope hard enough to, after while, tear loose his skin! They call the dance 'swinging to the pole.'

"Sometimes, instead of the rope and pole, the pulling is done by two buffalo skulls weighing about 20 pounds tied to strings at each end of the skewer. 'Dragging skulls' they call that. Yeah, m'lad, it's a bloody, ex-CRUciat-ing sight—but you never hear a groan from the men, though some do faint when the skin breaks loose from their chests..."

Maxwell spent the rest of the hour telling about the dozen-a-day ceremonies for four days—waterless, foodless days for the "Sun Dancers"—the rituals, body-painting, singing, smoking, dancing, feasting, speeching...until Randy stopped trying to keep up with words or events.

Kit Carson
Guild/Carter
p216

His mind wandered to Kit Carson and why Maxwell was his closest friend. Kit at 33 was 10 years or so older than Maxwell. Kit was short standing next to Maxwell, although his shoulder and arm muscles bulged just as big. Kit's talking was quiet and low. Kit got on a horse smooth and steady, and Maxwell jumped on with a rush, a leap, a bump. They were like...an antelope and a bear.

Well, he'd heard Kit say Maxwell was honest and true and goodhearted and openhanded, so that must be why Kit specially liked Maxwell and didn't seem to notice irritating things like how loud Maxwell talked when he talked at all.

Randy's ears caught some words that took hold of his curiosity..."first white man the 'Rapahoes saw a hundred or so years ago scared'um so bad they ran away. Old folks told me their grandparents thought the mysterious white-faced people had come out of the ground, or from a hole in a hill! 'Course that was when 'Rapahoes were settled farmers east of the

Cheyennes
Grinnell, II
p38

Mississippi, and had no guns or horses or wheels and carts."

With a short laugh, Fremont said, "What a change in the way they lived after whites and other Indians pushed them west to the prairie! They had to quit farming, by the mid-

Warriors of
the Plains.
C.Taylor,
p19,20

1700's got guns and horses like most other Indians. On the prairie, they moved their tent villages as they roamed the plains to kill buffalo. Making war on each other to capture more horses and guns became the major occupation, the way to status and wealth—horse wealth.

"When we came along, they made war and stole from us, too !" Maxwell added. He began talking about how the new way of life changed the personalities of the Plains Indian men. "I learned from them that the measure of a man was his daring during battles, how many times he got close enough to an enemy to touch him—a 'coo'—and got clean away. Back in camp he had to become a bragger, compete with other warriors in making a big drama out of every 'coo,' spend most of his day decorating his body in colored paints, feathers, animal claws, teeth and horns.

Pictorial History of Am.Indian. O.LaFarge, p156

"O, they've become up-tight, high-strung, competitive men, very artsy about dressing themselves for this new, exciting life. I include Arapahoes and Cheyennes, but to a lesser degree than the Sioux or the Crows."

Cheyennes. Grinnell II, p211-13

Randy looked around at the Cheyennes riding behind him. Had Maxwell's loud voicing of "Cheyenne" and "Arapaho" bothered them?

It seemed they hadn't noticed. All three had twisted themselves at the waist to look behind them at a more entertaining scene. Bernier, riding beside Mr. Preuss at the end of the line behind Ayot, Lajeunesse, the pack horse, and the packmule, was trying to show and tell his companion how NOT to lift himself above the saddle to ease his tortured bottom.

JF Report July 5 (Preuss's complaints)

Dr. Berney, as most of the men in camp had begun calling him after he yanked Carson's shoulder back in place, was speaking French, uncertain English, and no German in a sliding scale, nasal sing-song. Mr. Preuss was creating a duet with an unmelodic, lengthy line of, "No, no, no, no, no, no, no, no!"

His feet out of the stirrups, knees bent, hands grasping the saddle's pommel and back ridge, Mr. Preuss was trying to lift a leg at a time across the horse, turn his plump body sideways or even to face the rear of the animal. "Just for a change! Just for relief!" he kept adding to his "No, no, no" song while the horse kept moving along at Fremont's giddity-up pace.

"Monsieur Le Preuss! Stop! Stop!" shrilled Bernier reining his horse close to Preuss's side. "C'est impossible! Voo-goan deezmount, boom, to zee EART'!"

Mr. Preuss had just realized that. "Zo! vaht else can I do, Doctor?! Sitting backvard might feel better zan sitting zee vay I've been. My sore bottom vas constantly hitting zis saddle viz EVERY bounce of zee horse's five-mile-an-hour high step. Zis has put me in misery! I told zat foolish man, zat smarty Lieutenant, how I suffer riding a horse at even a slow valk, but he paid no attention, and now—"

"Monsieur Le Pro-ees! Say not bad t'ings of de grand Lieutenant!" Bernier flared, his voice running the musical scale top to bottom and back again. "Permettez-moi to geeve de coo-shion!" He pulled his blanket padding from under himself and handed it to Mr. Preuss. Face bright crimson, Mr. Preuss managed a French, "Merci," stood in his stirrups to pull the extra softening and extra height under his bottom.

Lajeunesse called to him, "Why didn't you bring your buffalo robe to sit on soft and high like a prince or an Indian and leave the saddle behind?!"

Mr. Preuss glared.

Lajeunesse laughed aloud, Yo grinned, the Indians shrugged, sat up straighter on their saddleless ponies, and Randy, giggling in the front line, turned to face forward again and listen to Maxwell.

Warriors of the Plains. C.Taylor p85(wars) p21(language)

"You wanted to know how Arapahoes and Cheyennes can live in the same territory and even camp side by side without fighting? Well, both tribes had for a long time hunted peacefully in the Bent's Fort area of the Santa Fe Trail on the edge of the plains. When Fort St. Vrain was built 200 miles northwest in the mountains four, no, five years ago, both tribes liked this TWO-fort area even more. They liked living on wooded streams close to the buffalo trails and also close to where robes and furs could be traded for white man's goods.

"But the Comanches, a big tribe in Texas, liked the same conveniences, made war to drive the two smaller tribes out and take their place. Arapahoes and Cheyennes had sense enough to join forces, beat the bowlegged Comanches in a big battle on Wolf Creek, chase them and their Apache allies back south.

"But, can you believe it, Lieutenant, two years later those same four tribes allied themselves to resist the whites if too many began coming, taking too many buffalo, too much land. Their Great Peace, as they call it, is bound to cause us a lot of trouble sooner or later."

"Surely not sooner," Fremont countered, "or Kit would have mentioned that to me."

"Not THIS soon!" laughed Maxwell. "The Great Peace is less than two years old! Besides, we have Pat and Mike who can hold off the Cheyennes, and you have ME to help Pat and Mike talk us out of any trouble with Arapahoes."

Fremont surmised that their languages must be similar. "They can understand each other? You can understand both languages, Max?"

Not knowing that his language skill would soon be put to a critical test, Maxwell lightly declared that, with the words he knew added to sign language, he could handle any problem—if they had any. "A bigger worry for you, Lieutenant, should be whether Pat's folks—I'm pretty sure we'll meet them—will serve you stewed dog! It's a serious insult if you don't eat what Indians offer you."

Maxwell, prompted by Fremont's questions, talked on about how the Indians bred and raised puppies to eat "the way we raise chickens," about dogfeasts he had enjoyed, about observing a dog-dinner preparation from the squaw's raised tomahawk-mallet through her singeing off the fur, dropping diced puppy, insides, skin, and all, into the boiling pot, and—

Oregon Trail.
F.Parkman,
p106
(dog stew)

Randy, overloaded with dog-eating details, suddenly reined his pony out of line and headed in the opposite direction, his nose and mouth crumpled with wrinkles. "Oh, something's going on back there about Mr. Preuss—just want to see what it is," he flung back to Fremont who'd turned his head questioningly. Fremont twisted around further to take a look at Mr. Preuss, too.

He was standing in his stirrups. His distant voice was pitched to the tone and rhythm of unresolvable complaints.

Fremont wheeled his horse out of the line and trotted to catch up with Randy, now close enough to Bernier to call out a question. "C'est serieux, Docteur?" Bernier made a helpless gesture with his hands. "C'est le derriere de Monsieur Pro-eess—il lui fait bien peine. Sitting in the saddle pains his bottom."

"Stop your horse, Mr. Preuss!" Fremont ordered. "Now, Mr. Preuss, is that better? Doctor Bernier says you're in much pain. One more hour before we stop for mid-day rest and food—can you bear to sit your saddle another hour?"

JF Report
July 5
(Preuss's
complaints)

Red-faced, grouchy as a snapping turtle, Mr. Preuss began a fervent analysis of his difficulty: It was his high bounce and fall in the saddle when the horse walked as fast as Fremont had set. It was also the distended belly of the horse—"so bulging my legs are in danger of being split off at ze groin or hip joint."

He eased his bottom down on his double cushion to demonstrate. His spraddled legs stuck out nearly straight from the sides of the horse, and he groaned miserably while pulling them close enough to toe into the stirrups. "Your leg joints are indeed quite stiff, and that's a pity, Mr. Preuss," Fremont observed. "But...Mr. Preuss, pardon a delicate question. Do you have hemorrhoids?"

The deepest red Fremont had ever seen on Mr. Preuss's face gave him the answer.

"We will march at our old, slower pace, Mr. Preuss. Stand in your stirrups as long as your leg muscles will

274

allow. I think I saw in the distance a tree by the river, so we should in less than an hour be able to stop in its shade for a rest."

Fremont cupped his hands around his mouth and shouted to the men ahead on their fast-pacing horses, "Column slow down!" He returned with Randy to the front of the line to lead a slower, kinder-to-the-bottom march.

Under the skimpy shade of three willows, they ate a handful of hard bread, drank their canteens dry while the animals, refreshed by Platte River water, grazed the plentiful browning grass. "Max will shoot the first buffalo we see, and we'll have a good supper of meat, fresh bread, and coffee with sugar," Fremont promised.

Slowly the ten men and twelve animals marched through the afternoon hours. Nobody talked. After two hours of boredom, Randy wished even Maxwell would start something, but he stayed humped over, silent, his interest in recounting Life Among the Arapahoes dried up. The silent, hot hours, minutes, seconds crept, dragged, even seemed to stop still. The landscape stayed the same old grass and distant hills, only more barren.

Fremont silently counted the miles he was short of his 40-mile goal. At the other end of the line, Mr. Preuss stayed press-lipped and soundless. Randy, looking back at him occasionally, saw him standing in his stirrups for long minutes at a stretch. "If we have to think about his bottom all ten days, I almost wish I hadn't begged to come," he thought to himself. Was anybody else thinking the same thing? he wondered.

Maxwell had to wade his horse across the river when the sun was nearing the horizon to come close to the only buffalo they'd seen in any direction—three long-bearded, slow-moving bulls. He shot and shot, and shot again before wounding one bull enough to stop it for a last, fatal shot. Max brought back the "boss"—fleshy, fat, back hump, exceedingly rich and tender and big as a man's head—the ribs and two-foot-long tongue, both favorites of hungry men—and the liver.

When he arrived at the little group of scraggly cottonwoods where Fremont had called a halt by the river, a wood and buffalo-chip fire was burning, cooking sticks had been sharpened, settled-out river water waited in the coffee pot. 'Yo,' the cook, was ready to throw coffee into the water and stir up bread dough.

JF Report
July 5
(Maxwell, hunter)
(no coffee,no salt)

"My god! I can't believe this!" shouted Lajeunesse digging through the mulepack. "Somebody who was told to pack coffee and sugar and flour packed NOTHING! If I could get my hands on the short-brained cook now on his way to the North Platte, I'd—I'd—I'd STARVE him!"

275

Fremont, angry and distressed, gritted his teeth as he looked around at his tired, hungry men and the young boy he shouldn't have allowed to come. He tried to sound calm. "At least Maxwell has brought in the meat," he said. "Let's get it cooking."

Even the hump of the old bull was stringy, and the rib meat required serious chewing. "Where's the salt?" "Ain't no salt." "Sacre bleu!" "Sunuva dawg." "This sure ain't nothing like last night's Fourth of July party." Silence while they chewed grouchily and long.

Some were still chewing when they took their blankets long before twilight and without a word to the others, lay down to sleep. Randy's last thought was of fruitcake made in St. Louis.

The first sound he heard was "Turn out!" The sun and Fremont were up, the fire was crackling, squares of bull's tongue and liver, the only chewable edibles left, were broiling at the ends of last night's long sticks. But the mood of the camp was so gloomy, Fremont decided to make his probably cheering announcement first thing.

"Good friends, in view of yesterday's miseries and mishaps, and also of the next nine days' considerable hardships, I have determined that it is the better part of wisdom to send our ailing Mr. Preuss back after breakfast to our column now no doubt marching along North Fork toward Laramie."

A noise sounding almost like the start of a spontaneous cheer, but quickly suppressed, greeted Fremont's decision. Mr. Preuss did not suppress his deep, loud sigh of relief. Fremont observed that Mr. Preuss's horse also appeared in no condition to support the rest of the South Platte journey, and therefore Doctor Bernier, "whom we all know as one of our most trusty men, will accompany and attend Mr. Preuss, make sure that he and his horse have a safe, slow, easy march north to intercept the main party. I expect the two will arrive today at the column's evening camp. If not, they will surely find the trail and rejoin the group tomorrow."

JF Report
July 6
(Preuss sent back to North Fork crew)

Buffalo liver never tasted so good. Good spirits restored, Fremont, Randy, Basil, Maxwell, Yo, and the three Cheyennes waved and waved and shouted, "Good luck!" many times to the two men riding away to the north. Mr. Preuss looked quite comfortable seated on one blanket. Doctor Bernier, seated on his own blanket again, waved back languidly, even wistfully, to the adventurers he was leaving behind.

With Mr. Preuss and Dr. Bernier gone to join the North Platte column, Fremont's party of six men and two boys rides west and south within sight of the nearly treeless South Platte. Arapaho interpreter Maxwell, Fremont, Randy, and, at his request, Tuesday, lead the way. Behind them, Lajeunesse keeps a wary eye on the hot, sandy, barren plain. Yo leads the pack animals, while Pat and Mike Cheyenne keep to themselves off to the side.

CHAPTER 26

WILD HORSES AND OLD BUFFALO BULLS

July 6-7, South Platte trail (Colorado)

Mr. Preuss and Dr. Bernier had not slow-walked their
horses away from camp for more than ten minutes before
Fremont made his second surprise announcement of the
day. "My assistant Mr.Preuss having departed, I am
appointing Randy Benton to replace him to help me carry
out the scientific duties of our expedition."

*Randy episodes
not in JF Report*

Seeing four mouths drop open and eyebrows curve
upward in surprise, Fremont quickly added, "Mr. Benton
(Randy's mouth widened further—MR. Benton!) is the only
one in our present party who has some training and experience in using the sextant to shoot the stars—that is, making
use of the light of the North Star, which appears to be sta-
tionary in the sky, to create an angle with us on the
ground. The sextant discovers the angle and measures it.
Its size is our Latitude, our distance NORTH of the
Equator—Earth's midwaist and Latitude zero baseline.

"Mr. Benton will also assist me in finding the exact spot
UPON our Latitude line where we are—that is, where we are
WEST of the Earth's TIME baseline. It's in England. As
you know, clocks measure time—and the number of hours
between us and England will measure how far apart we are
along an east-west line of latitude. To do this, Mr. Benton
and I must use TWO clocks—one showing the hour in
England, the other showing the hour where we are. We sub-
tract our hour from England's and the difference tells us
where is the exact spot on our line of Latitude for a dot
representing our camp!"

Maxwell, Yo, and Lajeunesse followed each word closely,
stared with new interest at Randy after Fremont's revelations—and others that followed. "Mr. Benton's years of
schooling in Washington and St. Louis have trained him in
arithmetic to a level high enough for him to help me with
calculations, and in reading to easily find information in
astronomical almanac tables.

"He is also proficient in holding a lantern when and
where I want it. Another job he will do is read and record
daily the heights of the mercury columns of both the

278

barometer and the thermometer."

Yo, Lajeunesse, and all the other workmen in the expedition, had heard weeks ago that Randy could read and write, something they—except for Maxwell and camp manager Lambert—had never been taught to do. Now Yo and Lajeunesse were hearing not only how Fremont used his mysterious scientific instruments, but ALSO that this 12-year-old Randy knew enough reading, writing, and 'rithmetic to take Mr. Preuss's place helping Fremont! They stared at Randy in silent wonder.

Randy, not used to hearing himself talked about as a scientist who knew just about everything, blushed, bit his lower lip, stared at the ground, and wondered if he really could do all those things John had said. But listen! John was saying Mr. Benton could do even more!

"I will take on Mr. Preuss's job of drawing a rough map of our travels," Fremont said. "I will rely on Mr. Benton to print neatly the names of rivers, mountains, and other geographic details. In short, Mr. Benton and I will together do the scientific work Mr. Preuss would be doing if his...umm, derriere had held up better."

Maxwell yelped with laughter so loud it seemed to echo from the hills. Basil and Yo added to the volume, the Cheyennes looked puzzled but on the verge of joining them, when Fremont began waving his hands, signaling them to quiet down. "Shhh! Not so noisy! Preuss'll hear this raucous laughing and think the worst—that we're making fun of him! That could make for future problems. He's not yet a mile away—moving very slowly you know.

"Let me say here that Mr. Preuss, for all his peculiarities, is a competent map maker, draws excellent landscapes—"

Randy blurted out, "I can't draw anything, John! But Tuesday can! Let him draw pictures of EVERYthing!"

"Well, Randy, if we happen upon a scene of such interest that my report will need it, I'll hand Tuesday some paper and a pencil," Fremont said.

"Something else you can do, Randy, is substitute for our weatherman, Moise Chardonnier. I wish I'd included him in our group. None of us will blame you, Mr. Benton, if the rain you predict turns into shine. We know you have only a barometer to guide you, not Moise's unmatchable sky and wind intuition."

Lajeunesse enthusiastically predicted that Mr. Benton would out-predict Moise and out-read, write, 'n'figure Mr.

Preuss. "Yessir, Lieutenant! Mr. Benton's appointment to dis scientific position has already improved de spirits of everybody, and de horses and packmule! Look how dey're watching, real interested like us, deir ears straight up!"

"Excellent start for my new assistant," Fremont declared, smiling at Randy. "Now, let's load up and start on our way."

Fremont took the lead with Maxwell on his right and Randy, feeling a little self-conscious as MR. Benton, on his left. "I'd like for Tuesday to ride next to me," Randy said. "Then call him up, Mr. Benton, call him up," Fremont and Maxwell said in unison.

"Where have all the buffalo gone?" Fremont asked after some minutes of looking around at the plains and hills. "This is the second day that the prairie's been empty. Have the herds all passed to the south—or can we expect more? I hate to think that we'll have nothing to eat but old bull like the one you killed yesterday. Or possibly not even old bull. It's a worry."

JF Report
July 6

"No buffalo herds means no Indians in the area are hunting them, alarming them into running away," Maxwell said. "For us, that's good—no run-ins with Indians who might be Oglalas or Pawnees, not Cheyennes or 'Rapahoes. But food WILL to be a worry if the plains stay empty many more days—which has been known to happen. Remember how many songs and dances the Indians have for begging the buffalo to show up and save them from starving?

"However," Maxwell continued, "during July, there'll be enough lone bulls showing up that WE won't go hungry. We may have aching jaws from chewing, but old bull meat will keep us alive and well."

"Why July for lone bulls, Maxwell?"

"Mating season. It's the time when young bulls will gang up on the Old Leader to end his long years as boss of the herd—the only bull having his pick of the females. If just ONE young bull attacks, an experienced old fellow can outwit and beat him—kill him even. But a gang-attack by six young bulls will end the old fellow's 20 or so glorious years as Top Bull.

Cheyennes.
Grinnell I, p269
(mating season)

Buffalo Book.
D.Darey, p145-
151 (old bulls)

"If he gets away alive, he daren't come back. He just staggers around wounded, alone, an outcast, until he topples over, or a wolf kills him, or a hungry hunter like me comes along. Back in the herd, fights among young bulls decide which one takes the Old Leader Bull's place."

Randy had leaned forward, listening intently. He blurted out a question. How old did Maxwell think the old bull was that he killed yesterday for supper? "Oh, years older than me. Probably older than Kit Carson. PROBABLY old as Mr. Preuss."

JF Report
July 6
("almost unendurably hot")

Burning heat of the sun shimmered over the featureless landscape, a sandy repeat of the day before. Monotonous rhythm of moving horse feet numbed the men's minds, dry air stiffened and silenced their tongues—until an unusual sight suddenly appeared.

It was a spot of green appearing in the distance away from the edge of the Platte. A creek! Water! Clear, perhaps cool water! Ahhh! it must be there in that little oasis of green trees, that tiny dot of green all alone on these blank expanses of short, dry grass reaching to the edge of the blue bowl of sky.

JF Report
July 6
(dry river)

At the first sighting of the green dot, Fremont had cried out the day's first "Gitty-UP!" and led the trot to the river. The closer they came, the less it looked like a river...or creek...or creeklet...or trickle. "It's a used-to-be river," Lajeunesse called it when they stopped by the wide ribbon of long-dried sand.

"It's a sometime river," Maxwell corrected him. "Comes a pouring rain and all of a sudden down that dry, flat bed of sand will roll a wall of water tall as a man, powerful as a herd of running buffalo. Run for your life! Flash flood!"

JF Report
July 6
("fort")

The green dot was real trees, a grove of large old willows. When the men pushed aside the hanging, curtain-like strands of leaves and led their horses through them to an open circle of space, they saw a puzzling structure. A fort? Upright sapling poles set close together in the ground fenced in a large oval area. Many poles soft with rot were sagging or had already collapsed. Just outside the stockade, scattered trees with branches still attached lay rotting on the ground.

Fremont guessed that a large band of warriors had attacked the Indians in the fort, and battled their way inside. "Killed—scalped—everybody?!" exclaimed Randy. Maxwell pointed out that there wasn't a single bone anywhere and no sign of fire. "Also, I've never seen an Indian village, not even a winter camp, enclosed by a big stockade fence."

Cheyennes.
Grinnell, I
p292 ("fort" is
deserted Indian
wild horse corral)

He spoke to Pat and Mike in Cheyenne, picturing the words with hand signs. Pat answered. Mike added more. "Now who woulda guessed it!" Maxwell said. "This must be an area where herds of wild horses roam. Pat and Mike tell me this 'fort' was a corral and trading post built by the Kiowa Indians, who used to roam and claim these parts. They caught wild horses, kept them in this corral to sell or trade to other Indians!

"Cheyennes and Arapahoes, moving down from the north, fought the Kiowas and Comanches, pushed them outta here about 15 or 20 years ago. So maybe 25 years ago, this quiet little grove of trees was a noisy place of business!"

Three hours farther on under the burning sun, they found a "here-and-now river" as Lajeunesse called it. Clear water running through hot, barren sands! Beautiful water flowing down a broad valley glowing with acres of yellow sunflowers! It seemed to Randy as he drank and splashed that such a dreamy place might have more vanishing power than staying power. Where did it come from?

JF Report
July 6
(Lodgepole R.)

Fremont repeated what Kit had told him the night Randy made his case for traveling the South Platte: "First for-sure stream you'll come to is Lodgepole Creek. Its water runs straight east 200 miles downhill from the Rockies into the South Platte."

Randy dried off in the heat, then wilted again as the horses plodded under a sun that aimed its scorching rays straighter and straighter at him. Head bowed, shoulders slumped, he didn't notice when the horses stopped hours later at midday. "Are you all right, Randy-boy?" he heard John say, and felt his hand on his shoulder.

"Oh. Yeah. Fine." Not the slightest whimper, he'd promised John. He slid off his pony and sat down under one of the spreading cottonwood trees by the river. No Randy-moan called attention to his giddy head, no sigh betrayed his queasy innards when Yo handed him crackers and water for lunch.

"You rest here in the shade," Fremont said. "I'll hang up the barometer and thermometer, and I'll call out the mercury heights for you to write down." He hung on a low tree limb the board with two attached, slender glass tubes, then gave Randy the pencil and record book.

Ency.Britannica.
11th ed.,Vol.2
p420)Barometer

"Ready? The barometer mercury in the glass has reached 26...umm...point 235 air pressure on the measuring scale. We'll convert that later into feet—our height above sea level. In the high mountains, air pressure is less, so it pushes the mercury column less high. Tomorrow when we're 40 miles farther west on this plain that looks flat but is gradually rising, you'll see that the mercury column won't quite reach today's 26.235 air pressure.

"Now for the thermometer measuring air temperature. Mercury column in the glass is up to...89 degrees? PHEW!! Felt a lot hotter out in the sun!—more like 99!"

Basil Lajeunesse and Yo had come close to watch Randy write down the words and numbers. "Oh dat's pretty, Randy. One of dese days I'm gonna study up how to do dat," Yo said, and Basil murmured, "Me, too."

Out in the sun, almost ready to leave, Fremont insisted on fitting his high-crown, broad-brim Army hat over Randy's small straw hat for two-layered insulation from the heat. Randy wanted to take it off—the Indians were laughing at him. "Keep it on, Mr. Benton. It makes you look older and wiser—AND you won't risk sunstroke."

Episode added.

"But Lieutenant! YOU're risking sunstroke if you go out dere bareheaded in dis heat! Can't let you do dat!" Basil snatched off his turban—his blue cotton shirt deftly rolled and wound—and pulled it firmly over Fremont's curls. "You look like a Sultan, Sir!" Before Fremont could protest, Basil had slipped off his red waistsash, was draping it over his own head, tying it under his chin, and striking a bullfighter's pose.

Everybody laughed—the Indians laughing the broadest and loudest anyone had ever seen them. Maxwell pulled the red bandana from around his neck, tied each corner into a knot, fitted it to Tuesday's head like a square, bill-less cap. Tuesday—and Pat and Mike—laughed and laughed until tears ran, while they bowed and bowed thanks with their hands.

"We look like a band of gypsies or a caravan out of Arabian Nights," Fremont said, then flapped his horse's reins, and clucked "go."

JF Report
July 6
(storm)

Two hours later, Fremont and Maxwell were conferring about emergency measures for the over-heated animals when a clap of thunder interrupted them. "I predict a rain storm!" Randy shouted. Within minutes, a blast of wind struck them, lightning flashed, thunder drummed across dark cloudheads rolling in on the back of a fierce wind. Squalls of rain powered by wind gusts slammed into men and animals, blinding them. "Halt!" came Fremont's voice wavering through the lashing water. "About face! Backs to the wind!" With wind and water pounding their backs, they waited, dreading the fiery flashes that could strike and kill, holding their soaked hats and turbans and headcovers until their arms ached.

In less than half-an-hour, the whirling winds had dragged away the bloated clouds and all the water and noisy terror they contained.

"So we've cooled off, had a bath, and the animals have revived," Fremont said. "We'll be dry by suppertime. Any sign of an old outcast bull, Maxwell?"

Near sunset, there was, and Maxwell brought the best cuts to cook at the camp they set up under trees on an island in the shallow Platte. "Dis bull must be no older dan I am," judged 20-year-old Yo, smacking his lips. "No, your appetite makes your teet' sharper," said Basil.

JF Report
July 6
Island

At sunset, Randy read the height of the barometer's column of mercury, and recorded it. "But it's a LOT less than it was this morning," Randy said, "and we aren't on top of a high hill! We haven't come any 40 miles west today either."

JF Report
July 6
lower air pressure

"It's not recording height this time," Fremont answered. "This fall in the mercury says 'low air pressure' for another reason—bad weather. Temperature's down, wind's rising, clouds could drop some rain. A low-pressure weather system is moving in. But if the wind beats off the clouds and clears the sky, I might possibly do some star shooting tonight. Think you'll feel up to it, Mr. Benton?"

Mr. Benton went with him carrying the lantern soon after the Cheyennes had lain down on the grass and Basil, Yo, and Maxwell were asleep rolled up in their blankets under a tree. Away from the trees, Mr. Benton held the lantern so John could see the sextant while he set the index arm to point at zero on its measuring arc.

By the time Fremont had focused the telescope on the North Star's twinkle in the mercury of the horizon box, finely adjusted the top mirror, and at last called for the lantern to light up the index arm and arc again, Mr. Benton's chin was sinking to his chest. He wrote down the angle number Fremont told him. "We're almost on the same line of latitude as Brady's Island," Fremont noted.

"I'd like to try determining our longitude by lunar distances and the chronometer," John said. "I brought the chronometer in my pocket, and I can use the telescope on the sextant. You can see your way without the lantern to our little makeshift tent, can't you? There's just room enough in the tent for both our heads and shoulders to have cover," Fremont said. "Our feet and legs will be sticking out, but at least half the body can keep dry if it rains.

JF Report
July 6
Longitude

JF Report
July 6
*(sleeping with
feet outside the
tent door)*

Go get some sleep, dear boy. I'll be there soon."

Into the A-shaped India-rubber-cloth tent held up by rifles, their butt ends on the ground, muzzle ends tied together above, Randy crawled with his blanket. No matter his feet and legs were outside the small shelter, in two seconds he was sound asleep, the wind moaning close by his head. He hardly noticed when Fremont scrambled inside, or when a light shower dampened his feet.

JF Report
July 7
*(buffalo,
wild horses)*

"The buffalo have come!" At sunrise, the words flew like a bugle call over the camp. Dozens of grazing buffalo herds, large and small, dotted the plains on both sides of the river. "No more worry about food!" exulted Fremont. "GOOD food, I'm talking about! A young fat cow! Right, Maxwell?"

"Right," Maxwell answered, but reminded Fremont that buffalo all around them meant hunters in the area were at work. Could be dangerous! Best to hurry on, get farther away. "Gitty-up!" Fremont called to his horse.

Randy enjoyed watching the buffalo so much the next few hours, he decided that plodding across barren plains wasn't boring at all as long as you could see other live creatures running and playing not far away.

More creatures came running in late morning—wild horses, a herd of them! The Indians saw them first in the river bottoms a mile or so away. The Cheyennes rushed back, began babbling to Maxwell, pointing to the pack horse, a spirited and fleet animal that Yo was leading.

"Mike says," Maxwell told Fremont, "he won't be able to face his people if he doesn't take home a big, fine horse—that the lead horse of this wild drove is a rare prize. To catch it, he needs a better mount than his small-size, short-legged Indian horse. He has his eye on our fleet-footed packhorse."

Fremont quickly said "Unload it! We'll rest here until Mike returns. Give him a rope to lasso the leader!"

The horse race was on! Randy moved out of line to join Tuesday and Pat across a half-mile of marly clay that today was underfoot, the sand of yesterday having almost suddenly disappeared. "Look at Mike run!" Randy yelled. "He's catching up—and they've not seen him! "NOW! THROW! QUICK!" Tuesday shouted, "NA-WA! NA-WA!" and began to swing his right arm sideways, his pointing finger tracing in the air a spiral like a twirling rope. "NA-WA!" he called to Mike. Pat leaned forward on his horse watching intently, one hand shading his eyes, but shouting no instructions to his brother.

Wah-To-Yah.
L.Garrard, p105
(Na-wah quick)

285

Based on Alfred Jacob Miller, 18--

"Throw the rope! Throw the rope! NOW!" Randy yells. But Mike's fleet horse thunders on, Mike's lasso twirling but unthrown. "They're getting away!" Randy cries. The herd disappears in a cloud of dust. Mike turns back. "Aww. He saved his big throw for the fine lead horse and lost them all," Randy fumes. "Wah-son-ne," murmurs Tuesday. Randy knows that means "foolish man." Soon he'll hear "wah-son-ne" again in a moment of great danger.

Mike easily overtook the closest animals of the group—and PASSED them! He was urging his horse on, thundering alongside the now alarmed and fleeing herd. "Throw the rope! Throw the rope! Quick!" Randy was yelling. Tuesday was yelling "Na-wa! Na-wa!" But Mike's fleet horse thundered on, Mike's lasso twirling, Mike's lasso unthrown.

JF Report
July 7
(lasso unused)

Pat called to Tuesday. The boy's excited expression melted into a frown. His shoulders slumped. Only Randy kept shouting at Mike. "Rope the closest one! What's the matter, Mike??!! They're all getting away! Throw the rope! Throw the rope!"

But the lead stallion in a burst of speed now far outstripped Mike's mount, leading the herd out of reach, disappearing in a cloud of dust. Mike's mount slowed to a walk, turned back toward Pat and two disappointed boys. The boys looked at each other, their faces showing the same message as their muttered words. "Foolish man." "Wah-son-ne."

Wah-To-Yah.
L.Garrard,p59
(wah-son-ne,
fool)

Randy clucked to his pony and headed back to camp. What would Pat be saying to his brother? Why did Pat stop Tuesday's yelling "Na-wa—Na-wa?"

During the afternoon, signs of a second animal drama appeared—puffs of dust rising behind a sandy ridge. Fremont stopped the column. "I hear buffalo bellowing over there!" Randy exclaimed.

A chorus of, "Let's go see!" and the whole party headed their horses for the ridge. At the crest, they looked down a slight slope at a crowd of young, fat bulls in a ring around a huge, gaunt, old bull on his knees, front legs folded under him. The young bulls had just knocked him down.

JF Report
July 7
(young bulls
attack old)

Buffalo Book.
D.Dary, p145-149
(young attack old)

He struggled almost to his feet, but fell again when the young bulls, bellowing in rage, struck him again with savage head butts and horn slashes, badly wounding him. "A few more of those and he'll be dead!" Maxwell declared. "This is the gang attack I told you about—and if we don't break it up, that old buffalo will never live to roam the plains again, even as an outcast!"

JF Report
July 7

"Aim and fire!" Fremont commanded.

Randy hauled his pistol from its holster and pulled back the hammer. Suppose he fired it and killed a buffalo?! Buffalo Boy! The thought was so overwhelming he lost track for a blank moment of what was going on.

Bang! Pow! Boom! all four—five?—men were firing and yelling. The young buffaloes paid no attention but continued butting and gashing the fallen old bull—until one young bull

Young buffalo bulls gang up on the Old Leader to end his many years as herd boss as well as mate to the females. Randy hears their bellowing and all Fremont's party comes to watch a half-dozen young bulls encircle a huge old bull, knock him down, slash him with their horns. "Aim and fire!" Fremont shouts. Young bulls run, Old Bull staggers off alone to finish life as an outcast. One young bull lies dead–from Randy's shot?

suddenly collapsed. Whose gunfire had struck him? Randy's pistol barrel felt hot to his hand. He saw the trigger had been pulled.

The young buffaloes were turning from Old Bull, then running away, bumping into each other, fighting as they fled in a gallop toward the river. Fremont and his men reloaded their rifles and rode after them. Randy and the Cheyennes, staying behind, watched the old, bloodied bull hobble away in the opposite direction, heard gunfire as young buffalo bulls and hunters disappeared behind a low ridge.

Randy and the Cheyennes dismounted and cautiously walked close to the young bull lying sprawled on the ground. Anxious to find out where the gunshot had entered the animal, Randy hoped he could tell whether it was from a pistol or rifle. Tuesday pointed to Randy's pistol, now secure in its holster, and his face and fingers asked the question: "Did you fire it?" Randy's cheeks reddened. Maybe. Yes, he must have when all the other guns went off. But did his bullet hit—kill—the buffalo?

Jeff Hengesbaugh
(size of shot wound)

The Cheyennes poked the buffalo with arrows to make certain the animal was truly dead before searching its huge body for the fatal wound. Randy saw the hole was big, made by a large rifle ball, not a bullet from his pistol.

Tuesday's eyes were asking the question. Randy shook his head. With a gesture, Tuesday said, "Too bad," and turned away.

Standing alone while the three Cheyennes examined the dead bull and murmured to each other, Randy thought of the day when Tuesday killed a bull, how he and Pat and Mike had danced and chanted and sung when they entered the camp circle. Nothing like that today for Randy Benton. He bit his lip in disappointment.

Just then, Yo rode up with the pack-animals in tow, and a babbled story about a near disaster he'd kept from happening. As he dismounted, he began rattling off the details of how it happened that he'd left the packhorse and mule alone, unsecured, when he got caught up in the buffalo excitement. "I wuz right up dere wid de Lieutenant chasing that pack of bulls! Forgot everyt'ing!

JF Report
(runaway animals)

"Dem packcritters saw dat and took it into deir heads to depart at a run! Dey wuz taking wid'um de Lieutenant's scientific instruments and all our baggage! Dey was gonna join up backpacks and all wid a herd of wild horses on de prairie for sure! Oh mon Dieu! Saw'um just in time!

"I cut loose from de buffalo chase and took after'um!

289

Dey wuz a mile away but dey wasn't running fast wid all dem heavy packs on deir backs. Dey wuz easy trotting 'long-side one anot'er so when my horse rushed up I could grab holda deir reins.

"Saints a-mercy, what a desperate t'ing if'n I hadn't seed'um in time! But I don't find not'ing in dem packs out of place or missing. Not'ing lost or broken, grace a Dieu!"

Heaving sighs of relief as he worked, Yo secured the pack-animals and his horse with hobbles, then turned his attention to the dead buffalo. "De Cheyennes got no knives? Dey can have mine, and Basil and Max'll be here in a minute wid deirs. Randy, have you found out whose shot killed dis buffalo?"

Fremont, Maxwell, and Lajeunesse riding leisurely over the ridge called out the same question. Randy nodded his head. "Hey! I bet it wuz yours!" Yo said. "I bet it turns out your aim wuz better'n' de rest of us, Randy!"

Randy cringed. "They'll find out soon enough," he said to himself, and made himself watch the bloody butchering of the young bull during the next half-hour.

Under a huge old cottonwood that stood alone by the Platte—"like an old outcast bull," Fremont said—the eight men cooked the tender juicy meat, ate long and in amazing quantities. Lajeunesse and Maxwell teased Yo about almost making them packless, but the Lieutenant stopped them with a sentence or two of praise for Yo's quick action and successful chase.

An almost silent Randy, his stomach full of food and a mind full of pictures of the day's dramas, and regrets, could hardly drag himself to follow Fremont and hold the lantern while he worked. No one, not even Fremont, could have predicted for Randy that the next day would overflow with even more excitement, danger, and astonishing dramas, one right after another.

Beth Berryman

Based on C. Russell (left), F. Remington (right)

"Indians darted into view at the tops of hills, (then) two to three hundred naked to the breech cloth (started) sweeping across the prairie. We (began crossing) the river, (but) before we could reach the bank, down came the Indians upon us! Our fingers were on (our gun) triggers when Maxwell recognized the leading Indian and shouted to him in Indian language! (Looking shocked) at the sound of his own language...(the Chief) passed us like an arrow...swerved...I rode out toward him. He gave me his hand, struck his breast, exclaiming, "ArapaHO!"

(From Fremont's Report)

CHAPTER 27

"BULL TAIL! YOU KNOW ME—MAX!"

Morning, July 8, South Platte trail (Colorado)

The dramas of the day began when they saw a wide stretch in their path where the sandy earth was churned by the tracks of many horses—hundreds of them, it seemed to all eight men. All agreed, too, that the tracks were fresh.

JF Report
July 8

"Indians!" announced Maxwell solemnly. "And they're close by. Look around—the buffalo herds we saw earlier are nowhere in sight. They've run away from hunters. From the looks of these horse tracks, and these going down to the river for water, the hunters number two, maybe three hundred."

A chill ran down Randy's spine. Three hundred Indians! Suppose they were bad Indians, not good Cheyennes who knew Pat and Mike, or Arapahoes that Maxwell could talk to?! Randy looked around. Himself and four men with rifles. Three Indians with bows and arrows. He patted the pistol in his belt holster to make sure it was there, just in case.

He heard Fremont asking a question. "How old do you think these horse tracks are—an hour? a day? more than a day?" Maxwell recalled "the crazy rain" of the day before, and guessed the tracks would have been washed away if they'd been made before the rain. "So these tracks are less than a day old. But that doesn't tell us where the Indians are by now. Nor what kind," mused Fremont.

"Right," agreed Maxwell. "This is the edge of Cheyenne and 'Rapaho hunting grounds. It's close enough to Sioux tribes like the Oglalas, Hunkpapas, Two Kettles, or Minniconjous that a big force of any of them might come this far south of the North Platte to hunt. Cheyennes, 'Rapahoes, and Sioux are friends, remember. But some of these Sioux tribes are NOT friendly to whites—depending on whether something happened last week or this morning or ten minutes ago to offend them."

*Warriors of
the Plains.*
C.Taylor,p1

City of Saints.
R.Burton, p 98

Maxwell studied the landscape for a moment. Then he pointed to the low hills a mile distant on the same side of the river they were traveling. "The horse tracks to this spot are coming from that low ridge. Here along our bank of the river, this mass of tracks goes right on west, same as we're going. They could be about 25 miles ahead of us by now—a day's march...unless they've crossed the river. Or they may have turned back toward us for some reason, in which case we'll soon meet."

Fremont rubbed his beard thoughtfully. Randy caught his breath and swallowed hard. Basil and Yo looked at each other, their expressions asking if Maxwell was reading de tracks right, knew what he wuz talking about.

Basil, at Fremont's request, pulled the spyglass from the instrument pouch on the packmule. Holding it to one eye, Fremont turned his horse slowly so as to gaze at the dune-like hills on the right, the larger sand hills on the left a mile away, at the trail ahead, at the sand-laden stream flowing briskly from the Rockies, at some tolerably large groves of trees on the opposite riverbank. No movement, no dust, no dark spots on the distant horizon or on the vast, sandy plain of short, suntanned grass.

JF Report
July 8

Randy suddenly felt a flash of impatience. Why didn't they ask Pat and Mike—or Tuesday? He announced his question. "Pat and Mike've been looking at the tracks and everything. They'd know if they were made by Cheyenne ponies and horses—wouldn't they?"

Pat and Mike, who usually rode a half-mile or more behind the group, had caught up, and were sitting quietly on their mounts, feet dangling, arms folded across their bare chests. "Well, I 'spect they'd've spoken up by now had they thought they were seeing things we couldn't see for ourselves," Maxwell answered.

Fremont nodded toward the Indians and said, "Ask them if they can tell from horse tracks what tribe the riders belonged to—no, just ask them the plain question: Did Cheyenne horses make these tracks here?"

JF Report
July 8
(not Cheyenne
horse tracks)

"Wah-hein," came the answer from Pat. No.

Mike added a short phrase, then another, raised both open hands, closed them, opened them.

"He says these're too many horses to be his people's. His band is small—only 20 teepees," Maxwell said. "Two hundred hunters means 200 or more teepees."

Fremont observed that turning back or hiding for a time in a grove of trees across the river would solve little or nothing—since they didn't know where the hunters had gone. "We'll move ahead along the river—but try to keep out of sight." He led them down the river's low bank to the sandy edge of the river bottom. The embankment and its weeds were barely high enough to conceal them from horse-

JF Report
July 8
(keep out of sight)

293

men on the adjacent plains.

An hour later, Fremont, standing high in his stirrups to peer over the river bank with his telescope, cried out, "I see an AMAZING scene! Out there across the river, the ground for MILES is dotted with buffalo carcasses! They're bloody skeletons stripped of skin and meat! Can't be more than a day old!" All the men rose in their stirrups and strained to look through the weeds at the plain beyond. They saw small specks, tiny black lumps on the ground all the way to the hills—or so it seemed.

Randy, grunting with amazement and horror, said, "Why did they kill so many?!"

"For food," Maxwell told him. "They need thousands of pounds of fresh meat to feed their 200 families now, and many more thousands of pounds of dried meat for winter. So they make big kills when they have a chance. Hunters made a surround here. Probably three or four hundred buffalo skeletons lying out there.

"The hunters encircle a small herd, or part of a big herd, kill ALL the animals, send for the women to come do most of the skinning and butchering. So, a surround means the women are close by—which means we don't have just 200 hunters, we have a whole village to face. A thousand people—or more!"

"Sacre bleu!" rumbled Basil."T'ink of dat many people crossing dese hot, sandy plains of de South Platte! It's more'n a hundred miles from de Forks to where we are down here! Ain't we come a hundred miles dese past t'ree days?—and we were already 40 miles from de Forks!"

"Don't think the Indians crossing these plains would be just grown-ups," Maxwell added. "The whole village moves, all the women and children riding horses, too. The village herds of horses, mostly stolen from other tribes, would amount to as many as 2,000. Some would be loaded with lodge poles and buffalo-hide teepee covers.

"A few hundred more carry household equipment and personal bundles for every man, woman, and child, bedding, war trophies, weapons, good-luck-medicine bags. Also, iron cookpots, baskets of dried food, water-filled buffalo bladders, and a long list of items we more'n likely couldn't identify. At least a thousand barking dogs would be running in and out among the horses and people. A whole village on the move is a sight you'll never forget!

"A crowd that big can't travel more'n twenty miles a day.

Oregon Trail.
F.Parkman,p86
(village move)

294

They musta been days ahead of us and moving behind the hills on our right, else we'd've seen the dust they were raising," Maxwell continued. "Whoever they are, they'd be settled by now into a big camp, probably by the river on the same side we're traveling. Their hunters musta come outta camp to look for buffalo behind the hills, circled back, came onto a herd, did the 'surround' killing yesterday."

Fremont nodded, saying Maxwell's story made sense. "But couldn't the hunters be Arapahoes—not Sioux traveling from the Forks—where everyone says buffalo abound?" Fremont asked. "Don't Arapahoes share this territory with the Cheyennes?"

Maxwell said, well, yes, but it would take several bands getting together to have 200 or more men going out for a hunt. "From what I know about Arapahoes, that seems unlikely. There're just too many rivalries and jealouses between bands of the same tribe—and competition for food."

Oregon Trail.
F.Parkman,p125
(rivalries)

After another look around the whole horizon through the telescope, Fremont said, "Since we don't know who these hunters are, and our Cheyennes think they're not Cheyennes, we'd best be very watchful for the next few hours. Let's hope that the number of trees and brush continues to increase along the opposite river bank so that very soon we can cross to them and move along behind them 'til we're 'way past the Indian camp, which our best guessing says is on this side. If the hunters show up before then, we'll have to lie against the riverbank and shoot from the edge."

The little group of four men, a boy, and three Cheyennes went on quickly and cautiously, keeping to the river bottom-land, keeping an eye on the low hills to their right, listening. In spite of the heat, Randy shivered now and again. Not knowing WHO these maybe-thousands of maybe-unfriendly Indians were, nor WHERE they were, nor WHEN they'd show up, made him feel shaky inside. He wondered if John was scared. He didn't look scared.

JF Report
(Basil's mare
exhausted)

After an hour in the blazing sun, Basil spoke sharply to his mount. She had stopped, head bowed. "Allons! Allons! Let's go! Une halte est une grande erreur a ce moment! Non, non, non, non!! No 'reste', s'il vous plait!! Giddyup! Giddyup! GIDDYUP, JE VOUS COMMANDE!"

The mare did not move. Its head drooped even lower. As the other four riders kept up their quick pace and left him behind, Basil stroked the animal's neck and said in a gentle, coaxing tone, "Je vous en prie—a genoux! On my knees, I beg you, giddyup, mon chere!" The animal sagged, eyelids half-closed.

"Mon Dieu! You goin' lie down?!" Seeing he'd be spilled from his saddle if the animal suddenly collapsed, Lajeunesse slid to the ground. "HEY! LIEUTENANT! Dis animal is res-tay—given out—won't move—can't move!"

Up ahead, the four riders stopped while Fremont and Maxwell conferred. When they started up again, Randy reined his horse out of line and rode toward Basil. The message he brought wasn't cheering.

"They said to tell you that the only way you can get a res-tay animal to walk is for you to get off it and walk, too. You walk either behind to push, or in front to pull.

"That's going to be very slow! they said. But they said it won't help you or the horse if all of us slow down. Instead, it'd give the Indians a better chance to fall on us and, and, and kill EVERYbody! John says if he sees through the spyglass ANYthing moving on the plain, you'll see us galloping toward the nearest trees. You should run, too, with or without the horse for some trees across the river, and be ready to shoot.

"They said the Cheyennes will soon catch up with you. All of you run when you see danger. That's the plan. Awww, Basil, I wish your old mare hadn't gone res-tay! What's gonna happen to you!?"

Message delivered, Randy hurried back to Fremont, Maxwell, and Yo. For an hour or so, he glanced back every other minute at Basil walking beside the mare, slapping her flanks, walking in front pulling on her bridle, persuading her to keep moving. Finally the Cheyennes caught up, rode their mounts alongside and in front of the mare. She lifted her head and straightened her ears, cheered and strengthened by their company.

The presence of the Indian ponies seem to inspire her to try to imitate their walking pace—but she was too weak to keep up. The Cheyennes halted their mounts every hundred yards and waited for the drooping mare and anxious Basil. Before long, to Basil and the Cheyennes, and, it seemed, the mare, the four horsemen ahead were small dots, all moving rapidly away.

The four horsemen ahead took turns standing in their stirrups, stretching as high as they could to look for any sign of Indians or buffalo on the open plain. Fremont stared through the telescope long and frequently at the low, dunelike hills on the right, and occasionally at hills farther away on their left across the shallow river.

Nothing stirred.

The cool morning with a breeze—the thermometer had stood at 70 degrees when Randy checked it at 6 o'clock—had melted away under a heightening sun. The heat, the silence, the tedium of looking and looking at an empty expanse, became stupefying. Randy had a fit of yawning.

In the middle of a yawn, his gaze drifted left across the river and beyond. Did he see something on a hill? A dark spot? No! TWO dark spots! THREE—!

"John! Look left! Across the river!"

John looked. Maxwell looked. The faraway dots were just dots, even seen through the telescope. They moved very slowly, or were they moving at all? "I'm pretty sure that the Indian camp is on this side of the river, not on the left," Maxwell declared. "Those dots across the river look to me like buffalo. They're just some loners grazing."

False alarm. They plodded on.

Randy settled down in his saddle. The men seemed relaxed, talked of the day's mileage—10? 15? 17? They guessed how many more miles it was to St.Vrain's Fort—75? 80? Randy relaxed, too, and had begun lightly dreaming of asking Mother if he could go swimming in Rock Creek at Georgetown, when he heard Maxwell yell, "INDIANS! MY GOD!—on the LEFT—across the river!"

Randy jerked to attention. He looked behind him for Basil, saw the three Cheyennes whipping up their ponies furiously, galloping to the lead group, leaving Basil still walking beside his exhausted mare.

"There's a clump of trees ahead a half-mile! Make for it! Ready your rifles!" Fremont shouted.

But the horses and packmule did not respond to "gid-dyups" and heel prods or whacks with the reins. They acted almost as tired as Basil's mare. The best they could do was a slow canter.

At first, the distant Indians appeared to be no more than 15 or 20 in number, but group after group darted into view at the tops of the nearest hills on the left until all those little heights seemed in motion.

In a few minutes, two or three hundred dark-skin men, naked to the breech cloth, were sweeping on galloping horses across the prairie toward Fremont and his men. In only

JF Report
July 8
*(dots on left
not Indians)*

JF Report
July 8
*(dots on left
ARE Indians)*

JF Report
July 8
*(200 Indians!
(Run! Run for
the tree grove
across the
river!)*

297

a few more minutes more, the lead horseman would reach the river!

Fremont, leading his men toward a grove of trees that looked to be just ahead at the river's bend, discovered the trees were actually on the opposite bank! On the prairie, two or three hundred yelling Indian horsemen were rapidly covering the distance to the river. A race! Which group of horsemen would reach and cross the river first—the Indian army with bows and arrows in hand, or the four white men with guns?!

Fremont's horse splashed into the water, heading for the grove of trees for whatever protection a few tree trunks might provide. Beside him rode Maxwell. Randy and Yo followed closely, with the Cheyennes some hundred yards behind them. Basil and mare waited and watched in the river bottom a half-mile away.

JF Report
July 8
(Maxwell knows the Arapahoe Chief!)

Just before Fremont reached the grove at the edge of the river, the lead Indian horse and rider splashed into the water at high speed. Swift as an arrow, the horse flashed past Fremont. "Guns ready!" Fremont shouted. At the same moment, Maxwell's voice yelling strange words cut through the air—and Maxwell's horse sprang suddenly into the path of the insurgent rider who was wheeling his horse around to face Fremont.

Maxwell was yelling more strange words and the Indian was pulling his horse to a halt, leaning toward Maxwell, then yelling and stretching out his arm and hand to grasp Maxwell's.

"They know each other!" Fremont shouted, and rode up to them, right hand extended. The Indian extended his. As their fingers touched, Fremont said, "Lieutenant John Fremont, United States Army!" The Indian, striking his breast with a fist, shouted, "ArapaHO!"

When Fremont had called "Guns ready!" he, Yo, and Randy had clicked back the hammers of their loaded weapons, set their forefingers against triggers, ready to aim and shoot a volley of lead as soon as Fremont yelled, "Fire!" Randy was breathing deep and fast when he pointed the pistol at the horse and rider splashing toward Fremont.

But now, the Indian rider was waving his hand high, signing "friend" and "halt" to his two hundred or so followers nearing the river, and he was shrieking to them, "MAX! MAX!" The message and name passed like a wave of wild wind over the acres of fierce, naked, mounted warriors on the prairie and brought them to a standstill.

Maxwell was quickly telling Fremont that Chief Bulltail was a good friend he knew well from living a year in and out of Arapaho villages close to Fort St. Vrain. "Praise our stars, Bull Tail recognized me quick!"

The Chief, Fremont noticed, was glaring at Randy. "Randy!" Fremont called sternly, "Aim at the ground! Holster your weapon!"

JF Report
July 8
(Cheyenne
families of Pat,
Mike,Tuesday
camp nearby
with Arapahoes!)

In a dreamlike state at the fast turn of events, Randy blushed fiery red as he put away his deadly threat to the Arapaho chief.

Fremont answered the Chief's many questions, Maxwell interpreting, especially about the three Indians the Chief saw splashing toward them. Cheyennes? Too bad. Bull Tail regretted they weren't Pawnees. His men would have enjoyed having a grand dance tonight around a Pawnee scalp. But Bull Tail was pleased to tell the Cheyennes that a band of 20 Cheyenne teepees was camped beside his 200 Arapaho.

He pointed upriver. His camp was in a big grove six miles ahead across the river, on the same bank the Fremont party had been traveling. Then he pointed to the same side at a small herd of buffalo slowly emerging from behind the nearest hills. He said his men were going to surround the animals. The hunters had made a large circuit from their camp, he said, crossing the river to approach the herd from that side to take advantage of the wind—when they saw the white men's four horses.

JF Report
July 8 Midday
(Chief's instructions)

"Look!" Randy suddenly called out. "Pat is riding straight into the crowd of 'Rapahoes! They might—" but then he saw several of the hunters slide from their mounts, Pat and Mike and Tuesday sliding from theirs, all beginning much back-slapping. "Looks like they're old friends—or relatives," Maxwell said, and turned back to listening to the Indian chief.

"He says," Maxwell interpreted for Fremont, "that he wants us to stay right where we are until the buffalo surround they're going to start now is completed. If we move, he thinks we might get into a wind shift that will carry our scent to the buffalo, causing them to run back behind the hills, escape before the hunters can surround them with the killing circle."

JF Report
July 8
(Temp.108

Fremont nodded agreement. "Glad just to watch this mass killing, and stay out of the way."

Fremont and his men, now including Basil and the Cheyennes—they had declined the chance to join their relatives in the surround—unsaddled their horses, hobbled them

before sitting down under a tree in the grove to view the
scene across the river.

JF Report
July 8

Randy, faithful to duty while satisfying curiosity, had
pulled the barometer-thermometer from the mule pack and
hung it on the end of a low branch of a cottonwood.
"John!" he called, "look at this! The temperature is up to
108 degrees in the shade!"

But Fremont's attention was on Maxwell and his answer
to a question just asked. "Max! What on earth did you yell
in Arapaho when you raced out to meet the Chief?" Maxwell
threw back his head in a burst of laughter. "I said, 'WAH-
SON-NE Bull Tail! You foolish man! MAX! Your friend!

Beth Berryman

Through a telescope, Randy sees a stream of galloping horses pour into the circle of Indians surrounding a herd of buffalo. The horsemen, screeching frighteningly, shoot a steady stream of arrows at the animals. The killing circle goes and goes until the last buffalo lies dead. Villages of hundreds of families depend on frequent "surrounds" for meat, fresh today, dried for winter.

301

CHAPTER 28

A SURROUND! 400 BUFFALO KILLED!

Noon July 8, South Platte trail (Colorado)

The grove of trees they had looked to as a place for defending themselves from hostile Indians became their shady front row seats for watching one of the prairie's most intense dramas, an Indian buffalo-surround.

"Yes, all of you stay here and watch," the Arapaho leader, Bull Tail, had told Maxwell. "Buffalo herd has emerged—you see it on other side of river? Distance makes it look small. My camp on same side is green dot, trees, far up river. You go there with me after surround. Now stay this place."

JF Report
July 8 Midday
(Arapahoes cross
river to surround
buffalo)

The naked hunters in single file had already begun crossing the sprawling, shallow Platte, accompanied by a troop of dogs that looked more like the wolf in them than like camp mongrel hounds. On arriving at the opposite bank, every other hunter proceeded in an extending line toward the hills, galloping over the prairie by the right edge of the herd. The other hunters turned left on the river bank and, single file, galloped around the left side of the buffalo herd.

The two lines meeting behind the herd kept the animals from running away, frightened them into huddling close together. "Ai-yay-yay-yay!" the men began yelling and arrows and spears started flying. Hundreds of close-packed buffalo crazed with fear turned to run in as many directions looking for an escape opening. They only succeeded in ramming into each other. Those on the outside edge of the herd bellowed as arrows pierced, spears punctured them, and they fell on their knees, mortally wounded.

Randy's attention was suddenly distracted from the scene when he heard Tuesday yell, saw Pat and Mike throw down their paint brushes of chewed twigs, their tin of red vermillion, and begin running full speed after one of their horses. It was the one they had temporarily loaded with all their old and newly acquired wealth—their spears, bows, quivers holding magic arrow and all, 'bacco, red flannels, calico shirts "borrowed" from men now on the trail to Fort Laramie, and a few begged trinkets for favored women in home camp.

The horse faded away into a speck that disappeared

between two dune-like hills across the river. Pat, Mike, and Tuesday had frantically splashed into the water on foot, no match for a swift, sturdy pony bred on the prairie and grabbing its chance to return to it forever.

JF Report
July 8
(runaway horse)
(JF loves his sorrel)

Pat, half his face streaked with celebratory lines of red vermillion, sought out Fremont and Maxwell to tell the heart-wrenching story. Yet at the end he bore the tragedy with philosophical laughter.

"Except—" he added, "all the Cheyennes in camp will laugh when we three who went out to steal horses from the Pawnees come back on FOOT," Pat added. "If you don't love your sorrel hunter—" he said to Fremont, who didn't wait for Max to finish his translating before responding, "My sorrel is the object of my intense affection!" The Lieutenant laughed as philosophically as an Indian before turning his attention to the hunters on the prairie.

Buffalo were still trying to break out of the tightly packed mass of animals but remained trapped by the closed circle of galloping horses, shrieking riders, hundreds of piercing arrows, and fallen, dying companions. The herd then tried to break into pieces. Buffalo groups turned crazily to the right, to the left, in circles—always to find the moving wall of hunters tightly circling around them, shooting death into their midst. One after another, buffalo stumbled over dead companions, tumbled, gushing blood, as the hooves of 200 wild-eyed horses thundered past.

Fremont, watching the scene through the telescope, was so spellbound he didn't notice Randy calling to him. "Let me look!" When at last Fremont lowered the tube from his eye, he seemed in a daze for a moment. "Too far away to hear anything! All silent and strange! And all's enveloped in dust so I can hardly see what's going on!"

With a start, he saw Randy, heard him repeat, "Let me look!" and handed him the spyglass. "Yes, yes, Randyboy, do look! It's a singular sight such as few other boys will see—IF the dust thins so you CAN see."

Through the roiling clouds of dust, luminous with sunlight, Randy could see only for a moment at a time a buffalo—or two—dashing frantically this way, that way, and close by it an Indian with a long spear, or a drawn bow. In a flash, a dust curtain closed over the picture. Immediately,

JF Report
July 8
(JF describes the surround)

he saw another buffalo, a horse and rider crowding it and sending it to its knees as dust rose around it. The dimly lit figures flitting by with such rapidity gave each scene the

303

aura of a dream, or of a picture seen through a thin curtain, a stage drama.

"You look a little dazed, Randy, the same way I felt," Fremont said when Randy gave him the spyglass.

They watched for perhaps an hour, all the men and the Cheyennes taking turns looking through the telescope—though the Cheyennes could hardly be persuaded to give it up when time was called. No one saw a single buffalo emerge from the dust cloud. "My estimate is 400 in the herd," Maxwell said, "and the circle of hunters goes and goes until every one of the animals lies dead on the ground. But'll they need a lot more than that to feed a thousand or more Arapahoes and Pat and Mike's Cheyenne kinfolks."

JF Report
Buffalo surround
400 killed!

Tuesday was the first to point far up the river to a long line of people walking on a trail that angled across the empty plain toward the acres of dead buffalo. The dustcloud had lifted and Randy could see the last dozen or so standing buffalo passively awaiting horsemen weaving toward them between black hulks on the ground. The horsemen arrived. Leisurely they fitted arrows to bows. The arrows flew. The last standing buffalo fell, and the surround was over.

"That line of people crossing the plain to the surround field is Arapaho women—and probably some Cheyenne women, too," Maxwell told Randy. "Looks like several hundred. They do most of the butchering and tote home a lot of the meat. But the hunters stay long enough to strip off a coupla hides apiece and pile them on their mounts. They'll stack heavy ribs and heads—they want the brains for tanning hides and the tongues to eat—on top of 'um and bring the load to camp."

Fremont wanted to know how long all this would take, and tugged thoughtfully at his beard when Maxwell guessed "about two hours." Randy wanted to know if Tuesday's mama would be in the long line of women going to do the butchering. Maxwell asked Tuesday's father, Pat. He said one long word, held his right hand, fingers extended and separated, over his heart, then rolled his wrist and hand back and forth several times. "He says, 'Maybe,'" Maxwell said. "He means he'd like to know, too."

"Since it's about a two-hour ride to the Indian camp," Fremont announced, "I think we should get started. Before we do, I must at least put on my Army hat—Randy, you can have it back later—and Army jacket, cinched by the holster belt with the big shiny buckle. Basil, will you pull them out of my bundle on the packhorse, please. And bring my boots, too. With Indians, it is not enough for a man to be called 'the leader,' he must also LOOK like 'the leader' even if his fine outfit cooks him in 108-degree heat."

Maxwell spoke for all—Randy, Basil, Yo, Tuesday, Pat, and Mike—when he said Fremont in his fine outfit looked like a Prince or Very Big Chief. "And especially compared to us," Basil grimaced. "I'm getting to be as ragged as de St. Louis-bound trappers we laughed at a mon'h ago when we met'um by de Platte River."

JF Report
July 8
(ride to Indian
camp)
They joked and laughed as they cantered their mounts and led their two packanimals across the wide expanse of hoof-deep water, clambered up the low river bank, and sauntered along it toward the spot of green six miles away. Soon they had the company of Indian after Indian laden with bleeding meat, women and men loping along the trail as fast as the visitors' horses, then some hunters leading horses, or trotting them past, all heaped with hides and heads, and blood-red ribs.

By the time Randy could see the teepees, the trail was jammed with returning horsemen streaked by dusty earth and sweat, laughing and yelling joyously. When Randy arrived in sight of the giant cottonwoods at the edge of the village, Arapaho Chief Bull Tail, Maxwell's old friend, his face, hair, and naked body dusted a dull sandy white, rode up beside him. He greeted Fremont and Maxwell, beckoned all Fremont's party, including the Cheyennes, to follow him.

Tuesday, Pat, and Mike had long kept their eyes on the slender line of women and returning hunters on the separate trail crossing the prairie from dead buffaloes to the far end of the lengthy Arapaho village. "That must be where the little Cheyenne village is!" Max declared. Tuesday, Pat, and Mike talked among themselves, their faces alternately glowing and grimacing. Their families! They resisted the urge to gallop to them.

They had already decided to stay with Fremont and his party, not rush off to their kin, reveal that they were still alive after an absence of two moons but bringing home less than they started with. Through Maxwell, Pat explained the humiliating situation.

"They will laugh to see me and the boy riding one horse. Not even the boy's buffalo kill will change that. But—they cannot laugh long when they see the white friends we have lived with, the great leader and his magic eye tube, the red-

305

"Arapaho women! Hurry to the surround field! The buffalo long for your knives!"
Quickly, hundreds of women walk the six miles to the place where 400 dead buffalo
are lying. They cut up the half-skinned animals, load themselves with meat, carry it to
the village. They'll spend days cooking stew, draping sliced, raw meat on drying frames.

haired boy that our boy loves—and Maxwell, not just ourselves, telling how our brave boy killed his first buffalo.

"Our kin will overlook our present condition when the
mother of the young buffalo-killer announces she will honor
her son by giving him the name of her hero grandfather.
Our kin will also forget Pawnee horses when the buffalo
killer's mother gives his horse to a worthy person who will
shout the new name of her son through the camp, and tell
of his great deed.

"Our kin will love us when we give to them the presents
our white friends have brought for them."

Maxwell winked at Fremont as he passed along the last
few words. "Better think of something," he said.

JF Report
July 8
(Arapaho camp)

Now Bull Tail was escorting Fremont and Maxwell, followed by Randy with Basil and Yo leading the pack-animals.
Tuesday and Pat on one horse, Mike on another, trailed
after them past the great spreading arms of two cottonwoods, gateway of the Arapaho village. Beyond their delicious shade stretched a broad street, both sides lined for a
mile with towering teepees and trees. Giant cottonwood
branches fully leafed made a canopy shading the line of 200
or more tall, cone-shaped tents of buffalo skins whitened
with rubbed-in marly clay and intense sunshine.

The street was crowded with platoons of women naked
from their knees down and their hipbones up, each one
bringing on her back from the killing field 50 pounds of
choice hump and loin buffalo meat, bending with the added
weights on her arms of baskets piled with livers, hearts,
lungs, kidneys, and guts large and small. A band of singing
hunters rode past them on horses draped in various heavily
boned buffalo parts. Each man had his own little cluster of
welcoming children, old men, women, shouting, singing,
beating their hands together or rapping small drums.

City of Saints
R.Burton,p86-7
(Indian teepees)

All made way for Chief Bull Tail and his guests. As they
proceeded with their noisy escorts along the avenue, Randy
stared in surprise at the handsome white teepees, their two
lines making irregular edges of the street. High above the
entrance flap, the open point of the cone-shaped teepee had
a covering flap propped open with a pole. Like a three-cor-
nered sail, it caught the breeze and funneled it inside.

Attracting Randy even more were the pictures drawn upon
some white teepee covers. "Look! Look!" he called to his companions and pointed ahead to a large teepee cover encircled
by black horizontal stripes enclosing a parade of buffalo. "I'll

Based on C. Bodmer, 18–

Indian village of teepees, homes for hundreds of families, travels with the buffalo hunters.

bet Tuesday drew those! Ask him, Max!" Tuesday told Max he didn't paint this Arapaho teepee, but had painted pictures on his family's Cheyenne teepee, and hoped Randy'd see them.

Abruptly, Bull Tail turned toward the teepee with the buffalo parade painting. On a tripod by the entrance, he hung his shield picturing a bull's head, fringed with tufts of buffalo hair and small pouches of protective magic–medicine. "Hook-ah-hay! Numwhit!" he said loudly, and with open hands and arms spread wide, indicated "welcome" to his home.

"He's also inviting all of us–I think–to eat with him," Maxwell turned in his saddle to inform the party, "so make the 'thank you' sign. He might take it as an insult if any of us refuse, especially if that man is one the chief considers low rank."

Pat and Mike, not hearing Maxwell's advice, in words and hand language politely asked Bull Tail to permit them to decline his invitation. They wanted to go home to the Cheyennes who were camping just a mile beyond the Arapahoes. Bull Tail nodded.

"I want to go with them!" Randy said urgently. "John! Remember?! Seeing where Tuesday lives was one big reason I wanted to come with you on the South Platte! Besides, Pat and Mike and Tuesday, too, need me to help them out if some of the Cheyennes laugh when they see no stolen horses. John! Pat, Mike 'n' Tuesday need ALL of US–'specially YOU in your uniform, and, and showing them the telescope–"

John and Maxwell reminded Randy that a white man

All the following episodes added. Not in JF Report, but it's probable that theJF party went with their Cheyenne friends to their camp next to the Arapahoes.

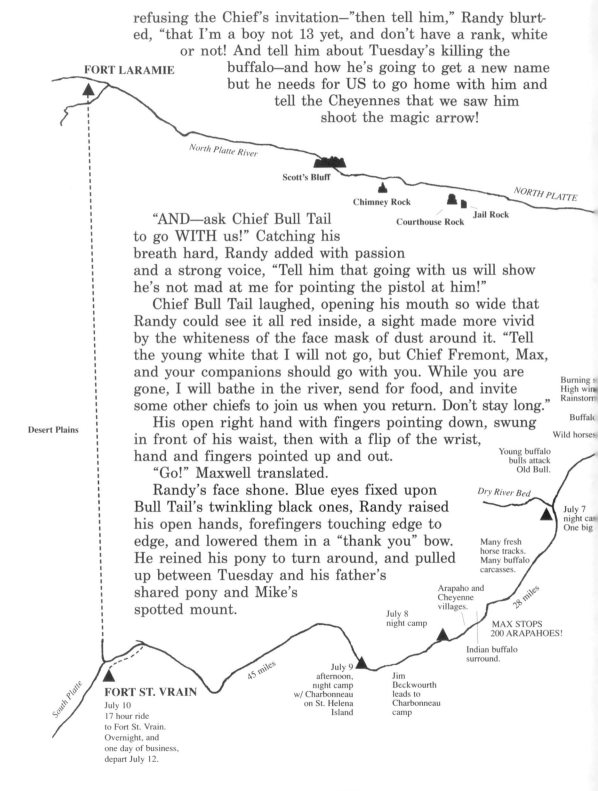

refusing the Chief's invitation—"then tell him," Randy blurted, "that I'm a boy not 13 yet, and don't have a rank, white or not! And tell him about Tuesday's killing the buffalo—and how he's going to get a new name but he needs for US to go home with him and tell the Cheyennes that we saw him shoot the magic arrow!

FORT LARAMIE

North Platte River

Scott's Bluff

Chimney Rock

Courthouse Rock

Jail Rock

NORTH PLATTE

"AND—ask Chief Bull Tail to go WITH us!" Catching his breath hard, Randy added with passion and a strong voice, "Tell him that going with us will show he's not mad at me for pointing the pistol at him!"

Chief Bull Tail laughed, opening his mouth so wide that Randy could see it all red inside, a sight made more vivid by the whiteness of the face mask of dust around it. "Tell the young white that I will not go, but Chief Fremont, Max, and your companions should go with you. While you are gone, I will bathe in the river, send for food, and invite some other chiefs to join us when you return. Don't stay long."

His open right hand with fingers pointing down, swung in front of his waist, then with a flip of the wrist, hand and fingers pointed up and out.

"Go!" Maxwell translated.

Randy's face shone. Blue eyes fixed upon Bull Tail's twinkling black ones, Randy raised his open hands, forefingers touching edge to edge, and lowered them in a "thank you" bow. He reined his pony to turn around, and pulled up between Tuesday and his father's shared pony and Mike's spotted mount.

Desert Plains

Burning s
High win
Rainstorm

Buffalo

Wild horses

Young buffalo
bulls attack
Old Bull.

Dry River Bed

July 7
night ca
One big

Many fresh
horse tracks.
Many buffalo
carcasses.

28 miles

Arapaho and
Cheyenne
villages.

July 8
night camp

MAX STOPS
200 ARAPAHOES!

Indian buffalo
surround.

45 miles

July 9
afternoon,
night camp
w/ Charbonneau
on St. Helena
Island

Jim
Beckwourth
leads to
Charbonneau
camp

South Platte

FORT ST. VRAIN
July 10
17 hour ride
to Fort St. Vrain.
Overnight, and
one day of business,
depart July 12.

With big smiles and joyous hand waggles, they started
down the long avenue toward the camp of the Cheyennes.
With a wave of his hand, Fremont took his place in the
line-up behind Randy and the three Cheyennes—himself and
Maxwell side by side, Basil and Yo leading the pack horse
and the pack mule.

They hadn't gone far when Fremont called a halt. "Let's
see if we can help Pat, Mike, and Tuesday more than a little. Can we arrange it so all three could come riding home,
each on a horse?"

With quiet excitement, they figured a way. Hand signs
and Maxwell's Arapaho words told Pat, Mike, and Tuesday,
who agreed with joyous enthusiasm.

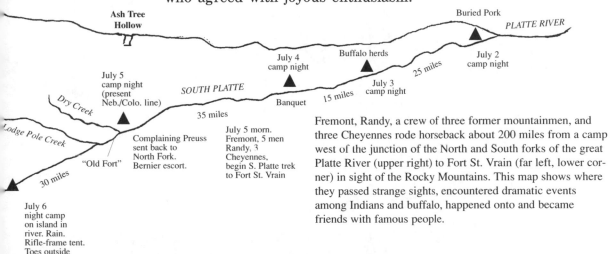

Fremont, Randy, a crew of three former mountainmen, and
three Cheyennes rode horseback about 200 miles from a camp
west of the junction of the North and South forks of the great
Platte River (upper right) to Fort St. Vrain (far left, lower corner) in sight of the Rocky Mountains. This map shows where
they passed strange sights, encountered dramatic events
among Indians and buffalo, happened onto and became
friends with famous people.

All three helped Basil, Maxwell, and Yo unload the pack
horse, and overload the pack mule. Fremont and Randy held
back with friendly hand signs a little army of tagalong
Arapaho children.

"While we're at it, we'd better dig out some 'gifts,'" Maxwell
said. Cheyenne smiles stretched even wider and Cheyenne eyes
glittered with anticipation on seeing the hand sign for "gift."

When they began to move forward again, Pat and Mike on
their ponies, Tuesday on Fremont's pack horse beside Randy
on "Spots," led the way. Behind them, Fremont was saying in
a low voice to Maxwell, "You are confident that Tuesday understands what he's to do—and will do it?" Maxwell nodded his
head vigorously.

"Because, if he doesn't," Fremont said, "I'll be obliged to inter-
vene—an unpleasant, even dangerous, situation—to forcibly TAKE
back a gift-horse we MUST have for the rest of our journey."

Within seconds of Pat, Mike, and Tuesday Cheyenne's riding into the village of the
Tsistsistas band, a cluster of kinfolks gathers about them, crying out excited welcomes.
Others come running, elated that the two warriors and the boy they believed dead have
come safely home. And see their escorts–five white men! Look!––one of them is a boy!
Had the whites saved the three long-lost Cheyennes? Did they bring any presents?
The shouting and hubbub bring Tuesday's mother to the teepee door. In a few minutes,
she will joyously reward her son's bravery and success during his first venture as a man.

311

CHAPTER 29

TUESDAY'S HOMECOMING, RANDY'S "SUNRISE"

Afternoon July 8, South Platte trail (Colorado)

During the slow trot of their mounts past the last tents on the long, very wide avenue of the Arapaho village, Tuesday turned his head to look beside him at Randy a half-dozen times. His increasingly stiff face and rigid posture told Randy he was uncertain about how his home-coming would turn out. At each glance from Tuesday, Randy smiled, nodded. Finally he looked behind him at Maxwell and asked how to hand sign "happy."

Maxwell held up his right hand, curled his thumb and index finger into a half-oval, then swept hand and arm up and to the right. "That's the closest I know to say 'happy' or 'everything's gonna be fine.' It's the sign for 'sunrise.' I sure hope it DOES turn out happy, for us as well as him."

When Randy turned back and made a sunrise sign to Tuesday, Maxwell called to him. "Randy, your friend has good reason to worry. His people call a man a 'poor rustler' if he comes back from a raid with no horses stolen from the enemy. The standing of the whole family drops."

Randy looked around, puzzled. "But he killed a cow buffalo on his first hunt!"

"See, it's this way," Maxwell said. "To look rich and to have a high standing in the tribe depends on how many horses, fine riding horses, a man has," Maxwell said.

Fremont interrupted. "Won't five whites bringing the three men home add as much to their status as stealing a few horses? Seems to me it will—and the glory coming from the boy's first kill and being given a tribal hero's name surely will outweigh the need to look rich."

Maxwell laughed, nodded, and told Randy to handsign another "sunrise" to Tuesday.

They passed all the Arapaho teepees and rode along the edge of the open plain stretching endlessly north from the cottonwoods lining the riverbank. Within minutes they saw ahead among the trees about 20 white teepees arranged in a circle. Cheyennes!

"Aiiiyeeee!" yelled Tuesday, bumping his heels against the

Episode added.
Not in JF Report.

Indian Sign Language.
W.Tomkins
(happy=sunrise)

Cheyennes.
E.Hoebel,p30
(poor rustler)

SUNRISE
(AND) HAPPINESS

Cheyennes.
Hoebel, p31
Cheyennes, I
Grinnell,p94
(band names,
camp circle)

pony to set it galloping. "HEVa-tanYEW!" His father and uncle shouted the name of their band and followed his lead. Leaving Randy behind, they bounded toward the white tents —"Buffalo-Hair-rope" village—a two-minute fast ride ahead.

"Now the Big Drama starts," Maxwell said loudly. "It better be 'sunrise' and we don't lose our horse—or time. How long do you figure you can spare for us to get done with everything we need to do for our Cheyennes, Lieutenant?"

Fremont declared they could spare no more than an hour before heading back to eat with Chief Bull Tail. "With an hour at Bull Tail's lodge for pipe-smoking and speeches, another hour or so for eating and talking and leave-taking, we'll be lucky to move out in time to complete a day of 20 miles."

Wah-To-Yah
L.Gerrard
p117(po-may,
Look yonder)

"Po-omey!" exclaimed Randy, using his newest Cheyenne word. "Yes! Look yonder!" echoed Maxwell.

"Our Cheyennes've stopped at a teepee with lots of pictures painted on it! Has t' be Tuesday's home!"

Am. Indian Art
N.Feder, p40

In the distance, the three Indians were sliding from their mounts into a gathering crowd that was growing larger by the second and babbling louder and louder. Suddenly a stooping figure came out of the low doorway. When she straightened, her arms flew wide open and her cry of joy rang through the air. She wrapped her arms around the boy who had jumped from his horse and run to her.

Pictorial History of
Am.Indians.
O.Lafarge, p150
(pictures on tents)

"Look! Tuesday's nearly tall as his mother!" Randy exclaimed. Maxwell said he'd probably grow to be a six-footer like Pat and many other Cheyenne men. Randy hardly heard. "Look! There's Pat putting just one arm around Tuesday's mother and pressing his cheek to hers! Isn't he going to KISS her?!"

"Far as I've seen, Indians don't kiss," Maxwell informed him. "Besides, she's too busy hugging Tuesday—well, now she's got ahold of her man, too. They're doing a three-way hug—but look! there's another woman coming up beside him, and she's wanting to get his attention. That's a knee-high baby holding on to her skirt. Lieutenant, did Kit ever mention to you that his old friend Pat has two wives?

Cheyennes.
Grinnell, I
p151, 3 wives
p153, 2 wives

"No? Well, of course Indian men can have as many wives as they can feed and steal horses for. They NEED at least two wives to pitch teepees, cook, have babies, dress buffalo skins, sew clothes and mocassins, butcher buffaloes, dry meat, get roots, berries, tend children and the sick—the worklist is endless!"

The five mounted white men stopped at the edge of the

crowd, immediately drawing all the children to look at them. Maxwell began calling out,"Wah-hein! Wah-hein! No! Don't do that!" to small, naked boys and tall striplings in breechcloths who were reaching for the baggage tied on the mule's back, fingering Maxwell's spurs and the fringe on Basil's trousers legs, stroking Randy's shiny saddle.

"Wah-hein! Wah-hein! Stop! Don't do that!" chorused Yo and Basil, then Fremont and Randy—then Pat and Mike, Tuesday and Tuesday's mother. All of Tuesday's family was now pressing through the gathering crowd of young women, old men, children, and a hundred dogs eager to see the five wihios—"mysterious ones."

More villagers kept coming—dust-coated naked hunters on horses laden with buffalo hides and meat, women just free of bloody backloads, or travois, or baskets. All rushed over, adding their yells to the jumble of voices crying out the names of the two men and a boy long thought lost. "Otoz-voutsi! Mah-keh-onih! Nawa-menoh-tou-wits!"

Arms and hands with fingers curved in a half-circle for the rising sun threw a thousand arcs of joy into the air .

"Those names mean Big Wolf, Mahkeh-onih—Pat—and Buck Deer, Otoz-voutsi—Mike. Quick Ornamenting Nawa-menoh-tou-wits—that's our artist, Tuesday!" Maxwell told his companions.

Then he shouted at Pat in Cheyenne words, "Nawa—quick! Mount your horse! Your people need to SEE you—they WANT to see you! Tell them who WE are! Tell them about the young killer of a fat cow! Nawa—hurry!" he said, chopping the air with the "hurry" hand-sign.

In a moment, Pat and Mike had remounted, quieted the noisy crowd, introduced Chief Fremont, Maxwell friend-of-Arapahoes, and Chief Fremont's "son" Randy. "Also here are sub-chiefs Yo and Basil. Our saviours—all of them," they told the villagers.

QUIET DOWN

"They fed us when we starved. They treated us with respect. We are friends of trust. We live together many days, many nights without fear. Tou-wits and red-haired boy big friends.

"We hunt buffalo with Chief, with Ki'Cars'n. My brother Buck Deer killed fat cow with one arrow flying through heart to grass on other side. Hear his name! Buck Deer! Mighty hunter!" The crowd applauded and shouted, "Otoz-voutsi! Otoz-voutsi! Mighty hunter!"

Pat signed "quiet," and shouted, "Nawa-menoh-tou-wits young mighty hunter! First hunt, first KILL! One arrow!

Not little calf, but big fat cow!" The crowd's "AAAHHHHH-HHH!" filled the village circle. "Ni-hi-ni! Yes! My son Tou-wits comes back in glory to Heva-tan-you village people! Tou-wits now a MAN, no more a child!

Cheyennes Grinnell (brave,123 I 1st hunt, II, 118-9)

"Brave Tou-wits deserves a great man's name! He should wear his grandfather's name, a hero name honored by all Cheyennes. Ohneh-oh, Smiling Moon, mother of Nawa menoh-tou-wits, give him the name!"

The villagers, most of them relatives of the young hero, clapped their hands and chanted his name, "Tou-wits! Tou-wits! Tou-wits!" But Tuesday clung to his Mother, speaking in her ear, then looking steadily into her eyes.

Randy, who had stayed mounted as Fremont had directed, was mumbling, "Awww, com'on, Tuesday, let go your mama!" when he saw Tuesday suddenly turn, and make signs to those in front of him to move back—make room for his mother so she could be seen. Then "be quiet," listen to what she's going to say.

Maxwell leaned toward Fremont, coughed and cleared his throat noisily to interrupt Fremont's rapt attention to the drama around them and another about to begin.

"Lieutenant! Did you see that?—Tuesday has done his part for getting us back our horse! We'll soon know if Mama does what he's told her to do—obediently carrying out orders from him now that he's a MAN."

With her husband Pat—Mahkeh-onih, Big Wolf—on one side and Tuesday on the other, Ohneh-oh, Smiling Moon, cried out to her village a joyous, quivering "Ayeyyyy yiiiiii!" from a trembling heart.

Flinging open her arms, she looked up at the sky and cried out thanks to Those Above Us. "My son, my man, his brother—all, home again! Quick flies my breath from happiness!" With a deep, gasping sigh, she composed herself. Fingers entwined, she held her hands against her breast and spoke loudly in a voice strong with pride.

Cheyennes. L. Hoebel, p93-4 (public ceremony for 1st kill)

"You have heard how the boy who left nearly two moons ago has come home a MAN, a BRAVE man who went among the buffalo and killed a fat cow with one arrow! Tell us, son-of-us-all, the whole story! Tell us and you will hear your new name repeated over and over among us Tsistsistas—We People—and your new name will be your Hero Grandfather's, the man you now are!"

Cheyennes. L.Hoebel,p1 (The People)

Randy leaned forward, quieting his pony with whispered words, staring in wonder at Tuesday, who, poised, shoulders straight, dignified, calm, began making his speech. Randy heard Tuesday's voice rise and fall, strong and confident, saw his hands and his acting making the story visible to the still growing crowd of his kinfolks, and enjoyed their "Ohhhhh!" and "Ahhhhhh!" responses, their open-mouthed admiration.

"What's Tuesday saying?" Randy loud-whispered behind his hand to Maxwell who answered, "Same story we know by heart—oh, now he's calling my name! Well, here goes. I'm gonna have to do a lot of acting and hand talking. Good thing Cheyenne talk is a lot like 'Rapaho."

Languages:
City of the Saints,
R.Burton, p143.
Warriors of
the Plains.
C.Taylor,p21

Maxwell clucked to his horse, moved close to Tuesday and his parents, and began to surprise his white-skinned companions with his graceful, vivid gestures, the flow of expressive, loud, incomprehensible baritone sounds. His audience listened entranced, and burst into applause and shouts when Maxwell's story came to a climax of fast words, fast handsigns, and a dramatic portrayal of an arrow aimed, released, a cow dropping her head, dying.

Fremont, Randy, and sub-chiefs Basil and Yo shouted and applauded, too. "De best show I been at since Saint Looie!" Basil declared very loudly.

Tears streaked the cheeks of Tuesday's mother, Pat hugged and hugged his son. Mike, whose magic arrow and advice had played a critical part in Tuesday's success, reached toward Maxwell, grabbed his hand, held on. He smiled and smiled, grateful that Maxwell had not skipped over his bravery and skill but, like Pat, had praised him.

Pat suddenly shouted that Smiling Moon was ready to give Nawa-menoh-tou-wits his new name, and also in celebration of his courage, and of his new status as a man, she would make a gift of his pony to a worthy person. An "Ahhhh!" of anticipation traveled among the two hundred kinfolks and friends now gathered.

Smiling Moon drew herself up and called out in her loudest voice, "My little boy has killed a buffalo! He has proved his bravery! He has proved he will be a good hunter, a good man. Now he leaves boyhood, I present him with his man name, the name of my hero father. All Cheyennes will from now on call him Tsis-tu-toh—"

Maxwell, leaning close to Fremont, whispered, "Cedar Tree—Tsis-tu-toh. Sounds as much like 'Tuesday' as 'Tou-wits' does, wouldn't you say?"

"—like my father Tsis-tu-toh who charged alone into the

316

Cheyennes.
Hoebel,p74
(hero's deeds)

camp of the enemy during The Great Battle against the Crows. Chief Tsis-tu-toh had only a trading-post long-knife but he struck mightily, killed many Crows without himself being touched. His bravery stirred the other Cheyenne warriors to follow his example. They charged, broke through the barriers, destroyed the enemy Crows.

Cheyennes.
Grinnell, I
p118,123
(horse gift)
Grinnell,II
p169(new adult
name for boy)

"My son, YOUR name is now Tsis-tu-toh! Do it honor! Ask the blessings of Those Above Us by giving away your own horse! Choose the most worthy man here to receive your gift!"

The crowd, tense and eager, leaned toward Tsis-tu-toh, expectant eyes upon him. His hands bowed "thank you" to his mother. He walked the few steps to his pony and declared in his strongest voice, "The most worthy man, the man whose kindness and generous heart saved me, my father, and my uncle when we had traveled six days without food, is this man—" he led the horse to Fremont, still seated on his horse, visible to all—"Chief Fremont!"

The crowd's cry, "AAhhhheee!" ended on a down note. Tsis-tu-toh quickly spoke even louder, "He has much strong medicine, this wihio! He used it for me and my father and uncle! He will use it for all of you—all of us—in the Hair-rope band! He and his men travel a long trail to trading posts and will do much good for us there.

"I wish to make sure he arrives at those places. He needs my horse. His ugly long-eared animal is bearing a heavy load and will fall on its knees without my gift-horse to share the weight.

"You, too, will gain from my gift to him! Chief Fremont promised me that he would show you his magic eyetube! I have looked into it! I saw hunters, horses, buffalo turn into giants! Also, Chief Fremont told me he has brought PRESENTS to give to US!"

The cry "Ayyyyyiiiiii!" from the crowd had a lilting end.

Wah-To-Yah,
Garrard
p98,269,115
(Cheyenne
leaders,1840's)

Maxwell had already signaled Basil to dismount and bring from the mulepack the spyglass and a package of presents assembled during the stop to pile the horse's pack atop the mule's. Already the leaders of the village—Ocum-who-wurst, old Chief Warritoria, and High Priest He-who-shows-how, had moved forward to stand beside Tsis-tu-toh.

Cheyennes.
Hoebel,p13
(priests names)

They were looking poised and dignified but pleased as they began chorusing, "Hookah-hay! Num-whit!" to the visitors. Howdy! Welcome!

Fremont took the modest bundle from Basil, and gave

the nod for Basil to take the spyglass to the leaders. "Just them—and Tuesday's mama. Ask them to tell the villagers that the magic of the glass wears thin, blurs, if stared at by too many eyes. Don't let it out of your sight for a second, and bring it quickly back to me."

Basil carefully did as he was told. Chief Warritoria described to the crowd all he'd ever heard about the mysterious behavior of the magic stick-held-before-one-eye, Basil focused and held the telescope so each chief and Tuesday's mama could see a teepee, greatly enlarged ("I see a bird sitting on a teepee pole!") on the far side of the village circle. The crowd repeated its leaders' cries—"Magic! Powerful medicine! The eye becomes a giant! How did the teepee change so?! Mysterious wihio stick!"

As soon as Tuesday's mother had made her cry of astonishment, Basil, with a sigh of relief, hurried the spyglass into Fremont's hand.

"Perfect job, Max," Fremont said. "Now for the delicate matter of presents." Bundle in hand, he rose to stand in his stirrups—he had kept himself and his men mounted to insure their departure within the time he had allotted.

Looking at the chiefs, he said to Maxwell, "Tell them we've been honored to have the friendship and company of the three brave Cheyenne hunters Pat, Mike, and Tuesday. We have enjoyed visiting their village and its people. We are grateful for the gift of the horse. Tell them, Max, in your most humble-Indian style that we wish to offer a few miserable gifts in farewell."

Maxwell repeated Fremont's message in hand signs and Cheyenne words mixed with Arapaho. The crowd noised its eagerness, and the chiefs smiled, mumbled to each other, nodded and nodded toward Fremont.

Fremont nodded back and began to undo the bundle. "For the chiefs—" he held up a fist-size pouch—"very good tobacco to make many pipesful of the best kinnikinik!"

The crowd, pressing in to see the gifts and hear Maxwell's words, murmured and sighed as Basil handed the pouch to the Chief, then, one after another, a gift to those Cheyennes whose names Fremont called out.

"For the daughter of hero Tsis-tou-toh, and mother of our brave young Tsis-tou-toh—a fine mirror and sharp scissors!" (Basil grimaced. He'd now have to borrow Fremont's equipment for beard-trimming.) "For the father of Tsis-tou-toh—my good friend Mah-keh-onih, known to me as Pat—these fine cotton trousers, and my regrets that they're not red!" (Yo silently hoped the ragged ones he was wearing would hold out another week.)

"For the young hero Tsis-tou-toh, best friend of the Red-Haired Wihio—here is red paint, a soft-lead pencil, and some pieces of paper he can ornament with his beautiful pictures!" (Fremont prayed he could buy more such writing materials at Fort St. Vrain.) "For O-toz-voutsi—Mike to us—whose now lost magic arrow meant so much to him, this bright blue shirt like one he has long admired!" (Yo closed his eyes, sorry to see it go.)

"This last gift is special from the Red-Haired Wihio for his friend of the heart, Tsis-tou-toh. He gives his tin drinking cup so that the boy he has known as Tuesday will think of him each time he sips water or broth or even medicine tea!" (Randy winked "thanks" to Max for agreeing to loan him his extra cup until they reached Laramie.)

The crowd, some with garish blood-smeared faces from eating warm buffalo liver in the field, produced a scattering of applause. But their faces and the low rumble of voices made it clear that they had hoped for, expected, at least a few white man's goods for themselves. Fremont saw and quickly spoke.

"I thank this village"—he bowed his hands to them—"for its hospitality. I will arrive at the trading post Fort St. Vrain in a day or two and there I will arrange with the Booshway to give to the first of your chiefs who arrives there three gifts to divide among your families. One gift is a big pouch of coffee to boil for the drink you like so much. ("Aaahhh!") The second is a big pouch of sugar for the coffee." (Applause! Smiles! Happy babbling!) The third gift is a big, big pouch of colored beads." (Applause! Smiles! Cheers!)

His gaze aimed straight at Fremont, Old Chief Warritoria began speaking in a high-pitched voice. "What's he saying?" Fremont asked Maxwell.

"He says, 'Many thanks, and never allow your heart to tire of giving so you'll always be loved and respected.'"

Chief Left Hand.
M.Coel, p6.
(giving)

Fremont saluted him, bowed his hands "thank you." Shouting, "Hookahay! Numwhit! Goodbye!" he quickly reined his horse in a turn away from the village. Waving his hat, he called, "Let's go, men!"

Randy wheeled his pony toward Fremont and cried out shrilly, "We ALL have to go with you?! I won't get to see inside Tuesday's tent?! Nor tell him a last goodbye?!

JOHHH-NN! I may never see him again!! Can't I stay here while you go smoke with that old 'rapaho chief? PLEEEASE, John!"

Basil and Yo rode up leading the pack animals. Basil spoke at once and fast. "Oui! Please! We sub-chiefs t'ink Chief Bull Tail would just as soon we of such low rank didn't come back to eat his buffalo stew. We could stay wid Randy and look 'round dis place wid him, den go 'long de river, find a good camp site, and wait for you dere."

His animated, beaming face was persuasive. "Yes, that's a better plan," Fremont said with an amused smile. "So— Maxwell, ask the chiefs for permission for Randy and two sub-chiefs to visit the village for an hour or so."

Shortly, Fremont was graciously bowing his thanks again, saying "Hookahay! Numwhit!" once more, and turning his sorrel in the direction of the Arapahoes. Maxwell reminded Basil and Yo not to leave the horses alone for a second. "Basil, your black beard looks more scary than Yo's pale one, so you hold onto the horses' trail-lines while Yo looks after Randy."

Maxwell laughed and added, "You noticed, I reckon, that nobody in the village asked Pat and Mike about the Pawnee horses they went to steal! So—all is 'sunrise!' Hookahay numwhit, everybody!" he called and giddy-upped his horse into a trot to catch Fremont.

Randy's feelings alternated between happy excitement—as long as he was looking at all the things and people in Tuesday's home and in the village—and a sad, sinking sensation in his middle—when he thought about leaving Tuesday, knowing he would never see him again. They waited to go inside the teepee as soon as everyone crowding around Pat, Mike, and Tuesday's mama had looked at, tried out, tried on, the gifts Pat's family had received, and ambled off to their own teepees.

Pat led Randy through the tent entrance. "What a BIG room!" he thought, his eyes wide, his mouth open. "And wide-open! And the floor so covered with—with—things spread out on it—and no tables, no chairs, no beds!"

Tuesday came in, his mother still holding his arm. Mike, his wife, and Yo followed them. When Tuesday's Mama moved to stir a cookpot hanging from a tripod in the middle of the room, Tuesday took Randy by the arm and led him around his circular home.

"Where do you sleep—which one of these?" Randy asked

Inside teepee:
Warriors of the Plains,
Taylor,p23,28
City of Saints
R.Burton,p98,
172,472.
Pictorial
Hist.Am.Indian
Lafarge. p49,92,155
Wah-To-Yah,
Garrard. p61,67,91
Am.Indian Art,
N.Feder.p39,47
Cheyennes,Grinnell.
Cheyennes, Hoebel

320

with hand gestures and a question sign. He'd counted eight
pallets of buffalo robes lying on the hard-packed ground by
the tent edges. Tuesday waved toward a pile, pointed to
himself, then another pile nearby, and pointed at Randy.

"His bed—and one for me? What's it like, sleeping in the
open space of a tent with seven other people? And two of
them Tuesday's Mama and Pat's Other-Wife? And Baby.
And Uncle Mike, his wife and baby. Oh my."

Tuesday's Mama beckoned to him to come taste the
stew in the iron pot hanging on the tripod. Uncertain about
what kind of meat in the stew was perfuming the air, and
whether it was the family's mealtime since no one else was
eating ("No mealtime," Yo told him later, "the stew's always
there and you eat when you're hungry") he accepted some
stew in a big spoon, once a mountain sheep's horn.

BUFFALO

Tuesday took a spoonful, too, and they stood together to
sip the hot, meaty liquid. Randy did more looking around
than sipping. He saw against the teepee wall by the
entrance large pots, large leather-wrapped bundles, and a
large bag tight with water, well-tied at the top. Tuesday
poked him, handsigned "buffalo," and patted his breechcloth. "Oh. A buffalo bladder," Randy decided.

He saw near the beds, near the cook fire, by the door,
tripods draped with clothing, bows, quivers, pouches. Under
the tripods sat baskets, leather boxes, pots, bowls, spoons,
firewood and buffalo chips.

On a walk around the tent circle, Tuesday showed him his
cold-weather clothes hanging on a tripod all his own next to
his bed. Randy inspected a fringed deerskin shirt, some leggings that at first looked like trousers until he saw they had
no seat or front panel. He resisted opening a small pouch, a
bigger pouch, both of antelope skin. He tried for size a pair
of mocassins with beaded designs and fringe—"very big,"
Randy's hands told Tuesday.

Finally, Tuesday took Randy to look at a section of tent
lining attached to the bottom four feet of the tent cover.
Randy leaned to look closer at some designs drawn and
painted on the wide skin canvas.

"Tuesday! That man killing those animals looks just like
Pat, Mah-kch-onih! Those are YOUR drawings—elk, buffalo,
antelope on grassy plains, and bears, cougars, mountain
sheep, and deer in the mountains! Just like some of the pictures you drew on the ground for me! I wish I could take
them home with me!"

Tuesday's mother can hardly let go of the son who left two moons ago as a boy and has returned a man worthy of bearing his hero grandfather's name. Pat and Mike, proud of Tuesday's new status and their impressive white friends, relieved to have arrived riding a horse each, and to have heard no questions about Pawnee horses they went to steal, wait to take Randy inside their teepee. Other Wife of Pat retreats into the tent with their baby.

There were scenes, too, of Pat on horseback making a "coo"—touching an enemy warrior while galloping past him, which took more bravery than simply killing the man. But here also was Pat waving a pole with six scalps dangling from it.

Then Tuesday led Randy to the snow scene at the edge of a woods. Some horses were running away from two cone-shaped Indian "forts" made of long poles. Three men were throwing snowballs at the horses, directing them to run together in the same direction.

"Hey! This man here looks like Kit Carson!" Randy exclaimed. "Ki'Cars'n!" Tuesday repeated. "And that one's Pat! and here's Mike!" Randy exclaimed. "It's the story Kit told me one day! I can't wait to tell Kit that while he was TELLING me about throwing snowballs when he took back stolen horses, a picture you made on your teepee wall was SHOWING the story!"

Suddenly Tuesday's mother, Pat, Mike, Other-Wife and child, Yo, and three chiefs newly arrived, were hovering around them, chattering and pointing to the stories on the tent lining. But they were talking about heat, not art. Pat and Mike began rolling up the bottom edge of the teepee cover, including the pictures, to let in cooler air.

Other Wife and child went to a bed and stretched out. Mama, tired looking but pretty with long flowing black hair, hugged and hugged Tuesday and Randy. She was still wearing her long buffalo-butchering dress smeared red with blood.

With one last squeeze, she led them to the stew pot where the three chiefs were already passing the huge horn-spoon back and forth. Randy was rescued when Yo nudged him with his elbow and said, "Cum'on, gotta go if you're gonna see anything else here. Already used up half the Lieutenant's 'hour-'r-so.' You do thanky signs and I'll say 'numwhit' so we can leave."

Trailed by ki-kun—small naked boys, doll-face little black-eyed girls in long dresses—along with the village dog-pack, several boys Randy's size, Pat, Mike, Mama, and the three chiefs, Randy and Tuesday arm-in-arm visited every teepee in the circle of tents. In his loudest voice, Randy "introduced" Tuesday by his new name, Tsis-tou-toh, at each one, listened to long singsongs of praise, smiled at the admiring body caresses—the rewards Tuesday liked best.

Inside the teepees and on the ground outside, Randy saw women in their short slaughter-house skirts standing or

Warriors of the Plains.
C.Taylor
p61,159
(*coup,"coo"*)

Carson story
Chapter 6
Westward Go!

Wah-To-Yah
L.Garrard
("*ki-kun,*"
=*children*)

Visit to Cheyenne camp added. Not in JF Report

Bent's Fort.
D.Lavender
p126
(*praise highest reward*)

crawling on the ground to hack, pull apart, slice, chop, drape on frames, or cook, hundreds of pounds of buffalo meat, bones, sinews, brains, and internal organs their men had killed that day.

On the ground also lay twenty buffalo hides waiting to be washed and scraped of flesh, fat, and hair. Skinny pole drying frames leaning against tree trunks were steadily being filled up with rows and rows of thin slices of dark red flesh to dry for two days and be stored. Over frontyard cook-fires, trading-post iron pots added hot steam and meaty odors to the hot air—stews that would be ready to eat when the hunters having watered and staked their horses, cleaned themselves in the river.

As Randy and companions came near the village entrance where Basil, holding the trail lines of the three horses, was watching half-grown boys in breechcloths wrestle, small naked boys roll and tumble with dogs, they saw the last arrival from the buffalo kill, a woman. Bent almost in half, she was staggering under a backpack that would have made a mule sink to its knees. She had finally reached home and began dropping her day's food and winter rations before her teepee door.

Tuesday's mama, Pat, and the village leaders told Randy "hookahay numwhit," hurried to help the woman, leaving Randy, Tuesday, and Yo at the door of the last teepee family in the village circle. Yo decided to depart, too, declaring he'd seen enough teepees, could just as well keep an eye on Randy from the place in sight where Basil and the horses were waiting.

Tuesday seemed to hesitate for a moment, then scratched on the teepee cover, lifted the flap, looked in, made a sign for Randy to enter. Inside, the scene was about the same as all the others, but in one way it was very different.

A young girl with smiling black eyes, shiny white teeth, short black hair across her forehead, long glossy hair to her waist, was tending the cook pot. She was wearing a spotless dress of antelope skin decorated with squares and stars made of dyed, colored quills of the porcupine. Long fringe on her blouse and skirt trembled over her arms and legs when she moved. Her mocassins' blue and gold beads sparkled in the cookfire light. Randy, the red-headed wihio, stared at her, deciding she was the prettiest girl he had ever seen in all his nearly 13 years.

Her mother, plump and pleasant, bedraggled from the

day's work, invited the boys to eat.

They sat down at the girl's feet and she served them stew in wooden bowls. It was burning-hot, Randy remembered later, and it may have been buffalo and good. The girl sat down facing him, watching with smiling interest his every movement. He smiled back, and stared, taking his time to empty his bowl.

He came to when he saw Yo at the tent opening and heard his call. "Randy! Lieutenant said 'an hour-'r-so.' You're taking too long. We gotta go. Basil's already on his horse. Finish your goodbyes! Hurry!"

Randy awkwardly scrambled to his feet. Tuesday was already standing, saying his thank-you's to the girl and her mother, and stooping to walk through the door. Randy, suddenly so flustered he couldn't remember fast enough how to sign "thank you," said it in English, and plunged through the tent opening.

Tuesday was just outside. "Ran-dee!" he said softly, and gave him a folded piece of paper. His hands touched his breast and spread open toward Randy: From me to you. "Hookahay. Nimwhit."

Randy squeezed the paper and bowed his thanks. He tried to say the Cheyenne hello-goodbye words that had always sounded so comical to him. They came out "Hookathanks."

"Numwhit," they said at the same instant and with a cry threw their arms around each other. They took one long, last look into each other's eyes, turned and walked away, Tuesday toward his family's teepee, Randy toward his horse. His watery gaze looking back found the eyes of the beautiful girl standing outside the tent. She smiled. Randy's hand flew to his heart. Quickly he turned, saw Tuesday had stopped, watching him. Randy waggled his hand for "question," gestured toward the girl. Her name?

He saw Tuesday blushing deep red as he made the sign for "Sunrise."

Based on C. Russell 18–

In Tuesday Cheyenne's village, women scrape buffalo hides staked to the ground, keep the buffalo stewpot boiling, watch after babies and camp dogs, slice and hang buffalo meat to dry. In one tent, Randy meets the most beautiful girl he's ever seen. In Indian sign-language, her name,"Sunrise," also means "happiness."

Beth Berryman

While Randy tours Cheyenneville, Fremont and Maxwell in Arapahotown visit Chief
Bull Tail and his associate chiefs in his teepee. Only the two visitors eat a skimpy meal
of buffalo meat and sip a mug of Platte River water. Maxwell, who knows some
Arapaho, and Left Hand, a young Indian who knows some English, do the interpreting.
They had little to do, for the associate chiefs said not a word, "just passed the pipe
around, smoked and smoked." Bull Tail asked a question once an hour or so. Three
hours passed very slowly with no way to politely depart.

CHAPTER 30

BULL TAIL'S DINNER, ROCKIES IN VIEW

July 8 - 9, South Platte trail (Colorado)

"Sunrise!" Randy turned to look at her, whispering "Sunrise, Sunrise—prettiest name, prettiest girl."

But her face was not there to look at again. He saw only the back-fringe at the bottom of her skirt disappearing as she bent to walk through the opening of the teepee. He almost took a step toward her.

Visit to Cheyenne camp added. Not in <u>JF Report.</u>

But...no, better not. He could feel Tuesday watching from twenty steps away and thinking that same message. She didn't beckon. All right. Good-bye, Sunrise, goodbye.

The boys looked at each other, stood still, staring. The last, last moment had come. Goodbye, Tuesday. Randy raised his right hand, two fingers upright side by side— "friend." He wanted to sign, "I'll remember you forever!" but could only lay one hand over his heart, point to his forehead with the other, then raise it high above his head and make large circles in the air. "Probably not real sign language," Randy thought, "but maybe he'll see what I mean." Tuesday saw, and with a tight-lipped smile, repeated all of Randy's signs.

"Hookahay!"

"Hookahay!"

"Hey! Randy! Come on!" Yo's shout turned Randy around and started him running. He brushed past the last little cluster of wide-eyed children, started to climb hastily into the saddle and was stopped by the crumpled, folded paper in his hand. "Tuesday probably drew a picture for me," he thought, and put it in his pocket. Up he swung into the saddle and clucked the pony into a quick walk. Just beyond the broad, open entrance to the camp circle, he looked back, half-raised his hand to wave. But there was no Tuesday in sight to wave to.

Randy put his mind to keeping up with Yo, and the two of them catching up with Basil and the pack animals. But that done, his thoughts leaped to pictures of Sunrise the first moment he saw her, to Tuesday, one hand on his heart, the other circling above his head, saying goodbye. Once more he toured inside Tuesday's cone-shaped, one room home, saw Tuesday with his arms around his mother, saw him riding Fremont's pack horse into the Cheyenne village, saw—

"Sacre diable! Lookit dat, garcon!" Basil's big baritone called loud and sharp, shattering Randy's memory-pictures, and Yo's supper-planning. "Up dere! in de sky!"

Basil wheeled his horse around and pointed to a thick, black cloud rolling toward them from the southeast. A jagged line of fire suddenly pierced it from top to bottom, lighting up its smoky inner parts for less than the flicker of an eyelid. Rmmmm! its voice rumbled to the edges of the world below.

"Look dere at de horizon, Randy, you and Yo—see how dis black cloud sits above a wide, bright blue strip, and how de cloud's bottom edge sprays water on de blue? Dat rain looks like scraggly hair hanging down over de blue forehead of de sky. De cloud'n rain're moving dis way—feel de wind rising? Let's get a move on—we've gotta find some kinda shelter quick!"

JF Report
July 8
("densely foliaged
old trees 3 miles
upriver")

They trotted the horses another two miles until they saw a grove of densely leafed old cottonwoods on the river bank. Under one tree lay the enormous trunk of a fallen, rotting tree. Hurriedly, they broke off dead branches and kindled a fire by the trunk side out of the wind.

"At least the wind has blown away the awful heat we've had all day—108 at midday, remember? Now, if we only had some of the Cheyennes' buffalo meat to cook! I'm hungry!" Randy declared.

"But we do have some!" announced Basil. "While I was waiting dose two hours for you to see every pot'n'pan in every teepee in Cheyenneyville, I made friends wid an Indian woman cutting up meat next t'me. I traded her my red kerchief for a hefty chunk of meat. See—it fills up our soup pot," he said, untying the pot from the packmule's overload.

"It's beautiful!" Randy exclaimed when he saw the size of the lean, red-raw meat. "Can't we start cooking right now? John and Max'll be here pretty soon, and they'll be glad we have supper ready for them! I'm starving! I was offered Cheyenne stew twenty times, but I didn't eat any—except the last little bowl. The others smelled kinda suspicious, and I figured it was dog stew that had to be eaten up before they could start cooking the buffalo meat—what's so funny?!"

Between laughing gulps, Yo told Randy the cook pots most likely DIDN'T have dogmeat stew in them on account

329

of Cheyennes cooked dogmeat stew only for special occasions. "I mean, like your mama will fry a chicken when the preacher's coming for dinner. Well, I spose you coulda been smelling PRAIRIE dog. When it's a-cooking, it smells just like, well, DOG!"

Randy didn't smile. Basil did, and added, "You know what de Cheyennes call prairie dogs, Randy—'o-noni-won-ski.'" Randy nodded vigorously and said he knew that, Tuesday had told him. "He tell you what it means?" Basil replied. Randy shook his head. "It means," Basil snickered, "'dey all look alike!' Dog puppies de Indians breed to cook, dey all look alike, too. 'Look-alike-o-noni-wonski stew' sounds real tasty, don'tcha t'ink?"

Randy made a face and thought, "John says Basil's his favorite man. He's mine, too, except when he teases."

They cut up buffalo meat for the pot's boiling water, stabbed long, pointed sticks through meatchunks and lined them up to roast hanging over the fire. Impatiently they waited for Fremont and Maxwell until near sunset.

When the black cloud rolled in with rain, Basil announced, "Let's eat! Dere's no need to wait longer for de Lieutenant, I t'ink. Old Mule Tail's prob'ly still smoking his pipe and saying six words every thirty minutes. De Lieutenant 'n' Max know better dan to get up 'n' leave 'til de Chief' 'n' de brudder chiefs rise to der feet."

It was nearly dark when Fremont and Maxwell, riding in from Bull Tail's, saw Randy's pony, the mule, and four horses staked and cropping grass next to a thick grove of trees. Wet and chilled from a cold shower and driving wind in the first half of their hour's ride, they reined into the leaf-sheltered camp. Behind the massive, fallen tree trunk they found their mostly-dry party lounging warm and well-fed around a flaming, crackling campfire.

"It seems hours and hours ago that we ate that roasted meat in Bull Tail's teepee," Fremont told them between bites of hot stew. "When we arrived at the Chief's teepee, he was all fresh and clean—had a steam bath, he said, in a little round-top sweat lodge after washing himself in the river. He spread out a robe for us to sit upon, and signaled his wife to bring the food. He then lit his pipe.

"He went through the routine of pointing the pipe stem to the sky, calling the name of the Wise Man Above, then to the ground to the underground god, then in four directions to the four powerful god-spirits—winds—by name. After

Oregon Trail.
F.Parkman, p106
(Puppy dinner as special honor)

Cheyennes.
Grinnell, I, p68.
(breed dogs to eat) (stew, II,190)

JF Report
July 8
("cold shower, driving rain")

Wah-To-Yah.
L.Garrard, p38-9
(sweat lodge)

Cheyennes.
Grinnell, p88 II
(pipe smoking)

blowing a puff to each god, he passed the pipe over to me, then to Maxwell. We did our best at doing what Bull Tail had done. Max even knew the names of the gods!

"Bull Tail's wife brought in and set before us a wooden dish of roasted squares of buffalo meat. Bull Tail told us to commence eating, and we were pleased to oblige, it being long past our meal-less midday. He kept on smoking. Gradually five or six other chiefs came in and, not saying a word, took their seats on the ground by the Chief. The pipe made the rounds to them. Each one pointed the pipestem up, down, to the four corners of the earth, took three draughts without exhaling, then blew out their nostrils huge streams of smoke! Quite amazing!"

Maxwell had known all the chiefs when he was working as a trader for St.Vrain's Fort. "But one of these today, the youngest, the six-footer, the very handsome one, isn't a chief—yet. His name is Niwot—Left Hand. You heard him repeating some of your English words, Lieutenant—mine, too—to learn them—and telling the chiefs in good 'Rapaho what I'd just told them in my not-so-good 'Rapaho.

Bent's Fort.
Lavender, p198.
Chief Left Hand.
M.Coel, p6,10,13

Left Hand might
have attended
since he knew
some English.
But no mention
in JF Report.

Arapahoe
Chiefsof 1840's:
Cheyennes.
Grinnell, I, p256,
335,340,
Bent's Fort.
D.Lavender,
p192,256

"Left Hand's about twenty years old, and I predict that in just a few years we'll be hearing about CHIEF Left Hand. His sister married a white trader and Left Hand's been learning English from him—and from anybody else who'll take the time. He's also one of the few men of any tribe who's cared to learn and speak another tribe's language. He talks Cheyenne and Sioux like one of them.

"Now let's see—the other Chiefs were Touching Cloud, Full Moon, Little Raven, and Buffalo Belly."

Randy giggled as he asked, "Buffalo Belly—why would anybody name their son 'Buffalo Belly?' I'm sure glad I don't have a funny name like that!"

Maxwell told him Arapaho boys, like Cheyenne boys, start out with a child-name, are given a grown-up name when they're about 13 years old.

"If a boy bravely shot an arrow into the belly of a charging buffalo, causing the animal to fall over wounded, so saving a hunter's life, he'd be PROUD when people called him 'Buffalo Belly.' It's an automatic, lifelong reminder to everybody of his great deed.

"Now suppose," Maxwell went on, "that YOU did a remarkable, valuable deed on this trip to the Rocky Mountains, and Lieutenant Fremont gave you the name of this deed—something like 'Just-in-Time-to-Save-Kit-from-a-

Broken-Neck.' Wouldn't you feel proud to hear everybody calling you 'Just-in-Time' from then on?"

Randy hunched his shoulders in thought before replying, "Kit knows I didn't DO anything to SAVE him from a broken neck. I'd probably get named what he said to me— 'What're-YOU-Doing-Out-Here?'"

Fremont raised both hands for attention, and broke off the teasing and laughter. "Whatever the names, Bull Tail and his associate chiefs didn't say a word nor eat a bite. They just smoked and smoked and looked dignified and solemn. Even when I gave them some important information of the highest interest for them, the chiefs' faces, like Bull Tail's, showed an unchanging grave expression, not a twitch of surprise or concern—or even interest! Only interpreter Left Hand's face showed interest, but not being a chief, he asked no questions.

JF Report
July 8
(silent chiefs, didn't eat)

"What I told them was this—and I did so in answer to Chief Bull Tail's asking me a question about the object of our journey. I wanted to see the country, I said, preparatory for the United States Army's coming out here to establish military posts on the way to the mountains. I didn't expect the news to please Chief Bull Tail, but not a muscle moved in his rather Oriental face to give me a clue to his thoughts. You know the Arapahoes call us whites 'the mysterious ones.' I think we could call Arapahoes 'the MOST mysterious ones.'

Arapahoes.
L.Fowler,p58,44
("Oriental."
Whites" mysterious ones")

"Max and I were the only diners. No food was brought for any others. Bull Tail asked a question about every hour or so, I would answer, Max and Left-Hand interpreted. That's all. Time passed very, very slowly. I confess I was quite uncomfortable in the midst of all that silence and smoky air—"

"And our legs were complaining about being sat upon for so long," interrupted Max. "Yes!" continued Fremont. "So when I heard drops of rain pattering on the teepee cover, saw Bulltail getting to his feet, Max and I got quickly to our feet, did thank-you signs, said 'hookahay,' and ran to spring upon our horses.

JF Report
July 8
(dining in Chief's teepee)

"What a pleasure to find you under a tolerable shelter, with buffalo stew cooked and ready to eat! These past four hours or so have frazzled me, and it seems a long, long time since I ate Bull Tail's not overly plentiful dinner. Max had a bundle of dried meat an Arapaho handed him as we were mounting our horses. But we didn't try eating any of

Among the Indians. H.Boller, p138,233 (jerky)

it while we rode here—Indian 'jerky' is too hard, dry, black, and tough.

"Now—tell us how you got along in the Cheyenne village. Did everything go well? Randy! What did you do after we left?"

Randy gave a quick summary of his tour of Tuesday's teepee and seeing Kit Carson's story in a picture Tuesday had painted on the teepee's inner lining. Fremont knew Kit would be mighty pleased to hear about that. Fremont had seen pictures on Bull Tail's inside walls, too, "several battle scenes showing Bull Tail dressed in a bonnet trailing long lines of feathers, a shirt trimmed with hair fringe and decorated with beads in colorful designs. A big shield decorated with bull heads and eagle feathers hung from a teepee pole behind Bull Tail, and he said the design and feathers on this special shield that stays in his tent protect him from harm."

"Well," Randy said thoughtfully, "I didn't see pictures on teepee inside walls anywhere else but Tuesday's. But I didn't go inside every teepee no matter what Basil says about my looking at every pot and pan." Cautiously Randy listed some of the sights he saw—the naked little boys, the women cutting meat, the very tall men, the boys wrestling with dogs and each other, one girl in the whole camp who was dressed in pretty clothes...

"Oh—and Tuesday gave me a goodbye present!"

He dug into his left trouser-pocket and pulled out the smudged, crumpled paper. As he was opening it, he announced his guess that it was a picture Tuesday had drawn, and his hope that it was a self-portrait. But when he looked at it, he stared hard, studying it in silence.

Added episode. Not in JF Report.

"Well?" Fremont prodded.

"It IS a portrait. But it's of me! It's the one he did in clay that day we camped by the hollow close to the Platte. He's drawn a map to show me where he hid it in some bushes. Remember when the men were gambling, losing, looking around for things to bet—and all of a sudden the clay head and Tuesday disappeared? He took it away and hid it.....and now it's his goodbye present.

"He knows we might camp there on our way home. Look at the beautiful drawing he's done of my clay head. Looks just like me, doesn't it?—only better. No freckles."

The piece of paper was passed around and the talk was all about Tuesday, his ability to draw anything and everything, how soon he'd be one of the chiefs of his Hair-rope band, whether Fremont could arrange with Mr. St. Vrain at

333

the fort to send news of Tuesday to him from time to time.

"If he would do that—!" Randy exclaimed, his eyes shining.

"First, we must get to Fort St. Vrain," Fremont said.

"We've advanced only 15 miles today, so we must rise with the sun and hurry on in the morning. Who will volunteer to stand guard tonight—I think we should take this precaution since more than a thousand Indians are within a short ride of us."

Basil stood up. "Lieutenant, me 'n' Yo were t'inking about our situation wid us being so near so many Indians. Dey friendly Indians, but it don't take but one sneaky friendly-Indian to do us some mischief. Me 'n' Yo offer a plan. We'd bring de MULE and our six horses to closeby grass on de prairie side o' de grove, stake'um in hearing of where we're rolled up in our blankets. Den we could ALL go to sleep.

Overland With Kit Carson. G.Bremerton, *p65 (mule sentry)*

"Everybody knows dat a MULE will snort 'n' move 'round to look toward any stranger coming near, specially in an unfamiliar situation. Seems dey can smell'um at a distance. Me 'n' Yo'll keep one ear open and our triggers set all night. De mule will keep watch, do de guarding, snort de alarm, and we'll do de jumping up'n shooting."

Fremont, first up at the dim greying of night sky, was first to pat the mule and whisper "thanks" into its long ear. He walked to the river edge of the grove, scrambled down the low bank, washed his face, and filled the camp canteen with water. He noted that the Platte was narrowing, current running fast, and its water an inch or so deeper than it was at the downstream crossing yesterday. When he stood up, he saw nearly opposite him the swirl of a large volume of water coming from the wide mouth of a creek into the South Platte. "Max will know its name—if it has one." He wondered who had named all the creeks and rivers.

He looked up the river, past a lone tree toward the west. The sun's first bright rays suddenly struck a spot on the far horizon and made it glitter. Fremont caught his breath. Could it be—?

He scrambled up the river bank and ran toward the campfire."Max! Everybody! Come out on the prairie with me and tell me if I saw what I think I saw!" They raced from the tree grove and looked west to the distant white spot on the horizon Fremont was pointing toward.

JF Report *July 9* *(Beaver Creek)*

"It looks like a little cloud," Randy said.

"Well, friends, it's actually the snowy summit of Long's

JF Report
July 9
(Long's Peak,
first view of the
Rockies)

Peak!" declared Maxwell. "It's faint, being about a hundred miles away from where Beaver Creek right by us here runs into the South Platte. We're seeing this minute our first glimpse of the Rocky Mountains!"

They ate their re-roasted chunks of buffalo meat, loaded packmule and packhorse, and set their thoughts on the distant, blurry height. Maxwell had said it was the highest peak he knew of in this area, and that it was said to be 40 miles due west of St. Vrain's Fort.

Randy had walked his pony out of the grove, fixed his eye on Long's peak, and was heading upriver when Yo called him back. "Hold on a minute! We have a problem.

Mule episode added.
Not in JF Report.

The mule's decided she won't budge. She's probably miffed that we made her stand guard all night, didn't give her a reward of any kind, just loaded her up for a full day's work." Randy came back, having heard about stubborn mules that held their ground for a half-day before being lashed into moving.

Basil was pulling on the mule's bridle and calling for Yo to give her a whack on the rump.

Obstinate mules:
Wah-To-Yah.
L.Garrard,p109
Overland With Kit
Carson, p.54-55
G.Bremerton,
Gr. Platte R. Road.
Mattes,p39.

The whack triggered her hind legs to flip up their hooves, and her front legs and hooves to cling more tenaciously to the ground. "Come up here 'n' try twisting her ears while I grab de reins and pull her forward!" Basil called to Yo. "Dat worked for me one time!"

Yo came and shortly was yelling, "Can't get ahold'uv her ears! She's snapping her teeth at me!"

Fremont thought she probably was objecting to the weight of her load, even though it was just half of the load she carried most of the afternoon before. "Maybe her back's sore. Take off the boxes of scientific instruments, put them on the horse."

The mule eyed them but held still while her load was lightened. Yet, she dug in her hooves and refused to move afterwards. Yo said, "Gonna have to give 'er the lash."

"No," Maxwell said, "there's one more thing we can try. When the Cheyennes herd into camp a bunch of wild ponies, they have a way to 'break 'um in' without beating or starving them. They loosely hobble the pony's front legs and tie its long neck-rein to the tail of a mare. She leads the pony around for a week or so. He eats when she eats. He watches a man petting and rubbing the mare, speaking to her softly.

"After a few days, when the man puts his hand on the wild pony, it doesn't resist being touched, petted, and rubbed, too. The next step is piling a buffalo robe on its back, and finally saddling and mounting the willing animal. Maybe if Muley here were tied to the tail of our packhorse but not hobbled, the mare's sympathetic nearness and her doing her work example might cause Muley to warm up to walking, following her."

Muley did warm up. Basil on his horse led the packhorse who led Muley, who led Randy, Fremont, Yo, and Maxwell out of the grove onto the prairie, heading toward the Rockies.

"Every day we just seem unable to keep to schedule," Fremont sighed. Maxwell thought there'd be nothing more in the way to hinder them today, and they could make up for yesterday's short mileage. "We should pace our horses a little faster."

Two hours later—seven miles across a half-dozen ravines lined with light brown sandstone—Randy, enjoying a lively gallop ahead of the others, wheeled his horse around and came back, yelling, "People coming!"

JF Report
July 9
(3 horsemen approach)

He swung his pony beside Fremont's and pointed to the other side of the river about a mile or so ahead.

"Three of them," Fremont and Maxwell said at the same time. "They aren't dressed like Indians," Fremont observed. "Look—they've seen us—they're turning in towards the river. Guns ready while we meet them and see who they are."

The strangers' horses splashed across the river and approached at a trot. "They're two whites and a black," Fremont said in a low voice.

"Mon dieu! Sacre diable!" burst out Basil, and pulled ahead at a gallop, yelling, "Beckwort'! Mon frere! You old batard! What you do'n here!"

He raced up to the dark mulatto man, both jumped down from their mounts, embraced with much back-slapping, cries of "Jeem!" "Baptiste! Brudder!" and jabbering in Virginia drawl and Canadian French. Right behind Basil had trotted Maxwell, grinning broadly, yelling, "Beckwith ole podner! What a surprise! Thought you were long gone from these parts!"

Autobiography of James Beckwourth. *(Lajeunesse) p50, 62-4,67-68,76,104, 113,122,142)*

Fremont rode up, but before he could speak, Basil's voice was shouting, "Dis man Jeem Beckwort', he's my brudder! I spent five years trapping in de mountains wid'im, not seen him since a mi'yun years! Dis meetin's a miracle, Lieutenant!"

Maxwell introduced Fremont to Beckwourth, and said, "Jim was working as a trader out of St. Vrain's Fort two years ago when I was there doing the same. Well, I'll be a son-of-a-gun! Where you fellows going today? Who're your

336

Bent's Fort.
D.Lavender
(Maxwell and
Beckwourth
traders at Fort
St.Vrain 1840)
JF doesn't
mention these connec-
tions.)

friends, podner?" Beckwourth introduced the two French Canadians, and returned to backslapping his brudder.

Randy and Yo hung back, eyes wide, mouths open in disbelief. How in the world could they just happen to meet ANYbody out here in the middle of an empty prairie a thousand miles from St. Louis! And especially a black man Basil was calling his brudder, and Max was calling his podner?!

More amazement came during the next two minutes of talk between Fremont and the two Canadians, whose names Randy didn't catch. "We can't linger," they said, "we've got to put in a quick search for a band of horses dat ran off from our camp. Camp's on an island in de Platte about ten miles from here.

JF Report
July 9
("Camp some miles
up-river in charge
of Mr. Jean Baptiste
Charbonard." JF
does not identify him
as Sacajawea's son
nor give any detail
about the appearance,
amazing life story
of the famous infant,
now 37 years old,who
made the trip with
Lewis and Clark)

"You should figger on stopping dere. Mr. Charbonar's de man in charge and he'll be sure to ask you to eat wid him and drink a mint julep."

Fremont looked puzzled. "Mr. Who?"

"Charbonar—Jean Baptiste Charbonar—you know, de baby de Indian woman toted on de trip wid Lewis and Clark. She was de wife of de half-bred Frenchman, Charbonar, a guide or interpreter or somet'ing, dat Clark hired. Her name was Sacajawea. She's de mama of our boss, Bap Charbonar."

Based on Worthington Whittredge, 1866

At a tentless camp in a grove of trees by the South Platte River, Fremont in early morning sees a flash of sunlight strike the snowy peak of Mt. Long, a hundred miles due west. First view of the Rockies! To Randy minutes later, the mountain's whiteness looks like a cloud. Fremont and his four companions expect this day's 30-mile trek will hold no such dramas as yesterday's stay with buffalo-hunting Arapahoes and Cheyennes in the present-day Brush, Colorado, area. But surprising events will again cut in half the mileage they hope to travel.

Chief, based on C. Russell
Women, on A.J. Miller

Randy hears one amazing, entertaining story after another from Jim Beckwourth after he happens along and joins Fremont's party. Son of a Virginia slave and her owner, Beckwourth became famous in the Rockies as Big Chief of the Crow Indians for six years. His exciting stories tell of his leading the Crows to victory in hundreds of battles with rival Indian tribes, and winning for himself ten wives. Now a trader working out of Fort St.Vrain, he knows Lajeunesse and Maxwell. He leads Fremont to his boss, "Mr.Charbonnar"—and mint juleps.

339

CHAPTER 31

MULATTO JIM, CHIEF OF THE CROWS

July 9 morning, South Platte trail (Colorado)

Early in the year, when Randy was arguing and pleading to go to the Rocky Mountains with his brother-in-law hero John Fremont, Randy's father had put into the argufier's hand a two-volume book. "You must read every word of both books before either you or I make the final decision about your going with John across two thousand miles of wilderness," Senator Benton had said.

Two weeks later, mid-February, Randy had read every page, all the words. They told the day-by-day story of the famous journey that Lewis and Clark had made on the Missouri River from its mouth on the Mississippi, across plains, through the Rocky Mountains to the Pacific Ocean nearly forty years before—when Tom Benton was a boy Randy's age.

The now-famous Senator hoped those early explorers' hardships—canoeing rough rivers, climbing dangerous mountains, enduring harsh weather, hunger, exhaustion, Indian scares, swarming mosquitoes and fleas, sleeping on the ground—would turn off Randy's passion to "go West with John!"

Traveling across the continent hadn't gotten any easier, the Senator made clear to Randy, and hardly anybody had tried it except some rough and tough "mountain men" eager to make a little money trapping beavers for the fur merchants of St. Louis.

But the two-volume details of Lewis and Clark's exhausting, exhilarating trip turned Randy on, not off. For two weeks, Senator Benton was greeted at every breakfast and dinner with Randy's high-speed, high-pitched voice full of excitement telling how a sudden, violent wind nearly turned Lewis's big canoe "tosa turva," and how the Indian girl, Sacajawea—"just fourteen—not much older than I am—" swam in the Missouri River to capture Lewis's journal while her French-Indian husband, Charbonneau, "a real old man more'n forty," hid in the listing boat—or how Captain Clark—"red-headed like you and me, and I remember seeing him when we went to dinner a long time ago at his house in St. Louis"—saw smoke signals in the mountains, then saw a lone

History of the Expedition of Lewis and Clark.(2vols.) Nicholas Biddle,ed.

Journals of Lewis and Clark. B. DeVoto (listing boat, May 14, 1805)

Sacajawea.
A.Waldo, p290
("white man"
Bap/Baptiste)

Into the Wilderness.
(NatGeoS book, chap5)
"Lewis and Clark"
Ron Fisher

Indian on a horse, and shouted at him in Sacajawea's Shoshoni Indian language, "Tab-ba-bone! Tab-ba-bone!"

"That means 'white man! white man!' and that Indian had never seen a white skin before!" Randy breathlessly informed the Senator. "And all the time going out and coming back for two years, Sacajawea carried her little baby boy Baptiste—she called him 'Pompy'—tied to her back! The trip didn't hurt him a bit!"

Randy's shining blue eyes and knowing smile told what he expected those statements to mean to his father. "But," Senator Benton observed with a suppressed smile, "You wouldn't have your mother along to take care of you."

"No, she can't. She's sick. But I'll have John and he's stronger than an Indian girl and I'm a lot bigger than a baby—my thirteenth birthday's November eleventh—and I can walk far and ride a horse much farther than Sacajawea! Nobody'll have to carry me either! Besides, we'll be out there just this one summer, not two whole years, and John says it's going to be flatland all the way. He'll go TO the Rockies, not up or through the Rockies."

Now, six months later, Randy on the South Platte approaching the Rockies was again smiling knowingly, eyes shining with excitement—and disbelief. "Did that man talking to John say 'Sacajawea' and 'Baptiste?'" he loud-whispered to Yo. "Sure did," Yo answered, not the least bit excited by names of people he'd never heard of.

Randy clucked discreetly to his pony, and guided it closer to Fremont and the two strangers still answering his questions. Maxwell, Lajeunesse, and Beckworth nearby were still talking fast, all at the same time, not stopping even during boisterous bursts of laughter and joyous shoulder slaps. Randy tuned his ears to hear the answers to Fremont's questions about Charbonneau.

"Yessir," the stocky, bald-topped French-Canadian was saying to Fremont, "dis Baptiste—we calls him 'Bap'—is dat baby what went on his mama's back up de Missouri River, over de Rockies, and to a beach longside de Pacific Ocean by de Columbia River mouth. But dat was a long time ago. Bap must be forty years old by now."

JF Report
July 9
(St.Helena)

Not quite, Fremont told him, and inquired what Bap was doing out here on the South Platte, how long he'd been here. "Don't rightly know how long—men out here move around so much, can't keep up wid'um.

"But what he does is work for Mr. Marcellin Sinverin, de

boss-on-the-spot, de booshway, at Fort Sinverin on de South Platte, and also for de Sinverin partner Mr. Bent at Bent's Fort on de Arkansas River down sout'. You know—Bent's Fort on de Santa Fe Trail. Bap takes Sinverin's furs and buffalo hides from de Fort—"

"You're talking about Marcellin St.Vrain and Fort St. Vrain, aren't you?" Fremont interrupted.

"Yessir, Sinverin. Marcellin Sinverin—he's de young one, only 20-something, a sparrow compared to his hawk-size brot'er Ceran Sinverin, de Big Boss—"

"Oh yes—Marcellin's the one whose reputation as a champion antelope hunter was reported to me in St. Louis," Fremont said. "I heard that he lures the animals by standing on his head and waving his legs in the air! Antelope curiosity brings the animals close to this strange sight, and boom! they're dead."

"Yessir, dat's harum-scarum Marcellin, heeheeheehee! But he don't have time to do much antelope hunting since he got married not long ago to Red. She's a 13-year-old Sioux girl. Some say she's a close relation, daughter maybe, of Chief Red Cloud. I dunno. Anyhow, it's Marcellin dat's running de trade post. Bap's his head-man of de crew rafting furs—only he's stuck wit' de low river right now. He rafts dem robes east on de Platte all de way to de Missouri and down de Mississippi to Saint Looie.

"He comes back by de Santa Fe Trail wit' horses and mules and wagonloads of trade goods, leaves some at Charlie and Will Bent's fort, brings de rest 200 miles north up de prairie to Fort Sinverin. Oh, Bap's a big man out here, yessir, near-bouta partner to de Bents and de Sinverins.

"But now, sir, we gotta get going to find dem horses. You won't have no trouble finding Bap's camp, being's it's on an island in de middle of de Platte. Just go straight on upriver. After a coupla miles you'll see Bijou creek entering de Platte. About eight miles after dat, you'll see Bap's tents on a big island. He's named it 'St. Helena.' Bap says he's like Napoleon—stranded on St. Helena! Heeheehee! Now, sir, we jes' GOTTA push on! So long ever'body!"

He and his impatient companion rode off calling to Beckworth to come on, too. But the bearded mulatto only waved at them. The grin on his devil-may-care, intelligent face stretched his bushy, teepee-shaped mustache into a straight line above shiny square teeth. Pushing his arched eyebrows into a higher arch and swishing his long, wavy

Bent's Fort, p223
D.Lavender
(Charbonneau on
St.Helena Island)

Bent's Fort, p195-8
D.Lavender.
(Marcellin St.Vrain:
standing on head,
wife is Red Cloud's
daughter)

Jim Beckwourth

JF Report
"The American
(Beckwourth)
turned back
with us."

hair side to side as he vigorously shook his head, he shouted, "I've gotta lead my brudder to St. Helena!"

Brown-faced, lean-muscled "Jim" confided to Fremont as
he, Maxwell, and Jim's one-time brudder Basil swung into
their saddles, "I can lead you to Bap Chabonard so fast
you'll have time for a mint julep before sitting in a CHAIR
at a TABLE to EAT!"

"Mint julep, eh?" Fremont said with a quizzical smile.
"With ice? Well, I hope it's worth putting a hole in our
mileage schedule. But mint julep or no, I can't pass by the
chance to meet and talk with the grown-up, famous baby who
traveled with Lewis and Clark." Laughing, the six horsemen
started off in high spirits, Maxwell, Fremont, and Beckworth
leading the way. "Lieutenant," Beckworth said, "You'll be
more likely to see a mint julep this midday than I was to see
you and a cavvy-boy this morning on the South Platte!"

"cavvy boy"
looked after the
spare mule,horses
on the trail.

Abruptly, Beckworth looked behind him at Randy and
called out gruffly, "Cavvy-boy! Come'ere! I need you right
here!" He flipped a hand at Randy to bring his pony up
next to him. Fremont's voice, loud and crisp, jarred everyone. "Sir!! That 'boy' is my brother-in-law! His name is
Randolph Benton, son of Senator Thomas Benton of
Missouri!" he snapped at the ebullient—or presumptious?—
44-year-old stranger beside him.

Randy, pulling his pony up beside Beckworth, saw a faint
flush of red under the brown skin of Beckworth's cheeks as
the mulatto responded, "Ohhh—sUUUh!! I BEEHH-guh yo'
pardon, Loo-tenant! I was born in Virginny and bred in
Mizzoori and MY name is Nan-kup-bah-pah—Medicine Calf—
Big Chief of the Crow Indian Nation of 16,000 warriors!"
He turned toward Randy a proud face, tense with temper,
black eyes cold with anger—until he saw Randy's bright blue
inquisitive eyes, the admiring smile on his flushed and
freckled face, and heard him say in his boy soprano, "I'll
bet you have some stories as good as Kit Carson's!"

The following stories
from Jim Beckwourth's
Autobiography are
not in JF Report. But
Beckwourth,braggart
and blabber, would
not have missed the
chance to tell his
stories during a
3-hour ride with a
new audience.

The Life and Adven-
tures of James
Beckwourth,
published 1856.
(autobiograpy as
told to Tom Bonner)
(Beckwourth was
Chief of Crow Tribe
during the 1830's)

"Better," he growled. "That's why I wanted you close by
me. I need a new audience." For the next few hours, he
held forth "almost without stopping to catch his breath," as
Yo said admiringly to Randy that afternoon. Randy got
Beckworth started by asking him how he got a scar across
the left upper corner of his forehead.

Beckworth bugged his eyes at Randy before twisting his
neck to look behind himself at Basil Lajeunesse. "There's
the man who can tell that story 'cause when it happened,

343

he was there and saved my scalp." Basil shook his head vigorously and waved the back of his hand toward Beckworth to say, "YOU tell it."

Beckwourth
Autobiography.
"Basil / Baptiste
Lajeunesse probably
the same man."

"Well, you can stop me if I get something wrong. There ARE some people who think I exaggerate," Beckworth said as he straightened, glancing at Fremont on the turn. "This happened in connection with the Rondy-voo on the south shore of Bear Lake quite a few years ago—right, brudder? Me and my Crow band—250 warriors and more than a thousand women and children—had set up camp by Bear Lake. "We'd been wandering in hostile Blackfeet country to trap beaver. Bear Lake's blue as blue can be, with a wide border of green, flat grassland and sort of yellow-brown clay hills behind it. The north tip of Great Salt Lake is maybe a day's fast ride west."

For the next quarter hour, Beckwith detailed the trapping, battles with Blackfeet Indians, and hardships of the weeks (or months?) leading up to arriving at Bear Lake. Finally, Randy heard him say, "We took up our traps and moved there after bumping into two white men who'd just arrived from Saint Looie. They told us that General Ashley, Big Boss of the American Fur Company, and 300 goods-toting packmules would get to the lake any day now to open up the annual Rondy-voo. You do know what a Rondy-voo is, don't you Randy?"

Randy knew very well that "rendezvous" was meeting a friend at a place and time you both knew. "But," he protested, "you didn't know the time and place—you accidentally found out—and what were the 300 packmules bringing?"

"All kinds of good things to eat—sugar, flour, coffee—and good things for us trappers to use, like guns, whiskey, lead 'n' powder, traps, clothes, tools, cookpots—AND things like beads, red cloth, knives, needles, fish hooks, things Indians wanted in exchange for the beaver and buffalo hides they brought us.

Beckwourth
Autobiography.
(Rondy des-
cription)

"Ashley was bringing these goods to hundreds of us trappers—though I MIGHT have been a little bit special since I was BOTH a hired mountain man of his company, AND a Crow Indian chief! I and all my Crow brudders caught beavers, and I and all my Crow brudders traded our pelts to the General instead of trading them with the British coming down from Canada!"

"What a big time I and the Crows, the whole tribe, would have every year at the Rondy-voo! Word would spread with the speed of plum blossom perfume all through the Rockies where to go for the Rondy, and when. The Green River—Seed-kee-dee the Crows called it—and Bear Lake were favorite places. Mountainmen and Indians would come from hundreds of miles—maybe 400 bearded, shaggy-haired white men and ONE mulatto —ME—all of us with Indian wives and children.

"Indians of many tribes came, maybe twenty thousand or more people with forty thousand horses, and even more dogs! Miles of Indian tents! Oh, it was noise, noise, noise day and night! A grand occasion! Like a big fair! It went on for a cou-pla weeks or more. Lotsa trading furs for white-man goods, and all day long eating, game-playing, contests and racing, dancing, singing, target-shooting—all sorts of frolic.

Jedidiah Smith.
D.Morgan, p228
(Rendezvous 1827,
Bear Lake)

"Well, here we were that year at Bear Lake as I was telling you, and almost the first arrivals. While we were waiting, we got word that some whites—26 men with women and children, maybe 75 people—were about 12 miles away, stranded, no ammunition for their guns, hiding from Blackfeet that wanted their scalps. I knew from smoke sig-nals I'd seen all over the prairie a few days before, when a thousand Blackfeet Indians had attacked us on the trail, that those whites would die if we didn't take shot and pow-der to them. I and two others rode out there with the ammunition.

Beckwourth
Autobiography

"I found out I knew some of those people! There was, first and foremost, my brudder Basil Lajeunesse! There was also one of the head men of the American Fur Company, which I worked for! What a disaster for ME as well as them had we decided NOT to bring them shot and powder, left them defenseless, let them be slaughtered!

"We were escorting them to the Rondy-voo camp when I heard singing 'way behind us, looked around, saw 500 mounted Indians racing toward us across the plain.

"Blackfeet!—the tribe that most highly prizes white scalps! I sent the horses with the women and children run-ning to a patch of willows six miles away, half-way to the Rondy camp.

"arrer"
(Autobiog.)

"We 29 men followed but halted now and again to shoot the frontmost Blackfeet when they came close enough to fling an arrer or a lance at us. An arrer did hit one of our men in the back. He fell from his horse, and the Indians were upon him in a flash to tear off his scalp."

Beckwourth
Autobiography

Randy, eyes and mouth stretching wider and wider as the vivid words made pictures in his mind, cried out, "Couldn't you save him?!"

"I and one other tried and it nearly cost both our lives. Yells from the advancing Indians told us they felt certain of their prey. To get away, we made our horses leap over a slough fifteen feet wide from bank to bank. More Indians over there! We charged through with the rapidity of pigeons, arrers whistling all 'round us, but we outran everything to reach the willow grove.

"If our ammunition had been plenty, we'd'uh shot the Blackfeet circling that grove 'til every last one was dead. But without plenty, we knew we'd have to charge through the Blackfeet circle, open a path for the women and children, escort them in a rush to the Rondy camp.

"'Hoo-ki-hi!!' Charge!! And ohhh! we charged mightily, killing and overturning everything in our way—until my horse was killed in his tracks. There I was on the ground, an arrer wound on my forehead"—he pointed to the scar Randy had noticed—"blood running down into my eye and ear. Yelling Blackfeet racing their horses toward me were coming from every direction.

"My brudder Basil—that very man riding right behind us here—saw my danger, called upon his comrades to help him save me, his brudder. They charged, firing, firing, driving away the Blackfeet. During that moment Basil rode up to me. Somehow, I sprang on the saddle behind him and he took me to safety among the willows."

Beckworth turned to look affectionately at Basil. "Now, I didn't exaggerate anything, did I, brudder?"

"Well," Basil said, "if you did, it was de part where I raced in, you leaped into de saddle wit' me and I galloped away saving you like in a fairytale. But taking de day as a whole, de worst story anybody tells about it can't be as bad, as scary, as de real event! You said yourself you'd never run such danger of losing your life and scalp as you did dat terrible day! I say de same! Bless de heavens dat help come in time from de Rondy camp to save us all!"

Beckwourth Autobiography

"Right, my brudder! Coming out alive made me decide I must be Indian-proof," Beckworth declared, thumping his broad chest with a fist. "I've had ten thousand adventures and Indian fights since that day—mostly because my Crow warriors couldn't bear idling around camp for long—they must have excitement and the excitement of war suited them the best. So I had to lead them to a good fight every few days. But I'm still alive! Scarred on my body here and there, but alive and well.

"Fact is, I fought so many battles, killed so many enemies, scored so many thousand 'coos,' heard so many hundred black-face scalp dances for victories, so many day-and-
night, weeks-long female grief-wailing and yowling—ou-ouuu-
ou-waaaaa—seen so much hair and finger-chopping, slashed
flesh bleeding for dead kindred, I couldn't stand Indian life
any longer. I decided to come back to the white man's world
no matter that my successes as a Crow warrior had raised
me from my Antelope name to six ever-higher names. Bull's
Robe! Enemy of Horses! Bobtail Horse! Red Fish! Bloody
Arm! and finally Medicine Calf, Chief of the Crow Nation—"

*Beckwourth
Autobiography
(six higher
names)*

Randy's shrill voice interrupted."I was born in Virginia
like you, Mr. Beckwith! I've lived half of every year in
Missouri where you lived! Will you ask the Crows to let me
come visit them next summer—"

"Ohh—son, you couldn't possibly qualify! You don't look
like a Crow—not the right color—I AM! You'll have to wait
ten years to grow up and show your talent as a warrior
before they'd invite you for a visit. Even then I'll bet your
freckles would turn purple the first time you saw a bloody
scalp yanked from a head!

"Besides all that, to get to live with the Crows, you'll
need a friend who can tell as big a lie to them, and as con-
vincingly, as my friend Greenwood did for me—no, Maxwell,
I'm NOT as good a liar as Greenwood! Here's what he did.

*Beckwourth
Autobiography*

"One day maybe a year or two before the Bear Lake
Rondy-voo, when some Crows came visiting a Snake Indian
camp we were trading in, the Crows began questioning my
friend Greenwood about me. They'd seen numerous scalps
of their Black Feet enemy hanging in my tent. Greenwood
took a notion to say to the Crows one day, 'Don't Jim look
like an Indian?' Then he told them I actually was a Crow!
'How can that be?' they said.

"Well, Greenwood recalled to them that many winters
ago, the Cheyennes fought the Crows, killed hundreds of
warriors, carried off many Crow women and children.
Greenwood said I was one of those children!

"Yes, he told them, the Cheyennes soon sold me to the
whites, I grew up to be a great warrior among them,
scalped hundreds, maybe thousandsa Black Feet, so Black
Feet now were scared to death of me."

Randy had gradually guided his pony so close to
Beckworth that their stirrups bumped briefly.

"Watch it, son," he said gently. To hear better, even Fremont had narrowed the space between his horse and the animated voice of Beckworth. Basil and Yo were leaning forward, mouths stretched into their widest smile line. Only Maxwell remained unmoved. He'd heard the story several times during the two years just past when both men were working at Fort St.Vrain.

"So! When Greenwood's joyful news was taken back to the Crow village," Beckworth continued, "all the older women wanted to see me, the lost child, the bar-ca-ta. Who would identify me, claim me as a son?

"But it would be a few days before I got to their camp and gave them a chance to look me over—as their prisoner, it turned out. See, I was about to steal a few of their horses from a herd that was acres in size—thought nobody'd see me. But they did—and grabbed me.

Beckwourth
Autobiography

"They recognized me and took me to a lodge, summoned all the women who'd lost a son in that dreadful battle with the Cheyennes long ago. Hundreds of old women, breathless with excitement, filled the lodge to overflowing. Squad by squad they examined me—arms, legs, face, neck, breast— every part thcy peered at closely, looking for some mark or peculiarity whereby to recognize their long-lost son.

"Finally, one old woman stared me in the eye and said, 'If this is my son, he has a mole on one of his eyelids.' My eyelids were pulled down as far as they would stretch—and sure enough, she discovered a mole on my left eyelid! Such shouts of joy! Such a woman-handling!

"I was swept along by the excited crowd to my father, Big Bowl, and presented with the eyelid evidence by Mrs. Big Bowl. In the next five minutes, my 'daddy' pointed to a pretty young girl prospect for my wife. When I said I accepted her, Still-water, that completed the marriage ceremony. Now I couldn't leave the Crows—I was married to them! I couldn't bear to tear myself away from their caresses."

Beckworth's audience was making so much noise beating hands together, cackling with laughter and making various appreciative sounds that Beckworth had to shush them so they could hear the end of his story:

Big Bowl
(Based on A.Miller)

"Trapper Jim Bridger happened to see some unidentified Indians take me prisoner, knew they would sacrifice me by the most improved torture. He spread the news. My friends spoke funeral eulogies never thinking that, while they were lamenting my untimely fall, I, renamed 'Morning

Star,' was being hugged and kissed to death by hundreds of my dear and near Crow relatives!"

So intent had Beckworth held his audience's' attention that looking up and seeing a campfire, bearded men with Indian women, and a swarm of very young, fat, naked boys tumbling about a camp on a rich bottomland of grass was a startlement to all six men.

JF Report
July 9
(trappers w/families camp.)

"Halloo!" "Halloo!" "Come join us!" they heard.

Fremont saw his men's horses pulling at their reins to bring their mouths down to the grass, heard Maxwell wonder if that was coffee boiling on the fire, and saw Randy's hopeful expression peering at him across Beckworth's saddle horn. "Out here, you can't just pass by other people without at least stopping to find out who they are," Fremont said amicably.

"We'll take a half-hour for the horses to eat and drink. We'll stretch our legs, chat with these folks, have a little coffee before pressing on for another hour to Charbonneau's island—and mint juleps."

It became clear very soon after Fremont and his companions were back in their saddles that Beckworth, who was now "Jim" to everyone, had done some thinking during this diverting half-hour stop with the five trapper families. "I have a little surprise for you," he began. His face looked set, even fierce. Randy's shoulders drew up with a small shudder as the thought crossed his mind that Jim was about to confess a shockingly bad misdeed.

The horses had not started moving, waiting on Fremont to take the lead. He turned to look at Jim. "What did you say?" he asked, his voice tinged with alarm. Abruptly, Jim slapped his thigh and bent over in laughter. "You all look so hard-knot worried! I feel sorry for you! So I'll tell you my almost-secret real quick. When we get to Bap's island, for sure the first person who'll run out to meet us will be— LADY Beckworth!"

"Awwww!" "Is she number fifteen or sixteen, Jim?!" "Hey—when did that happen?" "Is she the Crow girl? Is Lady Beckwith Still-Water, the pretty Crow girl you married?!" Randy's soprano rose above the others. Beckworth laughed and slapped his thigh again. "Lieutenant, I could waste you an hour here answering questions, so why don't we go back to my talking while everybody's riding—Sir!?"

"Thank you, Jim," Fremont said, and clucked giddy-up.

In a voice loud enough for everyone to hear every fascinating word, Jim proudly described Lady Beckworth as the former Senorita Louise Sandoval, a beautiful young Spanish woman of a prominent family in Taos, 60 miles north of Santa Fe.

"Max, you may remember her since you—and Kit Carson, too—call Taos home even if you don't spend much time there. You know when I quit St. Vrain a year ago, I took my accumulated money, a considerable sum, and set myself up in a small Taos tavern-store, headquarters for my Indian trade. I lived in it, too, very fast and happily, according to the manner—heh-heh-heh—of the other inhabitants.

"Among other doings, I courted Miss Sandoval and six months ago married her. There—you have it!

"This summer, we decided to go with a dozen or so trappers and their families to the Arkansas River somewhere and build our own trading post fort—"

Beckwourth Autobiography

"Now that's BIG news, Jim—that's the REAL surprise!" exclaimed Maxwell. "So what are you doing here, hanging around Bap's island?"

"I thought I and Louise would float with Bap and the furs to St. Louis, get paid for helping out, buy our trade goods and building tools, and walk our packmules safely west behind Bap's along the Santa Fe Trail. But—the Platte put sandbars in that plan. Instead, I and Bap've spent three months trying to arrange for a cloudburst!"

Randy, impatiently waiting to squeeze in a question, saw his chance and quickly blurted out, "But what happened to Still-Water?"

"Still-Water?" Jim repeated. "Oh—Still-Water! Well, let's see, that was a long, long time ago, wasn't it. And maybe you don't know about Indian marriage customs—"

"Like Tuesday's father had TWO wives?"

"Like Tuesday's father had two wives like every other Indian man, assuming this Tuesday-person's father was an Indian. Since I was a Crow CHIEF, I had seven—"

Beckwourth Autobiography

"SEVEN?!!"

"—and after a while I fell in love with and wanted Red Cherry for my wife, too. She was the most beautiful woman in the tribe, but also she was the wife of Big Rain, mayor of the village. However, I won her—wife number eight—no, nine—Little Wife was eight. But it cost me three lashings from Big Rain and his six sisters—AND it cost all 480 of my father and my horses as required by Crow law. AND it took a big contribution of guns, chief's coats, red cloth, new leggins 'n' mocassins from the Dog Soldier Society before MY sisters could brag that the most beautiful Crow woman lived in MY tent."

Fremont broke up the guffawing. "Gentlemen, you've noticed of course that the river hills appear to be sand, and that Platte water has lost its muddy character. The coarse gravel of the stream bed accounts for that, I think, and also for the very swift flow—despite a water depth of only a few inches. And, I'm very pleased to see more trees, bigger ones, and a profusion of shrubs on the banks."

JF Report
July 9
(landscape)

Not even Randy looked around to confirm these important observations. All eyes except Fremont's gazed steadily at Jim Beckworth, waiting for more revelations.

After a studied silent minute or two, Maxwell called out, "Jim, didn't you tell me that you actually had TEN wives—not just seven—or eight?"

Beckworth coughed and cleared his throat. "Ah yes. My tenth and last wife, Pine Leaf, was known as the 'heroine warrior of the Crows.' Now this is a story I love to tell. Picture this most remarkable Bar-chee-am-peh—Pine Leaf—a woman of extraordinary muscular strength, the agility of a cat, the speed of an antelope. Her intelligence charmed me, so great were her thinking powers and gift of speech. Her features were pleasing, her form also, she seemed incapable of fear, and she had few superiors in wielding the battle ax."

Beckwourth
Autobiography
(Pine Leaf,
p. 201-227)

Beckworth sighed loudly. "BUT. When she was twelve years old, her twin brother was killed in a battle with Blackfeet. She felt her loss so much that she vowed to become a warrior and kill ONE HUNDRED enemies to avenge her brother's death. She joined my warrior party. In no time, this girl was riding the speediest warhorse, firing a gun without flinching, and using Indian weapons with as much skill as the most accomplished warrior—me. I began to feel more than a common attachment toward her.

"So one day while riding leisurely along, I asked her to marry me. She said, 'You have too many wives already. Besides, I made a vow to the Man Above to avenge my brother's death.' I kept up my question until she said, 'Well, I will marry you—when the pine leaves turn yellow.' I thought she meant in autumn—until it dawned on me that pines are evergreens. Then she said, 'Well, when you find a red-haired Indian.'"

"Are there any?" Randy asked, running his fingers through his own red top.

351

"I looked for one during the next six years totally without luck. All that time she was fighting Blackfeet, Cheyennes, and Arapahoes with me and my party. To help her collect one hundred scalps, I never killed an enemy if she was close enough to kill him for me. In those dozens of battles, she occasionally rescued me, or killed the warrior who killed my horse—and she took scalps, took scalps. Three times she was wounded, once almost fatally. Only those three times did she paint her face in mourning color and wear it until she had a victory.

"Ah me—the more heroic deeds she did, the more lofty her bearing, the more ardent my attachment became. Her presence made me feel great courage and strength. But time and battles went on and her goal in scalps had not been reached. Only after she became bosom friends with Little Wife after my son, Black Panther, was born did Pine Leaf soften just a little toward me. She told Little Wife that IF she ever did decide to marry, she would marry ME." Randy's question started to break into the story. "Did you say—"

"SHHH!" hissed Basil behind him. "Hold on a minute," said Beckworth beside him, and went on with his story.

"A coupla years and several battles later, I told the Crows I'd been called to St. Louis on business, but I would return when the grass was green. Well, I went, thinking I might stay. But when the grass had been green for some weeks, the Fur Company sent me back to quiet down the Crows threatening to kill the whites in the Fort. Some 'fork-tongue' trappers had told the Crows that the St. Louis whites had killed me.

Beckwourth Autobiography

Beckwourth Autobiography

"When I arrived with the truth, Pine Leaf announced in a speech to the Crows, who'd gathered outside the fort, that she had fought her last battle, hurled her last lance. She had one hundred scalps and she would snatch no more. She would sacrifice her liberty by bestowing herself on Medicine Calf 'so he won't leave again.' I was thrilled, but not as thrilled as I would have been six years earlier.

"When she got out of her war costume and into a woman's decorated clothing, I hardly recognized her. Five weeks after she became my bride, and one week after my last horse-stealing, scalp-taking battle, I departed for good for the white man's world. I knew if I remained, it would be blood and destruction to the end of the chapter just to hold my reputation as a warrior. I had truly sickened of the job—"

Beckwourth Autobiography

Abruptly, Beckworth began shouting, "Halloo! Halloo!"

352

and all attention turned to the large island just ahead. They could see under the broad shade of a fine grove of cotton-woods that several people were running toward them from tents pitched there. "There's a cut in the embankment that we can take down to the water," Beckworth said, and clucked his horse into the lead.

Randy's "giddap" brought his pony beside Beckworth's. "Jim! The boy! Black Panther! You left him? What happened to him?"

"Yes, Randy, I had to leave him. He's with his mother, Little Wife, and his Grandpa, Big Bowl. When I last saw him, he was three years old. That was ten years ago. So now he's about your age. I expect to hear in another ten years that he's chief of the Crows." Beckworth hurried his horse down the gap and into the shallow water. "Halloo! Halloo!" he cried to the pretty young woman waving and smiling on the island shore.

Beckwourth
Autobiography
(Son: p.376,
383

353

Based on Alfred Jacob Miller, 1837

Beth Berryman

Pine Leaf, the Warrior Woman, could wield a battle ax with strength to match Jim's, ride the speediest horse, fight fearlessly, charm Jim with her thinking power and gift of speech–but not marry him. After six years of scalping enemies, she reached her goal of 100 to avenge her twin brother's death. Only then did she agree to sacrifice her liberty by "bestowing herself on Chief Medicine Calf"–his tenth, but not his last, wife.

Jean Baptiste Charbonneau, 37-year-old son of Sacajawea, who carried him on her back as
an infant during their two years with Lewis and Clark's Expedition, clinks his mint julep cup
against the cup of his guest, Lieutenant Fremont, leader of the Oregon Trail Mapping
Expedition. Randy makes-do with a cup of currants white with sugar. Maxwell exclaims,
and Basil and Yo echo, "Hail to the mint julep booshway!" But a short midday stop stretches
into all day and all night–by accident.

CHAPTER 32

SACAJAWEA' S SON SERVES MINT JULEPS

July 9-10, St. Helena Island, South Platte River, Colorado

Randy had reined his pony to a halt at the edge of the high embankment, and was watching with smiling fascination as Jim slid off his saddle into the embracing arms of Lady Beckwourth. The scene reminded him of one he'd seen at home—his 17-year-old just-married sister Jessie and husband John Fremont—and a scene he suddenly knew would happen again in just a few weeks at home in Washington, D.C.

Fremont's voice interrupted. "Well! Mr. Bap's camp looks like Father Bap in his big long tent with his family settled about him in teepees. Very patriarchal!"

From the trees behind them, a horseman shouted to them as he rode out at a fast trot. "He's speaking Spanish, first we've heard on this trip," Fremont said. "Probably a camp guard who's asking who we are. Max, bring out your Spanish."

Two minutes later, a smiling guard was leading them to the tent door of Jean Baptiste Charbonneau.

Randy was trying to imagine what Sacajawea's "Pomp" would look like now that he was an old man of 37. He fixed his gaze upon the wide-open flap of the big tent entrance where the guard had disappeared, and eased up beside Fremont. He wanted to be the first to see this person almost as famous as Lewis and Clark themselves. Fremont and Maxwell, then Randy, dismounted and stood waiting. No one came.

Fremont called to Basil and Yo to dismount and take charge of the animals. "Mr. Charbonneau should be coming out any minute. I'm hoping he really will invite us to eat a meal and drink a mint julep with him—we'll know soon."

Randy inched forward enough to peer through the opening into Bap's living quarters. On one end of the rectangular room lay a buffalo robe bed with blanket cover, a large canvas sack bulging with personal items. On the other end of the room sat a folding brass table, four folding wood chairs, and a knee-high stack of books.

The son of Sacagawea was not in sight.

Just then, the guard pushed through a flap in the back wall of the room. Booshway Bap had a two-room tent? The

JF Report
July 9
("patriarchal"
"first Spanish
seen")

Except for the mint juleps and lunch,none of the following episode is in JF's Report, but is a reconstruction of the day's most likely events.

Based on A.J. Miller

guard strode past Randy and spoke in Spanish to Maxwell. "He says Bap's in the warehouse back there where he keeps the furs and supplies," Maxwell reported. "He's on his way."

When Bap walked through the tent opening, he looked to Randy surprisingly like the lithe, trim, finely-featured, well-groomed, mannerly young men who clerked in Mr. Chouteau's outfitting store in St. Louis. He looked quite different from heavily bearded and mustached Fremont, Maxwell, Basil, and Yo. On Bap's handsome face, upper-lip hair and chin-hair were barely visible—more like an Indian face than like his half-French bearded father.

His face, neck, and arms looked as if he'd browned in the sun less than Fremont. Although his straight black hair was very long, he wore it neatly parted in the middle, drawn to the side and tied in a swag behind his neck. "He's better looking than John! and a teeny bit taller!" Randy thought, momentarily feeling disloyal and guilty.

"Welcome Lieutenant Fremont! Welcome young fellow — YOU're quite a surprise! Welcome, you other gentlemen. I'm especially glad to have company recently come from Saint Louis!" Brown eyes bright with intelligence and pleasure, wide smile sparkling with even, white teeth, Bap shook hands all around, and declared that they had arrived just in time to keep him company at midday meal. Fremont informed him that one of his own crew, Mr. Beckworth, met on the trail, had escorted the party hither and would no doubt also be interested in having a meal.

Bap guffawed. "His wife grabbed him on arrival? No doubt he's NOT interested in having a meal."

"Do you really make mint juleps?" Randy demanded. Another big Bap-guffaw. "Just give Pablo here five minutes to go pick the mint!" he said, and in Spanish added instructions for Pablo to deliver to the cook. "I'll take you and your crew on a quick tour of the camp, Lieutenant, while the julep is being minted," Bap said.

"The first place is right behind my own tent wall. The cargo stored in there is the reason we're stuck here, and the reason I'm sending a request to Mr. Bent at his fort on the Arkansas for horses and wagons.

"We can't move by boat our 900 buffalo robes and 500 salted buffalo tongues—altogether five tons weight, plus some weeks' provisions for a dozen or so people. No river water to float the boats! and we can't drag them nearly a thousand miles on river bottom to the Missouri! For trans-

Mountain Men and the Fur Trade.Vol.1 Hafen/Hafen,p213. (1840 shipment from fort next to Ft. St.Vrain: 700 robes, 400 tongues. In 1842 with all but one competitor gone, St.Vrain would have shipped larger quantities..)

357

port purposes, the Platte is dry."

Yo volunteered to stay with the animals, see that they had a long drink of river water. "I'll send someone to lead you to the pasture and help you hobble them," Bap said before beckoning Fremont, Maxwell, Basil, and Randy to follow him through his living room into the spacious room behind it, the warehouse.

They stopped in the middle of it to look around at the large piles of canvas-wrapped bundles, wooden boxes, barrels, kegs, and flat-bottom boats. "We thought we'd be in St. Louis six weeks ago, and back here by now," Bap said. "Instead, all the month of May, we dozen men, sometimes helped by Beckworth's wife and another man's wife—dragged our four loaded boats over endless sand-bars and shallows.

"We got this far—45 miles—from our starting place at St.Vrain's Fort. We were nearly dead from pulling and pushing from dawn to dusk, always wet, always angry at our incompetent river for not helping us."

Fremont, Maxwell, and Basil spoke at the same moment—"Just like the poor, ragged devils we met on the big Platte!" Fremont added, "They didn't wait it out—they started walking to St. Louis! No horses, no guns! Passed us on the way. That was two weeks ago." Basil described how they buried their buffalo robes, left their personal bundles of little furs "hanging high in de trees! Too weak to tote'um," he laughed.

Bap laughed, too, but declared that Will Bent and Ceran St.Vrain would fire him if he abandoned all their winter season's robes and buffalo tongues, a collection they could sell for $20,000.

"So, when I saw this big island and shady grove of trees, I called a halt for a few days. Well, we're still here ten weeks later. We're still waiting for big downpours of water. Even if Bent's wagons rescue us two weeks from now, it'll still be the mid-August before we pull into his Fort on the Arkansas. Then, wagons'll take six weeks on the Santa Fe Trail to move everything to the Missouri River. Still two weeks more, even with the current, to paddle to the Mississippi and St. Louis.

"What a dreary, expensive way to spend the summer! Sitting here day after day slapping mosquitoes, squashing bugs! Then creaking for weeks at wagon speed across dry, shadeless prairie! Augh!"

On their way through the "warehouse," Randy noticed a line of rectangular piles taller than himself—"100 robes in

Fort Laramie.
NatParkSer.
p46. (weight of
1 robe: 10 pounds)

Bent's Fort.
D,Lavender,
p115,92
(tongues in salt)

every pile"—a checkerboard of kegs—"buffalo tongues in salt"—five long, flat-bottom boats stacked bottom-to-bottom in pairs with oars inside one, another loaded with large, fat canvas sacks labeled "beans," "rice," "coffee" "sugar," "flour," 10-gallon tin buckets labelled "pilot-bread," and wooden boxes marked "bacon slabs."

Outside, they walked the circle of tents, and were politely introduced to the half-dozen men, Beckworth not among them, close by three cook-fires where coffeepots were steaming. "Ah—there's Pablo with a handful of mint!" Charbonneau announced. "He'll have our juleps ready to bring to us in a few minutes—almost by the time we reach my tent."

Bap hardly had time to answer Maxwell's question about the whiskey supply at Fort St. Vrain—"only a few gallons for the traders, none to sell to Indians"—when Randy noticed that Pablo, carrying a big pottery pitcher, and Yo bearing on his fingers some tin cups sprigged with green, were catching up with them. They arrived at Bap's tent door a half-running step ahead of Charbonneau and Fremont. Pablo quickly set the pitcher upon the brass table, hurried away, and Yo with a cheery, "One of camp's men is looking after our horses," unfingered five cups to sit by the pitcher.

Randy peered into the pitcher at a slightly brown liquid. He counted the five cups, looked around, and, lips moving but silent, counted, beginning with himself, SIX thirsty men. "Who won't get a cup?" he asked, impulsively speaking on top of Fremont's inquiring of Bap if he had any news of his mother.

Bap, carefully pouring liquid from pitcher to cups, answered Randy first. "You're not forgotten—Pablo has gone for your cup. It will be filled with ripe, wild currants white with sugar. Now, come sit on this fine ten-gallon bucket—it's just like one I like to sit on, adjustable in height by stacking books on it. You'd rather stand? Fine. Pablo and the currents are on their way.

"Now, Lieutenant, Maxwell, Lajeunesse, Ayot! Raise your cups with me to drink a toast to rain and easy travel, no matter the two sound contradictory!"

"Hear, hear!"

"Ahhh—Mr. Charbonneau, this South Platte mint julep will live forever in the memory of my taste buds," Fremont declared. "And mine—especially the second and third cup!" declared Maxwell. "What's your recipe, sir?" inquired Yo, smacking approval.

"Pure raw alcohol diluted but not too much with river water—it's clear and cold here, almost ice—stir in enough blackstrap molasses to give color and sweetness, send a man to grab some horsemint leaves before a horse's teeth chomps'um, crush and bruise the leaves with your hands to bring out the minty smell and taste, drop the mint in the cup of embracing liquid, give it a stir, and drink it down—but not too fast!"

"Hail to the julep booshway!" cried Maxwell, laughing and lifting his cup.

At that moment, Pablo returned bearing a large tray loaded with the second julep pitcher, three boiled buffalo tongues, each the size of wrestler Yo's arm, a heap of fried bread cakes, six tin plates and forks—and Randy's sugared currents. "When there's nothing left of the julep liquid to put in your cups, we have plenty of coffee to fill them, and as much sugar as you want," promised Bap.

JF Report
July 9
("mint gathered"
"very good julep
concocted," "buffalo
tongue, coffee
and sugar")

"Pull up a chair to the table, you four men. Randy and I will sit on the ten-gallon cans. Now, to answer your recent question, Lieutenant," Bap said as he cut the tongues into slices and laid a stack on each plate.

"There's no news of my mother, has been none since she disappeared nearly 20 years ago. I have no reason to think she's still alive. Once, a daft old woman croaked in my ear that she saw my mother living with Comanches in Texas. I couldn't believe that. My mother lived with whites in St. Louis too long to tolerate rough Comanche life even though the Comanches are Shoshoni cousins and speak a similar language.

Sacajawea.
A.Waldo
p 870

"No one—not even Captain Clark—has heard anything from her or about her since she rode away in the night from St. Louis. She rode away on my pa's best horse. I was 18 years old. She'd be past 50 by now."

Randy, puzzled, asked the question all the others were thinking but weren't sure how Bap would feel about it or react to it if they asked it. "But Mr. Bap! How could your mother leave you without saying where she was going, then never come back or write you a letter or anything?!"

Bap didn't look up from his carving. When he answered, his voice was flat, controlled. "She knew I was about to go to a faraway land across a great sea with the rich German Duke, and that I would be well taken care of. She didn't want to be abused by my pa any more. She didn't know how to write, she didn't know exactly where I was anyway.

Mountain Men
and the Fur
Trade. Vol.1
Ann Hafen
"J.Baptiste
Charbonneau".
Chapter,203-220

There now—the buffalo tongues are all sliced—bon appetit!"

He sat down on his 10-gallon can, gave Randy a quick smile, almost whispered, "My ma was the best," and began to eat. Emboldened Randy, curious about the word "Duke," whispered back, a touch of awe in his voice, "You went with a real DUKE?"

Bap chortled, swallowed, laid his fork down, and answered loud enough for all to hear, "You want to hear about that ?! Going to Europe with real German royalty and living there for six years—pretty amazing for an Indian boy, eh? Well, by that great piece of luck, I completed my 'white man's education' with the addition of the German language and royal world travel.

"It happened like this: One day when my pa and ma and I and some others were on a trapping and hunting trip near the junction of the Missouri and Kansas rivers—you know, Chouteau's near Westport—a boat with four men pulled up next to where we were camping. It was clear from his manner that the slim young man in the velvet coat and button-up leggings was the man in charge. He asked in German, which none of us knew, then in French for a hunting guide and interpreter.

"My pa got the job, but I got the invitation to accompany him—Duke Paul of Wurttemberg, Germany—when he went home at the end of the summer. The Duke picked me up in St. Louis where I'd lived 12 years with my ma—and my old-man pa once in a while—in a little log cabin of General Clark's."

"Excuse me," Fremont interrupted, "but I heard that Clark sent you to school during that time."

"True, Lieutenant. I had ten years of good tutoring from priests and preachers. General Clark's interest and support shaped my life! His death four years ago still grieves my heart. It is truly miraculous luck that two such powerful

men—the General and the Duke—took hold of my life at different stages and gave me, an Indian boy, a good education here and extraordinary years with royalty in Europe!"

Fremont waved his hand toward Bap. "Such 'luck,'" he said, "could happen only to an extraordinary person, Mr. Charbonneau!"

Nodding modestly, smiling to acknowledge the compliment, Bap said, "Randy, home for Duke Paul and me was a castle—"

"A CASTLE!" exclaimed Randy.

"—in Germany's Black Forest! And he was royalty in line

for the CROWN! But he told me he didn't want 'the purple' robe and power, that he would feel imprisoned, like a wild eagle in a gilded cage.

"Oh, he WAS a little wild—that is, very impulsive, very daring, very energetic, VERY intelligent, and always democratic. We hunted the deer and the wild boar in the castle woodland—he called me 'hunter extraordinary'—we collected plants—he wanted to be a botanist, not a military officer—and even set some traps to catch foxes. My woodland skills, which I learned from my trapper pa, delighted and fascinated him.

"We had a good time for six years. But then, at the end of our last long trip seeing the sights in Europe and North Africa—"

"AFRICA!" Randy exploded in astonishment.

"YES! Pyramids! Sahara Desert! Morroco! veiled women! No matter—I begged to go home, back to my own woodlands on the Missouri River. Duke Paul caught my home-to-America fever, and we took a ship to New Orleans. I was then 24, about the age the Duke was when I first met him on the Missouri.

"Well, we did a lot of buffalo, bear, and elk hunting up the Missouri again before he returned to his castle near Stuttgart, Germany. In St. Louis, I got a job as a hunter in 'Robidoux's Fur Brigade,' came west to the Rockies to live 'the simple life in vast silent places,' as the Duke liked to say. Here I am a dozen or so years later stuck on a dry river in a vast, silent prairie, 'a child of Nature,' as he called me, waiting for rain."

The hungry men had eaten their own buffalo tongue slices and half of Randy's besides, drunk "the second batch," weren't offered a third, but were invited to join a kickball game beginning to disturb the silence outside.

"But you, Lieutenant, stay here—take a walk around my island kingdom with me, and tell me about your expedition. I want to hear more about the mapping job Congress sent you to do." Fremont agreed to an hour's stay, "but we must then move on or else we'll be marching tomorrow most of the 45 miles to St.Vrain. Too much, too much for one day. Even arriving there tomorrow afternoon, we can stay only a day at the fort. We're due at Laramie BY the sixteenth—must arrive on the fifteenth."

Randy and Yo strolled onto the kickball field, watched a few minutes, kicked the ball when it fell nearby, and got a

Mountain Men and the Fur Trade. Vol.1 Ann Hafen "J.Baptiste Charbonneau". Chapter,203-220

*JF Report,*July 9, *abruptly ends with the mint julep lunch. He leaves the next day after breakfast. What happened in between?*

By staying over night, he had to ride 16 hours to cover 45 miles on July 10th to get to Fort St. Vrain by about 11pm. Events at Charbonneau's camp must have been temporarily disrupting to cause the stay. A disabled person whom JF did not want to name (Randy) or reveal his presence, is the most logical reason.

player's beckoned invitation to join the game. Between sprints and kicks, he saw Basil and Max following Pablo in a wade across the Platte to bring out their horses from the large drove grazing in the pasture. Randy also saw Fremont and Bap walking to the corral some distance behind the tents, their hands gesturing as they talked.

But before the hour was out, Randy had lost sight of all of them, and momentarily of everything.

It happened all of a sudden. There was the ball rolling toward him fast enough to have been shot from a ground-level cannon. Eye on the ball, he was running toward it—he was raising his foot to kick—he was kicking, when—WHAM!!

When he came-to, he was looking up into a circle of Mexican male faces. Yo was slapping his cheeks and calling, "Randy! Randy! Open your eyes!"

"What happened?" Randy squeaked.

"Two of you tried to kick de ball at de same time. You butted heads and flipped each ot'er over.

"Boy! am I glad you come-to quick! Let me help you up. Here—take my hands and I'll pull you to your feet," Yo said. A moment later, Randy was moaning "Owww" and grabbing for Yo's arm. "My ankle," Randy whispered, gritting his teeth. "My head hurts, too. Where's the man who ran into me? His head ought to be hurting."

"Well, he wasn't knocked out like you, just shookup. Some fellows are walking him to his tent." With Yo on one side and a stocky, muscular Mexican on the other, Randy limped to Bap's tent, sat in one chair and propped his lame leg on another.

"We need some strips of clot' to bandage your ankle," Yo said, "but I can't see where we're gonna get any." To the Mexican he said, "Go get de boss! Charbonneau! Booshway—bossman!" and pointed toward the door. The man ran.

Randy said, "You can cut off a few inches of my pants legs for a bandage."

"But I've got no b'ar grease to rub on your ankle," Yo said, "and a bandage won't do any good wit'out some b'ar grease, will it. But I'll cut off a t'ree-inch piece from bot' your pants legs anyway just in case somebody shows up wit' some kind of medicine."

He had barely completed slicing off the strips with the butcher knife he always wore in his belt when Fremont,

363

Bap, and three of the Mexicans crowded through the tent entrance. "I have bear grease right here in my pack!" Bap said, kneeling to dig in his necessaries-sack to find it. The three ex-kickball players were trying to show him small tin boxes and jabbering three-way Spanish. Fremont was asking at regular intervals, "How could this possibly have happened?!" Pablo arrived with a pitcher of cold water.

"Put some of everything on his ankle and bandage it tight!" Fremont ordered. "We have GOT to get started for St. Vrain Fort!"

Fifteen minutes later, Randy's ankle had been smeared with a layer of "red medicine, good for swelling," a layer of gray "motse paste, also good for swelling," a layer of "white-weed poultice salve, very good for swelling," and bandaged tightly with his pants-leg strip sticky with "b'ar" grease. "My ankle feels fine, nothing hurts, not even the knot on my head," Randy said with a grin. "Heap strong medicine! Plenny medicine men!"

Cheyennes.
Grinnell, p172,182,
185 (plants and
medicines)

Bap shook his head when Fremont told Yo to put Randy's mocassin on his foot and help him to his pony. "That's most unwise, I think," Bap advised. "A twisted ankle heals quicker if you don't use it for 24 hours. Using it now will make it worse, add days, even weeks, for it to recover. Also, he might possibly have had a concussion from the blow to his head.

"That needs watching overnight. He can sleep here in my bed, and all we men can sleep in one of the larger tents. We'll make room, and we have more than enough blankets to go around.

"Tomorrow morning, we'll have a five o'clock breakfast. If Randy seems quite all right, we'll get you started on your 45-mile day. I've done it in a day—but it was dark when I got there. Sorry about your accident, Randy, but it will, I hope, allow me the pleasure of talking a lot more with your Lieutenant."

JF Report
July 10
"We parted our
hospitable host
after breakfast
and reached St.
Vrain's Fort about
45 miles from St.
Helena late in the
evening."

And talk they did—the rest of the afternoon, through early supper, while settling Randy in bed soon afterwards, and after that while sitting at the table, Bap smoking his pipe. They talked about where to locate military forts, about Fort St.Vrain, about Bap's pa Toussaint "Tous" Charbonneau, about President John Tyler, Senator Benton, people wanting to escape the long-lasting economic depression by going to "rich lands in Oregon Territory."

The last words Randy heard as he was falling asleep

were Bap's. "What this trip means, Lieutenant, is that your published map and journal will make available to the general public the necessary details about how to cross the continent. What the public needs to know is presently locked up in the minds of illiterate hunters and trappers. Your map and journal will unlock for everybody a do-able trail to the Rockies.

In 1843, 500 people, with Fremont's map and report in hand, made the Oregon Trail journey in their covered wagons. In 1844..1000 In 1845..5000 By 1853, an estimated 250,000, including the Gold Rush crowd going south and west from South Pass to California, traveled the Oregon Trail. In 1856 famous John Fremont was the first presidential candidate chosen by the new Republican party.He lost: His opponents called him "a radical slavery abolitionist, a bastard born to unwed parents." The party's next presidential candidate was Abraham Lincoln.

"Congress's publishing and distributing your journal and map to all the newspapers and magazines in the country also means, Lieutenant, that John Fremont is soon going to be a very, very famous man—more famous than Lewis and Clark!"

John Fremont leaned back and laughed.

"But think of it, Lieutenant," Bap continued. "Lewis and Clark went by boat far north up the Missouri, then west through mountains as far as they could go, then on foot and on horseback through most difficult terrain. Their report said there's no 'northwest passage' to the Pacific by boats—or wagons. For 35 years, families have known they wouldn't be able to travel such a rugged route in the north to Oregon, and I've heard of no family that even tried it.

"They'll know from YOUR report they CAN go on horseback and wagons with their families on a southern prairie—not a desert—for a thousand miles to the Rockies. YOUR reliable map will show them a flat trail alongside the Platte River—plenty of water and grass for their animals. Trappers, they'll learn, can guide them to the river valleys cutting through the mountains to Oregon and the Pacific! They'll learn unexaggerated accounts of the Indians and the buffalo, the Great American Desert that isn't a desert!

"Families will come west by the hundreds—they WILL—carrying your map and daily journal in their hands! They'll be so grateful and you'll get so famous, they'll probably run you for President one day!"

Fremont smiled. "That seems most unlikely, son of Sacajawea. But I love your daydreaming."

Based on A.J. Miller, 1838

With Randy hoisted into his saddle, Maxwell tightening the pack mule's load, Basil and Yo mounted and raring to go, three famous men say their goodbyes. Gaudily attired Jim Beckwourth must finish a story from his life as Chief of the Crows, Fremont fidgets impatiently, thinking of the day's 45-mile, 17-hour ride to Fort St. Vrain. Sacajawea's son Bap Charbonneau enjoys to the last moment this visit of men from the outside world. He'll kill more weeks on his South Platte island, waiting for rain–or carts.

CHAPTER 33

AMAZING—TRUE?—JIM AND BAP STORIES

July 10, South Platte to Fort St.Vrain (Colorado)

"C'mon, Cut-Pants—yeah, you've earned yourself an Indian name—put your good left leg in the stirrup and I'll give you a hoist! Hey! Look at the knot on your fore'ed—your Indian name could just as well be Purple Polky-Dot Noggin! Good thing it's not a polky-dot INSIDE your skull, boy!"

Jim Beckworth, in his favorite fringed and beaded buckskin jacket, pants with six-inch fringe hanging on the outside seams, patted Randy's left ankle and looked up at his wistful, freckled face. "You take extra good care of this ankle while the other's out of commission. Sitting all day in the saddle, staying off your feet, is the best way to treat a sprain. With all that Indian medicine on it, you'll be fine by the time you get to the Fort tonight.

"Good luck at every twist and turn of your life, Randy-boy. You're the best audience I ever had."

"I'll never forget you, Chief Beckworth." To the pretty, bright-faced young woman beside Beckworth, Randy said, "Glad to meet you, Mrs. Chief."

JF Report
July10
("departed after break-fast")

Then they were waving and moving off, splashing through the Platte's thin veil of water, and up the embankment, this time on the south side of the river "same as the fort," Bap had advised them. Maxwell, Fremont, and Randy led, Basil and Yo close behind, all followed by the shouted good wishes and good-byes of Bap, Jim, Mrs. Jim, Pablo, and a dozen others.

"What a streak of good luck that was! Not one but TWO amazing characters!" Fremont was soon exclaiming. "Beckworth's stories and exuberant personality—oh my! More shocking, more daring, than a musketeer adventurer! And from the number of scars I saw on face and arms, I think he was telling the truth 90 percent of the time!"

Maxwell guffawed. "I'd lower that percentage to 70 at best, having heard him tell those tales, and more, several times during the two years he and I were working out of St.Vrain. But no matter. For all his noisy blather, Jim's very competent, very smart, trustworthy, a reliable friend. I suppose you might say the same for Mr. Charbonneau, Lieutenant, even though he told you stories as amazing as Jim's."

"Oh—I'm sure his account of himself is 100 percent true," Fremont countered.

"How do you tell whether a story's seventy, or a hundred, percent true?" Randy inquired. All the men chortled, having faced the question on many occasions and in many situations, some critical.

"Max, you care to answer that?" Fremont said.

"I've already answered the seventy percent part," Maxwell said, "but I'll say it again like this: If the story improves every time its hero tells it, you can keep knocking off truth percentage points."

Basil's "Well, I doan-know—" made Maxwell, Fremont, and Randy turn their heads to look back at him. "I doan-know as I'd be dat hard on my brudder Jim," Basil was saying. "He's a good shot to have on your side—remember my telling you 'bout how de two of us shot at a little noise in de dark in General Ashley's camp and de next morning we found two Indians dead?

"Besides knowing where to aim, Jim's a good-hearted man, which ought to count for sumt'ing. I'd give him...80 percent. See, Jim knows dat when you turn happenings into words—a story—you have to fix up de details to make a real clear, innersting picture, or nobody'll listen."

Randy nodded complete agreement. Maxwell said, "Now let's hear how you explain a full one hundred percent, Lieutenant."

Fremont began by noting that never before had he heard during one day two men telling stories so astounding that they raised the silent or spoken question, How much of either man's story is true?

"I'm not surprised," he said, "that a half-breed French-Indian's stories about living in a castle in Germany's Black Forest, with a Duke, for six years, touring the big sights of Europe and Africa, could sound just as low in truth as those of a half-breed from a slave state saying he lived six years with Indians on the buffalo plains, AND as the bravest warrior, rose to the top—Big Chief, boss of the whole tribe!"

Fremont's picturing of the two storytellers side by side for comparison excited an appreciative belly-laugh from Basil, a thigh slap and "Yessir!" from Yo, and a giggle from Randy. Even the sunken corners of Maxwell's mouth turned up a little.

"Max has told you how he arrived at 70-percent-true for the mulatto," Fremont began."Here's how I'm certain of a hundred percent truth for the half-breed Indian. Just in April in St. Louis, the MAIN facts Bap told us here I heard from a reliable source—none other than the respected merchant Pierre Chouteau, Jr. He happened to mention to me that he met Duke Paul when he came in to outfit young Bap just before they sailed for Europe about 25 years ago, and that six years later, the Duke and the Indian came back, had dinner with him in St. Louis.

"When I was in the balcony office of Chouteau's store arranging for supplies for this trip, he showed me a book the Duke wrote about his travels in America. I saw Jean Baptiste Charbonneau's name in the book! Chouteau and I made out the German words in the last pages telling how he took Bap to Germany at the end of his 1828 trip."

Journey in North America in the Years 1822-24.
Wilhelm Paul Friedrich, Herzog (Duke) von Wurttemberg (Entry for June 21, 1823)

"Hey—Bap's name and story got in print!? Doggone! I never for a minute t'ought Bap was stretching anyt'ing!"

"Yessir! I knowed you musta had plenny-a solid back-up for dat hundred percent, Lieutenant! Dat's de only-est way to nail down de troot'!"

Fremont looked around with a big smile at Yo and Basil. "So you've had occasion to learn the lesson about how to judge who's telling the truth?—that if there's no solid, confirming evidence, unusual stories may well be mostly entertainment? Faites attention, Randy!"

Randy's reply was a very serious, "Yessir." Quickly he added, "So, I could tell, couldn't I, from reading the book about Lewis and Clark's trip if Bap was saying 100 percent truth about what happened on the trip. Did he tell you any stories, John, remember anything exciting?"

"It's a question I asked him, Randy, and he reminded me that he wasn't even two years old when he and his mama got home at the END of the trip! He said he thinks he remembers seeing the 100-foot-long whale skeleton on an ocean beach, and being held up to look out through its ribs. But he wasn't even one year old then! Probably it was something his mother told him later, he said to me, not from his own memory. He also thinks he remembers a big black man and a big black dog who went on the trip.

Journals of Patrick Gass.
p249/note 470
Jan.5,1806
Sagajawea went with party to see "the monstrous fish(whale) and the ocean."

"Now, comrades, I'm getting the impression from some head jerks of my horse, and some pulling on the reins that our mounts think all this talking, laughing, and thigh slapping means 'gittity up.' So let's trot them while they're in the mood and get a mile or two ahead on our 45-mile day.

"Watch for prickly cactus—go around them—and circle your way around troughs that buffalo bulls've scraped out to flop in for a dirt bath!" They took off at a trot, keeping close to the shrubs and frequent trees on the river bank, ignoring the endless, open plain beside them, but eyeing distant, haze-blurred Long's Peak every few minutes.

JF Report
July 10
(cactus,wallows, Mt.Long)

When the heaving horses and deep-breathing, pink-cheeked riders had settled back into their steady three-mile-an-hour walk, Fremont declared that he couldn't get Bap off his mind. "In grade school, when I read about the Shoshoni girl with her infant boy, 'Pomp,' I never dreamed I would one day meet him as a grown man, hear his story, count him among my esteemed friends. If I hadn't seen, talked with him yesterday, drunk his julep, he would've remained an infant forever in my mind's picture gallery!

"He was quite a surprise to me, this mostly Indian man. He reads books, brings a stack every time he comes back here from St. Louis. He says when he and Jim Bridger meet up and have time to sit leisurely in sun or lantern light, Bridger asks Bap to read him Shakespeare! Imagine scruffy, lean-faced, hard-as-a-horseshoe old trapper Jim Bridger, who signs 'X' for his name, soaking up Shakespeare dramas, Bap playing all the characters!"

Maxwell added that while he was working out of St.Vrain's, he saw Bap off and on, but didn't know him well. "He was working out of Lupton's fort a few miles south. I heard about him—mostly that he was a great runner, the best man on foot in the plains or mountains."

Mountain Men in Am.Fur Trade, vol.I. *Hafen/Hafen* "J.B.Charbonneau" by *Ann Hafen.*

Randy suddenly exclaimed that Clark called baby Pomp "little dancing boy," so no wonder grown-up Pomp turned out to be the best runner in the West.

"Indian runner—when he could have been riding in royal coaches had he chosen to!" Fremont said. "But he chose the wilderness 'because,' he told me, 'my Indian's eye couldn't be satisfied with a DESCRIPTION of things—I must range the hills myself, be able to out-travel my horse, strip my wardrobe from the backs of deer and buffalo, feed on them, punish my enemy with my own hand. Otherwise, I'm no longer Indian, I'm going against the nature of my race.'"

Ummm-hunh, grunted Basil. "Well, wid a pappy half-Indian and a mammy full Indian, Bap's bound to feel de stronger pull of Indian blood, don'tcha t'ink? Bap wid his good head and good looks and, and people liking his company, well, he must take after his mama. You t'ink he might look like her in de face, Lieutenant?"

Fremont made a hands-up, who-knows gesture. "I could have asked him, I suppose. His features are quite handsome—straight nose, high cheek bones, deep-set eyes, medium brown hairless skin. Like other Indians, he probably plucks any hair that dares to appear. But these features could describe Indians generally, men or women, couldn't they?

"Still, nobody so far suggests that Papa Touse was any-

Sacajawea's husband Toussaint Charbonneau, father of Bap the booshway of St. Helena's Island in the South Platte, identifies for curious Indians about 1832 the Big Man of a visiting party, Prince Maximilian of Germany. An artist accompanying the Prince painted a picture of "Touse" pointing at the Prince and saying, mouth open, to a crowd of Indians that the small, fashionably dressed man beside him is a Big Chief. The Prince, like his kinsman, Duke Paul of Germany, hired French-Indian Touse as his interpreter and guide for a trip to wild, western America to see Indians and buffalo. Dark-skinned Touse, his black hair long, his eyes circled with red stain, wears winter garb of Indian or trapper of the time–rabbit's skin hat complete with its ears, long deerskin blouse with uneven edges flapping below his hips, flowing red sash, snug hip-leggings crossbound below the knees, and beaded mocassins. He has no weapon, but the whites with him–the Prince, the artist, attendants and fort guards watching from the top of a stockade wall, make a show of long-barreled guns they hold.

Beth Berryman

From Carl Bodmer, artist. Published 1843

where near handsome. Bap's good looks, then, might tell us what Sacajawea looked like."

"Right!" Basil agreed. "Bap looks and acts so sensible, so...polite and good, he COULDN'T have looked like or been like his papa. Ugly old Touse was a brute! Did you hear how Clark during his trip had to check Touse when he was hitting Sacajawea? Dat Touse was a scoundrel, a slob wid de manners 'n' sex'havior of a grizzly.

"I had to work in a crew wid Touse 'bout ten years ago, and I'll bet you he hadn't washed his hair in de 20 years before. And dat ain't all. He stank. Alla time. Musky beaver castoreum smell, kin to skunk. Augh! He stank so bad he had to pay twice as much red clot' and blue beads as any ot'er man to persuade Indian papas to send deir girls home wid him. Pity dat poor 13-year-old slave Sacajawea when

Journals of Patrick Gass (Lewis/Clark Expedition) p263 #685 note," Clark said Pomp (baby)' a beautiful, promising child." p239, #289 note," Clark checked Touse for striking his woman." Aug.14,1805

Touse won her in a gambling game.

"But come to t'ink of it, wonder how dat second German Duke, or Prince—whatever—Maximilian, who like Duke Paul came out west to look at de Indians and buffalo—how he got along wid guide Touse in his stinking clot'es?"

"That's easy," Maxwell drawled. "The Prince could've done what I expect the Duke did—take Touse to an outfitter's store, buy him his first change of clothes in five years, and throw in the river his pants and blouse so crusty with filth they'd stand up by themselves."

Fremont, who's been listening closely, half-turned in his saddle to look at Basil. "You've been speaking of Bap's pa in past tense. He's dead? Bap didn't mention it to me." Basil hesitated. "Oh. Ummm, maybe he hadn't heard. Uh, wasn't any occasion for me to mention it to him. See, I ran into trapper Charlie Larpenteur a few months ago, and he told me he heard when he was in Mandan country on de Missouri dat old Touse had recently died. It wasn't from small pox either, what most of de Mandans and Big Bellies—you know—Gros Ventres—died of some years back. Charlie heard tell dat de Blackfeet caught Touse and chopped him into little pieces.

"Another t'ing Charlie told me, dat not long ago when Touse was near'bout 80, he had a rip-roaring wedding wit' a 14-year-old Assiniboine slave he bought from anot'er tribe. Drums, pans, kettles beating, guns firing—an all-day-and-night whingding. De wonder is dat a character like Touse can breed a man like Bap!"

They discussed at length such an imponderable before stopping in a grove of cottonwoods for an early midday meal so as to water and graze the animals. Yo, who had held the leadropes of the packmule and packhorse all morning, dismounted, spoke sweetly near the mule's long ear as insurance against post rest-time reluctance, and started to lead it and the horse to the river.

"Cut-Pants!" he called, seeing Randy free a foot from his stirrups, swing his cut-pants leg over the horse's back, and cautiously slide both feet to the ground. "Want to come with me and the beasts to the river?" Randy held onto his stirrup strap and shook his head. Though reapplied this morning, the Indian herbs had not yet had a miraculous effect.

He had just enough time to swallow a little hard bread and sliced buffalo tongue Bap's cook had given them, drink a cup of water Yo brought from the river. Yo helped him climb back into the saddle.

"It hurts," he said to himself. "I took just a few steps,

Journals of Patrick Gass.
p230, 142n
(Sacajawea slave Touse won in gambling game.)

Touse torn to bits and scattered by Blackfeet Indians.

Sacajawea.
G.Hebard
p105 (Touse wedding)

and it hurt a lot." He looked out across the treeless, endless plain to the line between earth and sky and shuddered when he remembered Fremont saying long ago, "If you get seriously hurt during this trip, you're a thousand miles from a doctor."

The afternoon hours plodding the trail passed slowly. The only sounds were hoofs on earth, the creak of leather saddles, the fluttering of silvery cottonwood leaves in the lazy breeze, and the voices of Fremont and Maxwell. They were listing what they needed to do, observe, buy, ask about, arrange for, when they reached the fort.

"We have only ONE day, tomorrow, to do everything. Max, as you suggested, you can best take care of the horse business—checking out our animals, choosing a half-dozen mules and two or three horses. Basil and Yo can help you. I'll need you for a while when I'm buying provisions for our journey to Laramie, and to add to our supply carts at Laramie—coffee, sugar, flour—"

"And coffee, sugar, and beads we promised Tuesday's village!" Randy reminded him. "And give the Booshway my father's address in the Senate where he can send news of Tuesday!"

"Won't forget! And Max, we'll both find out more about the trail to Fort Laramie, though you probably know quite a bit already about the rivers and creeks we'll follow or cross. While you men work on your jobs, I shall be finding out about the 200-mile area from St.Vrain's south to Bent's Fort, talking with traders and trappers about the best locations for military forts.

"I want to find out if they think a line of Army posts that includes Bent's and St.Vrain's, all connected by a mapped, marked trail to Ft. Laramie, should be built to protect emigrants who are bound to come. But—I must also take some time to record in my journal our travel along the South Platte. AND, tomorrow night for sure—unless I have energy and a clear sky tonight—I MUST make star observations and update our map!"

Five drudgery hours later, Randy asked with a weary sigh, "Are we close to the fort now?" Hungrily he gulped the last bite of his hard bread and sliced buffalo tongue. "The sun's gett'n right low."

"Only five more hours ride," Maxwell said. "Your ankle doing all right, Randy?" "Y-Yeah. Sure."

"It's kinda discouraging dat Long's Peak we saw I-don't-know-how-many days and miles ago don't look ANY closer," said Yo. "Umm," agreed Basil.

"Looks like the desolate, grassy plains to the north are changing into more desolate distant plains with scant vegetation of any kind," Fremont said. "That's the desert we must ride across to get to Laramie. Lord help us if any of us has an accident or falls ill with sunstroke."

Randy cringed. He silently promised himself he'd douse his ankle tonight with double layers of Indian medicine, and never take off his hat during the day.

Fremont was saying, "At least the animals can grab a bite here near the river in places where buffalo haven't already cropped off the grass. It may look brown and dry, but see how quick the animals are to snatch it! They act as if it's been buttered and sugared."

"Wish they could have an hour to stop and eat," said Maxwell. Fremont shook his head.

The river curved southward, its banks higher, its current swifter. Cottonwoods marked its edges, patches of wild flowers sometimes spreading out from them. With each crushing step of horse hoofs, the flowers sent up to the men a welcoming perfume.

The sinking sun's golden glare behind the distant mountains backlighted their toothy edges rising above the massive wall. "An early explorer," Fremont said, "called the Rocky Mountains 'the shoreline of a great sea of sand traversed by the Platte River.' He was Army Major Stephen Long, and that's his name on the snow-capped mountain we've been watching—Long's Peak.

Expedition from Pittsburgh to the Rocky Mountains. Major Stephen Long. *p313-6*

"But look, Randy, at the clouds hanging over the mountains now that the sun is out of sight!" he said. All the little party of horsemen watched with open-mouthed pleasure as the flimsy white clouds above the mountains ignited into flaming sunset shades of crimson, pink, peach, and gold.

All the color had long been swallowed into twilight when Maxwell announced, "Right here we move away from the river. We bear left to climb a 5-mile slope slowly rising above the river. Fort St.Vrain sits at the slope's highest point, just before the hill sheers off above a flat grassland.

"So we've got about three slow hours of climbing in the dark before 'halloo-ing' Marcellin St.Vrain! It's a well-traveled path, we won't get lost. I've done this climb many a time—I feel like I've come home."

They finally saw flickering campfires at the far edge of deep darkness, then the faint outline of a low, wide, bulky shape. "That's Indian campfires outside the fort," Maxwell said. "We're just minutes from hollering 'open up' to the guard at the gate."

They began to climb the last thousand feet. They began to hear the tum-tum tum-tum of drums, the high-pitched sing-song voices rhythmically, continuously, repeating a one-line tune. "Most likely that'll be 'Rapahoes thanking Great Spirit for a buffalo kill. They might sing and dance all night."

Randy's soprano full of anxiety cut through the darkness. "Do we have to camp out there with them?!"

"No, Randy—Charlie Bent told me in St. Louis that Marcellin St.Vrain will take care of us inside the fort anytime and for free," Fremont said.

"Yes, and he'd better do it!" declared Maxwell, "or I'll threaten to visit every teepee and tell the Indians to take their robes and skins to Fort Lupton just up the river—do their trading there! Heh-heh-heh-ho! St.Vrain hates Lupton and his adobe fort! He's the only one of three rivals who built adobe forts close to St. Vrain's that St.Vrain hasn't been able, one way 'r' another, to put out of business. So never fear, Randy, Marcellin St. Vrain will be GLAD to put us up for the night!

Fort Laramie
L.Hafen/Young
p68,69,70
(rival forts)

"As for the Indians, all but a few 'invited' Indians stay outside ALL the time at this fort! St. Vrain and his hired-help go out to them in their teepees here or in their villages miles away to make the trades. Sometimes, they do business through a large hole in the fort's four-foot-thick wall—a wall 12 feet high! The hole's large and HIGH up from the ground, has a heavy door to close it, and heavy timber bars to secure it.

"Forts are built for protection, you know, protection for a handful of white traders and their goods sitting out here alone among thousands of Indians with intense urges and appetites."

Their five mounts, packmule, and packhorse walked in a line close to a side wall of the fort some distance from the campfires, the drum-beating, dancing and singing.

Randy strained to see the moving circle of shadowy figures, their feet lifting and falling to the rhythm of the drumbeats. The sounds, the violent movements of bodies passing in front of flames flickering across the darkness, made Randy feel he was riding into a mysterious dreamworld.

JF Report
July 10
("reached St. Vrain's
Fort about 45 miles
from St. Helana late in
the evening.")

The Big Man at Fort St. Vrain weighs 115 pounds and stands a few inches over five feet tall. At age 23, Booshway–"Boss" from French "bourgoise"–Marcellin St. Vrain, brother of ex-aristocrat Ceran St. Vrain of France, partner of the Bents of Bent's Fort, has managed for two years Fort St. Vrain Indian-trading post where Plains meet the Rocky Mountains. Traders working for the massive fort, which looks inside and outside much like Bent's Fort to the east and Fort Laramie to the north, call Marcellin's booshway style and fun-loving antics "harum-scarum." Fremont meets up with his style. Randy sees his most famous antic——standing on his head, waving his legs in the air.

Bent's Old Fort, La Junta, Colorado. NatPkSer.

377

CHAPTER 34

HARUM-SCARUM BOOSHWAY

July 11, Fort St. Vrain (Colorado)

Randy waked with a start. What was that strange noise? Where was he? Above him dry, hard clay that long ago had oozed through cracks when it was mud plopped on top of close-fitted roof poles, marked the ceiling with earthy lines. And there was that noise again!

Randy snickered. Just a rooster crowing! When had he heard a barnyard sound! It didn't belong in the prairie-camping, horseback-riding, Indian-trading-post scene.

He sat up and looked around at the small room: white-washed clay plaster, a tiny window high up, a wood-plank door with air, sunlight, and peeking-out spaces between the planks. On the hard, smooth clay floor across the room from him lay another bed of buffalo robes—empty, except for John Fremont's saddle, carry-all bag, and rifle. Where was John? Where was everybody!

Last night, the five of them, he recalled, had kept their distance from the dancing, noisy Indians, rounded a corner of the long, rectangular fort, and stopped in front of massive wooden doors.

"Halloooo!" Maxwell had shouted, directing his voice through cupped hands toward the watch tower. "Who goes there?!" came the reply. "Lucien Bonaparte Maxwell—that's Who! You sound like Bill New!" "Hey Max old man! Be right down!"

Randy remembered the sounds of bolts sliding, timbers lifted from holders, hinges squealing, then a lantern light making a bright circle in thick blackness, shining on Maxwell's face and the face of a smiling stranger.

The rest was a jumble—waiting in the dark for Mr. St. Vrain, hearing talking, talking while standing half-asleep beside his pony, trying to favor his not-quite-so-sore ankle, hearing, "Sacre bleu! There's five of you!" seeing the horses led off to the corral, being led off himself through a door by somebody with a lantern, and sinking onto soft, furry robes on the ground.

Now with morning light streaking through door cracks and little window, he levered himself into standing, testing the strength of his ankle. Suddenly the door latch snapped

JFReport
July 11
JF mentions no activities during one day at the fort, except hiring a Mexican to take care of horses and mules.

378

and Yo was walking in, sunlight from the courtyard streaming around him. "Look at you!" Yo said cheerily, "Cut-pants is now Warrior-Wit'-New-Leg!"

Randy winced. "It's not all that good." He took a small limping step as Yo said, "Aw, but it will be when you have some good ole buffalo meat inside you," and held out an elbow for Randy to hold on to.

"We saved some for you—wasn't easy, we were so all-fired hungry and fresh meat being so much easier to chew dan dried out buffalo tongue. Dem dancing 'Rapahoes we saw last night brought fresh-killed buffalo yesterday. Dey was 'specting to please Booshway St.Vrain into giving 'um some weehio MAH-PE—white man's fire-water—plain ole burn-your-gullet alcohol."

Wah-To-Yah
L.Garrard,
p269(mah-pe)

"Did he give them some?"

"A little—he said—but he told 'um—he said—two or t'ree times his usual warning, 'You put dis in your mout' and it will steal away your head.'

"All twenty Indians said, 'good, good,' passed de jug around and pretty soon started to dance, deir heads felt so good. Last night we t'ought dey were t'anking Great Spirit for good hunting, but dey were just t'anking de booshway, Marcellin St.Vrain, for good likker!

"But dey couldn't do enough likker-drinking to turn dem into demons. St.Vrain says he keeps a tight spigot on de fort's likker barrel, only half-filled de gallon jug he gave de 'Rapahoes. He says he allows his traders to take a few gallons only once or twice a year for a drunken orgy in an Indian village dats gotta have such entertainment.

Bent's Fort.
D.Lavender,
p160(alcohol)

"But yesterday, he was mighty glad to have fresh meat and turned de likker spigot a notch to pay for it. So—last night we got de dance show out by de fort, and today we get to eat a few mighty fine meals. Come on now, let's go across de placida, as they call dis courtyard, to de dining room and sit you down to breakfast."

They had already moved outside and Randy wanted to stop and look around. "This is the first building I've seen all summer, Yo! I just want to look at it! And I want to see the chickenyard! I know there IS one—a rooster crowing woke me up!"

Fort Laramie.
Hafen/Young
p121(chickens)

"Yeah—dat rooster waked me up about an hour earlier!" Yo laughed. "He lives wit' a bunch of hens in a fenced off corner of de corral. You know, Randy, you could have an EGG for breakfast!—and some milk from a coupla cows in de corral!"

Randy shook his head, his mind firmly set on grilled buffalo meat.

"Well, you can do a lot of looking whilst we walk—you're barely limping, Cut-Pants—to de eat'n table at de far end of dis long, long yard," Yo said as they strolled toward the opposite end of the walled-in open space. "Not'ing much going on here right now, St.Vrain says, especially since Bap and a lot of de fort crew left for St. Louis to sell last winter's haul of buffalo robe.

Bent's Fort.
D.Lavender, p184,199
(inside forts)

"In summer, y'know, buffaloes shed deir thick fur, so de Indians have only bare, scraped skins to trade. Not many skins left eit'er, after dey've made new teepee covers, mocassins, 'n' winter clot'es for demselves.

"St.Vrain says dem Indians who brought de meat live right outside de fort just about all year-round. Dey're gimme-a-handout relatives, he says, of de wives of some of de white traders living in de fort. See over dere at de foot of de stairs leading to de watch tower? Dat's a bunch of deir young'uns, half-breeds, playing in de dirt."

Randy looked long and with much curiosity at a swarm of toddlers and a half-dozen of their mamas. "They live in little rooms like the one I slept in? Just big enough for me and John! There's not enough room to spread more'n two robes and leave a little walking space."

"Oh, you're in a guest room," Yo said. "Traders wit' a family—a half-dozen or so people—have much bigger rooms." Yo pointed to the long back wall of the fort lined with sizeable clay-plastered, flat-roof rowhouses. Projecting roof poles fringed the front top edge of the long building. "Lotta front doors but none in de back against de fort wall. Little rooms like yours are workshops for carpenters, sadlers, shoemakers, seamstresses—anyt'ing.

Fort Laramie.
Hafen/Young,
p109 (rooms,
apartments)

Fort Laramie.
NatlPkSer,
p25-"dwellings, shops,
storehouses"

"A'course, de Booshway lives in de best rooms—a set of FOUR BIG rooms—two on top of two sitting above de dining room and kitchen. See up dere—TOP of de corner rooms we're heading for? See a staircase going up to a sort of tower-house? De highest rooms stand higher dan de fort walls! Marcellin, his wife, and baby live up dere.

Bent's Fort.
D.Lavender
33-35,334
(St.Vrain
apartment)

"Marcellin is said to be not much past twenty, a little fellow—short, 115 pounds—and wild. But he's brot'er to Ceran St.Vrain, partner of de Bents at Bent's Fort, so...

"His Sioux Indian wife's not much older dan you, Randy. Baby's a year old. And you know what—Marcellin told us at breakfast dat one of his four rooms is a billiard parlor and we can play dere! And up der on top of de wall is de clerk's

Wah-To-Yah
L. Garrard,
p42(spyglass,
billiards, eagle,
guestroom)

Ency.Brit. 11th ed.
Vol.3., Billiards
French Aristocracy
p939

Bent's Fort
D.Lavender,
p189(Marcel-
lin St.Vrain)

Lucien.Bonaparte
.Maxwell.
L.R.Murphy,
p30(Marcellin
St.Vrain)

office where you can look through a spyglass bigger dan de Lieutenant's! St. Vrain says you can almost see Bap's island !"

Randy had stopped listening to Yo, and begun mumbling to himself, "Billiard parlor!" He shook his head in wonder. "You sure found out a lot, Yo, by getting up an hour before me."

They had arrived under a porch at an open door of the long dining room in the ground level part of Marcellin's tower. Randy heard John's voice, smelled roasting meat, and began to pull away from Yo's supporting hand. But Yo held on. "Not so fast, Mr. Limping Cut-Pants. Stand still a minute and I'll point out De Store where you can buy all kind of t'ings. Look down dis long, long porch all de way to de corner. De corner rooms are De Store. You'll need to go dere to buy t'ings for de Cheyennes.

"Now go slow on dat foot to de eating table, Cut Pants. After you eat, if you're not limping much, come on out to de corral and blacksmit'ing shop behind de back wall of de fort. I'll be out dere—I've gotta help wit' de horses."

In a moment, Randy was hearing John say to a small, young man with curly black hair, a mobile, pleasantly attractive face, and a jawline marked by a narrow strip of short beard from temple to temple, "Mr. St. Vrain, this is Randy Benton, my brother-in-law. Like all our crew, he spent 17 hours on the trail yesterday, a rider as stalwart as any of us, no matter he had a bandaged sore ankle!"

With an exaggerated ceremonial air, Booshway Marcellin St. Vrain rose from his chair at the head of the long table to shake Randy's hand. He wasn't much bigger than Randy. He called in Spanish to a Mexican man at the metal-box stove and grill in a far corner, "Bring a big plate of meat and bread to this hungry adventurer! And milk! And coffee! With mucho sugar!"

Randy had hardly sat down on a long bench by the table before he blurted out as a question a worrisome matter on his mind. "Mr. St.Vrain, why do you allow a billiard PARLOR here?!"

"Randy!" Fremont's voice had a sharp edge."What kind of question is that?!"

"Billiard PARLOR?" laughed St.Vrain. "Not enough space around that big green table for a chair or a card table or even the spitoon required for a PARLOR! You think billiard balls can only be snookered in a PARLOR, Mr. Benton?"

"I don't know, Sir. I just know my mother talks about 'billiard parlors' in a certain tone of voice. I've never seen one because she says I must never go inside one of those 'dens of in—in—'"

"Iniquity?" St.Vrain prompted. "Yessir." "Because such parlors are VERRY bad, eh?" "Yessir."

"Well, Randy Benton, my grandfather as a member of the Royal Council frequently played billiards with the King of France—it was the King's favorite game—so my family got into the habit of keeping a billiard table handy to practice hitting the ball in case royalty called for a partner." Marcellin St. Vrain winked at Randy. "If we have time, I'll give you a lesson. Billiard playing is a quite respectable sport in France!"

Bent's Fort.
D.Lavender,
p49-51 (St. Vrain
family, Royal
council)

He added, looking at Fremont, "Here in the American wilderness, billiard playing is an entertaining time-killer for traders stuck with nothing to do in the slack season. However, for those like Mr. Benton who frown on billiards, there's another entertainment. In the guard tower attic, you can visit, but not play with, something quite unusual—a huge, live bald eagle! Randy, you might like to take lunch to this giant bird—no danger, Lieutenant, the critter's all tied up so it can't fly off its perch—aahh!—here's your breakfast. Bon appetit!"

Fremont was smiling and shaking his head. "From the Virginia mulatto Beckwith and his amazing stories about his years as Chief of the Crow Indians, to the son of Sacajawea who lived in Europe with German royalty, then to the grandson of a Chevalier who played billiards with King Louis of France—who'll be the next surprise-person we meet in this American wilderness!"

Marcellin was glad to have news of his friend Jim Beckwith. "Crow Chief Beckwith's stories are no more amazing than many another man who's lived years in the Rockies," Booshway Marcellin declared. "But my friend Jim Beckwith tells his stories better, LESS puffed up, than most others.

"All these mountainmen spent 20 or so years out-witting or out-lasting wild animals, Indians, weather, dangerous terrain, and desolate distances in this hard land. Jim Bridger, Kit Carson, Broken Hand Fitzpatrick, Joe Meek, the Bent brothers—each one can tell, and tell well, dozens of stories of narrow escapes, terrible hardships, hazardous journeys, bad luck from every direction.

"I have a few such stories myself from just a few years of living out here trading 25 cents worth of blue beads for an Indian's buffalo robe I can sell for $10 or $20 in St. Louis. Is it for MONEY I stay here? YES! I'm not like Bap Charbonneau. He told me he came back to the Indian way

Bent's Fort.
D.Lavender,
p171 (25c for
$6 robe)

382

of life because living the rough life here, on his own, suited him better than a luxurious life in the Old World leaning on someone else. I think it would suit me to make my fortune here and retire with it to an estate in southern France!"

The young booshway gave a cocky little laugh. Then seeing Randy was wiping his plate clean of meat juice with the last bite of bread, he said, "Have enough to eat, boy? Coffee sweet enough? Good. You're ready to explore the fort. You can do that by yourself while the rest of your party gets everything ready for you to leave tomorrow morning. That's much too soon, Lieutenant.

"If you'd stay a few days, you'd give me a chance to congratulate Maxwell on the prospect of becoming my brother-in-law by marriage! I've just heard that my brother Ceran plans to marry the sister of Maxwell's bride, Luz Beaubien! A brother-in-law of my brother is MY brother-in-law, too, ain't he? But I haven't had a chance to say six words to Max since you arrived. He seems to live in the corral with the horses. If you wait a few days, Lieutenant, we brothers-in-law could get together, and maybe the supply wagons will show up, too—a BIG advantage for you!

Bent's Fort.
D.Lavender
p197 (fort wall-
top walkway)

"Hey, Randy! You'd better get moving if you're going to inspect everything in this fort. You can ramble wherever you like—but stay IN the fort. If you want to look at Indians outside, stand on top of the wall."

"Yes, Sir. I'd like that—if my ankle will let me climb the stairs. But first, I'd like to see what you have in The Store, and before THAT I'd like sum'more real sugary coffee with cream."

St.Vrain called the order to the kitchen, complimented Randy for "saying what he wanted and exactly how he wanted it."

"Speaking of naming desired edibles," Fremont said, and began to list the provisions he wanted to buy. Randy saw St.Vrain frown for the first time. Hands and arms spreading in a tell-all, helpless gesture, he declared he had a serious shortage of everything.

JF Report
July 12
"no provisions
to spare"

"I just cannot sell you a doggone bit of flour, no more than a pound of coffee, and even less sugar. We're down to our last little handsful of everything, and no sign of the supply wagons from Bent's Fort. They're weeks overdue. I must feed 60 people here in the fort for I don't know how much longer. I may have to beg Bap to return some of his supplies. What an irony that you just visited his warehouse where so much of the fort supplies are sitting!"

Fremont looked at St.Vrain in stunned silence.

St.Vrain abruptly turned the talk to the situation John would find at Fort Laramie. "Did your friend Chouteau tell you he has a competing fort right by his doorstep? Fort Platte! The same trade leech, Mr. Lupton, who built a fort by MY doorstep, went up to Laramie a little over a year ago, and built himself another fort almost within sight of your friend Chouteau's Laramie! He's my friend Chouteau, too, since he and the Bents divided the trade territory between them and stopped fighting.

Fort Laramie.
Hafen/Young.
and
Fort Laramie.
Natl.Pk.Ser.
(Lupton forts)

"Now we're sharing the same competitor, Mr. Lupton. His new, imposing Fort Platte obliged Chouteau just last year to replace old Fort John's rotting timber building with an adobe Fort Laramie. And it had to be bigger than Lupton's! You'll see Lupton's fort by the North Platte on the way to Chouteau's new Fort Laramie just a mile away on Laramie Creek!"

Randy wasn't much interested in Mr. Lupton and his forts, though he wondered why anyone would want his fort so close to another. He finished his sugary coffee, said his thanks, stood up, and was about to walk away when he heard the Booshway say some Mexicans had just come into the fort. "When they heard a party was leaving tomorrow for Fort Laramie, they asked to travel with it. What do you think, Lieutenant? They're going for jobs."

JF Report
July 12
(Mexicans)

Randy stopped to listen. But Fremont didn't answer St.Vrain. Instead he spoke to Randy to tell him that The Store was just down at the corner, and he should inquire there about beads and red face paint for the Cheyennes—and then visit all the workshops in the fort. St.Vrain added that he'd find a woman in one of them who'd put some Indian medicine and a better bandage on his ankle.

By midday meal—"buffalo stew, and plenty of it!"—Randy had spent some hours looking at beads, paints, bolts of cloth, knives, hats, blankets, necklaces, rings, then writing out the list of promised items, and a few more, for the Hair Rope Cheyennes.

He had also spent an hour or so with "herb lady" Maria, who laughed and sang while she washed his ankle, drenched it with red, green, and brown liquids, pressed a large, wilted green-gray leaf around it before wrapping it tightly with strips of white cloth. "It feels much better already. Maybe this time, a miracle WILL happen." She answered in Spanish and laughter—then kissed the fading purple spot on his forehead.

After midday meal, Randy slowly walked into every workshop in the fort, sat for a little while in each one to watch what the people were doing...a Mexican shoeing Basil's horse...an Indian woman hauling on a rope to draw up a bucket of water from the well...a man whose massive arms and belly were rumpled with muscles, pulling on the biggest bellows in the world to pump air into a blacksmith's furnace...a saddler cutting and fitting a leather cover onto a wooden saddle...a carpenter repairing a chair...a seamstress who hemmed the edges of the legs of his cut-pants without his taking them off.

He clucked and crowed to the chickens, listened to Maxwell, Basil, and Yo discuss the personality and probable age of mules in the corral, groomed his pony, visited the sanitary-pit room.

Bent's Fort.
D.Lavender,
p78-9
and
Wah-To-Yah.
L.Gerrard,
p42-3
(fort life)

He saw young Indian wives carrying infants tied to backboards, mules and carts bringing from the prairie loads of "no-smoke" buffalo chips for the kitchen and blacksmith's shop, Mexican men sweeping, carrying out trash, running up the steep, long stairs to carry jugs of water and coffee to guards in the towers, lugging wooden pails of water to the kitchen, tending the cook fires.

He quietly decided against taking food to the eagle. When in late afternoon he half-limped into the dining room and asked for a little bread and milk, Fremont and St.Vrain had just arrived from "a tour to convince," as Marcellin called it. Flushed and grim, they weren't looking at each other, not talking as they stood, arms folded, by the table. St.Vrain called to the cook for a pitcher of water, and a bowl of currants just picked from bushes growing wild on the river bank.

Fremont broke the tense silence. "I'm still not convinced you can sell me only a tiny fraction of the provisions I need. I wouldn't have made this long, difficult diversion from my route to South Pass had I had the slightest inkling that I'd risk starvation for my men on the desert crossing from here to Laramie! I tell you again that in St. Louis, Charlie Bent practically guaranteed—"

"Charlie Bent has been booshway out here a lot longer than I have," Marcelline interrupted, "and he knows nobody can guarantee anything! You talked to him in April in St. Louis? Who knew in April that the South Platte wouldn't have enough water to float the robes—our year's income—to market?! Who knew in April whether Indians in June would wreck the supply train before it reached Bent's and Santa Fe and St. Vrain's?!"

"But surely Bent sends you supplies on a regular—"

385

Voice louder, higher, St. Vrain answered, "REGULAR? I just told you not even HE can get REGULAR wagon trains from St. Louis to his fort! Going and coming, we get things when we get them—and he knows that! I can't believe he'd guarantee you anything!"

Fremont exploded. "You're saying I'm LYING?! Well, I think you're lying when you say you can sell me practically nothing!! I just can't believe that! Listen to me, young man—I'm the head of a United States ARMY expedition—not some drop-in from the prairie! You are OBLIGED to give me help!"

"I'm not obliged to give you what I don't have!" St.Vrain hotly replied. "I'm not OBLIGED to risk starving my people in the fort to feed your people who're only a few days' march from plenty at Laramie! I'm not OBLIGED to feel sorry for you because you can't have flour for bread or coffee three times a day—with sugar! You did without them all the way on the South Platte—and you didn't starve! You won't starve on the way from here to Laramie! You can eat plenty of buffalo for the killing at every waterhole on the way!"

Just then, cook Conchita, who had speeded up the refreshments to match the speed of the argument, herself brought and sat on the table in front of St.Vrain a sizeable bowl of currants, three small bowls and bread. As she filled the little dishes, she spoke to the Booshway intently, in Spanish. The booshway raised his eyebrows at her. Then he said with stiff courtesy, "Gentlemen, be seated. Welcome to our humble dining table."

Minutes later, Randy laid down his spoon and restarted the talking. "Mr. St. Vrain, Conchita looked and sounded like she was telling you bad news. Was she?"

Marcellin's devil-may-care smiling face appeared. "She was giving me advice, Mr. Benton. She said, 'Be quiet and eat. A hungry man is an angry man.'" No one spoke while another few mouthsful of currants and bread were swallowed. The two men barely glanced at each other.

Randy emptied his bowl first and asked for a little bit more. He drank the last berry juice from the bowl before venturing to break the silence again. "Mr. St. Vrain, I'd like to see your billiard parlor."

"So you DO want to visit a billiard parlor, Mr. Benton! How about a look through the big telescope, too? If the smoke in the air clears up, we can see the white tip of Pike's Peak more than a hundred miles south, even the Twin Spanish Peaks beyond Pike's! And of course Long's Peak is much less far away, and to the west. You think it's

Argument with Marcellin not in JF Report. But JF not likely to accept defeat without resisting.

386

exciting to be within sight of the high Rockies?"

"Yes! Yes!" Randy agreed. "Can't we get going?" He climbed the stairs slowly on an ankle that felt weak under Maria's bandage but only slightly sore.

They couldn't see Pike's snowy peak through the smoky air, much less the more distant Twin Spanish Peaks. Marcellin told them that fires had been burning for months in the south. Snow on Long's Peak shone bright, looked close enough to be in the fort's side yard. The billiards table was just a big table with a rim around it to keep balls poked with a stick from rolling off.

Still, Randy got to see Marcellin's pretty Sioux wife nursing her baby. Afterwards when she stood beside her little husband, he saw she was taller and older at 14 than he was at past-20. In their bedroom, they had a real bedstead, mattress, and large armoir.

Marcellin led them walking along the top of the fort's thick wall to see the two cannon in the guard tower, and the chained eagle glowering on the shelf in the tower top. "We feed him live mice," said Bill New, summer-idled trader who preferred guard duty and the eagle's company to tending babies. Randy congratulated himself for his decision not to bring the eagle's afternoon snack.

After a supper of grilled buffalo meat, Fremont's four men and Marcellin used the dining table to pore over Fremont's journal and his sketched-out map, adding details, correcting errors. When darkness began to settle in and smoke still shut out the stars, Fremont called bedtime and a long sleep for his men.

"Yes," nodded Marcellin, "although tomorrow morning will be easy—you'll be riding 'longside the Platte. But for your next 75 miles north, you'll need faith and stamina. Water will be a problem—long stretches between streams. Strike out due north from the big bend of the Platte. You'll cross several dry rivers. Crow Creek is one of them, a big one. Its water stands in pools, has no continuous flow so it's called a salt stream—water too alkaline for animals—or people—to drink.

"But you'll find good water often enough, and grass, and buffalo—usually. A final 40 miles east along Horse Creek and its forks to the Platte is easy. Mountainmen used to travel this desert route enough that their comings and goings even got a name—'Trappers' Trail.' Get you to Laramie in three days easy."

Fremont gave him an almost invisible "if we haven't

starved" glance, excused himself and Randy, walked arm in arm with his brother-in-law to their beds on the hard clay floor of their tiny guestroom.

At the edge of the Great Plains, Fort Laramie beside Laramie Creek flowing into the North Platte a mile or so away, will be the take-off place for Fremont's last 300 miles to South Pass, the Rocky Mountain goal designated by Congress. To travel to Laramie from Fort St. Vrain, Fremont's small party must ride across present-day Colorado's northeast desert, and adjacent southeast Wyoming. After four dawn-to-dusk days, they finally reach Laramie's adobe walls. But they hear no jubliant welcome–only predictions of disaster.

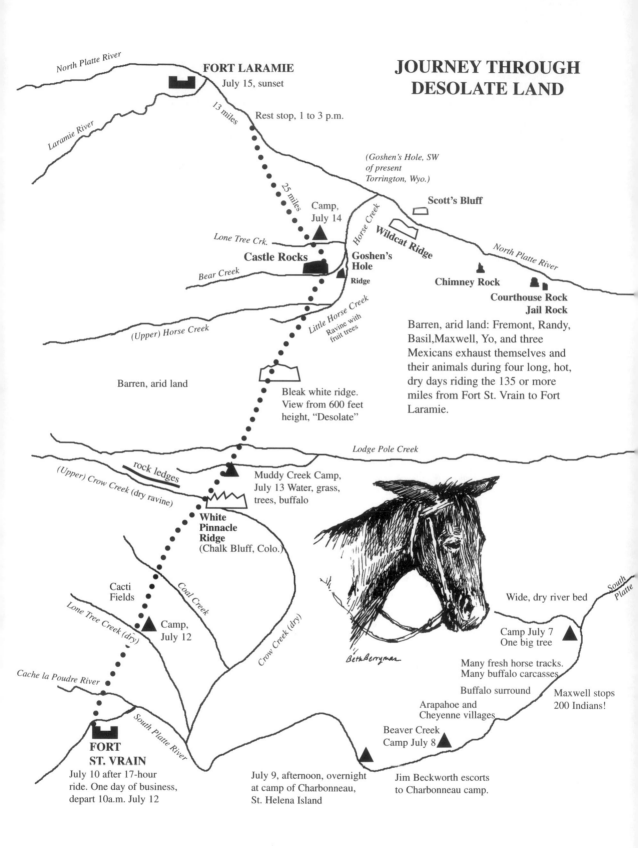

JOURNEY THROUGH DESOLATE LAND

North Platte River

FORT LARAMIE
July 15, sunset

13 miles

Rest stop, 1 to 3 p.m.

Laramie River

(Goshen's Hole, SW of present Torrington, Wyo.)

25 miles

Camp, July 14

Scott's Bluff

Lone Tree Crk.

Horse Creek

Wildcat Ridge

North Platte River

Castle Rocks

Goshen's Hole

Bear Creek

Ridge

Chimney Rock

Courthouse Rock
Jail Rock

Little Horse Creek

Ravine with fruit trees

(Upper) Horse Creek

Barren, arid land: Fremont, Randy, Basil, Maxwell, Yo, and three Mexicans exhaust themselves and their animals during four long, hot, dry days riding the 135 or more miles from Fort St. Vrain to Fort Laramie.

Barren, arid land

Bleak white ridge. View from 600 feet height, "Desolate"

Lodge Pole Creek

rock ledges

(Upper) Crow Creek (dry ravine)

Muddy Creek Camp, July 13 Water, grass, trees, buffalo

White Pinnacle Ridge
(Chalk Bluff, Colo.)

Cacti Fields

Coal Creek

Lone Tree Creek (dry)

Camp, July 12

Crow Creek (dry)

Wide, dry river bed

South Platte

Camp July 7
One big tree

Cache la Poudre River

Many fresh horse tracks. Many buffalo carcasses

Buffalo surround

Maxwell stops 200 Indians!

Arapahoe and Cheyenne villages

South Platte River

Beaver Creek
Camp July 8

FORT ST. VRAIN

July 10 after 17-hour ride. One day of business, depart 10a.m. July 12

July 9, afternoon, overnight at camp of Charbonneau, St. Helena Island

Jim Beckworth escorts to Charbonneau camp.

BethBerryman

CHAPTER 35

SHOCKS AT FORTS ST.VRAIN AND LARAMIE

July 12-15, Fort St.Vrain, desert trek to Laramie

At first cockcrow, Fremont had called, "Randy! Get-up
time! We must start early today, march our first 30 miles if
we're going to reach Fort Laramie in four days. We mustn't
be late, or Kit and our troops will worry that our topknots
are swinging at the top of an Indian scalp-stick."

Five hours later, Randy, Basil, Yo, and two eager
Mexicans holding their mules' reins were standing outside
the big gate of the fort, awaiting the arrival of Fremont and
Maxwell. Both men were still in the corral with Jose, the
Mexican hired for his magical skill with horses and mules.
Fremont was watching impatiently as Jose tried to bridle,
saddle, and mount the obstreperous mule that Fremont two
days before had named Vixen.

Despite walking 45 miles tied to a horse's tail, Vixen had
learned no manners or work ethic but gone back to kicking,
biting, rearing, and refusing to walk.

Jose had first tried his magical-friendly manner and
voice. Vixen treated them and him with scorn—tossing her
head, snorting, dancing the fandango. Thinking she was just
working off an ordinary morning show of individuality and
mule ego, Jose kept trying. When, twenty minutes later, she
rolled her eyes to see exactly where he was and let fly with
a foot that nicked the pants-leg covering his shin, Jose
decided he hadn't got through to her that he was Booshway
of Mules.

He went to his bedroll, opened it, lifted from its fold a
scissors-like wooden tool with very long, very blunt blades
ending in small discs. Fremont frowned. A special stick for
beating the animal? Jose brought the tool to Fremont. "Una
pinzas de nariz," he said, demonstrating its use with his
thumb and finger pinching the flesh divider of his own nostrils. Fremont seemed puzzled.

"Apparato de manejo y CONTROL, especial por una
tenazas. Animal NO suffriendo, NO herida. CONTROL sola-
mente," Jose explained.

Maxwell said he'd heard mule tenders talk about such a
"twitch" for controlling stubborn beasts. "Squeezing it a lit-

JF Report
July 12
(Vixen mule..
untractable..took
half-hour for Jose
to saddle)

Twitch use: Mule
experts:the late
Kenyon Whaley, and
Estelle Whaley
Hardison, Kinston,N.C.

tle as the animal stands still hurts very little. But when the critter moves sharply, the pain in this tenderest part of the nose becomes so intense, so exquisite, the animal quickly decides to stand perfectly still. I've been told that once a mule's been 'twitched,' it only has to SEE the tool to lose its ornery urges and obediently do its work." Fremont looked skeptical but nodded consent to Jose.

"Come here!" Jose called in Spanish to two laughing Mexicans who'd been watching the show. He directed them to grab the mule's headhalter, one man on each side. "Watch her front legs!" Jose, standing at arm's length in front of Vixen's muzzle, held up the tongs for Vixen to see. He worked the handles to open and close the blades. In his magical-friendly voice, Jose told Vixen the tool wouldn't hurt if she stood quietly. Still talking, Jose pressed the blades open a little, slowly stretched out his arm to deftly grasp the divider flesh of Vixen's nostrils between the discs at the ends of the twitch blades.

Vixen tried to pull away, but held fast by the men holding the halter she could move only enough to feel a sudden suggestion of pain inside her nose. Jose squeezed the handles to make the pinch more noticeable. Vixen started to bellow, quickly shut her mouth and carefully immobilized her head. She tested a few small leg and rump movements. The resulting pinches persuaded her to stand stockstill, not even rolling her eyes or switching her tail.

"Saddle and cinch!" Jose called to one helper. Then, "Bridle and bit!" he called to another. Vixen submitted to everything, hardly moving a muscle. "Take my place and hold the pinzas!" Jose ordered one helper, "but don't squeeze hard!" Jose hurried to swing up to the saddle and grab the reins. He called for the twitch. "Pull Vixen's head around a little so she can see me with her right eye! Bueno!" Jose, twitch in hand, extended his arm with the twitch into Vixen's view.

"Booshway Jose is always armed and ready, Senorita Vixen!" he said in his most enchantingly affectionate manner. He saw her pull her head away from the bridleman and nod.

Jose clucked "go." Vixen behaved as graciously as a long-eared lady should, walking sedately from the corral around the building to the big gate.

The Vixen-Jose duel, however, had added a half-hour to a leaving time already nearly three hours behind the time

Fremont had set. Two hours it had taken him to do all the necessary business—examine the 15 horses and mules Maxwell had selected, and choose eight of them...confer with the storekeeper and Randy about goods promised to the Cheyennes...write out delivery instruction and list...decide which of the additional five mules would carry how much baggage each. At last he and Maxwell and the 13 loaded and ready animals joined the others waiting at the gate.

Fremont sent word to St.Vrain, still in his apartment in the tower, that he was about to leave and wanted the fort workers to bring out all the provisions St. Vrain would allow him to buy.

But when the small, young Booshway came down to the gate, he exclaimed, "Lieutenant, I see you have brought out eight horses and five mules from our herd in the corral. We became so...involved...with the flour and coffee question yesterday we didn't take up the corral situation. That's regrettable since most of the animals in the corral belong to the men in the fort, and of course are not for sale. Of those few owned by the fort, I can spare you only ONE horse and ONE mule."

Fremont had not believed his ears yesterday—"No provisions!"—and he was no more able to believe them today—"ONE horse? ONE mule?!" Add to that the disappointing comments he'd collected about locating military posts along some 300 miles from Bent's Fort north through Fort St. Vrain to Fort Laramie.

White traders and Mexican workmen had all told him, "Station no military south of Laramie—except at Bent's where the Santa Fe Trail turns south. There, much white traffic, valuable goods, move along prairie miles swarming with roaming, thieving, murderous Pawnees, Comanches, and Kiowas, and protection is needed. But not here on the edge of the plains between Bent, St. Vrain, and Laramie where friendly Cheyennes and Arapahoes only worry the whites with petty thievery.

"A military fort west of Bent's Fort and hundreds of white soldiers with rifles and cannon could scare—insult—our Indian friends into becoming our enemies," they had said.

So one big reason for making his unauthorized sidetrip on the South Platte had produced nothing dramatic for U.S. Army planners. And now the other reasons he'd given to his party for the trip—more animals, more provisions—were facing Booshway Marcellin's talk of empty corral, hardly any

Bent's Fort D.Lavender, p263. No Army forts built. But Bent's Fort became "a handy substitute for an Army post by Spring 1845

392

provisions for a four-day trip.

"Marcellin," Fremont began beseechingly, suppressing his anger and disappointment, "we have a mare that was exhausted, reste, three days ago, and a horse also on the verge of collapse. I doubt we can make it to Laramie unless you sell us at least two good riding horses and three good packmules.

"At Laramie where the bigger part of my crew is awaiting us, we have no guarantee that we will be able to purchase either animals or provisions, particularly since we know that a 100 Oregon emigrants two or three weeks ahead of us may have cleaned out Laramie's warehouse, bought all the spare horses and mules.

"Your father's partner, Charles Bent, will be MORE than dismayed, Marcellin, if my lack of a few animals from Fort St.Vrain's corral, and our having to depart without enough provisions to feed six men during a four-day desert crossing, results in a disaster for an expedition sent by THE UNITED STATES CONGRESS!"

Not in *JF Report.* But JF would have used every strong point to press St. Vrain into complying.

Wearing his most sympathetic smile, Marcellin replied that Fremont should wait until the supply train arrived, and help persuade ITS booshway to part with one or two of HIS horses. "I'll work on him hard!" Marcellin declared, "so you can have TWO horses! But the mules—not much I can do—except—here's a possibility!

"Look there—two Mexicans and two mules that belong to them are still asking to ride with your party to Laramie. You might could make a deal with them. Tell them they can join your group on condition that they sell you their mules at Laramie!

"Oh—and let me assure you that when the supply wagons come, your order for your Cheyenne friends will be fully taken care of, and the bill sent with your other bills to Washington. Must excuse myself now—I hear my wife calling me frantically!"

"You know full well I can't delay departure!" Fremont flung after him.

At 10 o'chronometer when the Fremont caravan drew away from the massive wooden gates of Fort St.Vrain, Fremont, Maxwell, and Randy side by side led the way. Behind them rode Basil on the good St. Vrain horse, entrusted with five pounds of just-ground coffee beans. Yo riding beside him had ten pounds of dried buffalo meat, skimpy feed for eight men for one day, tied behind his saddle—all the edibles Marcellin would give up. No sugar, no flour.

Behind them rode Jose, entrusted with controlling Vixen's personality. The two Mexicans beside him on mules now contracted for sale to Fremont, held lead lines of Basil's recovering mare, and the one St. Vrain packhorse and the one St.Vrain mule carrying baggage. Basil and Yo held lead lines of Fremont's packanimals loaded with baggage and scientific instruments.

JF Report
July 14
*("couple of horses
and 3 good mules..
few pounds coffee,
dried meat for
one day")*

When Randy turned his head for a goodbye look at the fort, he saw a man standing on top of its thick, 12-foot high wall. "Look!" Randy called out, pointing and waving toward the fort. The man atop the wall waved back.

Bent's Fort
D.Lavender,
*p.195.(harum-
scarum Marcellin)*

Suddenly he moved quickly forward, arms outstretched to reach down and touch the flat wall top while legs and feet sprang straight up into the air and waved back and forth. Quickly he folded them down, jumped to his feet, waved, and hurried to the nearby tower apartment.

"That's harum-scarum Marcellin!" Maxwell laughed. "Booshwaying for years in the wild hasn't worn away his fun-loving streak!"

Not in JF Report.
*Marcellin's well-known
antic as a goodbye ges-
ture would have
amused Marcellin.*

Down the slope from the fort, they splashed across the shallow South Platte, came out of the cool shade of the trees lining the its bank to head north across sun-flooded fields of colorful, fragrant flowers. By the midday stop, they had crossed a small creek and the swift waters of a river, Cache a la Poudre, just before it joined the Platte at its big bend east. Under cottonwoods on Poudre's north bank, they watched the rushing stream, cold with snow melt from the high Rockies, and ate thin, hard, pieces of dried buffalo meat.

JFReport
July 12

When Fremont, food in hand, walked to the river's edge alone, Randy silently followed at a discreet distance. He thought Fremont had been not simple-silent after leaving the fort, but leave-me-alone silent. Is he mad at me for spending too much time and money buying presents to send to Tuesday? Did I take too much time with Maria getting a second dousing of Indian medicine and a bandage on my ankle, thanking her for a REAL miracle that made it well, and for making my forehead well with a kiss yesterday...and today? Will he fuss at me when he finds out I have two pockets full of sugar lumps Conchita gave me?

When Fremont stopped, stood gazing at the stream gurgling eastward over its rocky floor, Randy eased up beside him and in his most pleasing manner and casual tone asked, "Does this river have a name?"

Fremont silently continued chewing on the dry meat he'd just bitten off. He swallowed hard before answering. "St. Vrain and Maxwell say it's the Cache a la Poudre River— 'Hidden Powder'—no doubt gunpowder. Lot of water tumbling toward the Platte."

"Umm."

"It's so wide and swift," Fremont continued, "it must be cutting through high mountains, and on down through foothills, to get here. I wish I had time to go exploring to its source, see its valleys, how far it would take me across the snowy heights. Perhaps there's a pass—who knows? If so, this river, extending the South Platte west, might be a quicker way to Oregon than the North Platte." After a moment's silence, Fremont added in a half-whisper as if talking to himself, "I must come back and explore that interesting possibility."

JF Report
July 12
(Poudre– "better
way to Oregon?")

Shortly all were mostly dry and in their saddles watching Fremont consult a compass. The column began moving north, Jose having shown Vixen the twitch.

Five solitary hours later, having passed across flat miles of brown, dry grass, they halted at the edge of a wide but dry creek.

Fremont, Pathmarker.
A.Nevins, p189
(JF explored
Poudre River in
1843.

"What's this one?" Fremont inquired of Maxwell. "I think it's the Crow River, Lieutenant."

"But, Lieutenant, sir," Yo said, "I spoke to a trader named Dawson at the fort, and he told me the second creek we'd come to is called 'Lone Tree'—"

Consultant for JF's
journey between Forts
St.Vrain,Colo., and
Laramie, Wyo:
Lee Whiteley, Colorado
prairies historian,
Littleton, Colo. Author
of "The TrappersTrail"
in the Ore.Calif. Trail
Assoc.'s Overland
Journal, Winter
1998-99.

"No—it has to be the Crow!" declared Maxwell firmly. Blue eyes glaring in irritation at the two men, Fremont reminded them that they'd told him they'd worked in this area. "You must've traveled this trail to Laramie!" Yo squirmed and admitted he didn't rightly remember the details of one trip he'd made a long time ago on "The Trapper's Trail" between St. Vrain and Laramie.

"Maxwell!" Fremont snapped. "You worked out of the fort for two whole years, taking trade goods to Arapahoe villages in the South Platte area, you said. How could you NOT be familiar with these creeks!"

Maxwell's cheeks glowed with two red spots.

"SIR!" he stormed,"I told you I worked the OTHER bank of the South Platte—the side the fort's on! I had no business on this side! Beckwith was over here trading with the Cheyennes on this side! You should've hired HIM to guide you! Or you could've asked at the fort for somebody to draw you a map!"

Fremont drew himself up into his Army Officer pose, and was about to speak in a stiff manner reflecting his position, and in strong words reminding his subordinate of his place, when a boyish soprano asked plaintively, "Are we lost?"

Fremont laughed. Maxwell relaxed. Basil and Yo looked at each other and exhaled subdued phhews, while the puzzled Mexicans looked at each other and shrugged.

"Right, Randy!" Fremont said. "The right question is 'Are we lost?' and when the answer is, 'No, we're not,' we cluck to our horses, cross the dry bed, no matter its name, and move on! Giddap!"

On the slightly higher bank they were ascending, Randy caught a glimpse of light on water in a small bend of the river bed. "Look! A pool of water! That should mean THIS is Crow Creek—shouldn't it?"

Randy glanced around, hesitating. Seven faces looked at him as if they seriously awaited his decision. Fremont smiled. "What makes you think so, Randy?" Randy turned a knowing, smiling face to his companions. "I heard Mr. St. Vrain say that Crow Creek is a crazy river, that most of the time it doesn't flow, it just pools here and there—and even the water in the pools is crazy because it tastes bad and makes you sick if you drink it. Horses won't drink it, he said. So that pool over there's no use. But John—right here we're under the only tree in sight. Haven't we come enough miles today—Lieutenant?"

"Yaaay, Randy!" sang Yo, and all the others chorused, "Yaaay RANDY!" and joined the hand-clapping.

"We've been 28 miles, so 'yaay, Randy!' We'll camp by the tree on the crazy Crow for the night," John agreed.

Basil thought the creek's pool at the bend looked like a deep buffalo wallow the animals had pawed out of the river bed. Plentiful cakes of dry "bois de vache" in the area confirmed that many buffalo sometimes passed this way. Fremont gave to the Mexicans the job of collecting stacks of "bois" for the campfire despite Randy's offer to help. "See! Maria's doctoring has cured my ankle!"

When the smokeless "bois" campfire was crackling strongly, Yo announced happily, "Today for de first time on our South Platte trip, we'll have campfire-boiled COFFEE, de nectar of campers—even wit'out sugar!" He jauntily emptied a canteen of water into the kettle, poured in a small

JF Report
July 12
("I had great difficulty ascertaining what were the names of the streams we crossed..")

Camp probably on Long Tree Ck.,not Crow.

396

handful of Conchita-ground coffee, raised a fist to complete the ceremony.

"Hurray!" shouted five voices. "Vive!" added three more. As soon as the coffee was ready to pour, Randy passed by each man, hissed "shh," and dropped a fat sugar lump only slightly grimy into each cup. He collected a series of low but intense cries of "Vive Randy! Vive!"

By the time it was the turn of Fremont, last in the sugar line, Randy had decided to risk his questioning, even his disapproving. "Shh!" he hissed, drawing the sugar lump from his pocket, holding it over Fremont's cup. Lightning quick, Fremont plucked the lump from Randy's fingers. "Aha! Don't tell me you robbed Marcellin's sugar hoard in the kitchen pantry!"

"No, sir! The cook did it! No, no, I didn't mean the cook STOLE the sugar—the cook—Conchita—just filled my pockets with sugar lumps. She told me sugar would make my ankle strong!"

Sugar episode
not in JF Report

"You understood all her Spanish words, Randy?"

"I've gotten good at figuring out sign language, sir!"

Randy's brother-in-law dropped the cube into his coffee, said, "Vive! Vive Randy!" and smiled as he stirred the liquid with a piece of dry meat. His mood, and the mood of the camp brightened. The Mexicans began to sing, tapping the rhythms on their empty tin cups, luring the others into sending a rollicking "Ai-ai-yah-yaaay!" across the plains.

At dusk, Randy obeyed Fremont's order to "take care of that ankle," rolled himself up in his blanket and lay down near the campfire, now only a few fading red cinders. He heard Fremont and Maxwell's voices some distance away talking in amicable, getting-ready-to-shoot-the-North Star mumbles. He heard the other men speaking to the horses as they moved their stakes.

JFReport
July 12
("observation of the
night")

Darkness deepened, not even a thin crescent moon hung in the sky. Randy raised his head to see the sperm-candle lantern of the star-gazers bobbing on the right, and that of the horse tenders on the left.

Reassured, he stretched out and gazed upward. Look! Look! There crossing the middle of the clear, black sky shone the long cloud of fuzzy light that Tuesday called

Cheyennes.
Hoebel, p86
(Ekutsi Himmiyo,
Hanging Road:
Milky Way)

Ekutsi Him-miyo, The Hanging Road. "Tuesday said all Cheyennes go up there to the Milky Way when they die, and live the way they did on earth." Randy drifted off to sleep and dreamed of watching Tuesday draw his portrait on a sandy road inside a long tunnel, its walls made of millions of twinkling stars.

Beginning the next morning, for three more days the amount and type of a day's toil were one with the hatefulness of the land, the sun, and the wind. Riding began at six and ended 15 hours later as the sun was dropping out of sight.

The first of those three days, went on and on for 40 miles without a midday-meal stop. "We must make up for lost time," Fremont declared, "keep moving without interruption," so they stayed in the saddle and slogged on while gnawing meager leftovers of dry meat.

They had begun the 40 miles by picking their way through 12 long, blistering miles of spiny cactus, and were rewarded with water and grass in a small creek flowing in one of several ravines of a rumple of low knolls. In nearby ravines, little bands of buffalo grazed. On the west rose a plateau of layered white marl rising toward high mountains. But as tempting as the little creek and buffalo were, Fremont allowed only a one-minute stop to drink. The men chew their last bites of board-like meat as their horses labored on.

JF Report
July 13

Water, grass probably on Coal Ck. (present-day map)

Under the hot afternoon sun, their thirst and fatigue grew—and grew still more as they skirted past a high, white ridge broken into conical peaks topped with heaps of large boulders. They had seen it glittering in the sunshine for miles. As they passed its tall and short spires and cones, Randy decided a tornado must have whirled through this stone forest. "How else could piles of rocks have flown up and landed on the tiptops?"

Probably Chalk Bluffs (present-day map: 20m. east-southeast of Cheyenne, Wyo., west of Carpenter. North edge of Pawnee National Grasslands)

The ridge, they saw after rounding its northern end and crossing a dry streambed, was marked with gullies—dry—coming by frequent falls from ridge heights. Gullies joined the dry creekbed pointing southeast along the foot of the ridge. Its opposite bank soon became a high straight-up wall of layered white marl. As Randy, in passing, looked into the shut-in bed of a stream that didn't flow but maybe once a month—or year?—he shuddered, his mouth dry and stiff from breathing the completely moistureless hot air.

During the rest of the day, the draining hours dragged by with much of a sameness, nothing to see, nothing to feel but dry, dry, desolate, level prairie now whipped by hot, constant wind sweeping out of a fiery sky, sucking the last moisture from land, men, and animals.

Probably Upper Crow River. JF didn't know the course of the Crow, that, coming from North/NW of Cheyenne, Wyo. area, it makes a great bend south, enters S. Platte well east of where JF crossed Cache la Poudre River.

Toil, toil, toil, tongues stiff, eyes burning, buttocks numb. All canteens—dry. "We cannot stop until we find water," Fremont said, his voice hoarse, "and find it before these panting animals collapse."

At last, near day's blood-red sunset, a long, thin line of green! A creek! Water! Grass! Trees! And a miracle—a little band of buffalo! Food on four feet! Could this slender stream be Lodge Pole Creek? Or was it farther on, bigger with more buffalo, better grass?

Muddy Creek, trib. of Lodge Pole Ck. 12m.west of Pine Bluffs,Wyo., near Burns.(present-day map).

"Las bestias tienen mucha hambre, y la gente tambien," Jose croaked, a plea to stop here, end the day here. Fremont's tongue-dry reply was, "Yes, amigo, even if it's a small version of the place we've been dreaming about—trees, trickling water, fresh meat—a bigger one couldn't be better!"

Guns boomed, men brought to the campfire great chunks of fresh, bloody meat swinging in Fremont's prized sheet of India rubber. Eat! Eat! Drink! Drink! Cook more! Eat! Cook, eat! Cook at midnight, eat, eat!

"Alfonso, you're eating raw meat. Here, use this cooking stick."

"No, gracias. Trouble here." Alfonso patted his leg behind the knee. "Need raw meat. Need herbs."

Wah-To-Yah. *L.Garrard, p254 (pain behind knee, first sign of scurvy)*

"First sign of scurvy," Maxwell told Fremont. Fremont went looking for edible "herbs" with Alfonso. After dark, he checked and recorded the barometer's measure of altitude—5,440 feet above sealevel—and caught the North Star's twinkle in the sextant's mirrors.

At dawn, cooking, eating, drinking continued as long as Fremont permitted. "We must press on—I'm not sure of anything I've been told about this strange land, not even how much farther we must travel. We may come upon surprises that slow us down—more stone ridges, or other obstacles that pop out of the earth in this desert.

"By compass we have come north and a little east. How far? Forty miles from our camp on the Crow, 68 from Fort St.Vrain—perhaps half-way to Laramie."

JF Report July 14 (Lodge Pole Creek)

Desolate ridge: dividing ridge of North and South Platte drainage area.

They pressed on and shortly saw greenery framing a wide, full, rushing river. "THIS is the Lodge Pole!" cried Maxwell confidently. "Big, and going STRAIGHT east maybe 200 miles to the South Platte. Remember?—we saw its mouth at the start of our South Platte march."

But they did not stop.

They went on past two dry stream beds, faced at noon another surprise high-bleak-white ridge. Although longer, and blocking the way, the wider limestone and marl had no bizarre shapes like yesterday's ridge. Whipped by wind, Fremont led the climb up treacherous surfaces to the 600-foot-high top.

They paused to look down at a river and across arid, barren expanses of flatlands, ashgray-white like the ridge. The whipping wind suddenly turned chill, pushing and shoving the men and animals. Fremont, shivering and shuddering, spoke for all when he declared, "I have never seen anything that impressed so strongly on my mind a feeling of desolation!"

"Let's GO! Right NOW!" Randy said, teeth chattering.

Half-way down desolation ridge, they found another surprise, a dreamlike little paradise ravine of hothouse temperature, lavishly growing willows, grass, trees with ripe cherries, bushes with ripe gooseberries and currents, all by a tiny creek, its water running swift, clear, cool.

"Paradise" creek, Little Horse Ck., tributary of Horse River. Near LaGrange,Wyo. (present-day map)

Maxwell interrupted lunching berry pickers with a joyous cry, "Look! Look across there to the north! One, two, three, green lines—I'm sure they're tributaries of Horse Creek—the big creek that runs into North Platte!"

The paradise ravine and swift creek fed into the first green line, a Horse River stream. More trees! Water! Shade! The worst was over! The little column of horses, riders, and packanimals crossed it and another in comfort even though thermometer mercury rose to 104 degrees.

Horse River sequence of river and tributaries on present day map (JF had little info.about Horse R. and its"forks"):
1. Little Horse (trib.)
2. Horse River (western section)
3. Bear Creek (trib.)
4. Lone Tree Creek (trib. eastern section,entering north of Castle Rocks) JF camp July 14.

The third stream ran through a two-mile-wide gap between the ends of two ridges of steep hills. Yo remembered the place as the entrance into "Goshen's Hole," a 30-mile long prairie rimmed by a rocky ridge.

"See, with a ridge wrapped 'round a big prairie, you've got a flat, round, enclosed 'hole,'" Yo told Randy. "Mr. Goshen? Only heard-tell of him, Randy. Don't know who he was or what he did to deserve having his name on a 'hole,' but he musta been real important."

Great bastions of stone hundreds of feet high stood on both sides of the gap. Fremont favored the more northern side—it pointed north and it reminded him of a medieval walled city. Randy exclaimed, "It IS a town, John! See the church steeples and domes? I see watchtowers on top of the walls, too!"

JF Report

John shook his head and explained that winds and rains over a long period of time—"thousands, maybe millions of years"—had worn down a once-mighty ridge of limestone into these strange shapes. "The softer stone washed away

400

first leaving hard-stone steeples and domes, minarets and watchtowers. The same kind of weathering created the conical spires topped with 'hats' we saw when we passed the first white ridge."

Castle Rocks is west/ northwest of LaGrange, Wyo.

They called the yellow and red stone bastion "Castle Rocks." They called by numerous less romantic names the two miles of its shaled rock that had fallen from the "castle's" sides during eons of rain and ice. Such detritus, piled in heaps next to the "castle" wall, sloped outward hundreds of yards upon the prairie.

Yo remembered riding through the broken rock piles by following winding passages cut by water coursing down the "castle" walls. He and Fremont led the way, sometimes between walls of broken rock towering over paths scarcely wide enough for a horse to squeeze through.

In the hour or more that Randy and his pony slowly followed Fremont and Yo along the winding, water-cut path, through the sprawls and heaps of broken rocks, Randy rode silently, clenching his teeth, grabbing his saddlehorn when his tired pony's hooves slipped or stumbled. Behind him trailed Basil, Maxwell, the three Mexicans, and all the packanimals.

Well past the "castle" by sunset they caught a glimpse of water not far away. Horse Creek itself? A tributary? Last of the Horse Creek group? They camped on its bank.

Over the last of the coffee, Fremont calculated that the day's march covered 35 or more SLOW miles in 15 hours for a total of 103 miles in three days. "Today felt longer than yesterday's 40," weary Randy said to himself.

"Tomorrow," Fremont continued, "we'll be past this Goshen Hole and rim, so we'll race for the North Platte across the prairie. We'll continue about 25 miles north but bearing about fifteen or so degrees west of north so we can strike the Platte closer to Laramie."

"Hurray!" shouted Randy. "Just 25 miles to the Platte! Only half a day's march! No more packing and unpacking blankets or hobbling horses after tomorrow!"

JF Report, July 15

They could see the end of the rocky rim of Goshen's Hole in the distance the next dawn, plodded past it, and doggedly crossed rumpled prairieland for the next seven hours. The day turned extremely hot with a wind that seemed to have burst out of a vast furnace in the hills. Animals moved slower and slower, tongues lolling and dry. Two mares stopped, verging on collapse. Their riders dismounted, walked beside them, languidly leading them by the reins.

An hour past noon, the sight of Platte River cotton-woods in the distance thrilled the men into a weary shout—cut short by Fremont's announcement that they'd immediately turn north after watering the animals at the Platte, and continue to the Fort. "It's only a dozen more miles. We'll be there by 5 o'chronometer!"

"Please, sir," Basil appealed to Fremont, "we're all cooked, blasted to de bone by de sun, used up, in a bad way, drained, limp wid tiredness, falling off de collapsing animals. Please, sir! Relent a little. Give us and dese animals two hours to rest and eat. Maxwell here says it's 15 more miles to de fort. Dat's about six hours at de slow pace we'll be going if we don't rest at least two hours. Wid rest and food we may can speed up and get to de fort in four hours, well before dark. I speak for myself, Yo, Jose, Alonzo, Escalante, Randy, too, from his looks."

JF Report, July 15 ("reached N.Platte at 1 p.m.") "rested the animals, proceeded at 3 o'clock toward Laramie.

Fremont relented. "Two hours, then we move."

The long summer day had two more lighted hours when they passed Fort Platte, rival to Laramie. A quarter hour later, they saw the bigger white-washed walls and watchtower of Fort Laramie with an American flag flapping in the wind above it, and with dozens of Indian teepees in the trampled yard around it.

JF Report, July 15 (whitewashed Fort Laramie, many Sioux tents)

Clear, sharp sunlight behind Laramie Mountain strongly outlined the miles-away peak. The view and the sight of the fort inspired a small cheer, yaay!—mighty noise for such a worn-out party. Randy didn't dare look at the others for fear they'd see the tears in his eyes.

JF Report July 15 (delivered letters to Booshway Boudeau)

Fremont stopped a few minutes at the fort office to leave for the Booshway a letter he'd carried for weeks from the fort's owner, Pierre Chouteau in St. Louis. It informed the Booshway of the mission that Congress had given Fremont. Then he and his party cantered toward a grouping of tents and two-wheel carts by Laramie Creek.

Fremont tapped his horse into a gallup, and all at once his seven mounted men and all the animals on lead lines were flying with him into the open camp circle.

"They're here!! They're here!!" resounded from tent to tent, from man to man. Men suddenly were running from every direction toward the arrivals, crowding around their horses and shouting a jumbled message.

What were they saying?! Fremont's heart almost stopped. "Indians on warpath!!! Can't go west! Can't go!!"

Can five old Indian Chiefs persuade Lieutenant Fremont from leaving Fort Laramie and riding off toward South Pass? At the last minute, they crash Booshway Boudeau's farewell party to predict—Maxwell and Carson translating—that 300 warriors roaming that route looking for whites to kill will massacre Fremont and his men. That will bring Army troops to take revenge. They will destroy Indian villages, the Chiefs say, "So, you must not go and be killed."

403

CHAPTER 36

TALES OF DANGER—BUT WESTWARD GO!!

July 15-21, Fort Laramie (Wyoming)

Fremont, still in the saddle, looked at the circle of upturned faces, all drawn and marked with anxiety, many with open mouths reciting the news. In the muddled mixture of words, a few sounded loud again and again. "Indians!...He said!..Sioux!...two hundred!...Sioux!"

JF Report
July 15

Over their voices, Fremont called, "Where's Kit Carson?!" and pointed to camp manager Lambert for an answer. Lambert called back, "Gone to Fort Platte to find out what the booshway and traders have heard today!" Fremont looked at the men gathered around him. "Any of you who know some Spanish? Please take care of these three Mexicans. They need water, food, and rest. Jose here will need tent space to lay his blanket. The other two will be going to the fort to look for jobs.

"The rest of you men lend a hand to Maxwell, Basil, Yo, Randy, and our animals, including ALL the mules. The two Mexicans are selling me theirs. Now, I must talk to Lambert—"

"And me!" shouted Mr. Preuss, waving a hand high above the crowd. "And you!" Fremont responded as he dismounted and headed for his tent.

Randy carefully got off his pony and hurried to Fremont. "I want to go with you—I want to hear about what's happened. Please, John!" Fremont nodded.

For the next hour, while Fremont and Randy drank Laramie Creek water and quickly ate buffalo meat chunks, Lambert and Preuss "started at the beginning" of the story. "I kept a journal during ze ten days after I left you on ze Zowse Platte and caught up wiz our men on ze Norse Platte," Preuss informed him proudly. He handed Fremont several pieces of paper he'd written upon—in German. "Yah, yah, I vill SAY it all in English."

He began with details of the first three days of monotonous plodding towards Fort Laramie after he and Dr. Bernier caught up with the column. Late the third afternoon, advance scout Carson and two trappers or traders had galloped in from the north babbling about Indians on war path near Laramie.

Lambert broke in abruptly, saying that, a few minutes later "50 or 60 more traders and trappers showed up. The man in charge was none other than Jim Bridger!"

"Ah—famous Jim Bridger, mountain-man!" Fremont exclaimed. "No one who's traveled out here during the past twenty years could've missed hearing about or even seeing the legendary Jim Bridger!"

Preuss, his bulging blue eyes huge and staring, added, "He told us ve'd probably be all right as far as Fort Laramie, but going vest beyond ze fort vould be EXCEEDINGLY dangerous!" Preuss began to spill out details. "Bridger and his party of trappers and traders viz packhorses loaded down viz buffalo robes—but let me tell you NOW, or I'll forget, zat ve gave Bridger ze fur bundles ve took from ze trees, trusting him to take zem to Chouteau's store vhere Tulip's ragged trapper friends'll sooner or later show up—"

Lambert took over the story by loudly saying that Bridger told him how he and his men were having a trade rondyvoo with Snake Indians in Sweetwater Valley when he got wind that war parties of hundreds of Sioux, Cheyenne, and Gros Ventre warriors were scouring the country looking for them—"not to trade but to KILL!"

Mr. Preuss interrupted with some agitation. "At zat time, two veeks or so ago, ze var parties vere at Red Buttes, and moving vest along ze Platte toward its joining wiz ze Sveetvater !"

"So," boomed Lambert, "Bridger avoided the war parties by leaving the Sweetwater, not going by Red Buttes on the Platte to reach Laramie, but cutting east through the Black Hills instead!"

Preuss, his face red with excitement, said breathlessly, "Bridger said zose Indians had declared var upon any vhite person zey caught vest of Red Buttes—and ve'd be risking our lives to ride out zere any time soon! BUT, Jim Bridger said he'd turn 'round and accompany us to ze head of ze Sveetvater beyond Red Buttes—IF our leader vere viss us, but YOU VEREN'T! He vas assuming, I zink, zat ze var parties had gone farzer vest on Sveetvater."

Fremont ignoring the criticism, said, "Probably the Sioux did keep on moving west for some time until they realized their intended victims had escaped. Then what did they do? Stop, camp, hunt? Are they on their way back to the fort? What did they have against Bridger's 'big party of whites' that they wanted to kill them? How far is Red Buttes from Laramie?"

Lambert estimated 135 miles. He also estimated that by now, a full three weeks had passed since Bridger on the Sweetwater River learned the Indians were at Red Buttes on the Platte. "The Sioux've had time enough to go another 135 miles west, turn around, ride east two weeks along the Sweetwater and Platte, and be showing up at Laramie, say, day-after-tomorrow! They'll come to the fort since they've sent their families here for safety—camping outside the white man's fort!"

Mr. Preuss began waving his hands violently and spluttering. "I zink ze varriors could have camped for a veek to hunt! Zen zey vould be coming back just in time to meet US at Red Buttes or somevere! Zat is how all ze men, including Kit Carson, saw it ze night Bridger camped viz us. Zat is vy all of ze men except you, Mr. Lambert, and five ozzers, decided to pull out of zis expedition, join Bridger, go back to St.Louis!"

"WHAT!!!"

"Yah, Lieutenant! And one of ze biggest noises made for a turn-around came from ze mouse of zat useless boy, Henry Brant! Vhen ze Frenchies began saying in French, 'no more life for us if we continue to Laramie,' ze Brant boy began saying it in English."

Journal.
Preuss,
July 9 ("Brant
at the point of
going back
with the traders")

Fremont, astounded, demanded of Lambert, "Is that true?! Can that possibly be true!?? Our men would have deserted?!!"

Lambert patted Fremont's arm, quickly and calmly answered that they all changed their minds after a little talking-to, and nobody walked away with Bridger. "They're all here," he assured Fremont. "They're waiting to see what you decide. I predict that all will willingly do whatever you, Lieutenant Fremont, decide to do."

"But KIT CARSON wanted to turn back??!" Fremont was incredulous. Randy's shock echoed Fremont's. "And Cousin Henry did, too?!!"

Abruptly, Fremont started toward the tent door. "I must hurry to the Fort at once and speak to the bourgeoise, Mr. Boudeau. He's bound to know the facts from this end, and they may sound quite different from those Bridger told you, Lambert—and to Carson and the others. Come along, Randy, I want you to stay with me."

They rode their horses from the riverside camp to the massive adobe fort, through the tall, heavy wood gates of the corral to leave their horses. Fremont led the way inside the fort, across the inner court, and up the stairs to the office of Booshway Boudeau.

"Lieutenant Fremont, Mr. Boudeau! I left Mr. Chouteau's letter on your desk a half-hour ago as I arrived from Fort St.Vrain. You've read it? I have just heard from my crew in camp by the creek that Indians are out to kill all whites they catch on the Platte and Sweetwater Rivers! Is this true? What stirred them up?"

JF Report
July 15

Mr. Boudeau welcomed the Lieutenant and Randy, and confirmed the bad news. "As to what spark lit a fire under the Indians, well, it was the traders that Bridger and Fitzpatrick led here two weeks ago—"

"Fitzpatrick! 'Broken Hand' was with Bridger?!"

"Yes, indeed, Lieutenant, but he didn't go on to St. Louis with Bridger and the rest. Let me continue with the Indian war story, then I'll tell you about Fitzpatrick.

"The men with Bridger were the same ones who fought a big battle with the Sioux and Cheyennes last year about this time. Their leader then, Mr. Fraeb, and a few other whites were killed, but the Indians lost TEN warriors. They swore revenge not only against those traders, but against ALL whites!

"The three tribes—Oglala Sioux, northern Cheyennes, and Gros Ventres—last month after learning that the traders were coming to Sweetwater Valley, moved whole villages to the Sweetwater area. I've heard there's one of 800 tents! War parties began ranging the area from Laramie to South Pass, the Wind Mountains flanking the Pass, the whole Sweetwater Valley and the Platte Valley to Laramie expecting to catch the whites on their way to or from a trade rondyvoo with the Snakes, or Shoshonies.

"Just where the war parties are now since Bridger and Fitzpatrick and their men escaped, oh, about three weeks ago, there's no way to know for sure. What is for sure is that a Platte or Sweetwater traveler now has a good chance of bumping into an ill-tempered war party or two.

Broken Hand.
L.Hafen, p98
(emigrants)

"It's probably already happened! About the same day the Bridger-Fitz party arrived here from the West, a hundred people—men, women, and children—with 18 carts, herds of cattle, arrived from the East. Going to Oregon, their leader, preacher White, said—"

"That's the emigrants we've been following!"exclaimed Fremont. "We've camped where they'd camped, and once we saw a lot of furniture they unloaded and left behind!"

Randy exclaimed, "Did you see how many boys my age—nearly 13—they had?"

No, Mr. Boudeau hadn't had time to count children, he'd been too busy helping solve some of the big problems, very serious problems, the emigrant men and women had.

"They were pitiful, those people. They were greatly fatigued from their long and wearisome journey, disheartened, quarreling among themselves, and the feet of their cattle had become so worn they could scarcely walk. Then they learned from Bridger and Fitz that Indians were on warpath on the river trail, grasshoppers had eaten all the grass so their cattle would starve, that they'd find few or no buffalo on that route, and that their weakened animals could not possibly transport their heavy wagons across the mountains beyond South Pass.

"We advised them to trade their wagons and cattle at this fort, and at Fort Platte down-the-way, for riding horses and extra provisions. Fitz hired out to them as interpreter in case they met any Indians, and as guide through the mountains as far as Fort Hall 250 miles beyond South Pass. "I have to say we got better cattle from them than they got horses from us. We emptied the corral of good, not so good, even last-legs animals to make up the numbers. The only provisions they chose as part of the trade were coffee and sugar! They've been gone from here long enough to be somewhere near South Pass—IF a bunch of Sioux hasn't scalped them."

"NO!!" Randy cried out.

"Yes, m'lad—it's quite possible. Just a few days after they left on July 4, a war party of 350 braves set out after them. Their head war chief had lost some kin in that battle with the traders a year ago, and after the same traders gave him the slip two weeks ago, he swore he'd kill ANY whites he could catch.

"So, we have to assume they did catch the emigrants UNLESS Fitzpatrick managed to ward off a surprise attack, or, talked the Indians out of killing them."

Fremont asked tensely, "Is that likely—is it possible that Fitzpatrick can succeed in talking them out of it ?"

"Yes. Fitz—the Indians named him 'Broken Hand' because one of his hands was shattered long ago by the bursting of a gun—is greatly admired and trusted by the Indians. He's one of the few whites Indians will listen to."

Fremont grabbed at a sudden hope. "How about Kit

Carson?—is he trusted as much as Fitz? How about Maxwell—he stopped 200 Arapahoes in their tracks!"

"Possibly, I suppose. But don't count on it."

Randy had been picturing in his mind the movement of Bridger's party, Indians, emigrants—and suddenly saw Indians on their way back to Laramie waving 100 emigrant scalps at the top of long sticks. He swallowed hard. "Do Indians scalp children, too?" he asked loudly. "The emigrants had some boys—girls, too, didn't they? Some my age maybe. Would Indians scalp THEM?"

Mr. Boudeau thought they'd probably take them captive, keep them in their teepees, maybe sell them after a while. Randy thought of the scene in Tuesday's tent where all the family—Mama, Papa, Tuesday, Other Wife, baby, uncle, aunt, cousin, guests slept in one tent. And what if the Indians didn't like the white child. Would they be mean to him, or just SELL him, like Mr. Boudeau said, and like Sacajawea was sold?

He was about to express his feelings about scalping children, taking them captive, selling them, and how there should be a treaty that said captured children had to be taken right back to their families—when he heard Fremont say his name. "Just in case I decide to try my luck and go on toward South Pass, I must make arrangements with you, Mr. Boudeau, for room and board here inside the fort for RANDY and his eighteen-year-old cousin, Henry. It would be for about six weeks—"

JF Report
Randy and Henry
to stay at the Fort

Mr. Boudeau was nodding consent, but Randy began a noisy protest. Fremont waved a forefinger back and forth, and said in a very strong but affectionate manner, "Listen to me, dear lad. This is not like going on the South Platte where the Indians were friendly southern Cheyennes and Arapahoes, where the route was across flat plains, the time no more than ten days to go and return. The route to South Pass is a rough three to four hundred miles there and the same miles back, a journey of six weeks across some rough land and into the mountains.

"Most important, three tribes of Indians with murder in their hearts are lurking along the route. They will attack certainly, and they may kill some of us. I cannot risk that YOU might be killed—or captured. Mr. Boudeau is agreeing that you and Henry can live inside the fort until I return—I trust I WILL return—in, say, 40 days."

Mr. Boudeau took them to see a small room with a high

window and a plank door facing the big inner court—"just like St. Vrain." Most everything else looked like St. Vrain, except bigger and busier, Randy thought. But he was having feelings like those he had imagined for a captive child going off with strangers to live a strange way in a strange place for a long stretch of time, maybe forever if the Indians killed John.

"Now, we must hurry a mile down the river to Fort Platte—we have only an hour or so of daylight," John was saying. "I need to know what the Booshway there has heard, and I need to find and speak with Kit Carson."

On the way, Randy wanted to talk about how John could send back news to him during 40 days if he decided to go, but John said there was no way to do that. "Now I must do some thinking, Randy, and I'd like some quiet."

The first person they saw when they rode through the gate at Fort Platte was Kit Carson. Randy swung off his pony and broke into a run, shouting, "Kit! Kit! Kit!" until he reached Carson and grabbed him by the waist.

Fremont's greeting was almost formal. "I have been gathering information about the belief that Indians looking to kill whites are roaming our route to South Pass.

"I have run into the information, of course, that you not only believed everything Jim Bridger and his crowd told you about war parties, you were also among those who had to be persuaded not to join Bridger and return then and there to St. Louis—or, for you, Taos."

Carson gently detached the boy's hug and fastened his steady blue-grey gaze onto Fremont's hot blue glare. "Welcome to Laramie, Lieutenant. I'm glad you have completed your South Platte journey in safety, and regret that Laramie is the end of safe travel. I do fully support the opinion of Jim Bridger about the dangerous state of the country for the rest of your planned trip. It's my conviction that we cannot escape some sharp encounters with the Indians—if you decide to go ahead, regardless. Now, if Randy and you will excuse me, sir..."

JF Report
July 15
(Carson agrees with Bridger)

Fremont silent and frowning, went to pay his respects to the Booshway, heard a repeat of the Indian war party story, and found his way to the dining hall to ask for more opinions from traders lingering over coffee.

From his bench-seat, Randy looked through an open door across the inner court to the river. The unfinished fort, having only three walls, was open on the Laramie Creek side to

JF Report
July 15
(Fort Platte, 3 walls)

410

the view—and to Indians as well, the 12-year-old observed.

They sat among a half-dozen traders, all of whom had a detail to add to the war-party news. "I heard from some Indians that just showed up that the 350 braves going up the Platte to chase emigrants took off from a big village about twenty miles west of here. The whole village—lord knows how many hundred people, dogs, and horses—is now heading for HERE."

"We already have our share here, so we'll point the way to Fort Laramie. It needs some new customers, don't it—a few hundred women, children, old men?" joked a trader.

"I'm considering starting north up the Platte for Sweetwater and South Pass," Fremont said to a trader named Bissonette who was sitting beside him. "I'm United States Army Lieutenant John Fremont on a trail-mapping expedition for the U.S. Congress. My party is about two dozen strong, well-armed men, eight mulecarts, packhorses and mules, and a fair drove of spare animals. Jim Bridger, my guide Kit Carson, and some others advise me NOT to go. What do you think?"

"Why, Lieutenant, I think an Army officer and his men will have no trouble—provided you take with you somebody who can talk Sioux and Cheyenne to tell the warriors who you are—that is, a United States ARMY group. These warriors won't mess with the United States Army. Some've had a taste of the firepower from a few hundred soldiers and a piece or two of artillery, and they dread bringing upon themselves thousands of American soldiers and guns.

"Yessir, you take along an interpreter—I, for example, am fluent in Sioux and Cheyenne—and also take along two or three old men of the Indian village now on the way here, then you'll face no danger if you bump into a war party. I can go with you as far as Red Buttes, about 135 miles, where I could join up with warriors coming back from scalping emigrants, though old Fitz'll prob'ly talk'um outa that. I wanted to go up to the Buttes anyway to trade with them warriors."

JF Report
(accounts:
"Bissonette,
8 days $13 per day")

Fremont offered Bissonette $10 a day, agreed to pay $13, thus making his final decision to go.

"But I'm not ready to announce it, Randy. So help me keep the cover on for a few days while we repair and pack and strengthen up everything and everybody. I need to find out who among us, and how many, I can or can't depend on."

They rode the mile back to camp near dusk. Inside his tent by Laramie creek, Fremont and Randy found three old

411

Indian chiefs sitting on the ground to smoke their pipes in the light of white man's lantern, and Mr. Preuss grumbling about them. "Zese Indians! Vot irksome people! Pesky as children!"

JF Report
and *Preuss Journ.*
July 15
(Indian visitors)

Randy glared and his mouth and nose drew up in one tight wrinkle of silent protest. "Look zere!" Mr. Preuss went on. "Zey come into ze tent anytime day or night, sit down, smoke zeir pipes as if zey vere at home! Zese ones come EVERY day!" He made a noise expressing disgust as he rose from Fremont's chair and moved to clear the table.

Waiting beside the table stood two of the cart drivers, plump, big-eater Registe Larente, and Joe Ruelle, both looking rather uncomfortable. Fremont greeted them and asked if they'd come to talk to him about something. "Yessir," they replied together. Larente kept talking.

JF Report
July 15-17
(Larent asks
to leave)
(Carson made
his will)

"Lieutenant, we've come to speak for us eight cart drivers. Lieutenant, we want to be discharged from your party here and now. We don't want to go on and get kilt by the Indians, and Kit Carson is sure that's what's gonna happen. He's just had his will writ out, he's so sure he'll get kilt. He says him and Maxwell will go on if you say so, but he knows somebody will get kilt, maybe him. Maybe us. So we want out....sir."

Tight-lipped, Fremont had listened. Carson had made his will? And told everybody? increasing their alarm? Fremont felt a knot of disappointment in his stomach. Brave Kit, of all people.

Fremont drew himself up and said, "Nothing is settled. Tell the other drivers they and you can apply in three or four days if you're of the same mind. No matter what's decided on the matter of going ahead or not, repairs are needed in all our equipment—carts, tents, guns, horse gear—sorting and patching up our clothes and other belongings, grooming and shoeing our animals. As men still in my employ, do your best at these jobs. Good day."

For the next five days, Fremont repaired barometers, worked on the map with Mr. Preuss, made astronomical observations, patiently received and tried to satisfy the curiosity of an almost uninterrupted stream of Indian dignitaries. Several invited him and Randy to a feast of honor, a dog stew. Fremont went alone to one. He reported to Randy that the cooked flesh looked glutinous, tasted a little like mutton, and he politely emptied his dish despite feeling live puppies wriggling in a basket he was leaning against.

JF Report
July 15-20

Finally, near the end of the fifth day, the hour arrived for him to announce his decision. As the men sat around drinking their coffee and smoking after eating, Lajeunesse stood up and began blowing the Mama Deer whistle for attention. "Faites attention! Lieutenant Fremont wishes to speak on a matter of importance!"

JF Report
July 20
("We depart tomorrow")

Immediately that he faced the men, Fremont said, "I have determined that we SHALL proceed tomorrow toward South Pass." A breathy "Aah-uuh!" perhaps expressing relief, perhaps approval, perhaps not, greeted the news.

"I have taken every possible means to insure our safety—guns and ammunition, an interpreter who speaks Sioux and Cheyenne languages, and my U.S. Army uniform, which I shall wear every day, broiling sun or not. I have talked to many knowledgeable managers, clerks, and traders in both forts here, and I conclude that many stories that have been passed around are exaggerations or even fiction.

"A few of you have told me you wish to be released from the service you signed up for. They—all of us—heard in St. Louis about the unsettled conditions in the country we were to travel—so no one can claim ignorance of the present dangers as a reason for breaking his employment. Also, you have lived this kind of life where danger is expected in the ordinary course of a day—it's nothing new to any of you."

"Still, I am unwilling to take with me on a job of some possible danger any man on whose courage and loyalty I cannot rely. Any among you who are disposed to fear and cowardice, and are anxious to withdraw, you have but to come forward NOW and let it be known. You will be discharged at once with the amount due you for the time you have served."

Silence as each man looked around at his neighbors. A stir as one man rose to his feet. "Sir, I am sick and for that reason I had best not take on the hardships of, of, uh, the mountains."

"What kind of sickness, Mr. Larent?"

"Internal, sir."

"Could it be that you failed to swallow the daily laxative I handed you this morning?"

JF Report
July 20
(Larente dis-charged)

Hoots, laughter, from all of Larent's companions, who knew his eternal, internal weakness.

"You are hereby discharged from my service."

By 10 o'chronometer the next morning, the tents had been struck, carts loaded—some with supplies bought from

413

Booshway Boudeau—mules hitched up to carts or wrestled into packloads, horses saddled. All in readiness to depart, Fremont announced that interpreter Bissonette would join them when they passed his small trading post home a few miles beyond Laramie. "When we pick him up, we'll leave our cow, part of his pay, at her new home.

JF Report *(accounts: "cow to Bissonette")*

"Now we will all move horses and carts into the corral of Fort Laramie where there will be one last delay. We are invited by the Booshway to come to the fort dining room for a farewell 'stirrup cup' drink of an excellent home-brewed preparation!"

The "preparation" was stimulating, the stirrup cups had just been refilled, the good-luck wishes were at their peak— when suddenly, Randy, standing near the guard at the door, heard a loud-talking, body-shoving disturbance. Seconds later, the door guard was on the floor, Randy had jumped aside, and five large Indians with aged, wrinkled faces and hats or topknots of feathers were pushing through party guests, advancing relentlessly toward the Booshway and Fremont. The lead Indian stared hard at Fremont—"Bull Tail!" Fremont and Maxwell exclaimed at the same moment.

JF Report *July 21* *("a number of chiefs..forced their way into the room in spite of all opposition")*

Bull Tail nodded several times before speaking. "He says he heard yesterday that you had decided to go on to South Pass," Maxwell translated. "He hurried from his camp on North Platte to his friend Big Crow by the fort, found that Bissonette had visited him and written a letter to you from the chiefs. Bissonette agreed it's sure death if you go and this letter from the chiefs must stop you. Bull Tail says he's anxious to save the lives of his brothers Chief Fremont and Maxwell. Here is the letter."

JF Report *July 21* *(chiefs' letter signed by Bissonette)*

With raised eyebrows, Maxwell handed Fremont the letter. Dead silence held while Fremont read it.

"This letter written by our new interpreter, Joseph Bissonette," Fremont finally announced, "is signed with the names of these chiefs he wrote it for, and who have brought it here—Otter Hat, Breaker of Arrows, Black Night, and Mene-Seela. They—and Bull Tail who has joined them—prohibit our setting out before their warriors return—presumably meaning 'return from slaughtering emigrants.' Wait eight days, they say. They also say that the warriors will fire upon us as soon as they meet us—including meeting us here?"

Chief Bull Tail began to speak. He spoke a long time. Two others spoke. Booshway Boudeau, Kit Carson, and Maxwell agreed all were repeating the same things—they loved the whites, the warriors would kill Fremont's party and the Great White Father would then kill the Indians, the Great White Father is rich but sent no presents of guns, horses, or blankets. "We will keep you here until our warriors return!" they declared.

Fremont answered that the warriors would not harm the whites IF two or three of the chiefs would accompany the whites and talk to warriors when and if they meet on the trail. No, Chief Mene-Seela replied, we are too old to travel so far, we prefer to stay here, smoke our pipes in our lodges. Besides, the old chiefs feel afraid to try interfering with the young men.

JF Report
July 21
(chiefs refuse
to protect JF)

Fremont, drawing himself up to his fullest height, his polished brass shoulder bars and coat buttons gleaming against his dark blue Army jacket, spoke evenly, strongly, with resolve. "You say you love the whites, but you are not willing to ride a few days to save our lives. We do not believe anything you say, and we will not listen to you.

JF Report
July 21
(JF speech,
"We will not
turn back!")

"We are soldiers of the great chief, your father. He has told us to come here and see this country, and all the Indians, his children. We have thrown away—pledged—our bodies, our lives, to do the job our—and your—chief has commanded. We will not turn back.

"We are few and you are many and may kill us all. But there will be much crying in your villages, for many of your young men will fall to the rifles my skillful young men carry in their hands. Do you think our great chief would let us, his soldiers, die and forget to cover their graves? No! Before the snows melted again, his warriors would come and sweep away your villages as the fire sweeps away the prairie grass.

"See the place where we camped here! I have pulled down my white houses! My men are ready to leave! When the sun is one pace higher, we shall be marching west. "Attention, soldiers! Time to depart!! Form your column! Follow me! AAAAD-VANCE!!"

Poster of 1840's

WESTWARD WE GO!

416

Based on A.J. Miller, 1838

Beth Bergman

Randy stays in the safety of Fort Laramie for the month Fremont and his party will travel to the Rockies–and, with luck, return. Others arrive at the Fort seeking safety, too. In open acres by the fort's adobe walls, whole villages of Indian women, children, and old men set up their tents. Their Indian warriors sent them to the white man's fort while they roam rivers to the west looking for whites to kill. Randy joins in the life of the Fort and finds jobs to use his skills. Cousin Henry, also left at the fort, lives outside in a tent. He has questionable involvements with the Indians, sometimes draws Randy in. Always, for Randy, an awful question hangs over every day: Is John Fremont alive?

417

CHAPTER 37

RANDY'S 42 DAYS AT FORT LARAMIE

July 21- August 31, Fort Laramie (Wyoming)

Randy's pony kept pace beside Fremont's black charger briskly walking out of the corral and around the Fort past its massive front doors. Maxwell and Basil followed, Kit Carson and Ayot—reliable Hercules-Yo—rode directly behind them. The Fremont column was on the move!

JF Report
July 21

JF Report
Lajeunesse "my favorite man"

All the carts, horses, and mules had been crowded into the great, enclosed, almost empty corral of the fort while the men went for their good luck drink with the Booshway. Too risky to leave so many animals and so much interesting goods unguarded for even a quarter-hour at a campsite where a hundred teepees and 500 inquisitive Oglala Sioux women, old men, and nimble-fingered children had recently arrived.

On a well-padded seat of the lead cart of the departing caravan, Mr. Preuss sat comfortably beside the driver, Janisse. To soft-pillow the board seat, the mulatto on orders from Fremont had triple folded a buffalo half-robe, fur side out. Janisse had also been put in charge of installing in the small space between himself and Mr. Preuss a holder for a tall flagpole equipped with rope and pulley. In a last minute ceremony at the campsite by Laramie Creek, Mr. Preuss had hauled on the rope to run the flag up as the other 25 men and Randy cheered.

Now warmed by Booshway Boudeau's homemade "preparation," and by Fremont's spirited defiance of the five old chiefs, the caravan was marching north and west toward the west-bending North Platte. Randy hoped to ride beside Fremont at least a mile past the first naked sandhill and the graveyard for mountain men behind it. But just as he saw the tip of Laramie Peak above the dark knuckles of evergreen trees on the lower mountains, Fremont called a halt, saluted his brother in-law.

Laramie landscape:
Gr. Platte R. Rd.
J.M.Mattes,
p497,521
Oregon Trail.
F.Parkman,
p91,97

"This is your turn-back point, dear Randy. Pull your pony aside and wait for Cousin Henry to join you when he arrives with the last cart. I am charging you to believe firmly and unceasingly that our expedition will carry out its mission and return unharmed in forty days. I am also charging you to mind your manners and to respect the advice of Mr. Boudeau. He's promised he'll look after you.

JF Report
July 21
(wind clock)

"Remember every day to wind the spare chronometers I'm leaving behind. You know where to find them in the storage room with some other instruments, some baggage, and my field notes.

"The days will pass quickly if you keep busy, join in the life of the fort. Bring to your mind every day how much your young friends in Washington are going to envy you these weeks of living in a Rocky Mountain fort among hundreds of Sioux Indians in teepees! So! Until I see you in forty days, au revoir, be of good heart, Randy Benton!"

Fremont reined his horse back in line, clucked it into action, calling to his men, "For-WARD!"

JF Report
(accounts)
Mexican went
west with JF.
"Osea Harmigo,
113 days-July9
Oct31, 50c day"

Randy watched, his throat tight, as the flag on the lead cart vanished behind a bare hill, and finally the haunches and tail of the mule at the end of the column disappeared as Jose twisted in his saddle to wave a last goodbye.

Cousin Henry had left the column long before, and headed back to the fort. Randy poked his pony into a trot to catch up with him. "You didn't even say 'good luck' or anything to John, and you may never see him again!"

"Well, Randy, if John gets killed, it'll be his own fault for acting as if the stars he watches can tell him what's NOT going to happen when he meets 350 naked, screaming Sooozzz with battle axes. He has such a nice head of curly hair—it'll make a pretty scalp on a hoop. But the Indians would like your red hair better, Randy! I'll betcha that's why John wouldn't take you with him! He knew Indians would risk ten lives to snatch a red top-knot to wave on a stick, hee-heehee!

"Well, anyhow, WE have forty days to play around with the Indians, do whatever we want to without Mr.Preuss and a coupla dozen others staring at us. John moved you into the fort, but I'M gonna live in the tent! Alonzo and Escalante're out there by the river guarding it for me—for the three of us!"

Randy had heard John tell everybody that Henry had permission to keep the tent and live in it, and that the two Mexicans could live in it, too, to help keep the Indians out. "But," Randy reminded Henry, "when the Mexicans are working in the fort and you leave the tent for a while, the big Indian boys will sneak in and meddle in your clothes sack—they like our clothes, you know."

Henry had it all figured out. "I've made friends with the

guards up there in the watch tower—the fellows who fire the cannon. Indians are in mortal fear—that's what Mr. Boo-doh said—of the big-gun's power and 'loud talk.'

"I'm going to spread the word around teepeeville that if anything is EVER missing from my tent, from razor—I'm gonna start shaving—to rifle, the tower guards will turn the cannon on the whole swarm of them, while we turn the village upsidedown to find my things.

Gr.Platte R. Rd.
J.M.Mattes, p448
(Indians fear cannon)

"Oh—by the way—have you got any money? I may want to borrow some—I've got a plan for doing some trading—and I've got to show a few old bean-game men how to play a real gambling game with cards—stud poker, heeheehee."

Cousin Henry left Randy at the gate of the corral and rode off saying, "See you at the eating table in there — maybe. My Indian friends may feed me. I know two families real well now. Eating dog is better'n breaking my teeth on bonedry meat or swallowing the muck the cook at the fort makes out of it. Augh!"

Randy's thoughts and feelings as well as his eyes felt off-focus, swirly. Cousin Henry's wild talk addled him. How could he say such ugly things about scalping John—and his own red-headed cousin? And then laugh!

Randy decided before he passed from corral to courtyard that he was glad to be living inside the Fort, staying away from Cousin Henry's tent and company. He wouldn't have to hear about—or see—Cousin Henry's card gambling or dog-eating escapades among the Indians, or be addled by his talk.

No details in JF Report about Randy's—and Cousin Henry's— 42-days at Fort Laramie. Episodes will reflect accounts of the time about life in a fort, and describe how each boy might have taken part, according to his skills, character.

Randy Benton then said to himself that he'd keep busy forty days by getting himself a job, "Yessiree, I'm going right now to Mr. Boudeau and ask him to find me one in the fort. He might even pay me a little something."

He found stocky Mr. Boudeau and his clerk in the Booshway's office between the big gate and the trading goods store. Boudeau, his head bending low, was listening intently to the clerk read aloud a letter he had just written: "'Despite all warnings of danger,'" he read, "'the Fremont expedition departed today for South Pass, assuring us of a return in 40 days.

"'If we get any news of them by trader or Indian, I will send it on to you, Mr. Chouteau, by the next man departing for St. Louis. Your humble obedient servant, etc' and here's where we sign your name, Mr. Boudeau."

Randy, watching from the doorway, saw Boudeau's fingers hold the pen and the clerk's fingers guide the

James Bordeau
(Boudeau)

Booshway's to scratch a big "B" and a short line of squiggles on the paper. Randy licked his lips, understanding that Mr. Boudeau couldn't read or write. Might that mean a job possibility for himself? And didn't the clerk say Indians or traders might bring news about John ?

Oregon Trail.
F.Parkman,
p91,94,98,101
(Bordeaux at
Laramie)
p93(Bordeaux
can't read)
p97 (corral work)

He coughed to attract their attention. "Sir—!"

The two men looked up with a start. Hastily, Randy said, "Excuse me, Mr. Boudeau, but Lieutenant Fremont said I should tell you if I need anything while he's gone, and I need a job for forty days." The Booshway looked at the clerk. The clerk rubbed his forehead and said, "Right now, the only job I can think of that a boy could do is in the corral, Mr. Boudeau."

"All right, boy, report to Ramon at the corral gate. Tell'im I sent you. He'll tell you what to do."

"And Sir—NEWS about John—the Lieutenant. You think—?" Mr. Boudeau said, "Maybe. Don't know. Matter o'luck. Letcha know. Run along to Ramon at the corral."

So Randy led his pony to the corral, spoke as directed to Ramon, an old Mexican with deeply lined brow and cheeks, brown snaggled teeth, and long gray hair. He decided Randy could be the mule driver of a dumpcart. For next five days, he and the mule took the dumpcart to bare ground behind the first ridge. Randy unlatched the cart body and gave it a push. Out slid the not-dry bois-de-cheval that workers had shoveled up from the corral yard.

Back at the corral, Randy helped spread straw over the "just-cleaned" dirt floor of the corral. He helped curry the few ailing or just-arrived horses, ponies, and mules spending the day in the corral. He lugged buckets of water up the slope from the creek to drinking troughs, lugged to the kitchen a pail of milk Ramon squeezed out of the cows, threw kitchen scraps to the chickens, watered them, and picked up their daily two-egg production.

At sundown, he stood with a long pole beside the open corral gate to direct and nudge into it the running stream of 25 biting, shoving, kicking horses, ponies, and mules arriving from river bottom pastures for overnight safety.

Based on Oregon Trail
(Parkman) sketch

"But I didn't mind any of that—I got good'n tired 'n stopped thinking about Indians scalping John," he told Mr. Boudeau on the sixth day when he returned to the office to ask for a different job. "What bothers me is what the wild-horse breakers do to the mustangs.

"After they lasso them out on the plains, they starve them in a pen at the end of the corral. Then to 'break' them, they tie them with a rope to a post. They don't feed or water them for another day—or two. Then they'll harness the horse to a wagon and beat him—lash and lash and LASH him. He's never pulled a wagon, so he screams and kicks and lunges and bleeds, and gets lashed harder.

"After a long time, he looks droopy, stops kicking, takes a few steps that pull the wagon. That means he's broken, the men say, and I feel broken, too. Mustangs they want to saddle they beat the same way."

"Well, son, that's been the best way for a long time to tame them wild creatures," Boudeau said in his mild man-

Fort Laramie.
L.Hafen
(*Fort cows,*
 chickens)
Breaking Horses:
Wah-To-Yah,
Garrard, p11.
Oregon Trail..
Parkman, p26,31.
Spirit Magazine,
Apr.1966 story
"HorseWhisperer"

Based on C. Russell

"Buffalo hides worth four jugs whiskey!"   "No. Three. Take it or leave it."   "Augh!"

422

ner and squeaky voice. "Mexicans're the best wild horse breakers anywhere, ask anybody."

"Seems like there ought to be a better way," Randy said. "Max told us one time that some Indians he knew have a way to tame horses without beating them. If I was a pony, I'd buck and throw off anybody who treated me so mean. Mr. Boudeau, couldn't you give me a job in the store sweeping the floor or running errands? I can't stand hearing the whip crack, the screams when it hits a pony hide. I can't stand seeing blood running down their legs."

The next day he began working for Mr. Willet in the trading-goods store. The second day, four Indian men brought in two buffalo skins, white, soft, very beautiful. The spokesman said they wanted to trade them for liquor. Mr. Willet made an offer. It was turned down with a sneer. An argument started. Mr. Willet sent Randy for the Booshway.

During another round of arguefying, the Booshway sent Randy to summons the armed guards from the tower. Their arrival and the threat of making no trade at all brought agreement. The Indians left with three pint jugs of liquor, just what Mr. Willet had first offered.

Outside the big gate, three of the Indians claimed and held on tightly to one jug each. The fourth Indian violently protested and grabbed at one of the jugs. He fell when three jugs swinging at him suddenly struck his head.

He didn't get up. When the jug swingers saw he was dead, they sprinted to the hills with their liquor to brain-goof themselves the rest of the day and all night.

Cousin Henry heard what happened to them when the three hung-over men came home a day later. "The chiefs had them beaten with sticks until they couldn't walk for two days," he told Randy. "Then they were expelled from camp for 20 moons! Then the chiefs fined their families three horses each to give the dead man's family. One of the Sioux girls handsigned to me that those men would never marry because no girl in any band would consent to live with a man who'd kill a fellow tribesman."

Randy went with Cousin Henry to watch the scaffold-burial. The dead man, dressed in his best clothes, was lifted to a high platform built of small sapling trees. To the sound of a chorus of howls, wails, and sobs of women and men—many of them with blood streaming from cuts they were hacking into their arms and legs, or from fingers they were chopping off—the dead man's most cherished weapons, orna-

Journal.
C.Preuss,
Sept.3
"Randy and Brant
told about scaffold-
ing a dead Indian
and how he died."
(no details)

Based on Seth Eastman, 18--

Wailing mourners sit by the dead man's scaffold slashing their arms, cutting off fingers, chopping off hair. Two others bring his favorite garments to throw over the corpse, well-wrapped against scavenger birds.

ments, dried scalp trophies, blanket, and shield were all lifted and laid beside him. Howls and wails went on two weeks, day and night.

Cousin Henry complained about the noise every day. Randy was glad to be living behind thick adobe walls. In the fort, Randy at the end of three days of "work" in the store went again to the Booshway's office. "Mr. Boudeau, I don't seem to fit into store-keeping. It's either too scary or too boring." He waited for a response. When Mr. Boudeau didn't even look up, Randy took a deep breath and said

Indian grief:
Cut hair,
fingers, flesh.
Weeks of wailing.
Bent's Fort
D. Lavender
p.201

424

very fast a sentence he had spent some time composing and rehearsing.

"I could help with the reading, writing, and figuring in the office, sir. I finished the sixth reader at school, know the multiplication table and how to do long division. Lieutenant Fremont let me write while he dictated his journal one time, let me record barometer and thermometer readings, and said I did everything right."

Mr. Boudeau's expression had changed from a blank to surprise to disbelief to amazement-with-a-smile. "Sacre bleu! You learned how to do all that in twelve years?! MR. Benton, if what you say turns out in the next day or so to be true, you have a job with pay— in trade goods, of course— as long as you're here. Charlie, put him to work!"

Charlie Gilpin stood up to shake his new assistant's hand. "Grace a Dieu! An answer to my prayers. Philander, my assistant left the day before your Lieutenant did. Hard to get a man who knows how to read 'n write to come out here to work in an office and stay longer'n'a coupla months! All wanna be traders! At first chance, they buy beads, vermillion, n'liquor, run off to an Indian village to make a deal for buffalo robes!"

Before long, Randy had a part-time job, too, one he started after the evening meal. He got paid by the cook in extra bread, milk, boiled eggs, and sugar cubes. The job was playing his guitar in the courtyard, sometimes singing, most often strumming chords for the crowd to sing songs they knew. Traders, their women and children, and all the fort workmen who could would abandon their jobs for an hour to sing.

Tuneful sounds leaked out of the fort and into the hearing of those living in tents. One day as the after-supper concert was ending, Cousin Henry suddenly showed up—not for a meal or music, but to almost command Randy to come with him and play his guitar for "important" Indian friends.

"They're throwing a dance for two Sioux men who came home yesterday from I dunno where 'cause I don't understand Sioux talk. Or Cheyenne either—there's a coupla Cheyennes with them. Come on—have some fun."

Randy quickly jumped up and went off with Henry. "Sioux men? Are they waving around scalps on sticks?" Henry hadn't seen any. "Good! Since the families living around the fort are families of the Sioux men who went off to kill the emigrants," Randy reminded Cousin Henry, "these men just returning COULD've, on their way back, met John and our men and DIDN'T kill them! Maybe they'll tell us John and Kit and Basil and Max and Moise and Yo— everybody's all right !

"Henry! I've got to go tell Mr. Boudeau! He'll send one of the traders to talk Sioux to those men, find out if they saw a long line of men on horses, some carts, one with a red, white'n blue flag flying at the end of a pole!!"

Randy, guitar hanging on a strap across his shoulder, ran with Henry to the office, and both ran with Boudeau to find trader Freddy Lafou who talked Sioux the best, and all ran to the large teepee that Cousin Henry led them to. Henry leaned his head into its open front, called sweetly, "Rosebud! Weah Washtay! My Good Woman!"

Fort Laramie.
L.Hafen,p89.
(LaFou,trader)

In a moment, a plump, pretty young woman flanked by two tall, mostly naked warriors, their faces striped with red and yellow diagonal lines from temple to chin, stood in the opening. "Oh,"seemed to be all that Cousin Henry knew how to say. Freddy Lafou pushed forward and began speaking words that all ended with nasal sounds except for "Boo-doh" and after a while, "Loo-tenny."

All the while, Cousin Henry was smiling, staring at Rosebud, occasionally fluttering his fingers and hands to attract her attention. Her gaze held resolutely to a study of the guitar Randy was holding close against his chest.

But when the man on her left began to talk, her gaze shifted to his face, then to the face of the man on her right when he added a speech to the first. "Both are her brothers," LaFou quickly explained to Randy.

The Sioux-talking went on so long, Randy's need-to-know broke through his self-control. His question spilled out to LaFou. "Did they see him?! Ask them—did they see John and the men!?"

"Yes, Mr. Benton! They even talked to Bissonette. Hold on and I'll tell you all about it in a minute."

"Just tell me right now if they hurt anybody!"

"No, they didn't hurt anybody. Now let me finish hearing what these fellows are saying about what happened to the emigrants."

A few minutes later, Lafou announced, "They've invited us to join them in a homage-to-brave-warriors dance. Come on inside."

The first thing Randy saw hanging from a teepee pole was a scalp stretched on a bentwood hoop. Black hair as

426

long as his arm hung from it. Randy hardly had time to grimaced before being pulled by the elbow toward a tripod
where an iron pot hung steaming above a lively fire.

Rosebud poured a meaty stew from a gourd dipper into a
wooden bowl, and with a dazzling smile handed it to Randy.
Still smiling, she reached to touch a guitar string with one
finger. Ping! Her face lit up with joy.

Her eyebrows and a tilt of her head asked a question.
Could she hold the guitar, make lots of sounds? With his
free hand, Randy lifted it a little, the gesture inviting her to
rake her fingers across all the strings. Her smile was ecstat-
ic—and wistful.

But LaFou was nudging him with his elbow. "Let's eat
this grub so you can go on to the dance." Randy had a big
question. LaFou answered, "No, it's not dog, it's—it's—mountain goat."

With the help of LaFou and Boudeau— Henry was still
flirting with Rosebud— Randy managed to sit down on a
buffalo robe, secure his guitar with shoulder strap and left
arm, hold the bowl to his lips and slurp the stew. It hadn't
looked glutinous when he inspected it closely, and tasted
more like wild animal than village pet. He slurped more
rapidly. Suddenly, the gourd dipper was pouring more stew
into his dish, and Rosebud was stooping beside him, her
arm on his shoulder.

"She's VERY curious about that guitar," LaFou said.
"Why don't you say 'thank you for the stew' by playing a
tune. If you play a song we know, like 'Coming 'Round the
Mountain,' Mr. Boo and I can help you sing it."

Songs widely sung in U.S. pre-1842.

Rosebud, her two striped-face brothers and a stream of
Sioux of all ages squeezing through the front opening,
began to clap and stamp their feet when Randy stroked
chords and the four whites began singing merrily to the
lively beat of "Turkey in the Straw." Crowd noise said one
song wasn't enough, and Randy swung into "Yankee
Doodle," then "Shortening Bread." The Indians whooped
and hopped and flung themselves around.

Randy switched fast into "Up on the Housetop," sang
high soprano, with gusto, about Santa Claus, Little Nell,
and Little Will. "Ho,ho,ho!" sang the whites."HO,HO,HO!"
shouted the Sioux. "HOHOHOHOHO!" roared everybody.

All of a sudden, Randy saw four old men forming a line
in front of him—the same chiefs who tried to keep John
from leaving! They held up their hands to quiet the crowd.

Breaker of Arrows spoke in a loud voice, moving hands and arms toward Randy in graceful gestures. The crowd cried, "Hey,hey! hey,hey! heyhey!" Rosebud grabbed Randy around the waist.

"They're inviting you—they're insisting that you join them in the homage-to-the-warriors dance that's about to start. Rosebud wants to paint your face. Uh-oh—here comes Henry," LaFou said. "Well, you two tough it out—me and Boo-doh need to get back to Fort business. You're shore a big hit with these women—and warriors who rushed off three weeks ago to kill ALL whites they could find!"

JF Report
July 23
(emigrants)

Randy held out his guitar to LaFou, asked him to keep it safe in the fort while he turned Sioux dancer. "Oh—didn't get a chance to tell you," LaFou said as he took the guitar, "the two painted brothers said the emigrants were stopped by the Sioux army, and half of the warriors—including these returnees being honored with a dance you're invited to—wanted to kill'um all.

"But old Broken Hand Fitzpatrick argued hours for their lives in front of a big council. The council decided 'no attack,' and let the whites go on their way. Then the Sioux army broke up into small bands, scattered every which way, so that's why Rosebud's brothers came home.

"Listen, Randy, go ahead and dance with 'um, but come back to the fort no later than dusk. Don't try to stay to the end of the dance. Indians sometimes dance all night long once they get going."

Thomas Fitzpatrick
"Broken Hand"

Randy saw LaFou and Boudeau leaving the teepee with the Indian crowd, led by the four chiefs. Rosebud tugged at Randy's arm, held him back, and led him across the wide teepee circle to several women sitting in front of large flat-topped rocks, whacking and crushing colored sandstones, white marl, limestone, charcoal, bones bleached white. Others were grinding the fragments into powder with a pestle stone in a stone dish. They stopped to give Rosebud little cups of red, yellow, black, and white powders—and asked her if they could help paint Randy.

Cheyennes.
Grinnell,p265
(paint powder)

Between fits of laughter, Rosebud and the women streaked and dabbed the powdered colors on Randy's cheeks and around his eyes with pieces of buffalo fat held in their fingers. Henry squeezed in close and they painted his face, too—all black. They stripped off the boys' shirts and painted red and yellow zigzags on their glare-white arms, backs, chests, and bellies.

Giggling and tittering, they began to pull at Randy's pants. His face a glowing red, he held onto the top and showed them how to roll up pants legs from ankle to crotch. Giggling harder than ever, they streaked his and Cousin Henry's pasty white legs with yellow, black, and red wriggly lines.

Rosebud tied turkey feathers in Randy's hair, playfully admiring its red wavy length. She hung raven feathers by leather strings from Henry's ears.

Randy and Henry looked at each other and bent their colored belly stripes almost double with laughter—laughter as loud and joyous as the women encircling them. "A freckled Indian with raccoon eyes!" "Your whole face is black—and red stripes on your belly make it look like a painted clown face!" "Rosebud says black facepaint means 'joy!' and

Beth Berryman
Based on G. Catlin

With turkey feathers bouncing in his hair where Rosebud tied them, Randy stamps, hops, and spins his red, black, and yellow striped legs to the beat of drums and movements of the dance circle. Cousin Henry, his face painted in the color for victory—black—sways rhythmically and chants, getting into the spirit of the Tribute to Warriors. The two honored warriors have just returned from the kill-whites excursion on the route Fremont took to South Pass a month or so before.

'victory!'"

Tum-Tum-Tum-Tum! Tum-Tum-Tum-Tum! Homage to warriors! Randy and Cousin Henry with Rosebud showing them how, hop-danced out the teepee opening to join the circle of dancers.

Tum-tum-tum-tum beckoned the drums. Rosebud pushed the boys into the line of men jumping, wheeling, stamping, shaking their heads, war-whooping, in a circle around kneeling men drumming elbow-to-elbow on a giant drum. Tum-tum-tum-tum! tum-tum-tum-tum! their soft-padded sticks beat out monotonously.

Once in the moving line, the tum-tum-tumming rhythms vibrating through him, Randy felt an irresistible urge to stamp and hop and spin and yell. Suddenly, one voice cried "A-i-yi-yi-yi!" and a chorus of fifty voices took up the chant "A-i-yi-yi-yi!A-i-yi-yi-yi!" a thousand times, hypnotically. Randy felt the sounds, danced the rhythm, became part of the chant. He forgot all about Henry. He forgot everything except the movement and the chant going on forever.

When the drummers—how long afterwards?—laid down their sticks and the chanting-singing circle suddenly stopped, Randy as suddenly stopped, too. He was sweating and breathing fast. How long HAD he danced? For the length of a deep breath, he didn't recognize the world he was standing in, nor remember the world he'd just come from. Henry's voice summoned him.

"Hey, Randy! Sun's nearly down! You'd better be heading for the fort. Me 'n' Rosebud's going to my tent."

A dream, totally incomprehensible.

"Rosebud to your tent?"

"Yeah. Pretty exciting, huh? She's my squaw as of tonight. This morning, I traded with her Pa for her. He got my horse, I got Rosebud. Good trade,huh?"

"You mean you've married her and are gonna take her home to St. Louis with you?!"

"Naw. Indians don't marry. Out here, white men don't marry either. They just take squaws in their tents while they're here, and leave'um when they go off t' St. Looie. When you get to be eighteen, it'll all make sense to you."

Randy walked away in a silent daze. Surely the dance had transported him into a world he didn't know.

For the next three weeks, Randy stayed inside the fort copying traders' bills of lading, writing letters in his best hand as Mr. Boudeau slowly spoke the words, and playing the daily singsong for the fort crowd after supper. He also

Journal.
Preuss, Sept.5
"H.Brant (at the Fort) bartered a horse for an Indian woman. Lived with her 3 weeks."

spent a little time every day at the shop of the seamstress who was making him two pairs of pants and a shirt. John had told him to choose what he wanted and John would pay for it.

He wanted antelope leather pants to replace his cut-pants, which also had small holes in the seat and knees. He wanted even more a pullover shirt of antelope skin with fringed V-neck and fringed side and shoulder seams, and fringed bottom edge—just like the blouse Sunrise wore that day in Tuesday's camp.

Smiley, fat Mrs. Needle-Awl, also made mocassins. She was making Randy a pair with quill decorations.

He wanted to go swimming in Laramie creek, but he didn't. He wanted to go out to look at the scaffold to see whether the dead Indian was drying—or being eaten by birds. But he didn't go there either. He didn't want to chance seeing Henry OR HER. Whenever he thought about them, it befuddled him. The only contact he had with his cousin was through LaFou just after the Homage to Warriors dance. Henry had brought Randy's left-behind shirt and taken Rosebud's turkey feathers.

Randy had very carefully counted on the office calendar what day would be the fortieth day from July 21 when John had left the fort. When August 29 dawned, Randy was pacing the top of the fort wall scanning the northwestern bare ridges and mountains black with evergreens. No sign of a column of riders and carts.

On August 30, the forty-first day, he walked a mile along the trail, hoping, imagining the moment when he would catch the first sight of John leading the column over a rise. At the fort, he sat gazing out the window of the watch tower until he fell asleep. The guard roused him, led him to bed.

On August 31, the forty-second day, he was sure something terrible had happened to John, probably to all the men—Kit Carson, Basil, Yo, good old Moise —all, all! 'cause not a single one had escaped to bring news to the fort as to why they were late or weren't coming, ever.

Beginning at dawn, the watch tower guard let him sit at the window again, watching the trail, silent.

The Indians were watching, too. They knew the story about the Lieutenant from the four old chiefs, from the warriors who had returned, from LaFou who spoke their language, and even from Henry. From Henry?

Rosebud had left his tent three days ago, and Henry had

431

not gone to her papa's teepee to demand her return or the return of his horse. To the Sioux, that meant the Big Army man was about to arrive and Henry knew that a "runaway" horse would be easier to explain to him than a Rosebud in his tent. No hard feelings—until Henry two days after Rosebud left stole the horse while it was staked to graze, whisked it to the fort corral, and paid Old Ramon to tend it, guard it, keep the secret. Henry moved in with Randy inside the fort.

Late in the afternoon of the next day, the forty-second day, Randy at the guard tower window saw a running figure come over the nearest sandhill. It was an Indian, and he began shouting, waving his arms, pointing back toward the mountains. In minutes the Indian was at the fort gate, Lafou had his news and was shouting it to the guards in the tower. "Fire the cannon! He's here! This Sioux saw the flag moving among the trees in the hills!"

Randy flew down the stairs and out of the fort.

BOOM! The sound echoed once, twice. Silence.

Then Crack! Crack! Crack! Crack! Distant rifle fire!

"He's here! He's here! He's really here!" shouted Randy, racing up the trail to meet John Fremont.

JF Report
Aug.31
"Indians saw our flag as we wound among the hills. The fort(cannon) saluted us..we returned volleys of small arms."

JF Report
August 31
(arrival at Fort Laramie)

Based on Fort interior scene by Alfred Jacob Miller, 1838

Beth Berryman

"Lieutenant's back! Everybody alive!" BOOM!! The fort's cannon in the tower lets everybody at Laramie know the news! When will the Fort Booshway, traders, clerks, craftsmen and women, workcrews and families, hear what happened when Fremont's two dozen men met 300 Sioux, Gros Ventre, and North Cheyenne warriors? Fremont, planning to depart for St. Louis in two days, offers to tell the story at a gathering this same evening. Standing on the stairs to the guard tower, he relates the events of the six-weeks' journey. Beside him, Carson by hand signs translates Fremont's story for Indian chiefs, intensely curious to know how Fremont escaped death.

433

CHAPTER 38

ATTACKS? STARVATION? SOUTH PASS?

August 31, Fort Laramie Courtyard

Randy's joy and excitement spread through his body like warm waves from his pounding heart and heaving chest, sending surges of energy into his rapidly moving legs and feet. Up the slope and through the brush he ran—and at last there was the flag waving high and John Fremont on his horse ahead of it, leading his ragged, cheering men home.

JF Report
August 31
(arrival at Fort Laramie)

Fremont tapped his horse into a fast trot, and when it stopped, he swung out of the saddle and ran forward to catch Randy in his arms. "You're all right?" both asked at the same time, looked at each other through a film of tears, smiled, laughed, and hugged again.

"They treat you right at the Fort?"

"I reckon so. But I'll be glad to leave."

"Your Cousin Henry do all right?"

"Uh, yeah. But he might'n have a horse to ride home."

"What do you mean 'might not?' What's happened?"

"He traded it for a Sioux girl to live in his tent."

"WHAAAT! Is she still there?"

"No, she went home the day before you were supposed to come. But her Papa didn't give back the horse to Henry. Yesterday he stole the horse, hid her in the fort corral so the Indians couldn't steal her back. He's hiding himself in the fort day and night—mostly in my little room. He's scared the Indians know who took the horse, will grab him and beat him with sticks the way they do other horse thieves. Mr. Boudeau doesn't know what to do about Cousin Henry."

"Lordylord!" groaned Fremont. "I hope Henry's Mama — and your Mama—never hear about this. You come on now, brother-in-law. Let's get to the fort!" Fremont helped Randy clamber up to sit behind the saddle.

"Viva! Viva!" shouted the two dozen men approaching a hundred yards behind them. Fremont waved both hands to say "All's well!," tapped his horse to set the trotting pace for their triumphant last mile.

"Ai-ee-yayie-yahhh!" Hundreds of Indians ran to meet them. Hundreds more crowded outside the Fort's huge corral gates now swinging open to receive the little army of mounted men, carts, mules, packhorses, and spares.

Inside the fort, naked children, their mamas gaudily dressed in red calico, the men of the fort—everybody from Booshway Boudeau to cook Angelina, from trader LaFou to Francois the cannon man, Mrs. Needle-Awl to the black-smith—were cheering and waving as Fremont, Randy, and the bearded men of the Expedition entered the courtyard through the backdoor from the corral.

"To the kitchen, Angelina!" shouted Boudeau. "Set the pot to boiling, cook meat for thirty men, including me. Boil up gallons of coffee! Fill the cream pitchers, bring out a bag of sugar! AND! Set on the table a gallon jug of firewater for the Fremont men! They deserve a long swig each—a warm welcome to run around their insides! Now everybody else— OUT! OUT! This way, Lieutenant, lead your men to the mess-hall!"

While Fremont does not report that he told the assembled people at the Fort what happened on the trip to South Pass, it would have been unusual for him to have disappointed their expectations, their intense interest in him and the events of his journey.

"Hold on, Mr.Boudeau, hold on!" Fremont's voice matched the manager's in volume. "Let us pass to the campground for we are as weary as the animals you are so generously protecting for us these first moments of arrival. We need two hours to set up our tents, water our horses and mules, stake them in a grassy area before dipping our bodies in the river. Then if you'll send word that the stew is hot and the macaroni soft, we'll come back to eat—and to tell you what happened to us after we left this fort 42 days ago!"

"Yayyy! Yayy! Yay-yay-YAY!"

Three hours later, Fremont, well-fed, was standing on a low step of the stairs leading from the courtyard to second-floor apartments and watch towers. Carson, equally well-fed, stood one step down and to the side of Fremont, ready to translate Fremont's talk into Indian sign language. A hundred or so people living in the fort—white trappers, Mexican laborers, Indian wives, children—were noisily spreading robes on the ground, seating themselves, men first, behind Fremont's two dozen men still drinking coffee and smoking cigarillos.

On the ground closest to Fremont sat Randy on the front row, smiling, eyes shining, looking up at Fremont. Behind tall, broad-shouldered Yo sat Cousin Henry squnching down. All Fremont's men had rounded middles filled with macaroni cooked in the prairie traveler's old standby, buffalo stew. Their insides tingled a little from the whiskey

JF's speech at Fort Laramie not in his published Report.

appetizer while the comforting sweetness of sugary, creamy coffee clung to their tongues.

Two dozen half-naked Indians, chiefs of various activities within the several bands temporarily living in more than a hundred teepees outside the fort, sat on folded legs at the right of Fremont's men. At their left sat the four Chiefs—Bull Tail had long departed—who had tried to stop Fremont from going west six weeks before.

They had come by special invitation into the fort to hear Fremont's story. On their arrival, Fremont had looked directly at them, acknowledged their presence with a small, solemn bow. They nodded in unison at him.

From time to time, Fremont and his audience could hear a guard shout through a small window in the gate a polite, "Disperse, please!" to a hundred or more uninvited warriors outside. "Too many," Boudeau had told Fremont. "Can't let'um in. More 'n' more would yell to join'um. They'd all push us for firewater to celebrate. To refuse'um—risky. Tipsy jollification—worse."

Looking from one side of the crowd to the other, Fremont placed his fingers over his lips while bobbing his head forward. The crowd slowly obeyed his sign-language—just taught him by Carson—for silence.

SILENT

JF Report
July 21

"As you know," he began, and Carson's hands began to move, "the day we departed this place, we heard news of war parties out to kill us, of starvation for us since the buffalo had vanished, of starvation for our horses and mules since the drought had killed most of the grass, and grasshoppers had eaten the rest.

"Any one of those would have turned back the faint of heart and put a tremor of anxiety into the boldest. But my riflemen and I had a job to do for the Great White Father in the East. Having pledged our lives to do it, we marched away despite the dire predictions and grave warnings.

"You see us now! Whole and hearty! We met no attackers! We met bands of buffalo, killed many, ate our fill! We camped among patches of prele and rich grasses by two tree-lined rivers. We reached our goal, South Pass, the flat, broad, open passage into valleys of the snowy peaks. We have climbed some of those peaks, made a dangerous ride down a tumbling river.

"We have arrived here unharmed, only two days late, and not as hungry as cook Angelina expected. Only two men are missing—a coward who walked away, and a lame man who

Details taken from JF Report of the days July 31-August 31 when he and his men rode the trail by the Platte and Sweetwater Rivers to South Pass (in present-day western Wyoming)—and beyond.

finally could not walk at all. I sent him home with our interpreter, Bissonette, who lost his nerve after a week and returned home."

Lajeunesse was waving his hands and calling out, "Tell dem how dat pretend-guide led us de first day on a 'short-cut' t'rough de Black Hills near de Fort! We wore ourselves out stumbling over de roughest ravines 'n' weeds in de West! Den he 'splains he'd never traveled de hills before, always stayed in sight of de Fort! Aughh!"

The eight cart drivers spoke up almost in chorus to declare that they fared worse than the men on horseback during that trek, and every day after. "You didn't get shook up like us cart drivers did!" Johnny Janisse said emphatically. "We BOUNCED with every turn of the wheels over miles of miserable sage shrub. Every six inches there wuz a clumpy, tough, twisted, knee or ankle high bush, 'artey-missy-us,' as you call it, Lieutenant. It covered the ground all the way to South Pass, hundreds and hundreds of miles, across every plain—"

"Animals won't eat it, so what good is it," blustered young Ben Cadot, "'cept maybe to keep them sandy plains from blowing away! Oh happy day when de Lieutenant decided we'd unload the cyarts, take'um apart, hide the wheels and frames, put every cart driver on muleback to save our bones and time!"

Preuss Journal

Mr. Preuss cleared his throat loudly and stuttered,"A-a-a-and zey S-STANK, zose arty-missy-us plants! Ze air smelled like camphor and turpentine! Ven ze vind blew, it vas like ve're in a pharmacy!"

All the Indians began to laugh."What's funny?" Fremont asked Carson. "Oh, I had to find some way to translate Mr. Preuss's opinion—a simplified version—into sign language."

"Well?"

"Uhhh...'brush.'" Carson held out

BRUSH

his hands at waist height, palms up, curved fingers spread out before swinging his hands apart. "Now, 'smell.'" Two fingers clamped his nose. "Bad!" His fist opened as he flung it toward the ground. "'Taste! Bad!'" He stuck out his tongue, touched it with a left-hand finger while he flung groundward his opening right fist. The Indians tittered and snickered again. In a deadpan drawl, Carson said, "It's funny only when it's a WHITE man sticking his tongue out."

The audience's snickers and whispers ended when Boudeau called out, "Lieutenant, didn't your cart driver say you made most of the trip withOUT the CARTS?! How wuz that? How come??"

"Indians!" Maxwell exploded. "Stray Indians—only we didn't know but what a'coupla hundred more were coming up the next minute to join 'um. 'Scuse me, Lieutenant—didn't mean to jump in ahead of you.

Fremont gestured "go ahead."

"Y'see," Maxwell continued, "the second day out, when Kit and I went scouting, we saw on a rise what we thought was three Indians galloping our way. We hurried back to camp, and the Lieutenant ordered the carts to circle, horses and mules picketed inside the circle, men alert, guns loaded. That's a lot of work. And what showed up? Nobody but Bissonette and two long-faced Sioux.

"They hung around a while. Ole Bissy had found out these two Sioux had quarreled with their band and left it 'cause these two wanted to kill the emigrants they'd caught, but the rest of the band said 'no.' When we heard that, two of our men set their triggers to kill two Sooz then and there—but the Lieutenant stopped them. Well, them two Sooz looked at our guns and hard faces and rode off east with—and I'll never understand this, Lieutenant—chewing-tobacco plugs YOU gave'um."

Randy's shrill voice called out, "Two Sioux men came HERE—told us about the emigrants—told us they wanted to kill the emigrants, but the band let them go. So the two Sooz quit the band and came here to their families who had a dance for them. They invited me to the dance—maybe 'cause John gave 'um that chaw o' tobacky! "

"Well," said Lambert, "they were lucky to get home to dance. That day they paid us a visit, I was one of the ones with a finger itching to pull the trigger. All that barricading, hobbling and picketing for two sour Sooz, mad 'cause they didn't get to rip off some white folks scalps. I was mad when the Boss wouldn't let me pull the trigger.

"I was madder when a few hours after that, just as we'd set up for the night in a fine grassy place by the river, here come six more Indians! Unstake the horses and mules we'd just staked, drive'um inside the circle, put out the cook fires, stop everything, 'take your places by the carts, men! Guns ready!' Bissy talked to'um in Sioux, and they told him

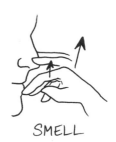

SMELL

JF Report
July 23

BAD

TASTE

JF Report
July 23

438

that a big party of warriors was camped just a few miles ahead of us. Maybe meant to scare us, turn us back.

"We didn't invite'um to stay for supper so they went on. We decided we were already set up for defense, and we could fight better if we cooked early, ate, and got some rest. I put on extra guards but nothing happened during the night. No sign next day of any Indians 'up the road.'"

"Instead," Fremont said loudly, "we saw a band of BUFFALO! Kit and Max went hunting, killed three fine cows for a feast. No uninvited warrior-guests showed up!"

"Oh, dat feast camp was sooo pretty—tres jolie!" exclaimed "prairie artist" Descouteau. "Red, red bluffs and big green arbres, de old makeshift fort where somebody fought der enemies long time ago—dis scene tres picturesque. All scenery getting better every day!"

JF Report
July 25

"I remember we ate half a cow for supper!" Maxwell boomed. "The other half at breakfast and midday! Kit and I killed SIX more cows next day—big band we come onto! All of us worked like slaves to slice and hang the meat to dry. 'Dried Meat Camp!' at a prettier-than-ever grove of trees by the river! Remember, men? ("Yaaay!")

"We dried enough meat to feed us TWO weeks. We were working 'til long after dark, kept the drying fires going all night. With fires snapping and blazing, men singing and dancing around—oh, it was like a country fair!" ("Yaaaaaaay!")

"But that was also the day the better of my two barometers got broken," Fremont said. "The one left couldn't measure higher altitudes, so it meant that from then on, we had to depend on a thermometer's registering the boiling point of water to determine our altitude."

"Yah," growled Mr. Preuss,"and zat vas MY job, and soon brought ME a miserable day."

Carson softly drawled to Fremont, "I'm obliged to skip hand-signing some parts of our story, Lieutenant. Right here I've got no sign for thermometer, or the idea of boiling water to tell land height above an ocean these Indians never saw or even heard of."

Fremont nodded, turned to Boudeau and said, "If anybody on his way to Oregon asks you about the trail ahead, you can tell him that, although altitude slowly increases all the way, the Platte River trail is FLAT—no big hills or mountains to climb! The mountains and colored sandstone cliffs—red, yellow, white, gray—are all to the distant sides of

439

the rivers, Platte or Sweetwater, and often picturesque, as Prairie Artist said. Well, I said the Platte's sandy river valley is flat, but I didn't mean it's FLAT flat. It's more like the surface of the ocean rippled by an ordinary breeze."

"EXCEPT!" added cart driver Cadot, waving a long arm, "don't forget that high, rocky ridge where the Sweetwater joins the Platte—AND on the prairie there's many a rainwater ravine to cross! Right OFTEN we had to circle with the mules and cyarts way 'round their real steep banks. 'N'don't leave out bumping over confounded sagebrush, old, dry, hard 'n' tough—wusser'n'stones!" ("Yaaa!")

Maxwell declared that sagebrush surely was a nuisance and hard on your bones and nerves, but it didn't keep you scared night and day, or worry you as a threat to your life like Indians—and hunger. "It may sound now that we just thought about Indian danger once in a while when a few showed up—but on the trail, both Indian danger and hunger were always on our mind. We never knew how a day would turn out 'til it was all over.

"Look what happened after Dried Meat Camp—one day plenty grass, next day zigzagging across the river searching out a little. BUT, at the same time, no Indians for four days. THEN, we come over a rise and run into a big bunch— a dozen or so of 'um! Quick! Make a cart circle, horses inside, guns ready!

"Kit, Bissy, and me, guns in hand real visible, went out to 'um to find out their attitude. They were Oglala Sioux, and they didn't act unfriendly—I think they were out of powder and lead and saw we weren't. We escorted them back to our camp to tell their story."

"Yes," Fremont said, "and their story scared Bissonette so bad, he said to me, 'Le meilleure avis que je pourrais vous donner c'est de virer de suite!'—'The best advice I can give you, is to turn back at once!'

"I told the company he said HE was going back, and we should go back, too, that the Indians were saying their big village of many thousands of people had left the area ahead to travel south—not on our path—we'd have nothing to fear from THEM. What the Indians were fighting, what we should fear, was STARVATION!

"Those Indians moving away from the area were trying to find grass and buffalo. Drought and grasshoppers had left not a blade of grass for the horses—or for the buffalo in this area, Bissy told us. What we'd see if went on would be

JF Report

440

skeletons of horses Indians had killed and eaten, and teepee poles they'd thrown away so as to move faster. 'A land of starvation you're heading into,' Bissy told us.

"So I asked my men," Fremont continued, "Shall we turn around, go back to Laramie?"

"NO!!" the men shouted up at Fremont standing on the fort steps above them. Lajeunesse yelled, "I told you, Lieutenant, we'll eat the mules if we have to!'" ("Yaaaah!")

"Not a man flinched!" Fremont said proudly, and began to clap his hands, applauding his men. The audience joined in. Indian chiefs looked at each other, at the applauding audience, and joined in, too.

Fremont asked for silence and said, "Bissonette and the Oglalas marched off toward Laramie. Our lame man, cook Dumes, and his collapsing horse limped behind them. The question for us now was, How can we reach our goal, South Pass, without our animals starving?

"We knew the grasshopper problem was real. Since Horseshoe Creek a week before, we'd seen parched grass, the ground alive with so many grasshoppers they made a little cloud around our feet when we walked.

"But, where we didn't find grass, we fed our animals on bark from cottonwood trees by the river. Horses and mules like it, can survive on it if there's no grass. For us men, we had 10 days of dried meat. Would that be enough if we didn't meet even one buffalo in the next 10 days? We had more than 200 miles to go — at least 20 miles a day. BUT...would we starve on the return trip to Laramie?

"If we turned back to Laramie now, I knew we'd not starve. But maybe we could go ahead to the Pass at double speed, then hurry back as far as Dried Meat Camp where we'd seen and killed buffalo! Well, the fact was we couldn't speed, not even a little. We couldn't go any faster than the carts.

"Ah— those carts! If only we could leave them behind. How? Where? Could we manage without all our baggage? Did we dare try?"

Beth Berryman

442

Beth Berryman

Based on Wm. H. Jackson painting

A weathered granite whale, Independence Rock lies all alone on the grassy prairie by
the Sweetwater River. Making camp near this half-mile long rock some 200 feet high,
Fremont set up his daguerreotype equipment to record a picture of the strange landmark. His picture-making, called "photography" or "light recording" is so new, Fremont
expects to make the first such pictures of western America. He'll try again at Devil's
Gap, the river-cut mountain opening he can see some miles away. Randy and Booshway
Boudeau listen entranced as Fremont tells his Fort Laramie audience how to capture a
near-magic picture on a copper plate.

CHAPTER 39

HOW MUCH FARTHER TO THE PASS, KIT?

August 31, Fort Laramie's Courtyard

Fremont paused, caught his breath sharply. "I had to make a decision, one that could mean success or failure, life or death, for me and two dozen friends. They had said, 'Go ahead!' but shouldn't I stop and think through the risks again?

"If we could only speed up! If only we didn't have to pace our travel by those lumbering carts, if we could relieve our mules of their hard work to pull them, we could give ourselves more chance to survive. I presented the question to my men.

"'Wouldn't we improve our chances if we left the carts here, traveled faster, took less time to go and return?' I asked them. 'We could take them apart as we did on the Kansas River, hide them and their loads among the trees and in the sand here, move quickly to South Pass, retrieve them on our return, save two days—or more.'

"'Raaay!' the cart drivers on the front row cheered, smiling up at the man on the fort stairs telling the story, applauding and shaking their fists above their heads in happy memory of Fremont's proposal and decision to have a "Cache Camp."

"Such enthusiastic workers you were," Fremont went on, "not minding the heat, emptying those carts, taking off their wheels, lugging them and the frames under the willows by the river, hiding them behind great tree trunks and thick curtains of leaves!" Fremont laughed. "Such willing, sweating ditchdiggers shoveling out huge holes in sand the river had washed up under the willows!

"We sorted our supplies and baggage, packed essentials on our animals, piled into the hole all else, covered them with our India-rubber sheets, filled the holes with sand, smoothed the top very, very carefully—"

"And zen came our reward!" growled Mr. Preuss. All the Fremont crew—except Mr.Preuss—laughed uproariously and slapped their thighs with glee. "It vas NOT funny!" barked the red-faced man.

Fremont tapped his lips for silence and said loudly over the fading chuckles and smirks, "No, no—it wasn't funny! It was dangerous—it could have been tragic. We'd set up the tent—we had only one giant tent we had borrowed to shelter all of us—and Mr. Preuss was inside it watching the thermometer in a pot of water beginning to boil on the fire—to determine our

In Fort Laramie's courtyard, Fremont tells the second half of the story about his journey to and beyond South Pass, wide door into the Rocky Mountains.

JF's speech at Fort Laramie not in his published Report.

Cache Camp July 28

Details from JF Report

altitude, of course.

"All of a sudden, the perfect calm was broken by a sudden blast of wind flying like an evil spirit down a nearby mountain. It whammed into the tent, collapsed it, began violently dragging it–and Mr. Preuss–away!

"Fortunately the spilled water killed the fire. A dozen men– I remember seeing Yo, Badeau, Lambert, Tulippe, Bernier, Lajeunesse–all strong, quick-thinking men, grabbing hold of the moving canvas. It dragged them along, then broke loose, leaving Mr. Preuss and all the others sprawled on the ground! The men jumped up, chased, recaptured the runaway tent, held it down until the wind died. I had run with them, and saved the barometer that had been inside the tent. It wasn't damaged, but the thermometer was broken. After Cache Camp, no more water boiling to tell altitude, Mr. Preuss!"

The red-faced man looking up at him, grimaced and shrugged. "And no more riding on a CART seat either. Oh my poor bottom," he murmured.

Red Buttes
July 29

"So with no one hurt, the tent undamaged, we went on, trusting to luck," Fremont continued. "With Bissonette gone, Kit Carson took over as guide since he'd lived in this part of the country during the beaver-catching years. We followed the Platte and came in a few miles to Red Buttes, that much talked-about place where Sioux warriors might be waiting to kill us.

"We saw towering hundreds of feet above the Platte and the prairie the famous free-standing red sandstones. Not a single Indian! Instead, our hunters saw a band of buffalo! and, through sagebrush six feet tall took after them! But! No feast for us–only a scare! Carson tumbled from his horse into a ravine–"

*Details taken
from JF Report*

A cry from Randy, "Your shoulder! You hurt it again!" stopped Fremont's words and Carson's hand-signing. "No, Randy, not this time," Kit said. "Landed on t'other side, in sand. I rubbed some b'ar grease on the bruise. It's fine."

Fremont quickly went on with the Indian story. "We saw signs of Indians the next day–but only signs–lodge poles, horse skeletons at a place where thousands of Indians and animals had crossed the river. A little farther on, we passed between white sandstone ridges 300 or more feet high. On the sandy flats by them was the campground where three tribes had set up a city-size camp of teepees–"

"Five zousand Indians! Probably a zousand tents!" Mr. Preuss declared emphatically.

"Yes," continued Fremont, "and the left-behind debris told a

445

From Picturesque America, Vol. II, published 1874

"(On the Laramie Plains) here and there the monotony of the horizon (is broken) by forms of castellated buttes standing out strongly against the sky. Most noteworthy and picturesque of these are the Red Buttes. They lift ragged edges above the prairie, looking lonely, weird, and strong. Among these shapes, the strangely pillarlike Dial Rocks tower up, four columns of scarred sandstone.."

grim story of hunger and haste. We went on a-ways until we saw the high stone rocky ridge we would have to climb and descend to reach the Sweetwater's entry into the Platte—unless we chose to stay with the Platte around a big bend through rough terrain. We took Kit Carson's wise advice to turn back a few miles, make camp on acres of grass on a Platte river island we'd passed, rest and prepare ourselves and the animals for the rocky ridge climb. Only heaven knows how the grasshoppers missed this lush island with its rich, crisp grass.

"We called our camp 'Goat Island' though the goats lived on nearby cliffs of red sandstone. We could hear volleys of stones rattling down as goats ran up and down 400-foot heights—"

"They were SHEEP!" called out long-time mountain man Latulippe. "They were GOATS!" answered Lambert.

"Name don't matter—they're good eating," declared Kit Carson. "We et at one sitting all three that Max and I killed on the cliffs and brought over to the island." Moise boomed, "Tasted like mutton t' me!"

Fremont stopped the debate with a description of winding their way next day to the summit of the ridge that slopes down from its crest to where the Sweet Water flows into the Platte. "Eight hundred feet high, bare and rocky—"

"Sure glad we didn't have them cyarts!"

"—but once past the top, a long, gradual slope led to the Sweet Water's mouth flowing into the Platte.. There on the plains we saw PLENTY of buffalo still finding enough grass to eat! No signs of Indians! So far, the dire attack warnings and no grass for the animals were false."

Mr. Preuss exclaimed emphatically, "I'd known all along it vas vindbag-talk!"

Fremont took no notice. "We went on without worry until we saw in the distance a landmark as famous as Red Buttes—Independence Rock— lying long and high all by itself on the flat grassy prairie! Quite a strange and breathtaking sight to come upon! Some of you who work out of the Fort may have roamed that far and seen it—a wide, brownish granite rock 200 feet high, nearly a half-mile long! It looks like the rounded top of an underground giant loaf of bread! Or the shell of a mammoth turtle! Curious sight—so curious, many travelers had climbed it to scratch their names on it."

"I did, too!" Maxwell called out. "Initials anyway. Didn't want to ruin my knife!" Several voices declared that their owners scratched their names. "But most of us," drawled Johnny Janisse, "stayed in camp a mile away hacking off, cutting up, and cooking the meat of two buffalo Max and Carson killed—

Harper's Magazine, 18—

Fremont's men and heavily loaded animals, carts having been buried and left behind, ascend a
rocky barrier 800 feet high separating the south-turning Platte River trail they're leaving and the
Sweetwater River they'll follow westward to South Pass. Once they labor past this height–the
only one they've had to climb in almost 800 miles of prairie–they'll ride down a long slope to
the Sweetwater.

much more important than showing the world you know how to write your name."

"For me, a special monument," Fremont declared happily. "It's the place where I set up a Daguerreotype picture-making apparatus and tried to make the FIRST sun-drawn picture of a landscape in the American West!"

("Yaaaayyyy!")

"I bought the boxes and chemicals in New York. It's the newest miracle invention! Nature paints, draws, imprints pictures when SUNLIGHT is beamed upon thin layers of chemicals on a metal plate! IF you do all the steps right, you'll see at the end a LASTING, exact picture of a scene glowing on a four-inch square of copper!

Daguerreotype consultant: Dr. Robert Shlaer, "The World's Only Full-time Professional Daguerreotypist." His van is a traveling daguerrean saloon based in Santa Fe, N.M. Author of a book on John Fremont's Deguerreotypes of the American West.

"I tried to do everything right, but my first picture looked more like a cloudy sky than Independence Rock. Next morning at another amazing landmark a few miles beyond The Rock, I think I did enough better that an artist-engraver in Washington may be able to make out the faint shape of Devil's Gate. Anyway, you men got to rest an hour, watching me labor with French magic!"

"More travel time lost," Mr. Preuss mumbled to himself, "and I didn't see any sign of a picture on your 'magic' plates."

Fort Manager Boudeau, who'd been leaning against the stairs, had jumped to attention at Fremont's last words, "French magic." Boudeau exclaimed, "Did you say French MAGIC? You made something happen by FRENCH magic? What does that mean?!"

Fremont looked around at him and announced to the wide-eyed crowd, "It means SUNLIGHT on CHEMICALS magic such as the world has never seen before! It's called 'DAGUERREOTYPE' for its French inventor, a Monsieur Daguerre. Since only a year or so ago, sets of his picture-making boxes, silver-surface metal plates, and chemicals have been available in New York for about $100."

At the audience's shocked gasp at the large price, Fremont explained that the picture-taking set had a number of boxes. "There's a main box—it's called a 'camera'—a chamber—about this big—" he measured with hands held apart a space the size of a man's dome-crown hat—"a folding three-legged stand to set it upon at waist-level. This main box, this 'camera,' has a brass tube sticking out its front side. It looks like a spyglass, and like a spyglass, it has a glass lens inside. This glass 'eye' will funnel light into the camera—light streaming from the landscape you want to picture.

"To catch and absorb this light, you must put inside the box

449

a square plate about the size of the palm of your hand. The plate is copper, and one side of it is coated with a thin layer of silver polished shiny bright and clean. I bought 25 plates, hoping to make that many pictures.

"Now for the starting step. I call it the 'iodine step.' The daguerreotype equipment includes a shallow box to lay the silver-coated plate in facedown. There in five minutes its silver coating collects an iodine coating from fumes coming off iodine crystals in the bottom of the box.

"Before you take the plate out of the fumes box, you must drape a jacket or blanket over your head, shoulders, and hands to shield the plate from light when you quickly slide the plate into the darkness of a holder-box. Even a sliver of light will ruin the silver-iodine surface, make it cloudy, so it can't change into a sunlight picture.

"Now you're ready to move the plate from holder-box into the camera. But first you must focus the light of the landscape into the camera— Mr. Boudeau, perhaps you'd like for me to skip over the details of how to focus—"

Mr. Boudeau took a step foward, waving his arms. "No, no, Lieutenant! I want to hear all about it! It'll take every detail before I can SEE these boxes and, and plates and chemicals— before I can BELIEVE you can juggle them around and make ordinary sunlight throw a picture into a box, then uh, uh, burn the picture into a piece of metal. Right now it sounds like some wild fairy tale!"

"Anybody else thinking like Booshway Boudeau?" Fremont said to his men and the fort crew.

"Yaaaayyy!"

"Then I'll go on with light focusing," Fremont said. "To make that job easy and accurate, the back side of the camera is an open, empty frame. Into that frame you slide a piece of GLASS! It's a special-viewing glass that lets you see the landscape the camera's spyglass tube is pointing at— and lets you see it as a picture the size of the metal plate you've just coated with iodine fumes.

"But you must gently push and pull the spyglass tube until the details of the scene you see on the viewing-glass show sharp and bright. That done, you remove the glass from the frame. You also cover the outside end of the spyglass tube with a cap to shut out the light.

"Now the moment has arrived for the sunlight picture you focused on the camera glass to fall upon the silver-iodine chemicals of the plate! All is ready for the plate, still in its holder, to go into the camera's backside frame where the viewing glass had been, and face the light tube!

"The frame of the camera's back side was specially designed for quickly sliding the plate HOLDER into it. This holder has a removable cover, so you pull it away, leaving behind the rest of the holder with the silver and iodine coated plate in the dark camera. Its coated side faces the end of the spyglass.

"Now's the moment for the sunlight picture you saw on the focusing glass to flow through the spyglass into the camera, and fall upon the silver-iodine chemicals of the plate!

"You reach—I should say you NERVOUSLY reach—to the camera front and lift off the spyglass cap.

"As light flows in through the spyglass directly in line with the plate, its focused light-picture falls on the plate's silver-iodine surface. You count slowly to 30— a half-minute is enough for the silver-iodine to absorb the light. Shut off the light by recapping the end of the spyglass.

"To protect the picture you've caught, you slide the COVER back onto the plate holder in the camera's back frame. With the plate now in the dark of the covered holder— light would destroy its invisible picture— the covered holder slid out of the camera and in hand, you hurry to the mercury box.

"It's an exciting moment! Have you done everything right? You won't know for a few minutes!

"To find out, get under your blanket, uncover the plate, lay it in the mercury box, and close it up. As soon as the fumes of the already-heated mercury touch the plate's silver-iodine surface, the plate's hidden light-picture will gradually develop, become visible!

"Wait only three minutes. When you lift the plate from the box, you'll see—if you've done everything right—a beautiful, radiant picture, every detail of the landscape! There's color, too— mostly bluish sky!

"What a magical moment—removing the plate, turning it over, seeing a picture of Devil's Gate, every stone, every cloud above it, in perfect clarity! Magic chemicals! Magic sunlight artist! Miraculous combination, isn't it?! Oh, but there is one more important step— fixing the picture onto the plate so it's permanent. Very simple to do. Just hold the plate by a corner and dribble all over it a bottled chemical called 'hypo' that comes in the daguerreo kit."

"Oh, I sure would like to see one of those pictures!" exclaimed Mr. Boudeau. "I can hardly believe sunlight can turn chemicals into pictures! Sounds absolutely crazy— begging your pardon, Lieutenant."

The audience murmured agreement. Fremont stroked his

beard and said he wished he had brought a daguerreotype to show to him. "Perhaps I can bring one tomorrow. I'm sure you— everybody who sees it— will be astounded! You'll want to rush to a big city daguerreotype studio to have your portraits made. Yes! those pictures will look EXACTLY like you— not just as good— or not so good— resemblance drawn by a person! I have a daguerreotype picture of my wife—and of myself! Both are mirror images of each of us!

"Next year when Congress publishes my report of our trip, I hope you will see printed engravings copied or derived from some of the scenes I tried to capture in daguerreotype sun-pictures. That's assuming that a few have miraculously come through difficult parts of our long journey without damage— I haven't had time to examine them since the last one I made of the Wind Mountains.

"Speaking of miracles, Devil's Gate is itself a quarter-mile-long miracle. The Sweet Water River during millions of years carved that wide gap through a granite ridge 400 feet high! Even if my picture of the gap isn't good enough to engrave and print in my Report, at least it is the first effort to make a daguerreotype sun-picture to show the world exactly— but exactly— what Devil's Gate looks like.

"I assure you that daguerreotype pictures will go down in history as one of the great inventions of the century! There's another word people are using when they talk about 'daguerreotype' pictures. It's 'photo-graph'—two Greek words meaning 'light-writing,' 'light-recording !'

"Let's leave it at that— get back on our Sweet Water track. At Devil's Gate, we still had a hundred miles or so before we'd arrive at South Pass. At the rate we were going, it could take another week! But we had no Indians to worry us, and we had enough food for men and beasts.

"It coulda taken twice as long if we'd-a had them cyarts!" a loud voice reminded everybody.

Fremont smiled at the persistent cart driver and began a description of the beauties of the valley and mountains on each side of the five-mile-wide Sweet Water Valley. "Tree-covered mountains edging a wide plain on the South side. But on the North side of the river, we saw rising abruptly from a narrow, flower-covered plain—very colorful—broken masses of jagged, bare granite peaks. Randy, I saw a grizzly bear scrambling up one of them!

"We glimpsed on the far side of the granite ridge a vast, desolate plain blanketed with wild sage. And soon we caught our first glimpse of the Wind Mountains, a low, dark ridge on the right, perhaps 100 miles away! As we moved toward it, heights on both sides of our riverside trail changed to shiny white sandstone and pudding-stone ridges nearly 200 feet high. Picturesque! Beautiful!"

"Vhat good is 'beautiful' ven ze place turns vet, cold, and miserable?" Mr. Preuss demanded, looking around at his audience. "Listen—in zat picturesque walley, ve slept in ze rain wiz no shelter— tent poles left at Cache Camp. Ve rode slowed-down-to-a-crawl in ze rain— cold, and vind-driven rain— FOUR days. Ve slept— tried to sleep— under vet bushes— all ze time smelling zat camphor-air! Augh! And ze Vind Mountains— BIG disappointment— nozzing like ze Alps! Zey vere molehills, even ven ze sun finally came and ve saw zem wiz snow tops!"

Moise, camp Weather Predictor, felt compelled to say that in his opinion, any miserable man could have kept warm if he'd dismounted and walked, kept drier if he'd worn the saddle blanket, or even the saddle, on his head.

Rain
August 6,7,8
Laughter squelched Mr. Preuss into a red-faced slump. He brightened a little when Fremont said, "Grass was plentiful, but weather WAS very, VERY bad. One day the wind was driving the rain so hard we had to stop and hide under willows tree curtains all night and half the next day— time lost," Fremont conceded.

"The next day was worse. Cold, wild wind and rain— and a five-mile march in Sweet Water Canyon picking our way among wild disorders of rocks and boulders. Above us, above the rushing, rising river loomed granite walls 500 feet high, jagged and pointed at the top.

"Carson had said the usual road bypassed the canyon by moving over to a sandy prairie road. But I thought I should know the course and nature of this river. I'd heard that it flowed south out of the Wind Mountains, ran into the Pass as it turned east. We stumbled wet and exhausted for FIVE hours through the canyon rocks— more time lost."

"Sure glad we didn't have them cyarts!"

"Right, Cadot," Fremont laughed. "So we finally came to a wall of hills in the canyon where the river disappeared. Thank you, Kit, for so patiently leading us up a ravine to the prairie. Prairie it is, a continuation of the plains of Nebraska— but not grassy, only sagebrush, sagebrush. At this high, dry, wind-blown end of the plain, very SMALL sage covers a hundred miles, every direction!

("Auggghh!")

"Marching over so much sagebrush prairie was more than ordinary-hateful by our being wet, tired, and having cold wind whipping rain into our faces. How much farther? I kept asking Kit. ('And WE kept asking!') Our patient guide kept saying, 'Just another day,' or 'When the prairie narrows from 50 miles to 30 miles.'

"On this next to the last day before the Pass, we had pushed ourselves to cross a little ridge. We were down-hearted, miserable, until Carson led us to a campsite on a little creek he knew. What a heaven it was! We found by this stream good grass, and a spot where Indians had recently left behind some teepee poles. At last we could raise our tent– at last we warmed ourselves by hot fires of oily sagebrush, reheated our cooked meat, slept dry.

"At dawn, the sun came out! I looked toward the Wind Mountains and nearly jumped for joy at the sight of their glistening white peaks emerging from four days of clouds and rain. While rain had fallen on us, snow had fallen on the peaks. The sight inspired me to speak to Carson.

"'We have one more day's march on this sagebrush plain?' I asked. He said, 'By camptime tomorrow, we'll be about six miles from the Continental Divide in the Pass.' I asked him if it was true the Pass is 30 miles wide. 'Well,' Carson said, 'some say 29.'

"In that case, I said, instead of heading for its center, let's approach along its north edge–"

"'That will put us on the reappearing Sweetwater.'"

"Good, I said–at the base of the Wind Mountains. That ought'n to lose us any time. Is there a trail of some sort by the river? Carson knew of a bridle path. I said I had a reason for wanting to be close to the Wind Mountains as we went through the Pass.

"Right off Kit said, 'After we go past the invisible bulge that's the Continental Divide– what then?' I asked him how we'd know we were even IN the Pass since being 29 miles wide, it would still look like prairie. Even more troublesome, how could we see we're at the summit when all around looks flat?"

"'You'll know you're there,' Carson said, 'when you see water running the wrong way– west. That highest little bulge you can't see is the water shed point between the Pacific and the Mississippi River.'

"Carson then quickly added, 'You'll be turning around there? You'll be starting back to Laramie, your map-making job for Congress done?'

"No, I said. I have something else in mind."

Based on Bayard Still illustration

South Pass! Journey's end! But why call it a 'pass' when it's 30 miles wide? And is the Lieutenant saying it's NOT journey's end? Wet, bedraggled men leading a long string of mules and horses have trudged during a week of bad weather across a vast flatland dotted with trillions of ankle-high bunches of tough sagebrush. They've seen Carson crawl on the ground in the Pass to find a nearly undiscernible "bulge," the Continental Divide, where rainwater trickles west on one side, east on the other. Now the Lieutenant wants to go on to the Wind Mountains north of the Pass, climb the highest peak before returning to Laramie.

CHAPTER 40

FROM PASS TO PINNACLE

August 31, Fort Laramie's Courtyard

Fremont's quiet words had hinted at something unexpected and dramatic yet to be revealed. First a motionless silence, then a rustle, a whispering murmur—"What's—?" rose from the little crowd.

Randy on the front row, mouth open, staring and frowning in puzzlement at Fremont, tried to recall what Fremont had said at the beginning of his talk. Was it CLIMBED snowy peaks? TUMBLED down a river? The Indian chiefs looked from Fremont to Carson, whose hands had said nothing for some minutes. They turned from Carson to the rows of whites, their Indian women, the Mexican workmen, a mixture of voices and languages buzzing louder and louder.

"BUT FIRST!" Fremont's voice rang out, "FIRST, as I told Carson that day—August eighth—I must do the job I was sent to do—pinpoint by land and sky the location of the Pass for our map! We could see the gap was flat and wide enough for hundreds of wagons side-by-side to travel. No narrow defile like those in the Alleghenies or Europe's Alps! The incline for a hundred-twenty-five miles— the length of the Sweetwater River— is as mild a rising grade as that in Washington, D.C., along Pennsylvania Avenue leading to the Capitol.

"But once you've gone past the invisible summit of South Pass, what's next? What does the pass lead to? Why is South Pass so important that Congress would make it our destination? I think Kit Carson can answer those questions better than anybody here," he said, gesturing toward Kit.

Carson hesitated, looked at the old Indian chiefs on one side of him, then at the younger chiefs on the other side. "Lieutenant," he half-whispered, "I'm gonna stop signing. These Chiefs already think we were a foolhardy two dozen men who left the fort in the face of 250 warriors looking to kill us. If I tell them about struggling for days up murderous peaks just to get to the top and look at other peaks, they'll be sure we're crazy.

"So I'm going to inform them that the places and people we're going to talk about are just faraway deserts and mountains not fit for people to hunt or live in, worth noth-

Fremont tells the second half of the story about his journey to and beyond South Pass, gateway to the Rocky Mountains.

JF's speech at Fort Laramie not in his published Report.

JF Report
Aug. 7

ing to them. And I'm going to ask Mr. Boudeau to agree for me to tell them that he'll give each chief a bit of firewater to SIP while waiting for us whites to finish our... I'll call it our 'goodbyes' to the Fort people."

"All right, I'll give them a SIP," Boudeau said. "Nothing bigger than an ounce apiece." Carson's explanation to the chiefs, and news of the reward for their patience while the whites bid each other farewell, excited much head-nodding of chiefs and pleased looks of anticipation.

"Well, now," Carson then began, rubbing his chin and looking out to the rows of bearded white men, Indian wives in their colorful dresses and jewelry, and dark-skinned Mexican youths. "Well, now, this here South Pass got to be known to, and regular used by, beaver trappers only eighteen years ago. Before then, they scoured the rivers on the east side of the Rocky Mountains for beaver, all the way from Canada and the Missouri River south to the Arkansas River and Bent's Fort on the Santa Fe Trail. Then, spring of '24, Jedediah Smith and Tom Fitzpatrick led a band of trappers to do what the Crows told'um to do and found South Pass—"

Mr. Boudeau interrupted. "Jedediah Smith! I know he's dead, killed by Comanches on the Santa Fe Trail, but I just heard all about him from 'Broken Hand' Fitzpatrick. He told me how Smith, his best friend of 20 years ago come to have such a messed-up up face. Terrible sight— eyebrow gone, ear out of shape and not sitting right—"

Jedediah Smith. D.Morgan, (discovery of South Pass,p89) (grizzly attack,84)

"A grizzly done that," Carson said. "A monster-size bear grabbed Smith's head INSIDE its mouth. Its teeth pulled scalp'n' hair back to the crown of Smith's head, chawed one ear clean off, tore away an eyebrow and eye socket skin. One of the trappers then and there sewed Smith's scalp, ear, and some face flesh back in place the best he could with an ordinary needle and thread.

"Well, that happened just one year before Smith, Fitzpatrick, and crew found South Pass. Lemme tell you how it's said to 've happened. They'd spent a real friendly winter with some Crow Indians on the east side of the Wind Mountains. At coming-on of spring, the Crows said, 'You want beavers? Many on other side of our mountains. Ride along our river down to a wide space betwix the end of this range and the beginning of the next.

"This wide gap opens into bigger wide space, but BAD space with no water, no animals, plenny sand. On the far

457

side of this big bad space is one VERY big beaver stream called Siskadee. So many beavers, don't need traps. Just walk along the river bank and knock a beaver in the head with every swing of your club.

"Smith, Fitzpatrick and crew rode south to the wide, flat gap— that's South Pass— survived its cold, raging winds two days 'n nights, four days with no food or water. They rode three days beyond the gap, across dry sand and wild barrens to get to the Siskadee River beavers. What the Crows had said wuz true! Swarms of beavers!

"So word spread about the high prairie pass, door to an open, dry, sandy circle 50 to 100 miles across, ringed by mountains but edged on the west by the beavers of Green River, as Siskadee come to be called. It flows south along the curve of the western side of the desert circle. It wuz Trapper Treasureland, a paradise where taking a hundred or so furs a week wuz easy. Many-a time I've trapped there and whooped it up at the Green River Rondyvoo when the supply wagons arrived from St. Louis."

Kit Carson Autobiography. p22-3,39,42,59 *(rendezvous)*

In a small lull when Carson's thoughts seemed to be lingering upon memories of days past, Fremont commented that Congress expected emigrants would soon take the place of now departed beavers and trappers.

"Well, the emigrants will soon learn," Carson said, "that South Pass is only halfway to Oregon Territory. But it's the Pass to most all the trails along river valleys through the Rockies. Whether they want to go north to Oregon, or south to The Great Salt Lake, or west to Spanish California, they'll find an out-of-a-job trapper in the area who's willing and able to serve as guide— for pay, of course. I heard last spring that Bridger, for one, is staying on in these mountains, and is about to start building a trading post-fort west of the Pass, maybe on the Green River."

Fremont beamed at Carson's mention of Oregon, Salt Lake, California— and exclaimed, "I want to travel to all of them!" Then with a nod to the future, he said, "But back to our present story of trails! We've just arrived at the invisible 'summit' of South Pass and Kit is slowly creeping along the ground in the RAIN looking at little gullies and tricklets of rainwater!"

August 7

Carson chuckled, saying it wasn't easy to see where a trickle of water is running toward the Pacific Ocean, and, an inch away, where a trickle of water is running east toward the Mississippi. "The dividing bulge is so small, the best eye can't see it. How do I know where to look in that miles-wide gap? First, I draw an imaginary line from the center of a low hill on the north side of the open space to a like-hill straight across 30 miles to the south.

August 7
Arrival at the
Continental Divide
"summit" in South Pass
(in western third of pre-
sent day Wyoming)

"Then I get down on my knees and crawl along our stop on that line. The day I wuz there with the Lieutenant, it wuz raining—which wuz a good thing since the direction water trickles is what I'm looking for. Once I wuz sure of a westward trickle, I knew I wuz looking at the gap summit, the Continental Divide. We didn't linger there in the rain but went on to camp where the Lieutenant could use his sextant and clock as soon as the sky wuz clear.

"About three hours travel west, then north, we camped on the Little Sandy River. The sun came out to dry us, the stars came out in a clear, black sky for the Lieutenant to shoot the stars for Congress—"

Fremont had listened avidly, his smile widening as Carson words came closer and closer to the final high moment of success. At the word "Congress," he raised both fists high and shouted joyously, "We made it, Senator Benton, we made it!!"

"That day at the Pass," Fremont declared with passion, "was a day I'd pictured in my mind for 100 days and 958 miles of sitting in a saddle! What a drama—standing upon the low hill on the north side of the Pass watching Carson inch along the ground fifty feet below us! Finally he stood up straight, pointed to his left foot on the west, right foot on the east! He was straddling The Divide!

"What a feeling of joy—exultation! That was a moment, like now is a moment, that called for a loud noise announc-

August 7

ing, 'We have arrived—we have survived—we have achieved our goal!' That day, we fired pistols! Today, we shout and applaud! Hip, hip, hooray!" he cried and beat his hands together enthusiastically.

"Yaaaaaayy!!" chorused his smiling men, standing up to vigorously clap their hands and cheer their leader. "HE done it—we just followed!" "Couldn't be no better booshway!" they chorused. "Yaaaaayy!" shouted fort-boss Boudeau, traders, workmen, all scrambling to their feet.

It was the perfect moment for two Mexican kitchen hands to arrive bearing trays of short, thick glasses, them-selves a wonder to the chiefs. Each glass contained a finger-width of clear, throat-burning liquid. The Chiefs beamed, stood, took a glass apiece, and joined the celebration with nods and smiles.

Quickly they revealed unfamiliarity with "sipping" but considerable skill at concealing small glasses. Arms folded over their chests, they sat down with eyes half-closed, enjoying the warm, inner spread of a gulp of firewater, and the special attention of handclaps and cheers they decided were meant for them.

"Now the moment had arrived when I must answer Kit's question, 'What now? Return to Laramie?'" Fremont commenced, his strong voice riding over the stir and talk in his audience. A murmured "Ahhh" of anticipation mixed with the rustle of resettling.

"It had been in my mind from the start," Fremont commenced, "that I should EXPERIENCE Rocky Mountain peaks—not just find the gap leading into them, not just look at them from a distance as I rode by.

"At the Pass, we were almost touching the base of the Wind Mountain range we had seen as a faint outline from many miles distance, then their snowcapped tops from 30 miles. We had talked about them, my men had laid bets on which was the highest.

"Now that the peaks stood so close we could ride to them in a few hours, I determined that we would not walk AWAY from this glorious opportunity to camp in the midst of their beauty, climb their rocks and ledges. I would measure their heights with a barometer, an instrument my men judged to be as true as the sun, one whose measurings are indisputable when settling bets.

JF Report
Decision to go north,
explore in the Wind
Mountains.

"This is the 'something else' I had in mind! We would explore this range, climb the highest peak, view the next ranges, the next plateaus—for as Mr. Preuss has keenly observed, the Rockies are not the solid wall we expected between East and West, they are numerous ranges separated by wide plateaus.

"In our exploring treks among the heights of the Wind Range, we might discover, even pinpoint astronomically for our map, the headwaters of great rivers—the Yellowstone flowing into the Missouri, the Green flowing into the Colorado, and others whose sources lie in this short Wind Mountain range.

"I asked Carson to guide us through the Pass westward to the first north-flowing river. At our Little Sandy River camp beyond the Divide, I told my men my plan. I said we could do it in less than a week—our schedule had just

Engraving published in Fremont's Report, 1843

At the foot of the Wind Mountains, more than a day's travel north of South Pass, Fremont chose a camp site near a lake that "looked like a glowing blue gem set in the mountains." Leaving horses, gear, and grub with a crew of guards, he and 14 others on muleback set off to climb a chaos of treacherous rocky heights in one day. It took five.

enough time.

"But the climb to the top of the highest peak took five exhausting, danger-filled days, not the one or two I'd allowed. We searched for no headwaters of rivers— that would have required another two weeks among rows and rows of ridges, precipices, and chaotic jumbles of rock I hadn't expected...."

Fremont sighed deeply, then straightened and declared forcefully, "But I believe the magnificent scenery and unusual experience repaid us well for the long prairie journey of a thousand miles we had marched. The instrument calculations we made of the altitude of the highest peak in the range will be of much use to the United States government's geological surveyors."

"Lieutenant!" called a bearded, bald-headed trader, vigorously waving a hairy arm. "Did you see buffalo in them mountains, or Indians we can trade with?"

"No buffalo. No Indians either—although one of their 'forts' of sapling poles stood near our camp by an unusually beautiful lake—oh! it looked like a glowing blue gem set in the mountain. The 'fort' was a sign that Indians came there from time to time, maybe to fish, there being no game to hunt." Fremont looked around at Carson, nodded for him to speak.

JF Report
Uninhabited
mountain area.
August 9

"The signs said these werz Blackfeet," Carson said," and I knowed they had villages at the north end of the range. I knowed Blackfeet Indians hate whites, so I recommended constant watch guards, no unnecessary gunfire.

"When the Lieutenant determined we'd make this place our basecamp and leave all our horses, gear, and grub with a crew of guards, we spent a day building a fort. We felled trees inside a grove of beech trees, made a breastwork of trunks and interwoven branches.

"Nearby, around the lake, the animals could graze a fine pasture—we'd seen no grass when we scouted the mountain paths. Besides that, horses constantly climbing up and down steep, rocky paths could easily fall, break a leg, have to be shot. So the plan changed to just a dozen or so of us on muleback working our way through the ridges to the peak the Lieutenant had chosen. Back at the camp, the horses would be safe and well-fed. Dr. Bernier wuz left in charge— he's the man who yanked my shoulder back into its socket—"

"Yes," Fremont added, "a man of most determined courage, and one of my most trustworthy men. ('Yaays' and backslapping of Dr. Bernier by those close to him.) Then," Fremont continued, "we mountain climbers on mules, 15 of us, went off thinking we'd be back the next morning."

JF Report
Bernier left in
charge of
base camp.

August 11

JF Report
JF repairs broken
barometer

Carson's mild tenor and Basil's bass suddenly overlapped with the same demand—"Don't leave out— Tell'um about—" "how you repaired—" "remember the broken barometer!!" ("Yaaayy!")

Fremont acquiesed with a broad smile. "All right. Remember we had to ford the stream feeding the lake where we camped. Boulders, beds of rocks, slabs, and angular fragments in the water caused our mounts to fall repeatedly into the frigid, swift current. Some men dismounted in waist-deep water to lead their stumbling mounts safely across."

Mr.Preuss mumbled that he froze stiff in ze icyvater.

"I heard many cries of dismay when I yelled, 'The barometer! It's broken!'" Fremont said. "The only means for finding the height of the snowy peaks was gone! As soon as camp was set up, I began to try to repair this object of my anxious solicitude night and day for a thousand miles. I succeeded!

"If ever any of you face such a problem, be sure you have handy a thin, transparent slice of Kit Carson's powderhorn to boil, stretch, and shape into a small tube, replacement for the barometer's broken glass! Be sure also to pack buffalo-hoof glue to hold the new tube together and attach it, and a vial of mercury to fill it!"

Fremont's men broke out with admiring comments, hand clapping, and fist-waving—Mr. Preuss excepted. The audience, listening open-mouthed, entranced if not totally comprehending, stirred and buzzed, clapped and smiled.

Signing for silence, Fremont picked up his story of the climb. "With barometer wrapped in a piece of buffalo robe and tied securely within my sight onto my own mule, we began our march into, and up, the Wind Mountains. The highest peak looked so close, so easy to reach and mount, we took just enough food for that day and half the next.

"We had seen from our Sandy River approach that these mountains rise abruptly thousands of feet high from the desert plain. At the lake camp, we could see three, we thought, rows of mountains, one behind the other, with the third one the tallest—a strangely serrated line of broken, jagged cones, now with snowy pinnacles.

"I had taken a daguerreotype of them as part of a breath-takingly beautiful scene when we first entered the range. Even Mr.Preuss called the rocks and pinnacles 'magnificent—never saw the like in Europe,' are his words—unexpected praise from a man who loves his Alps so devotedly.

"We advanced over the first ridge and camped. All was going well, all was beauty around us, the weather perfect, supper satisfying with hot coffee. We decided to leave all the mules and half-dozen men at this 'Mule Camp' in the morning, and nine of us would climb the next ridge. It looked adjacent to our highest peak, so we could quickly climb that pinnacle to its snowy tip, and be back at Mule Camp by dark."

Fremont smiled ruefully. "We walked our legs off all day long—up the ridge only to see another, down and up rocks, on slippery slopes, along narrow drop-off ledges—to come to yet another ridge to climb, each one bringing us a bit higher, but not close to the final pinnacle climb. Exhausted, we had to stop in late afternoon.

"The only flat place to rest, then try to sleep, was a broad, flat, COLD rock. Night came, a gale of wind blew in, freezing us—we'd brought no blankets. My head had begun a pounding ache. I was nauseous—perhaps from altitude—certainly not from food we'd eaten, for we'd brought none as part of our overly optimistic plan.

Booshway Boudeau and the English-speaking traders shook their heads and moaned in sympathy.

"Surely," Fremont went on, "SURELY, even without food we'd make it to the top this third morning, for we were already at the treeless snowline. But no. Everything got worse. We were walking on ice, along ledges of sheer walls, over massive stones, through tumbled rocks, around lakes and lakes and lakes, up slopes and down three times to achieve any height.

"I was in misery. Two more—Descouteau and Lambert—became ill. Mr. Preuss slipped on ice, slid on his bottom downhill 200 feet where huge rocks stopped him near the edge of a dropoff. Maxwell stumbled, was pitched toward the edge of a precipice, saved himself from going over by throwing all his weight flat to the ground."

"Aaaaaohhh," moaned Fremont's audience.

"When I heard Mr. Preuss 'hallo' from a point higher than mine, I sent Janisse to him with the barometer and instructions to take a reading there—perhaps the only one we'd ever get, I thought. But a little later I saw Kit waving from a higher point."

"There I was!" chortled Carson. "Finally able to look up and see the tallest peak towering a thousand feet directly above me—no ridge in the way!"

"We managed to join him, our goal within reach!" cried Fremont. "We could NOT give up now! But we were starving, three ill, all exhausted, and we'd have another freezing night in a few hours. What to do? 'Basil,' I said, 'Your powers of endurance resemble more a mountain goat than a man, and therefore you're the best to lead four of our nine men back to Mule Camp and return fast with mules and food and blankets.'

"They took off, and miracle of miracles they returned before sundown riding or leading enough mules for six of us! I never tasted a supper so good though it was only dried meat and a cup of coffee. We had blankets to sleep in, we three who were

JF Report
Details of 5 days of mountain climbing.
Aug. 11,12,13,14,15

ill had recovered, tomorrow we could ride our mules on the best route any of us had found, and at last begin to climb 'Snow Peak,' my name for the highest pinnacle."

On the front row, Randy, totally absorbed in Fremont's story, involuntarily sighed a very loud "Huuunh!" of relief. Moise seated behind him, patted him on the shoulder as an amused murmur circulated through the rows of Fremont's men and the fort traders.

Preuss Journal
Preuss says Fremont
and Kit had a dis-
agreement that created
a tension between
them.

"In early morning," Fremont went on, "I sent Carson and two men walking back to Mule Camp to prepare for the return of we six who'd make the climb."

Mr. Boudeau gave Carson a sharp, questioning look. Kit, arms folded across his chest, studiously looked at his feet.

"We six— Preuss, Janisse, Lambert, Basil, Descouteau, and myself," Fremont was saying, "on our mules began following a long defile by the base of the mountain. We expected it would lead to a spot where we'd dismount, climb the last half-mile straight up to the pinnacle. We did just that, thanks to the remarkable hoofs mules have!

"So surefooted! At one place they worked their way among angular, sharp rocks from three to ten feet across, leaping from one narrow point to another, almost always landing perfectly balanced. On rough or steep or slippery patches they hardly missed a step.

"Our six mules brought us in about three hours or so alongside a nearly vertical wall of granite two thousand feet high. Rising out of its top was the serrated line of broken, jagged cones—pinnacles. We rode beside the wall until we were below the tallest cone—my 'Snow Peak.'

"Now we must ascend the wall's irregular, steep surface for two thousand feet, then another 500 to the tip of its highest cone. We turned our mules loose in a patch of grass by three little lakes, and began our climbing.

"At one point I hurried past the others, who had sat down when they felt short of breath. I clambered rapidly up a buttress-like slab—until suddenly the only way to continue was to pass around a vertical side. I put my fingers and toes—I was wearing thin mocassins—in crevices to pull myself along. I'm here to tell you about it, but I almost wasn't.

JF Report
Climbing the
"highest peak."
Altitude 13,570

"Joining up with my companions, I began climbing the last few hundred feet—the spire. In a short time, I was springing upon the three-foot-square summit! What a thrill! But one more step and I'd've plunged into snow 500 feet below—a field with an icy dropoff to oblivion.

"But I stood still and firm on the pinnacle's slanted top in a space just big enough for one pair of feet at a time. I looked out over the dazzling scene. I could see the snowy heads of the Trois Tetons far to the north, and on every side sparkled distant source-lakes of great rivers. But the closer scene was shocking, one of terrible earth-shaking convulsions that had split ridges into chasms and fissures. Out of this wreckage rose our lofty granite wall topped by minarets, columns, and our pinnacle."

JF Report
August 15, 1842
(stood on highest pinnacle)

Fremont looked down at Randy who, with knees drawn up, arms wrapped around them, face bent over them, had made himself into a tense, round bundle.

"Randy," Fremont called softly, "are you asleep?"

Randy's head popped up. He shook it for "No," and said, "It was too scary—you standing up there so high and right where all that convulsing goes on."

Only Fremont laughed. "It didn't happen last week or last year but long, long years ago, and won't happen again— not anytime soon anyway," he said soothingly. "All five men with me came one at a time to the three-foot square tip to have a look at the chasms below. They can tell you they felt no shaking, except their own." Janisse, Basil, Lambert, and Descouteau chorused, "Not me!"

With the tension banished and the audience smiling, Fremont returned to his moments of standing on Snow Peak's pinnacle tip. "Mr. Preuss and I took turns reading the barometer mercury up there, and by my calculations, Snow Peak's altitude is 13,570 feet above the Gulf of Mexico. That fact recorded, we had our ceremony to celebrate being the first men to stand on this spot.

JF Report

"We fixed a ramrod in a crevice by our little platform, and unfurled the American flag to wave in the breeze where no flag ever waved before! Lambert fired his pistol, we all shouted 'Hurrah! Hurrah! Hurrah!' We became aware then of a profound silence, there so far away in height and distance from the rest of the world!

"All at once I heard a half-whisper from the level just below me. 'Sir,' the voice said, 'a bumble bee just landed on my knee."

JF Report
"A bumblebee just landed on my knee."

Descouteau's merry laughter and voice shouting "MY knee—it buzzed in from de east and took a rest on MY knee!" set off guffaws all around. Randy giggled noisily, rocking back and forth happily. Booshway Boudeau called to Descouteau, "What did you do with your bumbler?"

Descouteau called back, "I asked it what it was doing near'bout 14,000 feet from de wild flowers! It made a little noise like, 'Take me to Washington!' It's now in de Lieutenant's record book, on its way to visit Congress!"

Fremont raised a hand to quiet the laughter and hand-clapping and said, "The story of Lieutenant Fremont and how he had two dreams come true one right after the other, is now about to come to an end!

"This Lieutenant on his way back to Fort Laramie relived every night in his dreams that great moment in South Pass when he saw the continental watershed lying at his feet! And that other great moment on the tip-top of our world when he secured the rod bearing the flag of the United States of America, watched that symbol of our country fluttering above the Rocky Mountains! No man can be luckier and happier than Lieutenant John Charles Fremont!

"Goodnight good friends of the fort, goodnight my brave companion-friends— and goodnight patient Indian Chiefs!"

From a popular illustration of the 1840's

Based on Harper's Magazine, 18—

Kit Carson's going home to Taos, New Mexico, now that he's so close. Randy has misty eyes as Kit gallops off, heading South for Bent's Fort and Taos—and a beautiful girl waiting for him there, he hopes, "though I ain't been home for near'bout a year." Fremont's portrayal of Kit Carson in his Expedition Report as truthful, fearless, intelligent, daring, will create a national folk hero.

469

CHAPTER 41

LAST MIRACLE, INDIANS, GOODBYE TO KIT

August 31 - September 3, 1842, Fort Laramie

On the walk downslope from the Fort to the camp on the tree-lined creek, Randy skipped, jumped, flung his arms around, turned a cartwheel, then two, light-hearted and happy to have the presence again of John Fremont and good ole Kit. He caught only a word or two of the talk going on between Fremont and Carson just ahead, but that was all right—probably going over details of plans for starting home.

Oh happy home-heading day—hour—minute!

An exciting thought was stirred up as he pictured the route home along the Platte, that strange wading-pool river that looked like a great big lake, except long—600 miles long from Fort Laramie to the Missouri River.

He already had asked John to make sure they camped in the same Platte River hollow where Tuesday had secreted the clay head. What a great souvenir to take home and show to everybody. Souvenir! He suddenly pictured the buffalo skulls he had wanted to take home, skulls that instead became bull's-eye targets for Cousin Henry and his pals to shoot at.

Randy turned another cartwheel and sat down on the ground to think about what objection John might have to, say, ONE souvenir skull. There's empty space now in the carts, we'll be going downhill, we'll be going straight to the Missouri River to Sarpy's trading post at Bellevue, get there in about a month, ride on a boat all the way to St. Louis. One skull wouldn't be in the way or too heavy, would it?

Just then, Randy saw Moise near the end of the straggle of Fremont's men heading from the fort to their tents. I'll ask Moise what he thinks, Randy quickly decided, and scrambled to his feet.

"Moise! Don't you think—"

"Sh!" Moise signaled. "I want to hear what dose two behind me are saying." He did a quick head jerk backwards toward Mr. Preuss and Descouteau. Mr.Preuss was quite red in the face, and his words were flowing out emphatically, forcefully, almost without a stutter.

"Zis foolish little lieutenant didn't vant to let everybody know just how f-foolish he is—zat is ze real reason he didn't tell ze rest of ze story, ze BAD parts, to ze fort crowd. Zis childishly impulsive man who made us climb zis jumble of rocks to ze highest peak, knew nozzing about mountain climbing, took nozzing for us to eat or drink or to sleep varm in—STUPID!

"Zen he says he's sick, gets headache, sends ME ze barometer to do HIS vork finding ze altitude. He stupidly raves at Kid Carson—himself good for pronouncements about Indian danger just to make HIMself look important!"

"Now, Mr. Preuss, you ought'n say disrespectful t'ings, about anybody, 'specially about de Lieutenant," Descouteau interrupted, "'specially untrue t'ings like calling him child- ish or STUPID—or 'little' Lieutenant!"

Mr. Preuss blustered, "It is certainly STUPID of him to be so foolhardy to go, take us, vere ze terrain vas absolutely unknown!" His color brightening, Mr. Preuss spoke faster, with emphasis. "Ze mountain climb vasn't ze only stupidity— zere's ze boat accident he didn't even MENTION to ze fort people! I knew all ze time zis boating down ze river zrou zose canyons vas too dangerous! But not our know-it-all blockhead wiz his passion for zat two-ton rubber boat ve lugged 1200 miles! I'm glad it sank!"

Descouteau had stopped, stood facing Mr. Preuss, block- ing his way. Moise and Randy came to a stop, too, behind Descouteau. Randy, his face and shoulders stiff, asked Moise urgently, "Why is he saying ugly things about John? What's he talking about? Moise! Say something to him!"

Moise's voice roared. "Hey—you talking 'bout de seven men dat run de river in de rubber boat, ain't you? How dey hit de sharp rock in de narrows and spilled into de water? While I wasn't dere to see it, I know, and every man in dis camp knows—"

"Me, too!" declared Randy fiercely.

"—dat de Lieutenant is de most UNfoolish, good-thinking booshway any of us ever had, and you're gonna have a mass fight on your hands if you walk in camp and repeat what you just said. If dis boy wasn't here, I'd give you a rough piece of my mind right now!"

Descouteau began shaking his finger close to Mr. Preuss's flaming red nose and saying, "I WAS dere, and in de mountain climbing, too, same as you, and mishaps was no more de Lieutenant's fault dan yours!

471

"Take de riverboat flipflop—YOU was mighty pleased when we decided de seven of us would pump-up de rubber boat and FLOAT 12 miles downstream t'rou Platte River canyon to Goat Island. YOU didn't want to sit your bottom on a saddle to ride wid de ot'er men over de high rocks from Sweetwater to pick up de Platte trail, den ride more miles to Goat island! 'Oh my poor arse!' you whined about riding, and werz glad for a chance to float!"

JF Report
August 24

"B-b-b-but," Mr. Preuss said, "only AFTER ve started did he tell us zere vas a deadly 25-foot vaterfall—I vould have climbed on a horse—"

"You've forgotten sum'um!" Descouteau broke in. We made it t'rou half 'o'de canyon, we climbed 300 feet of canyon wall so as to look down de river lengt'. Not you, not me, not nary one of us saw ANY SUCH FALLS!"

"But I knew vhen we looked down zat river zat rubber boat couldn't stand up to ze rocks and rapids—"

"Augh, old man—if you knowed so much DEN, knowed it was foolish, dangerous, and we was bound to smash up in de rocks, dunk Lieutenant's precious books, records, instruments, chocolates—AND drown ME—'cept Lambert grabbed my hair, pulled me out—"

"Is THAT what happened!?" Randy almost screamed.

"Dat's what happened, Randy!" Descouteau said. "At first, de boat squeezed t'rou all de rocks in dat downhill river, skipped over de rapids like a duck in water. We was singing, dis man Proyce was BRAGGING on dis boat—when WHOMP! it hit a sharp, bull-size rock hiding in de water, whirled over, dumped us—everyt'ing—in de churning river, t'rowed all us 'ginst dat canyon's mile-high redstone wall!"

JF Report
August 24
(boat struck a
rock,turned
over in canyon
river)

"John got hurt!" Randy cried out. "He didn't tell me about the canyon—the boat! I saw a bruise spot on his forehead, but he said 'it's nothing'—"

"Not'ing serious, son," Descouteau assured him, and turned his most fierce glare on Mr. Preuss."When you wuz on top of the wall looking down de river and canyon, IF you could see AHEAD what was coming, how come you didn't refuse to go, den give us your whys and wherefors, save us a dunking and near-drowning??! I tell you why—'cause you like seeing people get hurt when you think you won't be hurt 'cause you're so smart!"

"NO! By zat time, it vas t-t-too—late! Ve couldn't go back and ve couldn't drag ze goods and boat up ze wall, zen tote zem miles to ze island! Nozzing to do but go back to ze boat, keep on going down ze river!"

Descouteau bristled and nearly snarled, "You wuz just hoping, wuzn't you, dat de boat would wreck so you could say you knew it would happen and de Lieutenant was stupid. ZE trouble WISS you is, you're always t'inking you're smarter dan anybody!

"Join dat to a mean heart and you get ANODDER Proyce-story dat's known all over camp—how YOU on de walk to Goat Island, after burning your mouth drinking hot water from a spring, you CALLED Benoist to drink, didn't tell him de water was boiling hot, just watched and laughed when he burned his lips!

JF Report August 24 Also, *Preuss Journal.* Preuss (how Benoist burned his mouth)

"Worse dan anyt'ing, you're puffed wid envy—t'ink YOU'd be a better Number One dan de Lieutenant! Dat's REALLY stupid as anybody in dis camp will tell you!"

"You're ze MOST stupid of all!" shouted Mr. Preuss at the top of his voice."YOU, Big Mouz Cook, are so stupid you can't cook anyzing so it's fit to eat!"

Descouteau snarled, clenched his teeth and balled his fist. Moise moved quickly in front of him. "Hey, hey, ami, Lieutenant won't like giving dis fellow le coup."

"Den, I tell you one t'ing, old man," Descouteau announced. "No matter I told you two days ago I'd wash your shirts for a little pay, I am NOT washing ANYT'ING for you for no kind o'pay! Ever! P-tou!" As soon as his spit hit the ground, Descouteau, eyes narrow, bottom lip protruding, fists clenched in anger, stomped off to build his cookfire. Mr. Preuss strode away huffily to walk alone on the prairie.

Journal. Preuss. p62-63 ("Descouteau won't wash my shirts")

Randy, eyes stretched wide, mouth dropped open, looked after each retreating man. "Good glory, Moise! They almost hit each other! I was right ready to help Prairie Artist—I'll bet if John had heard Mr. Preuss say those bad things about him, he'd've socked him, too."

Moise shook his head. "De Lieutenant got better ways to beat men dan wid a fist or stick. 'Member back when he had de hearing 'bout de buffalo skulls—how he punished Henry 'n' Preuss ? Dey can't stand each other, and de Lieutenant stuck'um to work toget'er at de end of de line."

"Well, all right," Randy agreed. "So just tell me what happened to the rubber boat—and did they really lose all the instruments, records, and baggage?"

Moise gave an accounting. The boat was torn, the air escaped. Useless, it was left behind. The list of lost valuables was long—one sextant, two compasses, large telescope, three other compasses, Fremont's pistols, and worst of all, some journals. "Mr. Preuss complained to anybody'd listen dat it was a pity de daguerrey plates hadn't drowned since dey had not'ing on 'um. He do enjoy making fun of de Lieutenant's daguerries."

Journal.
Preuss
p35,38,50,54
(makes fun
of JF's picture-
taking efforts)

As they walked on toward the riverside camp, Moise said, "Dey fished a lot out of de river—record books, tent, bedrolls, baggage, buffalo hides, Lieutenant's blue blanket coat. I saved his shotgun. Grabbed it in the water when I was drowning and Lambert was grabbing me.

"But one of Lieutenant's mocassins was washed away, and, like de ot'er men, he lost de shirt he'd taken off his back. Dey had all stripped down to half-naked at de start of de wet ride in de canyon. On de long walk to Goat Island, de Lieutenant wid only one moccasin wuz stopping every few minutes to pull out cactus t'orns. De whole way was one long cactus bed, and de t'orns stuck in his bare foot and t'rough de sole of his one moccasin."

JF Report
August 24
(half-naked,
walking with
cactus thorn
in his foot)

Randy exclaimed,"Ohh, oohh, cactus thorns! Even one hurts bad!" He stopped and looked so shocked that Moise hastily added, "His feet swelled, hurt bad for a few days, but dey're all well now. He's saving de moccasin wid de t'orns in it to take home to his wife as a souvenir of dis hard trip."

"Souvenir! Moise, that was what I wanted to ask you about when we got mixed up in the quarrel Mr. Preuss and Descouteau were having. If John says there's room in a cart to take a buffalo skull home to show everybody, where can we find a really good, clean, unbroken one?"

Moise thought the Indians camping around the fort might trade a buffalo skull—"maybe a big ole bull skull"—for whatever white-man goods were due Randy for his reading and writing work for the Booshway. "Near'bout every teepee has a skull or two hanging in it for good luck—and most any Indian'll trade a skull for a better-luck t'ing—like a knife," Moise advised.

When Randy told Mr. Boudeau he wanted some of his pay-in-trade to be a big knife to trade with the Indians, the Booshway inquired, "Trade for what? A BUFFALO SKULL?! There're millions of FREE ones on the prairie! I'll GIVE you a fine skull for a souvenir! Son, I'll give you another souvenir—a $5-bill for the good work you did for me and the Fort! Take it home and frame it, your pay as a part-time

JF Report
(accounts)
$20 a month
(cartdrivers)

474

working boy at Fort Laramie! It compares well to the $20 a month the cart drivers get for rough work full-time. If you frame it, you'll have a lasting souvenir of real VALUE long as you live!"

Fremont thought the safest way for the skull to ride inside a cart was to be buried among Latulippe's five, long-saved buffalo robes. Rolled and fitted into a barrel once packed with Pilot bread, the robes and his bundle of small furs had waited at Fort Laramie while Latulippe went to South Pass and back. Now, with Randy's buffalo skull fitted snugly in their midst, they were finally headed for St. Louis and a sale of $100, maybe more if Tulip could sell direct to customers for cash rather than to Chouteau for trade goods.

Fremont announced at breakfast the day after their arrival that the leaving date was September the third, early morning. "You have two days—today and tomorrow—to inspect, repair, replace our equipment and your personal belongings. Make every minute count!

"Anyone who wants to have new clothes made, there are two, no, three women in the Fort who are offering to do the work. They say they'll have pants or shirts of antelope skin ready by the time we leave. They've made a blouse and pants for Randy that're beautiful and fit well. Randy paid for them himself, the Booshway says, with his reading, writing, and arithmetic work in the fort office.

"Mr. Preuss, you might want to take advantage of the seamstresses' tailoring service. I notice you have on two pairs of trousers so that the top pair's smaller holes in the seat are covering larger holes underneath!"

Fremont's men tried to suppress their titters and snickers. Mr. Preuss, staring at nothing, blushed.

"Remember," Fremont hurried on, "we have about 600 miles—another month—of wear and tear before we reach Sarpy's Bellevue Trading Post on the Missouri. Then, another two weeks of floating and paddling down the Missouri to the Mississippi and St. Louis. Clean up, fix up, or replace your clothes so we'll look better than Latulippe's ragged St. Louis-bound trapper friends.

"Now to work! WE'LL be St. Louis-bound in 48 hours!"

As Randy and Moise were washing trousers and shirts at the edge of Laramie Creek, Descouteau strolled up. His face wore the steady smile of success. "You look like an Indian dat's just brought down a buffalo," Moise greeted him. "You could say dat," Descouteau said, smiling broader, "if you call de buffalo 'Mr. Preuss'. But I won't say I brought him down. A miracle hit'im!

"Dere I was talking to Lambert and here comes Preuss. Very courteous he says, 'Uh, pleze 'scuse me, Monsieur Descouteau, for interrupting, but I'm razzer pressed for time. I vant to give Lambert here my razor. I never use it, Clement. You lost yours in ze canyon vater and I know you like to be clean-shaven. Now scuse me, I'm on my vay to give Basil Lajeunesse zis coat I don't need. He lost his in ze same boat disaster.'"

Descouteau shrugged, grimaced, stretched out both hands, palms up. "Were Lambert's and my ears playing tricks on us?? I guess Mr. Preuss saw our mout's had dropped open and we werz staring at him, dumbfounded. He turns de reddest I ever seen him, he looks straight at me wid his pop-eyes, and he says, 'I have decided I should change my attitude and make myself more a-a-agreeable during ze rest of ze trip.' Den he walks off! Wha'do you t'ink of dat miracle?! How long do miracles last?"

Journal.
Preuss.
Aug.11 ("I must
make myself
more agreeable.")
Aug.26,Sept.5
(tries being agree-
able–gives away
his razor, his
coat)

The three men looked from one to the other. A long, silent moment later, Moise said, nodding his head, "I t'ink you got it right: A miracle hit Mr. Preuss. He'd a-done better had he let it hit him a long time ago."

"I dunno," Descouteau said. "Could just be dat he got afeared we'd tell de Lieutenant de bad t'ings he said, and den de Lieutenant would tell him he couldn't ride on de cart seat any more..."

On leaving day, as breakfast was ending at sunup, the deer whistle sounded. "Lieutenant Fremont has an important announcement!" Basil called.

Fremont in new trousers with six-inch fringe hanging from the side seams, his blue-blanket jacket buttoned against the first chill of autumn, held Carson by the arm as they walked to the gathering. "Men, my announcement this morning is one that will leave us all sad. Our most excellent guide and hunter, Kit Carson, will not be returning with us."

Kit Carson's
Autobiography.
p68 Left Fremont
Expedition,Sept.3.
(JF Report, Preuss
Journal do not
mention Carson's leav-
ing-taking.)

The men sitting on the ground got to their feet, and joined the others in a loud "Ahhwwwwhh!" or groaned a long "Noooo!" One voice said softy, "Can't stand us any more, Kit?" Fremont signed for quiet.

"I have tried to dissuade him from leaving us, but he has answered with a half-dozen good reasons why he must. He says we don't need a guide any more—we're retracing eastward the Platte River trail we marched westward on. For the eastern miles that're new to us, the Platte itself will be the only guide we need to bring us to the Missouri. Kit says he's a mountainman—not a river-man—not much good, he says, at paddling or guiding a Missouri flatboat 600 miles from Bellevue to St. Louis.

"I argued that we need his presence, no matter that we can make our way on our own! ("Yaaaayyy!!) We feel more secure, we feel less anxiety about Indians—and food! ("Yaaayaaayaaa!") 'Well, then,' Kit said, 'I guess I'll have to tell you my pressing personal reasons.'

"But let's hear from Kit himself what they are."

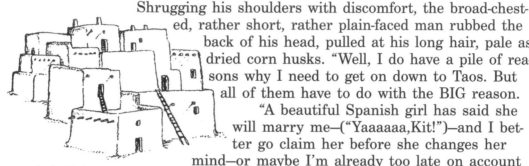

Shrugging his shoulders with discomfort, the broad-chested, rather short, rather plain-faced man rubbed the back of his head, pulled at his long hair, pale as dried corn husks. "Well, I do have a pile of reasons why I need to get on down to Taos. But all of them have to do with the BIG reason.

"A beautiful Spanish girl has said she will marry me—("Yaaaaaa,Kit!")—and I better go claim her before she changes her mind—or maybe I'm already too late on account of I've kept her waiting, that is, I ain't been home in near-bout a year. Now I'm this close to her, the pull is mighty powerful. I just HAVE TO GO, that's all.

Ancient Indian Pueblo of clay-plastered sundried brick at Taos, N.M.

"We've had a mighty successful trip across this country and got everything done, but that was on account of our daring, determined Lieutenant John Fremont. ("Yaaaaa!") I expect the history books will one day say this trip and the Lieutenant's map of our trail brought a lot of settlers out here, made a big difference in the size of the country.

"I'm gonna miss camping with you. But soon as I finish this cuppa coffee, I'm riding south to Bent's Fort on the Santa Fe Trail. Then it's south a good ways to the Cimmaron River and a long mountain gorge west straight into prairie town T'ous at the foot of snowy mountains. This here is my farewell and goodbye!"

Kit Carson drained his coffee cup, shook hands with Fremont, who embraced him briefly, hugged wet-eyed Randy, waved off everybody else, leaped upon his already bridled and saddled horse. Hauling on the rope of his pack-mule, he started off in a gallop toward the south.

Fremont laid his arm across Randy's shoulders and said loudly for all to hear, "There goes one of the world's most splendid characters—truthful, fearless, intelligent with good

477

judgment and humor, tough when necessary. I hope he's available next year and the next and the next for more exploring in the Rockies." Taking Randy by the arm, Fremont ended the session with a hand gesture and a reminder—"One more hour"—before walking away.

Randy asked him the question left in all the men's minds. "You're coming back next year and the next?"

"I think Congress will send me back to map the trail beyond South Pass to Oregon," Fremont softly murmured. He paused. "And probably California."

JF's Second Expedition 1843-44.
JF's Third Expedition 1845-47
JF's Fourth Expedition 1848-49
JF's Fifth Expedition 1853-54

Based on Harper's Magazine, 18--

In a few hours the word will come–"Advance!" The Fremont Expedition will jerk to a start, heading for Sarpy's Belleview Trading Post on the Missouri River, then a riverboat ride to the Mississippi and St. Louis. Mountain men, mules, tents, prairies, Indians, buffalo will in a few days become The Past– "sights and people I'll never see again probably– except John says Kit's invited to Washington." But just now Randy has a last-hour job John has asked him to do in the Indian camp. Will that turn into an exciting story? He wishes he'd written down every day's story, as Mr. Preuss had done– secretly.

479

CHAPTER 42

"EVERYBODY WAITS IMPATIENTLY FOR US"

Sept. 3-10, Ft. Laramie to a hollow on the Platte River Trail

Randy was still absorbing this startling news of future expeditions when Fremont abruptly changed the subject. "Now, dear fellow, there is one more task I must take care of during this hour before I give the order to begin our march homeward. I want you to help me with this task. It concerns Cousin Henry's behavior while I was gone.

"I am troubled by his 'bargain' with the Indian girl's father, the trade of a horse for a girl. I am additionally troubled by his later stealing the horse from the girl's father. If I let it slide, it'll send a message, one I dislike, to all the Indians and whites here—including our camp."

Why does he need my help—what will he ask me to do? thought Randy nervously.

"I have decided," Fremont went on, "that by giving Henry's horse back to the girl's father, we do right by the white man's bargain, even a bargain I disapprove of. What I want you to do will leave Henry without a horse, so he will ride home on a mule. He'll feel this as a demotion, and the crew will see it as punishment for bad behavior. Maybe Henry will, too."

Randy looked at Fremont with questioning eyes.

Fremont smiled. "What I need for the job of taking the horse Henry traded and stole back is for you to discreetly lead the animal from the fort corral to the girl's tent. I want the horse graciously presented to her and her father without stirring up a noticeable or emotional scene.

"To do this, I need a person who is obviously close to me, obviously carrying out my orders, and therefore cannot be challenged by anyone who might see you. You, Randy, are the only person for the job. Can you do it?"

Taking a deep breath, Randy choked out, "I don't know." Taking another deep breath, he said, "Will Cousin Henry let me take the horse? Does Mr. Boudeau know what you want to do and will he help me? Will Rosebud's papa know it's you, not me, giving back the horse?"

"'Yes' to all your questions," Fremont said. "Boudeau as

The following episode is not in JF's Report

...However, most certainly JF learned all the details of Brant's behavior as reported in Preuss's journal. The whole camp was talking about it, Preuss hints. Brant may not have stolen back his horse from the girl's father, but JF probably took some action to show the Indians and Brant that he disapproved of young white men trading an Army horse for a temporary live-in Indian maiden.

Journal.
Preuss, Sept.5
"H. Brant (at the Fort) bartered a horse for an Indian woman. Lived with her 3 weeks."

the boss of the fort has been quite put-out with Henry's hiding the stolen horse in the fort's corral, paying Old Ramon to keep watch, feed, and exercise it in secret. The Booshway also doesn't like Henry's moving into the fort, particularly since you moved out into a tent with us.

Episode not in JF Report

"I've told Mr. Boudeau the whole story and what I want to do about it. He's happy to get rid of both horse and Henry. So, he and a tower guard will escort you to the corral, hand you the reins. Mr. Boudeau'll send Henry with the tower guard to me. You'll lead the horse to Rosebud's teepee, hand the reins to her papa.

"As for informing Rosebud's papa that I'm the donor—well, all the Indians camping here know my name. You just say 'Fremont' very loud as you hand him the horse's reins. That should do it."

In the fort, Boudeau and the tower guard walked with Randy to the corral. Cousin Henry protested, Ramon looked frightened, the Booshway made it clear that Henry did not have the alternative of staying on. He gave the order and Henry walked away with the guard. Boudeau led the horse and Randy to the corral gate.

Boudeau gave Randy the horse's reins, but abruptly told him to wait a minute, ran back to his office, and returned in a few minutes with Randy's guitar. "You forgot this, son. Goodbye. I'm already missing you."

No one noticed Randy leaving the corral, leading the horse to the teepee where Rosebud and her father were living. No one was outside the teepee although a pot suspended on a tripod was steaming over a campfire.

"Why couldn't I just leave the horse and run," Randy thought, but then saw Rosebud opening the teepee flap and coming out.

"Ran-deeee!" she trilled. Arms open and reaching, she ran toward him. "She's getting 'motional!" he decided. He lost his nerve. Dropping the reins to the ground, he shouted, "FREMONT!" did a quick sweep of a hand from the top of his shoulder to his hip, the sign "give," and fled.

At a safe distance he glanced back. Rosebud was holding the horse's reins, her father beside her. Both were waving. On a sudden impulse, Randy stopped, held up the guitar Rosebud had admired so much that day of the dance. Again making the sign "give," he laid the instrument on the

GIVE

481

ground and raced toward the carts and horsemen of Fremont's Expedition. "Mr. Boudeau can tell LaFou to show her string tuning and fingering," Randy said to himself, and smiled at the thought of Rosebud striking her first chord.

The caravan had already begun moving, Maxwell, Basil, and clean-shaven Lambert in the lead. Behind them rode mule-driver Janisse and leather-trousered Mr. Preuss on the cart carrying Fremont's baggage and the scientific instruments—what few were left, the last barometer having been accidentally broken that morning.

JF Report

Fremont and Moise, mounted, were waiting with Randy's pony, standing near the extra horses, mules, and their tenders who would bring up the end of the column. Fremont had just said, "I hope nothing unpleasant and complicated happened when Randy met with the Indians. It should have helped that most other Sioux left yesterday—" when he saw Randy racing toward him. "Ah! there he is! Randy! Hurry!" he shouted.

Breathing hard, Randy shoved his foot into the stirrup, jumped into the saddle, grabbed his pony's reins from the tender, glanced at Fremont and panted, "I did what you said do, 'cept for the gracious part when I brought the horse to the teepee. I had to drop the reins and run, or get hugged and stir up a 'motional scene."

Trotting past the moving column, the three horsemen took their places with those leading the line.

On the way there, Randy glimpsed glum Cousin Henry riding a mule behind the last cart.

Past the cottonwoods and the tall grass of the bottom-lands of deep, clear Laramie Creek, the column turned southeast to follow the sandy shoreline of the Platte's North Fork. Like muddy orange soup, its shallow water trickled around strings of sand bars. Nothing much in the flat landscape to look at—just a long view across grasslands to the edge of earth's circle.

Views didn't matter to Randy Benton of St. Louis and Washington. The idea, the realization that he was actually leaving the Rocky Mountains and was on his way home kept his mind excited, his cheeks pink, his lips stretched into a smile. In a few days—he wasn't sure yet how many, not having come by this route to Fort Laramie—the column would reach the junction where North and South Forks came

Based on S.V. Hunt, 1860, after a painting by A. Bierstadt

Chimney Rock looms in the background near a Sioux village on the North Platte River.

together to flow east as one Platte River toward home.

Not much to see but plenty to feel—and wonder about. What had happened at home all summer? Did Mama get all right?—she'd fainted as he and John were leaving the house for the train station last April. Was sister Jessie and John's baby born yet? Would Father be angry when his guitar didn't come home?

Jessie Fremont
biog. by P. Herr

"Won't Billy and Joe and the rest of the bunch in Washington be open-mouthed and bug-eyed when I tell them all these Indian and buffalo and Fort Laramie and Fort St. Vrain stories! They'll think I'm lying like all mountainmen do—but maybe the buffalo skull and John's dagerries will prove my stories are true. But first, I'll have to see Cousin Henry's mama in St. Louis. I hope John won't say anything to her about Rosebud....I hope when I get home our cook will make flapjacks with honey for breakfast every morning for a year...."

He looked up when someone called, "Randy! Look over there—red rocks—Scott's Bluff! Another bunch of big, rocky fortresses!" And next day, "See far to the right there's a stone like a round muffin top with a candle standing in the middle?—that's Chimney Rock!"

JF Report
Sept. 5
("halted for
a short time
in a Sioux village
(whose) chiefs
we'd met in
Laramie.")

Soon afterwards, the column came upon a large Sioux village. Everyone—many whose faces he'd seen at Laramie—ran out to meet them. "Keep moving! Watch out for pilfering!" the word passed along from Lambert. Two Chiefs and three lesser chiefs who'd attended Fremont's speech called Fremont aside to invite him and the whole crew to an honorary dog feast.

The column had kept moving, and Fremont rejoined it, having tactfully declined the banquet honor. Finally, they lost sight of the acres of teepees, and shook off the last tagalong child.

Would he ever see another teepee town, or brown, leathery face of a chief, or naked brown children with eyes black and round as shoe buttons? His gaze turned upward from the sameness-scenery to the huge blue sky above. Blue, empty canvas for picturing places he was leaving behind— the prairie, the mountain peaks beyond St. Vrain, the desert and fortress rocks between St.Vrain and Laramie. "Some day I WILL see 'um again," he whispered.

He pictured the scenes he'd remember forever— Tuesday drawing portraits on the ground, Sunrise standing by her teepee, Rosebud painting his face...come to think of it, Rosebud looked sort of like Sunrise, something to think about some more....good ole Kit Carson galloping on his horse, Booshways Boudeau and Marcellin, Bap, mulatto Jim, Pat and Mike, Bull Tail....

He looked around at his special friends heading the column— Moise, Basil, Max, Yo, Lambert. And farther down the column Prairie Artist, Tulip, Johnny Janisse. He'd probably never see any of them again after the expedition disbanded in St. Louis. The thought made him feel lonesome. He'd miss having their company every day, seeing them doing their jobs every day, hearing them sing, listening to their stories.

But then came back in memory what he saw and felt when he was hungry, dead-tired, or scared, when being an explorer and traveling scientist felt so bad he was sure he didn't want to try it again. Still, how else could he see such curious and interesting mountains, rivers, sandhills, strange rocky shapes, exciting buffalo herds and hunts, forts—and people?! Maybe when he got as old as John he'd like even the miserable parts of wilderness exploring.

"Hey, Randy! Look right!" Basil was calling. "Out there by themselves on the plain are two blocks of rock—VERY big! Max says they look like a courthouse and a jail!"

Finally, "See the grove of trees between the stone pillars

Landmarks on the North Platte River: The Traveler's Guide to the Oregon Trail Julie Fanselow: Map p.79 Scotts Bluff Chimney Rock Courthouse Rock and Jail Rock Ash Hollow big as St. Louis hotels? That's the riverside end of the ash-tree canyon Kit told us about! At the other end, remember, the only way to get into it is working down a HIGH straight wall. Glad we didn't do that. Max says we're still two boring days from the North'n'South forks!"

It was all going too fast now. No, it was going too slow. They stopped to dig up the barrels of salted-pork buried two months before. After they forded the fork shallows, now more sand bars than water, John took two days for the men to weave willow switches into a basket boat, wrap it in fresh-killed buffalo skins, and try floating it down the river. It wouldn't. Randy helped drag it over sandbars for three miles, hoping they'd come to deeper water. They didn't.

JF Report
Preuss Diary
Sept. 13-15
(bull-boat)

They saw a two-minute excitement, a small herd of buffalo romping on the plains. Then, a camp excitement—Prairie Artist raising a couteau— knife— against Benoist who was raising a baton. Benoist won after Fremont reduced the sticks and knives fight to fisticuffs.

JF Report
Preuss Journal

Mr. Preuss had remained quiet, almost expressionless since Laramie, and spent much time scribbling in a notebook— letters to his wife?—while sitting long hours in cart-seat comfort beside Johnny Janisse.

At the hollow where Tuesday had made the clay head that Moise thought looked just like Randy, Randy got out the piece of paper Tuesday had handed him that day in Cheyenne village. The drawing showed the big tree with the gambling men facing each other near a long ravine—the hollow. On the near slope of the ravine was a group of three shrubs so close together their limbs entwined.

Clay head episode
not in JF Report

Tuesday had drawn a small head in their exact center.

Randy found the shrubs and clay head. It was just sitting there, dry and hard, no cover, but well sheltered by a thick tangle of scrub juniper limbs and their flat needles.

"I'd been wondering how Tuesday had kept it from getting messed up—it hadn't had time to dry when he took it away," Randy said to Fremont as they examined the clay head in Fremont's big tent. "If he'd tried to hide it in a hole in the ground, the dirt would have stuck to it and ruined it. But sitting outside, it dried hard. In a rain, the cover of bushes kept it from melting, but couldn't have been much rain, the river's almost dried up."

Randy held the clay portrait beside his face. "See? It

does look like me, doesn't it?"

"Exactly—even to a nose like your father's!" Fremont laughed. "I'll bet Tuesday made another for himself from memory after he got home. But this one he made for you should always remind you of one of the biggest successes of our mapping expedition to the Rocky Mountains—your friendship with Tuesday, the ways you and he found to communicate to make your friendship close and strong. I'm sure you'll see him again someday.

"Just as big—probably even bigger—is your success as a working member of the crew—living up to your word, uncomplaining, good-humored, your music and singing lifting the spirits of everybody. Your father will say your most important success was proving that families with children can safely make the first half of the trip to Oregon riding the trail we've mapped nearly a thousand miles across the prairie. Like you, they'll remember it as one of the Biggest Adventures of their lives!

"Randy, hold the clay head beside your face again," Fremont requested. "Yes, there—like that. When I think in the future of this expedition to the Rockies, the first picture I expect to come to mind will be this clay head beside your glowing face, happy from memories of your summer days in America's West, and especially those spent with your gifted artist friend, Tuesday Cheyenne."

Pleased, but a little embarrassed, Randy said, "Well, I have a first picture, too, and it's one I didn't even see, just heard you tell about. It's you waving the flag 'way up there high on the tip of the mountain peak. I wish somebody had made a daguerrie picture—I wish you'd made daguerrie pictures of EVERYTHING. I don't think Billy and Joe and the rest of the bunch at home are going to believe half the stories I TELL them."

"Yes, they will—when they and their fathers read in newspapers and magazines about my report to Congress," Fremont said, taking the clay head and wrapping it carefully in his old, worn-out trousers. "So will families all over America. They'll believe our Maps so much, and my day-by-day, camp-by-camp account showing that none of our crew—including a 12-year-old—died from injury, Indian attack, or disease, they'll start for Oregon 'by the thousands,' as your Father would say.

"So you see, Randy Benton, by traveling round-trip across two-thirds of the geography of the United States of America, you have helped open wide the Oregon Trail, the road that will stretch our country across the continent to the Pacific Ocean! As the only 12-year-old in the world who can say that, you can be very proud!

"Come now, saddle up. We must hurry on to Washington. Congress, your Father, all the families wanting to start for Oregon—the whole country—everybody—is impatiently waiting for us!"

JF Report
Lv. Laramie Sept. 3.
Arr. Bellevue on the
Missouri River
October 1.
Arr. St. Louis Oct. 17

THE END.

Within 10 years, an estimated 250,000 people, many with Fremont's Report and Map in hand, had crossed the continent to Oregon and California.

Popular illustration of 1840's

488

WHATEVER HAPPENED TO—

John Charles Fremont

The Fremont Report of the 1842 Oregon Trail Mapping Expedition caused nationwide excitement in 1843 when it was published and distributed by Congress, then reprinted by newspapers and magazines. Covered wagons began streaming that year across the prairie from Westport trading post, now Kansas City, Missouri, to Nebraska's Platte River. That cross-country waterway led them west across the Great Plains, north to Fort Laramie, west to Sweetwater River and South Pass, halfway across Wyoming. From there, out-of-job trappers would guide them through river valleys north and west to Oregon or, after gold was discovered, to California. During the 10 years after 1842, an estimated 250,000 people, many with Fremont's Report and map in hand, traveled the Oregon Trail to settle America's West.

Fremont led four more exploring and mapping expeditions in the west. One resulted in a court martial for his acting as the Army Captain on the spot, but without proper authority, to "take" California from Mexico for the United States. Two other Fremont Expeditions suffered wintertime near-disasters, and another was a total disaster.

As the most famous man in the United States, Fremont was chosen by the new Republican party to run for President in 1856. Branded a radical slavery-abolitionist and bastard son of an unmarried couple, he lost. The next Republican party candidate, Abraham Lincoln, won. Lincoln in 1861 appointed Fremont a Major-General commanding the Union Army of the West, then dismissed him 100 days later for issuing an unauthorized emancipation proclamation for the slaves of Missouri. For the next 25 years, Fremont's fame, finances, and reputation took turns soaring and collapsing until he died in poverty in 1890 at age 77.

Historians often fault Fremont as impulsive, insubordinate, arrogantly exceeding his orders, a man of poor judgment, even foolhardy. His crew members said otherwise. Alexis Godey, who went on three Fremont expeditions, described him as a leader of "daring energy, indomitable perseverance, and goodness of heart. More than any other man I ever knew, Fremont possessed the respect and affection of his men (and) ever lived on terms of familiarity with them. Yet never did commander possess more complete control...In his private character he is a model.....The truth of all these things can be attested by all of the old companions of Fremont."

Politicians   Women Agitators   Bums   Old Ladies   Catholics   Blacks   Fremont

THE GREAT REPUBLICAN REFORM PARTY 1856
Calling on their Presidential Candidate
Vote for the BEST Candidate-----Democrat James Buchanan

John Randolph Benton

Randy lived only 10 years after his great Western adventure in Summer 1842. A few comments about him in letters between his sister Jessie and his father, Senator Thomas Benton, reveal scattered bits about Randy's last 10 years of life.

Neither letter writer mentions Randy's own cloak of fame, particularly among his young friends and schoolmates, beginning in the Fall of 1842 when he returned with Fremont to Washington. But surely he basked in the attention, envy, and admiration of young friends who heard his stories about Indians, buffalo, and booshways in Rocky Mountain trading forts. His fame would have spread and enlarged with the publication in 1843 of Fremont's Report, when the boy's name and presence among the crew of the expedition became known throughout the country. However, no one appears to have written anything about him—at least, I found nothing during my search in the Libary of Congress card catalog.

The first recorded news I have been able to find about Randy appears, surprisingly, in a diary of October 1847 kept by President Polk! Even more surprising is Polk's assessment of 17-year old Randolph Benton: "(He's) in all respects worthless." Polk thought the young man had been drinking alcohol before coming to the White House, going in to see the President and announcing he wanted an appointment as a Lieutenant in the U.S. Army. When Polk gave him no definite answer, Randy jumped to his feet, became "impertinent," excited, demanded a yes-or-no answer. Polk still would not be definite—at which, Polk's diary says, "He banged out, swearing profanely 'By God' he'd do something!"

What had happened to Randy Benton in the five years between 1842 and 1847? What experiences could have resulted in the shocking incident at the White House? Perhaps the answer has its beginning in a drama that took place in April 1844 when Fremont and his Second Expedition party were riding from California across a Nevada desert. They came upon two Mexican families, including a boy named Pablo, whose herd of horses had been stolen by Indians. Kit and one other volunteer in a daring attack on the Indians regained the herd. But when they arrived where the Mexican couples were waiting, they found that Indians had killed and mutilated them.

Pablo, who had attached himself to Fremont's party, was suddenly an orphan. Fremont took him to Washington by the end of the Summer, where he lived for the next three years in the home of Senator Thomas Benton—and his son Randy only a year or so older than Pablo. Fremont describes Pablo as bright, eager to go to school, cheerful, fond of the Senator and his family. He surely would have spent much unsupervised time with Randy since Mr. Benton was busy being a Senator, Mrs. Benton was an invalid, sister Jessie had a small child to attend, Fremont was preparing for his third expedition, and the other three Bentons were young ladies of high society.

Then, Fremont relates in his Memoirs, "as Pablo was approaching manhood, he developed a capacity for evil." Presumably "approaching manhood" means at least 15—about 1847.

Randy's behavior in October 1847 in the White House indicates that Randy, 17, had fallen in with some of his long-time constant companion's "evil" doings, including a taste for alcohol and rude talk and manners—leading to Randy's audacity and profanity in the interview with President Polk. How did his father, Senator Benton, react to this impertinent behavior and the news that Randy appeared to be drinking alcohol? No doubt the Senator quickly heard Polk's story and complaint, and most likely he took immediate action. Fremont indicates that about that time, Pablo returned to Mexico, probably with a horse and a push from the Senator.

What did he do about Randy? A scrap of information from Randy's favorite sister may tell us, for Jessie wrote in 1848 that Randy was "away at boarding school." Nothing more until 1851 when she wrote how proud she was of Randy when she saw him complimented in newspaper articles for his excellent speech in perfect German at a public welcoming ceremony in Washington for exiled Louis Kossuth. The Hungarian Revolution leader, first and only elected head of the short-lived Hungarian Republic, visited Washington during a tour before settling in the United States.

Randy's skill in speaking German may be a clue about where he had been sent to boarding school—Lancaster County, Pennsylvania. Benton's biographer, William Chambers, mentions a letter Benton wrote some years earlier to his good friend then-Senator James Buchanan in Lancaster saying he'd like to send his young son Randolph for a visit some day so that he could learn the German language.

Less than a year after his 1851 speech in German to welcome Kossuth, Randy died. Jessie, strongly attached to her only brother, was "almost prostrated" when the news came to her and Fremont during their travels in Europe. She wrote then that Randolph was about to enter St. Louis University, and had "died when just entering into what promised to be a distinguished life."

Randy's father was so distressed at the death of his only son that "his firm nerves shook till he could hardly stand," a friend wrote. Randy's illness in March 1852 "had all the violence of cholera, though bilious, and quickly set his bowels on fire with inflammation," his father wrote Jessie. Randy died on the third day. It possibly could have been typhoid, the disease that killed Lincoln's young son a dozen years later. Typhoid had always been a danger in Washington where, until the 1870's drinking water came from pumps drawing water from springs, and where canalized Tiber Creek (now Constitution Avenue) was an open sewer.

As for Pablo, the Bentons never heard from him after he left for Mexico. But Fremont in his Memoirs says that a friend said years later that he got a close look at the infamous bandit Murietta of San Joaquin Valley, California, and recognized him. It was Pablo.

Christopher "Kit" Carson

Fremont's Report of his First Expedition, then his Second and Third, lavished praise on guide, hunter, Indian fighter Carson, and made him as famous as Pathmarker Fremont himself. By 1846, as the War with Mexico was beginning, a British naval officer who met Carson in California during Fremont's Third Expedition declared Carson was "as famous here as the Duke (of Wellington) is in Europe!" Carson, still in his 30's, quickly added to his fame by crawling miles through enemy positions to get help for Americans beseiged by Mexicans, and later by riding across the continent from time to time with important dispatches for the President in Washington. He spent most of the 1850's as the U.S. Indian agent at Taos, New Mexico, his hometown. During that time, he dictated his autobiography.

Having served as the Army's chief scout in the Southwest, and a rifleman when needed in Texas-New Mexico border fights, he was first made a Colonel in the Union Army during the Civil War, then a Brigadier-General of Volunteers. In 1863-64, Carson had the job of subduing the hostile Navajo Indians of New Mexico, taking them prisoner, and marching them hundreds of miles to a government camp. After the war, Carson commanded at two Army forts before he was mustered out. He settled his family at Boggsville, Colorado, before leaving on an exhausting trip to escort Indian chiefs to Washington, D.C. Two days after his return home, his wife Josefa gave birth to her seventh living child, and died a week or so later. A month afterwards, on May 23, 1868, Carson, age 59, died of a ruptured blood vessel (aorta) at Fort Lyon, Colorado. He had suffered severe internal injuries during a hunting trip about 10 years earlier and had never gotten over them. One of America's most well-known folk heroes, Carson, like his mentor Fremont, saw his name given to towns, counties, rivers, and mountains in many states.

Basil Lajeunesse

Fremont called him "my favorite man," and took him on his first three expeditions. During the third, on May 8, 1846, the party camped near Lake Klamath, Oregon, close to the present-day border of California. They'd mapped the Great Basin area from Great Salt Lake across present-day Nevada to Sutter's Fort in northern California, then turned north for Oregon Territory. A messenger from Washington caught up with them at their May 8 camp, and Fremont sat up late trying to decipher a letter. He decided it was telling him to return to California, that war with Mexico was about to begin. Soon after he lay down to sleep, he awakened at hearing Carson's voice calling, "Basil! What's the matter over there?!" He heard a groan, then Carson shouting, "Indians!" When the battle was over, they found Basil with his skull split open. The sound that had awakened Carson was a battle ax striking bone. Basil was 42 years old.

Lucien Napoleon Maxwell

Maxwell had just married teen-aged Luz, the daughter of Judge Charles Beaubien in Taos, when he joined Fremont's First Expedition crew. He went on two more Fremont expeditions, then, through his wife, became manager, later inheritor of 1,700,000 acres of land mostly in the northeast corner of New Mexico. The Maxwell Grant, as it became known, may be the largest private estate ever seen in the United States. Ted Turner's 1996 purchase of half-a-million acres of it, a slice from Cimarron on Cimarron River where Maxwell lived in kingly style for many years, to the Colorado border, only brought Turner's New Mexico estate within sight of Maxwell's original grant size. Maxwell had a reputation of brutality toward his hundreds of Mexican-American workers, but great generosity for his friends and guests. In 1870, he moved with his million dollars from the sale of The Maxwell Grant to a renovated old Army fort near Las Vegas, New Mexico, the same place Carson's defeated Navajos had inhabited for a few years before walking back home. Maxwell tried sheep raising, race horse breeding, railroad speculating, and banking. In Summer 1875 when he was 54, he died of uremic poisoning.

Charles Preuss

A native of Hohscheid in Waldeck, Germany, Preuss had lived in the United States for eight years when Fremont hired him as artist, skilled topographer and mapmaker for his First Expedition. In his secret journal, Preuss expressed his distaste for the hardships, the prairie monotony, the motley crew, and especially for Fremont. Preuss suppressed voicing his feelings it seems, for Fremont praised Preuss, and took him on his Second Expedition. During that journey, a serious quarrel occurred when Preuss refused to cut off his beard before a meeting with some distinguished officials. Fremont offered to accept Preuss's resignation. Preuss decided to stay on—perhaps even to shave? He did not go with Fremont's Third Expedition, but went on the near-disastrous Fourth in Fall and Winter 1848. He wanted to go in 1853 on the Fifth Expedition but his wife, remembering his sufferings on the previous trip, insisted he stay home. Soon afterwards, despondent Preuss hanged himself. A hundred years later, a descendant sold his journals, until then not known to exist, to a Berlin, Germany, library, which presented them to the Library of Congress in Washington. An English translation was published in 1955.

James Beckwourth

After a few years as an Indian trader in Colorado, Beckwourth (his preferred spelling though he was widely known as Beckwith) turned to running a hotel and saloon in Santa Fe in 1846, and in St. Louis in 1849. His business partner in St.Louis was "John Baptist Clark Chapineau," as Beckwourth's Autobiography spells Jean Baptiste Charbonneau, son of Sacajawea.

By 1851, he was on the adventure trail again, and is credited with the discovery of a High Sierra pass. Beckwourth Road and Pass became a major emigrant route into California. He spent 1854-55 at his California ranch, tradingpost-hotel on Feather River near present-day Portola dictating his autobiography, published the next year. By 1859 he had a job as clerk in a new store in a new town, Denver, Colorado, and was acting as mediator between the townsmen and local Cheyennes and Arapahoes. In 1860, at age 62, he married Elizabeth Lettbetter but left her four years later for an Indian woman and went back to Indian life in a tent. He was a man that "inactivity fatigued to death." Soon he was a footloose trapper, then guide, interpreter, and Indian-mediator for the Army. Various stories tell how he died at age 68 in 1866 in Montana while visiting Crow Indians. All the stories end the same way—that he was buried as a Crow Indian on a platform in a treetop.

Jean Baptiste Charbonneau

A few months after serving Fremont mint juleps on a South Platte River island, the son of Sacajawea hired on as a cart driver with the sport and hunt expedition of a rich, eccentric Scotsman, Sir William Drummond.

Another member of the 80-person party was Jefferson Clark, son of William Clark who had paid for Bap's education. Another member was artist Alfred Jacob Miller, several of whose drawings of that camping expedition inspired some illustrations for this book. For the next few years, Charbonneau worked as a guide for various groups, including the Mormon Battalion in 1846 on its march from Santa Fe to San Diego. He clerked in hotels, panned for gold with Jim Beckwourth and others in California, started in 1866 when he was 63 years old for Montana to mine gold in the area where he was born. On the way, he became ill with pneumonia and died. Markers at Inskip Ranch near Danner, Oregon, say he was buried there.

Tuesday Cheyenne

Like most of the men in Fremont's party, Randy's Indian friend has no recorded life story. If he was indeed a gifted artist as I have portrayed him, it would be easy to fit him as the artist-father into the true life story of a later Southern Cheyenne artist named Howling Wolf who was born in 1849 when Tuesday would have been about 20 years old—old enough to have married and fathered a son. Howling Wolf's father, who died in 1881, was called Minimic, "Eagle Head," after he became Council Chief. His son, Howling Wolf, about 1875 was one of a number of young Indian men taken prisoner by the U.S. Army at the end of a period of bitter warfare. During his three-year confinement, mostly in Florida, he and a few others spent their time drawing pictures with pencils, coloring them with crayons or colored pencils on lined, usually already-filled Army accountants' ledger pages. Howling Wolf became well-known as a "master ledger-artist," a favorite with tourists who bought his pictures. Back with his tribe on a reservation, he gave up drawing and painting pictures to work on attaining some leadership status. During his last decades, he turned to making money at doing whatever non-Indians would pay for. In 1927, at age 78, he died in an automobile accident in Houston where his job was dancing four times a day in a show for tourists. (Source: "Howling Wolf and the History of Ledger Art" by Joyce M. Szabo)